I0699656

THE DOOR TO NOWHERE

A SCIENCE-FICTION FANTASY NOVEL

BY

DB MARKHAM

BEDFORD TECHNOLOGY GROUP

VIRGINIA

ISBN 979-8-9910545-2-2

Library of Congress Control Number 2024913410

Some characters and events in this book are fictitious.

Any similarity to real persons, living or dead, is coincidental and not intended by the author.

Printed and bound in the USA.
First printing July 2024

Published by DB Markham
1800 Fescue Circle
Huddleston, VA 24104

To Melissa

I couldn't build you a statue
so I made you this

Acknowledgments

Many thanks to Jon Kern, Katrina Amenkowicz, James Grenning, and Bob Martin. Your help reviewing early drafts was invaluable.

Introduction

I've known the author for over a decade. We've created and delivered technical training material, sometimes very detailed. I was interested to see the first science-fiction book they wrote.

I found it intriguing! The mood oscillates between absurdity and forboding with no warning. It keeps me continuously off-balance. This is fun!

I enjoyed this. You'll enjoy it too.

Robert "Uncle Bob" Martin
Author *Clean Code, Clean Architecture*
Co-Autho *Agile Manifesto*
Editor-in-chief, *C++ Report*
Author UML For Java Programmers, Functional Design, Mor C++ Gems,
etc

2024

I. CODE OF THE DOWNTRODDEN

1.01

Avoiding Disaster

DEB HATED SUNSETS, and that was fucked up, but nowhere near as fucked up as the look on the pilot's face as their little Cessna's engine suddenly quit.

His grip tightened.

"Is that normal?" she asked.

The pilot's face struggled, finally deciding on a faint smile. He began searching around outside the plane, as if something outside the window was either the cause of their dilemma or the answer to it.

"I can do this," he said.

There had been 3,472 sunsets before this one,

123 had been while Deb had been flying. Most of those, a full 72%, had been under cloudy skies. The remaining 28%, while supposedly dramatic for their hazy orange sun and slow disappearance, had always been accompanied by some kind of painful drama. In 19 cases…

"I'm looking for a place to land," he said.

His knuckles turned white on the column. He held his breath.

"Might be something below us," she said.

His head abruptly turned to his left and downward.

"Yeah, of course," he righted himself squared his shoulders, "that's the airport."

He looked at Deb with an eyebrow raised.

"Our airport," he said.

Dickinson starts the poem simply:

"Our airport," she said.

The Lycoming engine remained quiet, the propeller making a whistling noise as it windmilled, the wind outside the cabin becoming the new normal.

This was C872GF. A recent article in Newsweek said that there were only 12,431 Cessna 172-Turbos left in the country, which, if compared to the aviation stats she read before boarding, was a 12% decrease in the last decade. This engine has 273 hours since rebuild, not an unusual number, certainly not a high one, and in only 3% of the cases of general aviation crashes had an engine under 300 hours failed, the most notable was….

"I've got this," he said. The plane tilted left and began a steep spiral.

She glanced at the instruments. Airspeed: 140 Knots Indicated.

"Are we going a little fast?" she asked.

There was a whoosh of air escaping his lungs. His smile relaxed. His grip loosened a bit.

"Well yeah, we are," he said, then began speaking as if reciting from a book, "airplanes each have their own speed for doing these kinds of things."

She nodded.

The nose pulled up a smidgen. The airspeed dropped. He looked over briefly, as if checking for an oncoming car at a busy intersection, "you have to do this the right way."

The airspeed stabilized at a number much lower, the wings began rocking. She could see the airport below them fast approaching.

She gently put her hand on the control column in front of her.

He did not notice.

He began flipping switches and pulling levers. There was the sound of an electric motor as the flaps extended besides them, to a full 40 degrees. The plane abruptly pitched up.

"Whoa! Wow! Forgot about that," he said to himself, then catching himself, "that's the flaps. We'll be landing in just a minute."

He was leaning forward, intent on watching the landscape twist outside the window. They couldn't be more than 300 feet off the ground now. The runway was fast approaching.

She grabbed her control column a little more. Whatever happened, he could never know her hand was there.

His feet were locked into blocks, knees locked in place. There had been no rudder control all the way down and she could feel the back end swishing and skewing the entire time. It almost made her nauseous. The plane vacillated from being uncoordinated one way to being uncoordinated the other way.

They crossed the runway threshold, still too hot and uncoordinated, but it looked like one was going to cancel out the other.

She let go of the column.

"Hey wow! Look at that," he said, surprised, "Right on the numbers!"

He had not landed "on the numbers", pilot speak for managing his energy correctly to achieve the landing spot he wanted. This was not the time, however.

She reached over and started the engine back up.

"You did a good job," she said, "A great job. Now let's taxi over and do the postmortem."

Debian Newbury was like everybody and nobody. She did not look like anybody special at all.

She was 19 years old, 1.8 meters tall, and had short, dark hair. She did not have tattoos. She did not have piercings. She did not speak with any sort of style or inflection. If she liked you, she was friendly and humorous, even animated. If not, she was quiet, plain, stoic, even flat and robotic. For everybody else, though, she was a wallflower. A piece of human decoration. She took up space.

Except for her clothes. There was no getting around that. Today she wore bright yellow flappy parachute pants with huge purple polka dots, a green wife beater t-shirt and orange flowery tennis shoes. Her bandanna was red. Her socks were blue and white. Her sister Sal told her once, "You look like you've been dressed by an insane colorblind clown trying to visually hurt people."

She liked that. She never wanted to hurt anybody, of course. People left her alone. People did not work correctly. That was fine with her, as long as they left her alone.

She watched her student go through the post-flight checklist. At the end, they got out.

From her feet, she heard a small thud. Oops!

Reaching down, she picked up the old, worn paperback. It's leaves were yellow and the cover colors had faded down to dusty orange and red.

She picked it up. Almost done. The front cover showed a beautiful ancient car. It was a Rolls-Royce Phantom. Running towards the camera was a shapely young woman. She was wearing a fur bikini.

Peaking over the mountains behind them were the upper torsos of two giant badgers, teeth at the ready. The cover announced, in all caps, and with four exclamation points at the end "GIANT BADGERS FROM

BEYOND TIME!!!!" In the woman's hand there appeared to be a Star Trek phaser.

She smiled. Put it back in her cargo pants.

He walked back to the tail to tie it down.

"How am I doing? Ready to solo yet?"

"You're an excellent student, Carl," she said. She watched the knot he was tying. Nicely done. "But I'm not going to tell you."

"Not yet? What else do I need to know?"

"It's not that. Instructors don't tell students when they're going to first solo." She thought that it would either be their next time or the lesson after that. "If we tell you, you'll worry about it. Instead, just come to each lesson and we'll have fun learning. One day will be the day. Don't worry about it."

"I worry about it."

"You've come a long ways. You're going to be a great pilot."

From the FBO they both heard yelling.

She frowned. He looked at the FBO then made himself turn back to her.

"Focus, Carl." She said. She patted the plane's wing. "Flying is all about focus, physics. You learn these steps like the power off drill today so that you don't panic. Panic will kill you a lot quicker than anything else."

"I'm not a panicky guy by nature," he said.

"We'll work on it. Meanwhile we'll just go through the drills. You'll find even when you do panic, like today…"

He made a face but did not interrupt.

"That the comfort of these drills and checklists will take you through it. Wings don't usually fall off planes, but pilots do stupid things that crash planes. Checklists keep us from being too supid."

"Too stupid."

They heard a loud pop from the FBO.

Was that a gunshot?

He didn't notice, or if he did notice he didn't show it.

There was another loud pop.

He noticed.

"Say, was that a.."

A third pop.

They both knew.

She looked around. The girl had brought the fuel truck over, ready to fuel up for the next lesson. She even had the hose out, but she was a statue at the front of the truck. She was frozen in time. Deb thought. She had received four Active Shooter lessons, one in elementary school, two in high school, and one as part of college admissions. They averaged 47.5 minutes each. The general consensus was run if possible, hide if necessary, and attack only if no other options. There was some debate over what signals to use to choose attack mode, with two of the lessons taking somewhat different approaches.

She felt a slight breeze. The tarmac plane parking area was only 50 meters or so. It was too closed in. A butterfly crossed her vision. They'd never make it the other side of the FBO without being seen.

Fuel truck.

"Hide."

She pointed to the truck 5 meters away.

She was closer, so she made it first. The girl must have heard her, for although she didn't run, she squatted, nozzle still in hand.

Carl was coming over, but he was not running. Instead she could see him visibly fight himself to not panic. He walked quickly, lurchingly, like a puppet unable to do an interesting trick.

His head exploded.

Blood and gristle splattered all over her.

From somewhere she thought that there were always exceptions to every rule.

The clanking alarmed her. She looked to the sound.

The fuel girl was shivering, the fuel nozzle clattering against the dark asphault.

"It'll be okay." She said. She placed her arm on the girls shoulder, smiled at her.

With her other arm she gently took the hose, placed it on the ground.

More yelling.

The girl brought herself to look at Deb.

"No it's not."

"Where is she!" she heard somebody yell.

The girl, she couldn't remember her name, bolted for the other side of the airport. Deb watched her run, flailing her arms and screaming. Running the angles through in her head, she had no idea why the girl had picked this direction. There were three other choices with higher probabilities of escape.

Not that it mattered. Within seconds there was another shot. The girl fell.

"Where is she!"

It was closer now.

Who did he mean?

The angles and physics just were never going to work out for the girl. Angles.

She looked under the truck, taking in the rest of the parking lot. People never thought of looking under things. Those were many times the best observation angles to have, depending on the topography, and visibility conditions, of course …

She saw sneakers, white socks, blue jeans. Whoever it was, they were walking toward her. Nope, not towards her, towards the girl, convulsing in her own blood.

A few more steps and he would be turned away from her and far enough away that she could make it. The office wasn't that far.

"Debian! Debian Newbury!"

Well there it was, she thought. Some equations were best left unsolved.

She scanned the rest of the area from under the truck.

She saw dead people. Carl behind her, the girl not yet dead to her right, and a couple more bodies by the front door.

Either this ends or more people will die.

He hasn't shot the girl yet, but he's moved out of position to observe Deb. It was either take a risk and run to hide, or…

She went to the front of the truck, not the back. His back was to her. He was about 4.9 meters away, moving at 2kph.

She jumped on his back.

"Arggghhhh!" he yelled.

She had one arm in a choke hold around his neck. The other arm was desperately trying to grab his gun arm. Her mental picture of this process was not mapping out to the actual execution.

He was much bigger and stronger than she was. She had seconds to live before he pointed the gun to his back and killed her. Less than ten seconds if she was looking at 50% confidence mark.

He yelled again.

She'll be shot at any moment.

It'll probably hurt.

The ground.

She bit him on the ear. She bit him as hard as she could.

A piece of his ear came off in her mouth.

"The hell!" he screamed, reaching for his ear instead of shooting her.

She took her break and scissored her legs, tripping them both up and putting them on the ground.

Now to keep from him getting on top. She could never overcome that weight differential, easily two-to-one.

He started bringing his pistol hand back, wanting this over with.

Checkmate, Deb thought.

She slammed his head on the pavement.

He was still yelling, so she did it again.

He stopped struggling and was still.

She slammed it a third time. Blood began pouring from his skull.

She let him go.

She could hear people moaning. her student's body, however was silent.

She kicked the man, pulled herself from under him, and pushed back.

Standing, she kicked him again.

Debian Newbury looked at the ground. Blood ran down her cheek. She listened to the sounds of approaching police cars. The body was inert on the ground in front of her. She stared at it, her face was blank.

She never told anybody that he shouted her name. It made too much sense. They would never believe her.

Teaming Up

"Here's twenty dollars for your car. Sorry, that's all I have."

Her waiter was barely twenty. His mouth hung open. He took the bill.

"How'd you know my car needs fixing?"

Deb smiled. She had this same kind of conversation many times. She pointed.

"The pin. You're wearing a 007 pin. There's only one car in the parking lot with a 007 sticker. It's got bald tires. The state inspection is past due. Sorry. Wish I had more."

"Do you know how many cars there…."

"Seventy-Six. There are 76 cars in the lot. It's changed by now, of course."

"But I've got…."

"I know you need the money because your clothes are more worn down than the other wait staff."

She stopped him before he could continue.

"And … there are eight other wait staff so far, including the nice red-head you seem to be attracted to."

"But…."

"I read a lot. Don't mention it. Always been this way. Hope the money helps. And so on. Et Cetera."

The boy escaped with the money. She watched him. He almost made it back to the kitchen before he turned around and came back.

He didn't speak. Instead he looked at her as if she were a tiger ready to pounce on him.

Finally he leaned forward carefully, "Buffet?"

"Yes. And iced tea. Thanks Hal. Hope your mom gets better."

He waited, speculating on another attack. He suddenly remembered his nametag, which did indeed say "Hal." He retreated.

Through the glass window she saw Timothy, her brother.

Tim parked under the big sign that read, "Fatso Roundup! Belly up!" There was a corpulent cartoon pig standing on its hind legs and wearing bib overalls. In one hand it held a spatula, in the other, a corncob pipe. It was wearing a straw hat. It had a big, stupid smile.

They had the best sushi in town.

"The clown returns from combat. My most fashionable relative."

She rose a bit.

He gave her a fist bump.

"The tiny runt of the litter, Timothy. Happy you're able to drive. You must feel like quite the big boy to be able to reach the steering wheel without cushions or books to sit on."

Tim was indeed the baby, three years younger. He was currently under the belief that he was a cross between a young Indiana Jones and Tom Cruise from Top Gun.

If you squinted just the right way, from a distance he could be a little brown-haired Arnold Schwarzenegger. He was muscular, smart, and adventurous, but he looked nothing like any movie star that ever appeared on any screen.

He never let it bother him. He knew it was a fantasy. He enjoyed it.

Throwing his leather jacket beside him and taking his aviator glasses off, he said, "Hope the sushi is fresh." Rubbing his hands together.

The waiter made another run at it, approaching again. He was wide-eyed. He took a step towards them, then another step. Leaned a tiny bit, unwilling to take any more.

Deb thought he looked like Bambi.

Tim looked betwixt the two trying to figure it out.

"You did the thing to him, didn't you."

"I gave the young man twenty dollars."

Tim smiled sweetly at the waiter who was older than both of them.

"Tea. Sweet. Buffet. Thank you."

He was confused at first, but happy to escape again, order update in hand.

"You did the thing. Again."

She shrugged.

"You really need to stop scaring the locals."

"I was trying to be nice."

From behind, "Well lookie here: if it isn't The Runt Man and his trusty sidekick, Clown Girl."

Tim glanced.

"Witch is here."

"Gathered."

Salomé Newbury was attractive, a normal girl in her early 20s. She was semi-popular in school but dedicated lately to becoming super internet famous, as soon as the world managed to figure out how awesome she was.

She had nice clothes, dyed hair, her ear to what was popular, and carried two phones at all times.

That was why she was never allowed in their house again. Mostly.

"Couldn't you just wear all one color?" she sat beside Deb, appraising her. "If you won't use the clothes with the little animals you can match up, could you at least just stick to one color each day?"

"I don't have any clothes that are just one color. Are you just going to continue giving me useless fashion advice? You're the only one with good advice? My advice is never ever useful?"

Sal picked up Deb's hat from the table the way a road worker might pick up an exceedingly ripe dead skunk from the hot summer asphalt. It was a pointy stocking cap, the kind people probably slept in when the year was 1880. But nobody wore anything like this back in 1880. It was dark blue with white human figures. The figures appeared to be doing all sorts of nasty and lewd things to one another. It was impossible to be completely sure.

She flicked it over in the corner past Deb.

"I promise to you, nay I swear to you, if you ever have any good advice, I'll take it."

"Deb," Tim said, "you don't want to talk about…"

"Nope."

"Good. Me first."

He left the table with carnivorous glee.

Five minutes later, "There's something a bit off with this tuna," chewing a piece of food as he sat, "I think they let it sit out too long."

"I'll be the judge of that."

Sal left, then Deb. Following behind her, Deb made a face at her big sister that all little sisters everywhere in the world know how to make.

"Wish we could pick up the DND game again, put the party back together. I miss it," he said when they returned.

"I could set one up online," Sal said, "We could stream. Might be an audience. For you, that is, not me."

"Yeah," Deb said, "But no. Count us out. It'd piss Dad off too much. His one golden rule."

"Don't start." Sal said.

"Can't we just eat?" Deb envied her food.

"I completely agree," Tim said, "Let's eat. Here, I brought some DND dice."

"Ok, runt, I'll just tell you straight. I'm not playing that stupid geek dork nerd doofus game no more," Sal said, "Why don't we do something smart, like a video interview about all the excitement Deb's been in?"

"Blah," Tim was unimpressed.

"Call me crazy," Deb said, "but isn't eating all you do, you know, while you eat?"

Nobody said it, but they all looked at her. They looked at her like she was crazy.

Five minutes passed. They ate silently.

"At the risk of making a clown cry, got some tough love for you, Debian. I think Dad and the rest are going to insist about you talking about, you know, the things. The thing that just happened. I know you. You want to stop going down that road before it starts. Maybe you can volunteer for some chatting? They got some kind of group, or survivors, or something around here? I don't know. I never see them online."

"I don't like people."

Tim pointed to Deb as if introducing her to a studio audience.

"And there's the tough part," he said, "True story. She doesn't like people."

"And I got nothing to talk about. It was horrible. It's over. It's done."

"Think about it. Maybe we can do stuff, like an interview. Two, three times a week for a few weeks. Maybe you and I can be a group. I'll run interference with Dad."

"Not in this universe," Tim said, "you can't. Interference? With Dad? You? Not happening."

They stopped. Tim continued.

"But I guess I could. Frack. Frickin' girls. Now you two are dragging me into this."

"Tim, you don't have to be on any kind of podcast. Trust me."

Tim tried to sound grown up.

"You know, we're all growing up, Debian."

"You know, there's a reason Sal's not allowed at home anymore, Tim."

She looked at Sal.

"I'm sorry."

"That's okay. The clown's probably right, runt."

"Blech!" Tim spat, "chicken's stale."

"Definitely not up to their usual high standards today," Deb agreed.

"That does it," he said, "whatever we're doing, we're not going to be meeting here. If we're actually going to be doing anything."

"Blech. Tim's right. I hate this sushi," Sal pushed her plate back. "In fact, I'm not eating this sushi. You cannot make me eat this sushi."

She stood dramatically, went to the trash, and dumped everything on her plate, all the while staring down the manager.

"Bad Yelp review coming," Tim said.

"I don't know what that is."

She took the plate and handed it to the manager.

Returning, "Remember this, children: If you want dramatic results, you're just going to have to take dramatic action."

The manager left, obviously to chew out somebody in the back.

"Certainly dramatic," Deb poked at her food, now unsure.

"Anybody remember our family hiking days with Dad?"

"Remember?" Sal said, "Hells yes. My feet still hurt."

"Remember what he said to do if we ever get attacked by killers in the woods?"

"I rememberm," Deb said.

"Was that during one of those four-hour interrogation sessions of Debian's where she came up with every kind of wild scenario she could and we all had to role-play responses?"

"Yes."

"Then I don't remember."

"Dad said," Deb explained, "if killers attack, everybody run off screaming at the top of your lungs in separate directions. It'd be too much to deal with and they'd most likely give up."

"Or just kill one of us. The slowest one," Sal said, "Yay. It's coming back now."

She rubbed her foot.

"Okay guys," Tim stopped eating, "where are the killers?"

"What do you mean? I don't get it."

She was obviously concerned they were going to open up the subject again that she didn't want to talk about.

"I mean lately we're all running off in separate directions, all doing our own thing as loud as we can. This is our first lunch in months. Why? Why don't we spend more time together? We can go to Sal's and do her podcast. Dad can just get mad. Let him. We either make a decision to come together and act on it, join together, or I don't think it's ever happening."

"I may talk to the manager again. We shouldn't have to pay for this," Sal seemed to be ignoring him, but Deb knew Sal could hear.

A man and his wife walked by on their way to their table. Beside them was a cute dog wearing a harness.

"Awww," Deb said, "It's a little puppy."

She reached to pet him.

"Don't you dare pet him!" Sal almost yelled, "He's a working dog, you moron."

"What kind of job could a dog have?"

The expressions Tim and Sal had were not happy. Deb was confused. She tried to take the conversation forward.

"I hate this touchy-feely nonsense, but I think Tim might be right," Deb reached out for Tim's hand but didn't take it, "Let's meet at Sal's. We can do this podcast thing you want. Everybody will be happy. But dad. We'll figure it out."

"I'm sorry, you can't."

Was that a tear? Did ice queen Sal have a tear in her eye?

"But you just said.." Tim started.

"I'm homeless. Pretty close. Let's call it homeless adjacent."

"The fuck you say."

"I didn't actually expect you guys to take me up on any of this. You both hate that kind of stuff."

She reached in her pocket. She tossed something on the table. It clanked.

"Here's all of my money."

They both looked.

It was a quarter and a nickel.

"That's it then," Tim hit the table, "You need help. We're going to give you help."

"Absolutely," Deb said.

"Thank you. It's not needed. I'm fine. I have my marketing job."

"Is that the one where you dress up like a gorilla, dance about wildly by the street corner, and hand out balloons?"

"Deb now," Tim chided, "I believe they call it an interpretive dance, and those were inflatable hominid andromorphic primates. It's educational."

"Right you are, Tim," Sal said, "See? Learn something like your brother. It's for the museum. Educational."

"I'm surprised you don't already have two or three houses with the money that gig has got to bring in. Or at least maybe a boyfriend gorilla."

"I'm good. I'm okay. Buzz off."

"How much time? Before you know?"

"I got this financial thing on my door yesterday. Some kind of eviction something-or-another. Just dumb paperwork. It's funny."

"I'm not laughing," Deb said. "I have officially stopped having fun."

"Give it time. I've had worse."

"Salomé," this time she did take her hand, "You should move back home."

"Even if fire falls from the sky and every shark has laser beams mounted on their heads, I will not do that. I will never do that. I am done with that man."

"Be like Tim. He and dad disagree a lot, about a lot of stuff, but he makes it all work. Learn to compartmentalize. He's got all kinds of stuff going on. He just puts it in different rooms."

"Wrong."

"Not helping. Tim. You are Tim, correct. My brother?"

"I know it looks like compartments, but all I really do is misdirect."

Sal pulled her hand back.

"Misdirect?"

"People want things from me, so I send them to a room that they think I'm in. I have little worlds created. But I'm not really there. It's just a room I created. They enjoy the fiction. I own the house; they get to visit little rooms."

He considered his thoughts. He waved his fork while doing so.

"I don't compartmentalize my experiences, I compartmentalize my relationships. Much healthier that way."

"I blame you," Sal glared at Deb. Deb couldn't tell if she was serious or joking, "He was never like that before. That's your fault. Used to just pick his nose and eat it."

"Blame me, huh." Debian scratched her chin, "Dramatic results some-times required dramatic actions you said, huh. Okay, here's a a dramatic action for you: stop being such a stuck-up witch and let go of your pride. Get off that broom of yours. Let's at least try to make this work."

"Whoa," Tim said.

"But I …."

"No buts. You said if I had good advice you'd take it. You swore to that. Well, Salomé, here it is."

Tim got very quiet. He looked at each sister in turn as if watching an especially intense chess match between gunfighters.

"BAM! Score one for the clown!" he finally couldn't hold back. Tim was only truly happy when he could watch sparring, people or ideas were equally fine, as long as there was fighting.

"Tonight's game night," she said before Sal could get started.

"It is indeedy-do," Tim was trying not to gloat. Victory was at hand.

"And I…."

"And you're coming."

Salomé started one last time, then stopped. She crumpled. She had lost. A loving thankful smile began fighting the previous stubborn grimace.

"Not sure. I think I have about four hundred dollars in my shoebox." Tim said, "It's yours. Come get it. At the house."

"I have $1,048.22 in my Einstein bust. That'll help."

"Rock on," Tim replied. They fist-bumped a second time.

Done, Deb stood up. She took Sal's boney elbow and helped her stand.

"Listen to me, you witch, right now you're coming home with me."

"Dad's going to freak."

"You're coming home for game night and you're not leaving until you take all of our money."

Sal shut up. She followed behind Deb meekly.

"Wait!" Tim said, turning back, still with a full plate, "Who's getting the check?"

They didn't stop. They didn't even slow down.

He looked around. Was there no help?

The waiter was hiding behind a plastic frond in the far corner, peeking.

He pushed his plate back.

"Freaking sisters. My. Freaking. Sisters."

He could hear yelling from the back. The manager.

He started putting his gear back on. He reached for his wallet.

Still grumbling to himself. People could probably hear. The waiter tried to hide further behind the fake plant.

1.03

Returning Home

"If I had my shotgun I'd blow that bastard to kingdom come."

Instead, the sheriff drew his service revolver, dropped into a modified Weaver stance and fired as many shots as quickly as he could.

Seven shots rang out like popping popcorn. The sheriff leered at the target of his anger.

Beau Martin was a big man. Six-foot-two and 270 pounds, he intimidated anybody he dealt with, even when he didn't want to. Most of the time he didn't want to.

He was also the most unkempt man on the police force, only not his uniform. His uniform was consistently immaculate. His desk, his car, his files; everything else was a mess. He got away with it. It didn't matter. People loved him. His doggedness was legendary.

"If you had your shotgun, you wouldn't be here."

Paul Newbury, Deb's dad, smiled at his friend Beau.

All seven of Beau's shots had missed the paper target 50 meters away. Beau wasn't much of a shooter.

"Watch and learn, my friend. Watch and learn."

Paul drew, fired his own seven shots in rapid succession. All of his shots hit in a six-inch circle, center-mass.

Deb's dad was a professor at the local college. He taught Computational Psycholinguistics.

He didn't own a gun.

Paul was an excellent shooter.

Paul Newbury was in his mid fifties. He was thin and fit with thick short white hair. Over the years he had developed a paunch. He was alternately ashamed of it and proud of it depending on his mood.

Paul and Beau had been friends since Paul's kids were little. Paul's wife had been Beau's boss back in the day. Both their wives had left them that same year, Paul's quite publicly and Beau's quite silently.

Over the following months, mutual grief had developed into mutual friendship. Beau would come by a couple of times a month for Newbury Game Night. Both of them liked history. They both liked target practice. Last week Paul had set up a makeshift range. He said it was cheaper than paying range fees.

Beau Martin was family.

He was also the sheriff.

"Why don't you call the kids over? Don't they like to shoot?"

"Sure. Tim would shoot me out of house and home if I let him. He loves it."

Paul grinned.

"And that is the secret reason why I put him on grill duty tonight for the first time. It's a distraction. I couldn't afford the ammo that kid would shoot. He loves all things combat-related. Takes after me."

"How about," Beau paused, choosing the right words, "the others?"

"Debian refuses to come. I strongly suspect it's because she can outshoot all of us. She gets in that zone of hers and get the hell out of her way."

"And the other?"

"Salomé isn't around, of course, but back when she was, she announced to all of us one day that target shooting was a tool of the patriarchy used to subdue the bourgeois."

"Yikes."

"I know, right? That was too much. I decided to wait until she's thirty and ask again."

Beau took the pistol back.

"Smart. Playing the long game."

Paul added, "If I ever see her again."

"My friend, I know this is a sore subject, but when I first heard of this Golden Rule of yours, frankly I thought it was dumb."

"Does this get better?"

"Now though? I really like it. It kind of grows on you. It's almost genius. Congratulations."

"The rule cause you any problems at work?"

"Me? Better not. I'm the boss." he thought. "Not sure I'd want anybody else following it."

"We'd better get moving. I smell something. Maybe dinner."

Tim was decked out in a Los Pollos Hermanos apron and captain's hat. He was dual-wielding black, non-stick spatulas and smiling like a banshee.

"How's the chicken coming?"

"Pretty good, Dad!"

Paul could feel the heat from six feet away.

He looked. There were little blackened lumps on the grill. The chicken. Without saying anything, he grabbed a fork and poked.

The fork could not puncture it.

He thought of rubber. Perhaps the chicken was made out of an old tire. Instead of criticizing, he smiled.

"Think they're done?"

Tim focused.

"Don't know. I don't want to undercook them. That could make people sick."

"They look great to me, Tim. They're done. Plate 'em up. Let's eat."

Paul glanced at the chicken again.

"You know, Tim, I like my chicken a little blackened. That's the way they do it down in Jamaica."

Tim started flipping chicken breasts onto a plate as if they were pancakes, watching them sail through the air.

"I made Jamaican Chicken. Woot!"

Beau took it all in.

"And if anybody doesn't like it, Timothy, don't listen to them."

"Hell no. I don't care if the chicken is just a little bit overcooked. I like it this way. I don't even think they need anything added. We don't have Jamaica Sauce."

"Then this is the way we'll eat them. Just like this. Stand up for your principles, Timothy."

Beau slapped Tim on the back.

Debian was sitting at the picnic table and spoke to Paul from across the patio.

"I didn't get my work done today."

Paul was very pleased to hear this. He looked at Beau.

"Before I even ask. She tells me before I even ask. This girl knows when to tell me bad news. Right away."

"Make way!"

Timothy ploughed around them holding the serving plate high.

They followed Tim to the table where he put the pile of blackened burnt poultry in front of Deb.

Concerned, she looked at the chicken. She looked at Beau and Paul. She looked at Tim. Back to the chicken. Back to Tim.

"Did you cook this?"

"Yup. It's Jamaican."

"Did you use a real Jamaican?"

"It's Jamaican Chicken, clown."

There was just a brief moment, a hitch, then she smiled.

"That's amazing Tim. I've never seen anything like this. Good job."

She attempted to spear a piece with her fork. Failing, she used the fork as a broom, sweeping a piece from the main plate to hers.

The smiled flickered for a second, then relit.

Tim was ecstatic.

"You should have another one. You're not on a diet, are you?"

"Nope."

Now the smile had gone on a bit too long, it was little too frozen for politeness sake, but Tim missed it in his enthusiasm. She fork-swept a second piece over.

"Yum."

She tried not to look up again, deep in her meditation with her dinner.

Tim wandered off.

"Debian."

Beau broke her concentration.

"I know you've got a lot on your mind, but can you come down one last time, go over what happened? I hate to ask, especially since your dad can't come along."

"I don't know. Can I, Dad?"

"Sure. As long as it doesn't interfere with your schoolwork. We've gotta push hard to get you into a good college. Remember the motto: full ride or bust."

"She can do it," Beau said, "smartest person I know, by a mile."

"Funny you should say that," Paul beamed at Deb while talking to Beau, "I'm running out of problems to give her. Last week I asked her to write assembly code to rebalance a red-black tree with 140 nodes. Know what she asked me?"

"I don't even know the question."

"She asked me why she should have to write a program for this. Couldn't she just give me the answer? And dang if she didn't. I don't even know how that's possible."

Tim had found his way back, grilling outfit gone.

"And yet she still can't remember names of stuff unless you tell her a lot."

"So you didn't work today," Paul said, changing the subject, "Are you slacking off?"

"Got busy."

"With what?"

Deb pointed to the backdoor of the house.

"With that."

Sal took a couple of steps into the yard.

Beau saw Sal.

"Uh-oh. This is going to be awkward."

Everybody turned. They all held their breath.

Paul took a minute to fully believe what he was seeing, then he finally said, "Salomé Oh my god, you're here!"

Sal shifted her weight back and forth. She was unable to speak.

Everybody could tell. She was afraid.

"Well don't just stand there, silly. Come over here."

He spread his arms wide wanting a hug.

"I'd take a picture," Beau said, "but we don't believe in cameras."

Paul almost hugged her, but held up.

"Did you follow the Golden Rule?"

"Yes."

"Then I am extremely happy to see you. Come here, you. Gimme a hug."

When they finished, she pushed back, looked into her dad's eyes. Searching.

"I need a place to stay, dad. I need to come home."

He pushed her away.

"Now," he said, "Now we have a problem."

Paul Newbury had one rule that could never, ever be broken. They all called it the Golden Rule. Nobody knew why it was called that.

There would be absolutely zero electronic communications gear anywhere on their property. It was an odd rule for somebody who was such an expert in computers.

Never.

Ever.

There were two exceptions. They had a landline. It was shielded and connected to one and only one 40-year-old phone on the wall in the kitchen. Nobody messed with the wire. If Paul was home, he was the only one that could answer it.

Beau was allowed to bring his police car to the house, but only under the condition he park it at the end of the driveway and leave his electronic gear in it.

It was a big deal when a year ago Paul had found a cell phone in the laundry room. Sal had been sneaking it in.

Things got much worse when he found out she had been recording videos around the house.

Paul had taken the phone outside. Then he had beaten it into tiny pieces on the sidewalk with a sledgehammer.

Paul hadn't been angry in the least. The rule was the rule. Sal had broken the rule. That was that.

Sal, on the other hand, was apoplectic. The more she thought about it, and Paul's rule, the crazier it made her. She was getting deeply plugged into social media.

There was a huge fight. Sal had left, swearing never to return.

And she hadn't — until tonight.

Paul tried to choose his next words carefully.

"I would do anything for you, Salomé, except this. This one thing I can't do."

"But why does it…"

He held up his hand for her to stop.

"I'm not going to argue this again. It won't end well."

Sal looked to Deb for help. Deb looked like she was working her way through an almost impossible math problem with her chicken. She looked at Tim. He shrugged and looked to his dad, as if to say he wanted to help but couldn't.

"Then I guess I'm leaving."

She went to get her stuff.

"Hey guys, Uncle Beau here. Remember me? Can I offer a suggestion?"

Tim said "sure" before Beau could finish his sentence.

"Please do," Deb added.

"Why don't you let her do it like I do it? Use her stuff, but only in the driveway?"

"Because you're a policeman, that's why."

"I like this," Sal was working it out as she spoke, "I could walk to the end of the driveway where Beau parks his car. I could go outside the privacy fence. That's not even our property. Outside the privacy fence isn't covered by the Golden Rule, is it?"

"Technically, no."

"And I could use the exercise. I'd probably go out a dozen times a day…"

"Hold up. Just where is all of this gear going to go when you're not using it? Not here."

Beau went to the serving plate, started poking at the chicken, trying to look as if he was ignoring the conversation.

"How about we make a lockbox?" he offered, continuing his poking, "I think I've got the material to do it. I'd be happy to help."

"Lockbox," Tim said, "Yeah Dad, we can put up a lockbox. A lockbox would work."

Paul looked them over.

"Lockbox," Tim said again, as if he were using a magic word.

"Does everybody think that will work?"

Nobody argued.

"Then it's settled. I trust, Salomé, that you will honor this deal. We're family. We work through these things. Let's try to move on. I have missed you terribly."

"You too. You have my word. But there is one more thing."

"What now?"

He almost yelled.

"Can I eat some chicken and play games?"

Paul grinned. The crisis was over.

"I'll join you. First let me get the electric knife."

Sal looked confused.

"It's a Jamaica thing. We're eating fancy tonight."

Tim cleaned up that night at cards. He insisted that the game would be eight-deck blackjack. Choosing a game with Deb around was always fraught with difficulty.

Beau stayed until 11. It was late for everybody.

They were happy.

Until the next day.

1.04

Trusting Dad

"No ma'am, I don't engage in mind control."

Paul waved Deb into his college office. He was on the phone.

He smiled, clearly talking to somebody who wouldn't understand anything technical he had to say. He tried anyway.

"It's Computational Psycholinguistics. I teach how to use computers to discover hidden relationships and patterns in all of the data and events that happen online."

He shifted a bit.

"No, I did not know the young boy who killed those people. It was horrible."

He made a "hurry up" motion. Whoever it was, they were obviously trying his patience.

"No ma'am. It's not astrology. Might be hard to understand, though. It might seem magical to some."

She sat down. Her dad rolled his eyes at whoever he was talking to.

"No, I don't sell anything. We're not a commercial venture. We're privately funded through charities."

His desk was always immaculate: papers perfectly square with the desk corners, books on a huge bookshelf with his own indexing system, old-fashioned landline positioned exactly square in the lower left, one picture, gold frame. He called it Spartan.

Nothing electronic was allowed.

"Yes, I'd be happy for an interview in person, just call my assistant."

He hung up, obviously relieved.

She reached over and picked up her favorite toy, Dad's extra magical magic eight-ball.

Several years back, Paul had created a giant eight-ball toy that was three-times the size of the original magic eight-ball sold from the 1970s. Instead of four sides, four possible answers, inside was a dodecahedron with 20 sides. On each side he had inscribed a popular meme from the internet. It was replaced yearly. The idea was that most memes would apply to most situations in one way or another if you try hard enough.

Almost as a synchronized dance, they both produced their brown paper bags. Office picnics with dad had become a favorite treat for both of them over the years. It was a chance to get caught up on Deb's self-schooling for him and time to spar a bit with the old man for her.

About a year ago, Paul had started encouraging Deb to explore areas in which she felt she had weaknesses, and to start thinking more about her future. Neither of these suggestions went down well. As the weeks went by, he realized that he had become her test dummy, needed to try out the new skills as she developed them.

He didn't like being a test dummy very much.

"Beau kept me a long, long time this morning, asking me questions about the shooting and even the family. There were a couple of other people there I didn't know."

"That's Beau, doing his job, being thorough," he said, dismissing the concern.

"Wants to talk again in the morning. Still on tomorrow?"

Now he seemed a bit more concerned.

"But barely. My week's exploded."

"Tell me. Phone's been ringing off the hook. We finally turned the ringer off."

"I've found the phone works a lot better with the ringer turned off."

"Aren't you going to tell me about your job problems, so, you know, I can help? I thought today I can be your counselor, your counselor Troi."

"Because of your extensive career knowledge."

"In the book I just finished, she held up a well-worn paperback, 'Exit the Tesseract', high EQ people lead the survivors of Earth to safety."

She looked as if this would explain everything.

"I'm working on my EQ."

"Your EQ."

"Emotional Quotient. It's like IQ but feelings. I can be a shoulder to lean on."

"I would love to help, but I'll pass. I'll be the dad. You be the kid. But thank you."

A lady cautiously stuck her head in the door.

"You're being called into a full board meeting later this week. You'll need all project supporting documents. Also bring the keys to all of the secure systems."

"Thanks."

Deb perked up, new problem to solve.

"Anything I should know about?" Deb asked as the lady left.

"Nope. Just office stuff."

"Would you tell me if it was?"

"Nope. Just office stuff," he repeated.

They emptied their lunch bags on the desk.

Deb stared her dad down. Her eyebrow raised in question.

"You been counting your carbs?"

"Of course. Religiously."

"Hmmm. I wonder," she glanced at his belly. Wary.

He rubbed it happily.

She handed her dad a letter.

"Here, check this out."

He started reading.

"A job offer from EigenCorp? Wow, that's a big deal, kiddo. I'm proud of you."

"Meh. I'm not going anywhere. I'm certainly not leaving town."

"I'd do it."

"How about you? What exactly are you going to do, Dad, for your future," she pointed around, "this job can't last forever."

"Yeah. Funding is year-to-year. I guess I always knew that things were going to change. Things always do."

"I wish Mom were here."

He had one picture in the entire office. It was a picture of her mom from fifteen years ago, before the incident. He had it propped up on his desk so that he could look at it while he worked.

"Me too, kiddo."

Lunch delivered, he carefully put his bag off to the side for later. Obviously there was something still in the bag.

"What's that? What's in the bag?"

"What? Stay on topic, Deb. You should take this job. It would be great for you."

"Okay, Pops, let's pretend I took this job."

"I would be happy."

"And now pretend it's five years later and I'm gone. Sal's gone. Timothy's almost gone right now and he's not even 18."

"That's a lot of changes to pretend about, and I haven't even had lunch."

"It is. And now your job ends and you've got nothing. There's nobody."

He took a bite of his pita and rubbed his belly again.

"At least I have my girlish figure."

"Unlikely. You look stressed already, and none of these pretend things have yet to happen."

"Daughter of mine, you just don't give up, do you. If you must know, I have been receiving threats. That's been a little stressful."

"And you think receiving threats should be kept secret?"

"These kinds of things happen all of the time. Collegiate life is always more dramatic than it needs to be. Nothing to worry about."

"Haven't you reported any of this? Beau seemed very interested in our family situation. Why not go to him?"

"There's nothing to report."

She started to reply. She even got up, as if angry. But instead of getting angry, she reached across the desk and grabbed his lunch bag.

Surprise attack successful. Achievement unlocked.

Looking in the bag, her eyes widened.

"Donuts?" she produced a wrapped donut from his bag, "Donuts? You are not supposed to be eating donuts, the doctor…"

"Don't push it with me, Debian. Stop it. I know you mean well, but enough. Lay off."

"Let's check the magic eight ball," she said, not backing off, "It'll know."

"Okay, I'll keep playing. What, pray tell, does our magic eight-ball say?"

Paul shook it, then flipped it over. He read the answer. All the answers were common quotes used online selected randomly.

"The question is: should Debian keep pestering her loving father?"

He shook it.

"And the answer is: Well, that escalated quickly."

"It has spoken. The Magic Eight-Ball has spoken," she said.

"Great. Now, give me my donut back."

"No."

He stood.

"Give me my donut back. I'm not kidding."

She clutched the donut closer.

"Not unless you let me be nice to you."

They both stood, eyeing the other, gunfighters in the hot sun on an empty, dusty street in an old western town. To one and only one victor would go the donut.

"Fine," Paul said.

He sat. He lost.

In magnanimous victory, Debian handed him his donut, as if giving a golden trophy to an Olympic athlete, closely watching if he would keep his word, open up to her a bit.

"Now Dad, could you lose your job?"

"I think that's a distinct possibility. This is a conservative town, the funding has always been tricky. They don't like scandal."

"Okay, that's one. Now two, do you need a lawyer?"

"Lawyer, for what? No, I don't need any lawyer."

"Maybe it's just me, but to me everything seems pretty serious."

"No, kiddo, it's not just you. Now let's do something fun." he said, biting into his winnings.

He never told her what the Magic Eight ball had actually said.

1.05

Accepting Opposites

"We are never going to make it through alive," Deb said as the single-engine aerobatic training plane pushed past takeoff speed and started floating gently above the runway.

"Stop being so dramatic," Paul said from behind her in the instructor's position. "It doesn't suit you. Why don't you open a window, get some air?"

"We've got no IFR gear," she said, opening her window and hanging her arm out, smiling a stupid smile, feeling like she was in a beat-up pickup truck heading out for a six-pack.

"Don't need IFR gear."

"It's overcast."

"Only at three-thousand. And not 100%. See that hole? See? Sunshine." There was indeed a small hole in the overcast sky, with sunshine beyond.

It was far away.

The clouds were moving.

She doubted they'd make it.

"Mr. Newbury." Deb deepened her voice and tried to sound official to Dad.

"Yes ma'am."

"You plan on flying through that hole?"

"Yes ma'am."

"VFR?"

"Yes ma'am."

"I must advise you that you're skirting the rules referenced in FAR Chapter Fourteen Section 91 where…."

"I'm a hellion. Watch and learn, kid."

They puttered on, the little plane slowly reaching into the sky, leaving the airport behind, heading to one of the training areas.

"So you're fine," Paul finally said.

"More than fine."

"You're ready to return back to work."

"Next week. You?"

"Don't know. Bunch of political bullshit."

"People fucked up."

'Yeah, I guess so, Deb. Everybody's broken somehow."

"Parks, the guy." She rummaged through her mind to provide her father the requested summary. "I'm not angry or scared. He was just another piece of the broken meat bags that are humans."

"I don't know. We're all broken, but completely broken? Maybe he was just acting normally in a way that made sense to him."

"Watch your speed, Dad. So you're saying he was alright?"

"We're fine. I can feel the flight envelope. I'm feeling for Vx. I'm saying if we make things too simple we miss the important stuff in life."

"My dad. The world's first ninja pilot .. and advice columnist."

"Don't forget the Kung-Fu. I know Kung-Fu."

She knew he was making a chopping motion back there. It was an old family joke.

She smiled. This time she didn't feel so silly.

Slowly and with exact precision the little two-seater Citabria corkscrewed its way through the hole and into the clear air above.

"Check the weather?" she said. They skittered through the puffballs on top of the overcast.

"Don't worry."

"I worry."

"Good. Now stop. I've got you."

Eventually she calmed. Flying always calmed her.

"This is good." Took a deep breath of air. Smiling. Relaxing. "Good."

"I love flying with you, Dad."

"Me too. There's isolation, solace, and beauty. The closest to it might be hiking, or sailing."

"Thinking about starting a new career as a sailor?"

"Humph. What I'm thinking about is putting the old girl through her paces. First up, kiddo, we're going to work on your slow flight and deep stall skills.

Deb made the universal sound of all kids everywhere, stretching one syllable out into a long whine.

"D-a-a-a-a-a-a-d…"

"Get moving. You have the plane."

She took the stick. She reflexively looked left and right for traffic.

"Now, execute."

There followed 32.7 minutes of blissful enjoyment consisting of equal parts complaining and encouragement as they wallowed the plane around trying to make it do things it was never designed to do.

When it was over, he patted her on the shoulder to let her know he was still there.

"Good, Deb. The falling leaf stalls are coming along nicely."

"I don't like it."

"Ice cream."

"I don't like constantly putting the plane into a spot I can't control."

"We'll get ice cream later."

"Dad. Seriously? Ice cream? I'm almost 20."

"Double fudge chocolate."

"Can we go right now?"

"Sure. I have the plane."

He banked almost ninety degrees, like a giant knife in the sky, then pulled hard to a heading back to the airport. He leveled off.

There was no airport.

There was nothing to be seen but solid white, nothing but cloud, white on white, from one horizon to the other.

They were stuck.

As usually was the case, above the cloud deck the day was beautiful and sunny, if cold.

Deb shut her window.

They flew on for a while.

Finally Paul changed his tone.

"You should grow up, Deb, move out, start dating. Get a life. You have the plane.

He let go with a jerk that made the wings wobble. She grabbed the stick again, checked for traffic again.

"Is this what dads are supposed to say when you don't have a mom?"

"I don't know. I worry about you, that's all. We all do."

"If the words 'biological clock' come out of your mouth next I'm leaving the plane."

"You're the one wanting to work on your EQ. I'm leading by example."

She mumbled to herself but not loudly enough for him to make out.

"God, Debian. What am I supposed to do? How can I help you grow? You've got more growing to do. I want you to have a full and happy life. Like normal people."

"Normal is overrated. Life is overrated."

"Really? Think so?"

"Can't we talk about this later? You work with what you've got, right? Isn't that what you're always saying?"

"Hmmm. Work with what you got." he considered for a moment, then "Okay then. I want you to take this plane, fly it through that cloud deck, and land us safely."

"There's no way. We'll die. You can't fly through by hand. Let's find an alternate."

"There's always a way."

"Nobody can stay oriented inside a pingpong ball. That's why planes have instruments. You can't train your instincts to act unnaturally. You lose track of up and down. Graveyard spiral. End story."

"There's always a way."

He tapped the fuel gauge in the wings.

"About twenty minutes of fuel. Think about it. Now, why don't we talk about something else."

"The tanks weren't full?"

"Couldn't be. You know that. Too much weight. Now, where do you see yourself in the future?"

Deb was scanning the few instruments quickly but with purpose, scanning the wings, scanning the cloud deck below, scanning the position of the sun.

"Near future? Easy. Funeral home."

He sighed.

"Kids today."

"Seriously, Dad. You okay? Lost your mind? Have a sudden death wish?"

"Work the problem, Newbury."

"Where'd you get this teaching style from?"

"School of hard knocks. Ninja school."

"Not laughing."

"Maybe not, but one thing's for sure. We're not going to stay up here forever."

She balled a fist. She hit herself in the leg.

"The hell with it. I'll just fly us right through this whether we can see anything or not. I can do it."

She started down. The cloud deck was less than fifty feet away.

"Deb."

"I'll just use the force."

"Deb. No. We would die. Stop."

She stopped descending.

"Don't you want to watch and learn, Dad? I could show you how to die."

"No thanks. I'm good."

"I have what I need. You say."

"I want you to have a normal life."

She was caught. Finally she turned and looked back at her dad, the hell with flying the plane.

"I have everything. I'm not …." she searched for the right word, "equipped for a normal life. You know that."

"I know nothing of the sort. Look around you, Debian. Everything you need is right in front of you."

She turned back to the second of her two problems: flying.

"I guess if I can't land the plane I won't have much to figure out anyway."

"Ten minutes of fuel. You couldn't make an alternate airport work now, even if you had one, which you don't, and even if you wanted to, which you did …"

She began rocking the wings, pulling up and down a bit. None of it did anything, but it felt good to do something.

"Since your mother left, I know that you've had problems."

"DAD!"

"No. Let me finish. Things got really rough for you. I know. Rougher than the rest of us. And we don't need to talk about it anymore."

"Ok. Let's not."

"But you have more healing to do. I can see that. You can do so much more."

She threw her hands up, done.

"I can't do this, dad. I need your help."

"Sometimes the best help is doing nothing."

"That's fucked up."

"You said it. People fucked up."

She wasn't sure, but she thought she heard something in his tone, like his eyes were twinkling or this was some cruel joke.

But Dad wasn't cruel. She knew that.

"But there's fucked up and then there's some other version of normal that just looks fucked up to outsiders."

His choice of phrase got her to briefly turn around again. Damn these trainers where you couldn't watch the guy, unless you were the instructor.

Her dad looked as if he were dying to say something but doing all he could to hold it in.

"Broken but normal."

His phrasing was awkward. There was a message here. She just knew it.

"Yup."

She tried restating.

"Totally wrong can actually be a complete kind of normal. It's sometimes right. It works. In it's own way."

None of this was working for her.

"Don't know" was all she got back.

"Break it to fix it."

"You're the pilot."

An incredibly crazy idea presented itself.

"I'm going to spin us in."

"You're going to crash the plane."

"You know better."

"Do I?"

He smiled but tried not to. She couldn't see him, but she knew with absolute certainty that he was fighting a smile back there.

She pulled the power all the way off.

It was quiet. The large, beer-can shaped glider that they were riding in didn't glide so well. The plane flew straight ahead, slowly sinking into the powder puffs just underneath them.

As they did, she pulled the stick back and the nose up. She waited a second, then pulled it up further.

They were staring into the open blue sky, like fighter pilots. They were kids headed off on a roller coaster ride.

As the nose came up, the sound of the wind whipping over the plane evaporated. There was the faintest whisper of wind left. Then it was completely silent. They were hanging in the sky, old suits caught on God's rusty coat hanger waiting for Goodwill day to be discarded with the rest.

She kicked the rudder. Hard.

Slowly the nose rolled over to the right. It fell. They went immediately from pointing at the sky to pointing straight down. The world fell out from underneath them and they were falling like a rock, looking straight down.

She held in right rudder, and instead of falling directly, they were now spinning like a top while they fell, maybe two revolutions a second, increasing.

She didn't have time to look at the airspeed indicator. She guessed they were dropping at something like five-thousand feet a minute, maybe ten. No visuals. Whatever was going to happen, it wouldn't take long.

She stared directly ahead at the nothingness. They felt the spin but from looking at the white, you couldn't even tell they were spinning. They were fully inside the ping pong ball.

They did not die.

Instead, within a few seconds, the white of the cloud in front of them faded out and brown earth took its place. They broke through the cloud deck. They had two thousand feet until they hit the ground.

Fifteen seconds.

Deb went through spin recovery, etched into her brain after many years of teaching it to others. Just might work. Key mnemonic: PARE.

Power-off. Ailerons neutral. Rudder to correct spin. Elevator to recover from dive. PARE.

There were not many times she wanted to actually hurt her dad. This was one of them.

He was behind her, though, and she couldn't reach him. Instead she recovered, then easily dead-stick landed the plane. The landing was perfect. As always.

They sat on the runway. She hadn't restarted the engine. There hadn't been time.

Looking straight ahead, she spoke to both of them.

"A spin is stable. The plane stays pointed the same way, down, but it is stable. It is its own gyroscope. You don't have to fly it. Just hang on."

"Yup. Uncomfortable, but yup. Sure. Stable can look really, really messed up."

"You can land a plane by beginning to crash it." She continued trying to summarize.

"Yup. You think they always had gyros? As long as you've got enough open space below, it works. Always. It's physics. Old biplane pilots used to do it like this. Hardcore."

"So this, this was just a stunt?" she turned back again and then back to her instruments. They needed to get the hell off the runway. "Do you realize how dangerous that was?"

"Do you realize how safe that was? We're in a cleared training area. We have known, stable weather. We're training."

"I didn't know we were training. Not like that."

"We're always training, Debian. This is the way. You train the same way with your students. You are broken, like you said. They are broken, like you said. Appropriate stress under the right conditions doesn't mean you beat all the differences out of them and make them all the same. It means you help them find some version of broken that may look awful fucked to everybody else but works for them."

He tapped her.

"They grow. You grow. Sometimes its scary or looks bad. Now get the hell off my runway."

1.06

Finding Dad

They found Dad beaten to a pulp at the airport in the back FOB lot, cowering behind an old green Nissan with missing hubcaps and coughing up blood.

He had a black eye. He was hugging his ribs. He had cuts and scratches down both arms. He was barefoot, semi-conscious. His pocket knife was wielded in his hand waiting for some further attack by some further attackers only he could fathom.

"There," Sal hit Tim as he drove by, "There he is. I see him moving. Over there behind that car. Pull in. Pull over, Tim! Tim!"

The headlights washed over the dusty gravel parking lot. They saw him moving behind the Nissan. His car was further down. Obviously he had been crawling his way to the control tower.

"Come back here! I'll cut you sons-of-bitches!"

Getting out of the car, they could see nobody.

Debian was first out, ran over to him. She stopped short seeing him still waving the knife.

"Hey Dad. How's it going?"

Her voice had the soothing monotone calm of a funeral director announcing prices.

"Debian? Salomé? Timothy?" The other two caught up.

Paul looked down the lot, across the dark field towards the runway.

"Those fuckers," the knife twitched.

"Come on, Dad," Tim soothed, "Put the knife down. Nobody's here. You're not in the Army anymore. Whoever they were, they're gone."

Paul dropped the knife. A fresh look of recognition.

"Dad was in the Army?" Sal asked.

"I'm alright. Had worse." Paul said.

Tim plopped down beside his dad. Deb was still watching.

"I don't know first aid. You two?"

She froze, thinking through the question.

Sal spoke first.

"ABC, right? Make sure the Airway is clear, then the Breathing is okay, then check for Spinal injuries and Concussion?"

"That's ABSC."

"Shut up, clown. We need to call somebody. Where's a phone? We don't know anything."

"Well, we know somebody did this."

Tim began checking his dad.

"It didn't happen on its own," Deb continued.

"Breathing's okay, if ragged," Tim offered, still checking.

"Could be a subdermal hematoma," Deb said, "We can only do so much."

"Stop making shit up, Deb. This isn't the time."

"I'm not making anything up," she said, then added "Runt."

"You two. Shut it." Sal said. "Either of you see anybody running away?"

"Nope."

"Not me."

Tim arranged himself, got up, shrugged.

"Just seems like the crap was beat out of him."

"Helpful, Tim," Sal said.

"We can't leave him like this," Deb pointed.

"We need to find out whoever did this and beat the living crap out of them. That'd help."

Paul moaned in reply.

Deb addressed her brother, "And how would we do that, Tim?"

Points around.

"See anybody?"

"I don't know. I guess no. Suppose you're right. Suppose there's nobody. Suppose it was just some random bunch of thugs, thought they could mug him."

Sal cleared her throat, shifted her weight. "Erm …"

Knowing their sister's signal, they both turned on her.

"I guess I should show you guys this."

She handed them the local newspaper.

Deb started scanning the front page.

"Professor's Homosexual Love Triangle Drives Airport Shooting."

"The hell?" Tim said

"Wha?" Paul tried to fully wake up. Shaking himself.

"Sal," Deb looked up, "When were you going to tell us this?"

"I was hoping never."

"Who comes up with these lies," Paul was trying to sit up, "What kind of person could do that?"

"Mr. James Padwin, Editor, looks like," Deb read, then to Tim, "That newspaper office is just down the hill, isn't it?"

"You know, sis, it sure is."

"I'm pretty sure the story was picked up on the wires, too." Sal said, "Not going to be that easy to waltz in somewhere and expect to find out where it started."

"Worth a shot," Tim was staring off.

All three looked. At the far end of the strip a little plane taxied into position. Its little engine cranked up, an angry bumblebee leaving the hive. It began rolling down the dark strip.

The lights and sounds were always pretty at the airport at night. Stark.

"We just can't leave him here," Tim said, "Somebody's going to have to do something."

"I'm doing something. I'll find a phone. Somebody needs to pay. This is wrong."

"I'm fine." Paul said.

Deb began picking her dad up.

"Come on. Give me a hand," she looked into her dad's beaten face, "We're going to get you some help."

"Sis, I got him. Back off."

Tim made his way through and effortlessly put his dad in a fireman's carry and started walking with Paul on his back. "Come on, old man. Let's get you to your car."

"All his things," Sal said, then began picking up his keys, wallet, and other things he lost on his way up the hill.

"All his things," quieter now.

Tim made it about halfway before taking a break.

"Whew. Give me a second."

"Good grief. This is going to be another police and media circus, all right here, at my job. Again." Deb said.

Tim looked up.

"And what's it going to accomplish? Nothing."

"Same as last time," Sal said, "Only more so. I wish there were some way not to go through that again. For any of us."

"Yeah. You and me both."

"Ow!"

Paul had somehow made it to his feet, wobbly. He went three steps. He sat back down.

"There. See."

Debian was unimpressed.

"We need to get moving."

"Good, I've got the call. There are phones in the FBO."

"I can get that editor."

"Leave me alone," Paul was sounding better. "You kids go home. I'm okay. I can make it on my own now. I'm good. Seriously."

He began to stand back up again, winced, then sat back down again. The kids looked at one another.

Nobody was impressed.

Sal studied her dad. Deb studied Sal. Deb thought that Sal would not like the worried, concerned look she was wearing.

"So. You got this, Dad?"

Paul said nothing, but in reply he stood weakly, this time without the wincing.

Tim moved. "Dad. Let me help you."

Paul pushed him away. He walked five more steps to the rear of his car, went to lean on it but fell down.

"I'm okay. Meant to do that. All good."

He began pulling himself back to standing.

"You're going to the hospital Dad," Deb said, "and that's that."

"I forbid it." Paul had found new strength, "If you love me. Please. Trust me. Let's go home. This has to stay quiet."

They watched as he made his way to the passenger door.

"Fine Dad. No cops," Tim said, "I'll just find that stupid editor and beat the bejesus out of him until he tells me who gave him that story. Somebody made this up. Somebody's doing this."

"Tim," Sal shoved him.

In reply, he shoved her back.

They began scuffling. Deb watched as her dad slumped against the door, giving up.

She went over, held him and slowly got him into the passenger side. Looking down, she saw him smiling. Thankful.

"Both of you!" Deb yelled, "Knock it off!"

She thought she heard her dad giggle, then realize that laughing hurt too much.

"Timothy, Dad was in the Army?" She looked at Tim, daring him to argue, then to her dad.

Paul nodded weakly.

"I thought you guys knew," Tim said, "Haven't you seen his tattoos? How'd you think he got those?"

Sal shook her head no. Deb looked at her dad.

He either didn't hear her or was ignoring her. He stared straight ahead.

"And Dad knows first aid."

"Yes," Paul answered.

Sal and Tim shrugged.

"And Dad says he is okay to go home."

Once again, they had no reply.

"Yes," she heard her dad say.

"And we love Dad."

No reply.

"Then that's it," Deb slammed the door, "We're going to go home. None of this happened. Officially."

She walked over to where the siblings had been arguing.

Tim put his hand out and touched her lightly, making sure their dad couldn't hear them.

"Are we going to fix this, or are we going to fix this?"

They both knew what he meant.

"Where do we even start?" Sal replied. Her voice was low. "Who would hate dad so much to screw him over like this?"

"Tim," Deb looked at Sal as she spoke, "We ARE going to fix this. Just not 'officially'". She made air quotes.

She folded Dad's knife and stuck it into her front pocket.

"And I know exactly where to start."

Blood from the knife seeped out and stained her favorite Hawaiian Hula-Hoop pants. She didn't realize that until many days later.

Library Losing

It was a six-foot giant stuffed gopher. Its eyes followed them wherever they went in the cramped room. It took up an entire corner.

Lego forts were set up in critically-strategic positions on the table.

The walls were bright colors. The light was harsh.

Little green army men stood frozen in time on the table, a diorama of one army's desperate struggle with another.

In the other corner was a large pile of little stuffed animals.

Dad was also frozen, frozen at home. Too weak to go to work, too stubborn to get help, he insisted he just needed a day or two to, "lick my wounds."

The Newbury children were on the move.

The library had one room available. It was the children's story room. They could make that work.

An inflated purple dinosaur encouraged them.

Sal found a stuffed badger in her seat and tossed it into the pile of little animals.

She sat.

"Beats sitting out in the open."

"Barely," Tim was next to her. He began playing with the army men, dancing them at one another.

"So," she clasped her hands together, "It's clear what's happening, and for those of you who don't understand social media," she looked at them as if they were infants, "The press is starting to create a narrative of a sad, lonely, troubled young student taken advantage of by an older professor, our dad. We have to destroy that narrative."

"Isn't there a bullshit button we can push somewhere," Deb said, "make all this stop. 'Cause I'll push it."

She pushed an imaginary button on the table. She frowned.

"Narratives get momentum and there's no stopping them. Instead, eventually everybody just moves on to some new narrative and it leaves destroyed lives as part of the permanent record."

Deb started playing with the army men too.

Sal was not sure she was getting through.

"That's the way this works."

"Army men to the rescue," Deb picked one up. Turning to her brother, "Remember we used to play?"

"I do. You made that chart of movement speed, attack, and defense damage. You made me set up supply chains. You made me declare my economic model. I had charts. I was seven."

"Yeah. It was fun."

"I guess so," he thought, then changed his mind, "No, you're right. Got me into gaming. I liked it, at least until the witch hid my army men under her pile of stuffed animals."

He gestured to Sal.

"Please. Children. Let's not start." Absent-minded Sal also grabbed an army man, looked at it. She began to play.

Catching herself, she waved the thought away.

"Yo, Tim!"

They all looked up.

A group of people were coming in, passing by their room.

"DM Tim! YOLO! Woot!" another yelled, "The man!"

He fist-pumped.

"Awesome," Tim whispered to himself.

Sal looked at six or seven very oddly dressed people walking by. Today Deb was her usual fashion disaster, of course, checkers of various shapes and colors, but this mob was all….thematic.

Thematically bad.

One man looked like a wizard. He had a pointed hat. Another man looked like an escapee from a nearby Renaissance Fair. (A place she knew about but would never be caught visiting.) One girl carried a plastic wand as if it were the real thing, pointing at people she met, saying gibberish. She appeared to be fencing imaginary people with it.

They made funny finger gestures to Tim. Still laughing, they continued into the library.

She looked at her brother.

"My old crew," he smiled, "You know…."

"I'm ignoring you."

"It was a tweet," Deb interrupted. She had been using the room computer, "User anon4815162342 tweeted about an hour after the incident. It was picked up by a couple dozen other accounts right away. That started the wave. Could be a bot farm."

"How'd you do that," Sal was amazed, "It's only been a minute or two."

"'Cause Dad's been teaching me, that's how."

Tim looked over her shoulder. Deb continued, pointing to the screen.

"Started off as a tweet storm. There's gotta be some real people in there somewhere, either suckers or accomplices."

Sal banged the table. She looked like a patron extremely unhappy with the happy meal that arrived.

"Social warfare it is, then. We'll divide the army. Deb, you continue chasing that tweet storm. Just not here."

She tossed her hand about vaguely. The minions must go elsewhere. I will be otherwise engaged.

Deb frowned.

"I call dibs," Sal pointed to the computer Deb was currently using.

Tim pointed at the door.

"That's my old DND crew. If this guy's any kind of nerd at all, they'd know him."

"Good," Sal said, "I'll work the opposite angle. I'll start with popular commentary and influencers and see where they got the news from. Some of them I might even know. I know people."

She smiled.

They were not impressed.

Tim wandered out of the room. He did not rush. He was afraid of approaching his old gang. He hung back, unsure.

As he got nearer, he heard them gossiping. It was about Dad.

Tim's face got red and hot. His muscles tightened. That's no good.

He gripped his fists. He made himself take several deep breaths.

He decided to stop being angry before anything else, so he walked over to the encyclopedias. He lurked. He tried very hard not to appear like he was lurking.

A small child saw him.

Embarrassed, he picked out a random encyclopedia and pretended to read it.

It took a while. He finally was able to approach his friends. They had moved on to another topic.

An hour later Deb stuck her head in the room to interrupt Sal.

"You getting anything done, or just learning new dance moves or cool kid stuff on your internet things."

Sal stopped her typing. She arched her back as if speaking to a classroom of dozens instead of just her sister.

"Being online is a discipline. It's like exercise. It takes practice. Not that you would know. Anything?"

Deb came in.

"Yeah, the guy looks pretty normal."

Sal put her hands in her lap. She started paying attention.

"You're saying that the guy wasn't one of those schizo people? With the voices? The crazy people?"

She made a rude gesture, circling her index finger around her temple. Realizing what she was doing, she looked around to make sure she hadn't been overheard or seen. She saw that the coast was clear.

Tim ducked in too, happy to be joining the party.

"Don't know what you guys found but I found that I could write this guy a job recommendation."

Both sat.

"Honestly? I wish I had known him," Deb added, "His online presence shows extreme intelligence."

Deb whispered, sharing a confidence.

"He was an anti-solipsist, you know."

Sal frowned.

"Was he gay?"

She shrugged.

"Not that I can tell. He didn't talk about sexuality."

"The only one. That's something, I guess. Anything good to share about Dad?"

"Rumor has it that he may have known Dad after all," Tim said, "but we know Dad's not gay."

Nobody commented. Nobody knew. They all just sat, deep in thought. Since the incident with Mom, Dad had never dated.

Finally Sal put her head in her hands.

"This is not helping."

Debian gently tapped her on the arm.

"He was big into body modification, cyborg stuff. That might help. Some of the things he was talking about were pretty hardcore, cutting edge. Cranial implant stuff. Subcutaneous Flipper Zero derivatives. Very tricky."

Sal considered.

"So we've found risky behavior. Got that. Good. But that's just victim attack stuff. We need more good things about Dad, we gotta create a more powerful counter-narrative. Don't we have any pictures of Dad feeding starving orphans? Can we make some?"

Tim shook his head.

"I thought we were here to plan and then go actually DO something, not just crank out a meme or complete some stupid book report. You guys are lame."

"There's his emails," Deb said, "I could break into the college network and get all his emails. I could get class data, his homework. From there it'd probably be pretty easy to get up into his phone."

"Do that," Sal instructed.

"No. I don't wanna."

Deb paused. She struggled to explain.

"It's dangerous."

Tim understood. He smiled, sad.

"You don't want attention."

He looked with shared compassion to Sal. Sal knew.

Sal was having none of it.

"She's just afraid she might get caught."

"You wish," Deb rose to the challenge, then realized Sal had tricked her into bragging. She swallowed. Her face colored.

"I don't want to get known for this kind of thing. That's all."

She pointed to the stuffed animals and story displays as if they were examples of computer systems she had broken into.

"There are bad things down that path. I don't want to go."

"Then don't," they both said simultaneously, surprised at the synchronization.

Sal leaned in.

"The only thing I want you to do, the only thing any of us wants, Debian, is for you to be comfortable. Don't push it."

Deb looked at Timothy. He nodded.

Breaking, they went back and worked until lunchtime. Again Deb was the one to pop in, coming back to the room.

"Ka-pla!" she said, entering again. She motioned Tim over.

When he got there, "Somebody he lived with was gossiping about him online."

"That's great." Tim looked bored. His eyebrow raised in question.

"So you found who started the rumor about Dad."

"Not sure if they started it," she admitted, "but somebody using his home router helped spread it, egged it on. That's the person we're looking for."

"Well we'll just find the guy, have a little talk with him," Tim hit his open hand with a fist.

"Tim, I love you," Sal said, "but we can't beat people up. Dad would come forth from his grave if he caught us using violence. You know that."

"Yeah runt," Deb patted him sympathetically, "Dad has always told me that we can't beat folks up, whether they deserve it or not. Sucks. But we can break into his system, find out everything personal and secret, blast that out to the world. That would be worse than beating him up. Much worse."

"Not as enjoyable, though."

"Agreed."

"Timothy, you are such a boy," Sal said, as if that explained everything.

"And now we're cyber hackers."

He slowly picked up one of the army men, rotating it around in his hand and inspecting it.

He gritted his teeth.

Deb continued.

"I don't see continuing my work here. I need another PC, another VPN, another location if we're going to do some serious hacking. There's too much traffic already from here. Given time, I could probably hack up a STINGRAY..."

Tim interrupted. He put his army man back.

"Me too. I'm leaving," he said, "as exciting as this sounds. The guys out there have a fun-looking pickup game going, and I've got an elf that needs more XP."

He looked them both over, judging.

"You two really frustrate me," he said. "And you're my favorite big sisters."

He left; not interested in anything else they had to say.

"What do you think the chances are he'll return," Sal asked.

"Zero."

"Deb, I'm not going with you to SeaWorld or doing whatever nerdy thing you got going with the computers."

"You couldn't."

"Nor would I want to," she pointed to the PC, "The answer is here. The answer has got to be online. The answer to everything is online."

"Fine. I'm going to the electronics store," she said, turning to leave, "You got this?"

Salomé nodded. She tried not to look dejected.

Over the next hour or so, school let out, the library became a lot busier, and the room's location by the entrance let Sal hear everybody coming and going.

"Shut up," she finally said to the empty room.

Her phones had been buzzing her all day, buzzing to get her attention, buzzing to get a response. Whatever the latest OS update was, it keep resetting her notifications. She'd turn them off. They'd turn themselves back on.

"Dammit."

Frustrated, she pulled them both out, turned them both off, set them back forcefully on the table.

"There. That'll show you."

Lights in the library went out, leaving her sitting in twilight darkness. Emergency lights kicked in.

She hesitated just a moment, then laughed at herself for being suspicious, for wondering about the timing between her phone and the lights.

"I guess that showed me, huh. Now I have to use the phones."

She turned each phone back on carefully, knowing that the phones and the lights were not related but still not completely sure. Sal was not superstitious, but like everybody else, she was superstitious.

With both of her phones on, she paused. She looked around, expecting light. Nope. Still dark. People began milling about. She counted to thirty.

Nothing. Nope.

She picked up the closest phone, bringing up her favorite app.

The lights came back on.

She threw it on the table as if it had electrocuted her.

It was bad. She looked around. It was a kid's room. The only thing here were kids' toys.

There was a pile of stuffed animals in the corner.

"Huh."

Taking both phones gingerly, she hid the phones under the pile. She pushed them as far back as she could.

Satisfied, she made the motion of cleaning her hands.

"Fixed that. Now, back to work."

The voices outside weren't too annoying, but one finally did make it through.

"Did you hear that Liz dyed her hair purple! And neon purple too!"

"Oh. My. God." The other person said as the voices died off.

Well, then. Liz? Purple? She just had to see that. Surely a little bit of social media wouldn't hurt. It was past 2pm, after all.

Hours later, the librarian finally started walking around, turning the lights out. She asked Sal to leave.

She had a dozen social media platforms she was active on. She had spent the last six hours working her network, creating, sorting, voting, responding.

She had learned several important new items about her favorite movie stars. There was a political scandal in a nearby town. One bunch of people had finally provoked another into a nasty flame war which drug more people in from all over. A famous content creator had committed suicide. A boat of puppies drowned in a lake but nobody was sure if it really happened or not.

All of that was important, interesting, and required her help, her insight. They needed her.

She did not get further towards her goal, though.

The librarian finally came again and tapped her on the shoulder, told her she had to leave, now.

Go.

Reluctantly she dug out her phones, walked out into the rapidly-cooling night.

Her phones buzzed.

1.08

Breaking Not-Bad

"On your life I must swear you to the utmost secrecy. This never happened. We were never here."

"It's an empty room."

Deb nodded.

"It's an empty apartment."

She said nothing.

"It's dark."

"Do I have your word?"

"The door was unlocked."

She stared.

"We are just standing here," he tried, "In an empty room, an empty apartment, in the dark."

Finally Tim relented.

"You have my word. I will not tell anybody that nothing happened."

"Good. You'd better mean it."

They were in the apartment where the shooter, Stetson Parks, had lived. Frustrated with the lack of action, Deb and Tim had decided to do some late night prowling. Break and enter as long as nobody else knew.

Tim was having difficulty preventing disappointment. A promised shared adventure turned into dullsville.

Deb had been eager to show her brother her lock-picking skills. She was quite proud of them. But he reached in as she got the picks out and turned the doorknob.

It was open.

This was the beginning of the failure.

"You act like there's nothing to find. This entire unit," she pointed, "was part of a crime investigation. Answers are here."

"And they cleaned it out. What's left?"

"Watch and learn, Tim. Watch and learn."

He was skeptical.

"First," she walked over, pointing, "we have these holes in the wall."

"Just holes. In the wall. I see them. Holes."

"No. Two holes, exactly 57mm apart. You may remember that 57mm is the new router mounting specs. This is where they mounted the router. It was also positioned towards the ceiling. There's no evidence of cabling, so somebody knew how to wire things. Professional installation, late-model router. These were computer people."

"Not sure that's rocket science."

"Three bedrooms, so there were at least three people, maybe more."

"Maybe."

"Since the shooter was only one person, something happened to the other two or more people. Perhaps there was a crime. Otherwise they'd still be here. Otherwise the police tape wouldn't be up. The place wouldn't be cleaned out. A crime."

"Maybe they just left. I'd leave. Horrible memories."

"This apartment had a computer with the MAC 74-46-A0-91-DD-8B IPv6 length 60 subnet. Somebody here spread horrible rumors from that PC. This wasn't a pleasant place. Things had to be bad. Whatever happened here, it's all very recent."

"There wasn't a shooting here. We know that. Otherwise we would have heard about it."

"Exactly. Finally, notice the smell in that one bedroom? Somebody here was a serious hardware hacker."

"I didn't smell anything."

"Exactly."

Tim wandered around in the back of the apartment, absent-mindedly pulling at still-empty drawers in the kitchen, testing them again, trying to find something he could add.

Finally, "Hey, really sorry we didn't have any locks to pick. That would have been awesome."

"No more locks anywhere in the apartment," she walked back to the kitchen, as if to find one there, "but perhaps that's best. I don't think the police take kindly to people picking locks or carrying around lock-picking kits."

"Crossing the police tape was probably bad."

"You don't get cookies for it."

"We don't need cookies," he smiled a little, still game to keep playing, "You know, with the right bit of flair, one day this could make the best story ever."

"What. What did you just swear to me? You don't tell people."

"Well, maybe fifty-years from now. That's okay, right? Fifty years?"

"Maybe. I was hoping that you and I put together something, a team, a system. We might be able to go out and do more work. A shadow crew." she said it as if she had just joined a black ops professional assassination team instead of wearing a Where's Waldo outfit around in an empty, dark apartment with her brother.

Tim was now fully-engaged.

"Woot! I would like that a lot."

"But you gotta keep your mouth shut."

"Mum's is the word. Nothing happened."

As he spoke, the room was bathed in blue flashing lights. They heard a chirp. Immediately they tried hiding. It was difficult. They finally found a space against the wall, beside the sliding front balcony doors.

The police were outside.

They peeked around the side of the sliding doors. They were careful.

In the parking lot, a police car had its lights on. A policeman was walking around. He had three young people against his car, searching them.

"Just guessing, that's bad," Tim said.

"Yeah."

They looked a bit longer. The young people were not handcuffed. The officer released them from the car and began talking to them. It looked like a lecture.

"You ask if that's bad. Such a smartass."

There were no curtains on the windows. There was no furniture in the apartment. They were on the second floor, almost even with the parking lot. There were no pictures. There was nothing. All they had was harsh light and them standing there like idiots.

Moving away from their hiding spot and to the front door was impossible without being seen.

Tim said, "I guess we could belly-crawl."

"And then, where do we go, out the front door? Into the parking lot? There?"

She gestured.

"Some of these older apartment buildings have maintenance doors on the ground floor in the back. It's a way for groundskeepers to get in and out without bothering the tenants."

"Does this have one?"

He shrugged.

He looked again into the lot.

"Hey, good news. That's Beau. It's Beau."

"That's anything but good news. That's awful news."

"Well, whoever it is, now they're here. We either need to try to sneak out the back or stay here and hope they don't come up."

"We leave."

"We stay. It's just now starting to get interesting. Why leave? Deb, you're on a roll. The cops are here. Who knows what we'll find in the next hour?"

"Who knows what'll happen if we don't leave." She pointed to the window.

A second police car pulled in.

Tim exhaled.

"This just keeps getting better and better. Here, take this."

He handed her something. It was a canvas bag of something lumpy.

"What is it?"

"It's a grappling hook and some rope. In case we need to rappel off one of the back windows."

"Thanks. I didn't know we were supposed to bring presents."

He took a second to remind himself that she wasn't joking.

"It's okay. I forgive you. So what's it going to be? Staying? Rappeling? Or do we try to make it to the ground floor and bet on finding a back door. Rappeling would be fun."

"I'm voting back door."

Deb started belly crawling towards the entrance, Tim behind her.

"This story is going to need a lot of work. In fifty years."

Eventually, they made it out the door and down the steps. Nobody heard. Nobody rushed them. Coming to the ground floor Deb pointed towards the back.

"You were right. There's your door."

"If that's Beau outside, let's just go talk to him. We can straighten it all out."

"No, you go home. I'll fix it with Beau."

"Not happening. I'm going with you."

She made an instantaneous decision.

Pivoting on her left foot, she swung her body around and grabbed Tim around the neck in a sleeper hold. Knowing she was seriously out-gunned, she dropped to the floor, dragging him with her.

"Seriously? You want me to hurt you?"

Lying there with her arms wrapped around his neck, with him on top of her, she thought he might laugh.

There was no doubt that he could hurt her. She squeezed a little bit, underlining her threat, painfully aware of their size difference and the futility of her bluff.

"Go home."

"I'm not going to fight my own sister."

"Go home."

"Okay. Okay already. Uncle. I have officially called Uncle."

She released.

He shuffled a foot or two away. She watched closely.

He sat quietly. She wondered if he was going to try a surprise attack. He did not.

In a quiet voice, as if he were in church, he said, "I want my grappling hook and rope back."

She conceded.

He didn't look back.

She heard the back door close. It sounded more like a slam.

After giving him five minutes, she walked up to Beau's police car as if she owned it.

"Hey, Beau."

"Hey there. What are you doing out?"

The first question immediately flummoxed her. Having no answer, she froze.

He waited for a while, maybe thirty seconds.

"Can't sleep?"

"It is true. I cannot."

She made no facial expression. She didn't move.

Beau shifted a bit, uncomfortable.

"You okay?"

There was a beat in which nothing happened, then she smiled. It looked and felt mechanical. She looked at him.

"I am fine. I am just out thinking things over."

"You too? Did you know that young boy lived around here, in these very apartments?"

"Really? Small world, huh."

She stood like a statue. He waited. He finally spoke again.

"My teams have been here all week, of course."

She was a statue.

"There's nothing left in the apartment. Just dust."

Still the statue.

She shot a glance at him. She was fearful of discovery. He knew. He had to know.

She knew he knew.

He made a sound like "Hmmppph." He didn't follow up.

"Hey, if you can't sleep either, why not go out for a cup of coffee? There is a case or two that I could use your help on."

She didn't need to check to make sure that her lockpicking kit was still in her cargo pocket.

"No. I have to go."

She instantaneously moved.

She turned and walked directly away. She wore no expression and was careful not to display any nuance in her gait.

She just left.

He did not come after her.

Instead of walking out, she walked behind, around back of the apartments. She wanted to make sure Tim had really left.

He was gone. She followed.

Seeing the door, she stopped after just a few steps. She looked at the door, the lock. She was missing something.

There was one more lock. It was obvious. She had forgotten all about it.

Still out-of-sight, she carefully crept back up the back way, back into the building.

She entered the landing area.

There. Bingo. Scanning to still make sure nobody was around, she got out the kit and picked the lock on the apartment's mailbox.

Breaking into mailboxes.

She was pretty sure that was a crime.

Finishing, she had to avoid the parking lot. In her hand, she had a letter she had found.

Going out the back door, she read the outside. It was addressed to that apartment, to a "Sam Featherstone."

It was from EigenCorp.

It was the same letter she had shown her dad. The one that had offered her the job.

She moved as quickly as she could, trying to make it to the intersection.

Made it to the end.

More blue lights.

Beau.

He rolled his window down. He waved. He had the wave of a cat to a mouse he'd caught out in the open.

"I should give you a ride home," he said, "Your dad would skin me alive if I didn't offer."

She walked closer. She smiled.

"No thank you. I am good."

He kept staring.

"Really I am."

He gave up.

"Just be careful, Deb. This is a small town, but it's not always safe at night."

She stepped back.

"I will try not to hurt anybody."

1.09

Fashionable Spying

"This is stupid. You are stupid. I do not want to go. I will hurt you if you make me go."

Sal scowled.

"Did you just escape from Dreamsicle Prison? Could you at least take the hat off? Please clown? I'll buy you a squirt flower."

"But you said one color."

"I didn't mean neon orange, and vertical white stripes. That's not even one color. You look like you're starring in a weird Japanese game show."

Deb took off her stocking cap, but not without a scowl of her own. She mumbled something about white not being a color.

They walked from their car to one of the many strip malls in town. In the middle was LGM comics. On one side was a new fashion place that Sal had been gushing about for the last week.

It was a compromise.

"This store," Deb pointed at the comic book place, "has the worst inventory and selection of any store within a hundred-mile radius. This, therefore, is stupid."

As if repeating to a small child, Sal said, "Remember, we said you go with me to my place, and I'll go with you to yours. Compromise. See?"

Salomé looked pleased, as if something great had been accomplished, like she had just finished an especially difficult casserole on a 1950s cooking show.

"My place first," Deb made an especially angry face, "I took my hat off."

She then looked at her sister up and down, trying to give her a similar inspection to what she just received.

"You sure you should be wearing those spiky things?"

"Shoes? They're called shoes. High-heeled shoes. This is the city. People dress that way here. They wear shoes."

"If you say so."

They entered the brightly-lit store. They were greeted by life-sized cardboard superheroes.

Sal knew none of them.

"Why don't you see if they have a sequel to that book you've been reading?"

"Psychopathic Robot Giraffes of Babylon?" I doubt it. The inventory here is always three months behind everywhere else. There's a standard deviation of 7.3 days, of course."

"Of course. How about some comic books? I mean graphic novels?"

She walked over to the shelf. She stared at it. After ten seconds she walked back.

"There are 11 authors I follow, all of which have both won awards and been in the top ten sellers list in the past five years. Of these, three they don't even carry. One gets sold out before I can make it here and …"

"Ok. Ok. I get it. No comic novels. My sister. Have I ever told you that you're a very hard person to make happy?"

"Really? I don't think so. What about you? Why don't you get something? Check the other side. Or this side. Maybe there's something you'd like."

"It's a sixty-foot shelf."

"We've got time."

"No, dear clown, this place is just for you."

"I've been here 17 times since they opened."

"Bet you have." Sal tried to move things along, "How about a rubber mask? Like to get a new mask?"

"I suspect," she lowered her voice to a whisper and looked around for eavesdroppers, "something's wrong here."

Sal lowered her voice as well.

"Aside from me being here? And your clothes?"

"The inventory movement pattern does not match up, even remotely, to similar shops in this genre."

Sal gave up whispering.

"How about we get a coffee later."

Sal joined Deb in looking about suspiciously. She was afraid too, afraid of being seen with her sister.

Finally she rubbed her face in weariness.

"Clown, it's impossible to keep track of all of the numeric trivia in that head of yours. If you want them to carry something else, why don't you just speak to the manager?"

"You think that's an option?"

"As long as you whisper, pretty sure."

"I'm not very good at persuasion."

"But you're good at math and numbers and such. You're great at arguing. How about a letter? We could write a letter."

"You can write the letter. I will tell you if it's correct or not. Yikes! There he is!"

Deb moved back a little bit behind Sal.

The manager came over. He had a plastic smile.

"Ladies, we're closing for 30 minutes." the balding, fat, sweaty middle-aged man said. He eyed them as if he were deathly afraid that at any minute they might start asking him questions.

Sal checked a phone.

"But it's only 2."

"Just for lunch. See?" he looked around, "I'm the only one here."

He left, flipping the sign on the door on the way back to the register, stopping before he got there, turning back to them.

"Feel free to make your purchases or whatnot," he emphasized whatnot, "I'll reopen in about 30 minutes."

His face scrunched.

"Sorry for the inconvenience."

"Thanks," Sal turned to Deb as the man tried to look like he was walking off, but ended up being a stalker, leering at them from behind the counter. "Could you just buy one of these comics or books of yours. Pick one."

"I told you. These are all dumb. I will not buy them. I am not here to buy them."

"You're exasperating. I give up. Why are you here?"

"Because I love you, Salomé, and I need your advice. You seem to enjoy this kind of thing. The shopping. Why are you here?"

"I need help moving all my stuff back home. Might need somebody to help with Dad again."

"Ladies!"

The manager who had been lurking shook his head in disgust and disappeared into the back of the shop.

"Alright," Sal said, "If you're not going to, I'll buy something."

She picked up a book at random.

"Here, this looks like something you would buy."

"Bonehead Mysteries #7? The Bonehead series doesn't even have a consistent magic system! Philistine!"

"Well, it'll have to do."

Debian almost ripped the book from her hand. She put it back, hesitated a second, then handed her another one.

"If you're going to read that kiddie fantasy porn, at least get a classic. Here. Read this one."

"Demonic Dingleberries of DarkTree?"

Deb pointed to the book, a hell yeah all over her face.

"Absolutely. The entire Demonic Dingleberry series is first class."

"You say so."

"I don't know if you know this, but in book three he explains the Fundamental Theorem of Calculus using unicorn livers."

"I can't wait."

They heard a sharp honking as a car sped by in front of the store, far too fast for a parking lot.

Deb stepped back again, trying to find something to busy herself in the back of the store while her sister chased down the little angry fat man. She wanted no part of that.

But instead Sal just looked out into the street.

"Is that who I think it is?"

"Who?"

"It's Dad across the street over by the coffee shop."

"Let me see."

Deb started over.

"You stay right there behind Iron Man."

"It's Insidious Invictus, Hero of the Lost Orphans."

"Whatever. A blind man could see you from the moon. Looks like he's talking to somebody. Let's see who it is."

"Do you know him?"

"No, but he looks familiar."

Glaring at Sal did not seem to make her respond. Deb decided on attacking her with single words.

"Well. Speak. What. Anything. Old? Young? Tall? Short? Data. Need. More. Data. Hey. You."

She threatened to walk over, taking a step. Sal noticed.

"Please produce data."

"Tom Ford."

"I've never met Tom Ford."

"It's a Tom Ford suit, stupid. The man's wearing a Tom Ford suit. Big hunk of money for that. And he's cute."

"That's great. Just what I wanted. Now that we've established his fashion sense and wallet size, what else? Did he come with anybody? Hair color? Just forget it. You're the worst spy ever."

Deb started walking to the window.

"Dealing with you is like trying to play chess using monkeys."

"Well, he's leaving now, so there."

She arrived at the window just in time to see the man turn the corner around the side of the building and leave.

"Drat. What's that Dad's carrying?"

"Nothing. Just one of those big envelopes. They traded large envelopes."

Debian sighed as loud as she could.

"And they say we're related."

From far away, they saw their dad turn. He spotted the bright orange that Deb was wearing from 300 yards away across a busy highway. He gave them a big wave overhead, a man seeing a fellow hiker from across a canyon.

They both made little small waves, their hands not rising above their bellies.

Sal looked at the book in her hand.

"Well, that went about as I expected."

She patted Deb on the hand the way you would a small child.

"What about you and I could cosplay? That might work for both of us. I can do costumes, you can do weirdo."

She watched her sister pay and return.

"I like it, Salomé. I'm thinking we go as one of those old-timey comedian pairs where they're always falling down or hitting each other accidentally. Remember The Three Stooges? We can do a lot of tossing pies and running around trains."

"Slapstick. It's called slapstick. I don't know. Maybe. Might be nice. That's a good idea. You have good ideas. Sometimes."

Sal smiled.

Deb remembered that hitting people was bad.

They stepped back out into the sunlight.

She looked at Sal.

"I've had some problems in the past obsessing about things."

"Have you? Haven't noticed. Shocked I am."

"I need your advice."

That stopped them from continuing. She stamped her foot in disgust. Tried summoning up the words again.

"I need your advice as a trusted older person."

Sal was expressionless. Deb continued.

"Much older. And dumber."

Deb looked across the street to where they had seen their dad.

"Is this going somewhere or are you just going to continue buttering me up?"

"Okay," Deb blew out like a person blowing up an imaginary balloon and all the words came at once, "weird stuff's happening how do I know if I'm going too far I need you to help."

It was all a jumble of words. Sal began parsing.

"There," Deb concluded.

Sal raised an eyebrow.

"Depends. What can you do for me? After this you'll help me finish my moving?"

"Yes. I will be your box mover slave troll. But just for the afternoon."

"Then I will be your spirit animal Obi Wan. I'll tell you if you're going too far."

They spit on their hands and shook, just like they had done since they were children.

Both looked at where they saw their father, each of them afraid to add any detail to the deal while the deal was still fresh.

Finally, Sal looked again at her newly bought book. It had a picture of a sheep's butt on the cover.

"Do I still have to read this?"

"Only if you know what's good for you. Yes."

"Now me. Your turn to butter me up. Let's go."

Sal escorted her to the new fashion store, excited to finally be experiencing it all.

Deb tailed along.

"How about the other part? You going to help with Dad if there's a problem?"

"Nope. Didn't agree to that. How about you. Will you help me find that envelope that he just got and see what's in there?"

"Nope. Didn't agree to that. Here, welcome. It is my people. It is … my happy placc."

She opened the door and went in first, the queen visiting the minions.

The lady in the fashion store looked at Sal. She smiled. Then Debian came in.

The lady saw her.

Debian thought the lady would have made the same face if she was the manager of a McDonalds and looked up one night to find an angry and hungry bear climbing through the drive-through window.

She slunk back again, trying to find shadows. There were none.

Sal would have none of it, instead dragging her back to the entrance.

"I will make your dreams come true. This store is your treasure, just pick something, anything."

She spread her arms as if showing off her vast empire.

"And I'll let you know if it's too expensive," she added.

Debian crossed her arms, looked about, then back to Sal.

"They got any top hats?"

"No."

"Squirt guns?"

"Definitely not."

"How about wizard wands, or mage staffs?"

"I'm pretty sure no."

"Glow-in-the-dark belts, plaid socks, rubber clown noses?"

"No, no, and no."

"Really don't have much here at all then, do they?"

She thought her older sister might have been angry from the way she was gritting her teeth, her eyes wide, her face dark red.

But it could have been some sort of allergic reaction. Deb remembered that it's best not to judge too quickly.

"Don't be like this. I don't know what you want. Just pick something, anything. My store card's still good, at least for a week or so. Play along with me."

Argghhh. Conflict. Emotion.

She looked back to the manager. If the lady had produced a tommy gun and began spraying bullets at them, it wouldn't surprise her.

"I don't. I can't. Please don't be angry. I am uncomfortable. I don't want anything here. I just want to leave. Can we please leave? The lady doesn't like us."

"Oh, nonsense," Sal said, then realized Deb was right.

The lady looked like she was about to pick up the phone and dial 9-1-1.

Sal's face got even redder and then, just like that, the storm passed. Deb knew that it was still going to be a rough ride for a bit. Her sister's temper flashed in like a storm and just as suddenly was gone. But lightning and thunder remained for while, warning all of those nearby that the shit might hit the fan yet again unless things went exactly as Sal expected them to.

It was both good to see and quite scary. She wondered how much she was in for.

Surprisingly, Sal gave up.

"I am going to beat you with a wet noodle. One day."

"This is stupid. You are stupid."

Deb let out her breath.

Oops. Too far again.

Sal balled her fists as if to strike Deb. That would have been okay. That made sense to Debian.

Instead she stamped her feet, made a loud noise, then stormed out with her sister close behind. Salomé Newbury stomped off to her certain death.

Almost.

As she stormed out, her heel caught on a defect in the sidewalk. She had been angry and not paying attention. It had only been approximately four millimeters deep, but that was enough.

She fell forward, her momentum carrying her into the road, just as a large truck went by at exactly 41.3 mph, far too fast.

Deb saw it all but was unable to speed up quickly enough.

She tried to catch her. She was too far behind.

Only by cartwheeling her arms and dropping her shoulder into a roll did Sal manage to avoid sudden death.

The driver didn't slow down. The truck continued barreling along without even brake lights flashing. Sal lay like a crab, frozen in fear, on her back, with her hands and feet up in the air.

"Damn it, Debian! You almost killed me!"

Sal was shaken, struggling to get up. She looked at her body as if she were afraid that pieces might be missing.

"Me?"

Deb wanted to do, say something. She wanted to grab her sister and shake her. She wanted to yell, at the top of her lungs, at her sister. She would yell at anything.

Instead she held out her hand.

Sal had decided on anger but as the seconds wore by and she glared at Deb, she realized there was nobody to be angry with.

So she took Deb's hand and got up.

All the way back to the car, Deb could not make Sal wear her bright orange stocking cap, even though she made a strong argument for it and it was quite obvious she was correct.

After a minute or two while the shakes wore off, Sal drove off. They were still arguing about the importance of safety versus fashion, the appropriate footwear for various kinds of activities, and the maintenance requirements of the average sidewalk as they went to her apartment.

Neither noticed the delivery truck following along, two cars and a hundred meters back.

1.10

Searching For Answers

The rock hurt her butt in ways she found unpleasant to contemplate, even to herself. Her heart, however, was deeply pleased by the front yard this morning, the sound of a breeze caressing the tall trees, squirrels, birds, and other wildlife going about their daily business. The overnight rain on the leaves smelled wonderful.

She thought that was a good trade.

Then the witch appeared.

"Say, whadya say we go for a walk?"

Sal stood with her hands on her hips, looking down on her. Sal looked at her as if Deb was a pile of dirty laundry that was going to have to be washed sooner or later.

"I like it here."

"We could go into town for breakfast."

"Thought you had to work."

"Quit."

Deb was surprised.

"I have stuff going on here that's more important."

"You didn't tell me."

"Don't tell you everything."

A county police car pulled into their long drive.

Deb pointed.

"Beau Martin's coming. I invited him over. To help."

"You didn't tell me."

"Don't tell you everything."

"Find the envelope?"

"Have any idea what this is?"

Deb held up a gray metal box. It was about half the size of a shoebox. It looked electronic.

"I have no idea. A CD collection?"

"I don't know either. It's electronic and sealed. I'll figure it out."

She put it in her cargo pocket.

Beau always managed to have junk food wrappers following him around, as if he were the unofficial pied piper of Cheez-Its. He got out of the car with a couple bags, wiped his mouth with a napkin, smiled, waved, and came over.

Deb studied him. He was out of breath. It had been a short walk.

"Beau, I've never asked you this, and apologies if I'm being rude, but doesn't your weight cause problems in the job?"

"Weight? What weight?"

"Moving along," Sal stepped between them and started going through the bags. "Oooh. Looks yummy! Thank you!"

She backed up a bit. She looked back at Deb. She was expectant. Deb accepted what was proffered.

Then, without looking at what she was holding, looked back-and-forth between the two, finally figuring out, "Thank you?"

Sal smiled to Beau as if she were showing off a new trick she had taught her puppy.

He pointed.

"There's coffee, pastries, and Slim Jims. Eat up."

"What? No tacos, fish sticks, or french fries?"

Beau looked for a second as if he was taking her seriously, instead he smiled.

"I could have brought lawyers, guns, and money, but things didn't look that bad."

"Why would we want guns?" Deb said, "To rob the lawyers?"

Sigh.

"Old, old. Lordy I'm old. The phrase 'bring lawyers, guns, and money' is before your time. Before my time, probably. It means there's an emergency. Big problems. We have troubles, problems, and questions, but no emergencies so far, right?"

Debian shrugged.

"Ask her," Sal pointed at Deb, "The Grand Wizard ChessMaster seems to be planning our day."

"GrandMaster. There is no such thing as a Grand Wizard."

"See?"

"I know you called me to try to help you both sort things out, but I've brought extra trouble. The Feds should be here any minute."

He looked back down the drive.

"Feds?" Deb cocked her head in confusion, "What for?"

"Your guess is as good as mine. Why would they tell the local Sheriff anything? No sense in that."

Sure enough, as he spoke the first cars started coming in the driveway. There were five, more on the way.

"I'm sorry," Deb said, "That sucks. They should have cleared it with you. Perhaps they thought there was a conflict of interest."

"Meh. Let's see where this is going."

He took a long pull of his coffee, warily watching the arrival.

"Who knows?" Deb continued. she smiled at Sal, then at Beau. "It could be fun! We've got nothing to hide. We'll probably learn more about them than they'll learn about us, and hell, maybe they can help. We're an open book, right?"

He only mumbled.

This was going to take a while. Sal sat.

"Ouch! This rock! Hanging out in my own front yard, pointy rocks, watching a platoon of cops toss the house for an hour or two. Not fun."

"Welp, I'm here. Here I be." He munched on a pastry. "I'm not going anywhere. Maybe we could get the cards out later, move this party to the picnic table."

A thin, angry man in a bad suit walked over. He looked at Beau.
"Paul Newbury?"

Sal made an expression like "look at this moron who can't tell the difference between the local sheriff and our dad, but before Sal could speak, Deb interrupted.

"He's away. Business. We're the daughters. We're both adults. We both live here."

The man turned to face them, checked his papers, then handed them off.

"You've been served. This is a search warrant. Anybody in the house?"

Sal slowly shook her head no.

"Tim's around back. I think."

"Good. We'll let you know when we're finished."

He then walked away. They all looked at one another like "get a load of that one."

Sal looked at the stack of papers.

"Didn't expect that."

Deb saw that there were nine cars in all. They were all the same model and parked equidistant from one another in the drive about 1.5 meters off-center, leaving enough space for other traffic to get by. A large white box truck came in last. Men got out in what Deb had heard people call "Bunny Suits" although they looked nothing like bunnies, nor were they suits. It was a question for another day.

"Hey Deb, let's you and me take these leftovers over to them, share a bit."

Beau stopped them.

"Probably not a good idea. I know how they work. They've eaten. They've already eaten and they've also probably got lunch and dinner pre-ordered from a local delivery service."

"Dinner?"

Beau nodded.

Deb didn't know her position. The entire concept of dozens of people filtering all over the house and yard until perhaps long after supper was beyond her ability to immediately compute.

Instead she said, "You're fat."

Sal looked for a brief moment as if she were being electrocuted, but Beau just laughed it off.

"I am. You know, I am. I'm what they call a bit chunky or large-boned. Slim Jim?"

He held it up as if he were having an idea.

She began staring at the ground in front of her.

"We're good, aren't we?" Sal asked a question but it was obvious that no answer was expected, so Deb continued working the problem.

"Is that our dolls …. I mean Action Figures? Who would want those old things?"

A female agent was carrying a cardboard box stuffed with Deb's figurines from her room.

"Awful weird," Beau said, "Why would anybody want that? What kind of investigation needs those?"

Deb sat motionless, her face blank, staring at the ground.

"I can call the lightning."

Beau reached for a small notepad.

"What. Say again. Lightning? Could that be why they're here?"

He gestured at the activity.

Deb kept staring straight ahead. Finally he waved his hand back-and-forth in front of her face.

"Anybody home? Debian?"

"Beau," Sal pointed at his notepad he was writing in, shaking her head no for him to stop, "Dad should be here."

"Why? She's not a minor. This isn't an interrogation."

"Serious."

Shrugged, put the pad away.

"It's just hard to figure out, that's all."

Deb must have heard him, broke her gaze, looked at Beau.

He continued.

"You know me, girls. I love you guys to pieces. Like you were my own. If I thought there were any kind of crime here, I wouldn't be here. It wouldn't be good for any of us."

"Ow! Damn it! I don't like this!" Sal stood up, rubbing her butt. "I ain't going to sit on this pointy stupid rock any more! Let's get some chairs or something. This is stupid! It's the modern world. We don't need rocks. Chairs."

She looked at Deb with a question on her face. Volley served.

Beau again reached for his notebook, realized what he was doing, and put his hand back.

Getting no response from her sister, Sal turned to assess Beau. Deb looked up, also recognizing the man.

"Beau, are you actually helping here?" she said.

Sal crossed her arms in agreement. She pointed to the people in the yard, looked back to him.

"Could you see if we can get an explanation?"

"I can," he subconsciously gripped his pistol, as if he might need to shoot the FBI agents, squared his shoulders. "And I will. I'll find out."

There followed an animated conversation out of earshot. Beau pointed at the girls. The agent pointed at the house. Beau looked quite angry. The man leaned back, listening, then said some things back.

Whatever it was, this made Beau even more animated. Finally, in a gesture of brotherly conspiracy, the man put his hands on Beau's shoulders, stooped down a bit. They both walked further away where the conversation continued.

Eventually, Beau pulled back, looked at the man as if the man had announced giant weasels existed and could fly.

The man nodded.

Beau blushed. He did not look back at the girls. Instead, head hung low, he walked back to the car. Just before he got in, he paused, reconsidered, then left.

"Didn't expect that," Sal said.

Deb went back to staring at the ground, the little ants working hard at their anthill.

Sal waited. There was no response.

"I guess cards are out of the question."

Still nothing.

"Whatdya say we…"

Deb tossed the remaining pastry at the ants. Then she reached over, took the entire box of remaining pastries, and hurled them at the anthill.

She still had no expression.

The ants started coming out to consume their newfound bonanza. Debian silently watched.

Sal looked worried.

Taking a deep breath, "That's it. Somebody has to. I'm going to figure out what's going on if nobody else is going to."

She waved the man over who had spoken to Beau. He walked over and she met him about halfway.

"Ms. Newbury."

One of the other agents walked over, saw Deb's pastry mess, made a sound of disgust, then started cleaning it up.

"Dickhead."

"Ma'am, if your language continues to be abusive, we're going to have problems. You don't need more problems."

Sal paused for a minute and gathered her thoughts.

The other agent finished picking up the pastries. Then he started squashing all the ants he could find, grinding them with his shoe. Methodically.

"Mr. FBI agent sir," Sal tried again, "We need an explanation about what's going on here."

There was a crash from inside the house. Something had fallen over.

"We asked our friend, the sheriff, to help us," Sal began, "obviously he couldn't stay…."

"Fuck!" some agent yelled from inside the house, no doubt a result of the crash.

It was obvious Sal had many snarky things to say. She did not say them.

"You know, that's an excellent idea," the skinny man said, looking over to Deb on her rock.

He closed the distance, addressed them both.

"Why don't I help? We could go to the office, I'll buy you both lunch. We can do an interview, I can get you up to speed on all of this. No problem."

He smiled, their new best friend.

Deb jerked to seriously stare at her sister.

"Money, guns, and ..."

Seeing where she was going, Sal finished the thought "Lawyers."

Deb quickly indicated yes.

Sal looked back at the agent. They had reached a conclusion.

"Lawyer."

The agent shifted his weight, cleared his throat. He stopped smiling.

"Okay then."

"But obviously we need to know what this warrant is for, why you're here."

He smiled a new smile. The smile was the smile the cat has for the mouse.

"Somebody needs to explain," Sal added.

He pointed to the papers.

"Lawyer."

Obviously thinking his banter was just hilarious, he left.

Deb stood up. Her butt still hurt. That might take a while.

The yard looked like a convention for 21st-century cop cosplayers. It was noisy, busy, and it stank. Their house and yard, normally empty of any electronics, was stuffed full of them.

She brushed off her butt.

"Where you going?"

"Anywhere alone."

"Not on your life. Come on, let's find Tim."

"You can't leave." the agent noticed them.

Deb stared.

"Don't wanna."

"Can't go in the house."

"I know."

Gritting their teeth, they left for the backyard, hoping to find Timothy.

1.11

Convincing Tim

Tim wanted to be left alone even more than Deb did.

He obviously needed cheering up.

They finally found him out by the creek way in the back, propped up against the old maple, reading "The Count of Monte Cristo."

"Go away."

He didn't look up.

"Aren't you curious about all the commotion out front?" Sal stood with her arms akimbo.

She looked like mom asking why his room wasn't clean.

Again, not looking up, "Ok, I'll bite. Why all the cops?"

Deb looked at Sal. Sal looked at the stack of papers she was holding. Sal shrugged.

"We don't know."

"Go away."

He went back to reading.

"He's right. We should leave Tim alone," Deb said.

She sat down next to him.

Sal sat on the other side.

"I agree."

Sal leaned over and spoke to Deb across their brother.

"Probably much too busy reading to talk to us."

"That's a good book," Deb said, pointing, "One of my favorites, Tim. Where'd you get it?"

He grunted a reply. He kept reading.

"Probably the basement," Sal said, "All kinds of junk down there. What a mess."

'Perhaps reading's not such a bad idea, Salomé." Deb said as formally as she could manage.

"And just sit by here doing nothing, listen to the creek? Might as well be a fish."

She threw a rock. She missed the creek. It was five feet away.

"What's there to do? And who are we, really, to do anything?"

Sal was much better at over acting than Deb was.

Tim still kept trying to read.

Deb looked from the book up into her brother's face.

"We just got started. We can't just give up. We can finish this."

"How about you two just let things play out," Tim said, "but why am I talking to you?"

"I know you both don't want to hear this," Sal said, leaning back and stretching, "but this kind of thing is perfect for a content streaming series. I know these things."

"Great idea," Deb replied, "You're right. Nobody wants to do that except you."

"Listen, we need to make noise, engage everybody. This is the kind of thing where bringing attention to yourself is a good thing. It could help set things right."

"The oracle of social media speaks," Tim said. He kept at his book. His brow furrowed.

Debian searched.

"I don't like us just sitting around reading; and I love reading."

Sal twisted the other way, stretching her back.

"I don't like nobody knowing nothing about what we're going through. Dad's getting screwed. It's just not right. It shouldn't be hidden. I hate it."

"Here's an idea," Tim said, trying even harder not to look up, "Why don't you each just get your own books? Try reading?"

He glanced up for a second. He did not look at them. Instead he looked down again.

"You could read. You both could read. Quietly. Somewhere else."

"Who wrote that book, 'The Count of Monte Cristo'?" Sal said, finally taking in the book, "Dum —- Ass? Seriously? This book was written by Dum … Ass?"

"I'm not playing with you." he said.

She was having none of it, though.

"So you just want to do nothing? Sit there and read your old dumbass book?"

That did it. Tim gave up. He closed his book, put his hands on his lap. He squared his shoulders.

"I'd like a little bit of control in life, thank you very much, something I'm not seeing so far today. Games aren't fun when you're just a piece on the board."

"Well, of course we can always read. Reading doesn't take much of nothing at all."

Deb leaned in, trying a different approach.

"Book's good, isn't it?"

Tim brightened. He engaged.

"Here's a guy that's definitely on a mission to make things right. He's bringing it."

"Both happy and sad. I liked it."

"Me too. At least so far."

Sal crossed her arms.

"Never heard of it. Does the author have any videos online?" she asked. "With a name like that, I bet they pick on him a lot."

"He's been dead a long time," Deb said.

"So like ten years? Fifteen?"

"He doesn't have videos, Sal." Tim said.

"Don't you think that we should at least try to make things right for Dad," Deb said, "even if we just gather together things that we might make into a video one day, who knows? Dad may need it, and we'll have it all ready."

Tim grimaced.

"Look around you. Take a good look. It's the federal government. This isn't some random visit, it's the result of a lot of research they've already done. We don't know what it is. Can either of you describe anything I can do that you can assure me will make a difference?"

Sal started to respond, but he kept going.

"And don't argue with me about whether it's important or not," he stopped them before they could reply, "I know it's important. My question is can we actually help or just churn things around at home more?"

"Why churn," Deb responded, "I think we stay here, set up a headquarters. We can organize what we already have."

"So, you mean hide." Sal said.

"Not hide, just limit our public exposure."

"The exact opposite of what we should do," Sal said.

"And the endless drama continues." Tim looked at his book, picked it back up again, but did not open it.

"Not his fault. Runts are always the unhappy puppies," Sal said. She winked. An inside joke.

"And witches are always stirring up things they don't need to," Deb said.

They both looked at Tim expectantly. He refused to take the bait.

Reaching in, Sal finally yanked the book from his lap.

"Pay attention."

Sal was the older sister. He was the brat.

Tim yanked it back. He dog-eared a corner where he was at and sat it down. He reconsidered, then he pushed it as far from his lap as he could reach, daring her to grab it again.

He returned to staring straight ahead at the stream, silent.

Finally he spoke.

"Where would we put anything? There's no computer. Nobody should carry stuff around, we couldn't share. But we can't just leave stuff willy-nilly lying around either. So where? How would we even decide what to collect, how to organize it, how to sort out the important from the trivial? This is not 'let's prove something is a lie' like we were doing. Whatever's happening here is involved, complex. This is much more about setting up an entire case file or something, a history of Dad."

"He's right," Sal finally admitted. "We haven't done much. I've got some information on the shooter's friends. Deb's hacked into his computer. But now if there's something bigger going on, it's going to get a lot tougher. Who knows how big it'll get. Gather and connect who knows how much more, and us with nothing. And there's always the fact that there may be nothing to find."

"Bad things happen," Deb said, "Yes, there could be nothing. But no, this looks somehow planned to me. There is a greater narrative to find. There's a big missing piece. Somehow. There's somebody else. I know it."

Tim looked at her, "Even if you're right, all we've got is unorganized tidbits, trivia, junk. We've never done anything like this. This is the kinda thing you hire a private investigator for."

"Tidbidts? Junk?" Sal said, "Like the basement?"

Deb looked to Tim.

"You think we could clear out enough space in the basement to put together a command post, a headquarters?"

He rubbed his chin. He looked sad. The conversation had overtaken his objections.

"Hmmm. Might work," he finally admitted.

"Great then," Sal said, standing, rubbing her hands together, "I'll be the General. The basement will be my throne."

"No," Tim replied, "That's not going to work."

She couldn't hide the hurt feelings.

"It's not that," Tim said, "You would be a great General, but we need you out working the public. That's your thing. It's what you're great at. Deb here can be our Sherlock Holmes."

"Cool. I will build a nest for us, our secret basement lair." Deb said, catching on, "but the Golden Rule stays in place. That's not negotiable. No tech."

She looked in disgust at the front yard where all the agents and technology had swarmed them.

"Then what do I do? How about me?" Tim asked.

He caught himself before he went too far. He rephrased.

"What is the minimum you guys require from me in order to leave me alone?"

"Spy," Deb answered immediately, "You need to be the spy. People naturally trust you. We can use that. You find out things. People things. I don't do people."

"Great," he tried it on, "Tim Newbury, Man of Letters."

"Do we all know what we're doing?"

They all moaned. Another one of Deb's famous recap times.

Sal started.

"I'm working outside resources on the condition that I eventually get to publish this stuff."

Tim almost jumped in to interrupt, but Deb hushed him.

"By outside resources, Sal, we mean the library, TV, college, newspapers, any public record or relations. How about you, Tim?"

"I'm interrogating people. I shouldn't be, but you two seem determined to drag me into this."

"Continue. Getting information where."

"That's, I'm guessing: Dad, Beau, the people Dad works with, and so on."

"Okay."

"But then I'm left out of it. Sure, I'll hang and gossip, but for the most part, after this, you're on your own. My official, secret agent position is this: knowing when to give up is the best part of playing any game. Now is that time. This is where we are."

"Message received. Fair enough."

He never got back to his book.

1.12

Watching The Watchers

The people of the little town of Liberty weren't ants, but that's what they looked like from far above.

From 15,000 feet, the operating altitude of a Mark II Lockheed-Martin 420K Aerostat, people were truly tiny, almost invisible without a high-resolution camera. The 420K had several. Each person and vehicle's movement could be tracked and recorded over time, sometimes for months. You could tell what they were wearing, lip-read what they were saying, determine details down to the level of the kinds of shoelaces they preferred.

It used simple, wide-angle telescopes, turned the other way, stuck in a balloon, and constantly recording.

In the late 1990s, an action-thriller movie titled "Enemy of the State" told a story about satellites always overhead watching everything everybody did. It was fiction, of course, but scientists and engineers watched the movie and wondered if such a thing was possible. As happens in so many cases, fiction became reality.

The War on Terror accelerated development. Weeks of everybody's actions on disk meant that if a bombing occurred, you played back the tape to see where the bomber came from, who he met with, where they came from. It was like being God.

For decades, satellites had been used for this kind of long-term surveillance. They worked well enough for observing people all of the time, but having so many in geosynchronous orbit got expensive, cumbersome. They were replaced by drones, then Lighter-Than-Air (LTA) vehicles. These helium balloon-based platforms were called Persistent Surveillance Systems (PSS). Way back in the 2010s, they became a hot product. Today, nobody knew how long any particular LTA PSS stayed in place, how many there were, or even where they patrolled, including the governments controlling the airspace overhead. They went higher. They adopted stealth. They had no motors. There was no heat signature. They had no radar signature. Their coloration made them invisible. They were much, much cheaper than satellites. Unless you owned and operated one, they were invisible to you. Nobody could tell where they were. They didn't exist.

The sun rose.

Whether being observed or not, the people of Liberty all went about their normal day. Teachers went to school. Lawyers went to court. Over a huge area, tens of thousands of people went about tens of thousands of ordinary lives in tens of thousands of ordinary ways.

Life was good.

On his way to work, Beau Martin looked forward to a day empty of meetings. It was a chance to get caught up on some old work.

Paul Newbury also looked forward to the day. He headed out of town to a board meeting at The Foundation. It was a chance to give project updates and feel the board out for how much future work there was.

Salomé was her usual perky, gregarious, and obsequious self. Preparing at the coffee shop, she armed herself with a double latte. She had a new outfit, a spring in her step and a song in her heart.

Now she just needed to sell it.

Timothy Newbury was not happy about his new role as a spy, but he liked talking to folks, and he figured there really wasn't much difference between chatting and spying. Both activities were just gathering information. How to use it happened later. It wasn't like he'd be parachuting at night into an Evil Villain's hideout. Dammit.

Debian waited outside the library until it opened, which happened at three minutes past the hour. Of the 31 times she had came to town in the last 1123 days, the doors had been late opening 19.35% of the time. She seriously considered writing an angry letter as Sal had showed her back at the comic book store. Instead, she decided to give it more time, gather more data. The letter might require a graph.

Back at the police station, Tim stopped in to see Beau. Beau wouldn't have agreed to meet anybody else aside from the Newbury family on such short notice. Even then, he didn't have much time. Very sorry. He was deep in a case. We'll figure something out.

"Any lunchtime this week, Tim," he offered, "Just drop by. We can catch up."

Watching Tim leave, Beau hoped he could help the boy. That family had been through hell, much of it brought on by themselves. Sad story.

The phone rang. Beau cursed quietly. The day was not turning out like it should.

Sal knew a dozen people hooked into all sorts of media and none of them were answering her texts. Fine, she could do it the hard way. She left the shop, fresh caffeine reload, and headed towards the car.

Many miles away, Paul sat in the conference room, mouth agape. He was being fired – or suspended – he couldn't exactly tell which. They used a lot of non-descriptive politician words and phrases, delivered with fake smiles.

It was effective immediately. Your pay will continue throughout the year. Your benefits are still good. We still believe in you. We still appreciate all the work you've done. You are our hero, a leader in the field.

We'll be in touch.

Don't call us, we'll call you.

It took some time to gather his things. He sat in the conference room by himself for the next half hour.

Back in town, Tim kicked the tire. Freaking piece of shit.

The car wouldn't start.

Worst part? It didn't matter. Beau was the third person he'd called on. None of them had time to chat. Everyone of them said later. None had given an actual time later. At least Beau had been nice, but even he looked pissed about something.

Now he had a new problem. Great.

At the library, Deb pushed back from the carousel. Two-Factor Authorization (TFA), the kind where you get a text message or use a hardware key to log-in, was required to get in the bank accounts.

Hardware security keys were always the toughest.

She cracked her knuckles. She was happy. Puzzles. Fun time.

She had a couple of tricks up her sleeve.

As each person worked on their projects, in the distance, Beau, Paul, Deb, and Sal all heard screeching, a crash, metal on metal. There was a horrible thump. Those outside saw flames shoot up. Black smoke followed.

Many of the townspeople came outside to see.

Beau got the call within minutes. An electric car had broken down in a bad spot. It had started updating and rebooting just as it was crossing the train tracks out by Miller's Crossing.

The passengers had gotten out, thankfully, but a fully loaded train had completely destroyed their car and the subsequent lithium-ion fire plus derailed train was going to be a big production; another big production.

He groaned.

He put the papers away. He frowned. He tried to take one last look. He felt like a kid cheating on an exam, spending time on one job that he should be spending on another.

Once something bugged him, something didn't add up on a case, he'd worry at it for years if necessary to tease out what was bothering him. This cold case bugged him like no other.

He had been working on it for years. A few more days wouldn't matter. Best to get out to the accident and help manage the work.

He grabbed his hat on the way out. He came immediately back in.

He almost forgot his morning XL energy drink and bag of corn chips. It was a close call.

On the other side of town, Paul was sitting in his car in a long line of cars, a half-mile of cars lined up for the wreck at the railroad crossing. He watched the black smoke. His grip tightened on the steering wheel. As he watched, even more fire trucks showed up. He thought he heard a helicopter.

What a mess.

He wasn't going to fight their suspension. At least he wouldn't fight it the way they expected. Instead, he had his own plans. His plans began with sorting out his family life. There were some serious problems there. Unless something was done, a big storm was on the way.

Up ahead, Tim had barely jumped out of his friend's EV in time before the train hit it. They took five minutes trying to get that stupid car rebooted.

Both had seen the light coming around the bend and heard the whistle. Both had been scared shitless, having problems just unlocking the doors in their haste to leave.

Who would make a car that would reboot while driving? How stupid is that?

Standing there deciding whether to wait on the cops or bounce, he decided that this wasn't working. He bailed out. He bounced, looking for a public phone. He was sure the suits would catch him for an interview. They did last time.

Being a spy sucked.

Deb did not go outside when the wreck happened. She didn't notice it.

She was absorbed in the work. Finishing up, she finally heard fire engines driving by. She gathered some printouts and wiped the PC. Nobody could clear online tracks, of course. There were a dozen tracking systems inside the walls of this library within twenty feet of her chair. Truly wiping your tracks was a Hollywood myth. But she went through the motions anyway. Like brushing her teeth, she believed in good hygiene.

She had accessed all the data she wanted from the banking systems associated with her dad, the student, and entities that intersected the two.

There was no pattern she could see. That meant there was no pattern, right?

Wasn't sure.

Take home.

More work needed.

An hour earlier, across town, Sal sat in an office talking to another dear friend on her list. She couldn't believe what she was hearing.

They needed an event to cover. An event. They didn't want stories that required a lot of work. Nobody had time for that. If they took an entire day to research a story? By the time they aired it a dozen other smaller stories would have broke online without them being able to pitch in. That "long tail" traffic, a bunch of little stories that still emotionally impacted people, just in smaller batches, would cumulatively generate a lot more interest than one big story no matter how good it was. They could afford maybe an hour, IF the story was already baked.

Before she could begin to figure out how that would work, all of their phones started buzzing and they ran off.

Some big fire across town. As if that were important.

Now what was she going to do?

Well, if they wanted an event, she'd give them an event.

A bit later, back at the house, Deb got home first. She headed immediately to their new lair.

She felt a bit like Batman. Maybe they could put in a pole.

Her mind began sorting.

There was something about the timing of the banking transactions. There was a TV show that had unusual air times back in the day. The neighbors had not been mowing the grass in the same schedule they had used in previous years. There was a statistical anomaly in the structure of the note she'd found that mom had left. Something was bugging her about a utensil she used recently. Phone calls to the house were dropping off, but in a statistically normal distribution pattern, unlikely at best. Could be poor modeling on the part of some programmer.

She shivered.

There was the other thing.

Things.

She hurried up the steps and locked the door at the top, leaving herself alone underground to deal with the demons.

Tim arrived next, having given up entirely on spying, at least for today. He went to his room, eager to start in again on the continuing adventure of the Count and his plans for revenge.

The witch returned, the oldest sister. The witch came to his room, of course. She annoyed him again to the point he put his book down, went downstairs, and made a sandwich. He ate it slowly. She sat across from him, talking.

He thought about a second sandwich.

He loved his oldest sister. He wasn't too sure he liked her being back home.

Sal's experience was similar to Tim's.

She got home. She was happy to have a plan she was developing. Lots of things to organize. She would need schedules, electricity, some odd knick-knacks. Perhaps she needed some construction work. It was nothing the runt couldn't help out with, though. Tim needed to make himself useful. He liked that kind of thing.

Only he was in another of his moods. He was in his room. He was continuing his recent uncharacteristic sullen attitude. It took ten minutes of badgering just to get him started on what needed to be done.

He was such a brat.

Paul got home last, much later, after dark. He'd been for a long walk.

He'd learned early in his career that if you always acted predictably, you become an easy target.

He wouldn't.

Time to mix it up some.

Beau Martin was also working late. The accident scene wore on, the NTSB had to be brought in. People had to be billeted, teams set up, communication plans made and approved. Train accidents always meant tons of work.

Taking his hat off, he cut the light on in his office. Papers were scattered everywhere. Three Styrofoam coffee cups were half filled, standing watch in various locations. The trash overflowed. A single tennis shoe sat on top of the filing cabinet. He knew Lois snuck in here when she shouldn't and cleaned. It was not worth complaining about.

He was glad nobody had gotten hurt.

Should he try to get back to the work he'd left? Should he try to call in outside help again? It hadn't worked out very well last time.

Letting out a long breath, making up his mind to try something new, he put his hat back on. He turned the lights back off and headed home.

Reality existed elsewhere.

The evening progressed. The people continued their plans. Cell phones, traffic cameras, License Plate Readers (LPRs) and thousands of other sensors dutifully collecting and recording everything: their gait, their clothes, location, sex lives, dinner choices, sleep patterns, menstrual cycles, TV selection, thoughts on topics of the day, hobbies, emotional triggers, purchase decisions, and much, much more.

No zoo animal in history or lab rat under the closest scientific study had ever been instrumented and recorded in such detail as the average human.

Over a million separate Large Language Models (LLMS) were updated. Trillions of linkages were established, strengthened, or weakened. No linkages were deleted. Never. Once data was recorded, it only grew in complexity. Data never went away and the linkages between things never, ever goes away. It just grows.

People continued enjoying their lives and dreams, both unaware and unable to grasp the world they lived in.

Night fell.

1.13

Crazy Interviewing

The only good thing that happened to Dad that day was that he wasn't there to see the destruction of his professional career, Deb thought later.

Tim and Dad had gotten up early, leaving only a note. "Hiking. Back by dark."

Would it have made a difference if they had been there for what happened? Or would the same things have happened only slower and with more pain?

She dwelled on it for years.

Left the note where she found it. Sal was primping. It was just like old times.

"Now that you're living here, think you could do the dishes?"

She passed her hand over her as if creating Deb from thin air.

"This look of yours. I'm guessing it's Jackson Pollack Drops Acid?"

"So? You really like it?"

"You look like you're the sole survivor of a horrendous explosion in a paint store."

"Thanks. This is my study/work outfit. We've got a lot of cleaning and research today. There's more to find out about Dad. A lot more. I'm sure of it. Tim needs to report in."

Not done, but giving up on improving perfection, Sal pushed past Deb and into the hall.

Deb trailed along.

"I've got a better idea," stopping to look back to make sure Deb was still there, then back to walking. "Let's do a press interview. I know people."

"No thanks."

Stopping by the door, Sal puts a jacket on.

"They should be setting up about now."

"You're joking. You have to be joking. Tell me you're joking."

Sal brushed dirt off Debian's clothes that only Sal could see.

"It's important. With what we know, you and I can set the record straight."

"Tell you what, you go. I'll watch on TV."

"No."

"What's wrong with you? Why can't we just do our separate things? Just go separate ways?"

"What, like a hermit?"

"No, like Dad and Tim."

"Exactly. We are doing our separate things. We're just doing them together, like Dad and Tim."

"Salomé. Big sister. Witch. We don't know enough to say anything to anybody."

"Sure we do. We know these gay love charges are ludicrous. We know where Dad's been and gone over the last couple of months. We know this Stetson Parks guy, the shooter, was into self body mutilation. You even said we could figure out who Parks was actually working with once we got up into his phone."

"Which I haven't done yet."

In reply, Sal opened the front door.

"Come on, let's go. We're ready for your close-up. Miss Newbury."

Deb physically held her sister to keep her from leaving.

"Me?" She pointed at herself. "The victim of a paint shop explosion?"

Sal slowly removed Deb's hand, then patted her as if she was a small child.

"Oh, pish posh. They'll love you. We all do. Just be yourself."

"Who else would I be?"

"See? That's great. Just keep doing that."

And she walked off again, making Deb chase along behind.

She finally had to run, get in front of Sal, physically stopping her with her body.

"Do you really think this is important?" They could already hear noises beyond the privacy fence.

"We need to control the narrative."

"I don't know what that means."

"You can do this, Deb."

"I don't wanna."

"For me. For Tim. For Dad."

"Then can we get back to actually working the problem?"

"Don't talk past the sale."

"I don't know what that means either."

"It means that once we do this, once we kill this horror show once and for all? Then we're done. We don't just keep digging up stuff. Our job is putting out fires, not starting new ones. The only thing more digging would do is just make it worse."

"Digging for what."

"Exactly. We have just a few topics to cover. We cover those, we nail it, we look sad, we plea for people to help. We're done. Nothing else. Easy as pie. I might cry some."

"And Dad, and Tim….."

"Are better off somewhere else. Doing their own thing. The meek and vulnerable need to do this, the victims, us. Hillary has to be the one baking the cookies."

"I don't want to know that," she finally relented, stepped aside. "Just get it over with."

Together they reached the privacy gates. Sal pushed them open.

Deb was completely unprepared for the road outside their fence.

She remembered a video she once saw of various mating dances. Some were simple, like fighting the other potential mates. Some were so elaborate and complex that there was no reasoning with how such a series of movements would ever come to happen.

This was the second kind.

First, the simple parts. There was a van. It had a large antenna on top, microwave. Probably 5 GHz range hitting a local repeater, but it'd been a while since she'd checked the specs. She had been only eight when she did radios. There were three people, umbrellas, lights, fold-out chairs, and a person with some kind of makeup gear futzing with a lady who looked about their age but only a large board stuck up her ass would explain her demeanor.

The makeup guy was smiling. The tech guy was whistling. Mrs. Board Butt's phone rang. Suddenly she smiled as well and began what appeared to be a happy conversation. Seeing them, she waved them over, pointed to three chairs set up.

They started over. The lights around the interview area flickered. The tech guy froze, as if hoping it wouldn't happen again.

"I said get those fucking lights right this time or we'll find somebody else," the reporter stood, phone still in hand. The man turned serious, hustled around checking wires again, obviously unable to figure out what was going on.

The reporter went back to smiling and talking on the phone, then hung up. She walked over, still smiling, and shook hands.

Deb thought of the snakehouse she'd seen once in a zoo.

She didn't think snakes had mating dances.

They started the interview right then and there, not even bothering to use the chairs, just standing in front of them. Sal, of course, was vivacious and animated.

Deb assumed the position that Sal always referred to as the "Garden Gnome" she used in their family pictures.

That might be a bad thing.

"You guys aren't hiding your dad back in there somewhere, are you?"

The reporter was all smiles, pointing to the privacy fence.

Deb smiled. Sal smiled more. She was better at it. Sal responded.

"No, hah, that's funny. All we've got is a yard to mow and dishes to wash. Dad and Tim are on a day trip."

"Let me tell you about our research," Deb said. She was trying to help. "It's really not that interesting."

She explained it all to the little lady in detail, much detail, taking about fifteen minutes. She thought her explanation of the Chi Square Law was especially pithy.

From the reporter's face, Deb could tell that she agreed. It was not that interesting. Finishing, Deb put her hands on her hips, daring her.

"Don't you believe me?"

"Of course I believe you, dear." The reporter produced another reptilian smile, "That's just yesterday's news."

"The news changes everyday?"

The lady gripped the mic better, obviously winding up for her big moment. The cameraman double-checked his gear, nervous.

"Do you or your sister have any comment on your father's rumored ties to organized crime?"

Deb looked at Sal. Deb was confused.

"We were not supposed to be talking about that."

"So there's something to talk about? About the ongoing federal investigation?"

Deb stopped movement. Sal pushed ahead.

"We need to stop this interview. Take a break."

"So, you admit that you know about your dad's involvement?"

Deb froze. Discontinued facial expressions. Backed up a bit, unsure of her next moves.

More questions.

Quiet.

Slowly backing up. The fence was somewhere back there.

She heard Sal yelling.

"THAT'S not what we talked about.

"I'm sorry, miss…"

Deb cut a hard glance to her sister, who was currently going berserk.

"There's your interview."

That stopped them. They both turned.

Pausing just a beat, the reporter picked it back up.

"So no further comments?"

She turned and started back towards the gate.

She heard Sal behind.

"Get off our land."

"This is a public street."

"Hey."

Sal stopped her while she was opening the gate.

"You okay?"

Quiet.

"Hey. Say something."

"Happy?"

She moved quickly to get through the gate, closed it behind her.

As soon as it closed, as she started walking up the drive, it opened again, Sal hot on her heels.

'You come back!"

She walked quicker.

"You have to come back! We have to finish this!"

Sal ran. They both reached their front door at the same time. Deb managed to make it through first.

Hot behind her, Sal said, "There's nothing there, Deb, just more slander."

"You think."

"Yeah. I think we need to go out there and have it out. Fight back. Don't let them picture you as guilty. They love that."

"How do you know?"

"That they love guilty people?"

"That there's nothing else there."

"Because Dad, our father, the man we've known our entire lives, is not some TV mobster, that's why."

"Don't exaggerate."

"I'm not exaggerating. That reporter's going on about some Janus Group that I've never heard of. It's ridiculous."

"Like Dad's tattoo?"

"He's got lots of tattoos."

"The one on his shoulder."

"He's got four on his shoulders. There's that weird guy with the pitchfork...."

"Not that one."

"That weird double-headed dude?"

"Yeah. Janus. That's Janus. He has a tattoo of Janus."

"How'd you know that's Janus and not some other two-headed guy?"

"Because I've been digging around by myself, doing the actual work of research, like a hermit."

"Being by yourself has never been good for you, Debian. You know that."

"What do you mean by that?"

"You really want me to bring it up? You want to talk about this? About the hospital?"

Deb clenched her fists at her sides. Her body tensed. Sal immediately saw.

"Didn't think so."

The two sisters continued staring, Deb with her hands clenched and Sal nervously fuming, nothing said.

Finally Deb attacked. She punctuated each word with a poke in the chest.

"You. Leave. Me. Alone."

Then she looked around the empty house for other people although nobody else was there.

"You all. You all just leave me alone."

She almost ripped the door to the downstairs off the hinges going through it, slamming it behind her, daring her sister to follow.

Debian spent the rest of the day in the basement, vowing never to go on any more adventures with Sal, a promise, sadly, she kept.

She didn't even come up for lunch, instead she slowly went through each piece of clothing and each school paper and old receipt carefully. At times she made notes to herself on her pad. The notes consisted entirely of numbers, the occasional punctuation mark or underline.

She kept coming back to that gray box. And Janus.

She mumbled.

The light through the windows faded bit-by-bit as night approached. She finally reached for the locked chest.

She thought about leaving, but didn't.

1.14

Fatso Showdown

"That is the fattest man I've ever seen in my life."

Tim tried not to stare.

"That's Big Jim. He's going to destroy all these people. Just watch."

Beau and Tim finally had their lunch. It was the day of Fatso Roundup's Third Annual Lasagna Eating Contest.

"You could take him, Beau."

"Perhaps. I don't compete anymore," it sounded like a practiced phrase. He rubbed his belly absent-mindedly, "I didn't feel it was right, me being the sheriff and all."

He glanced at Big Jim and then back to Tim.

"But I could take him." There was a twinkle in his eye.

He had the relaxed look of an aging, prize-winning champion being asked what it would be like to compete with amateurs again.

The restaurant was packed.

"Dad always said that he could easily win these eating contests too, but it'd be unfair to the others."

"Hurmmph," but he did not continue, "How is your dad?"

"Missing."

Beau checked his fork for dishwasher spots.

"He hasn't been returning my calls either."

"Another game night is coming up. He'll be around."

"Been grilling any more yummy chicken?"

Tim's eyes narrowed.

"Next time you come. I promise."

"Let's make it soon."

"A deal."

"You turn 18 next year," he said, "Thought about coming downtown to the station? We've got an opening for a dispatcher trainee. You might even make it into being an auxiliary."

"How about the SWAT team? Got any openings there?"

"Keep dreaming, young man."

They shared a smile.

"Don't know what I'm going to do. Have no idea. Blank slate. Thinking about the military, following Dad in his footsteps."

"Don't forget that your Mom was police. She was my boss. You sign on, we can get you a full ride to college, just as good as the military."

"Got a year. Need to think more."

"Fair enough. Always open. Long as you know."

Tim gave him a thumbs up. He looked uncomfortable.

"For a while there, I was expecting to have to break up a fight that night."

"Dad was ton-a more chill than I thought he'd be when Sal showed up."

"Things working out okay at home?"

"Haven't been any fights, if that's what you mean."

"See? Have faith in humanity, Timothy. Most people are mostly good."

He took a breath. "Most of the time."

That also sounded practiced, worn, stale.

In the background, some small group of people started chanting "Chug! Chug! Chug! Chug!"

"I live in a house of lunatics."

"Come now. Can't be that bad."

"Debian? She has a new favorite toy, did I tell you? It's a letter opener. Carries it around everywhere. Why? Don't know. Afraid to ask."

"Well, you know Deb's always been...."

"Salomé? How about this: she held a press conference. Can you imagine that?"

"I heard."

Beau frowned to himself, looking down. He picked up his glass, studying it.

"Went about as well as you'd expect. Thankfully Dad and I got out."

Beau sat his water back down.

"Everybody's from a crazy family, Tim. Don't sweat it."

Tim looked as if he were going to yell. Beau cut him off. A cop stopping a car in an intersection.

"Your family. Granted, your family is a bit crazier than most."

"I miss my mom. I wish I'd known her."

"I miss her too."

Beau looked as if he wanted to say something. Instead without responding he left the table for a second helping.

When he returned, Tim pointed at him with his fork.

"The feds at our house the other day. Why? I've heard Dad's version. What's yours?"

The large man simply shrugged.

"Can't tell."

"Can't tell or won't tell."

Beau scrunched his face, working through options.

"It's not my secret to tell. Wish I could."

"Is there an ongoing criminal case?"

"What does your dad say?"

Tim flicked a piece of food from the table onto the floor.

"Can't tell. That's not my secret to tell either, Beau."

People had gathered in the corner of the restaurant, leaving them mostly alone, sitting across from each other.

Fuming.

A man yelled, "And now it's Sudden Death! Gentlemen, prepare yourselves!"

"You know that the allegations against your dad are false, don't you Tim? About the relationship and such?"

"Of course."

"Your dad doesn't play for that team and even if he did, he wouldn't abuse somebody in his care. You need to know that."

"So why don't you clear him?"

"Because the Sheriff's Department doesn't get involved in people's sex lives, at least any more than they force us to, which is too much already."

"Am I supposed to say thanks?"

There was more cheering. Beau looked over. Tim recognized the look.

"You miss it. The competition."

He nodded. He kept watching.

"You should take Dad on a shooting contest, win some real money."

"Never seen anybody shoot like him," he continued watching.

"I'll come too. I can help you guys out. All I need is a little practice."

The commotion got louder. Tim half rose from his seat to see.

As he watched, Big Jim had a blue bucket and was busy barfing into it. The crowd applauded. Some whistled their approval.

"Oh man, that's disgusting!" he said. He sat back down.

Beau quit looking.

"Disqualifying, too. No purging allowed. Back in the day, his brother, Big Joe, used be the guy to beat. Big Joe went regional. No more."

"What happened?"

"Jim reported that he was purging, that's what. It made the committee set up all new rules about restroom use."

"He turned in his own brother?"

"He stopped a cheater, Tim."

Tim looked at Beau much more seriously.

"I guess that depends on how you look at it, doesn't it."

"How do you want to look at it?"

"I guess that depends," was all Tim had.

Beau held his finger up. One moment.

"Excuse me."

He stepped away a few feet from the table. Reaching on his shoulder for his microphone, he said some things that Tim couldn't hear. The radio squawked again. He spoke some more, then came back.

"Sorry about that. I requested an EMT. They really shouldn't be doing this without EMTs present. I'm surprised the insurance company let them."

"I think I'm going for more. I've got a strong stomach. I can do seconds."

Tim rose, but not all the way.

"Stay clear of the lasagna aisle. It could get ugly."

"Already pretty ugly," and he left.

Returning, his plate was loaded again. "It wasn't so bad. That bucket was awesome with the cleanup. That was a good move, very classy. They took the bucket right off. The entire lasagna section's empty, though. There's two guys almost fighting over a chicken leg over there next to the salad bar."

Beau waited for Tim to start eating again.

"I saw Debian the other night, son. It was late. She was by herself, walking. She didn't look good."

Tim nodded, swallowed. He stared at his food but didn't continue.

"Think we may be headed for more trouble. Another incident."

"And your dad gone missing too."

He clicked his tongue.

"Beau," Tim put his fork down, "she'd probably kill me if I said anything, but I was with her that night. It wasn't that bad. She wasn't by herself."

"You were both out walking in town in the middle of the night. And you didn't mention it. Is that supposed to look better?"

"We were there going to check out that apartment. That shooter. She's been obsessing again. It's like last time."

"You didn't break in, did you?"

Tim looked away. Tim chose his words carefully.

"We did not."

"Because, Timothy, if you two crossed a crime scene tape, I'd have to charge you."

"Have to."

"I'd have no choice."

"You say."

Tim pushed his plate away. It was still full.

"I don't think I'm hungry."

"I need to ask you a question," Beau pushed his plate away too, but not completely, not committed, "and I don't want you to go crazy. You do that?"

Tim nodded.

"What if your dad were to go to prison for a long, long time. Are you kids going to be able to make it?"

Tim squirmed.

"Deb's been in the basement for three days. She doesn't come out. Salomé won't stay home more than an hour because she can't have her cell phones around. Those two had a big fight. I'm not sure they're talking."

"I see."

"I don't think so. I don't think you see anything, Beau. It's bad and I don't know how I can change things."

The sheriff's radio squawked again.

He turned the volume down, embarrassed.

"Your mother wasn't perfect. You also need to know that. She takes after Deb. That laser focus. Amazing. But you take after your mom too, with your humor and sense of adventure."

Tim was having none of it.

"You think I'm playing games. I am trying to prevent disaster."

"We're all going to need to pull together."

It was a slogan from a motivational poster.

"I don't even know you. How can you refuse to tell us what you know?"

"Nobody knows nobody, Timothy," he shook his head, put his head in his hands. His eyes drooped.

Tim stared very closely at him.

"You didn't even like that chicken, did you. Tell me."

"Maybe."

"Maybe."

"It was bad," he held his hands up as if he were being robbed, "It was burnt, okay? Nasty. Ugly. It looked like lumps of charcoal encased in rubber. And the taste,.."

"Got it. No need to continue."

"We lied to you. We didn't want to hurt your feelings. It was a kindness."

"I know." he cleared his throat, swallowed, took a breath. "Perhaps hiding the truth every now and then isn't bad, is it?"

Beau pointed to his plate.

"This isn't chicken. Life isn't grilling chicken."

"I'm not the only one that needs lying, to, Beau. You oughtta consider that perhaps you need a kindness too. My family's dying. What can you do to help?

Beau thought. He rubbed his chin.

"I'll set something up with you and Sal. It may be time to release more of your mother's papers. I think that will let you kids understand more."

"You kept mom's stuff?"

"Your mother will always have sensitive and confidential material at the station that you can't see. The job."

"Why not release them to Dad?"

Beau was quiet.

Tim gritted his teeth.

"Because you don't trust Dad."

"A choosing point is coming, Timothy."

"And you fuckers think you're going to make me choose between you and Dad."

Beau had no response.

Tim stood, barely able to contain himself.

"Tim, it's not like…."

"Fuck you."

He almost ran to the door.

1.15

Adventuring Solo

"If you're not going with Sal and Tim to the library, can you at least come out of the basement, take a shower, talk to your loving dad. Maybe put down the knife?"

Paul had stuck his head partway down the steps.

"Letter opener, Dad."

"What are you doing with it?"

"I'm opening….." she looked around and realized there were no letters to open, just a bunch of scattered piles of their old junk she had been sorting through. "Studying it."

"I think it looks plenty sharp. Come on, kiddo."

He motioned.

Grumbling, she got up. She went up the stairs to the kitchen.

"Eat something," her dad met her. He pointed at the refrigerator, "No dishes in the sink. You need to eat. Eat. Eat something even if it's the leftover beans."

She got a bowl from the refrigerator, looked back at the table.

It was bare except for a whoopee cushion.

"Tim?"

"Tim." He agreed. "After the beans. He was planning ahead."

She sat. She picked up the gimmick designed to make farting sounds.

She held it in one hand, absently-mindedly reading the warning labels while eating with the other.

"He worries me when he plans too much," she said.

"You and me both. He announced this morning that with all of the family drama recently, he decided to run away to join the circus. He also acted like he didn't know me."

"Reasonable."

"Indeed. I reminded him there is no circus. Circuses don't exist. So he decided on going into town instead. With Sal."

"A man of action."

"Even when none is needed."

"Tim can find dragons to slay, dad, even when the dragons are long gone."

"Gets it honest. Know what they're doing?"

"Sal and I had a bit of a, um, thing. She's off to do some research."

"With books? Sal? Our Sal?"

"I guess. Stranger things have happened. The world is sometimes upside down, Daddo."

"And you? How are you doing? Upside down? Staying straight and level?"

"I am getting really tired of people asking how I'm doing."

"Just trying to figure you out."

"Well, got news for you. Instead, I've figured you out."

"Do tell. Why do I feel as if I'm the villain in one of those space detective novels you're always reading?"

"Space Opera, dad. Try to keep up. It's called SFF."

"If you've figured out I'm an alien, I feel that it's time I must confess. You have me. I am an alien."

"Cut the shit. What I've figured out is that you need to tell me what kind of heist you and your students were trying to pull before your criminal friends found you out."

"Nice theory; feels very Oceans 11. Fits the data?"

"Exactly. It all fits exactly, including this instrument." She held up the letter opener with the Roman God Janus on top. "This and your tattoo proves beyond a doubt that you're part of the organized crime group named after Janus."

"Do I look like a crime lord?"

"I'm not going to turn you in. You can relax."

"A relief. Are you serious? Do I now look like a relieved crime lord?"

"You look like something. Something's wrong here. I just fucking know it."

"No doubt. But what if it's you, not me? I own all sorts of various things with Roman gods. I'm a history nut. You know that. Not unusual."

"You just want me to stop poking around."

"On the contrary. I want you to keep poking around, only with a trusted guide. Have you thought about going back to Dr. Sykes?"

"That charlatan? Why would I need him?"

"I don't know. Seemed to help last time. We always talked about follow-up visits."

"I don't need a shrink."

"Could you humor me? Do a silly thing or two for your loving father?"

He tried to look angelic.

"Cooperate! Cooperate now! Or I will use my alien crime lord powers to mind control you."

"Sykes has been overbilling our insurance by 23.7%. I told you that last time we went."

"And I told you that every wrong in the universe doesn't need you to fix it."

"I know. And you were wrong."

"Need I remind you? Our last adventure ended with your threatening Sykes in his office. His secretary ran away. Not the picture of mental health."

"I simply told him I knew he was having an affair and to leave me alone."

"Mrs. Sykes wasn't too happy."

"But I said …"

"Especially when there was no affair."

"Because you told me to shut up…."

"To prevent a fistfight.."

She put her spoon down.

"He shouldn't have lied so much."

Rubbing his forehead.

"I am running out of patience. Remember the fire? A mess. Took me three months to get him to agree to see you again if you needed it."

"It's not needed."

"Hmmm."

"There are dark forces at work here, Dad, just like before, just like there always are."

"Oh god damn it, kid," he hit the table, "there are always dark forces at work, Deb. Always the dark forces with you."

She stared at her bowl, not wanting to continue eating nor wanting to continue talking either.

"You fret the living shit out of me. You know that?"

He continued.

"You tell me, then. Where does your imagination see this going? Your dad sent to prison? You finding your mom in a shallow grave out back or something? You tell me. What do you want here? I know what I want. I want you, Debian Newbury, to be happy. I want you to grow. I want you to see the doctor. What do you want? How about you?"

A small, tiny whine squeaked out from her butt.

They both tried very hard to ignore it, smiling to themselves, stopping themselves, not smiling together. Not smiling with the other one. Smiling at walls.

Deb finally gave in.

"More beans, Dad? There's a whole big container in there. You're welcome to them."

She repositioned the whoopee cushion as if it needed to be situated just so.

"I smell trouble ahead, for all of us."

Dad went from happy to sad, like he had run out of happy juice.

"Deb perhaps we should talk about the dark…."

"DON'T SAY IT."

There was a pause in which they both could hear the kitchen clock ticking off the seconds.

"You're holding that at my throat."

She caught herself. She put the letter opener back. She had realized. Caught herself. It was the problem. It was the main reason they gave her the medication.

She put the letter opener delicately in her pocket.

Her dad looked so sad.

Deciding.

"Ok, new plan. Promise me you'll stay here. I'll be back. Just give me a bit. I'll show you whatever it is you think I'm hiding from you in the basement. I promise. Just wait a bit."

He left. He did not come back. The rest of that day he did not return.

When he started out, she'd almost chased after him and stopped him, making it as far as the door, watching him walk to the car, not looking back. She wanted to yell.

But she reversed. She went back in, sat back down. She began fidgeting.

She was patient, but slowly, inexorably, the sun moved the shadows across the kitchen floor. She moved.

First she stayed where he'd left her in the kitchen. The beans got cold. She played with Tim's toy, making farting sounds. Poking at it.

Not fun.

She went to the door. She looked. She stood there. Not long. Maybe an hour.

She went to the top step of the stairs leading down, inside. She sat just inside the basement door.

She went down, drip by drip, bit by bit, only a step or two at a time. She always listened between moves. He might return.

She heard nothing. She was running out of steps. The hard concrete was right there. It had been 4.6 hours. Nothing. She went back to where she had started, by the locked chest. She held a rock-solid grip on the opener, back in the hand.

Just as she started thinking next moves, there finally was a noise. A knock, upstairs. A banging. At the door.

She stilled.

"Paul? Deb? Sal? Tim? Anybody home?"

It was Beau. God, what she wouldn't give to know what he knew.

Of course, he might be there for her. Maybe that's where Dad went. "Debian?"

He banged again. He used that police knock. It seemed like the whole house shook.

She hid.

It was 23.1 minutes until she heard his car pull out. She had been lazy not hearing it arrive. She hit herself in the knee.

Focus. Wake up, Debian.

A little bit at a time she toyed with the letter opener above the locked chest. She traced the edges. Surely a scratch or two here or there wouldn't be noticed.

She poked lightly at the hinge. Nope, they were metal, affixed somehow from inside with strong rivets.

She could pry them off, of course. Not that she wanted to, but she could pry them off.

If she wanted.

It'd be easy.

She listened again for sound above, sounds outside. Sounds in the house.

Nothing.

If she started breaking stuff and going through all of her family's things again, it'd be bad.

It'd be worse than the other time. After all, now she was an adult.

She ceased movement. She sat. She stared at the chest.

She thought about Timothy, his whoopee cushion, his sense of humor.

It wasn't funny. Nothing was funny. Tim always tried, though. Tim always thought it was worth trying.

Fuck it.

She took the Janus opener and started prying at the chest. She stabbed it.

It didn't give. Soon she snapped off the end of the opener struggling. Furious. Stabbing.

She kept going, though, never stopping to think about getting a better tool, beating her hands in frustration on the box, battling it open by sheer force of will.

The basement was just fine.

She was just fine.

Blood dripped from where she had cut herself with her improvised tool, but such things are to be expected when you need to stay in control.

Mom and Dad's things, their secret things, spread out in a half circle around her and the chest.

All to see.

It was just her now.

That was fine. Just fine.

She could do it all on her own.

She was the only one that could.

1.16

Kittens

That damned kitten had bitten her before she tossed it off the bridge. She was going to have to come to grips with that.

She wanted to yell. She wanted to cry. She wanted to jump headlong into the shallow water so far below.

He had to be alive, didn't he?

If Tim had come with her instead of planning to meet Dad, the kittens would have been fine.

But Tim was gone, Deb was hiding, and Sal knew that she and these kittens didn't have long before the train ran over them. She needed to do more.

It had been a long walk to town. She didn't usually take the railroad tracks through Fearsome Wallow. Fearsome Wallow was empty, dirty, and had poor cell coverage.

It smelled.

Fearsome Wallow Trestle had taken several lives over the years; people who thought they were daredevils. They stayed as long as they dared. They didn't make it off the bridge in time.

Sal was no daredevil. She didn't even take risks. All you had to do is listen. You had plenty of time.

She got out her money out and looked at it again. Dad had given her his last $50 for lunch and emergencies.

She remembered that Deb and Tim gave her all of their savings without saying as much as boo. She hadn't said thank you enough. They were brats. It made things tough.

They hadn't even posted about it online.

They all called her "witch" but they forgot how she wore the name with pride as they grew up. She was always trying to do sneaky nice things without them catching her. It was her magic spells. She was a secret good witch. Her magic made her happy.

When she had gotten her first phone, for a while she knew everything. She even knew things Dad and Deb didn't know. All she had to do was search.

When Tim had wanted to go treasure hunting, Sal went out and found a real, live treasure hunter. She interviewed him for her podcast. Afterwards she introduced the two as if it just occurred to her that Tim might be interested in a conversation.

When Deb had wanted something called an "astrolabe", she had found two brothers living in Portugal that made authentic ones. They had traded her one for free coverage from her and her friends.

She made it a present for Christmas. She had snuck out in the middle of the night and placed it under the tree and everything. She labeled the present "From Santa". Deb always thought it was from Dad.

Deb was wrong.

She smiled, remembering.

The little birds came.

She had found these little baby birds. They were in a ramshackle nest alongside the dryer vent. They were too close to the ground and the mama bird was never around.

She'd hid her new, secret phone in the laundry room. She got up each morning, quietly retrieved it, went outside. It was her first truly successful content series. She had tens of thousands of views. She took a video, talked about how cute they were, how much danger they might be in.

Her dad found the phone. She'd broken the Golden Rule.

And who was Dad, anyway, to tell her she couldn't have a phone?

All those years of helping out, pitching in, and she couldn't even exist? Fine for him. He already had a famous job. Deb wouldn't even have her picture taken, much less go online. Was Sal just supposed to be a nobody? A zero?

She started walking Fearsome Wallow Trestle, thinking about how to spin it, what a good hook would be, making sure she listened for the train, when she first heard the tin little meows. It sounded like kittens calling for their mom.

The breeze picked up. She held herself trying to stay warm. It would have been a good day for a jacket. Home was too far back.

Walking would help warm her. She started walking faster, still holding herself.

Then she saw the little tiny forms, stumbling around lost, hungry and desperately crying out to locate their mother. Through all of that, they still played.

Cats.

There was a burlap sack in the middle of the rails. It had come open and the kittens poured out of it.

Somebody had come to throw a bag of kittens into the river but had chickened out at the last minute, leaving them and the bag and running off.

She'd checked the surrounding area. She'd love to catch the scoundrels. She'd post their photos online and dox them as hard as anybody had ever been doxed.

As she approached them one of the kittens fell. It dropped a hundred feet to the water below.

She ran.

A lone dog barked. It was far off.

Still running, after a while there were two dogs, then three dogs barking. Somebody must have had hound dogs because then the hills became flooded with far-off howling.

She thought of the old werewolf movies Dad liked so much.

She made it.

Rain clouds scooted by close overhead. A light sprinkle began.

She was pleased: clouds and rain. Cloudy days made for the best videography and who wouldn't love and want to care for wet, defenseless kittens? There was nothing cuter. It was a goldmine.

That's when she heard the train.

She had just been setting up the selfie stick.

How many kittens were there? How far away was the whistle?

She knew none of these things.

She wasn't afraid. She had plenty of time.

The bag blew off the bridge, carried away by the breeze. She could see the rain dotting it as it floated down below.

Without the sack, she wasn't going to be able to get all of these kittens off this bridge before the train got here. She didn't have time to make two or three trips.

She had decisions to make.

That damn dog started up again.

One of the kittens had pounced on another. He teetered right on the edge of falling off.

She flashed out as fast as she could. She snatched him.

The little bastard bit her. Maybe he was scared. Maybe he was surprised. Maybe she was too rough because she was scared. Whatever it was, he bit down on her finger as hard as he could, sinking his teeth right up to the bone.

She wasn't thinking. She violently shook her hand as if it were on fire. He flew off.

Off the bridge.

Into the river.

To join his brother.

She didn't think. She scooped them all up in her arms, whether they were going to bite her or not. They were in this together.

She took off at a trot, then a run, weaving from side to side trying to maintain her balance.

She was doing it. She had six or seven kittens in her arms and she was running like crazy, jumping from one of those wooden things to another.

She was going to beat the train. She was going to get them all to safety. She had done it.

All she needed was one of the phones to record it all. Her running off a bridge saving kittens would be awesome.

As she ran, she tried to jostle around and lift a phone from her pocket. Her left phone was her best shot.

The kittens continued crying. They were crying louder now. A couple of them had made it to her shoulders. She wondered if they might bite her on the head like the other one had on her finger.

She fell.

She fell on two of the little kittens. She fell on the railroad track. She fell right at the end of the bridge.

She fell within ten feet of making it.

She fell on them. It was horrible.

The train kept coming.

She lay still. She wanted to be dead.

The birds had all died. Tim said he thought a dog had got them. Deb said the mama didn't come back because Sal was giving them too much attention.

She lay face-down, eyes-closed. She would have given everything in her life never to open them again.

Still the little ones cried. They were wandering off.

The ones that lived.

The train was closing.

She rolled off the tracks a few feet into the bush, eyes still closed.

As she reached safety, with horror she realized that she could have rolled over one of the other ones. She might have done it again, killed more.

She couldn't carry all of those kittens to town. It was too far. There were too many. The train was blowing by.

It made a horrendous screech. Metal ground against metal. Chains rattled.

She still might be able to shoot a video. She could move the good ones off to the side. She could shoot herself in close up.

The thought of it made her want to throw up.

She jumped up and opened her eyes, all in one move. She didn't want to look down, ever.

Taking a deep breath, she screamed with all of her might. She screamed looking straight up.

Nobody heard. Nobody cared.

The train continued off.

Standing there, legs apart, arms apart, fists balled, looking to the sky, it occurred to her that if she had a cape, she could be Super Girl. Why did she think these things? Why do these thoughts jump into the middle of her life, interrupting her?

Super Girl could fly off.

Super Girl could save all the kittens.

Super Girl wouldn't be crying.

She did look down. She had to. She shook her head no at the horror. This wasn't okay.

She walked as fast as she could to town for help. She would have run. Walking would get her there faster.

It rained.

The little sad mewing died off as she went. Begging for her.

She'd rescue them, but she wasn't going to pick winners and losers.

She wasn't going to play God.

She'd done enough of that.

Still walking, she saw the purple thing a long ways off. Purple hair. Bright neon purple hair.

She entered town realizing that Liz's house was one of the first houses she'd have to pass.

As she got closer, she could see that Liz was out in her yard. She was talking to somebody. The sky? No, Liz had a selfie stick, same as her. She had the same model phone, same eyeliner, same shoes.

She was just like Liz, only different.

She didn't want to talk to Liz. Ever.

If that wasn't good enough, tough. As she got nearer, the girl saw her. Liz saw the blood all over the front of her dress.

Kitten blood.

Unheeded, in her mind she could see the two tiny cute fluffs, wallowing around, their legs and spines clearly not working. They were twitching, jerking as they tried to make their small bodies work. Blood seeped out of their heads. They didn't cry. Their mouths just hung open.

"Oh my god, it's Sal Newbury!" like they had been longtime friends.

Two other girls appeared from the side yard. They had been shooting their own content.

"Were you in a fight? Was it your crazy sister? Who's blood is that?"

The questions continued.

She looked straight ahead.

She ignored them. They weren't important. At all. It was if they didn't exist, at least as real humans. They were stoplights. They were furniture in an old abandoned house. They were accessories.

She kept walking, fiercely. She was so angry she cried. She kept walking.

They didn't give up, at least at first. They just got more desperate.

"Hey Sal, I've got a million followers here!"

"Hey Sal let's add each other!"

"Hey Sal, I'll give you $100 for an interview."

She thought of Dad's $50, his last money. Deb and Tim giving their last money.

They followed. They didn't catch her. Slowly they started dropping off, uninterested. It wasn't worth the effort.

"You fucking bitch!"

"Bitch" for a second sounded like "witch".

Her phones began buzzing. Cell service had returned.

She was determined. She kept walking.

A buzz from one phone.

She reached up to throw her hat away. It was gone. It must have fallen off.

Had she worn a hat?

She was now entering the downtown streets. It wouldn't be long until she'd reach the police station. She would get help.

Now they both buzzed.

Waiting to cross the street, she saw herself in a store window. She was bloody, messed up, muddy, wild-eyed.

She found she didn't care.

It was always too much about her, she realized. Everything she did, good or bad, everything always had to have her in the center of it.

It hadn't started out that way. She never truly felt like that inside. But she was the oldest. She was the one who always had to do the things a mom would have done. She always had to be somebody else.

She didn't resent it. Just the opposite. She enjoyed it. She never wanted to admit it or get caught saying it, but being there and helping as part of her family was the happiest life she ever could imagine.

What had happened? How did she get this way over the last two years?

Life had happened. She had grown up. She had told herself that she deserved better. She had left home. She began finding her own way. It became all about Salomé.

No more.

She'd sell her car. She'd try to convince Dad to get legal help. He needed it. She would take herself out of the center of any good she might do. She'd try more to actually do good and not so much to feel good or to look good.

She would save the cats.

That was it.

Her phones buzzed a last time.

Happy, determined, she tossed both of her cellphones into the first dumpster she passed.

She had dignity. She had value.

She was happy.

She never saw the delivery truck coming.

Deducing Disaster

She was in a fistfight with Tim when they found out Sal had been killed.

It was the beginning of the end.

Maybe it was more of a wrestling match.

She had been studying the contents of the box. There were some papers from Mom, Dad's discharge papers, another odd grey box the size of a large external hard drive, a knife, some other things she hadn't catalogued yet, and a pistol.

A pistol. For the guy who wouldn't allow guns in the house, but loved shooting.

And what the hell was that gray box, anyway?

Tim had tossed a cardboard box from the steps on the floor between them.

"How'd you get in?"

"I'm like toenail fungus. Once I'm here, I never really leave."

The box was bright yellow. In the upper left corner it said "Rock'Em Sock 'Em Robots" Underneath that was "Knock His Block Off!"

The picture showed two kids controlling little plastic robots fighting in a tiny boxing ring.

The kids looked happy.

He winked. From behind his back he produced four large inflatable boxing gloves, the kind that could harm no one.

"I also brought these, just in case you want to fight like the big kids do."

He bounced a pair together the way boxers do before a big match.

"Funny. I promise, I'll beat you quick, make it easy."

Tim put the big inflated gloves on the top shelf behind him.

"Great. I was hoping you'd talk smack and lose quickly. Come at me, sis!"

He made the universal meme gesture of "Come at me, Bro!" which meant exactly nothing to Deb.

"Are you ready to play or is there some sort of dork fight dance you need to do first."

She began opening the game. "I could hum if it requires music."

Seeing his mistake, he took a seat opposite of his sister, doing his best to do so as if he were a Japanese warrior.

He looked at the basement for the first time. He quickly stopped.

"Perform an exorcism to get rid of the witch? Don't you two need a cauldron down here, a black cat? A spell book, maybe?"

"She's going to town to the station. Talk to Beau."

"I'm glad she's finally turning herself in. Public stupidity, I suppose. I'll miss her."

"Eat shit, scurvy runt. It's about some personal things of mom's Beau said we might be interested in. Might explain this smear campaign….If there is a smear campaign. If such a thing exists."

"Don't doubt yourself. Never change. Look how far its gotten you."

"I have been, to be honest. Doubting myself. Been starting to feel a little paranoid down here. Door locked. All these notes. Secret notes. The items."

One corner of the basement had a lot of organized material. It was the only one.

"I'm the red robot." He said. He looked around again. "I guess these kinds of activities could bother a person. Maybe you could get a butler."

"Things kept from me."

"Haven't found Atlantis yet, have you?"

"If I have, would you want to know?"

"How cute are the Atlantis girls?"

"Horrendous. Four noses each."

"Yikes! Don't let those assholes get you down, clown. Anybody dresses like you do," he pointed to her conservative green and orange tartan jumpsuit with a bright yellow ascot, "You have the kind of free spirit the rest of us would envy. Never forget that. You might need a little course correction from time-to-time, we all do, but always you be you."

"Dad said you're thinking about the circus."

"You've got that fancy job offer."

"Wanna trade? Witch told me this morning I was already dressed for the circus. How are you with Eigen Vectors? Octernians?"

"Do they bite?"

"Only if you commute with them."

"Cool. Never been much of a commuter. Never took communion. So I'm great. I will fight these octernians of yours."

She squared up the game between them.

"Spying going okay?"

"Yeah a bit."

He added nothing more.

"Usual stakes? Dishes for a week?"

"Make it interesting. How about we play for this nice, hundred-dollar lensatic compass?"

"Where'd you get that?"

"It was in Dad's old Army stuff."

She stopped getting ready.

"Bullshit. No it wasn't. Dad doesn't have old army stuff. All his army stuff was in that chest."

They both look at the completely demolished chest she had halfway hid in the corner.It had not just been opened; it had been torn apart piece-by-piece like a custom agent would tear up the suitcase of a suspected smuggler.

She looked back to him. Down to her robot. Back to him.

"You going to start in with the lies too?"

"Cool your jets. Dad gave it to me while we were hiking."

"Is that when he told you about Janus Group?"

"You've spoken with him?"

On the workbench were pictures, letters, post-its, note, numeric tags, labels, all in little piles.

They mesmerized him.

She looked to them now as well as if there were some answer to her question in the patterns on the bench.

"Ah," Tim presently said, "I thought not. You hadn't spoken. Nice. You got me."

She didn't look back.

"I'll figure it out anyway. It's pointless to resist."

It broke the spell.

"Who's resisting? I'm not James Bond. You're not the evil supervillain. This isn't a lair. It's a basement."

"So?"

"For real people, not movie people, there's a time and place for these conversations. And this isn't it."

"You don't get to decide that."

"So you, Deb. You're the one. You get to decide."

"Something really bad happened to Mom."

"Look around. See Mom? She's not here. So I'm going with 'yes', something really bad happened."

"I mean somebody came after her. It came for all of us."

"Oh fuck no. Oh gee, Debian. I am so sorry. Sal was right. You're back to this."

"There's something. It's just outside my ability to perceive."

"Please. Please don't. Listen to yourself. Do you realize how crazy you're sounding?"

He walked over to the wall. He picked a card at random. He started reading.

"The Three Stooges. In fact, they were not stooges and there was never three of them. They appeared on network TV an extra 27% above normal rates the year of the investigation usually in the off hours…"

He threw it down.

"Make sense? This is who you want to be? Some crazy chick hiding in her parent's basement her whole life stringing up weird factoids and making indecipherable notes?"

"I have a numeric semantic checkpoint system. It represents an ad-hoc cohort analysis…" Seeing his look and able to read it, "It's broken. Something here is broken, and only I can fix it."

"I agree, sis. Something is broken." He pointed around. "I can see."

"Fuck it." She stood. "I've had enough of this. I'm tired of it being broken."

She stood. She clenched her fists.

"And you're going to help me fix it even if I have to beat it out of you."

"Okay. Alright. I'm willing to go there. If you want, fuck it then. I can play hardball. If that's what it takes. Be just like old times."

He assumed a fighting stance. She had never seen him do that. Impressive.

"Like when we were little. But just like old time, you won't hurt me, your precious little baby brother, right?"

She relaxed. She would not give up, though.

"Never stopped me before."

"Fair point. I'll be gentle."

"You'll be the only one."

Instead of yet another reply or some masterful fighting move, he simply kicked her in the shins.

"Ouch!"

He stuck his tongue out and made a face at her.

Grimacing, she tried a one-two jab, feigning with her dominant right, pulling back, then a hard thrust with her left right at his head.

As Dad told her about one of her geometric proofs once, it wasn't even wrong. Tim's head dropped straight down before her fist could get there. He ducked low and spun like a little tiny ballerina just outside of her gaze.

Her clock speed had been too low. Frack.

As he spun, he stuck his leg out. His leg sweep took her completely by surprise. It took her off her feet. Feet up; head down. It had been too long, she thought on the way down, since she and Tim had sparred. He was getting good. Very good.

For an instant she thought he would pounce on her, finish her off. That's what she'd do.

Instead, he just stood back, resumed a normal posture. He brushed himself off. He looked at her lying there. He was amazed. He looked at her like he was amazed that she wasn't already dead.

"Why don't you come with me. Let's move out. We'll start over."

"Not going to happen."

"Okay. Plan B. How about Doc Sykes? He's not that bad. I kind of like him. The toupee is sick."

"And now you with the Sykes. You too."

She reached out to get a hand up. When he offered, she tried to pull him down with her.

It was a cheap move.

She caught a slight grin as if he were watching a puppy play. Keeping her hand, he dropped to a squat. He rolled. He flipped her over his shoulder and back towards the shelves.

Tim was going to kick her ass with these combat combinations she hadn't had time to file, no doubt. But how good was he at combinatorial physics modeling?

She picked up a brick she had fallen on. She carefully rose, holding it out like it was warding off an evil spell.

She held it out. It was her brick knife.

He indulged her. He dropped his hands but stayed alert. There was a faint smile. He was ready for this escalation. Want to beat me with a brick, his body seemed to say, go for it.

But she didn't attack with it. Instead, without looking, she threw it offhand off to the side, as if it was just more trash.

As hoped, he ignored it. The brick hit another shelf. The shelf shifted two inches to the left. She had categorized one of the supports as weak last month. As it shifted, a bowling ball fell off the top. They hadn't been bowling in years. She couldn't remember them ever bowling.

It dropped down to hit the old, dusty weight bench. That was the 63% risk. The big one. It was the riskiest part of the move, but he hadn't turned yet and she was already working on two backup plans using a similar modeling strategy. She had been tracking her plan execution with her ears, not daring to look over lest she give it away.

It rolled down the weight bench. It hit the hand weights. Tim had noticed by now, of course, but had not started reacting.

He was too slow.

They dropped on his foot.

"Ouch!"

Happy it had worked and unwilling to keep pushing her luck, she ran directly at him like one of those TV football people and tackled him.

He tried to resist. It was too much and it was too many odd things all at once for him to react. They fell in a pile.

She grabbed his head. She squeezed. She shook him.

"What have you and Dad been talking about?"

"Argghhhh." he looked caught between surprise and defeat, "We agreed. He's been telling me things. He needs somebody to talk to, I guess. We all do. Including you."

She tried again with different spacing.

"What. Were you. Two talking. About."

"We agreed. We've got just two choices."

She stopped squeezing and shaking. She pulled back.

"What?"

"Being quiet. Staying here, but no …. outside. Effectively hiding."

She started.

"Hiding from what?"

"Running away, Deb. Our second choice is running away. Then hiding. Or maybe not hiding so much."

She shook herself. What was he saying.

"Why do we have to pick one?"

The phone rang.

They stopped the struggle.

They listened.

Neither one of them cared what they listened for.

They listened as if expecting a bulldozer to appear and flatten the house on top of them.

It stopped.

Before she decided what was next, he rolled, did some kind of new judo thing.

Little runt.

His turn. He pinned her.

"I reject your choices."

She almost spat at him. But it was still Tim.

"Debian. My dear sister. Nobody is asking you."

She had one hand partially free. She reached and pulled the entire shelf down on top of both of them.

Even as she did it, she knew. It was suicidal.

Instinctively, both closed their eyes. This was going to hurt.

It was the inflatable gloves that saved them. That or something akin to godlike fortune. She replayed the move again several times later that week. She had not recorded each item on that shelf yet. Sal had been futzing over in that area before she left. She didn't know exactly how it happened. It happened.

The gloves saved them. They landed on their heads as a precursor to the paint cans, following immediately behind. Paint cans hitting your head are not good things, even with cushioning.

It hurt.

"How many people has Dad killed, or ordered killed?"

He slowly started getting off, disentangling. He was afraid. Neither one of them had any fight left.

Once he was free, "That's for Dad to tell you. It's not for me."

She started getting up.

"Our family can't keep keeping secrets."

The phone rang again.

"Well?"

"Get the damn phone, Timothy. Just get the fucking phone already."

Coming back, he took his time. She thought that he came down the steps like an old man going to his own cremation.

Said nothing. He just pointed at the ground.

They both knew. Quietly they both sat cross-legged. They faced one another.

He held both her hands in his.

"I have some hard news."

"I don't want to hear it."

"Dad and Beau are on their way here."

"I don't want to know."

She tried to pull away. She tried to look away.

She was feeble. She was weak. He was strong.

"Debian. Look at me."

Frozen. Frozen by his eyes.

"Salomé has been killed in a traffic accident."

She didn't reply.

She squeezed his hands as hard as she could.

Tim didn't grimace. He didn't reply.

He just sat there and took it.

1.18

Saving Beau

Beau didn't need to see the "psycho dungeon", as Tim called it, to know she needed to go to the funny farm again. Tim's general description, combined with both of them being so beat up, was enough.

Deb sat in the back of a police cruiser considering that police cars were the same as one of her airplane cockpits, with their own flashing lights, radio squawks, buttons and knobs. She could smell the gun oil from the recently-cleaned shotgun.

He'd apologized to her as he stuffed her into the back seat.

"I'm sorry, Debian, truly I am," he said, making sure her head didn't hit the top of the car, "I care about you. We all do. Sometimes when you care about people you have to do whatever it takes to keep them from hurting themselves and others."

Now he was arranging wrappers and other gear in the front seat. He looked to be delaying or putting off something.

"Your Dad's going to be another hour or two, so its just me and you," he said.

She thought he was trying to make some kind of apology.

He turned.

"Twinkie?"

"It's 8pm."

"So?"

"I thought you were on a diet."

"I'm doing what they call 'Food Journaling' I write everything down."

"Is this helping with the twinkies?"

"Sure. I just don't write those down. No entry, no problem."

"You should write a diet book."

He held up a blank notepad.

"I've already started."

He put the package and pad down, disappointed that his joking hadn't changed her mood.

"If it helps any, it was instantaneous. Delivery tuck blew a tire. I doubt she even knew anything was happening."

"Where?"

"Half-mile from the station."

"Doesn't help."

"Yeah, I know."

"Back to business. Unfortunately, Ms. Debian Newbury, you know the drill. You get a TDO, Temporary Detention Order. You talk to some nice people. You come back home in a couple of days. I don't have to worry about any more of your Family Circus stunts. At least for tonight."

"I'm not going on meds again."

"I'm not your doctor. Don't tell me. Tonight I'm just your chauffer."

Beau began fiddling with some gear she couldn't see.

"What's that?"

"We call it a wire. A bugging device you wear. We use it with CIs, that's Confidential Informants for you civilians, to gather information. We got a big Op later, but you didn't hear that from me, no sir."

He winked, sharing a confidence.

"People who sell out, huh? Who'd sell out their friends, get them arrested? Sounds pretty shitty."

"It's not always like that. Sometimes nobody gets arrested. Sometimes we're just gathering intelligence. Things are not always so clear cut."

"Not my thing."

"Me neither, but there are times that folks don't have a choice. There's no other way."

"I wouldn't be a very good policeman."

"Don't be so sure. Your mom was the best I've ever worked with. I can see her in you sometimes."

He began to put the car in gear. He stopped. He was obviously struggling with something.

"I don't want to do this. You guys deserve to be together, especially tonight. But this kind of incident, tearing up the basement, beating up your brother, breaking into stuff, it's not good."

"He started it with the robots."

"Not helping."

He continued poking and shuffling around in the front.

"Where'd my dang batteries go?"

"Tim isn't complaining. Doesn't want charges. Why don't we just forget it."

"Didn't need to. We've got physical violence, odd obsessions, concern from your family members, and a few other things you agreed to not do last time we had problems."

"I've been developing several new lines of evidence."

"I'm sure you have. I put your mother's things in a box by the back door. They'll be there and you can look through them when you return. You can continue your investigation or whatever you call it."

He cleared his throat.

"I had them, the things, your mom's things, you know, already ready, for her."

She saw that he didn't want to use Sal's name.

"What do you know about a large grey box about the size of a large paperback, looks like some kind of electronics? Found it in my parents things."

"Nothing. What do you know about an intrusion into the college network last week?"

"Nothing."

No one moved for a bit.

"Traffic accident," he repeated it as if trying to work through it. "Same thing happened to my aunt."

"I'm not crazy."

"Never said you were."

"Not crazy. I just know things."

"I don't think you're crazy, Deb. I think you're troubled. Big difference."

"What's wrong with you Beau? Don't you care there's something deeper going on with Dad, with Mom, with the shooting?"

He squirmed. She continued.

"I thought you were all about law and order. But not always? You a fake?"

"Call me troubled if it helps."

"You call that troubled? You're the one sitting in the front seat and I'm the one in the back. Not that it seems to matter to you."

He turned on her.

"I do care, Debian. I care very much. I'm not a fake friend, and I'm not a fake law enforcement officer. I've been convinced something stinks here since before your mom disappeared. A long time."

"You have? Then why haven't you said something?"

"Because I don't say things. I do things. And each time I tried to do something over the last ten years it ended up being the wrong thing. Just like with you."

She sat back.

"So now I just watch, pay attention, take notes."

He looked at his blank pad.

"You speak to my dad?"

"I did. He's not good with the news. I don't think Timothy's doing too well, either."

"Tim's like me. He doesn't do a lot of public emotion. But he's tough. He can handle it."

"He is. I'm thinking maybe we should wait for your dad."

"No."

"Damned batteries. They're here somewhere."

He continued mucking around.

"Am I troubled," she said, "just to want to find out things? The truth?"

He stopped and considered.

"I guess it depends on what you want to find out. I'm also trying to make peace with this situation. Everybody has things they don't want found out about them, sometimes they don't even want to know themselves."

"But how could...."

"It's people, sweet. They're like that. We see people guilty as shit one day, confessing everything, and three weeks later it was all somebody else's fault. And they believe it, too. People don't even want to know the truth about themselves, much less the truth about the world in general."

"So explain to me, how is it that it has to be me? Why am I the one that's got to go away?"

"Big question. I don't know. I guess you're only allowed to stir up so much shit, annoy society in general. Life sucks. Some things just need to end, Debian. The people around you decide that it needs to end. It's unhealthy. You hurt yourself and others. One way or another they just need to end. That's all."

The crackling of the car radio got louder.

Suddenly the opening to the song "Don't Fear The Reaper" started.

Beau punched the dash.

It stopped.

"Sorry. It's a short. Guy's supposed to fix it."

"It's annoying. It's got to stop."

"I stopped it. Look. You just kinda hit it. Makes it stop. Some kinda loose wire."

"No, Beau, I mean this. This pattern has to stop, so let's hit it. Let's do that thing with the wire, only with my dad."

"I don't think that's a very good idea. In fact that sounds downright horrible."

"It's been a horrible night, right? And he's not in good shape. So let me sit down with him and talk. I know he's already talking to Tim about some things. He'll talk to me."

"Debian, your sister. She died."

"So?"

"Doesn't that bother you? Doesn't it seem, well, a bit cold?"

"It'll bother me tomorrow. It'll bother me forever. But I'm not going to let it bother me now, not when I can end this."

"What if he says nothing?"

"Then I'll come back out and we can do your TDO. God knows we've already tried that once."

The song started playing again.

He hit the radio hard enough to crack the dash.

"Temper, temper."

"Point made. I guess in unusual times we can all have….moments. We lose control."

"Give me this shot. Please. I won't let you down."

"Good grief. You need to be sure. Like your mom. If he catches you or you catch him, either way it's not going to end well."

"It'll end. Isn't that you were talking about? Sometimes the only way is through."

"Fair warning: there was a time if we found something that was close to a crime but not completely, I could look the other way."

"I don't want you looking the other way."

"But I want to. I want to look the other way. And I can't. However this plays out, I can't be your friend, maybe for a long time. Maybe forever. I've lost too much already on this thing that's been bugging both of us.

I'll push just as hard as you will and I'll run over you to make this end. Don't tempt me."

"So give me the damned thing and I'll give it my own shot for both of us."

"I'll play along. Let's say I do. I'm not letting you out of this car, out of those handcuffs, unless you swear to me, swear, that nobody's going to get hurt."

"I swear it. I will not injure anyone. I promise."

"I've got a bad feeling."

He growled.

"Give me your stupid hands."

It was quiet when she got back inside the house.

She didn't hear the police car pull off from its hidden spot along the road. She didn't know that there was an all-hands emergency on the far side of town. She didn't know Beau had left and was unable to get a replacement.

She didn't know that she was on her own.

Tim was nowhere to be found. She hadn't bothered looking that hard.

She just sat, like she had throughout so much of her life, in a sad, empty room.

And waited.

1.19

Dancing Dad

"Right there? That's where we burned all of the computers. Everything electronic. It was the night of the fire."

She was standing at the back window. She hadn't bothered to notice her dad when he came into the house.

"Surprised you remember."

"The night Mom disappeared."

"Sal's dead. Your sister is dead. They told you, right?"

"Like Mom?"

Paul said nothing. He moved closer.

Tim had told her once to show people the things about yourself that you wanted them to see, take them to the little rooms in the bigger house that consisted of you.

She straightened up.

"Tim should be here."

"I know. We need to talk. We have plans to make."

"We have work to do."

He nodded.

"He doesn't want a service. I agree with him. We're private people. Sal would have wanted a parade, of course, but none of that is going to help her now. Funerals are for the living, not the dead. We're not public people."

"Not that kind of work."

"I hear you've been busy," he repositioned himself to try to get a look at her face.

"A bit."

"Clear my name yet?"

She turned to him. She skewered him with her eyes.

"Just the opposite. You weren't romantically involved with the shooter, although the newspapers said you were. You knew and worked with him, although you said you didn't."

"My memory isn't…"

"Is nowhere near that bad."

"There's a NDA."

"Which brings me to the organized crime allegations. They still haven't been resolved one way or another. There's the allegations of computer hackery and thievery that look likely to me but unproven. There's the body modifications the shooter made. He needed help and money for that. I don't trust you enough to even ask about it."

"I'm starting to feel a bit hunted."

"My guess is that you should have felt that way a long time ago."

"From your lack of emotion and expression, will this involve kick-boxing?"

Her face was bruised, yes, but it was also blank. Dead.

He started to reach for her, looked at her cold unblinking eyes. Stopped. There was danger there.

"Simply because you don't like having feelings doesn't mean you don't have feelings. I know better."

"I guess you're going to expect a tour of the basement."

"You have this deep need to figure things out, and the more you can't figure things out the more it bugs you."

"I may step over the line sometimes. If I do, I'm sorry. There, I said it."

"An apology – and your head didn't explode. Progress."

He looked around.

"Tell you what, let's sit and talk about this outside. It's a beautiful night. The birdbath is a lot nicer than that old firepit it replaced."

He invited. She accepted.

Five minutes later, they sat in old plastic discount-store chairs around the birdbath, giant birds looking for a midnight drink.

There was no light, only light seeping thirdhand from the house.

That was fine. She didn't need light.

Instinctively she felt for the knife in her pocket.

In the distance they heard police sirens, or maybe it was ambulances. She never could tell.

Disturbance gone, the tree frogs resumed singing.

"Sal told me that you and her were working on some kind of clues or history about the dark…."

He stopped. He saw the knife. It was at his throat. The point touched his Adam's apple.

She felt like she was a house made of ice. A wrecking ball had crashed into her and blown her apart into a million shards.

"Tell me, where'd you put Mom's body?"

"You're going down the same dark road she did."

Deb stuck the knife a bit harder. It hadn't punctured the neck yet. It was close.

Tears came from his eyes. He was crying. He was not weeping. The tears came. His composure remained. He cried and did not cry.

"It might be better for all of us just to kill me now."

"You're not going anywhere."

"Timothy is. He's gone."

She dropped the knife, but a bit.

"Is he coming back?"

"You should ask him when he calls. If he calls."

She refocused.

"Found some of Mom's things. She was concerned. Deb recited from memory,"Paul has put us all in great danger' that's what her notes say but I haven't zeroed in on exactly what that is yet."

Paul reached into his pocket. He had to stop and put his hands up, waiting for the slight nod that Deb gave so that he could continue pulling his wallet out, as if he would pull a gun on his own daughter. Once out. he delicately pulled out a yellowing handwritten note.

"Here. Your mom's handwriting, written that night. You can read it or I will. It says whatever happened, she made it happen. It was her, not me."

"But why didn't you…"

"Because it was inconclusive. It wouldn't have mattered, Debian. I didn't show anybody because it would have just made things worse, not better. You kids didn't need to know about her dark side. Nobody did."

He did not make the logical comparison, but they both were thinking the same thing.

"You could have told us. Maybe slowly. We deserved to know."

"No Debian, I couldn't."

"Why?"

Paul sat still. He said nothing. He was like a piece of stone. He was another concrete lawn ornament.

She withdrew the knife. You can't kill something that's already dead.

"Beau says there have been several deaths you've been around that have been suspicious. Suspicious deaths. Mom was police. That was her job."

"You've spoken to Beau? But of course you have."

"Tim said that you've told him about killing people. Is it true?"

"Tim's been talking. But of course he has. This is turning into a great evening."

He tensed.

"Fuck it. You want me to tell you, kiddo, I'll tell you."

He put his hands palm down in the bath, hands deep in the nasty water.

"I have been both directly and indirectly responsible for many deaths, Debian. It's true."

"Some were legal. Some were extrajudicial. I regret them all."

"Okay. I want you to tell me every one of them."

"Now? How about Sal? About arrangements? About you?"

She curtly nodded.

"After."

"Well, I'll walk you through, then. But there's a lot to tell. It'll take several hours. I'll need to show you what's in the chest downstairs."

"Already opened it."

"But of course you have. Lead the way. I'm warning you now: you're not going to believe most of what I have to say. I don't think you're going to like any of it. But you're old enough. Out of all the kids, you were the one I was most afraid of. The day I didn't want to arrive, has arrived. Lets get it over with."

They came back in. Too late, she heard the basement door shut, then lock behind her.

She ran up the steps anyway, tried. Locked.

Trapped.

She stood there, robotic, at the top of the steps. She listened. Her dad got something from the closet. He was trying to be quiet, knowing that she was listening. He left, softly opening and closing the door. The car started and was gone.

Beau should come and get her. Should.

And again she waited,. Beau did not come. Hopefully Dad hadn't done anything to him. Hopefully he hadn't done anything else.

Even though she knew Salomé was gone, it was still like she was right there.

Deb could speak aloud and almost perfectly predict what Sal's reply was going to be. She could even hear her.

She wanted to smile. She wanted to weep. Instead all that existed was this deep and vast emptiness.

"If you want dramatic results, you gotta take dramatic action." She could see Sal vamping the phrase in the restaurant, playing it for all it was worth, like she was right there.

Dad probably thought Deb had forgotten, but she remembered exactly. The box of road flares were in the basement, under the jack stands.

She also remembered where the lamp oil was.

She poured the gallon of lamp oil all over the notes and clues she had arranged, taking care to gather up the weird box and a couple of other things. She definitely wanted to get her Markov Blanket. She loved her Markov Blanket.

Then she dumped the road flares on the pile. Picking up one of the road flares, she struck it and tossed it in.

The flames immediately shot to the ceiling. Heat pressed her.

The house was going to burn and she was going to burn along with it, unless she could immediately find her way out of this locked room.

1.20

Counting

There were 4,873 steps from her front door to the bus station.
   There were 4,912 if she used the side entrance.
   That giant gopher at the library had a camera in it.
   Beau had started wearing a wire weeks ago.
   More Janus Group items were in the lockbox.
   There was a Janus Group combat knife.
   Sal began to believe organized crime was involved.
   Sal was dead.
   The phone had a tap and trace on it.
   She knew things she didn't mention.
   There was nobody to tell.
   All of them were in on it.
   Her next book was in her pocket.
   It was "Psychic Vampires Of Mars."
   The hero was also named Deb.
   She thought about how the book started.
   "As the fiery star disappeared behind the towering mountains, bathing the desolate plains with a final burst of warmth, Deb felt a sense of sadness and loss wash over her, for she realized that this was the moment she had been waiting for all her life, but now it was slipping away, consumed by the darkness. Yet, as she gazed upon the distant horizon, she saw a faint flicker of light, like a star being born, and she knew that this was her chance, her destiny, her salvation. So she set off towards that light, that beacon of hope, walking towards the unknown, walking towards her miracle."
   She walked.

The house burned.

II. PATTERNS OF FORCE

"We're going to need a bigger boat"

Jaws

2.01

Disturbing Coffee

Sᴀᴍ ꜰᴇᴀᴛʜᴇʀꜱᴛᴏɴᴇ ᴅɪᴅɴ'ᴛ ᴡᴀɴᴛ ᴛᴏ ᴋɪʟʟ ᴀɴʏʙᴏᴅʏ, and these two fuckers could just crawl back under the rock they crawled out of. Enough, already. He tried to reassure himself as he took the FBI credentials he'd just stolen back to the ancient, grimy bathroom.

He easily slid his 6'1" lanky frame into the cramped restroom, relic of city architecture from old times past. His dirty red hair and freckled face framed a smile that was always friendly, bemused. Sam was the type of guy who was best friends with whomever he met, eager to brighten up days and make life fun.

Inside, though, once the decrepit metal slide lock on the door was engaged, he almost broke into a shaky sweat. What the hell was he doing?

He got out his ten-year-old FOSS smart phone from the Faraday Bag he always kept it in. Time was limited. His only option was to document as much as he could and analyze it later.

Where to place things to snap pictures? Old bathrooms weren't very phone-friendly. They weren't anything friendly, for that matter. There's a reason they were called "water closets". It wasn't like there were shelves. There was a pull-flush toilet, a water stained sink and a tile floor. The tile floor was too nasty. This cool, antique rustic look was nice, but if you're running a coffee shop you should at least mop now and then.

He'd have to take his chances with placing things on the narrow rim of the sink.

Trickles of cold sweat broke out on his brow as he began sifting through this person's life. His hands began a small tremble. He forced himself to relax and focus as he got the driver's license and FBI badge from her purse.

There was a soft knock on the door.

Startled, he tilted the purse just a tad bit too much, almost dropping it. Over-correcting, he flipped it the other way. Before he could react, he had dumped the entire contents all over the tile floor.

"Hello?" a small voice from outside.

"Busy," he replied, trying not to sound nervous, but perhaps a bit hurried.

He heard somebody clear their throat.

There were personal items everywhere. What order were they in? How could he ever get it all back in there in the same order?

He scuffled up the cards first.

"Hello?" It was the same timid voice, child, it sounded like.

"I'm busy, kid. Sorry. Give me a minute."

"Er. Ummm."

Sam looked to the door. What next?

"I'll just, um. I'll just go somewhere else?" It was a question and not a question.

Ooof. Now, back to putting Humpty Dumpty back together again. Let's see. Cards obviously had a place. There were little slots for them. So did the Driver's License. The FBI credentials were in their own wallet.

Bam! Bam! Bam!

"Mr. Featherstone."

Uh-oh. No denying that. That was one of the agents, the female Shotwell.

The person banging on the door was the person who owned the wallet he was now holding. With the FBI credentials.

"Mr. Featherstone. Are you okay?"

This had to be the worst first day at work that any human ever had in the entire history of the universe.

How could it have started off so good?

Just an hour ago things were so pleasant. There was no sign at the building when Sam had reached it. EigenCorp owned the entire 20-story office building, but all that announced the corporate giant was a single, small, lower-case "eigencorp" on the single entrance along with the e-c-eyeball logo.

Low key.

The walk had been pleasant enough from the hotel. The day was opening up to be dry, sunny, warm, and he felt really good about being here. It was about time. He needed a reboot.

The last couple of months, the last couple of weeks especially, had been a nightmare. How could it have started so well?

He and his roomies had won CyberCon, breaking into an NSA system and beating all comers. Joe Middles, the guy who owns EigenCorp, the main man, had even stopped by. He took them all out for dinner. What a day.

Later that week he'd received a job offer from EigenCorp. College was ending, Sam was gaining prestige, he had a job with the number one cyber risk assessment firm in the world. EigenCorp had even agreed to pick up his student debt. Sam had been walking on air.

Then roomie, Stetson, started going haywire.

Stetson was the best of all three of them. He wasn't outstanding in just one area, like Sam was with Social Engineering, Stetson was strong in all of them.

After they won the contest, gone out to dinner, though, Stetson had grown more quiet, more fearful. He'd stayed to himself in his room more. He mumbled as he meandered through the apartment. He hid things from them, simple things like paperclips or pencils. He awoke some nights screaming.

At first they just ignored it, but as the weeks passed ignoring became impossible. Carl and Sam began openly talking about "What to do with Stetson," but neither had any experience, they didn't want to embarrass their friend, and they had no idea where the line was. They didn't even know who they should go to.

It was near the end of school. As much as Sam hated to admit it, by not deciding, they actually were making a decision: let's just get to the end of the year.

Sam had even started to use his close-up magic tricks and pick-pocketing skills on Stetson. Somehow Sam became Stetson's own Clown TV. He kept trying to keep him entertained, happy, distracted, if only for a bit. Hey, is this your $20? I'll bet you dish chores for a week I can make your phone disappear. How'd I do it? Figure it out, dude. What do you know, here's the phone numbers of those two cuties we saw last night. And so on.

Stetson knew what was going on. He appreciated Sam's effort. It even worked for almost a month. Sam did tricks and made puzzles. Stetson got distracted and tried to work them out.

Then it only worked while Sam was in the room.

Then it stopped working.

It had been a band-aid. Sam regretted not being honest with himself about it.

Now both Stetson and Carl were dead, killed at the airport.

But they'd made it to the end of the year. Yay them.

It was good for Sam to start over. It was time.

Much caffeine needed.

Walking along, enjoying the sunshine, looking for the closest coffee shop, he began whistling. It was the theme song to the ancient TV show "The Andy Griffith Show." His childhood. The show was about an idyllic small town where nothing very serious ever happened and people were all good friends with one another.

This town was no Mayberry, and the two or three people he passed on the sidewalk gave him odd looks, but he needed the music. Sam needed the dream.

After the shooting, life was anything but simple. He hadn't seen this many cops since he robbed that bank when he was seven. At least this time he wasn't the one in trouble.

He had been hard-headed as a kid, but Sam had eventually dialed it back over the years. He'd practice his magic tricks, help those he could, and try to make the world a happier place, but he was done with persuading, socializing, and being Mr. Popular Guy. Also the crimes. People didn't like the crimes.

It wasn't that he was bad at it. He was too good at it.

It hurt.

The sign on the door read "Ye Olde Coffeee Shoppe" in fancy lettering. In the storefront window he saw various antique coffee grinders and brewers. An old lamp stood in the middle of the window, bulb missing.

Pushing open the door, there wasn't a line. That was a relief. It was just a kitschy shop full of old and odd doodads. And two policemen.

The policemen were in plain clothes. They were facing the door. There was a football player sized man in his late 20s and an older, physically-fit lady with short hair. Both could probably kick his ass, maybe while blindfolded.

They smiled when they saw him. He was expected.

The man was the size of a college linebacker and when he shook Sam's hand, Sam thought his wrist would break. His grip was like a vise.

"I'm agent Jones and this is agent Shotwell," the man said.

"Pleasure," he replied, trying not to wince, wondering if the man would ever let go.

"We understand you knew the shooting suspect Stetson Parks. You were roommates."

It wasn't a question.

"For two years," Sam replied, finally getting his hand back.

"We need to cover a few details," Shotwell said. He thought the lady was smiling. His hand hurt too much to notice.

"I'm really kind of done with all of this. Perhaps if you spoke with Sheriff Martin or read my written statement ..."

The big man, hands like dinner plates, slapped him on the back.

"Have a seat. We won't be more than five or ten minutes. I promise."

"But it's my first day at work."

"I promise," he said again.

They sat at a tiny round table in the back corner of the shop. They sat in tiny wooden chairs that barely held them. Sam squirmed.

"Why now, guys?" he pleaded, "I've spent the last two weeks talking to you folks. What more could you possibly want?"

Shotwell placed her hands on the table.

"Mr. Featherstone, the investigation has sprawled out to involve," she shot a glance at Jones, "several other agencies. Some of these agencies will remain anonymous."

"So?"

"So," she replied, "we may not be done with you."

"What do you want now, blood samples?"

"Would you be willing to take a polygraph?"

Sam looked at the menu on the wall. Must have caffeine, he thought again.

He looked at the big dude, Jones. The man looked like one of his teachers in highschool asking if he had done his homework.

Sam never did his homework.

From a long ago TV show, he heard in his head, "Danger, Will Robinson. Danger!"

He took a deep breath and thought about this. Outwardly, he appeared to still be studying the wall menu.

FBI agents just don't come by for a friendly chat, everybody knew that. If they were here, they had a plan and a goal.

He needed to figure out what that was. He needed to do it without arousing suspicion. Get ahead of the game.

Some part of this conversation is bullshit. He knew it. He felt it. Which part?

He looked back to the lady cop.

"That's an interesting question," he said. He remembered from somewhere that you were supposed to say this when you're stumped.

Watching the cops, he realized that they knew this as well. They felt sorry for him, but that would change to suspicion pretty quickly unless he got moving, started managing the situation.

He frowned. The hits just kept coming, didn't they? The town of Liberty was like a black hole he was desperately trying to pull free of.

Could he get out?

He got out one of his decks of playing cards and began a one-handed shuffle.

Cards always relaxed him. There was something honest about playing cards, even marked ones.

"You know, I want to help you guys any way I can," he continued the shuffle, "I'm a little busy this morning, as I said, but I'm happy to continue this down at your office. I can bring Uncle Joe."

"Uncle Joe?" Shotwell was confused.

"The lawyer," he replied, "Uncle Joe the criminal lawyer. We can sort out whatever you'd like."

"Or we could just take you now. You could call him when we get there," she hit back.

Dammit.

"Either of you ever watch the Andy Griffith show?"

If they had, they'd never admit it. In return he got dead, blank stares.

"It was a good show," he said to nobody.

He caught a glance between the big man and the lady. They weren't prepared to go down this road. She had overstepped.

There was something else too. Maybe the two didn't know each other that well?

Time to raise the stakes a bit.

"Either of you two want to tell me now what this is all about," he looked between the two, studying their reactions, "before I leave."

Nothing.

"I don't think you're taking me very seriously," he said.

He looked back and forth again one last time. He could feel the conversation breaking.

"Good day, then,"

He began to rise.

Shotwell patted him on the arm, stopping him.

"Please sit, Featherstone."

He looked at her. He was not seated and not standing.

"Please," she repeated.

He sat.

Jones looked at Shotwell as if to say "What now?" In reply she raised her hands as if to say "What are we going to do now?"

Jones shrugged.

"It's your show, Shotwell," Jones said.

"We'd like for you to be our eyes and ears at EigenCorp." She looked Sam dead in the eye.

Welp, there it was. EigenCorp was famous for first day puzzles and tricks. Today they had come up with an especially nice one.

If he agreed, he was a security risk to the corporation. Who knew if these were actual cops or not? If he declined, he could be in trouble with Law Enforcement. The test would work best with real cops.

Heads I win. Tails you lose.

He was being asked how he would handle PERSEC, OPSEC, and LE interactions before he was briefed on what the corporation's official policy was. It was an especially nice test since some day in the future he might be playing the role of cop instead of victim, giving the test to some other noob.

Great. Now that he knew what the test was, what was he supposed to do?

What if it wasn't a test and these were real FBI agents?

A line from Star Wars came to mind unheeded, "I've got a bad feeling about this."

He certainly did.

He loved Star Wars, he loved this kind of back-and-forth human poker game, so he decided that this was going to be fun. Review options. Pull his phone out to check the credentials? Provide unnecessary SIGINT. Straight out refuse to talk? They'd keep pressuring him, up to a point. It was a bluff test.

The way he saw it, he only had one job: stall for time. Once he was briefed on security protocols at work today, he'd know what to do. Problem solved. That's probably why the female agent was trying to rush him. The other guy was probably a rental.

Of course, if he could turn the tables on the testers, get the identity of these two supposed agents without them knowing it? His first day would be outstanding. They'd talk about this for years to come.

Also, they might really be agents. He doubted it, but it was possible.

He didn't like using his magic like this, but hey, they started it.

"I'm here for caffeine and I need to use the bathroom. Can I get you guys something?"

As he stood, they both shook their heads no.

Moving towards the counter, he "accidentally" knocked the condiment tray to the floor. Little packets went everywhere.

"Gosh, I'm sorry," he said.

He stooped to pick them up. As they all looked at the mess, he palmed the purse of the lady and hid it.

"What a total doofus I am," shaking his head, he finished up and headed off.

And now here he was, ten minutes later trying to put all this back together and agent Shotwell banging on the door.

When in doubt, get up close. That's what his old magician mentor used to say. People don't observe that well when you're either very far away or extremely close. It's the middle ground that can be the death of any magic act if the magician doesn't manage it well.

He threw open the door and beamed at Shotwell, approaching and putting his arm on her shoulder. She tolerated this and did not kill him, so he kept going.

"Sorry, I'm a bit upset. I've been sick with nerves, my first day and all."

He grabbed his stomach a little bit.

She would take it as if Sam was overcompensating for nerves, which wasn't far from the truth. This would put her at ease.

"Say, has Jones already left?" he looked back to the dining room. She followed his gaze. This gave him about two seconds, which was all he needed.

"I guess so," she said, still looking. Her attention was easier to divert than he expected.

Delivery made.

Now to push through to the end. They either would let him go or his alternative course was throwing up all over them. Their choice. This job ain't beanbag.

He stepped forward, dropping his arm and looking at the entrance. Turning to her with a sheepish smile, he said, "Are we done here? I need to leave. I'm about out of time."

Just a flash. Oh, she didn't want to do this, he caught. This was a fighter, this one. But she smiled back.

"Of course," she shrugged, beginning to mimic his easy way, "Jones must have gone off somewhere. Of course, Mr. Featherstone."

"Sam."

She wasn't biting on that.

"Mr. Featherstone, here's my card. If you have any questions or there's anything I can do for you. Thank you for your time."

He shook her hand.

"Of course, this conversation is entirely confidential."

Sigh. "Of course Agent Shotwell."

"Mr. Featherstone."

Walking out on the street, he took a deep breath. The air was still fresh. The morning was still beautiful.

EigenCorp was only three blocks away, a nice interlude. He'd have to score some coffee when he got there. He was about to meet some of the cleverest, smartest, people on the planet. He was going to be making new best friends for life.

This was fun. This job was going to be fun.

He couldn't wait.

2.02

Hell Is A Real Place

He should have waited.

There was an insane person in the EigenCorp breakroom when Sam was ushered in by the receptionist. She was the only one there.

Medium height, athletic, short, cropped dirty-blond hair, about Sam's age. Sam thought the creature could have been attractive had it not been for the rest of her, the clothes.

Whoa.

She wore a baggy, button-up shirt, three-sizes too big, with diagonal red stripes on a blue background. Her jeans were normal and fit well, except for the neon orange belt, and the yellow polka-dots. She was wearing both a fedora and one of those Texas bowties.

A lunatic.

"What do you know about Janus Group?" she said before he could sit down.

"Nothing?" he replied. These EigenCorp tricksters just didn't give up, do they? Not going to work, my dudes.

An actress. It had to be an actress. EigenCorp had hired an actress for test number two. Ok. He could handle that. It'd be fun.

Today was going to be the best day of his life, he thought as he looked up to see some old guy enter. Maybe a janitor?

The old guy was about 65, ex-cop, although Sam didn't know why he felt that way. Something about the way ex-cops carried themselves: assured, inquisitive, and a bit combative.

"This must be Debian," he said, instantly destroying Sam's idea that he was a janitor, "and you must be Samuel. I'm Alexander McCulloch. You will call me Pops. I'm pleased to meet you."

147

Pops was dressed in what Sam would call "fake hipster". Jeans with a button-up flannel shirt, all pressed and starched, and just a wisp of a beard. The grooming was off, as if the man were a recluse playing the part of a fake nerd. If hipsters had an army, this man would be the genius general. That everybody avoided.

"What do you know about Janus Group," the girl immediately asked Pops.

Pops looked at Sam. Sam only shrugged. Good luck.

"Nothing," he said, "Should I know something?"

She considered.

"I don't know."

The older man accepted this in stride, sitting down at the table beside them, setting a large thermos in front.

"Coffee?" Sam lit up.

"Tea," he replied, "I make my own blend. If I don't sit it in front of me, I forget it."

"Same here. I bet you're the same way too," he looked at that new girl Deb.

"No," she didn't look up from the paperback she was reading.

"Debian," Pops began, "Samuel here, his team won CyberCon last year, best score ever. Sam, Deb came with the highest recommendations I've ever seen in an applicant."

Sam turned his smile up.

"Nice to …"

"I know," she said.

Back to the book.

His smile waivered a tiny bit.

Pops continued as if nothing happened.

"It wasn't a very big team, was it?"

"Nope," Sam was in his element, "Lotta interest. Just four."

"Nice work. We're still trying to figure out how you did it so quickly."

Sam looked at the girl to see if she had anything to say, perhaps by way of acknowledging how kick-ass Sam's accomplishment had been.

She did not.

She was reading an old, crappy paperback, with well-worn edges. It had a picture of a lot of bugs crawling around. The title was "Termites From the Fifth Dimension."

She kept reading, seemingly oblivious to anything else in the room.

The door opened and Joe Middles strode in. He looked just like Sam remembered: extremely fit, black shirt, black pants, short, black shoes, close haircut, and gold wire-framed glasses.

At least something was normal.

As odd as it all had been, so far today was everything Sam expected. He had been looking forward to this for years. He expected to be thrown some curveballs. The only thing different from his dream was that there weren't very many people. He'd expected scores of people, not just three.

"Good morning," Joe said. Sam thought they might wait for others to arrive, but this must be it, "The next couple of weeks will be intense classroom and practical application as we both evaluate and on-board you."

Sam thought Joe must have had this memorized.

"Computer programming," Middles said, beginning to pace across the room, "is dead. Back in the day when computers started, computer programming consisted of binary operations. Everything was yes or no. The light was either off or on. The program was either working or it was broken. Those days are effectively over. They've been over for a long, long time."

He stopped to face them.

"Decades ago, the Office of Personnel Management in the U.S. Government brought in a company to do a demo on a system that detected network intrusions. Not only was the demo successful, once they ran the program, during the demo, they discovered that the network was hacked, it had been for years. All of the sensitive personal information of every employee of the U.S. Government was lost, who knows where. As we speak, tens of billions of dollars per year are stolen from credit card companies. Losses for defective cryptocurrency runs in the hundreds of billions due to fraud and theft. The average patrol car has 14 pieces of malware in it. The average bank teller's terminal, 11. And that's assuming evil intent. When working as designed the risks are even greater because the risks can occur somewhere else, months or years later, not where you can see them. Data lives forever. This is a tremendous amount of damage and these are not dumb people creating and maintaining these systems."

"Sure, each little computer and each little program still works the way they used to, but we no longer live in a world with only one computer or only one program. Complexity itself changes everything, the sheer scale of computers involved. The average house has more than 200 microprocessors, and that's for people below the poverty line. Each of these computers can be running dozens or hundreds of programs. While each little piece of each little program is still yes or no, still working or broken, we don't interact with technology that way any more. The state of reality is far, far too complex for any person, programmer, team of programmers, or super-genius to ever figure out. For all intents and purposes, technology is effectively magic."

He smiled, reaching the punch line.

"And that's our job at EigenCorp: we evaluate magic here, because although it's all magic by now, people still need some kind of assurance, some educated auditing. Insurance companies still need to figure out how much to charge for policies. Cryptocurrency investors still need some assurance from an independent source about how risky a new cryptocurrency might be. We take the magic out of modern technology, or at least the best we can. Instead we replace it with a list of vulnerabilities, a calculated risk of failure, detailed reports of problems that need fixing. Cyber risk, and cyber risk underwriting, this is the future of all technology, whether it's controlling missiles or running the average home."

Sam squirmed in his seat.

"Sam and Deb, you'll be working together with Pops as a guide and master, at least until you're through your probationary period."

"Wait," Sam almost got out of his seat, "you mean this one is a real person?" he pointed his thumb at her.

"Of course I'm a real person. What the hell else would I be?" She said from beside him.

There was no smoke, but there was definitely a fire alarm. Sam knew something was on fire. He suspected it was him.

They all stared at Sam as if He had just farted loudly.

"And we've got to work together?" he had to do something. Something.

"That's how this works. You two are on the buddy system. Look to Pops for all of your training and to answer any questions."

"I'll make this as painless as possible, as long as you perform well," Pops said. He looked at his new charges as if not believing a thing he was saying. Sam knew the feeling.

Sam rubbed his head. "Isn't there a place I can get a cup of coffee? Please?"

Pops pointed, "Coffee clutch down the hall. A floor map is in your packet."

Now Sam just had to wait. Like a visit to the dentist, if he waited long enough, the pain would dissipate.

"You're not back home at school or with the buds," Pops said, "Things get real now. Buckle up."

"No. No way, Joe," Sam heard himself saying, "I can't work with her. I'm not that good."

"He's dumb," she added, "This one's defective. I'd like another one."

Sam held his hands up as if to say, "See? You want I should work with this?"

Joe crossed his arms, paced just a little back and forth, looking at them as if they were a car that wouldn't start and Joe was trying to figure out whether to call a tow truck or try to fix it himself.

"Well," he said finally, "If that's the way you want it, Sam, we can certainly find some study and research opportunities for you."

"Terrific, then that's what I want," Sam thought this wasn't going too badly.

"It'll mean you'll never work in the rest of the corporation." Joe said.

"Wait. What?"

"This is how we do things. We onboard people in teams, we work in teams. We train using the master-apprentice system. That's not up for discussion."

"If you want us to do this, Mr. Middles, I can do it." Deb said.

He hated her immediately.

Sam felt all the air suck out of the room. He slouched in his seat.

"Come on," Pops said to Deb, "Let's try to get you a team. I'll show you 'The Blackboard'."

They left. Sam watched them go. This was not going well.

After watching Sam for a minute or two, Joe finally said, "Should we get started on your new role?"

The breakroom felt very empty.

"Nope," he cleared his throat, "I've got this, Joe. I can do this. How hard can it be?"

Joe did not respond. He shrugged and gestured at the door where Pops and Deb had just exited.

Sam left the breakroom. He shuffled. He smiled until he got out of the room, of course, but once out he couldn't keep the smile going.

His fate awaited him.

His fate consisted of a round table with walled workstations pointing outwards, allowing both easy privacy and collaboration without having to get out of your seat. That was nice. Somebody had placed a potted plant. That was nice.

The girl Deb had already taken the workstation near the window, dammit. She'd also started putting her things on the shared table. If Sam didn't move now, there'd be no space for him. She was taking over the room.

He quickly grabbed another spot at the table, claimed his workstation, stuck his elbows on the table.

Pops spun around and pulled up to the shared table. He dropped a binder between the two.

"Both of you read that and we'll talk about it in a bit."

There was only one binder.

Sam turned the charm up, but Deb spoke first.

"I'll learn everything there is to know in here, Pops. No problem," she said, tapping the binder.

Sam pushed her hand off, tapped the binder as well.

"I love documentation."

"Both of you, is it possible to just dial it down a bit?" Pops asked.

They both frowned, glaring at the other.

"Absolutely. You got it. I plan on following your instructions to a T," Sam said.

"Tea. You forgot your tea," Deb looked at Sam as if he'd just lost a million-dollar poker game. To her.

Point Debian.

La-di-da. She had remembered something. Somebody play some trumpets.

Pops left, off to get his thermos, looking back one more time, unsure of leaving them without supervision.

Alone, the two new teammates stared at the other, then the binder, then each other again.

In his head Sam heard the theme song to "The Good, The Bad, and The Ugly."

Sam slid the binder over, "The man said we should both read this."

Deb slid it back.

"I will read it, then you can read it." She replied.

He slid it back to the middle.

"No, we can share. We can both read it."

Deb forcefully took it away again.

"I will read it. Then I will share it with you."

"Great Neptune's Ghost," he finally said. He tried to grab it. She held it firmly. Her knuckles whitened in her grip. Her frown was set in stone.

"Fine then," he slapped the table and stood. "Imma get more coffee." He looked down at her. She ignored him.

"Lots more coffee. Gonna need lots more coffee," he said, rubbing his head and wandering off, desperately sad.

2.03

That's Bananas

She came at him with the banana. Sam held the crowbar in hand. He'd gotten there early. Wasn't going to fall for that one again.

He was easily defeated, though. In the end, Sam felt that like the mighty and valorous opossum, his best option might be just to play dead and hope she left him alone.

It was a forlorn hope, easily dashed. It was all he had.

"Why do they call this room 'The Crowbar'," she came through the door, "when there's a picture of a hand on the outside?"

"Haven't you noticed? All the rooms are like that. The breakroom is 'The Stomach', our training area is 'The Ear'. This, for some reason, is 'The Crowbar'. I'm sitting here. This is my stuff. Leave me alone."

He spread his belongings out a bit more, trying not to look obvious.

It didn't work. He thought again of the possum, envied it. Opossums seemed happy.

She didn't leave him alone, but she also didn't ignore him. That was something. Instead, she came straight in, sat across from him, and jabbed at him with the banana as she spoke.

"What do you know about Stetson Parks?"

"My old roommate? Sad story. Horrible."

"What software were you running on your apartment router?"

"OpenWRT, whatever the latest version is. Are you going to greet me each day with random questions?"

She peered at him as if he were a spy.

"Does that bother you?"

"No more than yesterday."

She looked at her banana she pointed at him, as if Sam had just spoken to the banana and she was awaiting its reply. Without looking back at him, she sat the banana down. Finally she looked at him.

"I'm working on some things. That's all."

Back to the fruit.

She poked it.

He pointed at the things he'd already strategically placed around the table. He owned the table.

"I brought toys."

"Why would we need toys?"

"For one," he said, "gives you something to do besides abusing that banana. Watch this."

He began juggling, a simple three-ball cascade. Sam found juggling relaxing.

"You must be very proud of yourself," she said, then began eating her snack.

"Good morning," Pops said, entering the room, "This is 'The Crowbar'. It's where we take stuff apart."

Pops hefted up some large things in front of him.

"These are your backpacks. You'll carry them everywhere."

"Cool," Sam said, "I hope we get an Aston-Martin. Maybe with machineguns or smoke generators."

"There will be no cars in these backpacks," Pops said, "Empty them out now."

"What do you know about Stetson Parks?" Deb asked Pops before complying. Then she began emptying the pack.

"Nothing. Should I?"

She thought.

"I don't know," she said.

Pops began talking but she interrupted.

"Yet. Wow, what's this?" she said, holding something up.

"This," Pops said, "is your McGuffin. Everybody here has one and none of the tech will work without having it plugged up."

It was a small gray box, about half the size of an old metal lunchbox or hard drive.

"What's in it?" Sam asked.

"Nothing," the older man said, "That's what. Random noise. Each one is full of completely unique random noise, 100 terabytes worth. It's more than enough to record your entire life in holographic 3D and hide it from anybody else in the universe. Forever."

"Except the other McGuffin," Sam said, "It has a twin, right?"

"Very good, Sam. Right. These come in pairs, a key and lock. You'll never see the other one."

"McGuffin?" Deb asked, "Does this come with a McMeal or a McShake?"

"McGuffins, Deb," Sam was excited, "Never heard it? It's the old Alfred Hitchcock thing, right?"

Pops nodded.

"Hitchcock," Sam explained to her, "said every story needed a McGuffin. It's something the characters are trying to get. Hitchcock said it didn't matter what was in there."

"But we already have ours."

"Doesn't matter what's in there. It's just something you're trying to find." He tried again.

Pops smiled, "And, to Sam's point, this is both a tool and a honey trap. Try all you want. If you find one of these McGuffins? There's nothing there, just static. It's truly a bag of nothing."

Sam looked at his little grey box with admiration, "So attackers trying to hack into EigenCorp would be wanting one of these, thinking it's important. And even when they found it, there'd be nothing there."

"Kid's right," Pops said.

"One-time pad," Deb pointed at her box, "This is a One-Time Pad. One-time pads are probably the oldest still-secure secret code system. This is old."

"That's right, Deb. Moving along," Pops sat down, put his thermos on the table.

"Bulky, but totally secure," she finished.

"Also correct. That's why we use them. Storage costs are low. We can make a One-Time Pad for your entire life. We can hide you completely in statistical noise. Even better than quantum encryption."

"Then you should just call it a One-Time Pad," she said, putting hers down.

"I like McGuffin, Pops. Cool name." Sam said.

He tried to give Deb a corrective glance, but it was like making funny faces at an actively-erupting volcano.

Pops sighed.

Deb continued, "How about I hit you over the head, take this McGuffin thing, and I have all of your work?"

"No, Debian. That's what I'm trying to tell you. The pairs. Without both the exact machine or service and the machine pair, you've got a handful of nothing."

"This flips the script," Sam said, "Security happens completely server-side, not even any protocols needed."

"It does indeed. We used to make systems and try to secure them. Now, we just secure everything you say and we don't tell you which systems you're connecting to. It's like EigenCorp is a hotel with a million floors. We give you a key. You go to the elevator. When you get off, we know what floor it is but you don't. Your key works just fine. If somebody steals your key? Who cares? It'd be like somebody getting in the elevator trying to push all the buttons for a million floors, then trying to find what room they're in. Good luck with that."

"A McGuffin," Sam said, "My first McGuffin. I love it."

"Maybe Sam could buy it a little bonnet, write it a love poem," Deb said, "Perhaps he could enlighten us more about other things even tangentially useful that he also doesn't know."

Now Sam sighed, "Not here to teach you."

"Doubtful there's anything you can teach me."

"Didn't know what a McGuffin was, did you?" Sam felt suddenly very childish.

"No," she replied, "But that's nothing I wanted to know."

"This will be used for all of our communication," she tapped it soundly.

"This will be used for all of your communication," Pops agreed, emphasizing the word 'your'."

Sam leaned forward, "Wait, are there other ways of communicating here? Other cool stuff?"

"There are all sorts of things going on in all sorts of areas, Sam. We'll let you know if you need to know about them." Pops looked sad.

"Got it, manage the people first, the old professionals and amateurs thing." Sam said.

"Exactly," Pops responded.

"Exactly what?" Deb asked.

Sam straightened up, as if reciting poetry, "Professionals hack people. Amateurs hack technology. Pops is telling us that no matter what tech they give us, it's the human part that counts. Need to know."

"Sounds like something somebody who doesn't understand the technology would say," she replied, looking at the remains of her banana.

"I look forward to getting the org chart," Sam said. He wanted to change the subject, "See what I might want to do as I advance."

"We don't have org charts," Pops replied.

Sam didn't give up. "Or our first all-hands meeting."

"We don't have all-hands meetings," Pops replied.

"Or get to know some of the other people," Sam tried again.

"We work in cells," Pops replied.

"And yet somehow I just know this will be fun," Sam did not sound convincing even to himself, "Things are bound to change sooner or later. Debian will probably get assigned to the cyborg division, there she can really fit in."

Deb took him in, "And Sam will go where he can succeed with his 'skills', children's birthday parties or traveling minstrel shows."

"Neither of you," Pops' voice was starting to get strained, "are going anywhere at EigenCorp. You'll stay together in this team even after training. You'll stay together until I say otherwise. Get used to it. You two need to pay more attention, settle down."

Sam looked back down at the table, picked up the next item. It was a multitool in its case.

"Oooh, is this a combat knife?" he asked.

"No," Pops replied, "But if you want it to be, sure."

Sam smiled more, "Do these backpacks have satellite transmitters in them? USB charging? Are they flotation devices?"

"No, Sam, they're backpacks," Pops replied again, "but they are Faraday Cages. They keep radio signals from coming in or going out. That's kind of special. They do that."

Quickly moving his hand, a cigarette appeared in Sam's mouth. He tried his best to look super cool.

"I'm Featherstone. Sam Featherstone," Sam said in his best Sean Connery impersonation.

"Where'd you get that cigarette," Deb asked, "There's no smoking in here."

He took the prop from his mouth.

"I know," he said, "I don't smoke."

"Then why do you have a cigarette," she asked.

"It's part of the joke, the gag. Don't you ever joke around, have fun?" he asked her.

"I've had fun 17 times in the last year. I have plenty of fun." she said, "I am a fun person."

Now Pops leaned in. "Debian, is there something bothering you?"

She pushed back but didn't get up. "My father had one of these McGuffin things in his personal belongings. Before he left us."

"Made your own father run away," Sam blurted.

Realizing he'd gone too far, he quickly added, "That was too much. I apologize."

"I don't get it," Pops said, "Either of you two actually want to be here?"

They both nodded yes.

Pops did not appear to believe either one of them.

Sam tried pleading with Deb. "Can we please stop playing who's the biggest nerd?"

"I'm not playing anything," was the reply.

Sam glared at her. She continued. "I was at the airport, Samuel, ok? I was Carl's flight instructor. He died right beside me. Head exploded. I beat Stetson to a pulp, okay?"

"I'm so sorry," he was totally being the idiot today. He didn't know why, "I didn't know."

Sam struggled to put his thoughts into words, "Stetson," he said, "was unwell."

"Debian and Samuel," Pops said, now pulling back a bit, "We can do this tomorrow, or this afternoon. This is just a training session. There doesn't need to be so much drama. I had no idea that both of you had history."

"We don't," both said in unison.

"You struggle, don't you Deb," Sam was feeling his way forward, not knowing where this would go. You don't know the human side of this work, do you?"

"As much as I need to," she said. Was that a flicker of petulance?

Sam felt sedate. "If we're stuck together like Pops said, I've got a lot of work ahead. You and I have a lot to go over."

"I have some teaching," Pops said to the room, "Teaching, teaching, teaching. Anybody want teaching."

Pops sounded like a fishmonger, a terribly-depressed carnival barker.

Sam couldn't avoid it.

Pops sounded like Eeyore.

"Not now, Pops," Sam said without looking at their mentor.

"Excuse me?"

"The boy," Deb said the word as if Sam had just been found wearing a loincloth, feral in the deep jungle, "thinks he has something to say."

"Are you familiar with the seven leading personality modeling systems?" He asked.

"All of which are horseshit," she replied.

"Yeah yeah. Probably looking at them backwards, like a coder. They're lagging categorization systems, ontologies, not predictive models. But surely you've talked about using math to model people and groups, right? Yamir Moreno, Dawkins, memes, and epistemology, physics as social science, right?"

"Sure. Hari Seldon. Isaac Asimov and the Foundation Series of sci-fi books. You can use math to predict what people will do."

"Good books," he said, still studying her. He felt as if he were looking at a diamond with a million facets. Whatever was in there, he'd never see it.

"Extremely over-simplified, but okay for its time," She continued.

"You just don't give an inch, do you?" He started going berserko again.

"Who would I give an inch to?" She replied.

Sam started making a sound he'd never made before, something between a growl and a whimper.

"Ok, ok," Pops stood, "That's enough. Take five. You can leave. You can go grab a snack. Use the restroom. You can stay. But no more interaction between you two for the next five minutes. Got it?"

They got it.

Pops did not leave. He looked at them as if they were a bomb and the ticking had gotten too loud to ignore. In the silence, Deb picked up the Chinese Finger Puzzle Sam had brought and quickly got her fingers stuck.

Sam tried to ignore her. He didn't need a break, and hell if he was going to let her run him off. He could sit here quietly as good as she could. He began juggling some more. He started humming. He heard her groan as she pulled as hard as she could to escape the trap.

He hummed louder.

Pops crossed his arms, frowned.

She stomped her feet in exasperation.

Sam stopped juggling. He tried staring at the wall. He counted in his head. He started going through prime numbers. She began thrashing around, still fighting as hard as she could to get free.

"Dang it, enough," he said. He reached to both of her hands, pushed them together, releasing her from the trap.

"Things aren't all they appear to be," he said, hoping Pops didn't hear him. Pops was two feet away and it would have been impossible not to hear Sam. The teacher watched but said nothing.

Knowing he'd lost, he looked back at her, "You're really not so strong on inter-disciplinary cross-silo applications, are you."

"I don't know what you mean by that." she answered.

"Will you allow me to explain?"

She nodded.

It did not feel like winning. It did not feel like losing.

It felt like … relaxing.

"Well, eventually, of course, we're going to need to talk about Pan-psychism and IIT, Integrated Information Theory, but let's start with information leakage. People are always going to be a problem, even with these McGuffins."

"Really? Why's that?" Pops asked.

"It's like the wave-particle collapse function. Nothing can happen without being observed somewhere by somebody somewhere else. You can never ever really be alone in the universe, no matter how much you try to isolate yourself. The universe observes itself."

"That's good, Sam," Pops said, "that nerd stuff. Let's go with that. Deb, what do you think the risks are here?"

She picked up her McGuffin again and said, "That we're working with stone knives and bearskins, that's what. We're lucky we're not dancing around a fire with painted faces."

"Ooof," Sam said and immediately regretted it.

Sam kept talking.

Pops eventually sat down, poured himself some tea. Watched.

Deb listened a bit, and Pops never did get the morning training completed.

Donut Dating

Happily, Sam's next day did not begin with random questions from Debian. Instead, The Great Donut Scandal began. It marred much of Sam's work at EigenCorp.

Sam got to work first, which he considered a pretty good start. Pops, of course, was already there, but Sam had learned that days were better when he could gird his loins first, preferably with coffee, before the other one arrived.

Deb came in next, but instead of coming over, she started talking to the service lady about something. The conversation looked quite animated and Sam was glad he wasn't the service lady. It occurred to him that he was thinking of the latest assignment the wrong way. Instead of Initialization Vectors, he may be thinking of the protocol the wrong way, an error that was an order of magnitude more complicated.

Just as he began to refactor his strategy, he noticed Pops struggling over a notepad. Something big was coming.

Pops looked at his notepad the way a man might look at his last meal. "Go get Whiz Kid. We should start."

Deb was wearing what best might be described as golfer meets psychedelic experience. She had a foppy golfer hat on, golfer shoes and slacks. She was wearing a red and black checkered shirt, a flower on her hat. He could hear her lecturing the poor service lady as he approached them.

"All I'm saying is that according to the door logs, for the past three weeks you have been bringing donuts at 15 minutes past the hour, give or take a standard deviation of 2 minutes. That's seven minutes after the pastry truck shows up in front."

Deb pointed to the front of the building.

The girl had her arms crossed.

"They're here by 7:30. Every day."

She said this as if she had repeated it several times. Sam suspected she had.

"But not Thursdays," Deb said, "You usually add between seven and ten minutes. I'm sorry but I don't have enough data to give you a standard deviation yet."

The girl looked at Sam, helpless. Sam shrugged.

"Deb," he interrupted, "Pops needs us."

He pointed to the helper.

"Perhaps the case of the missing donuts can wait until later?"

"They're not missing. And it's not donuts."

"I know," he said. He turned to go back to the team room. He hoped she would follow. She eventually followed, slowly, not willing to give up the topic.

Pops was wrong. He didn't need them. Pops wasn't ready to start yet.

"Whatcha doing, Pops?"

"Trying to figure out what my online dating profile should be."

Sam looked up. Deb was on the way. Dating. Dating profile. Deb. On the way.

Red alert, Sam.

"You're trying to get into online dating?"

Pops looked up.

"I am. Can you help?"

Deb was almost there. Having Debian give any kind of dating advice would be like distributing cans of gasoline at a Pyromaniacs Anonymous meeting, loaded guns at Psychopaths Anonymous.

Run.

Sam grabbed his teacher and started walking him to the door. Passing Deb on the way, he said, "We'll be right back. Boy stuff."

"Great. I may need to write a letter."

She let them go. Escape. The day was looking up.

Leaving the building, he took in a big breath of city air, winked, and elbowed Pops conspiratorially.

"So Pops," he said, "Dating, huh. How long you been single? How long you been in the dating scene?"

"Ten years."

"If you've been dating for ten years, you don't need me, you're an old hand by now."

Pops stopped to look at Sam and clarify.

"Been single all my life," Pops said, "I haven't dated in ten years."

Sam ushered him on, trying to keep the mood light.

"So," Sam said, "What have you been doing? What are your hobbies?"

"I don't have any hobbies," Pops replied, "I've been training people."

Sam was a little taken back, "So it's just work for you, that's it?"

"How do you think I've developed my exciting personality?" the older man said.

Not for the first time, Sam thought that Pops looked like a dead fish, pretending to be a hipster.

"How about you, Sam," Pops said, "Do a lot of dating?"

"Dated the Homecoming Queen," he replied, trying to strike a balance between reassurance and showing off, "Kept three girlfriends going at the same time my freshman year in college."

"So you can help," Pops said as they approached the shop, "Good."

"Like riding a bike, Pops. We'll have fun. It'll be easy. You're a natural."

"Dating anybody now?" Pops tried not to look at Sam. Sam knew better. The man was nosey.

"Not in a couple of years," Sam replied.

"Why?"

"Dunno. Dating came very easy for me. Extremely. Eventually I realized that I didn't like what romantic relationships were doing to me. It was unpleasant."

"So, no dating now?" Pops asked.

He shook his head no.

"Gets pretty lonely," Pops replied.

Passing a panhandler by the coffee shop door, Sam handed him a bill.

"You give money?" Pops asked.

"Sometimes. You?" Sam replied.

"Never," Pops opened the door and they went inside.

"Nick, Nick, Bub-bick!" Sam fist-bumped the man behind the counter.

The man was obviously happy to see Sam.

"Usual, Sam?"

"As always, my man, and a double-coffee for my friend here," Sam replied. Sam handed him his credit card.

The man took the order, continuing the banter, "Thanks for helping with the phone. Thought I was going to have to get a new one."

"I live to serve," he replied, taking his card back.

They took their drinks. Sam said hello to two more people on the way to the table, each happy to see him. Sam had missed the gang.

"Come here often?" Pops said, pulling a chair out.

"Couple times a week. Since the offer."

Sam thought he saw one of the supposed FBI agents in the corner.

Sitting down, Pops laid out one of the EigenCorp burner phones.

"I've reserved this phone for the next month. I'm looking at installing this app called 'Let's Meet' Heard of it?"

"I have indeed," Sam said.

Wrong road. He was afraid of that.

"You don't look excited. Something wrong? Is there a better app?"

"Where do we start," Sam said, mostly to himself, wondering how things got all reversed. Again. Sam was the teacher.

"Let's do a little history," Sam said, "What's your dating history?"

"I was almost married once in my 20s," Pops replied.

"Oh. How'd that go?"

"She died."

Sam took a deep breath. Nothing was easy. "How about your 30s? Any serious dating?"

"Had a serious girlfriend in my mid-30s," Pops said.

"That's great," Sam replied, "How'd you meet? How'd that work out?"

Pops sighed before continuing, he was not enjoying any part of this. "She was an infiltration agent. Our meeting was a gimmick."

"Oh,"

"Let's just say it didn't end well," Pops frowned.

"Ok, well good," Sam said, "Your dating history is not as good as it could be. That's very common, especially with professionals. We can work with that."

"You're a tech guy," Pops looked up, "And single. You must have a list of the top ten things to do and say, right?"

"Doesn't work like that," Sam replied, "Dating isn't an outward-facing thing, it's an inward-facing thing. You learn to have fun, do it good enough, and other people want to jump in. I never use tricks on people. Relationships are hard enough without the tricks."

"But you said how good you were, surely there are patterns…"

"I'm a good schmoozer, Pops," Sam said, "That's it. Not a trickster, and we're going to make you a good schmoozer too, not a player."

He looked at his mentor. The man's face sagged today more than normal. His ears had hairs that were at least three inches long. He had the eyebrows of a mature camel. An unwashed camel. A mature, unwashed camel who did not like people, finding them all disappointing.

"If it's the last thing we do," Sam added.

Pops phone buzzed. He picked it up and started punching his fingers at it.

"Important?" Sam asked.

"Nyah. Damned notifications. You buy a phone to make sounds and the first thing you do is try to shut the damned thing up."

Sam looked at his teacher. He groaned. Still with the tech.

"I don't think this is going to go the way you want it to, Pops," Sam said.

"You recommend an app. You give me some tips. I get a date. What's so hard about that?"

"What indeed," Sam looked again at the phone, "Hmmm. Let's try this differently. How many serial killers do you think there are out there today?"

"At my age, not worried about a serial killer," Pops said.

"Nobody knows," Sam answered his own question, "That's how many. We can only guestimate based on the number of serial killers we've caught. The ones that don't get caught don't exist for us."

"I'm not a serial killer, Sam, I just don't date a lot," Pops said, "I'm very friendly."

"I know. Ideally I'd recommend three or more dating apps and we'd make about a dozen fake profiles on each. Then we'd start talking about creating an automated winnowing and vetting strategy."

"That's way too much for what I need," Pops said.

"Well yes and no," Sam replied, "When we engage with the universe using text and apps, we're playing a text and app game. The problem isn't what you need. The problem is how to make the app work for you. We have to have a different goal than the app, because the app definitely has a different goal than we do, whether we realize that or not. We've got to poison the model, stay ahead of the AI. Make it work in spite of itself."

"You're making this far too complicated, kid," Pops said.

"You'd think, wouldn't you?" Sam said, "I'd think so too, if I weren't in the business we're in. Why are so many things free online? Hmm. How do you prevent getting scammed on the telephone?"

"Things are free so they can sell you stuff," Pops said, "And you don't answer the phone if you don't want to get scammed."

Sam thought he saw an opening, "You don't answer the phone because there are a billion ways to get scammed and the only rational thing to do is just not play along. You'll never stay on top of them all. Yet here we are, you wanting an app and some tricks to get something simple done: meet new people. It's the same thing as answering some random telephone call."

"Bullshit," Pops said, "This isn't anything like answering the phone. I'm not giving anybody any money."

"Pops," Sam tried, "People think that apps are free because they want to sell you stuff. That's like telling folks not to answer the phone because they're going to want to sell you timeshares. It's just a tiny little example in an infinite sea of possibilities. Don't confuse a simple example and what you and I can reason about with reality. Data lives forever. You know that. Sure, they want to sell you things, but that's the thing you see. The universe is under no obligation to make sense to you. We only see the serial killers we catch."

"You're not going to help me, are you," Pops said, obviously dejected, "I can't take this."

He pushed the coffee cup away.

"Coffee? Why not?"

"Doc's orders," Pops said, "No coffee. The man's got it in for me."

Sam started to rise up, "I can get you…"

Pops motioned stop.

"I'm okay. This is why I bring tea. You didn't know. Couldn't know. We're okay. Sit down."

"I don't care what you have to say you son-of-a-bitch!"

Both looked over to see a middle-aged woman yelling at her phone, walking out the door.

"Yikes," Sam said, "not a good day for some folks."

"You don't know," Pops replied, "She may like relationships like that. Some folks do. They rarely admit it to themselves."

Pops looked at him as if making a point. What it was, Sam had no idea.

"If you insist, if you want me to give you the best dating app," Sam said, "I did a statistical study last year for some friends."

"Tell me," Pops said.

"Sure. Then you'll get fired for being a security risk in a couple of weeks, a month tops. Worse, they won't figure out you're a security risk and you'll just run on blindly being a firehose of sensitive data. This what you want?"

"Care to explain why?" Pops looked mildly engaged.

"I can give you examples, but the problem is never what you'd expect. Military folks are big into physical fitness, so they install fitness apps. Other folks, maybe three or four jumps later and a year or two down the road use the GPS that comes with the data to identify secret military bases, even estimate how many people are stationed there. Retailers who sell feminine products can tell when women get pregnant. People buy that data along with data from social media and other places to scare people into buying things to keep the baby from getting hurt. How do they know the things that scare you? Because people post about their fears on social media from some other source, perhaps posts they made ten years ago. Con artists online stopped trying to scam you directly. Now they use AIs to read your posts, like them, make good comments. After months or years of that, the AIs point you to some other thing that does the scam. If done well, you'll think it was your idea to contact the people who scammed you. They disappear and the scam continues. Hell, your AI friends will all commiserate with you about how sorry they are you got scammed, maybe offer advice about how to avoid scams in the future. It's always misdirection and never what you think, Pops."

He pulled a coin from Pops' ear, handed it to him.

"You never see the good ones. If you can expect it or figure it out, it doesn't work. That's showbiz. The internet is a huge magic act run by magicians playing games they'll never explain to you."

"You do this magic stuff while you were dating?" Pops handed him the coin back.

"No, why?"

"Didn't think so. At least you know about some of the things not to do. Maybe I should use different software."

Pops glanced at the phone, a puzzle yet to be solved.

Dang it. "No," Sam said, pulling the phone away from the man, "Apps are apps. People are people. Stop using apps to do people things. You're putting yourself at risk."

"Can I have my phone back?" Pops asked.

"No," Sam replied.

Pops glared.

"Would you like to see what I look like when I'm angry?"

"Also no," Sam replied.

Pops held his hand out. Sam slid the phone to the middle of the table. They both left it there.

"Watch this," Sam said.

He walked over to a group of women standing nearby. He began chatting, smiling profusely. They began smiling along. Laughter. A few minutes later he came back. He waved to them before sitting down. They waved back.

"See?" Sam said, "I got a phone number. You just gotta go practice talking to people."

Pops groaned, "I am never ever going to be able to do that," he looked at the girls, afraid, back to Sam, "Never ever."

Pops crossed his arms in either defiance or anger. Whatever it was, Sam didn't like it.

"This is hopeless," Sam finally gave up, "I can't train you. We can't find common ground."

"That's what I thought," Pops said, his voice even deeper and sadder, "Work too hard for too long, now I've got nothing."

"Everybody can learn to do something," Sam said. It was a reflex, but it was true.

"Can't teach an old dog new tricks. Might as well get used to it. Thank you for trying, Samuel."

"Teach. Hmmmm. I think that's it," Sam said.

"What?"

"You're going to teach yourself," Sam replied, "That's it. You're a teacher."

"I'm not going to teach myself to do something I don't know how to do. That's stupid," the older man said.

"Do you want to hear what I have to say?" Sam asked.

"No."

Sam tried again, "Will you at least try some new things with me?"

Pops realized that he was out of places to go. Try something now, or walk away from dating forever.

"Sure Sam," there was no optimism in his voice.

Sam took the phone, walked over to the nearest trashcan and threw it away.

Pops started up from the table, but before he could make a scene Sam said, "Come on, we're got work to do."

They spent the rest of the morning at the mall, the laundromat, the grocery store, and a half-dozen other random places. Sam would demonstrate, Pops would try. Most of the time he'd fail, but not always, and as the morning progressed, Pops had to admit he was finally meeting folks and failing. It wasn't a disaster.

Eventually, and most grudgingly, he also had to admit he was having fun. Towards the end, Sam hung back and let Pops do the work.

Turns out Pops could teach himself something he didn't know.

Pops was a pretty good teacher.

2.05

Testing Partnership

"You people actually get paid for this? This is a job?" Deb said to Sam as Pops entered the The Ears.

"We people get paid for all sorts of things," Pops said, taking a seat and nodding at them both, "I, for instance, get paid to take you puppies and try to make you into something useful And I'm happy to say that you two are my very last batch of puppies. So be good, wag your tails, and listen to instructions."

"We're honored," Sam replied, "Debian and I have been working a bit on our own on team-building."

"He showed me card tricks. They were stupid." Deb said.

"You're in luck. Today we're going to fix that," Pops said, "Today we have the last of our in-class exercises."

He dropped a huge stack of paper on the table.

"The exercise is to detect a network intrusion using only these server logs."

Sam guessed the stack was at least 400 pages thick.

"That'll build us into a team if anything will." he said.

"Sam is especially bad at things," Deb said.

"Things? Bad at what things?" Sam said.

"Anything," she replied. "All things."

"Still mad about that joke the other day?"

When she didn't respond, he looked at Pops and explained.

"I told a joke about the Fibonacci Series and clowns," he said, "It was my horrible mistake."

Sam held his palms up in a "who knows?" gesture.

Deb's lips turned white. Her jaw clenched.

"She doesn't like those things. She didn't speak to me the rest of the day."

"Can we please get on to why we are here?" Deb asked.

"Excellent idea. Today is going to be especially fun." Pops said. He rubbed his hands together in anticipation.

"Several years back, unsure if their network had been hacked, a client came to us. They were a research department studying auto-generated movies and associated plethysmographic telemetry. They were concerned about data quality." Pops said.

"Ah, the old wiener meter," Sam said.

They all looked at him.

"Plethysmographs are devices commonly used to measure sexual response."

They still stared.

"I read a lot. There was an NSA study years ago about using Viagra as a weapon against terrorists."

"There you go," Deb was thumbing through the top few pages and then tapping the stack, "Got it. They were right to worry. The research data was faked. Done. What's next?"

Pops cocked his head, "How can you tell?"

"The first digits in the data do not follow Benford's Law. Benford's Law says that when you collect a lot of data from the real world, the first digit will not always be random. Instead it follows a predictable pattern. People faking data pick random first digits, so they pick numbers that don't follow the pattern without realizing that they're giving themselves away."

"Yep," Sam said, "been used a lot in accounting fraud cases. Can't just make up fake numbers. Numbers don't work like that. I'm guessing PornHub was the client funding the research, and the data would have been all mucked-up anyway since it was college students."

"Do tell," Pops said.

Deb explained, "College students are notoriously bad for research. If you're not extremely careful, you end up with one bunch of college students measuring another. The age, education, and political bias are almost impossible to overcome even using de-confounding techniques."

"Don't you two want to scan the data into the system? Do an analysis?"

"No need to do all that," Deb said, continuing to look at the pages, "This was a network hack from the far East. Looks like North Korea."

Pops was amazed. "How can you possibly know that?"

"Well Pops," Deb said, "computerized hacking does follow a normal distribution, a bell curve. It usually follows a bell curve around both data collection and data consumption. Collection was Illinois, probably, and consumption was done in the Far East. The time zone can't be Japan, so it's one of the Koreas."

"It's an NPT NK." Sam said, "Asian countries are famous for the men worrying about penis size."

"Yup," Deb agreed, "and look here: we've got UDP packets during the experiment times."

Sam was surprised, "Wow. Funny. Hilarious even."

"Deb," Pops said, "How do you gather that data so quickly?"

Deb shrugged. "I don't know. Always been able to. But I'd worry about the perverts if I were you."

"Perverts?" Pops asked.

"Funny," Sam said again, "What Deb's saying is that a bunch of North Koreans not only hacked the data, they were surfing in and watching the porn as it was created. I doubt any of the training teams figured that out. I'm assuming the test you're giving is about good old data processing, right? Getting information into the machine, cleaning, slicing, dicing, running some R code. That's time-consuming. Deb's conclusions match up with the social situation, the behavioral model and ..." he found the page he was looking for, "Yup, the character set ISO numbers match. That was nicely done, Deb."

Deb shrugged again. "Deliberately excluding certain key-chords was a dead giveaway. Page 71."

"You'd think they'd all know about that one by now," Sam said.

Pops just kind of melted in his chair.

"I'm sorry," Sam said, reading Pops face, "We should have taken more time on that, shouldn't we? Could we start over?"

"Uh..." Pops said. It was the first time they'd seen him speechless.

"I'm doing my best to train Samuel," Deb offered. Now she also began looking uncomfortable.

Sam was also confused. Was that a joke? There was no timing and her expression was all wrong. WTF?

"I must admit that I'm enjoying myself," Deb said, "If it's possible to increase the complexity, this might even be entertaining."

"Small teams rock," Sam agreed, "I've never worked in a small team where we all didn't have a blast."

"Four or five orders of magnitude." Deb said.

"Both of you," Pops said, "obviously have talent. We need to harness that. Better. Somehow."

"It's Social Engineering, Pops. That's where all the action is. If you can work the people, you can do anything," Sam said.

"You are wrong. Again." Deb said, "Technology is the most important. We are all here, this entire building exists because of technology."

"Silly child. You can't see your nose for your face," Sam said with a flourish, "I know I'm right just like I know that there's an Ace of Spades underneath all of this paperwork."

Pops eyes narrowed, bemused.

Deb slid the remainder of the stack over and looked underneath.

There was indeed the Ace of Spades.

She didn't smile, pick up the card, be amazed, or anything Sam expected.

Instead, she gently put the stack back down. She sat back in her seat.

"You have to be the most artificial, fake person I've ever met," she said.

"I don't feel very artificial. I feel pretty real to me."

Sam looked at Pops. Sam smiled. This was obviously some kind of comedy routine Deb was starting. Sam could play along.

Sam thought that Pops looked very interested in Deb. Pops was not smiling.

"Ok, boys and girls," Pops said, "Something new. Get your chairs out. Put them in a circle."

They did so.

"We're going to have a team encounter session which I will facilitate. Since none of us seem to understand the other, I'm just going to call this exercise what it is: a Group Grope."

As Sam sat in his chair, it squeaked.

"One sec," he said.

"I hate that," he said as he replaced it at the table and got the last one remaining.

As he sat, they all heard that the new chair squeaked much worse than the first one.

Sam pretended not to notice.

"So," Pops said, trying to begin, "Let's start with something easy. What's your favorite part about EigenCorp so far?"

"Your confectionary delivery system is broken," Deb said almost immediately. She looked at both of them as if expecting immediate and overwhelming agreement. "But I like them. A lot. I also like the local-remote cloud configuration and your subnetting strategy."

Pops looked to Sam.

"Interesting people," Sam said, "I love the interesting people."

"You haven't met anybody. Neither of us have," Deb said.

"Well when I meet them, I'm sure they'll be interesting."

"Bullshit."

Sam tried to ignore her.

"And it isn't called Benford's Law," he said to Pops, "She was wrong. Again. It's the Law of Anomalous Numbers. There's another name .."

He looked around.

"Which we can talk about later, of course."

"This isn't working," the older man said, "Ok, switch gears. You," he quickly checked his notes, "Debian. Why are you here? What are your goals working here?"

Sam watched as she just sat there. He couldn't tell if she couldn't come up with an answer or was just off in some universe of her own. Or both.

Finally Pops answered his own question.

"Me? I'm here finishing up my career, taking my last team through training. After that? I'll do whatever the hell I want to do, that's what. Probably hang out here. Maybe I can build that resource center I've always wanted."

Pops paused. They both looked at Deb. She was exactly the same as before.

"I love it here," Pops continued, "I love the work and I love the people."

They looked at Deb some more.

Pops finally looked at Sam. Pops shrugged. Sam's turn.

"I'm here because this is my dream," Sam said. He was trying to be careful just to say things that Deb couldn't correct. "I love people and I love tech. I want to do well and get rewarded here. I wouldn't even mind doing what you do, Pops. I think I could train people."

Pops gave him a grandfatherly smile. The smile was maybe just a bit strained. Sam had overshot a bit.

"Somebody slandered my dad and framed him. My dad might be a criminal. My sister's dead. My brother's gone. My house burned down. I have nothing."

Sam knew his mouth was hanging open. He couldn't help it and he didn't care.

Deb continued.

"I'm here to find my family, ask my dad for answers. I don't care about any of you and I wish you'd all just leave me alone. Just tell me what you need me to do. I'll do it."

The room was silent.

"Hey! Who'd like to hear a joke? So there's this farmer, see," Sam started, "and he had a daughter .."

"Shut up," she said.

Sam shut up.

Deb moaned a bit. She massaged her temples.

"Are you okay?" Pops said.

"I'm fine. Just a headache," She replied.

Their mentor reached in his pocket.

"Here, take some aspirin."

Sam was intrigued.

"You carry aspirin around?" He asked.

"You get old, you carry all kinds of stuff around. Anybody want some nitroglycerin?"

"Not without detonators," Deb replied, swallowing the pills.

Sam leaned in. Again, joke or not?

"Debian, whatever your goals are, we can help each other out, right? You can help me with that amazing brain of yours and I can help you with friends."

"I don't have any friends," she replied.

Sam was excited, "See? We're all starting fresh here. I can help. We're beginning a great adventure. The world is our oyster."

"I don't have any friends. Anywhere." She had a fierce stare. Clear eyes. "No friends. Anywhere ever. All gone."

Pops shifted around in his seat.

"I have another exercise, if you two are up for it."

Neither spoke.

"Another time. I understand."

"Socialization skills are important," Sam said to his feet.

His feet did not reply.

"At least I don't have kittens as a desktop background," Deb said, also to her feet.

Sam felt his blood pressure building.

"What's the matter with you .. Wait a minute. How do you know what's on my background on my computer?"

Deb said nothing.

That little rat. That was enough.

"You broke into my computer."

He looked at Pops. Sam wanted his words to punch people.

"She broke into my freaking computer." Sam said.

"That's interesting," was all Pops said.

Back to the devil girl.

"How did you break into my computer.? He asked.

"It was defragging too much. I fixed it."

Sam spoke through clenched teeth. Nobody had ever broken into his computer. Ever.

"I have a 64-character," he stopped, "You're a fucking thief, that's what."

"And you're a fucking con man." she replied. Her face was red.

"What the hell good are you, Deb? Everybody here breaks into stuff. Why would you betray my trust and break into my stuff? Your own partner? All we have is trust. We are nothing without trust you stupid freaking Aspie Idiot."

In a tired voice, Pops said, "Not going well."

"You are not my partner," Deb muttered.

"I want her written up," Sam pointed at Deb, "Can't we do some kind of disciplinary thing?"

Deb would have none of it.

"I would rather go to Jail and be tortured by miniature unicorns than work with this fake-ass loser." she said.

"Team …" Pops began.

"I don't want to talk to you anymore."

Deb got up. She left. She didn't yell. She didn't slam the door. She didn't even make a face, besides the beet red one she was currently wearing.

Watching the door shut, Pops looked at Sam.

"You guys really are amazing. Do you realize how much you've just messed things up?"

"She means the rest of the day, Pops. This is the third time it's happened. She cools off."

Anger gone, Sam was just depressed.

Can't you figure out how to avoid it?" Pops asked.

"I'm trying," Sam said, "Trust me, I'm trying. I'm making a list of stuff not to talk about. I think I'm making progress. I hope."

Pops pushed his chair back. He started twiddling his thumbs.

"Why do you think you're here, Sam?"

"Because I'm good at this?" Sam answered.

"Oh you're good. Very good. But why you? There are a lot of people who are very good. Why did we pick you?" Pops asked.

"I don't know," Sam said, "You're the one who picked me. Why did you?"

"I don't know either, and there's something deeply wrong about that," the older man said.

"Not good enough?" Sam's day was spiraling down.

"Sam, I know everybody that comes through that door. I chair the candidate selection committee. I have to know them. I'm required to know them. But not you two."

"Both of us?" Sam was getting more confused by the minute. Was he being fired?

"Both of you were hand-picked by Joe himself. I don't know why and I don't want to know why. I started looking into it, quickly realized what a bad idea that was. But it's damned odd. I know that."

Sam struggled, "I just thought with the contest I won ..."

"Do you know that her dad, Deb's dad, is one of the leading researchers in predictive Large-Language Modeling?"

"He was one of my teachers," Sam said, "but no."

"Do you know Deb broke into the NRO six years ago?" Pops asked.

"But you can't do that. What was she, twelve? No. It can't happen."

Pops took a deep breath. "Said she wanted a better hiking map for one of their family's weekend adventures. National Reconnaissance Office. For a hiking map of a trail nearby."

"I don't understand," Sam said.

"Hmm. You're right about that. You're not alone. I don't understand either. Her dad covered for her. It's all hush-hush. If I didn't have a friend over there I wouldn't know. There are no records."

Maybe Sam could cry. He thought about crying. Instead he said, "Pops, she's not the easiest person to work with."

"I don't care," Pops replied, "Joe wants both of you guys. Make it work."

Sam left the training room looking for Deb. What a disaster. He had to do better.

He'd always heard that there's about one percent of people that you just can't get along with. He thought it was a myth. He knew hundreds, maybe thousands of people. He got along great with all of them. They enjoyed each other's company.

But this girl. This woman. She was this black, empty hole of humanity. She was the Death Star. He'd never seen anything like it, and he'd worked with a lot of people on the spectrum.

He shouldn't have called her names. That hurt him.

But Deb wasn't on the spectrum. That was the thing that made him nuts. He knew, he knew deep in his heart, that she wasn't, but hell if he knew anything else.

He had to help her or kill her. He really didn't care at this point.

He had to fix this. He could fix things. Maybe if he started off with some card tricks and a few jokes first?

2.06

Cutting Up On A Trip

"I'm taking you two on a field operation," Pops said as soon as they both got there that morning, "I don't want to. I think it's a mistake, but you're all that I've got and I've got to take you out of this pleasant, cushy cocoon sometime. Let's go."

"Wow, our first mission!" Sam said, "You can finally trust us."

"Did you not hear what I just said?" Pops replied, "It's not a mission. I do not trust you, not like that. Stay with me and try to stay out of the way. You don't do missions. We don't do missions here. All we're doing is picking up some folks at the beach and bringing them back to the office. It will be pretty dull. Plan on being bored. That's why I want you to pay close attention."

"Where's the documentation?" Deb asked, "Where's our list of goals? Our itinerary? Where's our list of learning objectives?"

Pops' normally sad face dropped a few inches more. He looked at Deb.

"I'm not your travel agent and you're not going to be taking a test."

Looking back to Sam, Pops continued, "Do you two think you can just follow orders and not be underfoot so much?"

They both nodded. Both were frowning.

Pops did not believe them.

Sam later wished he had kept his word on that one.

"I love field trips," Sam said on their way to the airport, "Say Pops, how come you're at the office everyday when I get there?"

"So? Who cares?"

"Don't you have other things to do?"

Pops looked to Deb to see if she had something to add. Deb ignored them.

The older man took a second to answer.

"I did, Sam, but I found over time that the company gave me every-thing I needed."

"That's sad," Deb said simply, still not looking at either of them. Her comment had neither mockery or sarcasm. It was as if she were recalling an especially interesting bug she saw once.

"You two can continue playing team psychologist on your own time. Today I want your eyes and ears open. While dull, there's still going to be a lot of things to learn about working outside the building and I can't remember them all. If you need something, ask me. I'll either tell you or get an answer for you, ok?"

Sam nodded eagerly. Deb did not respond.

Before Pops could call her on it, Sam asked "Is that our ride?"

"It is indeed."

The expensive jet sat on the tarmac fueled up and ready to go.

"Awesome ride, dude!" Sam said getting onto the plush jet, "I bet they'll even give you a complete bag of peanuts."

He sat in the first row, eager, hands on knees, leaning forward, as if waiting for a roller coaster ride to begin instead of the preflight.

Pop and Deb were both much more sedate, dullsville, passing him and going to the back.

After waiting three, maybe four minutes with no roller coaster ride starting, Sam said while turning back to them, "Who's up for some songs?"

They both looked to Sam as if they were dead inside.

"Or not," he said to nobody, "maybe on the way back," Sam turned back towards the front.

Landing an hour later, and after a brief drive, they reached the house.

Pops stopped them as they went in the door.

"Stay here," he said.

"Don't you want us to come with?" Sam said, "We can help."

"Do you want to go back to the car?" Pops sounded to Sam as if he were talking to a small child.

"No."

"Then do as you're told and stay here. I'll call you if I need you."

They waited a few minutes. Sam was too excited to do nothing, but he wanted to follow instructions.

"Maybe we should be scoping out the front of the house? Couldn't hurt to look around, right? We might find something useful to do while waiting."

"We're supposed to stay together," Deb said.

"You're right," Sam replied, "It's possible to overthink things. If we need to know or do something, Pops will tell us."

"That's not possible," she said.

"Pops is pretty good at giving directions," Sam replied.

"It's not possible for you to overthink something."

Once again, no snark, no humor, just a bland statement.

"Always so happy and cheerful?"

"I am not a people person," she turned to look at Sam, "Do you really think he's coming back?"

About to respond, Sam heard shouting from the far back yard, behind the small house.

Deb raised her eyebrows as if to ask "Now what?" but didn't speak.

Sam waited. After what could have been only seconds, he heard firecrackers.

No, not firecrackers. It was too loud.

He heard gunshots.

"We gotta go help him," he said.

"I'm not going anywhere."

"Screw you," he replied, pushing around her and into the house.

The house was a non-descript suburban bungalow a mile or two from the beach. It looked like the kind of cheap rental that several service workers would pitch in on and use for a crash pad

There was no place for a car. The yard was minimal, sandy.

If it hadn't been for the steel reinforced door that Sam just entered through, it could have been any house on that street.

Sam moved in, heading back to where he thought was the kitchen.

For some reason, the main lights were off. Blackout curtains were in the windows. Sam made his way by using dull, red emergency LED strips along the ceiling.

The entryway was full of plastic furniture, the kind you could buy at a box store. Reaching the kitchen, he realized he'd found the back door and not Pops.

Moving back the way he came, he took the second way out of the main room, into the dark hall. He heard the screech of a car peeling out and taking off somewhere close.

Sam moved quickly but quietly down the hall to the end. Pops needed help. Sam had no idea what he was going to do, but he knew he needed to be there.

As he approached the end, he could smell bullets. It reminded him of the Fourth of July.

There were no more gunshots. He reached the open door.

Should he run in? Should he peek in? Maybe he should just yell something and run away. He could be the decoy duck. There was as lot going on and Sam had no answers.

He stepped fully into the door and stopped. If they were going to kill him, now was the time. He either lived or died. From somewhere he remembered John Wayne at the end of the movie "The Searchers," standing in the doorway.

He didn't die. He was prepared for anything, but out of a million things he would have supposed, what he saw was nothing like any of them.

It was a small room, perhaps the size of a coffee shop. There were cafeteria tables set up. The tables had notebook computers on them.

It was still mostly dark. Nobody was at the computers. Instead they were all piled on the floor, dead.

Pops too.

No, Pops wasn't dead. Sam wasn't that lucky. Instead he found the older man kneeling down over one of the bodies.

Pops had a large, long knife and he had cut the man wide open from his neck down to his groin. Intestines splayed across the floor.

Pop still had the knife cutting into the man, gutting him. Pops was grunting.

"Are you okay," he heard himself say quite surprisingly.

Pops didn't look up. Instead he said, "Hand me that medical cooler."

He went to his teacher.

"Open it up."

He opened the cooler and held it open. From inside the man's guts Pops worked at something, digging the knife around. Sam didn't want to look. The older man finally pulled out a big hunk of plastic-like material, like a huge, hundred-tentacled octopus. Sam thought it was about two feet wide. It was just millimeters thick.

"Got it," Pops said, dropping it into the medical cooler and closing it. "Let's get out of here."

Sam heard some moaning in the next room. He started to move towards it.

"No Sam," Pops said, putting his hand on him gently.

"But."

"But there's nothing we can do. We have to go. The police will be here soon."

As they made their way back to the door, Pops started soothing him.

"This is not for you, kid. This has nothing at all to do with your job or anything. I had no idea. Do yourself a favor. Forget you were here."

Sam said, "Ok," but wondered if this was something that was part of Pops' job. He wondered what any of it had to do with EigenCorp.

Who was that dead man? What was Pops doing?

Ushering him out of the house, Pops asked, "Where's the other one? Weird clothes? Super nerd? The girl?"

Sam looked around. Deb wasn't at the door where he'd left her.

Sam was confused. Should he call for her?

Pops gave a weary sigh. Standing in the threshold of the house, he spoke in a completely normal voice but not directed at anybody. It was like he was speaking to the house itself.

"Come or stay, Debian. We're leaving. You'll probably want to leave too."

And with that, he left. Sam followed. Sure enough, about ten seconds later Deb came out of the house after them, walking, not hurrying, as if she had all the time in the world.

That's when Sam first noticed. He didn't say anything. He noticed that Pops was armed. Perhaps Pops had always been armed.

The second time in the plane was not so enjoyable.

He saw that they had lobster on the menu. Sam thought about ordering. Right now he could order a dinner that cost as much as he used to make in a week.

He wasn't hungry. Instead, he stared out the window at the sea below.

Eventually, bored almost to tears, he got up and found Deb in the far back of the plane. She was reading a paperback. It had a picture of an bright green lobster on the front.

He sat.

"Do you think we should confront Pops about what just happened?"

"No," she said, "I don't trust anything he has to say."

Nothing that ever came out of that girl's mouth ever made any sense to Sam.

"What else would you do?"

He could see her grit her teeth, then her entire demeanor, her body language … just went away. It was like turning off a light.

"I'm going to do my own research, that's what," she spoke in a monotone, "I'm going to look up all the corporate documents I can find on the system. I trust my own research more than anything else."

"I don't," Sam said, changing his mind about trying to talk and instead standing to leave, "I'm going to Pops with whatever problems I have. He'll help us. He's our guy."

She didn't say "Screw you" as he had said to her earlier. She didn't say "goodbye" or "so long". She just went back to her book as if he didn't exist.

He went back to his seat, unhappy. A couple of times during the flight back he almost did something about it. He could tell they all needed to talk. He had no idea how to start it.

Pops fixed the problem.

"You two, debrief," Pops said as they got into the car on the way back.

"You can talk about what happened today among yourselves and Joe, of course, but this is the kind of thing we don't talk about with any other people." Pops said.

Deb looked up. Her voice had no inflection.

"Because you committed a crime?"

"No," the older man said, "because if you do, bad things will happen."

Pops looked between the two as if to make sure they were still there.

"No crimes were committed by me today, at least no major crimes."

Sam knew in his heart the man was lying, but he also knew Pops was trying his best to care for them.

"If this kind of thing happens again, Pops," Deb said, "we're going to need better training. Or we'll need to escalate. We'll need to report."

Her observation startled Pops a bit. Not a lot, but enough that he pulled his head back a bit, considering.

"You're not going to get it, Newbury, Featherstone. We don't blackmail one another into telling things. That's not us."

"Pops, she probably meant escalate to Joe, report to Joe. That's all." Sam said. He hoped he was right.

"I am doing as you instructed," Deb said.

Pops looked as if somebody was trying to trick him.

"As instructed? Are you promising me that you're doing as instructed in the future or are you saying that you're currently doing as instructed?" Pops asked.

"Yes. You said if we had questions, ask and you would find out. My question is: why are you covered in blood carrying a cooler with some sort of biological or human organs inside it?"

"Ignore her," Sam said, "I'll talk to her. Only tell us if we need to know."

Sam didn't think he wanted to know. He knew she didn't.

Sam was wondering what would happen if Deb kept pushing the man. Pops obviously had a lot of capability for violence, but also for pain and sorrow. He didn't know if it would be worse for Pops to punch him or cry. Both options were very scary.

"I do not trust you," Deb said.

Pops started to say something then stopped. He crossed his arms. He took a deep breath then sighed loudly. He looked to the sky then back to them.

"This is going to be a problem, isn't it."

Simultaneously, Deb shook her head yes and Sam shook his head no.

Pops rolled his eyes. He hung his head and pinched his nose as he spoke.

"To think that I gave up bingo at a retirement home for this. Ok, I'll speak to Joe and see if we can get you both read into the program."

Neither Sam or Deb had a reply, each having different reasons for remaining silent.

The team made it back to the office just before supper.

Pops left them alone the rest of the evening. Deb disappeared.

Then all of the real trouble began.

Shotwell Shot Well

Sam was hiding. He had no qualms about admitting that to himself or anybody else if asked. The last few days had been stressful, and if Sam wanted to spend an hour or two at the coffee shop before going to work, he'd damned well do that.

It was that stupid, fake FBI agent, though. She sat behind him in the back corner. He could feel her eyes on his back. How could he enjoy down time being treated like that?

He couldn't, that's how. So he got his coffee, got up, and went back to face her head-on.

"Don't you have anything better to do?" He sat directly across from her.

"You don't know what I do, Mr. Featherstone," she said, putting her coffee down.

"Aren't you missing your pet gorilla?"

She deemed his comment unworthy of reply.

He noticed several sugar packets had been opened.

"That's a load of sugar, Shotwell," he said, "Never going to pass your annual physical woofing down that daily."

"I'm not the best of employees," she replied.

"You don't look too worried about it," he said.

"I am what I am," She said, "that's not changing."

There was a big slab of granite under those eyes. Somewhere this woman carried a lot of bedrock.

He sat back a bit in his seat, "Good thing I'm not looking for career advice."

This Shotwell lady was a fighter, he remembered. Dealing with her in the wrong way would be like fighting a mountain. Or having it fall on your head.

"You're really taking off at EigenCorp." She said, "I hear good things about you."

EigenCorp. She hears things from inside EigenCorp.

"I work hard," he replied, "I'm trying to make a life for myself, and you?"

She took a deep breath.

"Work is life," she said.

"Sorry to hear that," he replied, "You hang out in the coffee shop everyday waiting to see if I show up?"

"Oh, I get around."

"What, exactly is the department you work under, Shotwell? Who's your boss? You report to Joe?"

She glared at him. Her lips turned white.

"Where'd you go in the corporate jet recently, Featherstone?"

For a second or two, Sam thought he could engage in a staring contest with the lady. That was silly beyond measure, though, and he quickly looked away, as if her question never happened.

When he finally looked back, she continued.

"I've dug a bit into your past. It's quite the tale. Bank robbery, the school incident, the drugs."

He could feel his blood rising.

"Are you threatening me?"

"No. No. Not at all," she said, "I'm just pointing out that you're especially vulnerable here, that's all."

"And I suppose you're going to protect me," he said.

Now she'd pushed back in her seat, "I'm trying to be your friend, quite honestly."

He studied her.

"Agent Shotwell, if you are an agent, there are things I want to know and things I don't want to know. I don't get them mixed up. I suggest you don't either. I am not your friend."

"Samuel," she said, "The FBI is tasked both with international crime and foreign counter-surveillance."

"So?"

"So I don't want you trying to out guess us, what the government is up to. You'll almost certainly be wrong."

"That's it?" He said, "That's the only thing you're giving me?"

"Can't separate the two. You're acting like there's some wall or boundary we can put up between parts of our life, and we can't. Do you really want to know more about your boss, your company? Would you like to know about some of the seemingly-random violence that follows certain big EigenCorp jobs? How some of the intrusion work is being used to control media narratives?"

"I think …" he started. She stopped him.

"Be careful about your answer, Featherstone. You can't un-ring a bell. Have you thought any on what we talked about when we first met?"

"I have," he said.

"And?"

"That's not an option for me. That's never going to be an option for me," he said.

She looked at him, "Remember what they say: 'never say never'."

Sam could feel his heart racing. He hadn't even had that much coffee yet and already his adrenaline was going into overdrive, borderline out of control.

Breathe. Relax. Repeat.

It helped. It always helped.

"You're just going to keep pressuring me until I do what you want," he concluded.

"Not at all," she replied, "You're not that special. In fact, this may be the last time we see one another. I'm going to keep pressuring everybody until I crack this case open, and I don't give up. Your only choice is whether you're going to help or get in the way."

He remembered the credentials he'd photographed that first morning in the bathroom. If Shotwell was going to sift though his life, point out all the flaws? Two could play at that game.

"Hey, Sam!"

It was Nick, coming in.

"Hey, Nick!" he waved.

Thank god, Nick didn't come over. Instead he'd taken one look at Sam's companion and beat feet to the backroom. Nick must have been holding.

Small miracles.

She tapped on the table to get his attention.

"Instead of idly gossiping with me, Featherstone, you should look up some of the people that have retired from EigenCorp. The company's been around long enough for people to come and go. Surely people have left, right? They're already vetted. They'd be great for you to talk to. Maybe you'd listen to them."

Sam agreed, but he didn't want to.

She continued, "Only guess what? We can't find anybody. People leave EigenCorp and it's like they were zapped out of the universe. Nothing."

Sam was skeptical. "Not everybody has the engaging personality I do, Shotwell. People might not want to talk to you."

"Sure," she replied, "But we're very, very good at this, Sam. It's extremely hard to hide in the modern world, even for people who know the game. Folks always end up contacting loved ones or old friends. They'll get caught by facial recognition on an Uber or street cam. But nothing. Don't you find that kind of odd?"

He did indeed.

Something snapped inside him.

She looked at his large cup.

"Don't you like anything in your coffee?"

He glanced again at all of the sugar.

"Energy must always be conserved," he said.

"What does that mean?"

"It means the energy you get with that sugar you'll have to pay for later. There's always an accounting."

Or what I get with the coffee. Or the job, he thought.

She frowned, trying to make out what he was saying.

He stood.

"I'll sort this out on my on, thank you very much. Then I'll decide what I want to do."

She shrugged as if to say "so be it."

"Mr. Featherstone," she nodded curtly.

"Agent Shotwell," he replied.

He left, leaving the mostly un-drank coffee behind.

Coming out on the street, he walked with speed and purpose back to work. Sam didn't run from his past, and he sure as heck wasn't going to run from his future.

There was a difference between running away and hiding and just taking a break. He had been taking a break.

He went through the door and onto the lift.

And what the hell did she know, anyway? Yeah, there had been some problems in the past, but that was a long time ago.

Some things you took with you through life and some things you left. There were things in his life he had decided to leave. He wasn't ashamed of that. He wasn't going to be ashamed of that any freaking time soon.

"Joe, we've got to talk," he found his boss's boss in the hallway.

"Sam," Joe exclaimed, "I was just looking around, hoping I'd find you this morning."

"You were?"

"Absolutely," Joe said, "We've got a lot to talk about."

"We certainly do," Sam said, "wait, why did you want to talk to me?"

"I was talking to Pops earlier. He wanted to bring you two in on one of the biggest projects EigenCorp has ever been involved in. Groundbreaking stuff."

"Related to that trip?" Sam said, "That was awful."

Joe placed his hand on Sam's shoulders, fatherly.

"It was. Pops and I both are really sorry about that. If you want to see the EigenCorp therapist or you start experiencing any signs of PTSD let me know. We want to do whatever it takes to make this right by you."

Sam had to switch gears, somehow.

"Joe," Sam said, "Are you running some kind of extended loyalty test on me, maybe Debian?"

"Of course not," Joe replied, "Why would we do that? You've already been approved. You're here learning."

"I figured it was just some sort of cross-check, quality assurance maybe?" Sam replied. He was desperate.

"Sam," Joe said, "Have you been approached by any outsider looking for information?"

There was a long pause. Sam could hear the earth breathe.

Joe's outfit was perfect. His watch was perfect. His hair was perfect. Sam was certain the man liked him. The place was perfect.

He felt a deep, sharp unease. He tried to turn the smile up.

"Of course not, Joe," he said, "Nobody has asked me for information. I was only looking for some cheats, trying to figure out if anything was coming."

Joe smiled, relieved, "Good. Let's circle back on that. We're going to need to pick this up later because Pops has some really mind-bending stuff for you two this morning in The Crowbar."

It was a technicality. Nobody had directly asked him for any specific piece of information. He had not lied. It was technically true.

Watching his boss leave, Sam did not like resting so much of his life and career on such a little twig. He felt like he'd been fixing a dyke and he needed to shore it up one way or another or the ocean would rush in and drown him.

2.08

Inserts Encountered

Sam entered The Crowbar at precisely 8am, Deb was behind him with her standard banana. Sam held a reloaded espresso in a tight grip, ready for battle.

Pops was already there. He was wearing a body suit like mechanics use and poking at something on the table with a ballpoint pen. The medical cooler was beside it.

Sam moved in to get a better look. The first thing he noticed was that it was transparent, like a jellyfish, but it was obviously inorganic, like a 4 or 5 mm thick film of loose, floppy polyurethane. It was generally round and the shape and size of a manhole cover, but it was tentacle-ly round, like an amoebae, with a solid center circle approximately 3 cm across and fine 1-2 mm tentacles spread out taking up the rest of the area.

There was blood still on it.

It was what he'd seen Pops with the other day, in the back room of that house. Digging out.

Underneath it was a heating pad.

Blood and gristle both lay on, under, and around it from where it had been removed. Pops didn't seem to notice.

"That's disgusting," Deb said, peeling her banana and hanging out by the door.

"Well, it's certainly not a bacon croissant," Sam said. He walked over closer. He walked right up to the table, but he didn't set his coffee down. He sipped it and studied what Pops was doing.

Pops did not look up.

"You two have your McGuffins on you?"

"Just like you said." Sam patted his mostly-empty backpack.

Sam leaned in. He could see lots of complex *stuff* inside each tentacle.

"That's a truly bizarre and interesting piece of tech."

Pops grunted agreement.

"Good. How are you two holding up after our recent adventure?"

"Horror show," Deb said. "I'd go with horror show. Not adventure." she munched some more on her breakfast. "That was an adventure the same way 'Wizards from the Id' was an adventure'"

Pops kept poking at it.

"What is it?" Sam said.

"That's what we've been spending the last ten years trying to figure out. We're calling them 'Inserts' because they're inserted into the body. After that we're not so sure. They seem to form some sort of bio-mechanical function for the user."

The thing squirmed.

"Zoiks!" Deb said, "That thing's alive!"

Pops poked it harder. It did not move.

"Nope, that's just some kind of electro-mechanical reaction. Sometimes we get this response when poked, sometimes not."

"Don't be an idiot, Noob," Sam said. He did not look up from the Insert.

"How about 'don't be a dick', jerkface," she said.

Pops stopped poking and looked up, peering over his reading glasses.

"She's right. You were a dick. Cut it out."

He went back to the object.

"This is the longest we've kept one alive," he said, "not that it's alive, but it's the longest we've been able to get responses. It does indeed look alive, though, doesn't it? Took us a while to realize that all you see here is machine; hardware and not biology."

Deb finished the banana and walked over to the thing. She reached in and grabbed a tentacle, flipping it over.

"What are these metallic, er, channels?"

"Some Gallium-based compound. It's all through the thing."

"Why not just bring in an expert to look at it?"

"Because our primary mission here is security support, not research. Even if we figured it out, it wouldn't change our mission, and who wants to keep a research team onsite? Scientists write papers."

He put the pen down.

"We don't write papers."

She pulled the tentacle out more, holding it up to the light.

Sam finally set his mostly-finished coffee down. He picked up a piece and twisted it around.

"Betcha this is some kind of miniaturized CMOS derivative. Plasticized. Extremely low voltage."

"Agreed."

Pops cocked his head at the two.

"Newbury. Turn around."

The girl did as requested.

Pops took a post-it off her back. He held it up to both of them.

It read "kick me."

"Why you little.."

"Time out!" Pops stood. "Everybody. Shut. Up. Now."

"New rules," he said, "We're going to work like this from now on."

He started counting off on his fingers.

"One, Featherstone. No cornball magic or joking directed at us. What you do by yourself or in the privacy of your little mind is your own business. But no more cutting up. Two, Newbury. No snark or condescending derision. World's already got enough insult comedians. Don't need you. You both can kick puppies if you like on your days off but behave yourself here."

Both looked at Pops as if he had just suffered a terrible stroke and was unable to communicate in English any more.

He glared.

"Do. You. Understand."

Both nodded.

"Say it."

"No snark," Deb said.

"No fun," Sam changed it.

Pops did not look like a stroke victim. He looked like somebody who might hurt Sam.

"I mean no magic or joking directed at," Sam stammered. "the team."

"Look, I understand that neither of you are field agents," Pops said, "and I apologize for the recent unpleasantness. But I'll make you a deal. If you can keep from cutting into one another I'll keep you from any unpleasantness like that. If you feel like the other one is breaking these rules, or you feel physically threatened in any way, come to me. Don't jab back at your teammate. You're supposed to like one another. Put me in charge of any conflict. I'm used to it. But you two?"

Sad. He shook his head, disappointed.

They still had that stupid look.

"Not so much."

Pops thought a second, as if he were a foreigner trying to find exactly the right word in a translation book.

"Happy. Focus on happy." he said, "Happy happy."

Sam looked at Pops, then back to Deb. Nobody spoke. Finally he twisted the thing in his hand again, holding it up to the light like Deb had.

"Where's the power supply?"

"Ambient current generation, micro-RTG, piezo-electric, or thermal I bet. Perhaps all three."

"Can't imagine it staying on like that. That's not much current."

"Doesn't have to. Micro-supercapacitors or the like could store up a trickle charge over hours. It might only need significant current in small bursts."

"Supercapactiors, eh? Wouldn't want to shoot one."

Pops nodded. "The first few times we encountered these," he said, "it was even more unpleasant. Very messy. Too much force? Boom."

"Boom," Sam said.

"So," Deb said, "It doesn't run constantly, instead in bursts. It's powered by the human it's attached to."

"Are you thinking what I'm thinking," Sam asked.

"HSM," she said, "Microscope."

Pops got an optical microscope from a cabinet and brought it over. They cut off a small piece and put it on a slide.

"We tried microscopic analysis, at least as much as we could do, but nobody could figure it out."

"Yeah, aside from the Gallium it's all transparent. Excellent craftsmanship. Somehow they used the transparent flexible substrate as the PCB," she said.

"Let me see," Sam said. Deb offered him the scope.

"Yup, some kind of gallium crystal fluid. Capillary action. That's actually quite clever."

"Clever," Pops said, "HSM."

"Yeah," Sam stepped back looking at it, "This is the first Hardware Security Module I've ever seen that fully integrates into a human, packaged with a self-destruct. True biometrics. Game-changer."

"Either of you two speak English?"

"It's the first truly hack-proof technology," Sam said mostly to himself.

Deb smiled at Sam, then nodded. Turning to Pops she said, "You know the McGuffins we have, the devices that are capable of securely sending information in a hack-proof manner as long as you have one of the pairs?"

"Sure. As long as you know only two were made, and you have one and somebody else has the other, you two can communicate in ways that can never be hacked."

"Exactly."

"This is the next generation of that. Inserts are McGuffins Next Generation. Perfected." Sam was too excited to allow her to finish. She pretended not to notice.

"I prefer McGuffins plus plus, Uber-Guffin, or Super McGuffin. Guffin-O-Matic."

"So this, all this is, is a communications accessory?"

"Nope," Sam said. He pulled a small bit of plastic from his pocket. "Much more. This is a gateway to all technology. What's this?"

"That's mine," Deb said, "Give it back."

"Easy. It's a hardware device key, for using with a 2FA website. It's like the key to a lock." Pops said.

"Correct my good man," Sam said. "But it's just like a key. If you steal it, you can get into my online stuff."

Pops agreed. "So what? You're not going to plug this thing into a USB port. How'd that work?"

"Maybe not. Maybe so," Deb said. "It very well might be Bluetooth, could be low-energy Bluetooth, or have it's own protocol, but it's the same exact thing, just a lot more capable. But that's not the game-changing part."

"Which is?"

"This gallium metallic crystal is made into a liquid when attached inside people. Their body temperature is warm enough to make it into a harmless fluid. It's a conducting fluid. And it changes as you move. That creates a signal, a signature."

"Which is why we have the heating pad, Deb," Pops said, "We're ahead of you. Took us a bit, but we finally figured out that it had to be kept warm."

"Right, but even keeping it warm, you never got anything out of it, right?"

Pops nodded again. Deb continued.

"That's because as it's worn by a warm human host, the simple movement of the body pushes this metal, made liquid by body temperature, through these microchannels, combined with the dozens of these tentacles," she pointed with Pop's pen.

"Each section of the device expects to receive current on a regular basis in a very particular way due to body movement."

"Game changer."

"Exactly," Sam said, "What do these McGuffins, her hardware key, passwords, fingerprints, passphrases and the like all have in common?"

Pops stared.

"They exist outside the body," Sam said.

"Fingerprints don't exist outside the body."

"But the readers do. Every way we have of uniquely identifying a person, including these uncrackable McGuffins, are things that can be measured, recorded, intercepted, copied. I cut your hand off, I have your fingerprints. Fingerprints don't mean anything without a reader, and a reader is just another piece of electronic gear, like the credit card reader at the gas station. And any piece of electronic gear…"

"Is vulnerable."

"Exactly," Sam said. "Crytpocurrency was great until people started getting kidnapped, then threatened or their family threatened for the passphrases. This, however, this is a thing that is uniquely and permanently stuck inside a particular person, a thing that can never be hacked. You take it out?"

"It breaks."

"It breaks. I imagine it breaks permanently, as well, in order to prevent the type of unpleasant experiences we've had recently. You can kill the person and take the Insert, sure, but then it just becomes an inert blob. This is you. This super cool piece of tech gear can finally, and completely, make you, you, and nobody else you."

Pops frowned.

"We could create some kind of warming, auto-wiggler," Deb said.

Sam considered.

"I suspect not. It's all these tentacles, each with a slightly different places inside each host. We would have to out-learn a non-deterministic model which would be computationally extremely difficult if not impossible. Remember, not only does this thing require body warmth and human movement, to be worth a damn it would have to learn the unique body movement patterns of each host. People have their own unique signatures.

I sleep on my left side for instance, and turn at fairly predictable intervals. A change in the pattern?"

"It breaks."

"It breaks. This is a game changer because, if this does what we think it does, it allows for the first time for a real, live human to own something digitally that nobody else can get at. The host's body itself becomes the cryptographic elliptic curve, so to speak. The idea is that you'd have to disassemble a person and watch them go throughout their lives over time to outfox it. That's impossible. This allows people to be people again."

"Okay, so we just kidnap the person," Pops said.

"That's the only weakness I see," Deb said, "but my guess is that there are various practical protocols in effect, things like 'Hey, if you don't see or hear from Jim every day or so, don't communicate any more with him. Kidnapping would work, perhaps, but only for a very short time. And that's assuming there isn't a duress password, or biometrics stress monitoring, which I'm almost certain there is."

"A duress or panic password is a password that appears to work but actually limits the information available. It looks like you've hacked it but you haven't. I can almost guarantee this would have one. Stress-monitoring is already baked into this thing."

"So we're back to where we started," Pops said, "A lump of plastic that wiggles and some tech we haven't figured out yet."

"These Inserts are truly amazing," Deb said, "Now we know what it does, but not how, we've just gotten started."

She poked.

"Give us some time, Pops. Give us some time."

2.09

For Immediate Release

Conspiracy Theory Convention Cancelled Under Cloud of Suspicion
LAS VEGAS, NV - The 13th annual EnigmaCon due to start
next week in the Las Vegas Dodecahedron has been canceled,
organizers said in a statement today.
"Due to the recent death of many of the organizers, the fire in
the venue, the gorilla escape from the zoo, and the labor strike
under way by airline staff, we will be unable to hold the convention this year. We hope to pick it back up next year," the statement read.
The conference, which has been very well attended, was ex-
panding this year to include more academic work. Some of the
presenters will have nowhere else to present their papers.
"It's quite unfortunate," Dr. Beau Vine said in a telephone interview, "There's important information to share about the intersection of culture, fantasy, religion, superstition, and science
and no venue to present it in."
Dr. Vine said he hopes conferences such as EnigmaCon can
help mainstream the conspiracy community, which too often
has been presented as kooks and cranks.
"Religions and Conspiracy theories are a natural part of the
human existence. We believe that they're necessary to maintain
learning. It's time we fully accepted that. As the computer folks
say, it's not a bug, it's a feature."
Vine said both religion and conspiracies happen because of the
mind's inability to understand everything and need to control
the rate of learning.

"These control structures are most likely part of every sentient lifeform in the universe," he said, "Religions give us why things happen. They put us inside a narrative greater than ourselves that remains simple enough for us to understand. Conspiracies allow us to prevent new ideas from completely destroying our internal models of the world too often, leading to mental chaos. It's always us versus them, the ingroup and the outgroup, and the other groups are the ones acting in mysterious yet coordinated ways to prevent our true understanding and working towards our destruction. These are necessary shields. You can't have sentience without them. The only real question our research shows us is whether we can honestly acknowledge them or not. Honest humility is difficult, especially for the poorly educated, ignorant, and otherwise mentally feeble people."

Vine said he plans to resubmit his paper for consideration for next year's conference.

No further information was available on when and where that might occur. Repeated calls to organizers were unanswered. Mail was returned, no forwarding address given. A public relations officer for the Dodecahedron said there was no such conference and they had no evidence anything had been scheduled for that week.

Vine was also unable to be reached for comment.

# # #

2.10

Ducking Responsibility

The day Samuel Featherstone got the duck was the day he was almost fired.

It was also the day he got his first $20,000 watch.

He hated the conversation, but he loved the watch. He kept the duck for the rest of his life, one of a few precious possessions.

That morning, he hadn't even put his stuff down at his desk before Pops told him that Joe wanted to see him. Pops didn't say why, but he could tell by the man's demeanor it was something serious.

Joe's office was just like he remembered, opulent, sparse, tasteful, and neat.

Joe himself stood off to the side of his desk. He had a necktie. He was struggling to tie it.

"Crap," his boss said.

"Here, let me help."

He walked over and started tying the tie while Joe still wore it.

"Most folks would have a spouse that could do this," Joe said, "I never got the hang of it."

Sam didn't know if Joe meant spouses or tying ties. Finishing up, he patted the knot, job well done.

"Thanks."

"Benefits of a year in parochial school," he stepped back a bit double-checking the quality.

"That'll work. I'm also pretty good with polishing shoes, let me know."

Joe pulled the tie a bit as if expecting it to come undone.

"The tie is enough. I'm only willing to go so far for investors. Where are my manners? Here, have a seat."

They both sat. Sam steepled his hands in his lap under the desk.

Behind Joe on a special shelf were about a dozen rubber ducks.

"You're probably wondering what the ducks are."

"It crossed my mind."

"We don't have titles or roles at EigenCorp, and if I can help it, we never will."

He pointed back to the shelf.

"But we do have ducks, Sam. Various ducks show that you have demonstrated certain skills and are trusted with more responsibility."

"Cool idea," Sam said. He wondered if it was really cool or really strange. He suppressed.

"Since one person can have multiple ducks, it lets us self organize without creating hierarchies. Today, Sam, I'm happy to congratulate you on receiving your first duck, the sailor. It shows that you have completed all of your initial training and probation. You are ready to set sail into a bright new future. I'm going to tell Pops to start you doing some team lead work."

Reaching in his desk, he got out a duck.

"Thanks. I don't get excited about anything. Today I want you to know that I'm seriously pumped about being here."

"We think highly of you, Sam. You and Deb both. And we trust you, otherwise you wouldn't be here."

"I'm all in," Sam was beaming.

"We've also got a special gift for you back at your desk," Joe said, holding his hand up, "No need to say thank you. The gift is our thank you to you. You've earned it."

"I'm not going to learn a secret handshake, am I?"

"No," Joe replied, "But close. There'll be lots of other secrets. That's the job. Secrets, Samuel. Secrets are our business. We keep secrets. We test secrets. We find out other people's secrets."

Sam suspected that this was part of a standard Joe speech. He tried to look attentive, maybe worshipful.

"We work in the dark, by necessity. We don't talk about our secrets even to one another. This is what makes EigenCorp so special."

Looking up to the row of ducks and trying to look appropriately appreciative, Sam said, "You know I used to be able to juggle seven things at a time. Wonder how many ducks I could manage?"

"Used to? But not now?" Joe replied, "You can't juggle seven now? Why not?"

"Life got in the way."

"I feel you. Wise man. EigenCorp has been my life. I should have more hobbies."

"Based on what I've seen so far, Joe, I don't know why. This company is amazing. I can't think of any other place that does this type of work."

"Aren't any," Joe agreed, "We had competitors early on, sure, but we took them out."

Joe made a horizontal slashing motion with his hand to emphasize the point.

Scratching his chin, Sam said, "I can't even think of startups in this space."

"Nope," Joe agreed, "We keep an eye out, though. There's always something. It's important to stay aware. We have a special project team to eliminate upstarts. That something you might be interested in?"

From somewhere, Sam thought of a cartoon. It was Scooby Doo. Fred from Scooby Doo finally has the villain tied up. "Let's see who this is." Fred says, pulling the mask off and revealing the bad guy. The bad guy always said, "And I would have gotten away with it if it hadn't been for you meddling kids."

Joe didn't look much like a swamp monster or ghost. Joe was not a real-estate agent. Sam wasn't Fred. There was no Scooby.

"Hypothetically," Sam said, "Do these operations involve hurting people? Because I'm not in for that."

Joe laughed a bit. "Hypothetically no, Sam. Of course not. 'Eliminate the competition' is usually doing by acquihire. We hire them. We're just a bunch of computer geeks. We don't do violence."

"But the other day ..."

Joe waved him off.

"I'm not saying we're not around violence. We deal with powerful people and lots of money, that kind of work involves all kinds of things, good and bad, some very unpleasant. We're around it. We're around all kinds of things, but we ourselves don't do any of that kind of thing. Gosh no."

Sam heard a dog bark in the distance. Bring your pet to work day? Hmmm.

"Just to be clear, you're never going to ask me to hurt somebody."

"Absolutely not."

"And if we see crimes committed, we report them to the authorities."

"Absolutely not. We do not report. Anything. No sir."

"But …"

His boss shrugged.

"Secrets, Sam. This is our business. We don't look into what the secrets are, and if we accidentally stumble across a secret, we forget about it. We don't distinguish the good from the bad. We can't."

"That's awful," The words came out and Sam realized he shouldn't have said them.

Joe nodded.

"It's terrible, and this job, this company isn't for everybody. But how else could a business like this work? We're not the police. Our organization isn't geographically located, so it's not like there's regional or national laws that universally apply. If word were to ever get out that we were playing the role of police or actively helping them? If people start thinking we're sorting the good from the bad? We're done. Finished. Game over."

Sam toyed with the duck in his hand.

Decision made, Sam placed the duck on the desk in front of him. His movement was tentative. He stared at the duck, not his boss.

"You know, Joe, maybe I'm not ready for this promotion. After all, I'm still learning. I've still got a lot more to learn, right?"

He looked up at the older man.

Sam's normal smile returned.

"Sam," Joe said, "I don't want to play the heavy here, and if you're not ready yet, take your time. As you know, however, we have a strict 'up or out' policy."

Sam nodded. "So I either get promoted in a certain period of time or I'm fired."

Joe held his arms out in surrender.

"Remember, no promotions here, but yes, essentially correct. You've got plenty of time, though. Take a month or two. We can check in."

"I just want to do the right thing," Sam replied.

"As do I," Joe said. Joe took a moment considering something. "I admire and respect you, and you have the right to know why things are the way they are, so I'm going to need to tell you something confidential."

Sam sat up straighter in his chair.

"Sure."

"You have complete control here, as I said. You can leave, stay, get promoted, not get promoted. I hope we can be friends no matter how it plays out."

"I sense a big but coming," Sam said.

"But some of our customers might get really, really mad and even physically aggressive if we can't keep their secrets. Physical with us. Directly physical. Do you understand?"

"Understood."

Joe pulled the duck back, rejection taken amicably, but not sure yet if Sam meant it.

"So, you want me to slow things down," Joe said, "Take back the promotion? Take the gift back? Give you a couple of months to think this through? It's cool. We can delay, but today, right now we must decide whether we want to delay or not. Now's the time to decide, son."

Sam looked around the office again, admiring how fine it was. EigenCorp had been good to him. Everything so far had been awesome, almost perfect. Pops was even apologetic for all the horror that happened the other day. Tried to make it right. Joe's office was exactly the one he wanted one day.

There were no pictures of family. Joe had no family. That was the deal, Sam thought to himself.

Back to looking at his boss.

"Joe, I don't have anybody. You guys have been very kind."

Maybe not everything was kind. There was always Deb.

Sam stopped smiling. He was working it through in his head. He reached towards the duck but stopped.

"Your decision," Joe said again, "I've got your back either way. I'm here for you."

Inside, Sam felt as if he were having a tooth pulled without anesthesia. He took a couple of breaths. He was doing his relaxation exercise.

Behind the desk, Joe shifted in his seat a bit.

Sam snatched the duck, holding it to his chest. His precious.

Sam didn't say anything to Joe. Joe was quiet. Sam stood and started walking towards the door.

Before opening it, though, and still looking down at the duck, he stopped.

"Thank you," he said very simply then left.

He walked slowly back to his desk.

There was a gift box. It held an expensive watch.

The rest of the team wanted to know what happened, of course, but

Sam didn't feel like talking. Instead he swiveled his chair and scooted to the window, watching traffic in the city. Watching the sun come up.

He said nothing.

After an hour he went back to work.

He never told anyone what happened. He wouldn't know what to say.

2.11

Nick's Note

Nick with the note.

"Got this for you," Nick said, handing Sam his traditional four-shot espresso the next morning.

"Who's it from?"

"Don't know. It was here when I got here."

Leaving, heading to work, he opened it.

"Get your team and get out. Raid to occur NLT Monday COB."

He crumpled it up and threw it in the closest trashcan.

He'd never visit that coffee shop again.

2.12

Archons Depart

Sam wasn't going to let her get under his skin, he thought as the elevator arrived at his floor. Attitude was 90% of life, and he wasn't going to be the unwitting fool of some paranoid conspiracy monster.

"I will NOT submit to the tyranny of rubberized poultry!" was the first thing he heard Debian yell as he stepped out.

Debian yelling. That was new.

She and Joe were in the hall. Joe was holding out a tiny rubber duck, as if trying to feed a wild deer. Debian had her arms crossed and glaring at her boss, as if she were a victim of the Spanish Inquisition and feared more to come.

Another day at work.

"This is exactly how it starts," she said.

Sam approached, but cautious.

"How what starts?" Joe asked.

She looked at both men, horrified.

"Haven't either of you read 'Duck Dragons of Donobulus Seven'?"

Confusion.

"How they began their galactic imperial domination with the distribution of small rubberized duck idols?" She explained.

Hmmm.

"With the embedded nanites?"

Hmmm.

"Seemingly harmless? Seemingly?" She was done. She looked at the little duck as if Joe were handing out hand grenades at the mall.

Joe made another go at it, bless his heart.

"But that's what I was trying to say," he said, "These aren't meant to be offensive. Just the opposite. They're happy ducks."

Joe held the duck aloft as if none of them had ever seen one.

"See?" Joe said, "Cute?"

Sam stepped into it, trying to defuse a bomb that Joe had no idea was there.

"Joe," Sam said, "Debian is extremely well-read, far beyond any of us. I'm sure there's something important here that we're missing."

Both looked at Sam as if he'd just betrayed them.

Sam wondered what the hell he was talking about.

Books. Movies. Comic books. Novel. Space Opera.

"It occurs to me that this situation is just like Beta III in the C-111 system," Sam quietly, as if making a profound observation only he would understand, hoping she'd take the bait.

"Return of the Archons," she said immediately, memorized, "Landru. The Body. The Hour of Festival."

Bingo. He nodded sagely, not ready to actually engage. Wondering if this would work. Hoping.

"What are you two talking about?" Joe asked.

He looked at Joe. "An old Star Trek episode," doing his best nerdy 'but-actually' impersonation, "An abandoned computer runs a civilization."

Now he looked at Debian. She was still with him. He was a neurosurgeon asking a comrade for a concurring opinion.

"Well," Deb said, a professor beginning a lecture, "There are similarities. There were no ducks in that, of course. It would require more work to do a comparison."

Sam desperately wanted Joe to know and understand the ruse Sam was running but he dared not signal the confused man in any fashion.

"Why don't you earn another duck?" Joe asked, jerking the sailor duck back and putting it away as if were diseased, "You said you wanted to do infrastructure. We could use a good security analysis, find any anomalies, that kind of thing. We've got a librarian duck."

"It always starts so innocuously," she said, still untrusting of Joe, nodding.

Maybe if Sam could maneuver her to directly address Joe's concerns.

"Deb," Sam said, "Do you understand the difference between fantasy and reality?"

"Do you understand the difference between irrational and transcendental numbers?"

"Of course I do," Sam replied.

"I understand reality, Sam." she said.

"Debian, I understand the recent mission with Pops was unfortunate," Joe said, "even traumatic. We have services available if you need them."

It was Deb's turn to look at Joe as if she didn't understand a word he was saying.

Must stop.

"You're good at pattern recognition and network analysis," Sam interrupted, "How about we do some of that? I can help you get started."

"Don't need it," she said.

"You know, Debian and Samuel," Joe began, and Sam feared another Joe speech was on the way," You can see the room names: ears, hands, eyes. Sometimes I think of EigenCorp like a person, a super person if you will. We could use you to be part of the body, Come to the body, Debian."

Joe patted his pocket where he'd placed the duck. Problem solved.

Sam physically backed up. Of all the analogies for the man to use.

"If you think that I'm joining a poultry-based cult of bacchanalia and mind control, you've got another thing coming, mister." she said.

Joe's face froze. Sam thought Joe looked like somebody who'd just had his brain zapped out. Slowly he watched the man's visage blossom into a stupid, idiotic smile, the kind one uses on crazy people or very small children.

The first rule of stage magicians is to always smile and keep the damned thing moving. Never let them know something went wrong.

"Welp," Sam said, "I guess it's time we told him."

Deb yanked her head around to pin him down. "Told him what?"

Sam sighed as if having to share a terrible secret.

"Deb's been fudging a lot, and I've been helping." Sam said.

She looked at Sam as if he had revealed himself as Satan incarnate with lightning shooting from his fingertips.

He patted her, sad.

He continued.

"There's no shame, Debian. This kind of work isn't for everybody."

Her eyes were as wide as saucers. Her face darkening. Energy achieved, he began redirecting.

"Dragon Masters," he said, "Ducks swim in water. Reminds me of 'Secrets of the Water Dragon'"

"That doesn't make any sense at all. That's stupid." She said.

"Stupid is as stupid does," he waved around the room as if making some profound point, "Don't we need to stay on-mission, be loyal, things are not as they appear, right?"

Her face relaxed for the first time. There was a very small look of contentment there.

"You may be finally figuring it out," she said, "What's our next move?"

He tilted his head towards their work area, having no idea of what he'd figured out, "Next we do that intrusion analysis. That'll advance all of our missions."

He tried to look profound, a General announcing a very important mission for the troops.

Deb looked back to Joe, no longer angry.

"Thank you," she said simply, "Come on, Sam."

He and Joe exchanged looks.

It took him about ten minutes to get her set up. The entire time he thought about Joe.

Sam had a lot of explaining to do to Joe, a foreign, untrusted stranger lost deep in the land of Debian Newbury. Sam only wished he could be a better guide that had something useful to say.

2.13

Diving In

Sam's unexpected last weekend at EigenCorp began with a party and fireworks. There was a celebratory dinner. He received the praise and kudos of all his former teammates.

At least in his mind. In his mind, he was just starting down the path to a bright new future full of love and praise. Sam had just been given his second duck. Training was over. He was a tech lead. Life rocked.

He felt that way in his mind. This was before he actually began doing any of the wonderful things he was thinking about.

It was before Debian Newbury destroyed his life and career. It was before the dream died. It may have been the last day of the dream. It all started with such a simple question.

"Who's up for lunch?" He asked, coming over to the team area, "I'm moving up and out. Lunch is on me."

He'd just come from Joe's office.

"How can one company have so many customers," Deb asked. She didn't ask him. She didn't ask anybody. Her face was still in her computer and she was still typing.

He stood with his hands on her cubicle wall, waiting.

She kept typing.

"Say, that's my Chinese Finger Puzzle," he pointed, "And there's my Einstein bobble-head. And my nine-square Rubik's Cube."

"Solved it," Deb said and kept typing.

"And my Nun Chucker. And my USB Nerf Missile Launcher, and my…"

"Am I going to have to put both of you in time out," Pops pushed his chair back and looked at them both.

213

"She started it," Sam replied.

"He said I could play with his toys."

"Not all," Sam stopped. It wasn't worth it. Just give her the damned toys. He didn't have to play this game. Let it go, Sam.

"So, Pops," he said, "how's the online dating going?"

Debian's eyebrows raised and she stopped typing.

"Not well," Pops said, "Seems like everybody wants you to lie so much."

"Come on, Pops," he said, "surely you can lie a bit. Everybody lies, right?"

Deb frowned, then resumed coding.

"I can shade the truth," his mentor admitted, "I can refuse to tell you. But I'm not a believer in outright lying. It poisons things."

"What about practical jokes? White lies? Your mom asks you if that dress looks ugly, do you say yes? Do you …"

Pops stopped him.

"Long term, Sam. Long term lying. Not fudging around with the truth for a day or two." Now Pops was feeling uncomfortable, "Say, what's that chart on the wall."

He pointed at Deb's cubicle.

She kept working, in the zone.

Finally Sam said, "The must be the famous donut delivery observation log."

Pops frowned. Sam continued.

"Seems like there's been some problems with the variance falling outside the statistical norms by a Standard Deviation or two."

"Two," she kept going.

"You guys don't get out a lot, do you?"

"I'm trying Pops, I'm trying. Work with me here. Lunch." Sam begged.

Instead of replying, the older man looked at Deb as she continued typing. His brow furrowed.

"You two go on," she said, "I'm quite happy here."

Pops looked at Sam as if to say no, she's lying.

Sam looked at Deb again. Studied her.

"How long you been at this," he asked.

She kept working. Finally Pops answered.

"All this morning. I believe all through the night as well."

"Then we all need to take a breath. Come on, guys, let's go. It's on me."

Nobody moved.

"We're not having lunch, are we?" he asked himself.

Pops nodded no slowly. He looked back to Deb with a worried expression.

She finally stopped.

"I found out who broke into your apartment wifi and slandered my dad online."

"Who?" he asked.

"Us. EigenCorp."

Pops perked up, "But that ..."

She interrupted, "It was some group called 'beta team'. They also provided anonymous tips to the local newspaper. Another team, 'gamma team', seems to be responsible for a recent bank robbery in Taiwan. There's some money laundering, which I've yet to chase down."

"Wait just a damned minute," Pops spat, "That's impossible. We don't do that kind of thing at EigenCorp. That's not us."

Sam felt the world tilt.

In reply, she pointed at the screen.

"But, Deb," Sam said, "how do you know?"

She paused just a beat or two.

"I don't know exactly."

"Good grief," Sam began.

"What I know," she stopped him, "is that work orders come through, then these things happened, then the work orders were paid."

"Work orders? That's all just a coincidence, Debian," Pops said.

"Sure," she responded. She glanced at him momentarily, as if to make sure he was still there, then back to her terminal, "If there were only one or two incidents. But there are 23 such incidents and I haven't finished counting yet."

Pops leaned in to see better.

"You can keep track of 23 such arbitrary incidents in the real world and the dates and times of each?"

"Sure," she replied, "Can't everybody?"

Sam shook his head sadly.

Pops crossed his arms. "Maybe there are parts of this system you don't have access to yet. Think about that? You've only been admin for a day."

"I own it, Pops. Took me an hour."

Sam looked at Pops and shrugged. Deb continued, "The system was very well constructed. There was a problem with your key rotation. I fixed it."

"Still, Deb," Sam said, "so far all we really have is a statistical anomaly. We really don't have proof of anything.

Pops studied Sam as Sam continued.

"Without further investigation this can all just be considered a fluke, or hack. We don't know."

"But," Deb began.

Sam cut her off, "But clusters happen. We all know that. Intrusions happen."

Deb finally stopped completely. "Would you like to see my report?"

"What report?" Pops asked.

"Using the Bureau of Labor Statistics, I ran a regression study against industries in a similar field, and.."

"Just cut to the end," Pops replied.

"And it's not a fluke. The accounting data is pretty clear."

Sam glanced out the window. Today was food truck day. His stomach growled.

"Something's missing," he said, then turned away, "Well. There's your problem," he said, looking at Pops.

"I don't have a problem," Deb said.

Pops nodded slowly. Deb didn't look at either, she turned back to her computer, but she didn't start working again, either.

"What problem," she finally said.

"You're missing the people part of all of this, right? You've admitted it."

Pops nodded again. Deb still looked at the screen, as if she could magically type something in and people would pop out.

Finally, she committed. She completely turned her chair around to the two men.

"I don't understand," she said.

Pops cut his eyes to Sam for a second. When Sam said nothing, Pops explained.

"What Sam's trying to say is that what you have so far is okay, but all you have is access to the corporate org information: accounting, org charts, work orders, HR. Things like that. You don't really know what's going on. This won't tell you, no matter how much you poke at it."

"That doesn't make sense to me. Surely inference ..."

"Haven't you ever written a status report," Pops asked, "who believes those things? They're not lies, but they never cover the real work. They gloss over. A lot of this is fluff, information-free."

There was a long pause while Pops realized his mistake.

"Guess not. Your first job. Sorry."

"What Pops is trying to say," Sam thought he'd give it a shot, "I think, is that this is why we have the McGuffins. We use these for all the really sensitive stuff: work product, chats, socialization. The McGuffins cover all of the normal thrum of background noise. That's what you need to tell you what's really going on in any organization."

"Right on, Sam," Pops said, surprising them both, 'I know this beta team. I know gamma. I should. I trained them all."

Sam couldn't help himself, "How long have you been here, Pops?"

"Since the beginning."

"That's super cool," he said, thinking of all the things Pops must have seen.

"He's old," Deb said simply, "That's sad."

Both men stared at her.

"But it is also really cool as well."

Across the floor they heard the elevator ding as the doors opened.

"Of course you've got to report this, take it to Joe," Sam said, "She did good work, right Pops?"

"I don't know," Pops replied.

Sam felt sick.

Deb started gathering things. "I'm done here. I'm going to print this out and walk it out the door, take it to Joe's office."

"I can't let you do that, Debian," the older man said.

"I'm not asking for permission," she responded.

Sam nervously started pacing.

"You told us to take things like this to Joe."

"He told us," Deb said, "there was no illegal activity here."

"That's not exactly .." Pops started then left off, unsure how to end his thought.

Sam kept pacing. Finally he stuck his head around her wall, looking behind her monitor.

"Hey, you've got peanut butter crackers," he said.

He reached around her to get them from the back but was cut off. Watching her grab those crackers Sam felt like he was watching a snake strike a mouse on one of those nature shows.

Once she had the pack in her paws, she began eating them very slowly as Sam watched.

Sam made a squeaky, whiny sound. His stomach growled.

Pops got out of his chair and stood beside Deb's cube.

"I'm not going to leave either of you alone. I can't leave you like this. This project of Debian's has got to end one way or another. I'm doing as instructed. This is my job."

Sam didn't want to know what the two possible ways were.

Deb was insistent.

"My job is to find anomalies in the system. I have found anomalies. I'm not going anywhere."

Deb looked at Pops. Sam did not like the way Deb and Pops were looking at one another.

It was like watching lions pace in a circle, getting ready to fight.

If Pops was standing, Sam thought, it was time to sit. Sam rolled over a chair, turned it around backwards and sat in it. Just us teamies having a chat.

"I'm not going anywhere either, then," Sam said, "We're going to work this out peacefully."

Both looked at him for leadership. He could tell they were both worried. How could everybody like one another, really like one another, yet the situation be so dangerous?"

Oh yeah, he was the leader. He was the leader now and he hated it.

He sighed. He watched her eat more crackers.

"I hate being in charge," he said.

"You are not in charge," Deb replied.

He glanced at Pops. There was just a slight twinkle in the older man's eye.

"Welcome to the party, kid."

"Hey guys," they were interrupted, "What's up?"

All three turned to see Joe standing over them.

"Everybody looks so serious," Joe said, "Is everything okay?"

They both looked at Pops. Sam could feel his heart beginning to race.

There was a terrible, terrible pause. Then Pops said, "We're good, boss. The kids are just arguing over which version of Debian we're going to be working with."

Joe raised his eyebrows.

"Anything I can help with?" he asked, "How about lunch? My treat."

Sam slumped. If that damned girl opened that cracker-filled mouth and said just one damned word, they were all dead.

"Aren't you all done with this kind of thing Pops?" Joe asked Pops, "Shouldn't you be fishing? Cheer up, folks! You should be having fun! Work's fun!"

"We are," Pops said, "We are.. These two seem to have the most fun when it's all low-level. I'll finish it up here. Raincheck?"

Joe hesitated, then decided. CEO's don't ask twice.

"All right. Have fun!" He waved on his way out.

Once they were sure he was gone, Pops looked back and forth between them, as if watching a tennis match.

"Can't you two forget we ever found this?" He asked.

Both shook their heads no.

"Can't we have a break, lower the tension, let Sam buy us lunch?"

Both shook their heads no. Sam's stomach protested.

"I'm not going fishing, am I?"

Both shook their heads no.

"Good. I hate fishing."

Deb shook her head no a fourth time. There had not been a question.

"My patience has limits. I am done with both of you," She said.

"Both of us," Pops said. It was not a question.

"This company as well."

She looked around, although there was nothing on the empty floor to look at. She pointed to the elevator as if the elevator represented something specific.

"If this pattern of abuse and criminality continues as we investigate, I am going to go to the authorities."

"Golly fuck don't say that," Sam blurted.

They all looked at Deb's monitor. Pops was deep in thought about something.

"I'm not sure I can let that happen," he said again, emphasizing the word 'sure', as if testing it. He pulled his head back, "I don't know yet."

"May I suggest a compromise?" Sam said, "Let's work through the weekend, see how deep this hole goes, then we can all decide together. One big happy team."

"I don't like that idea," Deb said.

"Me neither," Pops said.

"I absolutely hate the idea," Sam agreed, "So obviously that's what we're going to be doing."

2.14

Pops

Sam did not like mushrooms on his pizza, he wanted to yell, watching his hand insert into his mouth the second slice of the second pizza on the second day of their work.

The other two loved mushroom pizza.

He put the slice back down on the paper plate. Unable.

"Where IS the other one," he asked Pops.

Pops was standing at the wall, holding a slice in one hand and moving cards and yarn with the other.

They had taken over The Crowbar for the weekend work. The room was large, and like all of the walls at EigenCorp, they were also whiteboards. Using dry-erase markers, small cards, and yarn, the team had taken a 36 x 12 wall and made it into an enormous evidence board.

Pops had let them use his McGuffin to pull more data from the system, but even Pops didn't have unlimited access.

Across the top of the wall, they had cards for projects. There were 173 projects they deemed to be of some interest. Down the left side, they had teams they were interested in. On the right hand side they had customers.

The system was simple. In the middle they placed cards indicating unusual behavior. Yarn came out from the card and joined up the customer, project, and team.

They were looking for patterns.

The pattern was that it looked like a mess, Sam thought of Mel Gibson in the movie "Conspiracy Theory" For some reason, a board of stuff on the wall with yarn and lines was the universal way to indicate crazy people.

Were they crazy?

Pops stopped for a second, done with the current work, "She's around somewhere. Came by while you were out. Seemed on to something if that helps."

"She's always like that," Sam said, then remembered, "Guess I should start wearing this. Check it out."

He got out his new watch and put it on. He held his wrist out and admired the gleam.

"Nice, kid," Pops said, "Looks good on you."

Sam moved his arm around, trying to hold the light, trying to make it look cooler.

"You think you could help me, er, sometime, help learn me some self-defense?"

"Sure," Pops replied, "But you're going to find that it's very similar to that magic stuff you're always practicing."

"I don't understand."

"You learn the basics," Pops replied, "you learn combinations, that goes into muscle memory. Fighting is a mental activity, Sam. You have to train the body, sure, but that's just the beginning."

"Think I've got a good mind for it?" Sam asked.

"No," Pops said without hesitation, without kindness.

"Thanks."

The older man smiled slightly. "Different minds are good at different things, Sam. Nothing to be ashamed of. I'd suck as a magician."

Sam looked around, still feeling down about the work so far.

"I'm sure if she were here, there would be some book that could apply," He said.

"She reads odd books," Pops replied.

"That she does."

"She's an odd person," Pops said.

"That she is. A massive understatement, Pops, but reality." Sam said.

"Look," Pops said, obviously having put something off as long as he could, "When we're ready to go to Joe, if that ever happens, we're going to need to walk him into this. No dramatic surprise confrontations. People don't like that."

"What if he already knows?" Sam said, "What if we're only telling him things he knows?"

"Our problem isn't Joe," Pops replied, "I know him. Our problem is Debian. She tends to be a bit …"

"Over the top," Sam finished.

Pops nodded.

"Ok, Pops," Sam said, "We'll assume positive intent unless we know differently and you and I are committed to slow-going."

"Agreed. But not sure it matters."

The older man backed up and looked at the entire wall. He put his hands on his hips.

"Let's review here," he said, "we can all admit that there's statistically unusual activity when comparing the EigenCorp work record to subsequent events, at least for these cards."

"For some definition of statistically significant, sure," Sam said, "and for some definition of interesting events."

"But with all this," Pops said, "We have yet to find direct evidence of wrongdoing on the scale Debian's been talking about."

"Agreed," Sam said, "and we've exhausted all of our data sources."

Pops took just a second to consider, then nodded. He turned back to the board.

"Then I think we're done, Sam. I don't see it."

Sam looked around the room for ideas.

"Anything? At all? Anywhere to go from here?" Pops asked.

"We've got another wall. We could use that." Sam replied.

"Ok," Pops said, "What goes there?"

"I don't know," Sam admitted.

Neither wanted to say anything about asking Deb, afraid she'd have an answer.

"Instead of all the boards," Sam said, "perhaps we create a clustered tagging system?"

"Didn't she say she was going to do that?" Pops asked.

"Yes."

"Then let her. It's a good idea, we'll never code it as fast as she can."

One of the pieces of yarn fell off. Pops stuck it back. It fell off again. They both looked at it.

Sam slumped.

"I don't know, Pops," Sam said, "I give up."

Pops did not want to hear that.

"What do you mean you give up?" he came at Sam, "We're in the middle of this thing."

"I'm not sure we're the right people for this." Sam said.

Pops held out his palm, "We never are. Don't you get it?"

Sam was confused. His mentor continued.

"Do you remember the first few days you were here, how I asked everybody why they're here, what they wanted to do?"

"Yeah," Sam said, "I remember you were ready for a change."

"You too. I remember," Pops said, "Well, guess what? Your change has arrived, Samuel. Welcome to it."

"It isn't what it's supposed to be," Sam said, "It isn't what I imagined."

"Never is," Pops shot back, "When the things that people imagine doing aligns with with what actually happens it's a damned rare occurrence. Get used to it."

"What's that mean?"

"Deal with the situation you've got," Pops said, "not the one you've imagined."

Looking at the table, Sam saw several more cards. He ignored them.

Pops walked over to the box, took a couple more slices and stuck it in a container.

"Doggy bag," Pops said.

"I love leftover pizza." Sam said.

Pops frowned a bit, but nodded, putting it away.

"Let's say we stop right here, Pops," Sam said, "tear it all down. What do you think she's going to do?"

"She's not giving up. I know that," Pops said.

"Me too," Sam nodded, "and as much as she drives me crazy, I think we owe her something."

"What?"

"I don't know," Sam admitted again, then looked up at his mentor sadly, "I think we're going to have to help Deb."

Sam paused, then continued, "Or get help for her."

The room was quiet as they both stared at the wall, neither wanting to continue.

"Life sucks," Sam finally said.

"Better suck it up, buttercup," Pops said.

The older man was smiling.

Sam stood.

"Analysis Paralysis, that's what," Sam said.

"Yeah," Pops replied. Sam could see his complexion darken further.

"Analysis Paralysis" refers to the tendency of technical teams, when faced with an unpleasant future, whether having a difficult conversation or actually beginning to work, to get caught in an endless cycle of continuing to talk about the technical details of the problem instead of solving it. Talking, diagramming, installing new tools, taking classes, and creating frameworks was always easier than actually recognizing and working the problem.

"All right," Sam said, "I'm calling it."

"Calling what?" Pops replied.

Sam looked at his watch.

"It's 6pm Sunday. We have until midnight, then I shut this thing down. That'll give us some time before Monday morning. We're not going to keep running out the clock."

"You going to do this?" Pops asked. "You going to do your job?"

"No, but yes." Sam replied.

Sam got the kind of "Are you crazy" stare he expected as soon as he heard his own words.

"I'm going to do whatever I need to do, Pops." Sam said.

"Can you tell Joe he's wrong? Confront him with severe problems?" Pops asked.

"I think so."

"Could you fire Debian?"

That was a good one.

"I don't know." Sam said.

"Could you fire yourself, leave EigenCorp if things weren't working out okay?"

Sam squirmed.

"Probably not," he admitted, "I'd probably just try harder."

"Then don't say you'll do whatever it takes, because you won't," Pops stopped as if considering his own words, "None of us will. What if she continues to see patterns when we don't?"

"Which you know she will," Sam said.

"And she becomes physically dangerous?" Pops asked.

"Unlikely, but possible," Sam admitted.

"We're going to have to do an intervention." Pops said.

"We?"

"I mean you," Pops replied, "That's your job now, Sam."

"Fuck me."

"Yeah."

Now Sam walked over to the board and tried to stare it into submission.

After a few minutes, he said, "I was wrong. We were wrong."

"About the data?" Pops asked.

"About Deb. Her brain will never let us walk her slowly into her admitting she's wrong. She's going to need confrontation."

"Sam," Pops said, "that just escalates other risks."

"Yeah, I know," Sam said, "but come midnight, we're going to have to spring it on her, try to force her to see reason."

He turned to face Pops.

"And we're going to have to be prepared for whatever happens after that."

"That's it. I'm done," Sam said. He took his new watch off and tossed it on the table. "Want a watch?"

Pops looked so dark it hurt to look at him.

Pops held out his arm.

"See a watch on this arm?" Pops asked.

He didn't.

"No thanks, Sam," Pops said, "I've got four more back at my place. They're nice. One's on my dresser. A couple are in a shoebox."

Staring at his watch, whatever the answer was, it wasn't in this room. There was signal here, something was off, but there was a lot of noise, too.

Sam thought that it was very difficult for most tech folks to deal with "I've got a hunch," but that's where the team was.

Sure, you could say "I've got a hunch" as a way of advancing the conversation, but at some point things have to shake out. The world must resolve. Computers must compute. Continuous ambiguity was not the world EigenCorp worked in.

He picked his slice back up. Maybe he could learn to love mushroom pizza.

"Let's find Debian," he finally said to Pops, "see what kind of new trouble she's getting us into."

He carefully put the slice back down without giving it another shot. He picked the watch up, put it back in his pocket. He thought of the man asking for money outside the coffee shop.

Now he knew exactly who he'd give the watch to.

2.15

Chamber Of Secrets

"I think it's time Pops showed us the Chamber of Secrets," Deb said, watching closely as Pops and Sam approached her cubicle.

"All this going on, and you want to go see a movie?" Sam said.

Pops searched the ceiling tiles for some sort of guidance. "Why do you two keep wanting to get fired? Don't you like me?"

"Get fired?" Sam asked, "Wait, is there something here I don't understand?"

"More than we would ever have time to go over," Deb said.

"What are you going on about now?" Pops gave up the ceiling and slouched just a bit against the wall.

"You going to make me show you? Fine."

She reached up to the wall of her cubicle.

"It's all here In the Confectionary Delivery Deviance Log."

"Oh God," Sam said, "Not back to donuts again. My life is hell."

She flipped the chart over to the back.

"I have been tracking the amount of time people spend in the break room."

Pops looked at Sam.

"I live a cursed life," Pops face did not move.

"Welcome to the party," Sam replied.

"Senior leadership," Deb continued, "spends more time in the break-room than all other employees."

"That's it?" Sam asked, "You've made a chart to prove that the bosses are slackers?"

"But when I compare that to the reverse chart," she flipped it back and forth, "Joe is always in the breakroom the days the confections are delayed."

"You're making a federal case out of proving that your boss likes talking to the service staff?" Pops asked.

"He does not," she said, "He mostly ignores them. What Joe likes is a certain kind of cannoli."

"Sherlock Newbury, Donut Detective," Sam said.

Ignoring him, she continued, "He gets them delivered on certain days in the breakroom, yet there is no evidence that they ever existed after the cart goes in there. They disappear. Along with Joe. He goes missing for up to 43.2 minutes at a time, entering the breakroom but not present when I check it."

"Aren't you keeping an eye on her," Pops asked Sam.

"She wanders off. We had a discussion last week about the possibility of genetically-engineering fire-breathing dragons and training them as programmers."

"I'm sitting right here, you guys," Deb said.

"There was a Powerpoint," Sam finished.

"This could be a good time to start that second chalk-talk exercise I was telling you about."

"Pop's stalling," Deb said to Sam.

Pops continued, "Which involves an electromechanical harness."

"Definitely changing the subject," Sam agreed.

Pops stopped. Sam continued, "But you know, I like him when he does that. It's endearing."

"It is annoying," Deb replied, "but also cute."

Pops eyebrows raised, "I'm standing right here too. And I know you didn't just call me cute."

"He started it."

Sam shifted uncomfortably, "Not cute. Definitely. Pops is a rough and tumble macho guy. Pops can't be cute."

"Did I ever tell you about when I worked in the military?"

"No,"

"Good. Let's keep it that way." Pops replied, "I know you two think you're Lords of the Universe, but with this little adventure, Deb's chart and all, we're playing for all the marbles. Keep that in mind. You need to be honest with yourselves."

"All I want to do," Sam said, "is learn and help out. That's all I ever wanted to do. It's the girl. The girl started all of this. Everything was fine before the girl showed up."

Deb grumbled before replying, "I have been honest with both of you since this started. I will continue to be honest until it ends."

Pops said, "My point is that you think we have a lot more control than we actually do. A little humility might be good for both of you."

"You're in charge, Pops," Sam said.

The older man looked at Deb. She nodded. Her face was set in stone.

"Okay then," Pops rubbed his arms as if he were cold although the room was warm, "Let's assume for a moment that there's another data repository. I know for a fact that there's no evidence for a crime there. So what good could it possibly be to break into somewhere at work where you're clearly forbidden to be? Just to find nothing?"

"Wait," Sam said, "There's a room? You mean The Cannoli Chick is actually on to something?"

"I said hypothetically."

Deb leaned forward, "How do you know there isn't evidence of crimes?"

"How about this," Pops said, "I'll pretend there's a room if you pretend there's nothing there. Why throw away your careers, your future?"

"Dammit," Sam said, "because here we are, that's why. Right? I hate to say this, but Debian has a point. Now that we're here we can't un-see the things we've seen. We can choose not to look anymore, but we can't choose to forget what we've seen, at least I can't."

"Did you just say I have a point?"

"Shut up."

She did.

"Hypothetically, Pops," Sam said, "I play the tuba. I'm not so sure this what-if, who-knows weaselly conversation is a good path to go down. This is getting real too quickly. If we're seeing things we can't un-see, we should stop looking around so much and speculating on what else there might be. It's either real or not."

"It's the only path you've got, it's the only path I'm offering you," Pops replied, putting his hand on Sam's shoulder, "Hypothetically or not."

"The problem with hypotheticals is that at some point they stop being so hypothetical," Sam replied.

"We could create a matrix," Deb said in a lower voice, "or a chart. We could make a list of the pros and cons of each hypothetical and the possible result."

"Write everything down," Pops said.

"Yes."

"Where there's a hard copy, written proof of all of our discussions. Proof that could be used by others in ways we wouldn't like."

"We could eat the paper after we're done," She replied.

Sam shook his head, "it's not happening, Deb. We don't want folks coming in where we'd have to bust them up."

He made a fist. He tried to flex the one muscle in his skinny, freckled arm.

"It's doubtful Sam could 'bust up' a small snail." She made air quotes.

"Smart people can fight, right Pops? There's a lot of science around fighting. Nerds fight too."

"Sam, that's great. You might be on to something," Pops said. "I think you're right. Let's talk about that. You're going to need a better understanding of hacking, attacking, and fighting if you're going to do this work because it's really nothing to do with computers."

"Sam's snail combat course," Deb said.

"If you two really want to work strategically, and not just spend your time bit-twiddling, we're going to need to talk about how intrusions and hacking always has to occur along OODA lines. You can't keep thinking so simple. You fight and control the enemy using OODA. Always. Ever heard of John Boyd and OODA?"

Blank stares.

Pops shrugged, "Boyd was one of the best combat pilots ever but there was no war, so they gave him the job of teaching classes to pilots on how to fight."

"You can't do that," Deb said.

Pops agreed. "I know. You're correct, but he had to do something, so he came up with this idea that every kind of fight boils down to four things, O-O-D-A, The memetic is OODA."

"More classes?" Sam said.

"This is not a class. This is your answer. OODA stands for Observe, Orient, Decide, and Act. No matter what kind of fight you're in, from fist-fighting on up to tanks and such, even companies fighting for market share, it's all OODA. You keep doing OODA over and over again as you try to fight. It's called the OODA loop."

"Pops," Deb said, "I don't understand what this has to do with EigenCorp."

"Just this," Pops replied, "Boyd said that the secret to fighting somebody wasn't necessarily to hurt them, it was to screw up that OODA loop they're doing: mess it up, give it false data. They call it getting inside the opponent's OODA loop. If you can influence how they Observe, Orient, Decide, or Act? You can make them fight themselves. You win."

"So," Sam frowned, "A boxer might hit somebody hard enough that they can't stay Oriented any more. They don't know where they are."

"That's good, Sam. Or a spy might get inside an organization and screw up how they Decide. All forms of any kind of combat involves an OODA Loop. It's always been like that. Boyd just listed the obvious."

"Observe. An army might create inflatable tanks to make the other army observing think they're bigger than they really are. I think I understand," Deb said, "Information beats action."

"Always. Explain it to him," Pops gave her the challenge.

She looked at Sam. "Pops is saying that we both can be right. EigenCorp may both be responsible for committing crimes and doing bad things and innocent of any direct criminal activity."

"Not just direct, any criminal activity at all," Pops insisted.

"The nature of what we do here, this type of work, it involves getting inside some other organization or person's OODA loop. We hack into how they Observe things. We figure out the secret of how they Orient themselves to the market. We read minutes and intercept comms to see or influence how they Decide. Some of the things we work with can actually control how they Act, like the code that runs power plants. But we're still just nerds. It's all just information."

"That's correct," Pops said, "By assessing cyber risk and running red teams, we're actually cutting into the way things work without actually doing anything. We just open things up."

"Once inside the system," Deb said, "we're inadvertently helping any other folks that want in. That's why there's so much security here, because what we do is so powerful, even though it doesn't look that way. By doing the things people want us to do and pay us for, we could be screwing all kinds of things up. We see the inside of the system that used to be invisible but in reality wasn't, just nobody knew. Now they do. It's like we're running a nerd fight club using OODA. We don't actually fight."

"Possibly," Pops said.

"EigenCorp is running an open bar and giving out free guns, but it doesn't want responsibility for anything bad happening." she concluded.

"No."

Pops got out a metal container and took some pills. Sam saw the man's hand tremble a bit.

Sam was worried. "You okay, Pops? Want to sit down?"

"I'm fine."

From his pocket, Pops pulled out a duck. Sam could see that it was a wizard duck. He'd never seen a wizard duck.

The man looked briefly at the duck then put it back.

"The ducks don't help," Pops said.

"I know," Sam replied.

"Debian," Pops said, "You got me stuck. I can't leave this job knowing that perhaps so many crimes might have been committed or even that we enabled so many crimes."

"Thank you."

"It wasn't a compliment."

Sam tried to sum it up, "I want to ignore this all and go on with our lives, forget it. Pops wants to acknowledge the problems we have and fix them but not keep poking around. And Deb wants to find out anything and everything she can until she's satisfied."

Agreement.

"Janus Group," Deb said quietly to herself.

The girl was a broken record.

"Ok, then I think we can work this out. Pops is a good person and Deb? Deb is what she is. Deb is also a person, I believe. Now that we know the nature of the problem, all that's left is resolution, and, lucky us, we specialize in this. How about we eat our own pudding. We can be our own customer. We can do a new security risk assessment, only on ourselves. We're certainly able to do it. Perhaps now we talk about deliverables."

To Sam, Pops looked so seriously at Deb that he could have been furious.

Pops grimaced.

"But I want you to explain one thing to me, Debian. If we do the right thing, all three of us, not only do we maybe catch some bad guys and fix some holes, we also blow up this entire company. Hundreds of families will go without dinner. People will curse our names for years to come. Is that okay with you, Debian?"

"Surely there's some way we can split the difference …" Sam began.

"No," Deb responded. "It's not. It's not okay, Pops. I agree. I don't want to cause even more pain. No more. Unless I have to."

"Well crap," Sam threw his arms up, "Ain't that just a kettle of fish."

"I'd like some fish," Deb said.

Pops didn't even look at her. "Not now."

"Come on you two," Sam had had enough. He led them to the breakroom.

"Now," he said simply, "Ok, Pops, show us where this room is."

Deb stuck her head in the way. "Sam, we shouldn't do this to Pops. He's right."

The older man took a deep breath and exhaled, the look of surrender slowly taking over.

Pops looked at Sam the way a condemned man might look at his best friend commanding his firing squad.

Sam shook his head no. "I can't let us keep circling. The only way out is through. Damn you all for making me make this choice."

"Pops?" She asked.

Sam thought it was the first time he'd seen her truly worried.

"Well Popster," Sam continued, "You want to show me, or should I just start tearing the place apart until I find it?"

"Ok," the older man said as he went over to one of the vending machines. He punched some buttons for snacks.

The machine front pivoted aside, a door opening up into a large room.

Entering, Sam was reminded of the main computer room in the movie, "Alien." It was quiet. The walls were cushioned and soundproofed. It was huge. The room had to be at least 10x40.

"Because of it's importance," Pops said, "We call this 'The Womb'. This Is the 'womb' of EigenCorp." He crossed his arms, "Everything you could possibly ask for is going to be here."

Above the door, one in a series of lights lit up.

Debian cocked her head. "What's that?"

Pops glanced, "Keycard alert. We've got this entire building wired up. Somebody just entered downstairs, swiped their keycard. Probably Joe. Probably back from dinner."

Sam looked at the light. "Where do you think he's heading?"

"Probably here," Pops replied.

The light went out.

"It won't be long, then," Deb said, still staring at the light, now out, "What are we going to do now?"

They both stared at their teacher.

But Sam was the one who answered, "We're going to need to stall him, distract him, probably for quite a bit of time. We need to investigate."

Pops shrugged, "Don't look at me. I can't stall people. You both just told me that I was bad at this kind of thing."

Sam put his hands on his hips, "I'll go with him."

They both frowned at him.

"What choice do we have?"

"Ok," Deb agreed, "I've got this part. Pick a location. I'll meet you in 24 hours with some results."

"No," Pops pointed at her as he replied, "you stay right here. We'll meet you in 8 hours to see where we are."

Deb remained.

Sam looked at his older friend as they left the breakroom.

"You really think we should leave her in there?" He asked.

"Why not?" Pops asked. "What kind of trouble can she get into?"

"It scares me just to imagine it," Sam said.

"Well, whatever it is, it won't be long. It's the weekend. Assuming we can handle Joe, and that's a big 'if', we've got until Monday morning. Then playtime's over."

"But we can still keep it hush-hush for a while."

"Nope. Womb entrance logs have already busted us. We're in it now, kid. The only way forward is directly though, like you said. You and Deb just made sure of that."

"Now the job's Joe." Sam said.

"Right. You and I have to keep him busy and distracted. Eight hours."

"You know," Sam offered, "A far as distractions, I can…"

"Don't mention magic."

Sam did not mention magic. Instead he asked Pops for more advice as they continued down the hall.

Debian did not get in trouble in 'The Womb'. Instead, after waiting 7.3 minutes from their departure, she came slowly out. She took the stairway down and went out into the street.

It was a beautiful day.

She asked an older lady who was walking by to borrow her phone.

Moving, dialing, speaking very deliberately she connected the call.

"Sheriff Beau Martin, please."

2.16

Trophies Of Pain

It was the guns that bothered Sam the most, the guns and the sadness. He could take anything but more of that infinite sadness.

Who knew how far the secrets of EigenCorp went?

"We need to stop by my apartment first," Pops said as they got into the elevator, "I have some things Joe will want to dive into."

"Don't have time for that," Sam said.

"Trust me, we do,"

Pops checked his watch and hit the button for Sublevel One. The watch beeped.

"Five minutes," Pops said, "Let's do this."

The lift stopped. The doors opened. Pops hit the switch. Fluorescents flickered into a secret life Sam would have never guessed.

On the far wall, an army cot. It was a large, mostly-empty area with some personal possessions over in a corner. Concrete floor. Bare. The rest was junk and machinery. On the end table by the cot was one of those old-fashioned wind-up alarm clocks. A couple of paperbacks. A musty lamp.

"You live here?" Sam couldn't believe it.

"Easier than buying a car," Pops replied, "We are now in 'The Feet'. Heat, light, mechanicals, interfaces, it all rests here. This is where it begins."

As they walked to the corner, Sam saw a label on Pops' cot. It said, "Big Toe. Here lies the little piggy that went to market."

Pops saw Sam noticing. He said, "What can I say? I'm always joking around."

"I like this," Sam said, walking over to some sort of hobby table, "You've got one of those stick models?"

He touched the model.

It completely fell apart, hours of work lost.

"I did," Pops replied. "Not anymore."

Walking quickly away and over to the wall, Sam saw a 50s movie poster. Beside it was an autographed picture of a very young Pops shaking hands with a movie star.

"Movies. I always thought of you as a classical music and red wine kind of guy," Sam said.

Pops replied, "I have a couple of bottles around here somewhere. I collect things. Always have."

"How do you choose what to collect?" Sam asked.

"That's the fun part," Pops said, "each one starts a story."

"Look here, that is truly amazing," Sam couldn't help himself, he felt he was visiting a museum of oddities, looking around some more "You've been everywhere. If these walls could only talk, right? I bet you've got some great stories to tell."

"I do," Pops said, "Some might be good. Some I might be able to tell you. Pops also looked around, obviously impressed at his collection, adding"one day."

Pops winked. He looked back at Sam who was still admiring the layout.

"You should help Debian out more. She needs you," Pops said.

Sam stopped looking, the mood ruined, "I'd rather keep a giant, rabid, angry polar bear as a house pet. It's nicer."

Sam turned to Pops as the older man replied, "Maybe so, but there's something there. I can see it."

"We're friends, Pop, aren't we?" He asked.

"Yes," Pops replied.

"Then please shut up."

Pops studied Sam for a long second, then nodded, "Ok, but let me say one thing, and that's all, okay?"

Sam nodded, suddenly afraid.

"Sam," Pops began "I've never seen anybody like you. You made a good point these last few weeks, it's people. I think you could break into just about anywhere given enough contact with the people in charge. You're special."

Sam was confused, "If you're going to keep flattering me, I'm sure as heck not going to fight you off."

"But," Pops held his finger up, "I've also never seen anything like

Debian, either. I can't give her a computational puzzle that she can't figure out. I find that bizarre, weird, scary. Disturbing."

"So far we agree." Sam said, "We can leave it there."

Pops concluded, "But stranger than all of that is the way you two interact."

"Please be quiet," Sam said.

"There's something there, that's all I'm saying."

"And now you've said it," Sam replied, "Something. Yup. Something. Moving on. What's this, a filing cabinet?"

Pops nodded. Sam moved over to it, wondering what goodies it contained.

Filing cabinet. What to say about a filing cabinet, Sam thought. Must say something, anything. Filing cabinet.

"You're old school, Popster. A crazy man. And what are these?"

It was a glass case, the kind people might keep bowling trophies in. Instead of trophies, though, there were weapons: pistols, rifles, little short guns like they use on TV, knives, and many other things Sam couldn't recognize.

"When I do things," Pops took a beat, "that I need to remember. I put a record here."

Sam thought of the beach house and the horror that was there. There, he saw the knife. He almost pointed but stopped himself.

Sam shivered.

These were unpleasant things, these trophies.

"Sorry," Sam said, "Didn't mean to pry."

"Yes you did," Pops replied, "Friends pry. They should. This is my third case. The other two are already full."

Pops looked back to the filing cabinet, "Joe was interested in some irregularities in EigenCorp's initial investors. If we give them my research," he pulled a drawer out and started thumbing, "That'll keep him busy for a couple of hours, easy. You can do your thing and ask a bunch of annoying questions and make inane observations. We might be able to stretch it out."

Sam wasn't ready to take the folder yet. He was still inspired by the trophy case. "Maybe we should tool up, arm ourselves."

Here was a lot of visceral power. He could feel the cold metal in the air.

Pops turned to look. Dark eyes. Maybe a tiny twitch.

"I don't think you should be given sharp objects. Leave the tooling up to the mechanics."

The chimes of a clock interrupted.

"Whoa, you've got a grandfather clock?"

"Grandmother clock, Sam," he checked his watch, "two minutes remaining."

"But you have so much here," Sam couldn't help chasing this down, "You make really good money. You could live anywhere. Why all this? Why here?"

"Man's gotta live somewhere," Pops said.

"Why the files? Why the guns in the case?"

"What can I say," Pops held his hands out in surrender, "I'm a hoarder, Sam."

Sam pointed to the bed, "Big toe. This little piggy went to market. What happened to the other four piggies? There were other people?"

"They retired," Pops said, "They left."

"Still talk to them?"

"No," Pops started looking like his mood was heading the wrong way.

But Sam couldn't help himself, "And that doesn't strike you as odd?"

"It's an odd place, Sam," Pops said. "Everything here strikes me as odd."

Having enough, the older man walked over to his cot, his teeth clenched and groaning, obviously in pain.

"You alright?" Sam said.

Pops sat. He rolled up his pants. His leg had a brace which he tightened, saying "I'm fine. Old injury. Just need to keep it tight."

"Sure I can't help?"

"Got a new leg?" Pops joked, finishing up and patting his trousers.

"No," Sam replied.

"Then you can't," Pops said, beginning to stand up but thinking better and remaining on the cot.

The watch beeped.

"One minute," Pops said, town crier.

Pops placed his hands on his knees, considering giving standing up another shot.

"Maybe you should do this, not me," Pops said, "I'm not giving up, Sam. It needs to be done and I'll help, but aside from taking the consequences, perhaps I should hang back. This kind of thing might be better for younger people. I'll just slow you down."

Pops looked around at his things once more, taking them in, not as proud as before.

Sam hadn't seen this mood before in his teacher and it bothered him.

"Come on. We're just getting started, Pops. Remember? You've got a fantastic world of dating ahead of you. You still have important work to do. You're not an invalid. Uncertainty and doubt? This isn't you."

Pops tapped his piggy label, "I miss my friends, Sam," he pointed.

Sam saw a picture of a much younger Pops and five other people in front of an entrance to a hiking trail. They all had backpacks and camping gear. They looked very close. Happy.

"You talking about retirement?" Sam said, "That what you want?"

"No," Pops had also been looking at the picture but turned back to face Sam, "You're right, but that's what I've got. If I don't have my friends, I don't have anything. Might be time to join them."

Sam thought about agent Shotwell and the people disappearing, never to be heard from again.

The damp room felt ever damper. Sam felt he was walking down a dark, foggy path late at night. Alone.

"Okay," Sam said, "If that's what you want. I'm not going to ask you to take any more hits for me. I've got this."

Pops' watch started beeping.

"Time's up," Sam said.

Aside from turning the alarm off, Pops didn't move. He stared at the floor, then the wall again, then back to the floor, each time becoming slower. He didn't move. Back to the wall of memories, trophies of pain.

Sam thought Pops was the saddest person he'd ever seen.

It hurt Sam.

"I can't leave you like this," Sam said, surprising himself, "I won't leave you like this."

Sam cleared his throat, "You've been denying any EigenCorp problems all along. The guns. The files. When are you going to admit that there's been something really rotten here?"

"Sam," Pops looked up, "There's a difference between keeping secrets and hiding from reality."

"So?" Sam replied.

The old man sighed, "I have forgotten exactly where the line is."

Pops looked back at the floor, unable to make contact as he finished, "A long, long time ago."

"Alright then," Sam stepped up and took his friend's shoulder, "We're going to find it, together, you and me, got it?"

The older man nodded, clinched his jaw. Sam thought Pops looked like an arctic explorer, having lost the rest of his party, Pops looked out into the frozen abyss, the sad lonely day of night, prepared to finish it.

"They eat their dogs," Sam said, trying to lighten things up.

"What?" Pops was at least breaking his mood.

"Arctic explorers. In the end, they eat their dogs."

Sam nodded knowingly. They were in this together. He smiled at Pops, trying to cheer him up. A little bit of silliness.. It was all just an adventure they could handle together.

"I'm not eating Spot," Pops replied.

"You have a dog?" Sam asked.

Pops nodded, "He's around here somewhere."

Sam looked around, didn't see a dog. He saw a chest of drawers. There was another picture on it. Was there a dog?

"Wait a minute," Sam said, "Since when did you know Professor Newbury?"

"Paul and I go way back," Pops replied, "Almost as far back as the founding of the company. Joe introduced us when we met with all of the initial investors."

Sam was at sea, "Joe knows Deb's dad?"

"Sure. He used to be Paul's grad student. I thought you knew that."

"Oh my geesh," Sam said, "This is a hit."

He looked at his mentor. Sam was now joining Pops on his arctic suicide march.

"We have to tell her," Sam said.

"Oh boy," Pops said.

"Yeah. Oh boy." Sam replied. He walked over, picked the picture up, examined it as if it were a fake, "Maybe we wait a bit on that."

"Sam," Pops replied, "If this continues to go south, and I suspect it will, we don't need to drag everybody we've ever known into this train wreck. Our main job at some point has to be damage control."

"Yeah," Sam agreed, "But if we don't tell her, she'll never forgive us."

That got him going. Pops stood up. He looked around the room.

"This is all I've got, Sam," He said.

Sam placed his hand on Pops with compassion. With his other hand he pointed.

"I know, but one day you're going to have our pictures on the wall.

You've got us now. We're here for you. We can be your piggies." It was uncomfortable to say.

Sam saw the worry on his friend's face. Worry didn't suit the older man. None of this suited him, and Sam was going to make it right.

He started walking towards the case on the way out. Pops began following along, at first slowly, then gaining speed.

Sam pointed to the case. "These are tools. You're right. We're going to need our tools. We can't stay here," he pointed around, "in the past. We have to make a future, use the tools, maybe not these, but we're going to need a lever, a big, big lever. And I need your help using it."

"Okay Sam, we go forward," Pops said, looking back for just a second, "You win."

Sam stopped him.

"It's not a contest. Nobody wins. If Joe and Deb's dad are working together, even know one another, we're going to need to find Deb, tell her. She's going to have to move forward too. That'll change her entire analysis. Maybe she's the lever. I hate this."

"What about finding Joe, delaying him?" Pops asked.

"I don't know," Sam admitted, "But I know if Deb's doing the heavy lifting, getting her squared away has to come before anything else, even Joe."

"I have an idea about Joe," Pops said.

"What?"

"It'll work better if you don't know." Pops said.

"I don't like the sound of that," Sam said.

"I don't like the sound of any of it," Pops agreed.

They got back in the lift. There was just a brief pause as Pops gathered himself, tightening, then working quickly.

Neither Pops or Sam ever saw The Foot again, and for that Sam was truly and deeply sad for a very long time.

2.17

Meeting The Maker

"She's not here," Pops said, as they both came through the secret door into the empty Womb.

"I don't want to tell you I told you so but .." Sam said,

Sam didn't finish. He couldn't.

"What now?" the older man said.

Sam realized that no matter how much incompetence he faked, people were going to come to him for leadership. It was that way at school. It was that way his whole life. The stars may fall from heaven. The sun may go red giant. He could find another secretive company full of arrogant, smart people. They'd still end up leaning on him.

Except Devil Girl.

"We leave and find her, that's what. I don't see any other choice."

Pops looked out into the empty breakroom.

"There'll be more trouble if we stay," he said.

"It's decided then," Sam said, "If there's more trouble here at Eigen-Corp, then here at EigenCorp is where Debian Newbury is going to be."

They went by her cubicle first.

"That little rat," Sam said as they got there.

There were over a dozen ducks assembled into some kind of pattern on her desk.

"She's got them all," he was beside himself, "She's stolen all the stupid ducks. Unbelievable."

"Stealing is a strong word," Pops replied, studying the pattern, "I wouldn't use it. That's not what this is."

"What is it then?"

Pops looked closer.

"She's organizing, collating. Once she's done, she'll put them all back; never be interested in them again. Ever."

"I don't like it," Sam said.

Pops looked to him and frowned.

Sam pointed.

"I don't like it," he said again, "I don't like it because I think you're right. It's not stealing."

They both started towards the elevator but Pops stopped.

"This isn't going to work."

"I thought we agreed we had to find her," Sam replied.

"She's a moving target," Pops replied, "That's going to require a bit of thought."

"Does this building have some sort of lockdown mode?"

"It does," Pops rubbed his chin, "We might get away with using it for an hour or two without setting off a major alarm. First, though, let me show you the Brain Room. That's another place she's not supposed to be."

"Good. She's probably there, then," Sam agreed.

Walking down the hall, Pops began quizzing Sam.

"Why do you keep doing all of that silly magic stuff anyway?" he asked, not looking at Sam, "You're a smart guy."

Sam considered, not breaking his stride.

"I don't know, it's just always something I've been good at, getting people's attention and directing it places. Figured I might as well have some fun, right?"

"Then why are you so bad at it?" Pops said.

"That, Pops is a much better question."

Sam did not answer it.

"You need to start thinking about your long-term future, both you and Deb," Pops said.

"I don't think about Deb at all."

"Um-hmm," was all Pops said.

Pops stared at him with those dead eyes of his.

"Why don't we go into business, Pops," Sam asked, "just you and me. Batman and Robin."

"I'm not going to wear tights. I'm too old, and you're going to need to negotiate your way forward, not fantasize about it. Learn to compromise. Like the rest of us."

"Here we are," Sam pointed at the hall ahead as they walked, "Walking around, looking for Deb, actually doing things, not fantasizing."

"We are indeed," Pops replied, finally stopping, "here we are."

Pops looked at a closed door.

No secret panel covered the door to the Brain Room. There was no label, no picture of a brain. There was no eye scanner, complex lock, slide, or bat-pole to use. It was just a simple metal door with a mechanical keypad lock and double deadbolts.

Walking by, Sam would have thought it was just a broom closet or supply room, perhaps containing expensive or dangerous items. It was the kind of door you'd see in a rental cottage or an AirBnB.

"Get on in, Sam," Pops pointed after opening it, "time to meet the maker."

Inside, Sam thought immediately of a home theater. It was a large, mostly-square room. There were couches, a bar, chairs. There was a wall-sized monitor, carpet, and lots of shelves.

There were expensive 3D printers, Christmas Tree Machines, of a type he'd never seen before.

Lying around on the shelves were all kinds of creative tech. There were several different video games. There were more than a few AR/VR headsets.

But there was one thing. It was a scalp interface with electrodes and goggles. He'd know that anywhere. It had a small power pack. Sat next to electrode jelly.

Sam knew that one. He'd only seen it in one place: being used by Stetson, his old roommate, in the weeks before Stetson went crazy and shot all of those people at the airport.

"Some of this I know," he said, trying to look at everything and not just the thing that was freaking him out, "some of this I've never seen before."

"This is where we make everything," Pops said, obviously proud, "It's the maker room, the brain. Joe keeps all his secret projects in here, at least until they're ready to prototype."

"Dag Pops, you're right, this is 'The Brain', the maker room. I bet all the bigshots hang out here. I'd love to be a fly on the wall."

Pops shook his head no. "Joe and me, that's all, and I make it a point not to come very often."

They heard a sound from one of the side rooms.

Sam started, but Pops held him back.

"I've got it."

Pops went to the door, opened it slowly and looked inside.

His face fell when he looked back at Sam. Something was wrong.

Joe came out into the large room.

"Joe," Sam saw no point in gushing over the gear. Or the man.

"Sam," Joe said, looking around to see if there were anybody else, "You're not supposed to be here."

"I know."

Joe sniffed.

"I'm going to have to ask you to restrain him, Pops," Joe looked at Sam, a loving father coming home and being disappointed in Sam about some trivial domestic incident.

Pops sighed, took it in, looked back to Sam.

"I'm afraid he's correct. Come on."

Before starting, Pops looked back to Joe.

"You sure?"

Joe nodded. "They're going to want to interview them all. If we help tidy up, we might make it through in one piece."

Sighing a second time, and not looking pleased at the whole affair, his teacher tied him up.

But not tightly. It wasn't obvious, but Sam could tell his friend had gave him plenty of slack. Sam still had options.

"What about the police?" Pops asked Joe.

"They're on their way here too," Joe said. He shook his head and waved his arms around. This room is a mess! he seemed to say. "But that's not for us. Let them all sort it out. Now might be a good time to break out your go-bag."

Pops looked again at Sam but spoke to Joe, "It's under my desk. We'll need to find the other one. She's here somewhere."

"They're like mice," Joe replied, "I'm sure she's scurrying about. She'll turn up, probably looking for him."

Sam felt very small.

"Are you armed?" Joe asked Pops.

"Always."

"Good. Let's hope we don't need it."

Pops looked back to Sam and knelt.

"You okay? That's not causing you any pain, is it?"

Sam nodded a tiny yes as he regarded Joe, 'I'm okay. Thank you."

"Here, let me help with the gear," Pops and Joe left to the back room.

Sam had his ropes undone within seconds. He stood.

Should he leave? Joe and Pops were in the other room. Pops would have to pay for setting Sam free.

Disgusted, Sam went to the open door the men just went through. He could hear them talking. Hearing the voices get nearer, he plastered himself against the wall and was very quiet.

As he'd hoped, Joe was the first one through.

Sam leapt upon the man like a pouncing cat.

At least he hoped it was like a pouncing cat.

It was not like a pouncing cat.

Joe simply pivoted and twisted to the side. Sam overshot him, missed him, and fell into the shelves on the wall, his arms windmilling.

"Get him!" He yelled on the way down.

Rubbing the new knot on his head and looking back, Pops had indeed grabbed Joe.

Victory!

Pops did not look victorious.

"Now what?" Pops asked.

Fuck if he knew.

"Do the math, Sam," Joe said, "Things are bad. I'm your ticket out of here."

"I don't want a ticket. I want an answer."

"Go fish," Joe said, "I don't do answers. You're not getting anything."

Sam looked at his mentor. "Pops?"

"Joe's not the talkative type," was the response, "at least when it doesn't suit him.

Sam wasn't about to give up yet. He'd come too far.

"I say we tie him up! Sweat it out of him!" He'd heard that on a cop show one time. Sweat, for some reason, was a powerful persuader.

He imagined millions of Norwegians, sitting in saunas and telling one another every secret of their lives.

Pops did not look happy. He let Joe go and moved closer. "You're moving into kidnapping territory. You sure?"

"I've decided. We're going to bust this man up." Sam shook his fist. From somewhere he heard Deb laughing.

He shouldn't have done that.

By stepping forward, Pops had shown his back to his longtime friend Joe.

Sam heard the loud crackle and pop of electricity and the old man fell to the ground.

Behind him, Joe was holding a taser, a big industrial model, the kind that cops use.

Frack.

Joe pulled the trigger.

Some time later, groggy, Sam shook himself awake. Joe had zapped him too.

Opening his eyes, there was Joe, right in his face.

"Good, you're awake."

Joe grabbed Sam's chin in his hand and tilted Sam's head back-and-forth. It was the way you might look at a new bowling trophy once you got it home and wanted to relive the glory.

"I'm sorry it didn't work out," Joe said, still studying Sam's skull, "You could have been somebody."

Pleased that Sam was awake, and looking just a bit disappointed, Joe went back to the other room again.

Sam let out a deep breath and thought about how much he hated his life.

Back in the chair, the cords were tight this time.

Joe had been in the other room for a while.

Pops begin stirring.

"Pops," he whispered, "Pops."

He knew it wasn't loud, but Joe stuck his head in the doorway anyway. Joe looked at Pops.

"I'll get to you in a minute. Stay right there," he told Sam as if Sam could go anywhere.

Very funny.

Joe left again.

Sam didn't see much chance of becoming Batman or Robin. He didn't have a ray gun so becoming Buck Rogers wasn't going to work.

He had a chair. The chair was near the exit.

He had a boss in the other room, worried about finding Deb, probably to tie her up too.

He had a friend and mentor, slowly moving about on the ground, trying to come to.

He rocked the chair back-and-forth, making a tapping sound on the door.

"Deb, is that you? Run away, Joe's here."

He whispered just loud enough that Joe could hear him, but no louder. He hoped.

He had to get Joe out of the Brain Room before Pops became fully alert. He had to. That was his Ace.

With no reaction, he made the knocking sound again.

"Deb?" he whispered, as if desperate.

It worked. Joe came out, almost running. He went past Sam, opened the door, then looked both ways down the hallway.

This was it. Would Joe chase or go back to what he was doing?

Chase. Chase. Chase chase chase, Sam thought.

He took the bait. He went fully out into the hall, door closing behind him, off to find Deb.

"Pops," Sam was as loud as he dared, "Pops. Come on, Pops. Wake up."

The older man got to his hands and knees. He began to rub his head.

"Pops!"

Pops just moaned.

Sam was almost in a panic. "Come on, Pops. Come on. We gotta get out of here."

Pops got to his feet, unsteady, rubbing his eyes.

"What? Is that you, Sam?"

That's when the door opened behind his chair.

It felt to Sam like the floor dropped from under him. The walls disappeared. He was alone in empty space. There was nothing.

"That's not going to work," Joe said, as if he'd accidentally got out the wrong colored socks for an evening out.

Coming fully into the room, Joe walked over to Pops and zapped him again.

The man screamed and fell like a sack of rocks.

"Nicely done, Sam," Joe said without looking at him, going back to whatever he was doing before.

Sam struggled with his bindings. The more he struggled, the tighter they became. He believed they called this being "hog-tied."

"That's another fine mess you've gotten us into," he could see the old-time black-and-white comedians Laurel and Hardy doing some skit in a movie.

It was indeed another fine mess.

In the other room he could hear Joe rummaging around, drawers opening and closing. Probably packing up to run off, he thought. He had no idea why he thought that. It was just as likely his boss was preparing a large deep-fryer to turn Sam into fricassees.

He finally looked down. God dammit he finally looked down.

"He's not dead, he's just pining for the fjords," A Monty Python skit flew through his mind.

Pops was dead, though. He lay still. He didn't breathe. His skin was turning white, his lips blue.

He had lost control of his bowels, his bladder.

Sam tried to control his breathing. He tried not to cry, or panic.

Joe kept rummaging and Sam didn't want to look down anymore.

2.18

Lion Bearding

Joe should have never shut the door behind him. He also should have read Sam's bio before hiring him.

Given time, Sam was able to meditate himself through fear and panic. As a teenager, Sam had also been a fan of Harry Houdini, and Joe didn't know much about knots. Houdini had been the ultimate escape artist.

Escape was what Sam was all about. The only thing he wanted to do first is secure the scene so that Joe couldn't get away.

Like the Chinese Finger Puzzle, he needed to push, pop his joint out, not keep pulling. That was the trick.

Freeing himself, he crept over to the closed door.

Sam would manage, he would win. He'd been through too much to let this get to him.

He started turning the lock quietly, locking Joe in.

He owed Stetson and Carl this much, his old roomies back at school. They had died horribly. One of the three would have to make it. This is what they'd wanted.

The lock clicked quietly into place.

Resources, resources, there were always resources. Joe didn't know about Sam's magic habit. What else didn't he know?

Ignoring the body, he scanned the room.

There was nothing here, nothing he could use or take with him.

Well crap. He stepped back towards the entrance door. Stay or leave.

And what did Sam owe anybody, anyway?

He glanced down.

He owed Pops a lot. This was awful.

He owed his former team a lot.

Did he owe his current workmates anything?

He had to do something for Pops. The other one not so much.

But did he owe Pops what Pops wanted for him or what Sam imagined Pops might want?

He looked at the exit.

Sam had no problem running away. If he had to dress like a giant chicken and make clucking sounds as he ran like a frightened child, that was fine with him.

He had read every word of the policy manual he got that first day. He could quote it. None of it said anything about what was happening right now. So he felt free to run away, and he was good with that, no matter how it looked.

He glanced back at the door he'd just locked.

Joe, on the other hand, had to be locked up, one way or another. That's the way Sam saw it. This was messed up.

And he'd done that. Yay him. Now GTFO, Sam.

That's when he heard the scratching and clicking at the door leading out to the hallway.

The knob rattled some more. He heard more scratching sounds. The first deadbolt released.

It wouldn't be long now. What did he have? Rope? A chair? Pithy rejoinders?

The second deadbolt released.

He held the chair in front of him. He supposed he looked like a lion tamer. He needed a whip.

It was unlikely that a lion opening the door. Instead, after a few seconds more, the final lock gave way.

The door opened and there stood Deb. The girl. She was casually putting some tools away in a lock-pick kit.

"You have to be fucking kidding me," was all he managed.

"I'm here to rescue you." was the reply.

"You're the only person I know that breaks into a prison."

"What happened here?" She stepped in and looked left and right, "What is this place?"

"This is the Master Maker Room, The Brain. Joe's the maker. Joe killed Pops."

He knew she could accept this information only as bullet points.

"So? Then where's Joe?"

He gestured back to the door he'd just locked.

She took another step in. "Good. We should clean up, gather intel."

"Good? What is wrong with you?" he said, "And keep your voice down."

He heard a beep from her pocket.

"You've got a cellphone?"

"It's nothing," she said, "just ignore it."

She walked over and started rummaging through Pops' clothes.

"What the hell are you doing now?" he asked.

Finding what she wanted, she held it up.

"Getting his McGuffin."

Sam shook his hands in frustration. "Wrong. We need to leave all of this right where it is until the authorities get here."

"What authorities?" she replied, "You want me to call an ambulance?" She touched her pocket, admitting the phone she'd just denied.

"Don't worry about it. I've got everything I need here already and I've got it all handled," he replied.

"Do you know what's wrong with the work orders and jobs EigenCorp has been doing?"

"No."

"Do you know how these criminal activities are occurring?"

"No."

"Do you have any physical evidence that we could use in some fashion?"

"No."

"What are you doing here, then? Are you in this room to play video games? Perhaps 3D print an action figure or an ornate teacup?"

"So smartass, what about you?" he said.

"Now that I have this McGuffin, I have all of those things."

"Really?" Sam tried to smirk.

"Really. I know for sure."

He remembered that Joe had been packing stuff to take off, and Joe wouldn't have been leaving with it if it weren't important.

She didn't know nothing.

"Deb, I have some contacts in the government. This whole place is going down. We'll need to talk to them."

"Really?", she replied, "So have I. I have been working with Law Enforcement. For some time, actually."

"You duplicitous piece of shit," he'd had enough, "talking to the cops. Sold us out. Figures."

"And you, running the long con as always," she said, "That's Sam. How'd you get Pops killed?"

"Pops died while trying to help us," he said, looking to his dead friend again, pleading, "both of us."

Her expression didn't change.

"Well? Don't you have anything to say?" he asked.

"No," and nothing else.

He shook his head sadly. "You're a real piece of work, Debian Newbury."

He felt his lips quivering, a new wave of grief set to crash over him.

Breathe. Relax through it.

He closed his eyes, then slowly opened them. The grief did not destroy him. For that he was thankful.

She pointed at the open door.

"Why don't you just leave?" she said, ""You're not needed here anymore. You can't handle yourself and you're just going to get in the way."

"Screw you," he replied, "Why don't you just leave? What's keeping you around? You've sold us all out. Obviously, other folks will handle it. Don't need you."

"I'm almost through the research. I told you. I'd explain, but it's nothing you would understand."

Ugh.

"So, do you know why Stetson shot all those people at the airport?"

"No."

"Do you know what Joe's plans are?"

"No."

"Do you have any idea who the silent partners are here?"

"No."

"I guess you don't know much, then. Why don't you go figure that out, Girl Genius."

He involuntarily glanced at the door Joe was behind. Joe had that device Stetson had been using. She didn't catch him looking.

Sure, Joe had ran off with it. But he could fix that. She didn't know.

"Run along, little girl. I have to get some things. Important things. You'd just get in the way."

He opened the door to the hall and held it open, as if he were the doorman at a fine hotel and she was some urchin that had wandered in off the street.

He tried to hurt her by staring at her. It didn't work.

Amazingly, he managed to get her out in the hall, but the little fucker still didn't leave, at least just yet.

"You've got more work to do?" She asked.

"Yup."

"In there?" she pointed over his shoulder.

"Yup."

"How you planning on getting in there?"

He looked back. The stupid door had closed behind him.

Arrrghhhhh.

She held up her lock pick set. She tilted her head just a tiny bit. There was a faint smile.

He looked back at her, back to the door, back to her.

"Please," was all he could get out.

She sighed loudly, the queen having to visit her tiny little peasants, perhaps get her gown dirty. The horror.

But she stepped forward, started opening the door again.

Finishing, she held it open, much as he had just held it open for her.

"Idiot," she said.

He felt …. Sam didn't know how he felt. It was unpleasant.

The lights dimmed to about 10%.

"Now what?" he asked.

"That's lockdown," she replied, letting go of the door for him to take it, "We're now on lockdown."

"Joe triggered an alarm," Sam said, "You'll find exterior doors and elevators won't work.

"You've trapped Joe. And now you've trapped us. Idiot."

"Good grief, Debian," he said, "If you'd stop being such a lone wolf, we might have made it out of here."

"I have been fixing things I'll have you know," she replied, "fixing things for both of us." repeating the words he'd just said about Pops.

"Bullshit," he said, "Maybe there's no 'I' in team, but there's sure as hell no 'Deb' in team, either. I know that."

"Double bullshit on you."

"Fuck you, Deb. Just fuck you. I've had enough. Fuck you for turning me around."

"Turning you around? Where were you headed to? The cubicle with the window? The corner office? Parking space? A bowtie?"

Sam tried to speak very carefully.

"Get out of my face you dumb shit. Right now. Leave me alone. I never want to speak to you ever again. Ever."

He pointed down the hall.

"Get."

What was that? Did he see a twinge of hurt? Pain? Had he hurt her feelings? Could he do that? No, it couldn't be.

She spun around on her feet and left. He could see her fists tightened into balls by her sides as she walked.

He didn't wait for her to leave his sight. He turned and strode back into the Brain Room.

He put his hands on his hips, staring at the door Joe was behind.

His wrists were still sore from being tied-up.

Lesson learned, he thought, purposefully walking to the lock he'd just fastened. There was no yelling behind the door or sounds of movement, but that didn't tell him anything.

He put his hands on his hips, preparing himself mentally.

Ok, fucker, game on.

This time he wasn't going to try his Pouncing Cat Attack. He also wasn't going to get up close enough to get tased again, either.

He checked the room for a third time. There was a boom mic. He could use that as a spear or club. But that would mean getting in closer. No, he needed to be able to stand back.

There was only one option, and he didn't like it. He went and knelt by his dead friend. Now he was looting a corpse just like Deb had done.

Sam wasn't an expert in guns by any means, but there was a gun, and it had bullets in it.

Could he shoot Joe? He decided not to think about that anymore. He would do whatever he had to do.

Could Joe shoot him? Did Joe have a gun, a real gun?

He shook it off. This game of what-ifs could destroy him. If Joe had a gun, Sam would have to shoot him, and Sam just wanted it over with, one way or the other.

He listened again at the door. He heard nothing. Slowly and as quietly as he could, he unlocked it.

There was no magic phrase or special ninja move for Sam to make. Instead, just like back at the beach house, he just opened the door and stood there, holding the gun out front and wondering what the next few moments held.

2.19

Getting Roofied

Like a Native American, Sam sneaked across the carpeted floor. He'd read somewhere that they did that to prevent twigs and logs from rustling, giving away their position.

There were no twigs and logs. It was a carpet.

'What am I doing?' The thought came to him once and once it arrived, it kept on repeat. What-am-I-doing What-am-I-doing What-am-I-doing What-am-I-doing What-am-I-doing What-am-I-doing.

He stopped it.

He was doing the right thing, that's what, he lied to himself. He was doing the work Deb couldn't do. That was closer.

In his mind he could see her smirking that smirk of hers. That smirky smirk.

Smirker.

Sam was making sure that Deb didn't do better than he did.

Ouch. It almost hurt. Closer.

But no, it was worse than that.

Committing. For the first time in his life, Sam was actually committing to something. Not working hard or reaching for the dream, but committing. There was a difference. He knew that now.

There was nobody, just an empty room with a metal emergency door at the end with a push-bar on it. A sign on the top said "Roof Access."

Gun back in pocket. Of course it was empty. No sounds. No Joe. Nothing.

The room looked like somebody's hobby closet after a hurricane. There was stuff everywhere.

Ain't nobody got time for that. He moved immediately to the door.

As he expected, beyond that door was about a dozen concrete steps that led to another metal door. the sign on it said, "Roof."

He climbed the steps slowly, with purpose. He squared his shoulders. Smart people could fight too. Pops was right.

Sam had been known to bust a move or two, he lied again to himself. Lying to himself made him happy.

Only moves that Sam ever busted involved hats, rabbits, cards, coins, shock boxes, and other jokey magic stuff. Those also made him happy.

He pushed open the door to the bright sunshine.

Joe was 20, 30 feet away. He was clearing a bunch of loose metal rods off of a large painted square. They were the kind of rods used in construction work.

"Sam," Joe said, "I was so worried about you."

He sounded happy. He didn't even stop.

Sam let the door close behind him and simply stood there, wondering what he should do next.

Joe finally stopped and turned to face him. His boss smiled and put his hands on his hips, obviously impressed.

"That's really quite amazing, outstanding even," Joe said, "How'd you get up here? How'd you get loose?"

Okay. Sam could play it that way too.

"A misspent youth, boss," he said, "was kinda wondering what you were doing up here, all by yourself. Leaving without us."

Joe still seemed amused. "You've got it all wrong, Sam. I'm saving what I can, making it safe. That way we can pick it all up down the road. I'm saving your future, Samuel."

"Didn't feel that way when I got tased."

"Well, change can be difficult," was the reply.

"Pops is dead, Joe," Sam said, "He couldn't stand the tasing."

"Oh no," Joe said, "His heart."

Sam nodded, studying the man.

"I loved Pops. He was like a father. Sure we can't get help?"

For a man hearing terrible news, there was no urgency.

"Far too late," Sam replied, "now we just need to do what Pops would have wanted us to do."

"I agree," Joe replied, then went back to whatever it had been that he was doing.

"Joe," Sam said, "We're all going to have to have some answers. You can't run off. You've got to be accountable for something. For Pops if nothing else."

"I'm very sorry about Pops," Joe replied, and Sam didn't believe a word of it.

"I'm not going anywhere until we settle this, Joe," Sam said, "put too much work into it to allow this to be the end."

"You know that you're one of my favorites, Samuel," Joe said.

Sam tried pleading.

"Joe, let's make this work. There's some unpleasantness here, sure, but if we hang together, it can't be that bad, can it?"

Sam stepped a bit forward, held his hand out. "Come on, Joe, I know that we can work our way through this."

Joe returned the favor by stepping a bit forward himself. Both men were smiling. It was extremely unpleasant.

"Sam," Joe said, "We might have gotten off to the wrong foot. With the tasing and all. It was all too fast for you. I know that. Why don't you come with me? You can take the place of Pops, be number two. We could do a lot together."

Sam looked away briefly, then back.

"That's not going to happen, Joe. How about you give me the few things I need, answer a few questions? Maybe give me a piece of gear or two. Come with me, get this all sorted out."

"That's not going to happen, Sam," his boss said, "Whatever we do here, it's not going to matter, right? In the long run, it doesn't matter. Let me show you a world you never knew existed."

Joe held up his bag of gear.

"I've got things in here that will blow your mind," Joe said.

Sam was getting fretted. "What do you know about Janus Group?"

"Nothing. Should consider my offer," Joe replied.

"What did you do to Stetson?"

"Stetson didn't ….." Joe caught himself going too far, "I'm not going to spill my guts to you, Sam, it's the only thing I have. The only thing any of us have is information arbitrage."

"What the hell is that headset, then?" Sam tried to keep the bitterness out of his voice. "I've looked in the bag." He lied again.

"It's a door. Come with me and we'll both step through it. It takes you magical places."

"You're on a roof," Sam replied, "You're not going anywhere."

"Try me," Joe said, "Watch and learn."

Sam reached in, took out his sailor duck, looked at it. He thought of Pops, put it back.

"You know," Joe said, "this could be your next level. You're capable. We can do this. Together."

Sam's smile dimmed. "I think we're done with that by now."

"I can write you a letter of recommendation."

Sam stared.

Joe stopped smiling. "Probably done with that, too. Oh well. So be it."

Joe made the washing motion with his hands, as if to say, if that's the way you want it. "As long as you're sure."

His boss wiggled a bit, adjusted the straps of the pack he was carrying.

"Damn, this pack gets heavy."

Sam ground to a halt. He searched Joe's face.

"Wait a minute," Sam said, "why are you up here, Joe? Why are you picking all this up? Why are you leaving?"

"Somebody broke into The Womb. They hacked into our system. I suspect it was you and Debian."

Deb mostly, he thought. But just hours ago he had been the one who decided to hack into everything. That was on him.

"So?" He said, "Who cares? That's what we do here. We were trying to help."

Joe was beside himself, "Help?" he couldn't complete the sentence, finally saying, "Don't you get it? You gave everything away. It's all gone now."

"You crazy? We did no such thing," he had stopped smiling, "Why'd you hurt my friend Stetson?"

Joe was so angry he spat out a laugh, "You're just clueless, aren't you? Babe in the woods. Why do you think this is here, Sam, all of this, all that happened?"

Joe waved his arms as if describing the entire universe.

Hmm.

Sam replied, "You're out to make a buck, that's what. I think you hurt my friend just to make a buck."

Joe flinched for a second. Sam had gotten close, but not yet. It didn't stop the man.

"Debian. You and Debian," Joe said, "You're responsible for all of this and you don't even know why, do you?"

What the hell was he talking about.

Sam was concluding that Joe had completely gone round the bend, lost his mind, and that made Joe very dangerous.

Joe continued, "And would you like me to tell you why? I would, because I can't tell. HAHAHA."

Sam became very, very worried about his future.

POW!

Sam jumped.

It was a car backfiring. Somewhere on the street. Sam was truly going off his rocker hanging out on the stupid roof with Joe.

Unconsciously, he rubbed his sore wrists.

Joe noticed, "Sorry about that. I didn't mean to tie those ropes so tight."

"Yes you did."

Joe started fumbling around in his pocket.

Uh-oh. Here it comes.

"Don't tase me, Joe," Sam said.

Sam reached into his own pocket, reassuring himself. Joe made another half-crazy laugh, as if Sam were faking.

Changing his mind, Joe moved towards him. He took his hands out of his pocket as if to say see, no danger. Instead, he reached down and picked up one of the metal rods.

"I'm not going to tase you, Sam," Joe said, "I'm going to beat the living shit out of you so that I can get away before you destroy what's left of my life."

Sam stepped forward again. He wasn't afraid. He kept his hand in his pocket.

"Don't make me hurt you," Sam said.

"With what, your finger?" Joe held the rod up. He was getting close now.

"I mean it."

Sam pulled out the gun.

That got his attention, but only for a second. Joe ran at him.

Sam pulled the trigger.

Nothing happened.

Was it a safety? Was he supposed to put bullet into something? Could he …

All of his questions were cut short when, as promised, Joe swung the rod and started beating the living shit out of Sam.

Getting beat up was a lot worse than Sam expected. He would hold his hands up to protect his head. Joe would hit him in the ribs. He would try to grab the stick. Joe would hit him in the head.

Head shots made his teeth rattle. His vision blurred. Body shots were numb at first, blossoming into a deep and dark pain.

It went quickly. After four or five hits, he lost count, somehow he was no longer standing up, much to his own surprise.

In fact, for a little bit, he wasn't even sure where he was today. Had that been a second? An hour? A day? He didn't know that either.

He was taking a vacation to pain that he only wanted to stop.

It was a helipad, he realized, climbing to his hands and knees. The pain had stopped. Or took a break. Maybe it was on vacation too. They were building a helipad.

That's why Joe was up here. That's why he didn't know the door was locked. Joe was waiting on a ride.

Well, if he wanted a ride, Sam would give him one.

Still trying to blink the blood out of his eyes, and still on his hands and knees, he crawled as fast as he could over to the center of the helipad, looking like a giant toddler just escaping his playpen. I'm free.

If Joe wanted out, he'd first have to come through him.

It might be good to stand up first.

"This had gone about the way all of my other fights have gone," he mostly mumbled, believing he was thinking to himself.

"We're no good at this, Sam," Joe said. He paused, rephrased. "You, especially, are no good at this."

Man had a point.

"Ummmm," was all he managed. Some teeth may be coming out soon.

"Come on, Sam, give up," Joe said, "Just lie down."

"But I'm having so much fun," he got his mouth to work, kinda.

"Don't make me finish you off."

Sam barely made it to his feet. Was gun was over by the door, lost early in the beating. His head rang like a bell and his legs were wobbling so badly he was afraid they might quit without warning.

But it was sunny. There were nice clouds. He thought he heard a bird sing, traffic honk.

It wasn't that bad of a day for it.

"I'm afraid you're going to have to," he tried to sound fierce but he wondered if Joe could even make out his words.

It wasn't that bad of a day to die.

He pulled his shirt down, straightening his clothes, as if getting ready to go into a formal dance. The world swayed.

"But first," he said, "I've got something you're definitely going to want to see."

Sam tried to smile. His face was bleeding. There came the tooth. He spat it out.

Joe raised the rod, threatening him.

Sam tried his normal smile. "Nyah, it's okay, man. It's all good. See?"

Sam pulled his fist out and held it closed between them.

Joe started that crazy smile again. "What is it you have in your hand that you think I want to see? You can barely stand up."

"You'll love this."

He opened his fist. There was a handful of powder.

With as much breath as he could manage, he blew the itching powder directly into the man's eyes, then backed up, afraid of getting hit again.

Yeah, Joe took a good swing at him. Sam could hear the whoosh as the metal stick flew by his nose. Stepping back was a good call.

But Joe also screamed. And he dropped the rod. Joe grabbed his eyes and kept hollering.

Sam picked up the rod. He hit Joe across the face, testing the stick out. Testing himself out.

Joe started waving his arms around. If Joe got a hold on him, he'd kill Sam, of that Sam had no doubt.

Sam whacked him a couple more times, trying all the time to stay out of his reach. Sam did not have much power, but he was trying.

"Come on, Joe," Sam said, "Give it up. You've lost."

He shouldn't have said anything. Like an evil game of Marco Polo, Joe took the voice as a way to echolocate where Sam was.

Sam couldn't keep this up for long. He hit Joe again. He hit him in the shoulder, as hard as he still could. Sam's breath was ragged. He could hardly see Joe.

Joe screamed again. Tears were streaming out of his eyes.

Joe could still move quicker than Sam. Sam had seconds remaining. If he was lucky.

He swung again, hitting Joe in the legs as hard as he could, almost falling down in the process.

Joe fell down. That was it. Sam was all spent. Fortunately it looked like a tie. Sam was still standing, though. He slowly stepped up to stand over his former boss, trying to enunciate and holding the stick in a death grip.

"Come on, Joe. Enough."

This was the end. Joe was still struggling. Sam was going to have to kill him.

That's when Sam heard the first shot. Joe had a pistol and was pointing it pretty closely to Sam's head. Joe's fat lip, bloody face, missing teeth, and evil insane grin made the man look like something out of a horror movie.

Sam dropped the rod and immediately started running away, an old man hobbling as fast as he could to make it to the bathroom in time. Again, he was expecting to die any minute. He could make the door. Could he make the door?

Gun, then door.

Another shot. It couldn't have been more than inches away. Joe knew where Sam was going and Sam had no other option but to go there. Joe's blindness would be gone in seconds, a minute tops.

He tried to hobble faster.

Shot three. Sam dropped.

He had the gun. He started crawling towards the door. Joe would think he'd shot Sam and Sam was crawling around pathetically.

It wasn't far from the truth.

"Come here you little shit," Joe said, shooting again. This time it wasn't close. Was that good or bad?

Sam took the chance and glanced back. His former boss was wallowing around, making his way to standing, rubbing his face with one hand and waving the gun around with the other.

Sam was at the door. He started opening it, swinging around, using the doorknob as a crutch to pull himself up.

Shot number something. Why was Sam counting? "He looked to the right. Just inches away was a ding where the bullet had hit.

He swung around, getting inside and pivoting using the door, dancing with the door as if he were at a square dance.

Shot bing. Hit the door again. Joe was improving rapidly.

Sam started shutting the door like a drunk man coming home at 3am. Joe would just hunt him down and shoot him. Wouldn't take too long.

Bam! Shot again.

Safety. Safety. It was the stupid safety.

"Dammit," His boss yelled.

Sam stuck his head around the door and started pulling the trigger over and over again.

The gun was working.

Bam!

Close!

He pulled back his head. Maybe not so smart. But he left his hand poking around the edge and pulled the trigger until his gun didn't shoot again. Still he kept pulling the trigger, yet nothing happened.

He withdrew his hand.

He stood perfectly still. There were no sounds coming from the roof. He didn't want to open the door and see what he'd done so he didn't. Either way he couldn't handle it.

When all the bigwigs came, they would collect whatever was left up there. Whatever he'd done, he'd done.

Move, Sam.

He'd fallen down again at some point on the steps. He didn't remember doing it. Maybe he passed out.

Ok, he stood up. It hurt. He brushed himself off. It still hurt, but he was moving.

The only loose end left, the only thing he knew he had to do before it all ended, was speak to his teammate. Tell her. Apologize. Maybe.

Whatever happened, Sam didn't want to leave without making sure Deb was okay.

2.20

Safely Screwed

"You look like shit," Deb told him when he found her in 'The Womb.'

"I feel worse," Sam replied, "I think I killed Joe."

"You also have gathered exactly zero evidence, I see, but that's the least of our problems."

"The cops will be here any minute, Deb. Look, it's been good working with you. I thought I'd find you and tell you that before whatever happens next. I thought I should say that. Sorry about the other stuff."

"You're not listening. We're not surrendering to the cops."

"I'm going to need a better explanation than just a simple command."

"It was an observation, not a .." Deb started, but Sam interrupted her. He held his hand up.

"Being nice. Enough. Explain."

"You're not going to like this."

"Now that's something I can believe. Find something?"

"I did. Switching to people and money, and using these McGuffins, I found out several interesting things."

He waited.

Finally he said, "Well? What were they?"

"Which one would you like to know more about?"

"How in the hell should I know? You haven't told me yet."

"Dumbass. Which general category of things would you like to know about?"

"God. Damn. You continue to be an open sore on the fat ass of my happiness."

Palms up, he shook his hands up and down as if asking a crowd for a round of applause.

He said the next words very slowly, as if speaking to a small child.

"I want to know what you think we need to do next and why." he spat, spittle and blood coming out of his mouth.

"You aren't going to be happy."

"I am beat up. I am homeless. I'm probably a felon, perhaps a murderer. I'm already fairly unhappy."

"I'm sorry. By the way, I've returned all of your toys to your desk."

Ok, he was going to have to let her get to this in her own time. He could die, be arrested, get shot, collapse, a giant meteor could strike, but he had all the time in the world. She wanted distraction, Deb wanted to meander. Sam had to let it happen. He was learning.

As best he could, he straightened himself, trying to appear pleased to be having this encounter.

"Thank you, Debian. You got family?"

"No."

"Me neither," he replied.

"I'm not in this for the long haul," she said.

"In what?"

"This life."

Now? Now Deb has an existential crisis? If he could have made his head explode at that moment, he would have done so. It would have made him happy.

Possum.

"Ummm. Gee, Deb. You just need to learn how to reinvent yourself, right, that's all."

He made a popping sound with his mouth. He didn't know why. He liked the sound.

"Fair enough," he replied, "I see your point. Granted that a lot of things we do is just by default. But that doesn't mean we can't change things. We're not machines."

"No. We work with them."

"You know, Debian, just between us, I don't think EigenCorp is going to work out for either of us."

Was that a smile?

Wat?!?

It was gone. That was nice.

Sam tried to shake it off. He was a boxer who'd just taken a hard hit. He must really be messed up to have seen something like that.

"Also, we don't seem to work very well together," he said, "I take responsibility for that."

There was a long pause.

"You are good with people," she said. She looked him up and down. "Also you wear sensible shoes."

"The next few days or weeks for us are not going to be easy," he said.

"You have no idea."

"Could you please get to the point?"

"I hate you."

"Good point. You're not exactly a bowl of cherries."

She frowned.

"Why would I want to be a bowl of cherries? What sense would that make?" she said.

"It's just a saying, Deb. An expression."

"Do you like cherries?"

"I do not," he replied.

"Good, because we're going to be stuck together for a while."

There it is. She wants something.

Talking to this woman was like reaching into a dark gunny sack full of corncobs trying to find a turd.

He searched around. It was a big room.

"How much stuff is in here? There must be hundreds of items to check out."

"More than I can manage," She agreed.

A-ha, we've finally got there. She doesn't want to admit she needs help.

"I can help. Let me help. Maybe we should lock ourselves in for a few hours and go through it all before turning ourselves in?"

"It's more than both of us could do in a month. Definitely possible in a year. For both of us, current estimate is 47 days with error bars of ten days on either side."

"Perhaps I can help you gather some of this together, take some drives? Maybe hide them for later?"

"That's impossible. You know this. Without the matching McGuffin you have nothing. And if we're going to need Inserts, even the McGuffins aren't useful."

"Yeah. I know."

From overhead, a soft voice began repeating, "Perimeter alert. Perimeter alert."

"Ever sing the song 'There's a hole in the bottom of the sea'?" she asked.

"Yes, but .."

"Each verse, you add another item in there. Each singer has to remember all of the items that came before and their relationship to each other. 'There's a frog on the knot on the log in the hole in the bottom of the sea.' And so on."

"Your point?"

Please have a point. Please, please.

Please.

"A person with good memory might make it to 10, even 20 items, remembering how they're joined. The McKenzie Foundation is funding research into using long chains like this as an attack vector using OODA, not a direct attack. They were funding my dad's work. Until all the things happened."

"Multiple intersecting causality chains, LLMs as an attack vector? Whoa. Crazy."

"It is non-rational," she agreed, using an odd word.

"It would be like singing six or seven songs like this all at the same time," Sam said, "trying to keep track of all that stuff."

"The monkey begins to understand."

Ignoring her, "Who could do that? Who could track all that stuff at once?"

"Almost nobody, that's who."

"So it's just theoretical. You're just bullshitting. It's not actually being used as an attack vector, a weapon."

"You missed it. Nobody. 'No Body', Sam, not 'No Thing'. Even a moderate AI chip could handle seventeen of these at one time, or a hundred. It's far, far beyond anything people have experience with. I've found both the silent partner and the evil cabal."

He took a deep breath. He let it slowly out, refocusing.

"Oh, you are you. Of course you did. Now I have absolutely no idea what to do. Pops could help," he said, "Fuck. We need Pops. I miss him. He'd know what to do."

She considered.

"I miss Pops too. Also there may be explosives in the walls, but I'm not sure."

"Really should have lead with that. Important. Going to need to leave.

Right now. Leave. Narrows choices. Leave. Take what we have and go to the authorities. Lucky us, they're already here. Did I mention leave?"

"Go to jail?"

"Not going to run from the authorities. Not happening," he said, thinking "Move it, Deb."

"I don't want to," She replied, "but just for a minute, what do you think will happen?"

"Getting arrested? It won't be that bad," he sighed, "Sure, we might do a little jail time, but we'll get out. We can start over. We can each start over. Each of us. On our own. By ourselves."

"You are wrong."

"Might even be better," he continued, "look here at what you've discovered. We might be able to break an incredibly huge case, with this new cyber attack vector. This could be a big win for us. Heck, we might not even go to jail. We could be famous."

"Ok, so we go to jail," she replied, "we start becoming famous. What do you think the people behind these attacks, the people building this invisible weapon, are going to do?"

"They're not going to be happy."

"And?"

He continued, "And they'll strike back against the cops themselves, the legal system, trying to hurt us through them, getting inside their OODA loop. And since they have a predictive, non-rational weapon…"

"And the cops will never even see it coming, by the way."

His mood got even darker.

"And since they have a predictive weapon …" Sam said.

Deb continued.

"There is a very real chance we might not make it out of this building alive, Sam. Who knows what they currently think about us? In their minds, we might be suicidal, heavily-armed terrorists."

"Come on, that's a bit…"

"Or nothing that elaborate. We could just get hit by an auto-drive car," she thought for a moment, "or a delivery truck."

She frowned, thinking sad things only Deb could think.

"Shit," he said.

"Shit," she agreed.

"Didn't you find any other people in all of your research? People we could ask for help?"

"Yes."

"Great. Then let's do that."

"They're all either dead or missing. There's nobody to find."

Sam leaned against the wall, his legs becoming unsteady.

"We're going to be working together, aren't we. God help me."

Deb sighed, "I am sad. I told you that you would not like this."

He winced, "I think my ribs are bruised."

"I have a rash. Sometimes it itches."

"Thanks for letting me know. With the right gear, could you mount a counter-attack? Figure out what's going on? Shut them down? Something? Do your thing? Do your stuff?"

She considered.

"I could."

"Great."

"But not with any of the gear here."

"Terrible."

"It's worse than that," she said, "since somebody's using a predictive model to attack us, the more data we provide, even by just walking around in the world, the more accurate the attack will become. Simply by breaking in here, we've given data to the model."

He thought of Joe telling him that he'd ruined it all.

"The universe observes itself. So the more we fight, the worse it gets for us?"

"Correct."

"This is like a Greek tragedy," he said, "It's our own Kobayashi Maru."

"And we cannot reprogram the simulation. If it helps, Socrates solved the problem by taking poison," she said.

"Say, that's not a bad idea."

"You want to take poison?" Her voice was flat.

"No, I want to poison the model they're using."

Deb replied, "There's no way we could poison an AI model built on the entire internet using unknown parameters. You have to know what they're modeling and how in order to fight it. It's not like we're copyrighting images. To erase or camouflage us across the net would require at least ten thousand data capture devices, perhaps a billion new pieces of crafted poisoned input."

"And what does genius think we should do now?" he asked.

"Investigate and attack the money flow, this McKenzie Foundation.

There's a leverage point there, I'm sure of it. We find the money. We find the people."

"And does that involve us appearing in public places and doing things that would provide even more data to our attackers?"

"Well of course it does, Sam. How would …"

Sam interrupted, "Hang on. Couldn't somebody do that for us? We could use people as proxies, puppets." much the same as they've probably been using us, he thought.

"Sam, assuming we find people who would do our work for us, they could be modeled, attacked, and used just like the cops could. It's the same problem, just different people."

"Not if we randomly pick dumb, crazy, stupid people, people who act in seemingly random and haphazard ways. We're not stuck poisoning the data. Not all the data, Deb. We have the advantage of being able to narrow things down to whatever we choose. We can poison everything we touch along just one line of action, secret to us, a direction only we know, or at least try to. That's a plan."

"You want us to find the biggest bunch of crazy, stupid oddballs we can."

"Yes."

"That would be willing to act as proxies, and could research this McKenzie Foundation for us."

"Yes."

"While we hide."

"Yes."

"You are so stupid it might work. I know who we need to talk to."

"I was afraid I might have a good idea," he replied.

She missed it.

"We're stuck," she said.

They did not look at one another. Instead, each stared straight ahead. Combat veterans called it the "thousand-yard stare." Each in their own way, they were gathering their strength to jump out of the foxhole and charge the machinegun nest.

"God hates me," Sam finally said.

"He may indeed," she finally replied, "I haven't asked him."

Sam's face scrunched. He was a man playing chess, realizing that no matter what he did or how he looked at the board he had lost.

He slapped his hands to his legs, decision made.

He looked at her and smiled.

"Looks like we're putting the band back together. Who knows? Maybe one day you'll write a book about this. Now just need to find our minions, our rubes."

"Life with asshole," she said.

"What?"

"The book's title will be 'Life with Asshole'," she replied.

"I'm sure," he said, moving his hands, "Leave. Move. Let's go. Before this place blows up, figuratively or literally."

She joined him leaving but continued talking.

"Also I do not play a musical instrument."

"I know."

"And I do not want to be in your band."

"Got it."

They disappeared down the hall. Sam trying to hurry her as best he could.

Flashbangs started below as the multiple SWAT teams in position began raiding the building.

III. STRANGE ATTRACTORS

Scooby Doo

3.01

Saving The Cat

It was the cat. The cat started everything. If it was a cat.

It was hot.

They acted like teenagers. They were grown men, one old and two young. They worked in the yard of a house that was really a plantation. They did yard work although they were not landscapers or professionals of any type. They pretended to be detectives. They weren't very good at it.

"You tell her," Steve asked Jupiter as he returned to the back yard from Mrs. McKenzie's front porch.

"I told her."

Steve had a rake in his hand, a pile of leaves by his feet. Pete had stopped shoveling and edging the sidewalk and was looking at all of the work remaining. Steve wiped the sweat from his brow, looked up at the cloudy sky.

Muggy.

"He didn't tell her," Steve said.

None of them could ignore the wheelbarrow. A tarp was covering a small lump.

"I told her that based on our investigation this morning," he said, "Mr. Cuddles is unlikely to return to her domicile."

"He didn't tell her," Jim said.

"I told her," he said again. "Mostly."

The three stood around in a large yard that had obviously been let go many years ago, gardening tools in hand.

"Based on our investigation? Unlikely to return? What, did you tell Mrs. Mckenzie that precious Mr. Cuddles joined the French Foreign Legion? Spending time up the river for running a cat gambling operation?"

Jupiter glowered.

"I'll tell her," Jim said, sticking the shovel firmly in the ground in front of him as if he had been the first one to discover the East Pole. "If somebody needs to tell her. I'll do it."

"She knows," Jupiter countered. "She knows. It's a grief process. Give it time. I'm not about to go tell an 80-year-old lady that her only cat is dead. I told her he was lonely and maybe needed a friend."

He pointed to the wheelbarrow.

"So what happened?"

"She offered me five dollars for our work so far. She told me there'd be twenty 'nice big one dollar bills' for us when we finished the yard."

Jim groaned.

"That's not all. She has even more work," Jupe said. "She wants to know if we can come back later this week to help clear out her basement. I take it she may be downsizing."

Jim groaned again. Steve pointed the rake at Jupiter.

"We've been at this four hours already!" he said, "Isn't it enough to be forced into submission by the capitalist overlords! Now we hide their lies —" he pointed to the tarp and the very dead Mr. Cuddles under it, "from them as well? Lies! Lies I say!"

"Decaf," Jim said to no on in particular, then, "You take the money?"

Jupiter shook his head no.

"Good."

"What!" Steve said.

"On the positive side," Jupiter continued, "Check out what I was working on last night."

He reached into his jacket pocket and produced a business card.

"Take a gander."

The boys gathered around. The card said:

Jim smiled.

"I like it!"

Steve agreed, trying to edge his way in front of Jim.

Jupe stepped back, letting the two boys hold the card.

"Taking payment from poor old Mrs. McKenzie is something The Three Investigators would never do," he said. He thought for a moment. "It's not in our character. It's not our milieu."

Steve cringed.

"I thought we were broke."

"And we've still got another hour of work here," Jim said. "And what are we going to do about the cat?"

It started lightly sprinkling.

Jupiter groaned. Steve returned to looking at the sky, now betrayed.

"Now what are we going to do?" he said. He pointed to the driveway. "Our bikes are going to get wet."

In the driveway was a 30-year-old conversion van, the kind used by contractors. It was mostly white, with rust spots running along the bottom. In some places the rust had eaten through into large holes. On top of the van were three bikes tied down with bungie cords.

"We'll put them in our van," Jupiter said.

"Well then, Mr. Smarty Pants," Steve said, "Why didn't we put them in there to begin with?"

Jim looked at the van. Frowned. Looked back at Steve and Jupe.

"We've discussed this already. The Three Investigators in all the books had bicycles, not a van. Bicycles. We do not have a van!"

The van sat in the driveway.

"You know who got a van?" Steve asked.

Jupiter shut him down. "I don't want to talk about it."

"They got a cartoon, a theme song, dog, and everything."

Just then a beautiful, shiny, brand new convertible pulled up, stopped. The automatic top started coming up. The car honked twice.

"Hey assholes!" somebody yelled.

The boys looked over. In the car's windows a couple of bare butts showed. They were being mooned.

"Those fucking Hardy Boys," Jim said.

"Language!"

Steve was incandescent.

'What the hell? How can they be the Hardy Boys? They're girls! And there's three of them!"

"Well, in fairness one of them is transitioning…"

"But three! There's three! The Hardy Boys did not have three people!"

"Wasn't there a third?" Jupiter asked. "Or was that the Three Stooges?"

"Actually, there were five actors who played the Three Stooges," Jim said, reciting, "depending on how you count."

"It's not okay," Jupiter said, looking at Jim.

Jim nodded. "It's not okay," he agreed and they both then looked to Steve for a reply.

"Yeah," Steve agreed. He looked lost, a man in the middle of a journey to the other side of the house that forgot where he was going.

The car honked its horn again, sped off. They could hear loud music as it left.

Jupiter looked back at the tarp.

Steve went, pulled the tarp back. A squashed tabby cat lay there. They had shoveled him off the pavement two hours ago.

"He dead"

Jupe nodded.

"Agreed. It does not appear that he will be joining the French Foreign Legion anytime soon."

Jim covered the cat again.

"Let's go put the bikes in the van. Then we can bury Mr. Cuddles before it gets soaking wet or Mrs. McKenzie finds him."

They all looked at the house. Afraid.

As they finished with the bikes, Steve's phone pinged. He looked at it and scowled.

"It's those fu.." He caught himself, "Scooby Doo people, reminding us we have bowling league tonight."

"Tonight we can take them. We can take them this time," Jim said, shutting the door.

Steve smiled.

"Shaggy's got a weak knee. He's also got that glass eye. And I don't think Velma's ever bowled before in her life."

Jupe nodded. Then he looked back at the tarp.

"Agreed. It is time."

Eventually, the rain stopped.

The men stood around a fresh pile of dirt in the back corner of Mrs. McKenzie's yard, far from where she could see, hands clasped in reverence.

"Mr. Cuddles was a good cat," Jupiter said, "He was alone in the universe, at least the universe of Mrs. McKenzie's house, but he did not despair. That was not in his nature."

Jim and Steve looked at Jupiter as if he might start sprouting leprechauns from his head.

Jupiter ignored them.

"Through my many paths in life I have met many a cat not as happy or adjusted as Mrs. Cuddles…"

"Thought it was Mr. Cuddles. Who's up for lunch?" Steve said.

"That cat had no penis!" Jim said, "Not that I looked."

"But there comes a time for every man, er cat, to come to grips with his life, such that it is, and realize that no, there will be no other mouse, no new bag of catnip."

"I hear it's Taco Tuesday at the grill," Steve said.

Jim had been lured enough. "Yum! Let's go!"

Jupiter was going to say something else. While they were working he had worked out a nice soliloquy based on Julius Caesar. He hadn't got the meter exactly right, but saw his friends walking off and stopped.

"Hey guys! Wait for me! If it's Taco Tuesday, I'm buying!"

Both men stopped and turned.

"I thought you were broke," Jim said. "Where'd you get money?"

As quietly as he could say while still being heard, "I took the money" Steve winked at Jim.

"Took the money. Told ya. It's all forgotten. Who's up for milkshakes."

Steve put his arms around both of his friends.

"It had a penis," Steve said.

The teenagers who were not teenagers finished burying the boy cat who may have been a girl cat. The landsccapers who were not landscapers ,the detectives who were not detectives finished the yard work which was not finished. They left.

But the cat wasn't dead.

$$3.02$$

Starting The Agency

The Three Investigators were ready for their first case by the time Autumn arrived. The junkyard was covered in the smell of rotting dead raccoons. They could never mention their obsession to others, but after long discussion the topic of complaining about racoons was determined to be on-topic.

The men had chosen not to live in reality, just not in the way the surrounding town thought.

It was the books. The books said The Three Investigators needed a junkyard, so Jupiter bought a junkyard. The books said they needed a house trailer for a secret headquarters, so they bought a house trailer. The books said they needed a periscope, so they found a periscope. The books said they needed to bury the house trailer under junk, so that's what they did.

The townsfolk didn't know what to make of this. Drug addicts. Meth lab. They all agreed on one thing: something really odd was going on.

Nothing good could come from this.

Jupiter Froststrike had never taken drugs in his life.

Jupe barely lumped his way into the old trailer from the secret tunnel they had just made, his large, old, pot-bellied, out-of-shape body finally squeezing through the trapdoor made from an old refrigerator door and barbeque grill, grinning from ear-to-ear "A client! We've finally have a client!"

Steve Byers looked up from his phone. His phone beeped. He was angry. "The WiFi here sucks"

"We don't have WiFi," Jupiter said.

"We need WiFi," Steve said.

Jim Cincinnati looked up at Jupiter. "That's what I told him. We don't have WiFi. He won't listen."

Jim had been constructing something out of wood on the narrow trailer floor. He had placed his tools about him in an ordered, geometric pattern.

Jupe looked over. "What's that?"

"I know we don't have WiFi," Steve didn't even bother looking up from his phone this time. "Jim's being a jackass again."

Jupe looked around. Jupiter Froststrike looked like a MC at a circus, the worst, most cheap and bad circus in the world. The acts were not going as planned. The crowd angry. The kids were eager and excited. The MC was ramping up. The animals were on strike and refused to perform for him.

"Didn't you guys even hear me? We've got a client!"

He tried smiling. He directed his attention to Jim. He smiled as hard as he could right at him. By way of answer, Jim just shrugged. Satisfied enough to consider that a victory, he then tried to stare down Steve. After poking a few more times at the screen, Steve finally looked up from his phone.

"A client," Steve said. "So what. Whoop-de-shit."

"A client," he repeated, "A real client and watch your language."

Jupiter was in his late 50s, overweight, bald. He wore a suede jacket with elbow patches. A pipe stuck out from his front pocket. The pipe was four times as large as it should be, immediately drawing attention and making him look something like a cartoon figure. His face was round and fat, shaven, and showed the telltale pockmarks of a bad experience with acne as a child. He was clearly out-of-breath.

Jim and Steve were both in their mid 20s. Jim was wearing a button-up shirt with slacks. Steve had a baseball cap on his head turned backward, black gym shorts, and a bright red t-shirt with "Ok Boomer" on the front with the raised fist of power underneath.

"Ok, he's a moron then," Steve said.

Jim raised his hands in the universal "What do I do now?" gesture, "We don't have WiFi. We're in the middle of a junkyard buried under a dozen or so junk cars, we're in a house trailer, we even have a periscope (he points), a wall map from somewhere around 1950 (points again), and we have to climb through a 40-foot tunnel to get here which could probably kill us at any moment. We don't have WiFi, and you're never going to be able to get cell reception to work here."

Steve growled, put the phone down. The phone beeped again.

"Who ever thought this was a good idea?"

Jupe sighed, "We all did. I bought this place. We decided. We all did. We thought that it was going to be fun. Remember?"

"Ok Ok enough. Tell us about the client," Jim said. He rubbed his hands together. "A cat again? Please no. No Mrs. McKenzie. This will be the third time! I'm still sore from last time."

Jupe sat down in the nearest roll chair. Living in a junkyard had its advantages. They found this beauty underneath a wrecked septic tank truck. The cracked leather strained, the rusted metal squeaked. As he settled in, the chair made a threatening cracking sound. In response he leaned forward, moving his weight off the chair and towards the boys. His face widened.

"It all began late last night when I received an email from frankledoo47@yahoo.com."

"Tell us the job," Steve said.

Jupe stared down Steve. Steve refused to blink, so Jupiter switched to glaring at Jim which seemed to work better. His raised his eyebrows. He looked around like a librarian at a room full of kids during story hour. He waited for the right moment.

He was the master storyteller. This was his element.

"It was last night, late last night" he said, holding his arms apart as if drawing forth a painting from the air, "It was dark and rainy. Did I mention that? It was a dark and rainy night. I got out of the car, thinking about that dame I met last week with the cat. The old dame. The wind whipped around me as I sauntered towards the open door…"

Steve went back to poking at his phone.

Jupiter stopped. He looked up at the sky. His name was Jupiter. Was it too much to ask to ask the universe to be able to call lightning bolts from the sky?

"What?"

"It's a bookshelf," Jim said.

"What?"

"This is a bookshelf. I'm building a bookshelf," Jim pointed at the construction debris and an empty spot on the wall, "If we're going to have only one ethernet cable and we're not going to have WiFi, then we're going to need research materials. We're going to need all of our Three Investigators books, whether we have them memorized or not. Hence, a bookshelf."

The sacred books sat in a stack next to the shelf being created: every book in the Alfred Hitchcock "The Three Investigators" series.

These three men had decided that they would become The Three Investigators. Nothing would stop them.

He pointed to the empty spot on the wall.

"We haven't decided whether it's just going to be one connection or what, for all I care" Jupiter said, "The guy's coming tomorrow. We could wire up the whole place. Put jacks in every room. Sometime later. Not now."

He smiled as if he were looking out over a vast plantation with thousands of acres of crops, deciding where to plant a new orchard or divert a river, instead of the 60x12 foot, four-room trailer from 1962 that they were actually in.

"We need WiFi," Steve said again.

"Now Steve," Jim said, "See here. We all decided last month before Jupe bought the place that phones and other wireless devices wasn't going to look very Three Investigator-ish. All of this has to be perfect."

Steve looked up. "What's the client? Jilted husband?"

"It's a General, actually," Jupiter nodded. He surveyed his audience. "An Air Force General. It's quite a delicate matter, in fact."

"Doesn't sound like a cat," Jim said. "There's that."

Steve took a breath and puffed up his chest.

"Finally! What, is this some National Security issue? Are we going to be helping root out some right-wing terrorist in the military?"

He stopped. He was confused.

"Wait, what the hell could three dudes Live Action Role-Playing some ancient kid detective novels be able to do to help the Air Force? Or an Air Force General, for that matter?"

"It must be a private thing," Jim said.

"It is." Jupe said, teasing. He waited a bit more, disappointed that he did not have the time he felt was necessary to present the surprise. "His daughter is being blackmailed."

"Blackmailed? That's great! By who?" Steve asked, "Is it a pastor she once had an affair with who is really a Mormon fundamentalist and is the secret love child of a rich industrialist? Is there a love child? Did they plan to run off before they were found out by the church elders? What about the Mormons?"

The world stopped. There was a giant reset. Jim and Jupiter froze. They were the antelope caught out in the open seeing a cheetah they had missed before. Steve was the cheetah. Without moving their heads, they glanced at Steve. Maybe if everybody stayed still, this could work out.

"It was in this show I was watching last night," Steve said.

The silence continued. In the dark gloom of the trailer, they all heard the quiet tick-tick-ticking of the black cat wall clock in what remained of the kitchen. Jupiter and Jim remained frozen. They shifted from looking at Steve to looking at each other, eyes dancing, bodies still. Jupe sighed. Unimpressed with his own performance, he sighed again as dramatically as he could.

"It was really good," Steve said.

The world began moving again. Jupiter shifted in his seat. He began to speak, thought better of it, shifted back in place, then began again.

"Eight-part series," Steve said.

"I want." Jupiter looked at Jim. "No. Let's try this. She's in college. She just dropped out. Dad's very upset. Could be drugs or emotional issues."

"Wow!" Jim stood up. "Finally! Real human tragedy and disaster Steven! This is what we've been waiting for!"

Jim and Steve grinned at one another.

Steve said, "I know right?" and elbowed Jim. Good times.

Now it was Jim's turn. "Do they want money? Are we supposed to do the drop or whatever? That thing where we pay the kidnappers? With the bag and everything? We could be the bag men?"

Jupiter for his part frowned. He was an algebra teacher having to repeat a recent and rudimentary lesson. It was painful to do so.

"No. There's no ransom. There's no kidnapping. There's no kidnappers. It's not a kidnapping. No Mormons. Nothing. There's just a dad, a daughter, and some anonymous rando that threatened them both."

"Threatened them with what?" Jim asked, "asked for what? Where is the daughter? Will we have to travel?"

Jupiter stood.

"That, my friends, is where this mystery begins and where our adventure starts! I shall call this the Mystery of the Gallant General"

"Jesus fucking Christ," Steve said.

"Language!"

Jim shook his head no. He frowned, mumbled to himself.

Steve and Jim began to go back to what they were doing, but Jupiter held his hands for them to hold up.

"Look, I don't know some things," he finally admitted. "I don't know anything else. But I do know one thing." He immediately contradicted himself.

"What?" Jim said.

"That we're supposed to meet him at his house tomorrow to get answers to all of these questions. At least the ones he knows the answers to."

"Okay, fine," Jim said, still muttering.

"Is that awesome or what, Jim? Also, almost forgot. I know another thing."

Jim, "What?"

"I know that before we do any of that, first we have to go help Mrs. McKenzie finish up her back yard."

They both sighed loudly, and Jupiter was forced to admit that they sighed better than he did.

"She called on my way here. She was crying. You know how she gets."

Steve threw his phone at Jupe. The phone beeped.

3.03

Interviewing The General

"I've lived a very dissolute life," the old General said from his wheelchair, "and if there's some final accounting in the hereafter, I deserve all the punishment I get."

They watched intently as things took a hard turn. "But my daughter? She's as bad as I've ever been. Worse even. It's not right that she should get blackmailed and I didn't."

It was a leisurely drive to the General's house and beautiful to boot: long paved roads with farm houses converted to mansions sitting well back from the roads and huge magnificent horse barns nearby, expensive cars in the driveway.

The General's house was unlike the others, although it was far enough off-the-road not to notice. The end of a cul-de-sac led to a long gravel drive. It ended in a huge Federal brick mansion, but in the middle of the well-manicured front yard was a forty-foot-tall dinosaur, the kind you might see in old movies or at a miniature golf course. The head pivoted to track their van as it arrived.

"That, my friend," Steve said, "is living," from the back of the van.

"That's certainly something," Jupe agreed, getting out of the driver's side, eyeing the mechanical beast with suspicion.

There was debate over whether or not they were wearing the appropriate Three Investigators clothes, which happily ended when the General's live-in healthcare worker, a shifty-looking man dressed impeccably as an aide, met them at the door.

The General would see them in the rose garden.

Jupiter didn't see any roses. He didn't see a garden. They were in a large, brick-floored greenhouse-type thing extending off the back of the house. Covered in dirt, here and there were little planters of weeds scattered about. Nothing bloomed and there was very little green for a greenhouse.

The General was in his late 70s, smartly dressed, and sitting with a heavy blanket over his legs even though temperatures were easily in the 80s.

"It's not fair that she should be blackmailed and I shouldn't," he said again. He made an odd hand gesture and the in-home worker approached with a vitamin shake. The worker then returned to the edge of the garden where he'd been all along, unnoticed.

"My daughter is the most important thing in my life," he said, handing them a framed picture from under the blanket, "I'm afraid she's fallen in with some bad people. I don't know, maybe drugs or a cult. Need to find out who's doing this."

"How'd they contact you," Jim asked, "was there a shifty man in a raincoat?"

"No, just a note at the door," the General handed Jim a piece of paper.

"We will ruin you and your family if you don't pay us one million dollars by Friday. Details to follow." Jim read.

"Well there's your problem right there," Steve said. He and Jupiter both had been peering over Jim's shoulder. "It's the cry of the oppressed, the downtrodden. What'd you do to these people anyway? Who might hate you enough to do this?"

"Nobody, at least recently," he said, "I haven't been on my game since I lost my legs. Since June's mother died, we've been living here very quietly. Six, seven years now. June had a lot of problems in school, but we managed to get her into an apartment and enrolled in college."

He wheeled over to the nearest planter.

"I had hoped that June would have come around, helped me maintain the garden she and her mother loved so much," he absent mindedly poked at the dirt, "but all I seemed to have grown is weeds and anthills."

Jupiter couldn't help feel sorry for the old guy, even he did admit to being a lout.

The General was an odd one.

"We'll do what we can, sir," Jim said, "Do you have any more printed information about her? Perhaps a credit report or utility bills? Does she have a computer we could look at?"

"No, no computer. Left with everything. Got a credit report, though. Figured you would need that. Some bills going back a ways. Ought to have them! I'm the one payin' them."

He waved to the aide who left the room.

"What makes you think drugs?" Jupiter asked.

"I don't know," he said, "and that's job one for you: figuring out what they have on my daughter. Job two would be locating the aliens so I can deal with them."

"Aliens?"

The worker returned with a folder which he gave to Jupiter. Out of sight of the General, the aide gave a wan smile as if to say, "He's like that."

Jupiter handed the folder to Jim. Jupiter found something extremely interesting on a weed nearby.

"Got any pictures of these aliens?" Steve asked.

"Of course not. They're invisible. Everybody knows that."

"How about the person who left the note? Do you have a doorbell camera? Some security system that might have recorded them?" Jim asked, flipping through the file.

"No. No. No. The dinosaur was turned off that day, unfortunately. Routine maintenance. The remote-controlled squirrel system as well. I suspect they'd been watching the dinosaur."

"They do that," he looked at them, sharing secrets.

"Aliens," Jim said, "Watching the dinosaur." He handed the file to Steve. Jim began hiding behind his pencil taking notes.

Conversely, Steve looked very interested in the man, slowly nodding in agreement as he told his story.

"This alien part may be a little more difficult for us," Jupe said.

"Of course, of course! But all that's down the road. Humans can neither see nor interact with the aliens, so I fully expect that to be a bit of work. Of course! Right now we need to know the stakes! What's the tactical situation? What does anybody have on my daughter? What proof? If this is a real threat, might be, they haven't told us on-purpose, their next move will be some revelation. That will be a disaster in itself. We need to be ahead of them. Seize initiative men!"

He slapped his blanket.

Jupe began looking through the material.

"This looks very thorough, sir. This helps us quite a bit."

"Now to brass tacks. How much do you charge?"

Jim had stopped taking notes and was poking at an anthill.

"Maybe we split the job into two parts," he said. Jim didn't look up.

"Excellent idea, young man. I propose that you take three days to figure out what they have on my daughter. Pay you whatever you want. After that, a monthly retainer since the second part may be ….. well, a bit more complicated. Can you do this? Are you men enough?"

"No," Jupiter said. He looked at Jim and Steve who were both nodding yes.

Trying to cover his mistake, Jupiter immediately nodded yes. Off to the side he heard Jim and Steve say "no."

Jupe tried to look like this was planned.

"We'll get back to you. Later?"

The General agreed. They left, much more in a hurry than they had been when they arrived.

They hadn't even made it to the van before the bickering began again.

"We can't take this man's money to find aliens," Jupe said.

Steve stopped and turned back.

"Why not? Who else is going to find them? I don't see that Nancy Drew bunch doing anything this serious. And I'm sure not letting those X-Files jerks anywhere near this guy."

"You guys are looking at this all wrong," Jim said.

"I'm being honest," Jupe replied, "taking money from old senile people isn't something the Three Investigators would ever do. Full stop."

Jim shook his head.

"Still wrong."

Steve held up the files as if they were Excalibur and he was King Arthur.

"Why not?" he said, "We got this. There's plenty enough information in here to clearly identify girl and report back to the old guy. The Three Investigators sure could do that."

"What about the aliens?"

"You guys are talking about the Fermi Paradox, the Parable of the Ant," Jim said.

"The Parable of the Ant?"

"Sure. Back in the day, there was a genius physicist named Enrico Fermi. One day, like smart people do, they were kicking around the idea of intelligent life in the universe while eating lunch. With a universe so big, full of so many suns and so many planets where life may thrive, there should be other intelligences, right? In fact, there should be millions, maybe billions of other intelligent life forms. Intelligent life should be everywhere. So Fermi asked aloud what everybody had been thinking, if there are other intelligent life forms, where is everybody? That's the Fermi Paradox. The answer? In the ants."

"Ate the ants, didn't he," Steve said. "This is one of those stories where a nice intelligent person goes crazy and starts eating bugs, maybe even pretending that he's an insect? 'Cause I don't think the old guy here eats bugs."

Jim looked at Steve as if he were a gauge on a power plant that might need fixing.

He continued.

"People struggled with the paradox for ages, even, but just like Bertrand Russell's Paradox and many others, the answer is actually in the way the question is worded. People have fun with paradoxes because most of them are language games. They're worded such that the entire paradox can't be figured out even though the words and terms make total sense in isolation and the question seems simple enough. Paradoxes sound like simple questions and should have simple answers but they're not."

Jupiter thought that crazy might be catching.

"The ant."

"Right! Right! Yes, so to figure out where Fermi was wrong, where the trick is, just picture an ant on an anthill on an island in the middle of the ocean. One day the ant climbs up to the top of his anthill and says something like: there must be other ants in the world. Surely we are not alone. Ants should be everywhere. So where are they? The ant's making what they call category errors although he doesn't realize it. Just check out all the assumptions layered in which are unspoken. The ant assumes other intelligence would be antlike, he assumes that the things he can observe are the only things, he assumes that the failure of observation means the failure of existence and so forth. In fact, the ant might be being observed by dozens of other intelligent creatures, perhaps even other ants *while he's asking the question.* He just doesn't know any better. He can't. It could be that he's in a zoo on the island and other creatures are observing him to study him. It could be other creatures that observe him care nothing of him and just observe him as they pass by. Maybe ants on other islands have invented telescopes to look around and this ant doesn't have one. It could be that he's purposefully being ignored. It could be a bunch of other things. It doesn't matter. The ant's error is in assuming that he's asking a question that he is able to answer. He is not."

Jupiter looked at him.

"What does this…"

"Look it. All I'm saying is you're reading more into the General's problem than you need to. Let's assume that you, Jupiter Froststrike, also live on this island with the ants. One day as you walk by, you see our little friend on his anthill, our little General, the ant, and through some kind of miracle, you understand his question: where are all of the other sentient lifeforms?"

"Dr. Doolittle," Steve grinned. He began humming the "If I could speak to the animals" song from the movie.

"So," Jim said, "You want to help the little guy answer his question. How could you? Even if by some kind of miracle you were able to communicate with him, how would you explain islands, oceans, people, and so forth? How could he explain to you pheromones, or the importance of the queen? What it's like to be an insect? And even if you could do all of that, you've never left your island. As far as you know, you have the same question, for the same reasons. Maybe he's right. Maybe he's wrong. It's not that there's an answer to the paradox, it's that there can never be an answer. Superior intellectual and sentient creatures work at a higher level of being able to see and interact with things, they're not just smarter. Higher level of consciousness can never make sense to the lower levels, to those creatures beneath them. You'll never explain yourself to one of your brain cells. That's the universe. So the General says there are aliens that are invisible. Maybe so. Who cares? If they're invisible, he can't see them. Same as the little ant. You can never prove or disprove something that you can't observe one way or the other."

Jupiter started nodding.

"So you're suggesting…"

"Take his money, find his daughter. We'll get the scoop," Jim said, "then tell him the aliens are a separate matter which we can't help with one way or another, a true statement, by the way. We refuse to take his money for anything to do with that. We can do a lot of things, nice old man, but we are completely incompetent when it comes to aliens. We don't have to confront you about your beliefs, Mr. General Sir, it's just all us, we're just incompetent."

"Yeah, completely incompetent," Steve agreed, "I'm telling you we can do that. Yeah."

Unfortunately, that made sense, which bugged Jupiter to no end, but he could find no argument, dang it, so that's what they did.

And so, *The Story of The Gallant General* began.

Getting New Clients

"Janus Group. What do you know about Janus Group?"

Weirdo. Jupiter was not an unkind man. Jupiter Frostsrike would never stoop to name-calling, but he saw the girl and thought: weirdo. He could not make the thought go away.

The girl was making her voice as deep as she could. Jupiter thought she looked a bit silly. She didn't seem to think so.

"We are completely incompetent when it comes to aliens," Jim said to the weirdo who was suddenly in their face. "Just so you know that."

The girl frowned.

"Who said anything about aliens? Are you incompetent in other areas as well?"

"Sure," Steve said, "We're flexible."

The lanky man held the girl back.

"Maybe we're off to a bad start," he said. "I'm Samuel Featherstone. This is Debian Newbury. We're interested in employing your investigative firm."

"You are," Jupe looked at them.

"Yup. Deb and I are," the lanky man smiled at the girl. She did not smile back. "Investors. We're investors. Interested in employing a detective agency. Due diligence. Want to invest but we don't know the company's background or the officers. You come highly recommended."

"This isn't some ... domestic situation, is it? You guys have some personal situation?"

Jupiter tried to pay attention to the tall, freckly one instead of the girl.

"Gosh no. Just corporate research and a couple background checks. That's all. Easy schmeesy."

It was almost dark by the time they arrived back at the junkyard, excited from their visit with the General. The chill was just setting in and the two new people had obviously found their way in and built a small fire. Interlopers. Interlopers! Before Jupiter could toss them on their ear out they started in with this Janus Group thing.

"So you want us to investigate Janus Group."

The girl started to speak but the man held her back again, saying "Nope. EigenCorp. Big cyber security company. Joe Middles is the CEO. They want us to invest. We're just not sure if they're completely on the up-and-up."

"Also Janus Group," she said.

Sam nodded but remained quiet and did not break eye contact with Jupiter.

Jim pointed to the paperback sticking out of the girl's cargo pocket.

"Hey, that's a good series. How far along are you?"

The girl pulled it out. Jupiter peered over and read the title aloud.

"Rabid Vampire Monkey Accountants," Jupiter said, "That's a book."

She put it back.

"'I am 47.2% complete."

Jupiter wrinkled his nose. Jim continued.

"I won't spoil it for you, but the next one? Let's just say inventory control doesn't work out the way anybody thought. And just wait until the werewolf auditors show up; you'll love this whole thing."

"What is this? What are you guys burning here, a tire or something?" Steve asked. "Y-O-M-G. Don't you know the kind of pollution that causes? There's soot everywhere. Don't you care about the trees? The children?"

"I do, actually, and I told Deb that it was a bad idea, but we are in a bit of a hurry. It was getting cold. We didn't know how long you'd be."

Jupe noticed that not only did the girl not respond, she looked very still, like a mannequin.

"Where's your car?"

Samuel did not seem phased.

"We don't use cars."

"Don't use cars?"

"Yes. Very bad for the environment."

"Hells to the yes. Finally some normal people." Steve said and went for the high five. Nobody took him up on it. He continued to hold his hand up for an uncomfortable moment then put it down.

"I appreciate your dedication to finding us," Jupiter said, "You made a good choice, however you got here.."

He adjusted his jacket, searched around for his pipe. Dang! Must have left it in the van.

"You do not have permission to build a fire though. Steven's right. You're going to have to put that out. Right away."

"Of course. Yes. Absolutely."

Sam began kicking dirt on the coals. It only made the smoke and pollution much worse. He tried to hold back a cough.

Tying to ignore Samuel, Jupiter said, "Gimme your email. We can set up a pre-engagement interview at your convenience …"

"Nope. We'll be staying here. As well. Part of the engagement."

Sam pointed to the junk cars all around them.

Steve seemed to really be getting into the newcomers.

"It's because of the aliens, isn't it. Did they do experiments? Do you have pictures? Sexual experiments? Only asking because it's important people know."

"Ignore him," Jim said, "Why would anyone want to stay in a junkyard?"

"That's a very good question," Sam said, looking around the junkyard as if he had just seen it for the very first time, "And I can see why you would ask it. Good job!"

Sam then turned his back to them and looked out over the yard. He said nothing.

"And?" Jupiter was thinking that perhaps they needed to re-do their advertising strategy if all the clients were going to be like this. "Why?"

Sam turned back, reached into his pocket.

"You see, we're on a bit of a pilgrimage for reasons we'd rather not discuss."

He pulled out a large folded stack of $100 bills.

"But we're prepared to pay you guys rent, and we promise to stay out of the way."

"We don't need your stinking money," Steve said.

"Hang on. We'll take the money, but just for a week or two. That's it," Jupe replied.

Jupe stuck his hand out.

"A thousand a week, paid up-front."

"Absolutely. We're gone in a month, tops."

Sam began counting.

"And you promise to stay out of the way."

"Me and Debian, we're just like mice."

"We are not like mice," Deb said, "We are nothing like mice."

"What's up with the bandages?" he had to ask. "You guys in a fight?"

Each of them had a couple of black bandaids on their face. The man Samuel walked with a limp.

"A bit. What about the work? Take our case?"

He shifted on his feet.

Jupiter stared at the money.

"I'm sorry. Rent yes, but we don't do corporate work. And this looks a bit … mmm too uncertain for us. I don't think we can take it."

"Maybe you should just explain yourselves more, stop being so secretive," Jim said. "You can tell us. We are the soul of discretion. So what is it? Tell us! You guys hiding out? On the lamb? Got the coppers after you? In dutch? In a bit of a pickle? Did somebody drop a dime? Just get out of the hoosegow?"

Deb seemed puzzled at Jim's questions.

"We have no copper for you. Nor is there a lamb we are currently riding. As you can see. I do not have a goose-cow. Does the lamb come with the goose? Should we have brought a cow?"

"Just ignore her. Not really much of a people-person per se," Sam said, making air quotes, "Deb's looking for her father, Paul Newbury. We think he was involved with a couple of organizations, one of which we were just employed at: EigenCorp. That's how we got to the Janus stuff."

"EigenCorp. Never heard of it," Jupe said.

"Well, we interned there for a while," Sam explained, "Made a bit of money. Did so well they asked us to invest. We just don't know whether to do it or not. That's a big decision."

Sam shook his head yes as if agreeing with somebody. There was nobody.

"I'm sure you didn't hear about it, Jupe," Jim said, "It's only the best blue-green crypto InfoSec risk team on the planet. Wow, you two were really in it, huh?"

"Came into a bit of money," Jupe said, thinking aloud.

Steve stepped forward a bit.

"You worked at that corporate monstrosity," Steve said of the place he had not heard of just one minute earlier, "You should be thankful you got out. Why do you need us to investigate it? Crimes?"

"Another good question!" Sam said, "You guys are really on the ball tonight! Great questions. As it turns out, EigenCorp was involved with a lot of shady stuff, and so was Deb's father. Oh, we're not in trouble with anybody, of course, nor were any crimes committed, everything's fine, but we'd like as much information as we can get so that we don't end up in trouble later on. Deb's father was somehow involved with this Middles guy who runs the place and this group, Janus Group, blah-blah-blah seems to keep popping up wherever we look. That's it."

Sam put his money away. They had obviously been prying too much.

"Don't overthink it, guys. It's a simple research gig. In the time we're here, you guys can knock it out, make even more money."

Jupe looked at the gang, dubious.

"I don't know. We haven't discussed this kind of thing before."

He then looked back to the two newcomers.

"Ten times our normal rate, Mr. Featherstone, if we even take the job, and that's not including expenses. Easy. Hmmm. That money in your stack is not going to cover it."

"We have money."

Deb said it. He saw Sam cut her a sharp look.

"You know, Mr. Froststrike," Sam said, stepping forward a bit, firming his stance up, "Perhaps we're wrong. Perhaps you're not the guys for us. It doesn't sound like your firm has done much investigating. After all, this is a junkyard, not a fancy building."

"Well," Steve said, You're actually looking at our…" he began.

Jim elbowed Steve. He stopped talking.

Jupiter could see that it was time to give his pitch. He saw a guy in a movie once call it "closing the sale." That was a good movie. He saw it twice, so he had to be an expert in it.

"Actually, Sam," he said. He squared his shoulders and gave his best professional look. Stuck his chin out. Dang he missed that pipe. Now was the exact time for the pipe! "We've done quite a bit of work in all kinds of non-corporate situations. What you see here is our long-term plan working exactly as we wanted."

Sam looked around.

"A junkyard."

Sam looked to Deb as if to say. "How's that? Good enough?"

"I don't know. They look incompetent." Deb said. Her expression did not change. She was completely blank. She didn't even look back to Sam when he spoke to her. Weirdo.

"You might think that," Jupe said, "but you'd be wrong. We've had many clients over the last year or so. Why we even have an ongoing arrangement with a large landowner around to help with location services and barrier-security organization."

"Location services?"

"Oh yes. Of a feline nature." he said, speeding up to move on to some other topic. "James here works at the local library and is a world-class researcher. Steve's dad is a leading expert in FX and is called to consult on locations all around the world."

"Library. His *dad*,"Sam said, stressing the word dad, "Gotta admit guys, I like hearing that, but I'm still not so sure."

"Where are my manners?" Jupiter said, "I forgot to tell you about myself. I'm a Fields Recipient and former Chief Naval Investigator. Spent my entire career chasing down the ill-mannered and disentangling their nefarious motives and operendi."

Noting Jupe's exaggeration, Jim looked at Jupe. Jim looked betrayed.

"Never thought I'd see you do that."

"It's true," Jupiter continued, "I was a recipient and all that. Don't like to talk about it."

Steve began to speak but Jim gave him another elbow.

Deb moved. She looked at Steve then to Jupiter.

"It's not working out. Let's leave. These are not the right people," she said.

"Well then, I agree. You could leave," Jupiter said, "You could leave … or … perhaps cutting our rate might help. I have a soft spot. I feel quite sorry for you. We might could make an exception."

The two interlopers looked at one another.

"I don't know…" Sam said.

Jupe pointed at Sam. He was careful to use two fingers, otherwise it would be rude. Damn that pipe being gone.

"We're going to need some kind of reasonable explanation of why somebody with all this money can't stay somewhere reasonable like a hotel."

Samuel smiled the biggest smile Jupe had ever seen.

"That's reasonable, don't you think so, hon?"

He did not give Deb time to continue but Samuel kept going.

"Deb and I are actually a couple. She's my girlfriend."

He took her hand.

"We are not," she said, staring straight ahead.

"And we fight some, we do."

"We do…"

Deb looked as if she wanted to bite Sam. Both of their knuckles whitened, the muscles tensing in the joined wrists and arms, but they kept holding hands.

"That's my little chickadee. Little Debian. We fight, a lover's thing. And right now we're on a tour across the country, replicating one of our favorite books. It's kind of our first vacation for us."

"Ah! So you're role playing a favorite book!" Jupiter said. "That is truly amazing! You should have said something. That's awesome. What's the book?"

Sam's smile faltered for a second.

"Another good question," Jupiter thought Sam looked very sad as he continued, "You tell him, hon. You do it so much better than I do."

"Furious Devil Furries of the Ethereal Frontier," she said, then "Unabridged." Then, "Original Czechoslovakian edition."

"I don't remember that one," Jim said.

"It's out of print."

"Yup. That's it. Very rare. In either case," Sam said, "We need a junkyard, so we're staying here or in some other junkyard. You guys have an investigative service. We've also got some work for somebody with an investigative service, and we've got some work for somebody already with a junkyard. Sure'd be nice to kill two birds with one stone."

"I will not assist in any form of avian assaults. The birds have done nothing to us," she said, then, leaning in, "recently, of course."

"Come on Jupe, why not?" Jim said.

"Yeah," Steve said, "I want to hear more about this evil EigenCorp and the overlords."

"Might make a good research project. We could use some in-depth work," Jim said. "Also that Furious Devil Furries sounds incredible."

He smiled at Deb. If she saw it, she did not indicate it.

"Alright guys, dang it," Jupe said, "but for anybody living and working this close to us, there's one absolute, invariable condition."

"What is it?"

"You can never tell anyone about our secret headquarters."

"Sure," Sam said, "Where is it?"

"It's right here, guys!" Steve said. "Didn't guess that, did ya? Is this cool or what?"

"Wow," Deb said. Her head jerked left, then right, then back to neutral.

She looked at Steve. "These may actually be the exact kind of people we were looking for."

"It is certainly something." Sam said, mulling it over, "They have a secret headquarters."

"I know, right!" Steve smiled.

"Absolute oath, guys, no kidding," Jim added.

"Of course."

"We should make them take an oath, like in court," Steve said. "Anybody have a bible, a DM Guide?"

"I don't think so," Jupe said.

"Swear on something. Swear on the grave of your favorite pet! That's it! The pet!"

Deb said "I don't have a…" but Sam interjected "It's okay. Remember Spot The Puppy? Very sad."

"Spot is not dead."

"He was sick. Spot was very sick. Obviously dead by now, or very close to it. We agree," Sam held up his hand in an oath, "We swear. Poor Spot."

"Now tell me about this super-secret headquarters you have here," Sam said, leading Jupiter away.

As the two men left, Deb, Jim and Steve were left to stare at one another. Deb found something about a freckle on her left wrist that needed her attention. Steve jangled the coins in his pocket and started checking out the fenceline. Jim finally spoke.

"You got a luggage, backpack, storage building, wheelbarrow? Anything we can help with?"

"Donuts. We need donuts. And coffee. Make sure they are bad."

She crinkled her nose. She looked to make sure Sam was out of earshot.

"You want disgusting donuts and coffee?"

"Not disgusting. Very good coffee. But old. Bad. Crusty. Except for maybe the coffee. The pastries. I don't suppose they make coffee crusty."

"I suppose not," Steve said, "So you must get old donuts and good coffee, and you have no luggage."

"Also I will not like the donuts. Perhaps you can tell me that no other beverage or desserts are available."

Deb looked blankly at the young man.

"I am not good with people."

Jim looked at her.

"I don't suppose so. We'll see what we can do."

And so, *The Story That Will Never Be Told* began, much to the eventual sadness of everyone involved.

3.045

For Immediate Release

Market Experiences Large Drop

New York, NY - The stock market today experienced it's most dramatic drop in one day since the banking crisis of the last decade, losing on average over 30% of their value before circuit breakers set in.

When contacted for comment, Albert Allred, professor of economics at City College, explained that the loss was most likely due to hidden risk in complex derivatives, the same problem that precipitated the last crisis.

"We don't know for sure, but I expect over the next decade or two economists will work it out. You know the old saying, if you have two economists you'll have at least three opinions."

Allred was asked during a press conference if the downward trend could be expected to continue.

"We don't know. Economics is a lagging indicator. We see people trading and doing things with money, we come up with theories. Sometimes they're useful for the future, sometimes not, but none of them are actually true. All models are over-simplified and wrong in some way. If we could predict the future, all economists would be billionaires, right? Economics is astrology for people who know calculus."

The press conference was cut short by college organizers, but Allred did have one last question.

"The real question is why the circuit breakers took so long to kick in. It's never supposed to do that."

# # #

Staking Out

"All I'm saying is that we should have never left newcomers alone at our super secret headquarters on our first day on a job," Jupe said, scanning his rearview mirror for Jim and Steve's response.

They were in the old van, heading to the girl's apartment. It had been too far for the bikes, unfortunately, so they strapped them on top again. There had been some discussion about parking a few blocks away and riding the last bit, but the argument died down in favor of the current topic: how much do we trust the newcomers?

"Super. Secret. That's our headquarters for sure. But we still don't have any WiFi," Steve said, "so there's that."

"Stop with the WiFi!" Jupe said. He turned into the large apartment complex's parking lot, "Let's not start that again. Please."

"Would you look at that." Jim pointed from the back.

There was barely room to get into the lot and find a space. Most of the existing space had been taken up by police cars. From a distance it appeared that an old blue station wagon had been driven off the road somehow, careened across the open grass, and struck some bushes by the front entrance to one of the buildings.

"We're not getting anywhere close to that," Steve said, "and there's people involved too. Casualties."

An ambulance came in behind them.

"I'm not even sure we're getting out," Jupe looked around the way they had come. "If we wanted to get out."

People had started approaching on foot from the other buildings. Police began putting up tape. It was a thing.

"Must have just happened," Steve said, snapping a couple of pictures with his cell, "and good luck getting any stake-out work in all of this."

"We're going to need to gear up, guys," Jim said, handing out lab notebooks and pencils.

Steve took his. He looked at the small black notebook and pencil as if Jim had just handed him a bug. Or a calculus book.

"What's this? Do we have to write? We've got phones."

"Lab notebooks. For recording our surveillance notes."

"So where's the 3D VR helmet cams?" Steve asked.

Jupe turned to look back at the two.

"The what?"

"Helmet cams. 3D. Nobody brought the helmet cams?"

"We don't have helmet cams. I'm not buying helmet cams for anybody," Jupiter said.

"And now we don't have helmet cams," Steve looked at his notebook, "But we have sketch books. I don't even know what planet you people come from."

Subject must be changed, Jupiter thought.

"What are the notebooks for?"

"The stakeout procedure," Jim said, "The three-part document. Didn't you guys get my email?"

"I don't check my email much," Jupe offered.

"No WiFi," Steve seemed overly happy to say this.

"Shut up Steve. This is good, Jim. Excellent, in fact. These notes can form the basis of our next novel, 'The Gallant General'. I already have some artwork started. I was thinking we need something with a lighthouse, maybe a hunchback."

"Notes? Novel?" Steve asked, "What's a novel? We're doing a video game, right? MMRPG? We're doing the whole thing, no? This is part of an immersive world AR experience that.."

Jupiter frowned at Jim.

"Can you translate that?"

"He's saying that books are old school. He wants to take The Three Investigators to the next level."

"Oh. That again. Before we go down that road," Jupe said, "can we just all agree that now, right now, we're on a stakeout? Just shake your head yes or no. No comments. You can do this."

Yes.

"Ok, very good. Now yes or no again. Can we agree that we need to take notes, record things when you're on a stakeout? And that everybody has their own way of doing that."

"I don't have cams. 3D cams."

"So next time you'll have them. For now, we wait. Stake-outs are mostly about waiting and boredom. Let's practice being bored, see how we do."

Steve put his notebook down. He reached in his bag and produced a large hardcover book and began to read.

Jupiter turned back to watch the ongoing commotion outside. He began formulating some great tips to share about stakeouts and the importance of disguises, but Jim interrupted before he could begin telling them all about it.

"What the hell is this, Steve? Harry Potter? A Harry Potter book? You're reading? You read Harry Potter?"

"I never read the last one. I hear it's pretty good."

"You never read the last Harry Potter."

"That's exactly right. If the author of those books had only realized…"

"Shut up, Steve!" They both said at once.

From far away was the sound of a helicopter. Slowly it came in, circled, and landed on a field across the main road which had been blocked off.

"Must be pretty bad," Jupiter said to the two in the back.

"Yeah," Steve agreed, "See the tarp they're holding over next to the entrance? They only do that when it's not pretty. Trust me, you don't want to see that. Been there."

"Accidents. Vans. No bikes. Tarps. Helicopters. Corporations. This isn't much like The Three Investigators," Jim said, "I don't see a lighthouse anywhere."

"No," Jupiter glared at Steve's book.

"What? I can't read my book now? Not okay for me to read? Was that in the memo?"

"Of course you can read, Steve. Read the book. It's a good book. I'm just not so sure about all this 3D business."

Steve stopped, closed the book.

"See this? A book. I read books. Love books. Just nobody else does. Look around. It's not 1714 anymore."

He considered, turning back, watching the rescue team wheel the first victim to the waiting helicopter.

"We argue a lot," Jupiter finally said.

"That we do," Jim said, "way too much. But sometimes it's important. Jupe, I've been thinking that the work is important. We need to get a lot more disciplined about where this is all headed. What will the Gallant General be? Book, mystery, film, game, series, song? If we don't know where we're headed how can we get there?"

"Good point, Jim. I'm just not so sure about tech," he replied, "I think once we start focusing on the tech it's easy to get ahead of the story, lose the important parts, that's all."

Steve had been holding his phone in the air trying to get a better signal. As the gurney came by the front of the van, the tarp dropped. By reflex, he snapped a picture.

"That's disgusting, Steve," Jim said, "taking pictures of beat-up people now? This is what we're doing?"

Steve looked at his phone.

"My dudes. Whoa. That's her. That's our girl."

Steve held the phone and they both looked.

He took his phone back, still looking.

"Now what."

Jim snatched the phone from Steve, horrified.

Jupiter looked at the two boys. He tried to assess their emotions. It wasn't good. They were keyed-up. No matter what his body language, Steve was primed for another emotional jag and Jim looked like he lost his best friend. He needed to get this back on-track.

"Now we continue our stakeout, gentlemen, because we're professionals. I'll start recording this in my case notebook here. This procedural thingy. The doohickey."

Jim didn't look up or correct him.

"Stakeouts are usually pretty boring, men. We must take all the notes we can, right?"

"I suppose you know this from your time as a Naval Investigator. Fields Medal recipient." Jim still didn't look up from Steve's phone and the image on it. "Did you also cure cancer?"

Steve seemed completely oblivious to Jim's emotional state or his accusation that Jupiter was a liar.

"The book's great so far. They don't do stakeouts in Harry Potter, that's for sure."

"Shut up," Jim said, but he was still transfixed what he saw on the phone.

It was ugly.

"Wonder if this stupid radio works," Jupe said, turning the knobs this way and that. It didn't work.

"They've stopped CPR," Steve said. He was peeking out the side mirror again. Jim still had his phone. "That's usually it. The end. Game over."

Steve looked back to his partners.

"She's dead."

Jim bit his lip.

Steve finally woke up to what was going on, pressed his back against the van wall, looked at his friend.

"It's okay, Jim. We didn't do this. We couldn't have stopped it. It was already here when we got here."

Jim continued to struggle with not crying. In Jupiter's experience, sometimes that worked. Sometime it just made it worse.

"Steve's right, Jim. It is very, very sad. A horrible thing."

He could see Jim pinching his leg. Jim gave Steve his phone back.

"Our first real case," was all he said. His lip twitched.

"I guess I can get out and take regular old 2D video now since we don't have to worry about getting busted," Steve started fiddling with his phone.

"You have to be kidding me!" Jim said.

"Don't we still have a job to do?" Steve said. "Isn't recording things part of our job?"

"Not now, Steve," he said, looking at Jim, "it is a good thought, though. We do still have a case. We must be professionals about it. Discretion."

Steve lowered his phone.

"I'm not saying we have to go all 'futuristic' making air quotes for Jupiter's benefit. But we're going to have to get with the times. We're going to have to be more modern if we want others to join us."

"You're right."

"Could you say that again?"

Steve looked slapped by the compliment. That got Jim's attention, distracted him.

"Steve's right. We're going to have to do something to go with the times. I agree." Jupe continued.

Jim crossed his arms.

"So, guys, what kind of tech we need to tell our first client that his daughter's dead? Got any ideas about that?"

It was quiet. They spent several minutes watching the helicopter take off. The police crime investigators begin working.

"We're going to have to figure out how to tell him," he didn't look away, "and it's not going to be a video or a printed report. We need to do this in-person."

"Isn't going away," Jim said. "It's permanent."

Jim looked away from them afraid to meet their eyes.

Steve picked his small black notebook back up but didn't open it.

"Jupiter, I don't see how this fits into our Three Investigator system at all," Steve said, "There was nothing like this in the books."

"Steve's right again," he said, counting off on his fingers, "So let's work through this. I see that we have one of three options. One, quit the entire Three Investigators thing and go do something else. Maybe we go into the junkyard business."

Both kids looked horrified. He continued to count off.

"Two, ignore that it happened. We just do nothing. We let the General find out on his own. We look away."

"I like that," Jim said, looking away.

"And pass on the money. Option three, figure out how The Three Investigators would have handled it even if there's no canon to help us. We ad lib. That would be fun."

Jim shook his head no. "fun" was probably not the word Jupiter should have used.

"Jupe, nobody ever died in a Three Investigators book. It never happened. It never *could* happen."

The other two could not make eye contact with Jim.

"I've had enough. I'm out of here," Jim said. He began to leave.

Steve put the little book down and started reading the big hardback.

Jupiter looked around the old van. The world was moving in slow motion.

He held both hands high to the sky looking like an Evangelic TV minister.

"Steve's right again!"

That stopped them. Now what.

Jupiter looked around conspiratorially. There was a secret he had to share. Steve looked barely interested. There was a danger of him going back to reading. Both would lose interest quickly. This moment would pass. They could lose it.

He could really use Steve's help. That stupid book. Freaking Steve.

"You know what we need? We need to have a super special emergency backup LARP, that's what!" Jupe concluded.

"A backup LARP?" Jim stopped leaving. "Super special? How would that work?"

"Well, like you said, Jim, this kind of situation would never work with the Investigators, yet if we really want to be detectives we're going to have to have a way of dealing with bad news, and more, um, adult situations. Right?"

"How exactly would this work, Jupe?" Steve cocked his head.

"Well, you're right again, Steve. Our special super backup LARP will be …"

He waited for effect.

"Harry Potter!"

Steve lit up in a smile.

"Yeah. Awesome! That makes sense. We could do that. What do you think, Jim? They killed all kinds of people in those books. Cool clothes. Plus we get spells."

Jim considered the plan. He shrugged. He nodded, keeping a wary eye on Steve.

"Might work. Perhaps we could pick an alternate canon, sort of a backup. Lots of shows and books did mix ups. Crossovers. Why not."

"It's decided then," Jupiter went to start the van and get out of there before any more drama happened. "We'll be Harry, Ron, and Hermione."

It finally started and he got it turned around, away from the wreck. The policeman motioned him through.

"This is going to be a blast, guys! We're going to love this!" Jupe tried as they made the road and began to pick up speed.

"Freaking A, man!" Steve agreed. "I've always wanted to be Harry Potter."

"You? Harry Potter? I don't think so." Jim said, "I'm Harry Potter. You're more like a Rita Skeeter."

"Well I'm certainly not being Hermione!"

The van became firmly established in traffic, coughing as it did. He headed for headquarters, crisis averted.

For now.

Battling Fate

"That man is watching us," Debian said, looking through the periscope out into the junkyard.

Sam called from the other room.

"What man?"

"Gone now."

But there was a sound.

The sound was calamitous, a schizophrenic Santa sliding up in a broken diesel-powered sleigh.

With angry elves.

All had been quiet. The black cat clock slowly ticked off the minutes in the dim fluorescent trailer light. Deb had been reading. Sam was back in what was left of the bathroom. He had almost perfected his new trick.

The dim jangle of a fence sliding back. The dissonant diesel engine noise. The silent crunch of tires on gravel.

The engine stopped. Doors open and shut. Voices far away.

Then a clanking. Perhaps the tunnel entrance? The voices got louder. There was an almost-shout, the silence.

Sam walked into the old living room where the refrigerator had been repurposed as a trapdoor. It started jostling. The whole room started jostling. The entire thin trailer floor was heaving to and fro as Jupiter Froststrike fought his way in through the trapdoor.

Sam thought that he looked like a fat man trying to break into a candy store using a small window.

"Golly frack!"

There was a struggle as the pot-bellied man finally arrived, brushing himself off. Jupiter looked down in concern as the other two followed.

"Still here, eh?" Jupiter looked around to Sam and Deb as if he'd just noticed them and they hadn't been watching them the entire time. Everything was the same inside as they had left it.

"We are," Sam said.

The girl Deb turned the last page of her paperback.

"Did you bring donuts?"

"Yup. Here you go," Steve handed her a box. "All they had was yesterday's donuts and this old coffee."

Steve looked at the lady as if asking a question. She nodded. She weakly smiled as if Steve were a moron. Jupiter thought that might count as an emotional outburst for her.

"These donuts are disgusting," she looked to Sam as if expecting a reply, but he ignored her.

The girl frowned, much more than a simple crusty breakfast pastry would cause.

"We saw an accident today," Jim looked from one to the other and back. Jim was a child telling a parent a story and unsure how he was supposed to feel about it "it was horrible."

"I bet so," Sam said. He put a hand on Jim's arm. "Sorry to hear about that. Are you guys okay? Would you like to talk about it?"

Jim shook his head no curtly. Neither of the other two responded. Deb stepped forward.

"I got these from your mailbox. Appears nobody's received the mail in a while."

She handed him a stack of envelopes. The ones on top were red.

"Utility bills look important," she said, then got back down, mission accomplished.

Jupiter took them quickly and put them on the counter behind them. "Nothing special."

"Yeah, aren't they always annoying ya," Sam looked at the other two Investigators, sharing a happy memory, "We used to get these all the time when I was growing up. These utility folks. Always trying to sell you something new."

Jupe needed something to say; his mind came up empty.

"How about I go with you tomorrow," Sam continued, "If we can run by one of these places, I can show you how to get them to stop with all the junk mail."

"No. We're fine. We have an important client meeting tomorrow," Jupe looked at the other two. "We have a report to deliver and we're going to get paid."

Sam looked around their lair. He pointed to the clock.

"Put some batteries in the clock. Cleaned up what was left of the bathroom, blocked off the toilet because hey! You don't want to be using that. Not connected to anything."

Jim deflated, looking at the ground. Jupe saw that Sam noticed.

"I feel really awful," Sam said.

"I do not feel awful." Deb said.

"We feel really awful," Sam said more slowly as if explaining things to a small child, "because there's nothing for us to do around here all day. Why don't we help you out more? Frankly, this is boring as shit."

"Language!" bunch of damned newcomers with the profanity, Jupe thought. What assholes.

"Oops. Sorry. You can ask Deb. I'm always careful about language. Profanity is a tool of the uneducated, that's what I always say. Sometimes I make mistakes."

Deb looked at the paperback she had just finished.

"Say," he said, "you guys got started on our case yet? Made a visit to the library? Do some online research?"

"There is no internet here," Deb said, looking up.

"I know, right?" Steve said.

"That's good."

"It is?"

Steve looked befuddled. Deb produced another weak smile. She looked like she'd just been told that there's going to be a bit of a wait for an extremely unpleasant upcoming dental procedure.

Sam glanced back at the unpaid bills.

"Yup. In fact, we were going to ask you guys if you could hold-off on installing any internet."

"We're not ready to start your case yet," Jupe said, "First thing tomorrow."

"After this client thing. The meeting," Sam nodded.

"Yes. The meeting."

Jim shuddered a bit. Deb stuck her hand out for him to take it. It held a book.

"I just finished. You'll like this. By the same author of 'Rabid Vampire

Monkey Accountants' that I finished last night. Just came out. First edition. Supposed to be part of the ISO-9000 universe."

Jim took it. He smiled.

"Wow! Thanks! 'Crypt Monsters of City Zoo' Can't wait to read it!"

Sam winked at Jupe where the two boys couldn't observe.

"Serials are awesome,"Jim said, "where they expand the franchise, do crossovers, deepen the universe. You really get a feel for how the characters work."

"Working is good," Deb said. They waited but she didn't continue.

"You know," Jim picked up the thread. "You guys could stay here after the case. We could join up."

"We cannot, sadly. I need to locate my father and brother. Sam needs to, um, file this paperwork. The research. We have, um, a lot left to do."

"On our own," Sam said, looking to Deb, "Each of us."

"Did you guys break up?" Steve asked, a little too eagerly in Jupe's opinion.

"Yes," Sam said at the exact same time Deb shrugged a "maybe."

"Are we that bad? Why not hang out with us a bit?" Jim continued his pitch. "Make some money."

"We have money," she said, "money is not a problem."

Sam looked at Jupe as if to say, "See? Anything we can do for you?"

"We don't want your money. We'll do the work. You pay us. Start tomorrow. We don't need charity."

Sam briefly looked away, down at the floor, then back to Jupe.

"Got some problems with the barn door?"

"Excuse me?" Jupe began shifting from foot-to-foot.

Sam pointed at Jupiter's zipper. He quickly zipped it up.

"You wouldn't notice it," Sam said.

Jupe shifted a bit more. He tried to gain some control.

"Just try not to damage anything while we're off working for you, okay?"

A picture fell from the wall.

Everybody looked around to see if another picture would fall.

"How about this," Sam said, "How about we do some carpentry work while you're busy? We can fix stuff up."

"We don't know carpentry work," Deb said.

"We know carpentry work," Jupe noticed that it had gotten so that Sam ignored her, or at least tried. Maybe these spats were normal.

"Sure we do," Sam said. He pressed against the flimsy wood paneling. "We can shore these things up. Hang these pictures better."

He pushed a bit against the wall, testing it. Another picture fell in one of the bedrooms. He was afraid.

"Look, young man," Jupe said. "Everything here has an exact place and reason for being here. It's all very important, and it's not something I'd expect somebody like you to understand."

The two were confused.

"There's a lot we can't go into right now," Jupe said, "a lot of important things. But I suspect we're your best shot right now, for answers to the…."

Jupiter looked around in confusion. He was startled.

The what? He looked around again. Oh my god! They didn't have a name! They almost took a case without having a name!

Jim spoke up.

"It's 'The Corporate Conundrum'," he said, "The Case of the Corporate Conundrum."

"The Case of the Corporate Conundrum," Steve said, "I like it! With the Cask of the Mysterious Potion!"

Steve pointed to the box of old coffee he'd brought.

They looked more confused than ever

"The case … so there's nothing we can do to help you?" Sam asked, "… with things."

"We are fine," he said. He examined the two as if they were action figures on his shelf, "You guys just wouldn't fit in."

"There's only three of us," Jim said, "We could use some professors or something. Maybe we could chop the nose off of one of them, shave their head."

"They can't pay their bills," Deb said, looking to Sam, "They're incompetent, most likely insane, and this makes them broke as well."

Sam didn't respond, maintaining eye contact with Jupe.

"Is that true?" Steve asked.

Jupe finally broke contact. "Yes. It's true. Perhaps we've encountered an unexpected kind of parsimonious penury, perchance even perilous," Seeing that this wasn't working, he continued, "The money thing. I've been meaning to tell you, but with all that's going on…"

"They can't pay their bills," Sam looked to Deb, "and they won't take money from us."

"No we won't," he told them all, "like I said, we get paid tomorrow."

"If the General even pays us," Jim said.

There was a click, and it was dark.

"Hmm," Sam said. Jupiter could tell that Sam was about to say even more things he didn't want to hear.

"The power is now off," Deb said from somewhere in the darkness.

"Genius. A team," Steve said. "She's the brains of you two, huh."

Deb turned on a light. "Maybe so. I have a flashlight. Do you?"

He did not.

Steve looked at Jim.

"Whaddya think, Jimbo? She just produced light. Pretty cool, huh? She could put that flashlight on a stick. We could tape it. There's some aluminium foil around here somewhere. I could find a robe."

"Maybe so," Jim looked back at the two, "Could you guys work out some better outfits? How are you on your Latin? Know any spells? Done any theater work?"

Their frowns only deepened.

"If you touch me, I will hurt you," Debian said.

"I'll just come out right and say it," Jim said, "Could you be wizards?"

"Must they be alien wizards?" Deb asked, "Remember, we didn't bring the cow."

"I don't know. I haven't thought of that. Very interesting." Steve rubbed his chin, "There was rumor of a secret sequel…."

"STOP! Right now!"

The room shocked itself into stillness. They looked at Jupiter.

"We need to completely shut the hell down any of this," Jupiter gathered the word, "meta nonsense. I mean it. I didn't do all of this work, cash out my savings, almost deplete my retirement, if we're going to act like this."

"You cashed out your…"

"Stop! We don't talk idioms with outsiders. Means and methods. This is important to me, and I would appreciate it if we could maintain the ambiance and genre…"

"But Jupe," Steve began again.

"I mean it. And I'll kick your ass if you keep pushing it."

"He's weird," Deb said, "they all are. Very weird."

They all looked at her in astonishment.

She adjusted the plastic flower she was wearing on one sleeve. Her sailor hat looked a little too tilted on her head.

"And old," she looked at them as if it were obvious.

"I think Steve could take him," she finished, then, looking to Jupiter, "You will not be kicking anybody's ass."

"Guys," Sam began, "I have more money. We can get you money. You need money we can get it."

"Yes," Deb said, "We have money. If that's all you require."

They all looked at Jupe.

"But I doubt it," Deb finished.

"Jupiter, please. Let me take you to my bank and get you caught up. You can pay me later."

"I think this is a good idea, Jupe," Jim said, "if you want this to continue."

That was it. Jim had nailed it.

This was a horrible night for him. A horrible day. Whatever.

"I guess so."

With that, it was like the trailer ran out of energy. Everybody went to their corner. Deb started another paperback. Sam went to the bathroom and shut the door. Eventually the boys left.

After a time, realizing his lie was up, Jupiter crawled back through the long tunnel of junk and found the old office in the back of the junkyard. There was a cot in the back.

The power was off. It was quiet, and he curled up to sleep in the dark.

Those two still never told him why they dressed so weird, the clothes and the band-aids.

Calling them weird. He knew they weren't as weird as those two were.

Thinking some more, he also knew now that he had some special work for Jim to do off-the-books.

3.07

Telling The General

"You guys have fun. Anybody want to tell me about the dinosaur?" Sam asked as they pulled into the General's driveway.

"We can't. Lawyer-client privilege," Steve said.

"Lawyer what?"

"What Steve means," Jim said, "is that it's part of our engagement which should remain privileged."

Jupe looked at the man in the passenger seat beside him.

"It's part of a security system, Sam, but the boys are right. We need to be more careful."

"Careful? With me? I thought we took the sacred oath and all of that," Sam said, "The puppy? Remember the puppy? I swore on little Spot!"

He considered Sam's words. It was going to be very difficult to have folks around them all the time and not let them in more. But enough is enough. He had to admit Sam was likeable, but he wasn't supposed to be here. Yet Jupiter had no idea what to do about it.

"Like I said last night, we're closing up a case. You really want to be part of the circle of trust on this?"

"No, but I think I need to know what's going on anyway," Sam frowned.

"You sure about that?" Jupe opened the door and they all started to get out. "We've got some really sad news and this is not going to be pleasant."

Sam looked back over to him over the hood of the van as they all got out.

"The way my life has been going lately; sad news is really not that unusual."

Sam waited by the passenger door, waiting for the others to lead.

"I can help with sad news," Sam said, "I've spent some time learning how to cheer people up. Worked as a clown for a while in college."

"His daughter's dead," Jim said from behind Sam. "He asked us to do a stake-out and research on what kinds of trouble she might be in, and she was dead when we got there."

"Oh god," Sam said, "I'm so sorry. So this is what had you guys all stirred up last night."

"Yeah," Steve said, "Come on, guys. This isn't getting easier."

The dinosaur's head pivoted to watch them as they came down the sidewalk. Jupe stopped the group before they made the door.

"I won't lie, Sam, we could use your emotional support if you're able. We've never done this. You don't have to say or do anything, just be there."

"Of course, guys," Sam said, "I would be honored. Happy to be part of the team."

They started again.

"For a while."

Before he rang the bell, Jim looked at his friends.

"How *are* we going to tell him, anyway?"

"I think the only thing to do is come straight out and tell him." Jupe said.

"Jupe's right," Steve said, "I've been through this a few times when I volunteered Rescue. You just have to rip that band-aid off. There's no right way. Make it quick."

"Your show," Sam said. Jupiter noticed that the man still had black bandaids on his face, but they were in a different position this morning. He really needed to ask those two about that.

"It's unanimous then," Jupe said, then rang the bell.

The aide met them at the door again, and without so much as a howdy-do escorted them back to the rose garden where the General again waited.

The man looked angry. He had been expecting them.

"Did you bring the bullshit?"

Three responses fought with one another in Jupiter's brain. Finally there was a winner.

"Good morning, General. What were we supposed to bring?"

"Cow manure, nincompoops, for the roses! Bring it?"

He pointed at the planters. Some work had been done, but he couldn't see any roses.

"Sir we have some bad news and we're not really sure how to tell you."

"Well man, then get on with it." he pointed to some bags of topsoil. "Those will need to go in those planters over there once you clean them out."

Nobody moved.

"Aren't you here to help me with my garden? I DO so wish June would come back. She was so good with the plants."

"Sir, this is about June," Jupiter felt like a trapped animal.

"Of course it is. We're not going to win the rose contest this year if we don't straighten up. We need to get moving, men!"

"Sir, General, Sir," Steve said, "things aren't so good."

"You're telling me!" the man in the wheelchair said, "I told that aide that he either needs to start helping me with my garden or I'd find some-body who would!"

They heard a sigh. The aide appeared and handed the General some pills and another health shake. He looked at the gang, shrugged, then disappeared back to his observation post by the door.

"He said some kind of nonsense about just being a healthcare worker. Nonsense, I say. What could be more healthy than a healthy garden?"

Jupiter watched Sam go to the man, kneel down.

"I notice you have some tomatoes you want to plant. Have you tried planting them alongside basil?"

"Tried just that last year, young man," the General said, "best tomatoes I've had in a long time."

Jupe couldn't tell whether it was last year, ten years ago, or if it even ever happened.

Sam moved a little closer, looked in rapt attention at the General as the man continued.

"Got those stinging beetles, though. Those little guys are the dickens!"

"Yes sir, they are." He took the man's hands.

The General looked around as if they had just arrived.

"Who are you, again?"

Sam released him and stood back up. He pointed to a planter behind them. He gave the Three Investigators a sad smile as he continued.

"Say look, here's a rose. A volunteer. This garden must not be in such bad shape after all."

"Thank you," the General said, "We get a lot of compliments. Won an award last year. Have I told you that? It's so hard to get good help."

Jupiter nodded. He was interested in how Sam was doing this. The anger was gone. Maybe the lanky man really could help. The General stopped looking at Sam, though, and back to the gang.

"My wife died."

"Yes sir."

"Killed by the aliens."

"Of course, sir."

"Not that anybody did anything about it."

"There's a lot going on here, Mr. General Sir, that we need to investigate," Steve said.

The General shook, almost in a fit, but only for a second.

"Exactly. Now, gentlemen, where are you on the background investigation of my daughter?"

"She's dead," Steve said.

"What!"

"Car accident," Jim said, "4:07 pm, yesterday."

"Very sorry," Jupe said, "You have our condolences. Terrible tragedy."

"You have to leave."

The General looked trapped, confused, as if they were about ready to attack him.

"Sir?"

"I hired you to observe my daughter and instead you get her killed. This has been a horrible mistake. Leave."

"But sir," Jim said, "If you'd only let us finish our report, wrap up the case. My friend Steve is correct. There are things going on."

"Things."

"Yes sir, things. We had only begun the investigation and stakeout. You'll want answers. If I were you, I'd want answers," Jim said.

"You sat there in that dumb van of yours and watched as my daughter died. Didn't even talk to the authorities to find out what happened. Get out. Just get out."

"It was the wizards, sir," Jupiter said, "dark arts. We didn't want to say that because most people, frankly, wouldn't believe it. But it was wizards. Alien wizards. You can be sure of that."

"I can see why …" Sam said. Thankfully he said no more. There was a sadness in the room that went beyond the daughter's death.

"Of all the cockamamie stories," the General looked at the Investigators. "This is what you three are telling me. You too?"

He looked at Sam.

"Just an observer, sir. This is the first I'm hearing this. Take this slowly, sir. You're okay."

"Were they wearing rings? Did they have wands? Did you recognize any?"

"Sir?"

"These wizards. How many were there?"

"It was quite crowded, sir," Jim offered. "I counted several dozen people in all."

That was true.

"There was even a helicopter," Steve said, sounding a bit too much like somebody telling a child about the Easter Bunny.

Sam knelt down again next to the old man.

"What's this on your shirt?" Sam said, then reached beside the man's head, "Say look! A flower! This can be your garden's first magically-created flower!"

The man looked confused for a bit,. but he settled.

"It's about time! Now that they're all showing up, how about doing the rest of the garden! We were going to have to do it all the old-fashioned way for heaven's sake! Took you long enough!"

From his kneeling position, Sam looked back at them as if to say "This is what we're working with."

"I can say that I'm quite amazed at these three so far," Sam said, standing again, leaving the silk flower in the General's hand. "Every day seems to be a completely new adventure with this bunch."

He looked down at the man.

"I'm sure they did the best job possible for you. They're not your enemy."

The General's eyes drooped.

"Very well, then, men." He made another gesture for the aide, "I'll see to it that you're mailed a check this month."

This month!

Jupiter looked at the aide. The man seemed unsure of whether to come back into the room or not.

"We'll see ourselves out. Once again sorry."

He started, then stopped, "General, are you going to be okay?"

The old man woke up a bit.

"Why certainly, son! I'm never anything but okay!"

They started to leave.

"Say," Sam said, "What were you a General in, anyway? The Air Force? Army?"

"NCRO, son, but I'm not supposed to talk about that. Three Stooges and all."

The General pointed a finger to the sky as if they were being recorded.

"Three Stooges?"

"Of course," Jupiter nodded knowingly.

"Time for the General's nap," the aide was immediately beside the wheelchair, kicking the brakes off, getting it ready to move.

"Sam," Jupiter said, "We should go."

Sam looked confused, but came along. "Of course we should."

"Poor man." Jim agreed

As they left for their next stop, Jim spoke up.

"I don't understand," Jim said, "He's the one that told the story to us. How did he know anything about what happened?"

3.08

Envying

"You're saying that there's no money left in my account."

"No sir. The latest tax lien took all of it … as I explained … a half hour ago."

"Come on, guy, let's get moving!"

Jupiter glared at the man behind him in line.

The man just shrugged.

It was a slog back to the van forty-feet away. On the way, he heard a familiar beep beep.

The Hardy Boys and their convertible pulled in. The car was new, shiny. They were impeccably dressed in character, even, yes, if there were three of them. They smiled and waved.

He ignored them. Opened the van door.

"This didn't work out."

"Want to talk about it?" Sam asked.

"No."

He shuffled his hands around through his clothes.

"Can't even find my stupid keys."

"Let me help. I'm good at finding lost things. Hold this while I look."

Sam handed him another fake flower.

He watched Sam as the man made a show of looking around the van interior. Could he have taken his keys? He didn't think so, but this one was full of surprises.

"Here ya go. Besides the driver's side seat. Stuff always ends up there."

"Look at those assholes," Jim said. He had been peeking out the window at the expensive convertible.

Jim saw that he was going to be corrected, and quickly said, "Sorry. I know, language."

"Those jerks are really flush," Steve said.

"Nyah," Sam replied, "there's more to it than that," but did not explain.

"Next stop your bank?" he looked at Sam.

Sam nodded, said nothing, thankfully.

It took even longer to get to Sam's bank. Jupiter dreaded it. The van was creaky, smelly. It shook at speed. At least that part was enjoyable, much more than the next part.

When they got there, Sam got out, remaining mute. Jupiter checked the boys. He sure hoped they weren't afraid of him. Jupe had gotten a little loud last night, probably out-of-hand. He knew better.

It certainly wasn't in character. Jupiter Jones would never do or say the things Jupiter Froststrike did last night.

Just plough through it, he kept thinking. Just keep on putting one foot in front of the other. That's how we get there.

There were two good gigs they had going. Each of them promised a payday. Just needed to make it there.

"Fuck if those assholes aren't here again!" Steve said.

"Language!" he yelled, "Come on, you two!"

But sure enough, as they waited on Sam at the next bank, there was the flashy gorgeous convertible again, the Hardy Boys, pulling in beside them. Again.

"We're better than that," he said in a quiet voice.

He didn't know who he was talking to.

"We should call them out for the fakers they are," Jim said, "that car is a rare collectible. Like the Hardy Boys would ever have something like that."

How long was Sam going to take?

"Steve!" he heard Jim yell.

Turning, he saw Steve, pants down, naked butt sticking in the window.

"Steve!" he almost hit the boy, pulled back. "Steve!"

Steve stopped. Pulled his pants back on.

"Payback's a bitch," he said, then "Weiners!"

Steve waggled his fingers and stuck his tongue out.

"We're better than that," Jupe said, "Come on, guys. We shouldn't do that anymore. Please? Let's try just a bit harder to stay in character, okay?"

The fake Hardy Boys didn't notice, thankfully.

"Hardy Boys," Steve grumbled. "Hardly Boys more like it."

"Seriously? Straighten up."

"Have you seen their social media presence? They're everywhere. I bet you they've got four hundred thousand followers. In just two months!"

"They do seem to be kicking our butt online," Jim said, then added, "and in other ways."

Jupiter let it go.

"I'll go see what's keeping Sam," he said and left.

Sam was finishing up when he got in, meeting him at the door. Sam nodded to the Hardy Boys in line.

"You know they're running a scam, right?" Sam whispered, "didn't you see all of that surveillance gear they're carting around? That's not investigative work. Some kind of honey trap, probably."

He didn't know what those words meant and hadn't seen anything.

"Watch this."

Sam walked over to the closest one.

"Any of you miss a micro surveillance cam?" he said.

The girl closest to Sam reached directly over to him, into Sam's pocket, and produced a small black object.

"You mean this cam? The one you palmed when we came in the door? This one?"

They started laughing. It was too much. Jupiter went to the bathroom.

He stood there in the bathroom. He listened to the silence. After what he thought was five minutes or so, he came back out.

The "Hardly Boys" were at the counter. Sam had gone back to the van. Thankfully nobody saw Jupe come out.

He didn't feel very Jupiter Jones. He was beginning not to feel much anything.

And they were running some kind of scam! Making money illegally.

"All a fucking gimmick," he said quietly to himself leaving. He didn't care if anybody heard him or not.

As he pushed open the door, coming out of the bank, he felt his van keys in his pocket. He looked at the convertible and beyond that the old van.

Got the keys out. Looked at them. Decided to walk around behind the back of the convertible instead of in front.

On the way over, he keyed the convertible owned by the Hardy Boys, as hard as he could. He left a long, deep scratch down the side.

He began whistling. Got into the driver's seat all smiles.

Jim smiled back.

"What made you so happy?"

He smiled all the way back, whistling, thinking about how nice it was to have money.

He whistled, "Put one foot in front of the other."

3.09

Debating Snacks

"After a morning like today," Jupiter Froststrike said, walking into the supermarket, "we deserve a snack tray. Anybody would deserve one."

"You got paid," Steve said, "You get paid, you party."

"Sam gave me enough for a week. He said the rest would follow once we give them our research."

Sam had stayed in the van when they went into the grocery store. For such a friendly guy, Sam seemed oddly shy of public places.

"Nothing says victory like a pound of cold cuts," Jim said, trying to hold back a smirk, "Bologna, salami …"

Instead of smiling, Steve grimmaced.

"But this? This is not right. We got paid. And now we will make animals suffer for our hunger? Or do we just slaughter them for our pleasure now? Who will stop the genocide?"

Jupe looked around to see what yummy food was available.

"Or maybe not. Maybe something else," he said.

"People celebrate in different ways," Jim said, "Did you know that in a small town in Spain, folks get into a massive tomato fight every August to celebrate the harvest. In Japan they have a penis festival. In one city in Spain…"

Jupe looked at Steve.

"Was salami that bad? Couldn't you just let it go?"

"… the men dress up like devils and jump on babies," Jim finished.

"Uh-oh," Jim pointed at the floor. He stopped talking and picked up a wallet that the other two missed.

"Hang on," he said, walking over to Customer Service.

Jupiter and Steve watched Jim go, smiling in spite of themselves. Jim was their paladin.

"We could use a celebration, Steven," Jupiter said to him when Jim was out of earshot. "Been a tough week. We deserve a victory lap. Loosen up. I know you're teasing. I've seen you gnaw down many a cheeseburger, but sometimes you might take it a bit too far. Jim doesn't always spot it, or feel like sparring."

"Maybe so, Jupe," Steve agreed, "I'll dial it back. Salami isn't that bad, as long as it's a free-range salami."

Jim returned, rubbing his hands together.

"I'm starving! Let's find some chow."

"Jupe and I agree: if you want a meat tray, we can do that," Steve said.

"Nope, guys, Steve's right. We should stick to veggies. Celebrations work best with veggies."

Sigh.

"May I help you?" the manager seemingly appeared out of nowhere.

"Save yourself. Run away," Jupe told him.

It didn't work. The man looked at Jupiter as if Jupiter had Tourette's Syndrome.

"I'm not throwing tomatoes at anybody," Steve said.

The man looked confused.

"That's good? Are you gentlemen looking for tomatoes? We have a wonderful organic selection over in produce."

He pointed.

"We're having a celebration," Steve said, "I was just explaining my limits. Man's gotta know his limitations."

"We all have limits I suppose," the manager said, reconsidering, "So a party tray then? Good choice. Today's delivery day. Apologies that the shelves aren't stocked. There's still a nice olive tray, though. We can do a custom one, of course. Is this some sort of cultural thing?"

"Got something that wizards and investigators both would serve?" Jim asked.

"Wizards? Like Harry Potter?"

"The show with the owls," Jupe offered.

"I'm not dressing up like a penis. I might could eat an owl though," Steve said. He then muttered something about free range.

"We don't have any owl dishes, at least prepared."

"The calorie density of olives are quite high," Jim said, He picked up a tray. "This is something that I think would work for anybody."

"That's a plastic demo tray, sir," the man said. He looked as if he'd just woken up in a maze with a giant Minotaur lurking nearby, "Ah! You're here! Thank goodness!"

A delivery man wheeled in a large selection of trays. It was salvation.

"We've got it from here,"Jupe told the manager, "Thank you. You can go. Please go. You should go."

The man did not seem happy. The man went. Jupiter couldn't help but notice that the man became happier the farther away he got.

Jim put the plastic demo back, unfazed. "There were three times in the Three Investigator books that they served snacks, the first one…"

"This one works," Jupiter said, picking up the top tray the man was bringing in, right off the hand-truck. "This work for you?"

They did not reply. This made him quite happy for some reason.

"It's settled, then. We'll have this."

Ten minutes later they were leaving the store, plastic bag swinging as they made their way to the van. Jim was already explaining his strategy for their client presentation to Deb and Sam. Steve was already complaining about having to do the "grunt work" of operating the flip chart.

In the back of the store, though, the delivery man left and went back to his truck. It was a warm day and a breeze had picked up.

The delivery truck started to leave. On the back was a picture of a basket of pickles. Around the edges of the basket were the corporate slogans "Happy Valley Pickle Company" and "We're the Pickle You'll Love to Stay in!"

The Three Investigators didn't notice it following them.

＃ 3.10

Boundaries

They never should have agreed to show these two the mansion, Jupiter realized as he sat in the driver's seat, studying the windshield, but once Jim mentioned it, they were quite interested. His hands were on the steering wheel, gripping it in impatience, waiting for Jim to come back. Sam had paid them, nobody else had, and Sam and Deb had simply wanted to drop by huge house, look around, and meet Mrs. McKenzie.

There was really no way he could say no. Was there?

Now here he was, looking at an ambulance and police car in her driveway.

"It was the cat," Jim told them, returning to the van, "She was outside putting out food for Mr. Cuddles when some kids jumped her."

Steve steamed, "Mrs. Cuddles."

"Back when all this started, I told you that all of this talk about pining for the fjords thing or joining the French Foreign Legion wasn't a good idea," he said, "Of course nobody listens."

They were all crammed inside the van parked outside the wrought iron fence surrounding Mrs. McKenzie's property. The light rain that had been off and on that week continued. The gate was open. Several first responder vehicles had pulled up to the house.

There was a very fancy and expensive sign that said "McKenzie Manor."

"Is she okay?" Deb asked.

"She's dead, not that we could be honest about it All of this 'abandoning the domicile' bit and hemming and hawing. Sneaking off in the backyard with a shovel. I knew all along this would end badly." Steve replied.

Sam leaned forward a bit. "What happened?" he asked, "How did it happen?"

"Hit by a car," Jim said, "Flat as a pancake."

"Why would somebody run over an old lady feeding her cat with a shovel? How big is this cat?" Deb said.

Jupiter stopped Steve before he could reply. He tried to explain.

"The cat, Mr. Cuddles. The cat was run over."

"That cat did not have a penis," Steve said, "Don't lie to the girl."

"Okay," Jupe said, "It may have been Mrs. Cuddles, but it was not Mrs. McKenzie. We don't know about Mrs. McKenzie."

"Yeah we do," Jim said, "They said that they're taking her to the hospital."

Sam frowned. "You know, for investigators, you three seem to have a hard time figuring things out."

"And for a romantic couple," Jupiter said, "you two don't seem to like one another very much."

Sam took Debian's hand and squeezed. She squeezed back. Both hands turned white as they tightened their grip.

"You guys buy this van all on your own?" Sam said, obviously trying to change the subject, "It's nice."

A piece of rust fell on his head.

Jupiter smiled slightly.

"Came with the junkyard, can you believe that?"

Then, seeing Sam flick the rust off, Jim shrugged, "Told Jupe I'd fix it up, change the oil and tune-up. He wouldn't let me."

"We don't need a van," Jupe was firm, "Bicycles are enough."

Steve would have none of it. "You know who got a van?"

"Shut up," Jupiter replied.

But Steve would not.

"They got a talking dog, a stoner dude, free cookies, a theme song, a cool paint job ..."

"I said shut up," Jupe said again.

Sam shuffled a bit. Trying not to be obvious, he spoke as he pried his hand from Debian, pointing to the front.

"Does the radio work?" Sam asked.

"Sure," Jupiter replied. He twisted the knob.

Nothing happened.

"NPR," Jupe said, pointing, as if that explained everything, "This week they're doing that documentary series on silent movies."

"You three want a dog?" Debian asked, "Doesn't talk, but I know where…"

Before she could continue, Jupe increased his volume, "We are NOT going to have any kind of dog in …"

"Jupiter," Jim patted his friend, "Enough."

The older man stopped, but he visibly fidgeted as he struggled to do so.

Looking at the EMTs carry out a stretcher, Debian said, "We've crossed some kind of ethical boundaries here, Samuel."

Sam looked to her. She stopped and returned his stare. Sam looked away empty.

"Maybe so."

Instead of Sam continuing, Jim answered, and to Jupiter, "We shouldn't be introducing these two to Mrs. McKenzie, not with their history."

It was now Jupiter who said nothing, instead staring away.

"Our history," Sam said, but nobody responded.

A policeman walked over with his flashlight. He gently tapped on the driver's side window.

Jupe rolled it down. "Good evening, officer."

"Can I ask why you're here?"

"We're investigators," Jupe puffed out his chest a bit, "The Three Investigators, actually, at your service."

The man backed up and took in the entire scene.

"Why are you parked here? Why do you have bicycles on your roof? In the rain?" he asked.

"Because they wouldn't fit inside the van, obviously." Jupe replied, "Here you go," and handed the man a card.

Jupiter smiled as if he'd just made an especially good chess move.

"Obviously."

The officer peeked in. He glanced at the business card Jupiter had given him.

"The Three Investigators. But there's five of you." he said.

"We're working for Mrs. McKenzie," Jupe continued.

"All five?"

"Yes sir."

"Investigating?"

"Perimeter re-organization and general security consultation," Jupe replied, then when that this didn't work, "Lawn work and helping out."

The policeman backed up again, scratched his ear, then tapped again on the van, this time on the door.

"Move it along," he said, "I don't want to see you here when I come back."

"Yes sir," Jupiter replied. Jupiter saluted the man.

The policeman took another beat, looking at them, puzzled, then glanced at the card again.

Shaking his head, he went back to Mrs. McKenzie's house.

Deb made a wrinkle with her nose. Five people stuck in a van in the rain for any length of time was not pleasant.

Jupe sighed, "Was Sherlock Holmes such a bad guy? I had choices once."

"What do you mean?" Debian asked.

"Never had problems with coppers." Jupe said, "It could have been a different life."

"What's wrong with you?" Jim butted in, "Does none of this mean anything?"

Jim looked around the smelly old van as if it had profound meaning for all of them.

Jupe's grip tightened on the wheel, but he didn't reply.

The light rain became heavy rain. The wind began gusting.

He finally spoke.

"Problem's the fence, the boundary," Jupiter Frostrike said. He was almost wistful, looking out the window at the finely wrought fence, "What we'll do. What we won't do. What we know. What we don't know. Socrates Attack."

"Excuse me?" for some reason Debian was now interested. She was the only one.

"It's about what each group has words for. They call it a Socrates Attack: Any threat to a species that cannot be written down in words is, by definition, an extinction level, existential threat to that species."

"Jupiter," Jim said, "I can't tell if you're making that up or not."

"Exactly," he replied, "And you don't need to. We have our own group of trust here, and when we define our groups we define what will destroy us."

As they tried to process that, the ambulance came through the gate and sped up the street away from them. The lights were not on.

Jupiter tried starting the van. It took several attempts, but it finally caught.

He didn't put it in gear, waiting for something, nobody knew what.

After a bit, Sam said, "I know, guys. What about this: We want to see the big house, and you guys are friends with this Mrs. McKenzie. So why don't we wait until all these cars leave, come back and look through the it. No point in bothering her. Or waiting until she gets back. If she gets back."

Steve said, "Yes!" while Debian said "No."

Sam looked at her.

"I've had some bad luck with that kind of thing in the past. Going into people's houses. Sam has too."

He waited. He thought for sure she was going to say something else.

Instead, she broke eye contact and went back to staring at nobody.

"That's a terrible idea," Jupiter said, "It's not something The Three Investigators would ever do. Ever."

Silence resumed as the van's engine kept struggling to stay alive.

"Well, okay," Sam said, "This is all kinds of fun, am I right? Who's up for some charades?"

Deb glared at him.

"Singing?" he tried.

"How about 'There's a hole in the bottom of the sea'," she said, spitting it out.

Sam hung his head.

Weirdo, Jupiter thought again. It made him struggle with his conscience. It was not right to think such a thing. She was just different. They all were.

"Get out," Jim nudged him, "I'm driving."

All out of juice, Jupiter simply complied. The men switched places in the front.

Jim put it in gear, pausing to make sure it wasn't going to die.

"Where are we going?" Jupiter asked.

Jim pointed to the scene in front of them.

"We can't stay here," he said, "We'll get arrested."

"Okay," Jupiter agreed, "then where to?"

Jim looked back and forth, slowly letting his foot off the brake.

"I don't know," he said, "Back to base."

"Can we get arrested there?" Steve asked, hopeful.

"Let's hope not," Debian replied.

"How long have you had this company?" Sam tried again.

"Many, many years," Jupiter said.

"About a month," Jim said.

It looked like Jupiter was going to go at them again. Instead he stuck his chin out. He assumed what Sam began thinking of as "the pose."

"By Grapthar's Hammer, we're going to need to sort this trust issue out, and I mean right now. We'll never get anything done if we don't."

Nobody replied.

The old van's engine completely stopped. Jim managed to get it mostly out of traffic, but not completely.

As the van completed its dying process, Jim struggling with the steering and then struggling to get it started, they remained in silence, each lost in thought.

Horns began honking, and the faint sound of people yelling profanities permeated their private space as other drivers had to find a way around them.

Jupiter began shuffling in his seat, not willing to stay and not willing to leave. Leaving would mean defeat.

Seeing him, Jim asked, "Can I fix it now? Please Jupe?"

"Can you make Steven shut up about those," he glared at Steve as he continued although Steve hadn't done anything, "Ghost-infested jejune delinquents insidiously butchering the entire genre and leaving it a flaming pile of dog poop in an empty alley of forlorn despair and disquisitive balderdash?"

Confusion.

Seeing nobody got it, Jupiter finally said it quickly, "No Scooby."

He pointed his thumb at Steve.

"No," Jim admitted, "I can't get him to shut up about anything, but I can try."

Grudgingly, Jupiter nodded. Steve, to his credit, remained silent.

When Jim finally got back in, Sam asked, "I don't understand. Why didn't you just fix the van when you first got it?"

"Ask him," Steve replied, obviously hurt, nodding towards Jupiter.

"There are rules." Jupe said.

"Don't you have to bend these rules sometimes?" Sam replied.

It must have been a sore subject, because there was no answer. Eventually Deb nudged him. He looked at her.

"How about us, Sam? Don't we have to bend our rules sometimes?"

Sam considered.

"Maybe it's time to lay more of our cards on the table. All of us."

Everybody agreed by doing or saying nothing. It had to happen.

"I propose, then, that we all talk about this first thing tomorrow," Sam said, "after breakfast. It's been a long day. This kind of thing needs a fresh start. We've got a lot to go over."

"All I'm saying,"Steve replied, "Is that Mr. Cuddles did not have a penis," as if announcing that a peace treaty had been signed between major powers.

"Except that one topic," Sam finished.

"65,536," Deb said.

"Excuse me?" Jupiter looked back.

"65,536 probabilistic node linkages around this house that are anomalous. It's a semantic desert. I know it."

They all frowned. Then they looked to Sam, the interpreter.

Sam smiled and nodded as if all of this had been pre-planned.

"Is she good with math or what?" He asked.

Nobody made eye contact. Nobody ventured forth any questions or conclusions. Nobody did anything all the way back to the junkyard.

Then they continued to do nothing, and were happy for it.

3.11

Dreaming

Jupiter laid in the dim, musty junkyard office staring at the ceiling.

He didn't have a home. He'd sold everything he owned to finance where they were today. He was never going to tell them.

The tabletop oscillating fan was useless without power, but it was cool enough. Eventually he drifted off to sleep.

He was standing besides his bed. Hadn't he got in already?

But it was *different*, somehow. Looking around his usually dim room, everything had a slight glow to it. He touched the nightstand. It was solid and it wasn't. As he pushed against it, it held up, but pushing forward allowed his hand to push into the wood.

He was taken back. That was different.

What else was different?

He hopped a little bit. Up he came a couple of inches off the ground and down he went, just like always, his weight shaking the little work shack that ran the place. But it was a little higher than normal, and he hadn't tried that much, so he jumped a little higher, only it wasn't just a little higher. He jumped through the ceiling and came back. He had seen the night sky, stars and all.

Was he some kind of ghost, floating in the astral plane?

Ok, he was either dreaming or he had ascended like Daniel Jackson in Stargate and either way he wasn't going to let this one pass him up. He jumped as hard as he could. His body shot up 20 or 30 feet into the air. He could see the entire junkyard.

Coming back down, he popped back through the roof and then, somehow, kind of bounced on and through the floor, returning to normal, like a weight on a spring.

If he could go through walls and the floor, how could he stand on anything? It was something that had bothered him since he'd read stories as a small boy. Going through walls is great, but wouldn't you just fall through the floor into the center of the Earth?

There was really only one answer that made any sense to him, and it was the answer the small child in The Matrix had given in the waiting room for The Oracle: there was no floor. These things existed because he could see them and his mind accepted them as reality.

There was only way to test this.

He jumped again, as high as he could. Once he reached his peak, he thought to himself: I'm just going to stay up here, floating and zooming as I wish.

It almost worked. He floated, just a bit, and his fall back to his dingy room was delayed and slowed, more and more, as he slowly got the hang of it. Once inside his room, he simply stopped thinking about what things were and where he wanted to go. In response, his body stayed on the floor. Things felt mostly normal. By not thinking about the floor, just accepting it as reality, it became reality.

It took him three or four tries, but eventually he worked it out where he could hang in the air, like a giant Jupiter Frostrike balloon, bobbing about. Then, after a bit more work, he could float around. After about an hour of this, he figured out how he could zoom around, just like Superman.

Well, this was the most amazing dream ever, even though he'd never been fond of Superman and always thought Batman could beat him. The Flash could beat him easily. But was it a super cool dream, or perhaps was it some kind of astral travel, the way DND characters with psionics do?

He decided to pop in on Steven, see if he could see him sleeping.

Slowly he floated up, he allowed himself to feel a wide area, then zoomed down to the house nearby where Steve lived. He felt bad about intruding in on his friend, but it might just be a dream, so it was okay.

There he was, lying on his right side, snoring softly, underneath his Chairman Mao and Che Guevera posters. He wasn't sure that proved anything, since it was pretty easy to imagine Steve sleeping. As he stood there watching, though, he noticed something he couldn't have imagined.

There was little bit of glowing light, some kind of fluid, leaking out from his friend's head. It was faint glowing blue. Was there a blacklight here? But no, it was dimmer than that. He gently poked at the small stream. It wasn't a fluid, any more than Jupiter was a person, yet it slowly, bit by bit dripped from Steven's head, down the bed, and onto the floor. As he began seeing it better, he saw it had formed a small stream flowing out the door.

He went out into the main area of their house. Now that he adjusted himself to see it, he could see other small streams, made by the other people living there. coming into a larger stream, flowing out into the street.

Was this everywhere?

He made himself jump out and hover over the house.

Each house on the block had similar glowing streams, all just like this, flowing out and joining into a small stream.

Was every house like this? Was he like this? Where was it all going?

Over the next hour or so, he really wasn't sure of time, he floated around his hometown. He found out that yes, every house with people dreaming had these streams coming out, joining into a small river flowing through then out of town.

It was like their dreams, their fantasies, their subconscious thoughts were coming together into some new thing.

Jupiter remembered reading somewhere that during the night, while you slept, your mind re-organized your mental linkages, strengthening some patterns and memories, letting others go.

If the mind kept some things, what happened to the others? You never remembered dreams, so what happened, then? Where did your unused thoughts, emotions, feelings, loves, fears, and the rest of you go when they no longer stayed with you?

You lived in your mind. We all do. So where does all of the other existence live?

He slowly followed the stream, needing to know where it all ended up. As he feared, it joined with other streams, other dreams and fears, and eventually became a mighty glowing dark river.

It joined a sea, or a lake, or something that was so enormous and profound his mind couldn't imagine it, even in a dream.

He stood on a rocky shore under a starlit darkness and watched as the pieces of everything around him, everything that existed and had thoughts, flowed into this Jungian metaphysical void of shared existence.

Then he saw the rowboat.

Did he want to get in and take flight on this endless void? He did not. Couldn't he just fly over it? He didn't know. He didn't want to think about it. He wanted to go back home, right then, right now, right away.

And yet.

And yet.

And yet he felt there was something here he wanted to see. Maybe it was something he was supposed to see. Maybe something called him.

He walked, old-fashioned walking, to the edge.

He remembered as a boy going with his father to the bait shop. His dad fancied himself as a fisherman and every week they'd go to the bait shop on their way out. It always had a pier where the customers would feed the fish, and there were always the most interesting fish to see. Some would come right out of the water begging for snacks. Dozens of big fish with their gaping mouths open sticking out of the water.

He peered down into the shallows. What fish swam these depths? What creatures waited, hungry, eager to come out? Eager to be fed?

He thought he saw movement in the dark water, and that was enough for him. He jumped and zoomed all the way back to his junkyard and his safety.

The night had felt beautiful at first. Natural, like a mother's womb. Now it felt like a dark abyss teaming with unseen life that he had no truck with. He was the monster here. He was the cancer, the simple single-celled organism that for some horrific trick of science had grown and grown, eventually getting large enough for the body to attack, to cut out.

He had to hide. Right now.

He floated over his shack. His mind held only one thought: how can I never ever have this kind of dream again?

That's when he saw his first glowing man. He had no other words for it. There, just outside the gate, a man was walking towards town. At least it might be a man. It was like a human, it seemed to walk or float.

It was made out of whatever dreams and fears that came from the townsfolk.

No. Fuck that.

He willed himself go back in. He went inside that room and stood by his sleeping body.

He did not wake up. Over the next bit, he simply faded into nothingness, all the while staring at himself and his own life.

When he awoke the next day, it was gone. He was left with only a dim memory of dreaming about a glowing man, about going fishing with his dad. Soon, that also faded off into nothingness, nowhere.

And yet.

Closing The Case

The power had come back on. A bare, old-timey incandescent bulb lit the room. An extension cord snaked out the window.

"We've been working on our own, and we've got answers for you," Jupe told them the next morning, "You're not going to like them. Steve: flip chart."

Steve grumbled but said nothing, instead bringing a flip chart into the kitchen where they all could participate. Jupiter had teased Steven about being a "version zero slide projector," but he wasn't sure the words meant anything to the boy.

He took the stage, gestured. Steve flipped the first page. There was a crude drawing of a giraffe wearing a hat.

"Is that your logo?" Deb asked.

"We didn't have any markers," Steve explained, "So we're just using what somebody left on here."

Jupiter gestured to the line-drawn giraffe.

"EigenCorp is not owned by Joe Middles."

Steve flipped it again. There was a bunch of squiggles. Stick men stood around looking at them.

"But we were there," Sam said, " I saw it. He was the CEO."

"Sure, he is the 'de facto' CEO," Jim made air quotes but managed not to upstage Jupiter. "But there's a series of shell companies. It certainly looks privately-held and he's the guy, but nope, only a puppet."

"So who owns EigenCorp?" Sam asked, "We never saw anybody else."

"Initially, the McKenzie Foundation was a major investor," Jupiter said, "but then they bought Middles out. The trail doesn't end there, however. Middles has a perfect record, spotless. Too perfect. McKenzie Foundation is also a front, but never fear; fellow countrymen. We've ascertained who's behind it all. We've also got some ideas about follow-up work if you'd like."

"They're not criminals," Deb said, "Please continue."

"Oh, I suspect just the opposite," Jupe said, "they are incapable of crime. They are beyond it."

Deb frowned.

Steve flipped the chart again. The next page had a sun setting over mountains and a stream. It was drawn in crayon.

"It's the Defense Department," Jim said, "Can we tell them it's the Defense Department? Is that okay now? The intelligence apparatus? Five Eyes? That's it."

"Just did, jackass," Steve said, "way to kill the suspense."

Before he could call Steve out, Deb said, "I thought you said it was this McKenzie thing. The McKenzie Foundation. I thought that was the key part."

She picked up an old shoebox and started thumbing through it.

"It may have been originally, may still be, but McKenzie is completely owned by various intelligence organizations, DoD, DARPA." Jupiter said, "Good news, though, we happen to know the executor of the McKenzie Foundation. Know her very well, in fact. You've even been to the mansion."

"We don't know anybody," Steve said. He thought for a minute. "McKenzie? Mrs. McKenzie?"

"Exactly right," Jim said. Jim looked around the room as if he had just won the lottery. "Used to go by Willows, Crystal Willows. In fact it's not much of a pseudonym since her real last name is on…"

"I'll be damned," Sam said, standing, "So EigenCorp is clean? Pops was right all along?"

"Squeaky, at least as far as you care," Jupiter agreed, "Unless you want us to start chasing theories that the DoD and some nice old lady are actually cahooting. I doubt it. It's a funding pipe. That's it."

"They're clean," Sam said again, mostly to himself, "How does that make sense. We can't start investigating the U.S. intelligence apparatus. That's it. We're done."

"That's exactly what we're going to do," Deb said.

Everybody looked at her. She continued looking in the shoebox.

"Next steps. Instead of just meeting her and going through McKenzie Manor, we're going to investigate this lady, We need to demand the truth from her."

Sam looked at her.

"But why, Debian? This is it. We're not part of anything. We're nobodys. Found the money. Found the people behind the money. We can show people. We're cool. No crime."

Deb held up the shoe box. She pointed to it as if explaining trivial things.

"Clue. Here is a clue for you."

"What's this?" He asked.

"The detritus of a lost life serving the oppressor," Steve said, looking at the shoebox, "Probably not even recycled cardboard."

He flipped the page and there was a huge smiley face. The ears were far too big.

"It was one of several boxes Mrs. McKenzie gave us when we helped clean up her yard. That's hers. That's the lady we've been talking about." Jim said.

"The Executioner," Steven concluded, "But no cahooting. Just the one hooter."

"Mrs. McKenzie much of an oppressor?" Sam asked.

"Mrs. McKenzie is a very nice lady that I've known for most of my life," Jupiter said, "She's our neighbor. We try to help her when we can. As we should."

"Oppressor." Deb asked the room, "Executor. She somehow ended up an executor. This average person."

Jupiter leaned over to look in the box.

"Perhaps her husband was in some kind of DoD think tank or something," Jupiter continued, "I imagine that's how she ended up being executor. She'd love to talk to us. She's no criminal, I know that, as long as we're nice to her, we can certainly talk to her."

Steve grabbed the box.

"Lemme see that. There are probably plans in here to wipe out the planet with smallpox or something. Maybe there's a Nazi Smurf collection. Could be aliens in there, like Area 51."

He looked around the room for support.

"They'd have to be very tiny, of course," He looked deeper.

"We don't do aliens, remember?" Jim said, then, peeking some more, "Incompetent. This looks like a bunch of drawings."

"Don't you have a flipchart to flip?" Jupiter elbowed his way past Steve and took back the box.

"Not a bad horse," Sam said, looking at the first paper Jim picked up. "And that's a reasonable unicorn."

Steve flipped the chart again. Nobody paid any attention.

"It's sketches. It's a sketch collection." Deb said. "That's what I was talking about. That's your clue."

"Clue," she said holding the box out to Jupe and Jim.

Debian looked like somebody suffering under an extremely long and boring courtroom drama.

Jupiter nodded. Jim continued going through the drawings.

"Wait a minute," Sam said, "What's that one?"

Underneath the unicorn, in black-and-white pencil, was a god with two heads, each facing a different direction.

Janus.

Sam looked to Deb in surprise.

"We're going to need to talk to Mrs. McKenzie," Deb said, "We're going to need answers from Mrs. McKenzie."

"Just to be clear, the beat-up lady in the hospital: our friend." Jim said.

"Hold up. Background investigating using these guys is one thing," Sam said, "Debian, but this is another thing entirely. We're not going to go on some fishing expedition with a 70-year-old lady living by herself. You have specific questions? Fine. But remember that we're the good guys."

"She'll talk your ear off," Jupe said, "But Sam's right. Absolutely no sketchy third-degree nonsense. We don't even know if they're her drawings. Even if they are, god knows how many years ago they were sketched. There's a sketch of a cow in there, for goodness sakes. Could have been she had a kid, or ran a daycare, The house is huge."

They all looked at Sam. Sam looked at Deb.

"This is the first Janus thing I've seen, okay? There's also a unicorn. There was a pig. Looked like a pretty good Zeus. We need to stay focused. We wanted something, we got it."

"I could begin another file," Jim said, "We could start a new case. That might be fun."

"No," Jupiter said, "We need to finish one thing before we start another. Otherwise how would it work in the new book? These are episodic, for the love of Pete, not a serial. We're in the home stretch, fellow investigators! We just completed our first client presentation. Steady on, men."

They heard Steve flip the chart again.

"You have nothing," Deb said, "Fine. You do whatever you want,

Samuel. I am going to go talk to this Mrs. McKenzie whether the rest of you want to go or not."

"She's sweet," Jupe protested, "She bakes us cookies. She'll love talking to us, but if we don't keep this light and friendly," he stared at Deb again, "it could traumatize her, that's all. We need to do the talking. If you have questions, you tell us."

"I don't understand why all the fighting," Jim said, "Why don't I go to the library, visit Mrs. McKenzie in the hospital, find out whatever you want. We'll need it for our case file anyway."

"Case file," Sam looked at Deb, "They need to write it down."

Jim seemed confused, "How else could we write up the book and publish it?"

"Then it's settled. We're going," Steve said.

To Jupiter, it looked as if Samuel and Debian wanted to continue fighting, or to argue with the gang, but instead they went suddenly quiet.

Jupiter, Jim, and Steve spent the next hour discussing what exact requirements were needed for the clothes they wore for their next mission. Jupiter argued that they should stick to a classic 60s motif like the gang did in the books. Steve thought just the opposite; it was only by bringing it as modern as possible that they could bring life to the gang. Jim reminded them that if they stayed as classic as possible, it would preclude most modern blended fabrics.

"Maybe we should ask our guests," Jim said.

They looked at the couple. Deb and Sam had spent their time organizing some of the boxes. Deb had tried to hang a picture but when she started the nail plaster started falling from the ceiling. Sam was wearing the same clothes he came in. Deb was wearing a green and orange ensemble with a white belt. She stopped sorting.

"Clothes? Like my advice?"

"No," they all said at once, including Sam.

Nobody saw the charcoal sketch of the god Janus that Steve had flipped through while they were distracted, at least not right away.

3.13

Visiting The Sick

Deb noticed the sketch, though. She wouldn't let them leave without searching all the boxes. Even then, she stopped them in the junkyard before they got in the van.

"Questions," she said, looking at Sam, "Ask questions. You deserve answers."

Finally, Jupiter thought, it's about time.

"Why the band-aids?"

"Fools facial recognition."

"But the clothes?"

Deb looked down. She had changed into a bow-tie, black, green shirt, button-up, and brown/tan checkered pants.

"Yes. They're clothes."

"I lost my family. Everything I owned. I am sad," as if that explained her wardrobe.

Now Jim and Steve turned to stare at Deb.

"I have to admit," Sam said, "Janus keeps popping up in places. If you guys remember the attack in the islands a while back, that might have been them?"

Sam said it as if he was just now thinking it for the first time. He frowned.

"My sister is dead," Deb said, "My brother is missing. My father is involved."

"So you see, guys," Sam said, "There's a lot going on here."

He shot a glance at Deb, meaning a lot going on here with Deb.

"We've been trying to limit your exposure. This could be dangerous business," he continued.

Deb remained quiet. Jupiter spoke.

"I'm very sorry for you, Debian," he said, "but all we have is a couple of sketches. They're just drawings. The EigenCorp information comes up clean. Frankly, this Janus thing of yours looks like vapor, imagination."

"This is the exact center of a Janus Group semantic desert," she said, "I don't see how I could be any clearer than that."

Jupe looked at Sam. Sam's eyes were fixed on Deb. He did not move.

"I don't know what that means, but I know Mrs. McKenzie isn't responsible," Jupiter said.

"Be careful exactly what you say, Debian," Sam finally said, "because this will be on us if things go wrong again."

"Mr. McKenzie would have been about the right age to have worked with my father before I was born, perhaps as a supervisor."

"Saw a lot of military stuff in the house, in the attic," Steve added, "I thought maybe her husband was a gun nut or one of them militia dudes. Probably a right-wing terrorist."

"Remember the mailbox? The house number? This house number was mentioned in my father's papers."

"This street address? And house number?" Jim asked.

Deb faltered.

"I am unsure of the street name. I have difficulties with names. I am good with math."

She cut a glance to Sam who said nothing.

"It might be time to expose this charade for what it really is," Jupiter said, grabbing lapels that his shirt did not currently possess.

"This may be a bad time," Jim said.

"Nail 'em, Jupe!" Steve said.

"We know things too. In our research we have found things we initially weren't going to bring up," Jupiter continued, "on you two. We were afraid this was going to be another 'Mummy's Curse' scenario"

"Mummy's Curse," Sam repeated.

Jim perked up.

"That's where the Three Investigators were actually hired by the criminals who wanted to scare away potential investors so that they could set up an amusement park. It was especially interesting because it was the first book…"

"Shut up," Steve said. He nodded to Jupiter. "Tell 'em."

"Tell us what?"

"Well, we know that Ms. Newbury here was involved in an arson investigation recently in her hometown. We also know she was involved in a federal investigation of a mass murder. A B&E. Tragic, really."

"Yeah," Sam said, "but we're not charged with anything. We already told you that. Nobody's looking to arrest us."

"Harummph," Jupe said, overriding Sam. "We also know that Eigen-Corp was just last week raided by the Secret Service."

"I thought you said they were clean?"

"They are. We believe they raided it because of you two," Jupe continued, "You did not tell us that you were wanted for questioning in a murder," Jupiter said. He pulled out a small notebook. "At EigenCorp. A Mr. McCulloch."

"Told you," Deb said simply.

Sam unconsciously fiddled with the duck in his pocket. He said nothing.

"You two," Jupiter said, "have been the criminals all along! Ha-HA!"

"Yeah!" Steve said.

Sam furrowed his brow.

"How does that work? We're the criminals and we're asking you to investigate us? This is your theory simply because some official people want to talk to us? Some curse?"

"Mummy's Curse," Steve pointed at Sam and Deb, victorious. "I knew it! Told you!"

"It does not work," Deb said. "This is more stupid. I wanted bottom of the barrel. These three are not in the barrel."

She pointed at them.

"You are outside the barrel."

Jim took her in, not impressed.

"You have hired us to investigate these imaginary mob ties to your old company and past so that we can alibi you out. That was the plan all along," He said, "but we figured you out."

Jim smiled at the word "alibi."

"You're an idiot," Deb said. She looked to Sam. "He's an idiot."

They all stopped and stared.

"There is a Janus group," she said, "my father worked for it. I know it for a fact."

Sam sighed.

"There are criminal connections in EigenCorp, all though it, actually.

Sam knows that. Sam and I were lucky to get out of there alive. You just couldn't find them. You are bad."

"If there are, it's the government committing the crimes," Jupiter said.

"Maybe dial it back a bit," Sam said to Debian. "These guys are a bit new to the kind of drama you bring to things."

She stomped her foot. She made fists by her sides.

"And you. You … fuckwads … are the worst private investigators ever! Which is exactly why we hired you. You want to know? You're so bad that no reasonable person would ever suspect you're actually investigating anything at all in the real world! That's why we needed you!"

"Or not," Sam said. "We could also not dial it back, see how that works. I'm voting for dial it back."

He raised his hand, looked around.

"We have been trying to keep you off the grid and engaged as much as possible without putting you in danger," she continued, "not that this has worked at all. It's been like feeding fish to an ocelot, knarding a shrawl without a beeflax, or trying to find prime numbers by simply counting."

"Ocelot?" Steve said, "Is that like an owl?"

"Look folks," Sam said, "instead of having it out here in the yard like a bunch of punks, can we take this somewhere else?"

"So that's why we never got the WiFi set up?!? That's why you never wanted it?" Steve asked.

Sam nodded.

"We wanted to be nowhere public. Nowhere noticed."

Jupe nodded, rubbing his chin, as if he had expected this all along.

"Of course! I expected this all along! I thought they were just being eccentric. It was the WiFi. WiFi really doesn't match our milieu. That gave it away. I've been saying that all along. I was right. Told you."

"You fucker," Steve said, "you piece of shit. We're not getting a milieu, not if we can't even get 3D helmet cams."

"Can we at least get an ocelot?" Jim asked, "Nobody else has an ocelot. Maybe Barnaby Jones."

"Or not," Sam said. He lowered his hand.

"Dialing it back might not work," Sam became interested in the fence. Sam was a man in a POW camp yearning to break out, knowing they'd gun him down before he got far. Still dreaming.

"So you think that these connections are real," Jupiter said.

Deb nodded.

"But to find them, we can't let on in any kind of online way what we're up to. We were used as stalking horses, to get online and go out in the world in your place."

She nodded again.

"The causality linkages may be too much for your small minds to figure out," she said, "But anything you found out would have helped us without us making so much noise."

Sam looked down while slowly shaking his head.

Steven's face turned red.

"What! You mean that the one major case we finally have and we can't even tell anybody about it?"

Sam looked up, frowned.

"Not unless you want to end up like all of those other people we've been telling you about."

"Dead," Deb said.

"Yeah, I got that part," Jupiter said, "We are really going to need to work on our communications skills."

He made a gesture back and forth between the two groups.

Jim's eyebrows went up.

"So we're not going to call the cops? I thought this was going to end with the cops showing up. I'd already started on an ending."

Jupe shook his head no.

"And we're not going to get into a chase? Fistfight, maybe?"

No.

"Cross-country adventure? Hot air balloons?"

No.

"Now what?"

Jupiter began, but it was Debian that replied.

"Now we start investigating Mrs. McKenzie, like I said. Janus is important. It's not just me."

Deb glared at Sam, dared him, then returned to the three in front of her.

"In a nice way," she added. "We should always be nice. To older people."

There was silence. Jupiter finally cleared his throat.

Still no one talked.

"I am nice," she looked back and forth to all of them.

They appeared in shock, but Jim was keeping up with the latest news. He nodded. He was the sage. He knew all along.

"You guys go on," Sam said, "I'm not going. I'll stay here. I need some time."

He simply sat where he was. He put his head in his hands.

• • •

The hospital was slow for this time of day and its size. Debian announced that she had calculated this based on the square footage and population density. It should have been roughly 14% busier than it was. There must have been a missing variable somewhere. Perhaps a thousand variables.

She'd barely got out of that junkyard without hitting Samuel. He was getting to know too much, getting too close. She was immensely glad he hadn't come along.

The old lady struggled in her hospital bed, just released from ICU. Somebody had found her a good gown, helped her with her hair.

"What do you know about the Janus Group," Debian asked, standing in the doorway.

"Excuse me," Jupiter had slipped around her, "Mrs. McKenzie, how are you doing? Sounds like you've had quite the adventure."

Jupiter glared at her. Perhaps he was angry about something?

"Oh my!" she said, She instantly perked up. "It's my favorite investigators!"

Jim and Steve also filtered past her as she stood there.

They chatted idly about various topics Deb found unimportant. She came into the room a bit. Most people were like chickens, pecking around a barnyard. Four-hundred seventeen words of tripe. She began a five minute timer in her head. As she reached the 4:19 mark, she realized they were all staring at her.

"Mrs. McKenzie, this is Debian Newbury," Jupiter said, "Deb's one of our very first clients."

Deb nodded, looking back and forth. Was a nod expected? Is there some sort of dance she should perform? What did chickens do? She nodded quickly, bobbing four times. Pecking. Then she went back to staring out the window.

"Deb, you want to ask her about the sketch you saw? In the box there? That you're carrying?"

She pulled out some papers, pointed one of them at this McKenzie character.

"What do you know about Janus Group?" She stuck the sketch out for them. Again they made her say it. These people were slow.

The sketch showed Janus.

"That's just one of my sketches, sweetie," she said, "I also do a very nice walrus if you turn to the back."

"I think this is about the McKenzie Foundation," Steve said. Steve bounced from foot-to-foot. "Were you one of the, er, secret overlords? Puppet masters? An executioner?"

"Oh that, pshaw! Overlords! Goodness gracious. McKenzie Group? That old thing? It was a trust executor job that I picked up a long, long time ago, way back when I ran the real-estate agency."

"Can I keep this?"

The gang looked at her in horror, but Mrs. McKenzie smiled.

"Why of course, dear. Which leads me to something I need to tell you boys," she patted Jim's hand on her bed, "I'm not going to be around much longer. Going to have to prepare."

"What do you mean?" Jim said, "are you sick? Is there anything we can do? Do we need to call a doctor?"

He looked around in desperation.

"Should we help find missing relatives?" Jupe asked, stepping up to hold her hand.

"Nothing like that! Heavens no! I'm just making a change in life, moving to a retirement facility. That's all. That big old house was too much for me anyhow. You all know that."

"Need help moving? We can help moving." Jim seemed much happier.

"Why I do, but first I need help sorting! Who among you big, strong men are going to go through my house and take all of that junk to the thrifters?"

She patted Jupiter on the arm.

"I will," Deb said immediately.

This seemed to shock the old lady though Deb had no idea why she would care. She needed help and Deb was offering it. In the last year alone, there had been 17 times …

"We can do that," Jupiter said. He looked back at Deb. "Maybe her. Deb, would you like to come along? Perhaps you have more work for us? Would that be okay, Mrs. McKenzie?"

Debian looked at him.

"Just the normal work. Like we discussed. Back when we started."

She held the picture up for the room to see. Again.

"Mr. Featherstone said that our work was over. We were paid this morning. So this is a new engagement?" Jim asked.

"A what? Sam said the work was over?" She was surprised.

"Ya," Jim said, "Sam's packing up to leave. I thought he told you."

"He was trying to be nice," Jupe said.

She did not ask the old lady any more questions. She gave Jupiter all the money in her pocket on the way out, sketches and box firmly under her arm.

She hitched a ride back to the junkyard.

3.14

Chickening Out

"What in the living hell are you doing?"

She found Sam at the end of the escape tunnel, two of the black backpacks stacked by his feet.

"And that's my backpack."

"Leaving, that's what," he said. He patted the file under his arm that the Investigators had given them. "We know we're innocent of the murders. We did nothing. Maybe assault, that's it. Pops did nothing. We're just rubes, just like these guys. We're the real dummies, not these three. We're done here. I'm taking this to the press, taking it online. I'm out."

"But what about Janus Group? What about Pops, his legacy? What would he want us to do? What about what happened at work?"

"Not my problem. Not your problem, for that matter. And don't you even get started on Pops. That's going to have to be good enough. Let it go, Debian."

Her hand balled into a fist. She gripped it tight enough to make her knuckles white.

He pointed at one of the packs.

"Left you something."

He backed up, smiling.

"Guess what I did while you were gone. Got a present for you. You'll never guess. Guess."

"If I can never guess, I will not. Probably some sort of thing where you go to the bathroom and drop playing cards, then curse at yourself."

He ignored her.

"I went on a little field trip to Mrs. McKenzie's house. The trip that nobody could agree on. I figured what nobody knew wouldn't hurt them."

"You broke into a nice old lady's house."

"Oh knock it off, Debian. You'd do the same. And for the record, I went into an unlocked house to make sure it was secure while the owner was in the hospital. I fed the cat, okay? Didn't know how much time I had. Timed myself to 30 minutes. Found that in the basement."

He pointed to the backpack again.

"In the pack?" She asked.

"It gets even better. Here's your get-out-of-jail free card."

He bent over, unzipped it, pulled out a large blob.

It was an Insert.

She knelt down to inspect it.

"Sam, this is slightly different from the ones we saw. Rougher. This may be an earlier model. It's even got production stamps on it. Numbers, Sam. Trackable numbers."

"Might be an earlier model. Don't know. Don't care. Once again, not our problem. Let the cops sort it."

She almost punched him before she caught herself. Somehow he had anticipated it and backed away.

"Whoa! Noob! You might have a live load of charged supercapacitors in there somewhere. Cool down!"

She backed off, but still stared alternatively between the pack and Sam.

"It's because of the things I see."

He rolled his eyes. He looked at the clouds. He made the hurry-up gesture.

"Like we talked about. At work. Sure."

She shook her head yes, afraid to say anything. Then she shook her head no, fearful.

"They make you hurt people, right? You see things, hear voices, then want to hurt people. Yadda yadda. There's drugs for that."

She glared.

"Look, you don't want to talk, fine by me," Sam said.

"What is wrong with you? No, they don't make me hurt people. I don't hurt people. I'm not crazy."

He gave her an "if you say so" look. She didn't know a lot of looks, but she knew that one. Too well.

"You have to understand, Sam. I've been under attack since around the time my mother left. Since I was a child."

"Under attack." It was a question.

"Under attack. I've learned to be peaceful about it. A truce. I'm just defending myself."

"You're defending yourself against me, some red-haired beanpole guy with an awesome smile and engaging personality?"

Her fists started clenching again. She took deep breaths.

"It's the duh…"

She beat herself several times on her legs with both clenched fists, a tiny kid trying to gain self-control. To his credit, Sam said nothing.

She'd never felt this way. The more she tried to speak, the more she couldn't. She felt like she was literally going to explode if she continued.

But she had to.

Finally he made a tiny step towards her. He lightly touched her upper arm.

"Hey. I've got an idea. I think I've got just the thing for you."

She lunged, but caught herself. He leaned away, expecting another attack, but did not step away.

Once she had slowed for a few more breaths, he reached inside his loose jacket.

"Here's a small rubber chicken."

She began to respond, but he stopped her.

"It's a chicken, not a duck," he said, "Chickens are our friends."

He handed it to her.

"That's your trick. Handing me a chicken. You hand me a chicken. That's your brilliant idea. That was the worst trick ever, Sam."

"This is something I learned In therapy. Yes, I've been in therapy. It's the idea, not the chicken. Just listen and learn."

She looked at the chicken.

"Look at the chicken. Squeeze the chicken. Think of nothing but the chicken."

She started to interrupt but he wouldn't let her. Morons.

"Only say one word at a time. Don't think of the entire sentence. If stressed, squeeze the chicken. If that doesn't work, take ten deep square breaths. If that doesn't work, cycle through again. Take all the time you need. Do you know how to square breathe?"

She nodded.

"They."

Squeeze squeeze squeeze.

"Are."

More squeezes. a round of breathing
"Coming."
She went through the cycle three times.
"They? What's coming, Deb? Who's 'they'"
"Duh…."
More stress. More stress. Sam waited. He looked concerned.
"Darklings."
Rubber chicken firmly in hand, she punched Sam as hard as she could right in the face.

3.15

Finding A Rat

The old conversion van struggled into the junkyard, backfiring bangs giving them a ten-minute lead.

Deb watched as Jim jumped out of the passenger side.

"We've done it! Woohoo!"

Still looking at the van, but speaking to Sam, "I gave them all of my money."

Jupiter gathered them in front of the van. He had out that pipe of his and was chewing on it. Deb had never seen him light it.

"Thank you for the money," Jupiter said.

Maybe it blew bubbles.

Odd people.

"We have, indeed, my fellow investigators!"

Sam and Jim high-fived.

"Yeah, just wait until those Nancy Drew guys get a load of what we've been up to," Jim said.

Sam rubbed the new bruise on his cheek.

"Debian and I have something. One more job. Nothing big. Just a day, maybe two. Maybe it's only a few hours."

"We need to continue looking through Mrs. McKenzie's possessions," she said, "somehow we've been compromised."

She grabbed something, the thing, in her pocket and gently squeezed it.

"Maybe Mrs. McKenzie wasn't just attacked for no reason," Sam explained, "Maybe they were looking to rob it, or get something out of her, that's all."

"It was us," she said, "This all happened because you took us as clients."

"The new job is important," Sam added, "to both of us. It has to do with a guy named Pops. Don't ask."

"How could anybody really know anything about you guys?" Jim asked.

"Yeah, you've forbidden us actually doing our job, creating our new content," Steve said, "That's what you wanted. It's typical imperial over-reach, if you ask me. The invisible masses are always trampled on …"

"So this is the extra work we were talking about at the hospital," Jupiter said, "with the house."

"Kinda," Sam said, "What did you talk about?"

"Yes," Deb said.

She looked at them. Nobody seemed to be moving. They always seemed like statues. People were so slow. It was painful.

"Sam found. A thing," She started.

"Don't go there," Sam said and shut her down.

"You found a thing and now you want us to help you go through Mrs. McKenzie's possessions." Jupe said, "that's not sketchy at all."

"Mrs. McKenzie has already given us permission," she said, "Technically."

"Us," Jupiter replied, point to the other two investigators, "not you two."

"What?" Sam asked, "Spring cleaning or something? If we're cleaning, things gotta go, right?"

"Sam," Jupiter said, "are you happy with the job we've done?"

"I am. You know that."

"And would you write us a recommendation for our next clients, provide an online review?"

"I would."

"Then we're done."

"You and me both, brother. That's what I thought," Sam agreed, "Welcome to two hours ago."

"I'm going to Mrs. McKenzie's as I promised her to help clean," Deb said, "Sam, are you coming with or not?"

"We didn't say that, not like that. I don't want you going there without us. It's not right." Jupe said.

She started walking. Behind her she heard Jim.

"Packed up already, Sam? Leaving right away?"

"Doesn't look like it, does it."

• • •

The house looked bad. Smelled bad. Sam came in directly behind Deb. The group spent a few hours in the yard cleaning up first. Fairly soon, though, they found their way into the attic where she and Sam had set up shop, boxes scattered about.

Jim muttered something about "server logs" and left the other two, going back down the steps and continuing his muttering.

After all the commotion that day and summer heat, Sam found it hard to concentrate. He said he was "meditating" for a bit and propped himself up against a support beam, eyes closed.

"So now we gotta dig though those papers?" Steve asked.

Deb nodded.

"Working with papers constantly, wooden papers! With printing! It's like it's 2020 up in here!"

Jupiter stepped closer, looked at what they found.

"Steve has a point," he said, "while certainly analyzing some data is part of the detective's work, we're made to be out in the field! Interviewing people! Finding clues!"

He shrugged, "Ok. We should clean up, then go do some of that, our calling. Our true calling."

"We've already started. There's only two boxes Sam and I care about," she pointed, "That should help. This looks like a bunch of memorabilia around some place called BCI and it's in a handwriting style that does not match up to the others."

"Mrs. McKenzie? Her husband? Your father?"

"Maybe. Looks very ornate and feminine, though."

"You guys see this?" They heard Jim before they saw him, climbing slowly down the stairs holding a big sheaf of papers in one hand and something furry in the other.

"That's a cat," Deb said.

"She went to school," Sam added, briefly opening his eyes, "does math and everything."

"This. This is Mr. Cuddles," Jim said.

Steve and Jupiter looked at one another like Jim had discovered dynamite instead of a tabby.

"Yep," Sam said, "I fed him."

"Check that cat for a penis!" Steve jumped up, yelled, and pointed.

She looked at Steven, "You really seem obsessed with cat penises."

Jim held the papers out.

"Ran some reports while I was upstairs. I ran with your idea of somehow it getting out that you were involved with us," Jim said.

Sam started back to sleep again.

Deb kicked him.

He yawned, unimpressed, but he didn't close his eyes again.

Deb nodded. "What's the bad news?"

"As you know," Jim said to the other two investigators, "I keep several alerts on my searches for anything involving The Three Investigators."

Jupiter interrupted, "It's part of our media strategy. We've agreed that eventually we want to go to full time streaming…"

Deb glared at him.

"And celebrity endorsements."

Jupiter stopped talking.

"Well, that's just it," Jim said, "Somebody has been recording everything we're doing and already streaming it online. We're already streaming."

"WHAT?" Sam was now fully awake.

"Not live streaming," Jim blushed. "More like recording what we're doing and then posting it the next day."

Steve's phone dinged.

"But we're not," Deb sat forward, "When did this begin?"

"Best I can tell, couple days ago," Jim replied

"Give me those logs," She said, taking the sheets.

Sam leaned over the papers.

"Yup, that's BitTorrent," he said, "Wow. Old school."

She nodded, still scanning.

"I know some of these IP addresses," she said, "This one is a reverse proxy on a Chinese NGO. This one is NSA. That one is Amnesty International. Here's NCRO."

"How does she know that" Jim asked.

Sam shrugged. "School. Does math."

"This one is actually a German communications satellite…"

"Who's hosting the torrent?" Sam asked.

"Let me see," she said, thumbing through the papers. "That would be."

She mumbled something to herself, then she looked up.

"Him," she said, pointing at Steve, "That's where it starts."

Steve held his hands out, palms forward. He backed up.

"We have to stand for something, guys!" he said, "I think we might be on to something important. Folks need to know what's going on!"

"You were right" Deb said, "This was a bad idea, Sam."

Steve continued.

"Yes," he said, "Starting a while back, I decided to record what we were doing. But I didn't share it with anybody. It's locked up."

Jim looked at the papers.

"That's not what the logs show."

"Interesting" Jupiter said. He got that dumb paper back out.

Deb went back to the server logs in her lap.

"Wonder if there are any poison sites," she said, "Wonder if there's anybody who doesn't want this shared."

Steve continued.

"I did not betray us," he said, "I only wanted to set up the recording so that it would be ready once we wrap the case up. It's important to record these things. This is our moment, guys."

"You didn't share it," Jupiter said, "Yet here are all of these…downloaders. People taking our work."

"407," Jim said.

"407 downloaders," Jupiter repeated. He rubbed his chin. "What gear did you use? You have one of those 3D cams?"

"Just this. Just the phone. This one," Steve said, patting his cell phone. "It doesn't even have a good connection. You know that. I couldn't have shared that much."

He stuck the phone out in front of him.

"It's locked up." he said again.

"Sure doesn't look that way," Jim said, "I looked at those logs. There's a ton of servers, all starting with you, and you don't even have a good connection. The only reason I spotted it is that you named it 'The Three Investigators and the Villainous Village'."

They all looked at Steve.

"Well, I wanted to remember what it was. It was catchy."

"Steven, That's enough. You're out of line," Jupiter told him, "That's it. I can't do this."

Before Steve could reply, Jim said "Jupe's right, he made a T-shape with his hands,"Time out, guys. This entire thing is getting much more stressful than I wanted, and now I don't know whether to trust anything Steve says or not."

Jupiter shut Steve down again before he could start, "Steven, James and I are going to take some time. Stay here, oversee what they're doing, leave, whatever you want. Frankly I don't want to know. This is not working out. Not like I wanted. We agreed to a media strategy and now even that agreement isn't enough for you. Nothing. Nothing is working."

He shook his head. He started to say something else, shook his head again, and left.

She watched Jim and Jupiter leave, Jim taking the logs and their reports, the case file he'd made with all his research. She expected more arguing, but Steve was strangely silent. She looked back at Sam.

"Now what?"

Sam looked around, "those logs were the key," he said, pointing at the steps, "They just walked out the door. We need them back. And our case files."

"I'm not worried. They'll be back. Meanwhile we've got his phone. That's not nothing. We may be in a position to know something they don't."

"Who's 'they'?" Steve asked, finally coming back.

"Don't ask," Sam said.

She felt herself tense up.

"But Steve has a point," Sam blurted, "have you thought about how you're going to deal with something you can't even name? Like with other people? Normal people?"

"Only every day."

"Yes," I'm beginning to realize that you have a problem with certain names or nouns."

"Adjectives and Adverbs are fine."

Instead of replying, he searched his memory.

"Ok, how about this trick," Sam said, "I have another trick. New rule: we only deal with numbers. Server logs, dates, times. Numbers are okay, right? You like numbers, right? I need some help here, Debian. If you want me to help you, I need some help."

She nodded. She started forcing herself through the exercise he had showed her. Breathing slowing.

"Then that's what we'll do," he said," what can numbers do for us now that we've lost whatever was left of our, um, 'the official Investigative Team'."

"They're not even simulated investigators."

Steve didn't fight back. He looked like the human version of a mylar party balloon, held by a frightened and lost child, waiting on a lonely street corner for an evil clown to blow him back up again.

Sam looked at Steve for a minute. She could tell he was debating how to approach Steve. Sam was like that. Finally he looked back at the shoeboxes.

"Wait! Maybe that's it! Logs! Simulations! I can simulate traffic. We've got his phone. We can use your phone, can't we, Steve?"

Steve nodded, happy to be of use.

Deb grabbed the phone.

"Then let's move up to the dining room, there's table space there. I've got an idea."

"Dinner?"

"No. Bait."

They left Steve, sullen and angry, in the damp basement below, staring at a lost world long gone.

3.16

Searching For Sentiment

"Not a lot but sketches and doodles," Deb said three hours later.

Sam tossed some of the papers on the table.

"Spot on. None of this has anything to do with EigenCorp or our old jobs. According to the manufacturing stamps, this BCI place started all of this. It made the tech, at the least the early prototypes," He agreed, "but that's ancient history. Mrs. McKenzie doesn't look like much of a wonk, so I don't think there's going to be any good bits with the rest of it. Attic was mostly real-estate stuff."

"Yet here she is in the middle of it all," Deb said. "With that prototype, we're getting really close to being able to crack one of these Inserts if we can catch it before it self-destructs by being out of the body."

Sam shrugged.

They heard the van again. It was the van. It was people talking outside. She assumed the gang had somehow worked it out.

"We don't have to stay," she told Sam before they got there, "we've set Steve's phone up so we can monitor who's getting the data and posting it. With Steve's phone as a honeypot, as long as we keep it running and connected, we can work anywhere."

"Here's your stupid files." It was the first thing Jim said before Sam could speak. He entered through the kitchen. "I'm sorry I took them. It was unintentional."

Jupiter was next in, followed by Steve. Debian thought Steven looked like a beaten dog.

"Of course there'll be an additional charge for all of this," Jupiter said, pointing at the dining room table. She did not want to buy a dining room table.

As Sam reached into his pocket, Deb asked, "Work it out?"

Steve perked up, came forward.

"We did. This gig?" he circled his hands as if describing something in front of him, "we decided. This is our practice gig."

Steve checked the other two to make sure he was correct.

"A mulligan," Jupiter corrected. "We learned lessons." Jupiter looked at Jim, frowned, then Steve. "All of us. Myself included. Some lessons were painful."

The kitchen phone rang.

Nobody moved.

"Does it do that a lot?" Jim asked.

"It's a phone," she said, "they do that."

She studied Jim. He looked afraid. This puzzled her.

"Seven times in the previous four hours, with a mean time between rings of 31.2 minutes. Does that help?"

"Hmmmm." Steve rubbed his chin. His chin probably itched. She suspected the culprit was the pollen count in the air which was extraordinarily high today.

Perhaps they had difficulty understanding how to work telephones.

The phone rang again. Nobody went to it.

"I do not understand the purpose of a telephone if nobody answers it," she said.

"Just leave it," Steve said, conclusion made. "All of it."

"Steven's right," Sam said. "We've got what we needed. Aside from this one pile, I think we should leave everything here. Let Mrs. McKenzie decide. Get out, make up some pretense. She's obviously got money."

Deb noticed that Sam did not mention the things he had put in his backpack from the attic. She was going to bring it up, but she suspected another one of his magic tricks.

Sam smiled at the gang.

"Time to bounce, my dudes."

"I would like to take these notes with us," she said, "as long as we're all working together, we can return it later if needed. I think it's important to finding my dad and my brother. I still need that."

Jupiter was perplexed, "She couldn't have meant for us to thrift everything. Surely something is important. We should have asked more questions, another lesson."

"Important? Who knows?" Sam said, "One person's trash is another person's treasure and all that." He put on his smile. She did not like that version of his smile. She had counted 28 versions of his smile so far. This was the only one she didn't like. The others were … nice.

For some reason, this made Jupiter angry.

"Here's a news flash for …"

The kitchen phone rang. Again.

Jupe growled, turned to look at the open kitchen door and the phone just behind it.

"Dang it! Tell you guys what. I'll just call her. We'll work this out in five minutes easy."

"Earlier today," Jim said as Jupiter went to the phone, "You were just gonna leave your partner like that to find her family. Here in the middle of nowhere. Man, that's cold."

"It's not like…."

Jupiter came back into the room.

"She's dead. Mrs. McKenzie is dead."

"But we were just there," Jim said.

"She was old, Jim," Deb said, "You're right. We were just there, but people in hospitals tend to be very sick."

"Mrs. McKenzie," was all Jim had. He suddenly started looking blankly at the space ahead of him. His lips began some sort of involuntary twitching.

"How about this, guys?" Sam said. He waved his hands across the dining room table, "Let's find something to do, find some work. Get busy. Get our minds off of things," Sam looked at Jim, his intent clear, "Take a few hours, do some detective things and stuff. You guys are great detectives, right? Maybe you can teach us some of your detective skills. We can sit and talk a bit," he looked at Jim, "while doing something else. Purposeful distraction. Talk therapy."

"But what about her?" Jim said, not looking at any of them, "Mrs. McKenzie?"

"It's not like she's going anywhere," Steve said.

Jim hit him, not hard, more like an annoyed brother.

"I think all Steven meant was that it was not time sensitive," she was starting to stiffen up. Very uncomfortable. "Did she have family?"

She looked around for anybody to help.

"No, just us." Jupiter smiled. He was sad. "She never mentioned anybody."

"That's a great idea," Sam said, rubbing his hands together, agreeing with himself, "logs, logs. Where are those server logs?"

He picked up some papers Jim had dropped. Jim came over.

"I could help with the data collation."

Jupiter began to pace.

"Guys?"

"If Jupe thinks we have the time," Steve said. He glanced back to Jupe. "I'm in. How 'bout you, Jim?"

"The time," Jupiter said. He got his pipe back out. "Has anybody checked the time?"

"It is 18:47:30 hours, assuming you're not on UTC."

Nobody responded, which she thought rude, but Jupiter did walk over to where Sam was sorting.

"I mean the times on the logs. Instead of just looking at how many servers did what, or where they were, what times did things happen?"

"Checking the times on the server logs. Who could have come up with such a thing?" She asked Sam.

Sam shared a frank look. Could these morons actually solve a case?

"Looks like it all started sometime during our visit to town," Jupe said, shoulder surfing. "Deb, did you go online while we were gone?"

"I don't go online. Ever. Not like that."

"Not surprising." Now the investigators shared the same look that Sam and Deb just had. Could these morons actually know anything about computers? Debian started a background task working on an appropriately pithy response. It was not a huge priority.

"You said you wanted to stay off the grid," Jim poked at one of Sam's band-aids he was wearing, "perhaps facial recognition got you. Or a trace from your bank account."

"Don't think so, chief," Sam said, "I know enough to fake both of those out. Done it before. That wasn't it."

"It was the dinosaur. The General named it 'The Dinosaur', of course," Jim explained, continuing to scan the logs.

Steve looked like a small bulb suddenly given too much voltage.

"O-M-G. The dinosaur got him. We gotta find that squirrel, before it comes for us too."

"Fuck, you know, you're right. It was the General," Sam said, catching the profanity only too late, "I walked right into that one, but that's not when the streaming started. Looks like Steve started it much earlier."

Steve looked around. He was trapped. He said nothing.

"So the General, specifically his dinosaur, hacked into Steve's phone," Jim said.

"Are there other dinosaurs?" she looked at Jupiter.

He shrugged.

"Did the General hack the phone? Can we meet the dinosaur? Does the dinosaur talk? How many squirrels are there?"

"I'm not sure," Steve said, He leaned in, lowered his voice. "Never saw him talk. He probably does, though. Bastard. Who knows what he could get up to. All he did was watch me with those beady eyes of his. Never saw no squirrel, but you can believe he was always there, somehow."

Steven looked around the room as if seeing it for the first time.

"In the shadows. Could be a lot of them. I've seen things."

Staring straight ahead seemed like a good idea. She did that. She turned off facial expressions. We were back to dangerous ground again. The last 38.2 days had been insane. Walking the razor's edge.

She started squeezing her chicken under the table.

Out of the corner of her eye she thought she saw them make faces, faces at her, but she wasn't falling for that one again. She kept looking ahead.

Jim started, "but why do we want…"

"Once again," Jupiter said, "Can't we just call? I'll ask the General if we can come over. I'll ask him if he knows about Steve's phone being hacked. Easy."

Jupiter left, decision made.

As Jupiter stepped back to get the phone, Jim said, "but what about the other papers? Did we decide what to do about these, um, perhaps valuable papers?"

"I'm still taking my toys and going home, guys." Sam said. "If we're not going to stay here for a few hours and work, if this is all about," he shrugged, "your drama. I'm not part of it. Not my thing. Here you go, Deb, Janus Group and the General: what you wanted, but it's never enough, is it?"

"He loves the idea," Jupiter came back, "he said 'the more the merrier', 'be sure to remember June', 'the usual bullshit would be nice', and, I quote: 'I never trusted that damned dinosaur in the first place'."

"You guys have fun," Sam said.

"Back to leaving again?" Jim asked.

"That was always the plan."

"Seriously. What are you going to do, Samuel," Jim said.

"There's no harm in quitting."

She thought Jim gestured to her but he spoke to Sam, "Isn't there?"

This had to be redirected.

"I need somebody to go with me to find this General of the Dinosaurs," she stated the obvious.

She didn't look at any of them, but she knew Jim had given one of those "you see?" looks. She hated that.

"Perhaps his squirrel army."

She continued to pump the chicken under the table.

She was pretty sure they were talking about her.

"So Sam," Jupiter sounded amazingly calm, "Debian's getting what she wanted. Now it's your turn. What kind of story do you want to leave? The guy who got what he wanted and just ran out on his friends? Or the guy who stuck with them through thick-and-thin. What kind of trophies do you want on your life's wall?"

"Trophies. You motherfucker."

Deb stopped. The relaxing had helped. Jupiter had somehow fixed things. She looked at Jupiter who was smiling, but angry?

"Language!"

"Guys! Do you really think the General is going to help us?" Sam said, "That man couldn't hack a mystery-of-the-week from TV show from the 70s, much less Steve's phone."

"Barnaby Jones," Jim said quietly. They looked at him.

He pointed to Sam, "Just saying. Or Perry Mason."

Now it was Sam that held their attention. Deb had achieved relaxation, perhaps something close to happiness.

He gave up. He hit the table hard with both hands while standing up.

"But I guess, gentlemen, and crypt monster," he looked at Deb, "that's where we're going."

She stood. She was happy. She did not smile. She would never do that.

As they left, Deb and Sam came last. She pointed to the back of Jupiter.

"He does it better than you. He's much better at arguing and persuading people."

He glared.

"The chicken?" He asked, looking at her pocket. "You should stop focusing so hard. The chicken makes a squeaking sound when you squeeze it like that."

3.17

General Mayhem

"He's dead, Jim." Steve said, smiling. "Always wanted to say that."

He certainly was. The man they had referred to as "The General" appeared to be old, in a wheelchair, covered in a blanket, well-dressed, and very dead. His head lolled gently to the side. He sat in an unused garden. Planters with weeds and materials for gardening were strewn about the 517 square-foot room. There were fourteen electrical outlets. Eight-hundred watts of illumination available.

Nobody responded. Steve stopped smiling. He bent over the man. He looked almost tender, checking for a pulse, feeling his head for injuries.

"Somebody show me the dinosaur control system," Deb said.

The four men either shrugged or looked at one another.

"But of course nobody knows where the control system is. Okay. We need to begin looking for PCs and start on a spectrum scan."

"A spectrum scan should prove very interesting," Sam said, pulling out a R&S FSH handheld spectrum analyzer.

Steve, still kneeling, closed the General's eyes. He patted him on the blanket.

"Poor guy, probably had a bad ticker. He's cold. It's been a while."

"Don't you have another cold and callous joke?" Jim asked, clearly shocked. Jupiter was patting him on the back. She didn't think Jim noticed.

Steve stood, his cursory examination completed.

"No. There are things we can do and things we can't. Work the rescue squad for a while and you'll know. DRT."

Sam was still getting set up. He stopped.

"Say, where's that other guy, the home health nurse aide person?"

More shrugs. What a bunch.

Maybe she could help prompt them.

"Was he a person like the dinosaur is a person," she said, "or was he a person that walked around? Unlike the General?"

"Nowhere," Jupiter said to Samuel, backing up and looking around the surrounding area. "That aide was never far."

Jim stepped closer to the dead man.

"But I guess we can find his contact information. I'm sure he came through some kind of temp agency. Do we really want to go through a dead friend's papers? Seems like grave robbing."

"Sure," she said.

Jim clenched his arms.

"Like Mrs. McKenzie's house?"

"Don't worry, James," Jupiter said, "We're not grave robbers. We're employed by this man, just like Mrs. McKenzie. We'll call the authorities. We'll get it all organized. The way he would have wanted."

She wanted to say "That is not going to work." Instead she locked-up, started breathing. She thought about the chicken, then thought about punching Sam in the face again. Either one would make her very happy.

"Jupiter's right," Steve said, "SOP, Standard Operating Procedure. This will be handled by First Responders."

"Wait one," Sam said. Sam was looking at his RF frequency analyzer. "Steven's recordings were stolen from here and put on BitTorrent but I'm also seeing a lot of poison pills, even locally."

"Speak English?"

"Somebody here or somebody else using a computer here didn't want Steve's stolen streams going public. DDOS here and a lot of port scanning."

He looked around. They still didn't get it.

"The General or somebody who hacked into his house was stealing Steve's recordings. But somebody else didn't want any of it to get out."

The breathing seemed to help. Jim had relaxed also, going over to Sam.

"Shouldn't we go online and start doing some reverse lookups?"

"Nyah. We need to start thinking SIGINT," Sam replied, "Probably a lot of cross-talk on the WAN. Might need to start packet sniffing at the NAT. Let me think. Steve's phone might be useful. We already know it's pwned. Maybe it was open season for whomever wanted in there and the guys we're looking for also took up shop. Long-shot, but it might work. It'd be the easiest to check, and it's the kind of thing attackers would overlook."

"Hey! I want my phone back!"

She went to the old guy, started looking carefully at his wheelchair. "We should do a thorough examination for evidence."

"Agreed," Sam said, coming over.

"Are you two even paying attention here?" Jupe asked, "This is a situation. We have a situation. We shouldn't touch anything."

"Too late," she said. She was holding the General's wallet. Searching through it, there was nothing interesting. She put it back.

"My phone!" Steve said. Perhaps Steve thought his communication deserved an ACK. She wondered what CRC algo she would need to use.

'Very soon," Sam said. "Very, very soon."

Sam started looking under the chair. The man truly had a gift for finding hiding places.

"Nothing in the clothes," she said. She looked over at him.

Sam crossed his arms.

"You thinking what I'm thinking? We should thoroughly feel his skin. Let's get his shirt off."

"Are you sure that's appropriate?" Steve asked. "That's messed up," he changed his mind mid-sentence.

"Absolutely, Steve," Sam said, cutting off any of the others. "I thought about that also. But you know the General, right? I bet that he would have loved this kind of thing! Wasn't he excited about all of it on the phone?"

Jupiter nodded in reply, but he was frowning.

"So I honestly feel like we're only doing what the General himself would want us to do," Sam put his arm around the dead man, his new best friend, "if he were still with us."

"I managed to reach around," she said. Perhaps that would calm things down. "I can't feel anything on the upper torso."

'You know I'm not so sure you'd be able to feel something anyway," Sam said, "kind of defeats the purpose. Perhaps if it were an earlier model."

"Pops would know."

"He would indeed."

"Okay, I got something," Jim said. He had been examining Steve's phone, much to Steve's unhappiness.

"Wow, let me see!" Sam said.

She wanted to leave immediately, but for some reason she suspected somebody would be quite angry if she left the General disheveled with his shirt half-off. So she started cleaning him up as best she could.

Sam scanned Jim's work.

"Awesome, Jim!" Sam said, "that's it, right there," then he looked at Debian, "But don't say a word. We're going to need to check for forbidden words."

The gang looked at one another.

"Oh boy," she heard Sam say. "I don't think we can't talk about this. Not in front of her."

"What do you mean?" Jupiter asked.

"I want my phone back!" Steve yelled.

She stood, looking at them.

Sam was holding Steve's phone to his chest, looking at her.

"Debian has seemed, um, upset about some things for a while…"

She couldn't close the distance in time to hit him, plus the others were in the way.

She tightened. He was betraying her. Like he always did.

"Let's just say there are phrases and terms we have agreed never to mention."

She desperately wanted, needed to freeze up. The man also drove her so crazy she wanted to kill him. She tried glaring hard enough to determine if laser beams would shoot out from her eyes. It was worth a shot.

They did not. Maybe she really didn't want them to.

"Debian," Sam pointed to his nose, then to her, "we're not going to do this. We're not going to say the things. But I need to ask you a couple of questions. Can you do that? Nod yes or no."

Yes.

"Stay with me. The thing we don't talk about. Were pickles on the list?"

Yes. A shrug. Perhaps.

"A warehouse or factory? With pickles?"

Yes. She got it. It came together.

"What is wrong with you two," Jim asked, "Is this some sort of code? Should we call for some," he glanced at Deb, "Does she need some kind of help?"

No.

"No no no," Sam agreed. "We're fine. We're working through it. It's a process. We're doing this. We've got it."

He rubbed his cheek, then continued explaining to the gang.

She locked up. Deep inside she was impressed that she had held out that long.

"Best way I can explain it is that there are certain words or phrases…"

Her eyebrow twitched. Without her permission. Things bad. Maintain.

"That, for lack of a better phrase, make her berserko."

Steve walked over to her, looked all around her face as if she were going to, indeed, physically explode at any moment.

"That would have been good to know," Jupiter said, "I don't think we can make that part of our standard pre-engagement interview questions, though. Not a lesson for us."

"People with extremely powerful triggers might be unusual, agreed," Jim said. "We could just ask them which words make them angry."

Steve left her, going back to his team.

"And how would you do that, Einstein? You're going to ask new clients to tell you things they can't tell you?"

"True. It is quite a conundrum," Jupe agreed, reaching for his pipe, "There was this one book …"

"Before you guys continue, can I just request that you let me be the only one to use certain words and phrases, and only when I've set them up for her appropriately?"

"How would you tell us these words?" Jupe asked, looking at her.

Sam waved his hands around his head as if trying to get rid of a gnat.

"Deb. The reverse lookup tracks back to some stupid pickle place."

Squeeze squeeze. Breathe.

"Happy Valley Pickle Company."

Sam placed his hand on her shoulder. He looked at her closely.

"The truck," She said, "almost ran over my sister. The truck. Did run over my sister. The truck. From the place."

"So, this place, with the cucumber things, is our next stop?" Jim asked.

Amazingly, Steve upchucked the entire thing, "We're going to Happy Valley Pickle Company."

Everybody looked at her, expecting what, she had no idea.

She relaxed. Sam's stupid system was working. Freaking chicken.

She nodded slowly.

"Yes," Sam said, looking at Steve, "Yes we are."

Sam gently took her arm. She allowed him to. They began walking out.

She felt herself begin loosening up.

"We're going with them," Steve told the gang, "Cool."

"We are?" Jim asked.

"If this is practice," Steve said, "It's even more important to follow-through, gotta go to the end. How else we gonna know what's working or not?"

"Steven's right. We're going." Jupe retorted.

On the way out, she led the way, pulling free of Sam and daring not to stop lest things got bad again.

She heard them talking, though. James was whispering.

"So Sam, Deb had all these problem with words, right? And you seem to be the only one here that can help her, right? And yet you were going to leave her with us without any fiddly doodle about what was going on."

There was silence.

"We'll call the authorities once we get in the van," Jupiter said, a little too loudly. "Tell them that we're employees, the boss passed away, but we're called away on an emergency A close friend has just died."

Mrs. McKenzie wasn't the first or last.

3.18

Kidnapping Endelman

The excitement was there was no excitement. It was just a stupid pickle plant. They arrived at Happy Valley only to find a few cars in the lot, the doors open, and most of the plant ran by bots. In fact, they were finding it impossible to find anybody to question or secretly observe.

Things were going well. That did not make sense to her, but she stayed quiet. They made as little noise as possible. Jim scouted ahead of the group, peeking around corners to make sure they were safe before waving them on. Jupiter followed behind, taking his time to read signs and pick random things up to be inspected with his magnifying glass. This fretted Deb, it was taking too long, but she maintained her silence. Steve stayed in the back, staying close to her, her new best friend.

Sam was not so patient, however, eventually moving past Jupe and catching up to Jim, then waving them on to what Jim had found. It was a small wooden paneled room constructed in the back corner of the plant. The door said "Office."

Sam smiled. He nodded to Deb. They were here.

She almost smiled. She stopped.

He noticed.

Asshole.

She hurried Jupiter along. Jim, however, did not wait, throwing open the door and rushing in. She heard signs of a scuffle. Sam ran in after him.

Seeing Jim disappear and hearing the scuffle, both of the remaining investigators ran after their friend. Deb did not run, however, instead trying to be careful that nobody saw them or heard what was going on.

She did walk faster, though.

—

The first thing she smelled was the sawdust, slowing taking over the pickle brine smell when she entered the small administrative office. There was an earthy smell lingering.

From the outside the office looked thrown together out of scrap wood from the plant floor, but on the inside the first thing she noticed was a large world map on the far wall. She smelled cheap cologne. To her left, Jupiter was studying whiteboards and posters. Sam was busy trying to figure out what the map was for. To her left, Jim was tying up a tall man in a cheap chair with electric cord. The broken lamp lay beside them.

Steve was pacing back-and-forth.

"Now we've finally put the bag on this conspiracy," he said. "The cabal has been conquered! We've won!"

She closed the door, first checking again that nobody saw them. The nature of this trip had obviously changed from chatting up somebody, anybody to interrogating somebody, this particular man. She could do that. She automatically checked the room for cameras as she approached the man. On the old wooden desk was what looked like a motorcycle helmet, gloves, and some keys.

The man was 1.9 meters tall. Thin. He wore glasses. His white hair was thinning out on top. He had a button-up shirt with two pens in the shirt-pocket. He had a white t-shirt. He had black, durable boots, the kind you see on hikers.

He looked scared.

Jim backed away from his tying. Then he leaned in towards the man.

"How does that feel? Hopefully not too tight. Can I get you some water?"

"Water!" Steve did not stop pacing. "You want to get this guy a glass of water!"

"You might want to see this," Jupiter said.

She turned to look. He was holding up a plaque with a bunch of names on it. It looked like one of those team pictures you might take after an especially good bowling season. The people were smiling, dressed in military clothes.

Etched in the center of the wooden plaque, underneath the picture, was the double-headed god, the laurel wreath circling him.

Janus.

The label said, "Janus Group," with a date from five years ago.

This man tied up in the chair was in the middle of them, out front, their leader.

"This must be the Janus Group," Jupiter said, "Deb, looks like you were on to something after all. These were all military."

The man shot a look at Sam. She could not decipher what it was.

"That's them," Sam said without looking. He continued to study the map.

"You kids should just leave," the man said. He struggled with his bindings.

Steve finally stopped pacing.

"Who is this guy?"

Jim crossed his arms, leaned back looking at the man struggle a bit more. He smiled. Then he reached over to the desk and picked up a nameplate.

"This man here looks like a 'George Endelman'" he said, putting it back, "Plant Manager."

"In a pig's ear," Sam said.

"Look," Endelman said, "I don't know you guys. I don't know why you're here. We don't have any money. My wallet is in my back pocket. I think there's a hundred dollars you're welcome to have. Just take it and we'll call it even. I'm friendly."

She walked up to him, leaned over, and studied his face.

"Janus Group. What do you know about Janus Group?"

"What? I don't know what you're talking about."

Jupiter cleared his throat, held the picture higher for the man.

"Oh that," he said after trying to make it out. "That's just a college club we had. It was like a Sorority. That's all. We liked Greek gods. It was fun."

"Where is my dad?" she said, "My brother?"

The man shifted in his seat. He strained against the cords.

"Look it. So far, all you've done is break and enter," the man said, "Tied me up. I don't know what you're going on about. I've offered you all of my money. I've offered you a way out. Forgive and forget, I always say. Take some pickles."

"Where's my father?"

The man ignored her.

"Let's call it even," He said, "Hey, mistakes were made, right?"

Sam didn't stop searching, but he spoke, "I can't stop it, mister. You'd better listen to her."

He struggled more, pleading to Deb with his eyes.

"But if you keep going? I don't think you're going to like it. In fact, with the silent alarm set off, cops'll be here any minute anyway."

"He's bluffing," Steve said. Steve pointed his finger at the man. "The lying bastard. I didn't hear any silent alarm. Why would a pickle plant have an alarm? Who would steal pickles?"

"Am I?"

Sam stopped studying the map. He came over to join the rest of them studying the man.

"There's a lot going on here," he said to nobody in particular, "And Janus was a Roman god, not a Greek one."

"Who knew? Really?" the man said, "People making pickles? Distributing them? Picture on a wall? This is your idea of a lot going on? That sound sane to you?"

Sam frowned. The man continued.

"And what are you so upset about anyway? Why are you here?"

"Fucker," Deb said. She pulled a pistol from under her shirt and pointed it at the man.

The man's eyebrows flew up. He struggled even more, desperate now. Jim backed away from the man as if he were on fire. He looked at Deb.

"Wait a minute," he said.

Sam took a step.

"Hey Deb," he said, "whatcha doing there? How you feeling?"

"There's gotta be more information," Jim said. He looked away. He went behind the desk and started rifling through the drawers.

"This is not what I expected," Jupiter said. There was no inflection at all in his voice.

"Yeah," Steve agreed. He looked back at Sam who was still intently staring at Deb. "We're going to catch the guy, get answers, not shoot anybody."

Jim stopped looking through the desk. He nodded, then resumed. He didn't look. It was like he was afraid to look.

"We're the good guys, right?" He said, head down.

Sam stopped staring at his partner, his concentration broke. Instead he looked at the Investigators.

"You're exactly right, Jim. This is not going at all how we expected."

"You're going to tell me where my father and brother is or I'm going to shoot you in the head," Debian said to the man.

Sam looked back over her. His face widened. He spoke to Deb as if reminding her.

"We are the good guys. And we're sorry about tying you up."

"I am not sorry," Deb said.

The man looked up at her. He was afraid. She continued.

"Do not think I won't shoot you."

"Jupe," Jim said, "no case is worth this. I want no part of this."

Jupiter nodded. He did not say anything but walked closer to Debian and Endelmann.

"Deborah," he said. "Deborah Newbian. Put the gun down. Let's wait on the police."

"And let him walk out of here? And let the authorities gather up all of this?"

She pointed around the room.

"We'll never see any of it again. And it's Debian, not Deborah."

"Hey guys," Jim said. He pointed at the top of the desk. "This isn't motorcycle gear. This is ATV gear. This guy came here on an ATV."

"But there wasn't an ATV in the parking lot," Sam said.

Jupiter went to the desk.

"That's right. There wasn't. And there weren't any ATVs in the plant."

"You can't ride ATVs on public roads," Steve said.

"A-Ha!" Jupiter said. He had difficulty controlling himself, completely forgetting about both the gun and Endelman. "This man has an ATV. This man arrived on an ATV, and there's no ATV to be found. Therefore it logically follows that there is a secret panel somewhere, perhaps in this very office, perhaps even a cave in which to escape in case of emergencies! Maybe even a lighthouse! Or a hunchback!"

"Fuck," the man said.

They all looked at him. Deb guessed he looked embarrassed.

"You got me." He said, "We might have been doing some things we should've done here."

The man paused. She growled while he continued.

"Perhaps even breaking a few customs or import-export laws."

"I knew it." Jupiter said.

Jim abandoned his desk search and went over to the far wall.

"I bet it's over here somewhere. I felt a breeze earlier. Probably behind this filing cabinet."

Endelman struggled more. Gave up.

"There is a door. He's right," he said nodding towards Jupiter. "You got me. Fair and square. You guys are good."

"And he was going to escape." Steve said. "When the cops came."

The man looked from one of them to the other.

Endelmann spoke to Jim. "There's a switch. It's right behind the map. You should be able to feel it."

He switched to Sam.

"There's money in the tunnel. Enough for all of you. You can have it. Just take it and leave. Nobody has to know anything."

Jim began feeling behind the map.

"Gotta be here somewhere," he said.

"I have no beef with you," the man said. "Let's not start something we can't stop. They're coming. You know that, don't you? You need to know that."

The lights dimmed. She heard an electric snap. A pop. Nearby.

Deb had never heard a scream like she heard. Jim screamed all he could. He fell to the floor.

Behind the map a bit of blue smoke puffed up.

"Oh! Sorry! There's some wiring problems back there," the man said, "I should have told you. My goodness. Is he okay? We really should fix that."

Steven immediately went to Jim. He knelt and started taking vital signs.

Steven looked different. A completely different boy. All business. He moved on to different measurements.

Jupiter's looked back to where Jim had been.

"What?" he said, walking over to the corner.

Steve looked up. "He's okay. He's breathing and has a strong pulse, but I don't know what happened. I strongly suggest we get him to a hospital. Right away."

There was a loud bang on the factory floor.

Endelman started laughing.

"Fools," he said. "It's all going to be over soon. I tried to let you go. Deborah, I did the best I could for you."

"It's Debian, asshole."

"I know."

She hit him in the head with the pistol.

"It's not my dad," she said. "It may never have been my dad."

She tried to work through the logic of this room, this situation. There had to be a way out. She could feel it.

Nobody said anything to her.

They heard the click of electric locks locking all of the doors in the factory. The smell of pickle brine hung in the air.

Steve walked to the wall and kicked it as hard as he could.

There.

A door opened where a solid wall had been.

"We're leaving," Jupiter said. "Steve, grab Jim. We're leaving. We are leaving with or without you two."

Sam broke. He looked to Jupiter. He looked back to Deb, then back to Jupiter. He nodded.

"We are. We're coming," Sam said, "Debian is coming along, but one thing first."

"We are never coming back," he said, "I need to take a minute or two and make sure we're not missing something important. I'll catch up."

Jim's breath came ragged. He moaned.

Looking at Jim, Sam shook his head no, some internal conversation ended.

"No, that's it. That's not important. Jim's important."

Deb slumped, but she still held the gun. Noticing that they were noticing, she put it away.

"This is what he wanted," Jupiter said, "This is what he was afraid of. He wanted you to attack him, Deb. I don't know why."

Steve looked away.

"There is a Janus Group," was all he said. He said it again, quieter.

"There was," Jupiter said. "Or is. Whoever they are, I know we don't want to meet them."

He looked up and around.

Steven finally snapped out of it.

"I don't want to be here anymore," he said, looking at Jim groaning. "I hate this."

"Yup," Jupe said. He jerked the papers back from Sam. Sam started to fight but saw something in Jupiter's eyes. Jupiter pointed at Sam.

"You. Steve. Pick Jim up. We are done here. Now. No delays."

They did so. There was no argument. They carried Jim through the secret door.

"He's coming with us," Debian wheeled the old office chair with the man in it to the secret door.

"There is no cabal, Debian," Jupiter said. He did not argue with her. Sam and Jim paid them no attention.

"This is all just old news."

She looked at him. She gritted her teeth.

"Maybe there is no cabal, but there is something. There is/was a Janus Group."

"I know."

"I've grown to like you and Samuel both quite a bit."

"So?"

Somewhere in the plant they heard men yelling.

"You and Sam," Jupe said, "are no good for us, maybe not even good for each other. I'm afraid."

He cleared his throat.

"You make me afraid."

Jupiter looked away.

She didn't flinch, but she tensed her muscles.

There was the sound of a gunshot, or maybe it was a big door slamming shut.

"Well then, give me a hand with this Endelman creep."

They both finally began leaving, Endelman in his chair in-tow, the secret door closing. But before it completely closed, it was her turn to stop him.

"Jupiter, I'm afraid too. That's why I can't stop."

3.19

Questioning Torture

The door shut automatically behind them. That was the start of it, not that they noticed right away.

There were lights on, strip LEDs along the edges of the ceiling. That was good.

She had to remind herself of the good things because the bad was all so very obvious. It wasn't going away.

It wasn't a tunnel. There wasn't an ATV. There was no way out. It was a box, a cage. She would have guessed "storage closet" but that would have been off by a factor of two or three

The room was a cube, fifteen-feet on each edge, making for 225 square feet. Plenty of room for the five of them plus Endelman. Looking about, she noticed that it didn't have walls, at least not in the traditional sense. Everything was a tiny cabinet with a protruding 80cm shelf.. The walls were bookshelves, with little cabinets in the back of them.. Each shelf had books, magazines, pamphlets, newspapers, knick-knacks, and loose-leaf reports. Who knew what were in the cabinets. All the doors were closed. She noticed all of the problems right away.

But it was well-lit.

"This room is approximately 3375 cubic feet. It appears to be stuffed with all sorts of random and useless things. There are 4,500 locations where various items might be found. Half of them might be locked or not. It will take some time to discover anything of value in here, assuming there is anything of value to be found."

"Which was the entire purpose," Sam said, arms akimbo. "Security by obfuscation. Can't crack a puzzle you can't find. Plus a time-waster."

"Look for wear marks," She said, "Where people consistently touch and use things."

"Nyah," he replied, "Too easy. A place this automated, they'd have a bot shuffle it all regularly."

He continued looking around, studying their options.

"How's he doing?" Jupiter asked Steve, who was still hunched over their friend.

"I don't know, Jupe. I'm not a doctor," Steve said, "Breathing's good, pulse strong, I don't think he's concussed. He's just out. What do I know? Getting knocked out is always a very bad thing. It's never like the movies."

Steve rolled up his jacket and tenderly placed it under Jim's head.

"He's as good as I can make him."

More sirens. Should be quite a show.

Jupe crossed his arms, addressed her.

"Wonder if this door is still visible from the office side," he said.

Sam felt the shelves that covered the hidden door. A cat looking for a hidden mouse. A contestant on a rigged game show.

"I don't think so. The cover was spring-loaded. It would have been built to reset after entry."

"It won't be long until we find out," she said. She looked down at Endelman unconscious in the chair.

They all heard the sirens, louder.

"We're stuck," Jupe said, "Cops show up, find us. Or the cops show up and are sent away. That might be worse. Who's to say anybody else knows how to get in here. All anybody knows is that an alarm got tripped. Maybe."

"That's not going to work with James," Steve said, standing up but still looking at his friend.

"Unlikely to work with whoever's coming also," she said, "assuming they can get in. And that's not considering Endelman here."

"How about just go back the way we come in?" Sam said, "If we're quick enough, we can backtrack the way we come in, then run, or go as fast as we can. Escape, confuse. Out there at least we have options. We're not trapped animals like we are now."

"Sam's right. Let's go back," Steve said.

"You are both wrong," she said.

"Notice something?" Jupiter said. He pointed at the wall where they had come in. It was all bookshelves, just like every other wall.

"There's no door," Steve said, "It resets both sides. Soon as you walk away, you can't see anything."

He was right. It was invisible.

Sam agreed, a new appraisal of Endelman, "Nicely done." He ran his hand along the edges of the closest bookshelf, "We're not going anywhere."

"We are exactly like trapped like animals," She said, "Samuel was wrong. We may die in here."

'But we are in luck," Jupe said.

They all looked at him.

"We know where we came in at. It's in that wall somewhere. Therefor we know there's a door back there somewhere. We just have to find it. That's a clue."

"Yessirree," Sam kept feeling up the shelves, "Here we go. This shelf looks screwed into some kind of pivoting door with the map on the other side. Since it's all spring-loaded and we know the magic, we just need to get to the pivot to get it working. Possible."

"I saw the pivot," she said. She was still studying Endelman, trying to figure out what to do with him. Dragging a grown man around in a 1983 roller chair didn't seem like much of a plan. "before we came in. The hinges are 4 feet from the right wall. Door's a meter wide. Probably standard framing."

Sam had been continuing as she spoke. He found something or another. The door swung open.

As it swung open, instead of the office they saw a steel wall and a keypad on the reverse side of the door they had come through.

"One step forward," Sam said, "two steps back. But we are here. Somewhere."

He began searching the door and wall around the keypad.

"Any lock can be picked. Given enough time and the proper tools."

"Keypads," Jupiter said. "Odds are a lot of things in this place have keypads, including our way out, if there's a way out."

"It's a closet," Steve said, "this whole place is a closet. But it's not a closet. Just supposed to look that way."

"Flytrap," Sam concluded, "and we're the flies."

"Exactly," she said, "we all need to be looking for the exit if we want to leave soon. We don't want to go back the way we came."

Steve walked over to the opposite wall.

"Easy then, the other door will just be exactly opposite."

"Unlikely, Steve," Sam said. "Symmetry works in houses, not in secret rooms. That's the last thing they'd do, especially if they're trying to waste our time. Could even be in the ceiling or floor."

Sam took off his backpack, started getting out the papers from Mrs. McKenzie's.

"Let's see. I remember some keys in here somewhere."

"There were four 128-character alphanumeric keys on page seven on the third stack we looked at. Which one are you interested in?"

She thought Sam looked at her as if he were scared. Weird.

"You mean that you can remember pages of source code, notes, and passkeys in papers you saw only for a minute or two?"

"Seventeen seconds."

"You saw that page for seventeen seconds. You know what's on there."

"Yes. I took some time on it. There was significantly more data of interest on that page. I can give you the key, just tell me which one."

She looked around. They all looked angry or scared. Weird.

She hated people.

"Can't you do that too, Sam? I thought that's why we got the jobs. Why were you there?"

Sam made some weird shivering motion, but the temperature had not changed.

"We all have our special skills," Jupiter said. He got his pipe out and started chewing on it. "We are the Three Investigators."

"Two," she corrected.

"Two Investigators then, at least currently," He said. "We can certainly deduce our way out. This should be trivial."

Jupiter stared at Endelman as if expecting the man to both wake up and immediately start giving up his secrets, neither of which seemed likely.

Sam had gathered some dust bunnies. Holding his arms as high as he could, he dropped them. They drifted slightly.

"There's the breeze Steve. Very slight. I was guessing that they didn't make this room airtight. James felt a breeze on the other side. Airtight rooms tend to be bad on the health. You also couldn't ventilate it. That means you'd have to create some pressure differential along with some planned air leaks."

He pointed.

"Bet there's another door, on the left side there." he watched the bunnies some more. "Towards the back."

"So somewhere on that fifteen-feet wall," she said, "That's good. Better than not knowing."

"The problem is that either I find another trick switch like on the first one, or we're going to have to disassemble that entire wall."

"And it's unlikely you find a switch."

"Perhaps. I'm pretty good. But even if I find a switch, behind it, most likely we're back to keypads."

"Those codes were backdoors, master IVs," She said, quietly, "I know it."

He pointed to the entrance door.

"We need codes for alphanumeric keypads. None of which are going to be 128 characters. The papers won't help. Much too old."

"Well, my friends, if we're going to start taking apart things," Jupiter held his pipe out to punctuate the point. "We're going to need tools."

"Which we don't have, Jupe," Steve said.

"Agreed," she said, "those were initialization vectors, seeds, not keypad codes. That'd be just the start, the way in, then we'd need the actual data."

Jupiter made a funny face, took an odd pose. Then he started unscrewing his pipe. He revealed a multitool embedded in the oversized pipe.

"Elementary my dear Steven."

"A trick pipe!" Sam smiled. "That's awesome! I want one!"

"Mine," was all Jupiter said, then went to the shelves covering the exit.

"This should only take about an hour or two."

"That's the best I can do." Jupiter smiled again at her. Deb felt simultaneously extremely annoyed and kind towards this older, fat man with obvious mental and emotional problems. She shut that down. Not useful.

"You don't want to hear this, Sam, but we need everybody here looking for McGuffins. I believe the vectors at Mrs. McKenzie's were for the McGuffins. Or Inserts. Part of the prototype paperwork."

"You're right. I don't want to hear it. It's also not something they need to know."

Their conversation stopped Jupiter's work. He looked back at them.

"Is this something you two can talk about," he looked at her. He was definitely fearful this time. "Or is it one of those other things."

She looked to Sam for agreement.

"We're going to need to brief Jupiter, at least a little more than we have so far, if we're going to want to get out of here in any reasonable amount of time."

They heard the firetruck horns, the universal city sound of "Get the hell out of the way!"

Sam nodded. She trusted Sam, yet did not trust him. Sam was all they had.

Asshole.

"So we haven't told you everything," Sam said, in a lilting voice, sounding like a lady giving a Tupperware dinner, "Funny story, it wasn't just crime we were worried about. It was crypto folks. Maybe doing things they shouldn't."

He made a scary face, as if telling a toddler a fairytale about an angry bear hiding in the woods.

"Crypto folks. You were having us investigate international currency smugglers."

"Yeah, but good news! You guys showed us that it wasn't those guys. It was the U.S. Government."

"That's the good news?" Jupiter went back to working on the shelves.

"Yes. No harm, no foul. You guys got it all cleared up." Sam looked around as if expecting applause. "Good job, guys!"

"This isn't much of a briefing, Sam."

Sam glanced at her, then back to Jupe.

"Let me do this," he held up his hand to stop her, "No, it's not. There's all the crypto stuff. Jupe, Steve, time to fess up: We're crypto dudes. Codebreakers. We specialize in getting things out of computers that other people can't find and that the owners want locked up. That's our job."

"That certainly explains Rainman over there," Steve said, gesturing to her.

She didn't know what that meant. She was certainly not an aboriginal shaman, or male, although she'd also heard that "making it rain" meant making money. There was also naked dancing.

There were seven other paths of possible meaning. She kept processing them while Sam went on.

"On our latest job, with EigenCorp, we had these black boxes we kept locked up. We made them in pairs, and with one you could talk to the other in an unhackable, totally-secure way."

"McGuffin," She said, "OTP." They wouldn't understand either one.

"Secret box that lets you talk to people," Steve said, "Trippy."

"Yes again! It's a bright group today!" Maybe he would start giving out stickers.

"You want us to look in here for, um, McGuffins?" Steve said. He started glancing at the walls, overcome with the options, "What'd they look like?"

"It's the size of a very large external hard-drive. In fact, that's what it should look like for all intents and purposes." she said. The seven other semantic paths for "rainman" were not panning out so she abandoned them bookmarking where she left off. She wasn't about to start dancing.

"And that should get us into this!" Jupiter seemed extremely pleased with himself. The shelf pivoted open and there was a second keypad. And another door. It was the exit, perhaps.

One step forward. A second keypad.

"Hopefully," she said, but she doubted it. Still, it was better to have them doing something.

She started feeling around inside Endelman's clothes, searching for a bump, knot, or anything out of the ordinary.

"Deb?" Jupiter asked. "Is there a reason you keep feeling up strange men?"

He looked at Sam.

"Well, funny enough, that's exactly what we needed to tell you. There's also an internal version of the McGuffin. We call them Inserts.

Steve's mouth hung open.

"Internal. To people? You mean inside people? Sewed in? Like alien face-hugger eggs?"

"Yeah, kinda sorta, that's really all there is. Nothing else to tell you. Just some hardware, nerdy stuff, that people might have inside them. Very technical," he waved his hand around, "Nerdy. Very nerdy stuff. Technical technical."

"They can get messages," She added.

"Probably not a good thing to tell them, Deb. Let's stop the briefing here."

She decided the dork face was right. If they liked these guys, they should contiue to ty to keep information to a minimum. Find this. Go there, and so forth. They did not seem very good working even at this level, though.

Jupiter looked at the exit door and the keypad he'd just found.

"So you think the exit key is in some McGuffin around here?"

"Yes, I do, Jupiter," she said, "Once we apply the master keys to either the McGuffin or the Insert if there is one."

"Wait. Presuming it's an Insert, Deb, how do we work it? Even if we backdoor our way in, all we're going to get is noise," Sam asked, "Never seen an Insert work, and Endelman here is unlikely to help out."

"If we can find a McGuffin or Insert," she said, "I can figure out what's in there, as long as we do it before the gallium security system locks us out."

"Without heating pads, what's that? Five, ten minutes?"

"Approximately," she said, "It's all a simple matter of running the decryption code mentally. The melting point of Gallium is 29.76 Celcius."

More astonished stares. Maybe it was a club.

"What? I doubt it's anything more than AES256. It's old tech, ancient."

Sam shook his head as if trying to clear it again.

She pressed against Endelman's chest. The man moaned. He might be coming around. She heard snoring from Jim.

"There's something here. I can feel it. It's subtle, but it's not natural."

She pressed again, this time harder.

"Deb," Jupe said, pointing at the keypad. "If you're so good at this, why don't you just give us the number so we use the keypad to get out."

"Look guys, I need this," She pointed at Endelman, "I can't guess huge, truly random numbers, at least not ones that will be useful to you."

"But you could guess huge truly random numbers?" Jupe asked.

"Leave it," Sam pointed at Jupe, He walked over to Endelman, felt where she indicated.

"I agree," he felt around, "We've got an Insert here." he said, "Whoah. Very cool."

"Which she can read,"

"She can," Sam said. "It appears she can. But not like this."

Endelman came to. Looking around, he began screaming.

Deb backed away from the man, considering. There were twelve current options. One of the rainman searches was coming up with an ancient movie she had never seen.

"We'll need to get to it," she said.

"Well then by all means, get to it!" Jupiter said, "We're running out of time! Move it along! Now!"

"You know, Deb, I'm not sure…" Sam began.

She pulled out the pistol and shot George Endelman in the head, just as she had promised him in his office 12.7 minutes ago.

Things got worse.

3.20

Reading Endelman

There was nothing. Amazed silence. Smoke took over. It was the smell of fireworks on the Fourth of July. Pleasant.

Sam pulled out a knife she didn't know he carried.

This was a day for surprises.

"We're going to have to cut him. You two may not want to look at this."

They said nothing. They did not move. Sam pulled open Endelman's shirt the rest of the way. Blood was shooting out from the back of the man's head, spraying the shelves behind him, running down his back, dripping, splattering on the shelving. It was like a fountain, but weak, intermittent, the kind you would see in a rundown city park.

"Isn't it enough she shot him?" Steve said as Sam began trying to make a small cut, "Now you gotta cut him too? He might be okay. He might make it."

"Never enough, Steven." Jupiter said in a quiet voice. He tossed his pipe multitool to Steve.

"Get that keypad apart. We get the hell out of here one way or another."

Jupiter was looking directly at Deb. She put the gun away.

"Perhaps if you made a small incision," she said.

"I can try. I've never done this before."

Sam poked hesitantly at the dead man with the tip of the knife.

"We have left any sort of reasonable Three Investigators story," Jupiter said, still in a quiet voice, talking to himself, "a long, long time ago. This is a horror show."

"Come on, now," Steve was poking at the keypad in frustration.

"We absolutely, positively have to turn you in. There's no other way. There's no running or calling later, of any of that. This is over."

Deb studied him. It was not pleasant.

"Sirens? Do you hear any more sirens?"

Jupe looked up. "Nope."

"Perhaps they're already here," Steve said. Deb thought he sounded panicked. Somehow they were both broken, wooden, weak. Like the man.

"No. They are not here. The sound reached a maximum volume and then slowly died off, the Doppler Effect."

There had to be something else she could help Sam with.

"They. They were never coming here?"

She shook her head no.

"So, this was never going to end with the police arriving?"

She shook her head no again. She heard a "blech" from Sam, then a loud swallow. The sound of someone beginning to throw up, then stopping themselves.

"But the alarm." Steve said.

She looked again at Sam, then back to those two.

"There was an alarm, certainly. *Somebody* is coming. It just was never the authorities."

"Endelman was bluffing." Jupiter said. His vocal volume level had increased 22%.

"Agreed. I don't think anything Endleman said was in any way accurate. He was bluffing, lying."

"He knew you, Deb," Sam said, still trying to minimize his cutting, and failing. "That wasn't a bluff."

"But he got my name wrong, perhaps deliberately. He was expecting somebody," she said, "and he was prepared to bring somebody or something to us. He also considered it an emergency, otherwise no alarm."

"I don't like where this is going," Jupe said.

"He was going to kill us," Sam concluded. He had stopped cutting. "The only thing worse than an unconscious Endelman was a speaking one. Had we done nothing, Endelman would have certainly killed us all."

She shook her head yes.

"Probably after a most-unpleasant conversation, probably in this very room. This was a trap. He was never our prisoner. We were his. Who knows what else is in these cabinets."

He bore down on the knife, beginning to use all his strength.

"You saved us." Sam said, "Debian, you actually saved us."

"Don't look so surprised, rock-head. Keep working. You're not going to want to meet whoever that alarm was for. He was right about somebody coming."

She caught herself shivering, like Samuel, must be some sort of biological bug. Not worth investigating.

"She's right," Steve said, "We need the code. I can destroy this thing with the screwdriver. Maybe Sam could pick it. But the code would work right now."

"That's not happening," Sam said to himself, "I can't get to the port. It's too —- warm, yucky, smelly, slimy. Pick one."

"Bloody," Jupiter said.

"Do I have to do everything?" she said to Sam.

"Immoral," Steve said to nobody.

"Ghouls," Jupiter said.

Sam looked up, knife in hand.

"You remember in the lab. The port is underneath in the back, next to the sternum."

"So it's all gotta come out."

"Now," Sam said. "This is made specifically to prevent this kind of hit-and-run data theft. We're on a clock. We gotta move."

She grabbed the knife, pushed Sam out of the way. She began hacking and sawing in ernest.

"I'm just hoping we both know all of the possible countermeasures at play," he said, "Exploding bodies would be disgusting."

"I don't see how this gets any worse," Steve said. Had everybody lost all emotion, she wondered? Were they just really bad at this?

"But I might be new at this," he continued.

She continued gutting the man, spreading his skin wide, reaching inside his chest cavity and pulling out the Insert. It looked the same as the ones they had seen in the EigenCorp lab.

"I've got the interface," Sam said, pulling a ruggedized display-only tablet from his backpack. "But we'll need the master keys, if there are any. We'll need it decoded. Which I can't do. Not without the right gear."

"Here. Let me show you."

She took Sam's device, extended the cable to the Insert still inside Endelman's chest. She entered the passkey, started working through the cipertext. It was a bit of work, 2.7 minutes. She gave it back to him.

"Wow. I'm amazed."

He did not sound amazed.

"Here we go. Coming in now," Sam looked at his screen, being sure to hold it where she couldn't see, "Looks like a lot of orders, like military orders."

"This man was in the military," Jupiter said, flat. "That's great. This wasn't the far past."

He did not seem to think it was great.

"Records only go back a couple of months. Must be some wipeout or auto-clean at work."

"We need the passkey. For the keypad."

"That'd be over in long-term storage. Hang on."

Sam's fingers flew over the keys.

"Just tell me what to type in so we can get the hell out of here." Steve said, coming closer.

"Here," Sam unplugged the device and briefly showed it to Steve. "type that in."

Then he did something unexpected. He held both of her hands. They were both bloody. He looked at her with much more concentration than he ever had before.

"Debian, we're going to need to talk about some things that may make you upset. Do you have your chicken?"

She pulled the chicken out. He held her and the chicken.

"Remember the breathing."

She started the breathing cycle.

"Give me your gun."

She hesitated.

"Trust me or not. Pick one."

She handed him her dad's pistol.

"These military orders were from a place called MELLO just over the mountain. National Cyber Reconnaissance Office. It's close. We can go. I'm pretty sure your dad's there."

"How can you be so sure?"

"Because he was the one issuing the orders."

Her mouth hung open. He continued from memory.

He now held her face in his hands, said gently, "Some of these orders were for your sister's death. Signed by Colonel Paul Newbury. NCRO."

3.21

Growing Up

Sam had to drive. The Three Investigators would move a bit, get angry, mumble to themselves, then go wooden again. Steven got the exit door opened. They stood there. Sam and Deb eventually ushered them through a normal hallway, no rock tunnel, no ATV, no money, no lighthouse. Deb felt like it was helping an old person to the cafeteria. At one point Jupiter said something about a hunchback. There was no hunchback.

The tunnel ended in a utility service panel in the far parking lot. They found the van. Nothing going on but the usual background urban activity. Sam drove for about an hour until the Investigators had all came to enough that he could pull over.

The dilapidated conversion van sat by itself in the gravel parking lot at the top of Afton mountain in the dark. The late light was barely enough for Deb to see the abandoned motel behind them. They parked next to a rusted-out food stand. A large rusted sign promised "Fresh Popcorn!" The fog prevented her from seeing much else besides Sam by the main road on a satellite phone.

He hung up the phone and put it back in the Faraday Bag.

"We've got twenty minutes before our ride for Mrs. Ketchupface gets here," he said. He walked back to where she was talking to Jupiter.

"Ketchupface?"

"It was all I had. I'm going through the condiments for fake names." She turned to the older man.

"Is Jim going to be okay?"

"I think so," Jupiter said, nodding.

Sam gestured towards the van with Steven and James in it.

"He wasn't out that long. I'm not sure he was completely unconscious.

I certainly hope he didn't hear anything. He's alert. His vitals are good. He's complaining."

"Really?" She asked.

"I saw him in the mirror on the drive up. He was taking notes, writing in his detective journal."

They considered that.

Jupiter finally cleared his throat.

"You may have noticed that I'm a bit fond of making speeches," he said.

He paused waiting for them to argue with him.

"So I'm not going to do that."

He glanced back at the van, then back to them. She immediately had 147 pithy rejoinders to that, without doing a search. She remained quiet.

"In fact, I really don't have anything to say."

"You need to leave," Sam said quietly. Jupiter began nodding as Sam continued. "Before our ride gets here. You know they all have dashcams, the drivers have smart phones, and so on."

"We do have to leave," Jupiter agreed. "We've got our bowling league this evening with those degenerate Scooby Doo jackanapes, a cadre of lickspittle carbuncular rapscallions."

From inside the van they could hear the muffled sounds of arguing. Sam smiled.

"I want to make this right for you, Jupe," he finally said.

He took his backpack off.

"What do I owe you?"

"You owe us nothing more," Jupe said. He looked at the backpack as Sam put it on the ground.

"But another bit of remuneration might be nice to fix up the van."

Sam smiled again. He reached into his backpack.

"Here. You know, I've been rethinking your online presence and this case. I think perhaps the 'Case of the Purloined Pickles' went quite well," Sam said, making air quotes, giving Jupe the money. "You found an evil gang, you found their hideout. Smugglers. There was even a secret door and a tunnel! Just leave off four or five details and it'd work nicely. You could turn Deb here into a hunchback."

"Oh, where's my manners? We have new business cards! I made them on the way."

He handed one to Deb.

From behind them, Steve blew the horn twice, then a final time.

"Fuck," Jupiter said.

"Language," Deb said.

She smiled at Jupiter. He smiled back.

"Yeah." He stood a little better, taller, "Correct you are, my young Debian."

Sam began putting the pack back on.

"Do you have any more ammo," she asked, "Also, I am willing to be a hunchback for your book. I will not dance naked."

Sam stopped. He quickly shook his head no, then continued putting on the pack.

Jupiter's face darkened.

"In all seriousness, Jupe," he said. He did not look at Jupiter. Instead he kept at his work. "I think you guys should take what you have and go public, like Steve has been saying all along. Play it up big. You can be safe by being loud. This is a situation where that strategy has a good chance of succeeding."

"You do?"

He stood.

"Yeah. After all, you don't know that much, really. Dump everything you know online. Make a big deal out of it, then nobody has any reason to come after you. If they did, they'd just give you more attention and credibility. I think this works great as fanfic. I guess you've been trying to make fanfic but don't tell me, it'll spoil it. Make your lack of knowledge work for you, not against you."

Jupiter's face darkened more. He looked intently at Deb.

"Steve's father is a drunk. His mom ran off on them a few years back."

"You don't need to tell us this."

"I know I don't. Jim's dad died when he was fourteen. His mom is in and out of the psych ward."

"Jupiter, please."

"We love one another. I think we love one another. At least as much as people can love one another."

He glanced at Sam.

"I want you to promise me that's there's going to be no more violence."

She thought Sam looked very sad as he adjusted the pack and smiled back at Jupiter.

"All we've had is violence, Jupe. Ever since this started."

Sam looked at her. He was still sad, but he was no longer smiling.

"I don't know," Jupe said. He looked down.

Deb replied, "I don't either."

He thought for a second then looked back up at her.

"I think that's the problem. You do know."

"I don't understand," Sam said.

"Look," he said, "I'm just a sixty-year-old retired High School English teacher. These guys?"

He nodded his head towards the van.

"They're just friends. Former students. Family. We're having fun and solving problems. This has been a joy for me."

"But?"

"But you two? You are involved and see things that most of us can't. We find cats. That's us. The Three Investigators. We're the cat guys."

He smiled again, took them both in.

"I am quite concerned about two things. The first is that you're on to something here operating at a global level that I feel is, truly, nothing more than violence, and lots of it, at least for normal folks. I worry about you."

"Jupe," Sam shook Jupiter's hand. They both started walking back toward the driver's side door. Sam put his hand on Jupiter's back, "Just forget that. We don't need to talk anymore. Trust me, you don't want to know any more. Leave out the Insert and McGuffin thing. Make it invisible writing or some such. Maybe it's a lighthouse when the secret message only becomes visible in the searchlight, and only on certain nights."

Jupiter gave them a short, sharp nod, then pivoted. He opened the door.

"Wait," Deb said.

Both turned.

"What was the second thing. Jupiter. I have to know."

The old man sighed, took a step away from the door.

"Yeah, you do," he was very quiet as he wiped his face, "I'm sorry."

"My mom died of cancer," he said, "I hate fucking cancer."

He mumbled something to himself, started back towards the door but stopped before getting in.

"Here it is. The second thing I'm afraid of is this: some of the most evil, vile things in life, the things we hate and despise? They're the things we never truly understand. That doesn't make them any less worth fighting. Or less dangerous."

They heard some more arguing.

"You may never understand. I'm afraid you'll die without ever knowing why it happened, without ever understanding," he paused, "like the rest of us."

He looked as if he might say something else. Instead, he got in the van.

She looked at the business card he gave her. At the top it said "The Three Investigators. We Investigate Anything" Under that was three question marks. At the bottom were their names and contact information. In careful all-cap printed letters, somebody had written between the middle and bottom in all capital letters. "NO MURDERS!!!"

The van left them, its bad suspension jostling through the potholes, creaking as it went. The taillights flickered with each bump. Eventually it got enough gumption to make it on to the main road. It picked up speed. Deb saw the license plate as it went down the road. DFR-2342. They had been in the parking lot approximately 12.5 minutes. This was the 83rd foggy evening she had experienced.

To nobody in particular, she said, "He's wrong. This can be understood."

They were alone.

It was dark.

It was quiet.

The abyss awaited.

IV. POLYNOMIAL ROOTS

"All happy families are alike; each unhappy family is unhappy in its own way."

Tolstoy

4.01

Explaining The Girl

PAUL HATED EXPLAINING to his wife that he killed that woman, especially since he'd just apologized that morning for leaving the toilet seat up. What a day.

Now the boss and everybody else was here at the Piggly Wiggly, and that was that. Lights everywhere. blood everywhere. police tape everywhere, cameras.

Everywhere.

It was a production. Boy, he was going to hear about this later. Probably never hear the end of it.

"General Ramirez, can you tell me why you're here?"

"Please. Just Sonya. I haven't been a General in a long time," Sonya Ramirez said to Mary Newbury, "Our funding partners require us to do our own investigation when any sort of violent crime occurs. Completely out of your hair, of course."

They all looked at the dead Asian lady in raggedy clothes sprawled out next to the green beans, her head twisted almost off her body.

"Which obviously this is."

"Mary," he caught his mistake, "Lieutenant Newbury, why are you here? Am I going to be charged with anything? Should I get a lawyer?"

There's also "can we afford a lawyer," but he left that off. Probably better said later that day when and if they ever let him go home.

"Let's clear the air here, be perfectly blunt about boundaries," she said, "I'm not here investigating. I'm not even here as your wife. I'm here because of this lug."

She gestured to a man in plain clothes standing behind her. The man tried to either smile or frown. He did a bad job at both. So he shrugged.

408

"This is Detective Martin's first week. He's the primary. I want to make no mistake that we all understand that. But I'm also his supervisor. And he and I are the only detective game in town. Paul's my husband. Everybody knows. I'm not going to say anything to Paul about this case unless it's in front of multiple witnesses, hopefully being recorded. That's the best I can do."

She thought a moment.

"For now. I'm certainly not going to call in any outsiders … at this point."

He heard the hesitation. He wanted to interrupt, ask about the going to jail thing, but he knew better than getting in the way when she was on a roll.

"As far as charging, we don't know. I think it's fair to say," she glanced back at Martin, then back to he and Ramirez, "that if the events occurred the way Mr. Newbury said, then this was self defense, at least under this state's laws. But we don't do charging, anyway. We do investigations."

Martin nodded, but hesitantly. He suddenly found out he had a note-pad and looked at it.

"I've got unis picking up the surveillance cams. Looks like about a dozen. Nobody knows the victim, so far."

For the fifth time, Paul said, "Came out of nowhere. Never before saw her in my life. Pulled that big knife on me."

It was a SOG EDC combat knife, but there was no need bringing that up, or that he had his own strapped to his leg.

There was a lot not to say. Mary knew that.

He cut a look at Mary. She didn't look worried. He knew better.

Time to drop the hammer.

"I made many statements here to you nice folks," he said. He was probably overplaying the niceness. Fuck 'em.

"And I'm happy to write this all down and sign it. I know you're all just getting started. I am happy to help any way I can."

"But?"

Martin was picking it up. Maybe he'll work out after all. He hoped so. Mary had a dickens of a time trying to find somebody to promote.

"But from here on out I'm lawyering up. I apologize that this is going to be a pain in the ass for everybody, but as I understand it, that's what I need to do."

He looked worriedly at the body again.

"That girl almost killed me. Scared me to death."

Don't overplay it!

Freaking Martin frowned. He wasn't buying it.

But that was Martin's job.

In Search, Evasion, Resistance, and Escape (SERE) school, the first thing they taught you was "survive the ordeal."

He had done that.

The second thing they taught you was how to lie.

In progress. So far, so good.

"Well, then, let's get you to the hospital," Mary said, taking him by the arm.

She was mad. Ramirez was mad. Martin looked mad. Everybody was mad.

Paul had survived. What a day.

4.02

Comforting Debian

"So you see, little Debian Newbury, there are no monsters under the bed. Just us."

"Yeah, huh," was all she offered.

Paul got home first, so he was the one to pay Mrs. Withers and put the kids to sleep. He loved story hour. The kids did too.

But they struggled. He noticed as they grew more and more cognitive capacity, their emerging personalities started making preferences known.

For the last six months, the main difference of opinion was book selection. Tim was very happy with "Goodnight Moon", "Jerry the Jet", and "The Monster at the End of This Book," Salomé, being the oldest, wanted "The Hunger Games."

Middle child Debian?

First it was "One, Two, Three Infinity," about how different cultures had different number systems. Then it was" Gödel, Escher, Bach" about a bunch of things, including how patterns naturally repeat across a number of sciences. Then it was "Introduction to Electronic Circuits."

Now we were on to Harry Potter.

Reading to Tim took 15 minutes. Sal took a half hour, and with sadness in his heart, he realized that there weren't too many story nights ahead for her. Sal's face had begun screaming "boring."

Debian could go two hours if he'd let her. She loved learning in a preternatural way. Her common complaint was that he didn't spend enough time telling her the stories.

He tried.

For each book she made him show her all the diagrams, or any pictures, which she looked at quite closely for ten seconds. Then she was done. Never asked to see them again. Sometimes he would read a passage she especially loved and she would ask to look at the page, just page. She studied the pages just as much as the diagrams.

Seven years old.

Of course, this meant everybody got separate stories. Fine by him. Tim first, then Sal, finally Debian. He announced up front that she only got an hour. He needed to talk to mommy when she got home.

"Come here, let me show you."

He took her little hand and they both peered underneath.

"See? No monsters."

"I can see that," she said, "but I didn't think they were here."

"But you said."

"I said there were monsters underneath."

"Underneath what, dear?"

"Underneath us."

He didn't chase this down, mainly because Debian was wonderfully creative, and had the ability to talk at length about anything, for any length of time. He loved her ability both to understand and imagine. He never wanted to ruin that.

"Well, we've covered the area under the bed," he winked at her, "So that's that. You want to continue the book or not?"

"Book!"

4.03

Placating Ramirez

"I want to know why my chief of research killed somebody yesterday morning in a Piggly-Wiggly," Ramirez said the first thing the next day.

Ramirez stood in the doorway to the team's common room. She was short and extremely fit. She had a short haircut. Grey hair. Paul thought she always looked like she had a board stuck up her butt and was perpetually angry about something. Never unpleasant, she was terminally polite, but never dull, either. There was always fire behind those eyes. She always seemed in charge, too. She was an opinionated butler, the one that guests could easily dismiss but who actually owns the mansion.

He respected her.

"Sorry chief. At the time I thought the other options were suboptimal. I didn't think that being dead was a good way to start my day."

The plaque on the desk read "Paul Newbury, Computational Psycho linguistics." He'd wanted it to read HMFIC but Sonya vetoed him. On the wall was an X-Files poster of a UFO and the caption "The Truth is Out There." He had a second nameplate that he flipped up when he saw her. It said, "Paul Newbury, Director BCI."

She sighed and looked at him the way one might look at a wayward toddler.

You can take a General out of the Army but you can't take the Army out of a General.

Sonya sat across his desk from him, board stiff. Relaxing.

"How are you doing, Paul?"

"I'm well, Sonya. Not my first kill, as you know. Hopefully the last one."

"Was your statement accurate to the police?"

413

He waggled his head in a "kind of" gesture. "Mostly. Homeless woman attacked me in a Piggly-Wiggly. I broke her neck."

"What parts were not exactly accurate?" She said, "I need to know."

"You saw. Mid 30s maybe. Looked homeless, perhaps mentally-ill. But she knew knife-fighting, she knew her CQ, so that wasn't her. She wasn't what she appeared to be, it was just camouflage. That's why she almost killed me. She was good. Very good."

"Military training? Chinese National?"

"Out of my pay grade, General. I'm out. I'm just the research guy. That's for you to worry about. Maybe."

"Which is why I'm here."

"Fuck. Me."

"Yeah, you know where this is going. We're going to need an incident report. We're going to need this woman investigated. We need to liaise with local police."

"You mean my wife. You want me to run interference between BCI and Mary."

"Not going to be me. I don't want anything. I'm a one-digit midget. 3 more months and I'm gone," Ramirez said. "All I want is a better margarita recipe."

"Sonya. General. Friday is the end of Phase One. I've got the two sponsors showing up for the big presentation."

"About that."

"Again fuck me."

"I contacted higher ups after the, um, incident. They feel like this could be a security issue."

"Jesus. Nothing ever changes with these assholes."

She held him back from speaking further.

"Bear with me. They wanted to increase the size of the presentation to twelve. I talked them down to seven."

"um."

"They also wanted to send a team of operators to work the security issue."

"Argh."

"I talked them down to sending one person, at least for now. They can do the security work, liaise, as long as you promise to get them up to speed."

"Active duty?"

"Most likely."

"Well, as long as they don't outrank me, that seems reasonable. Or get in the way. Thanks chief."

"Hmmm," she studied him, "you ready for Phase II?"

"I was never onboard for Phase II. You know that."

"You could get a brand-new SCIF, a promotion, might even get my job."

"Phase II? How would that even look?"

"You're in luck. That's what we pay you for. That's what you also need to do. You've got until Friday. How *would* that even look. Tell me."

"Then I guess I'm coming up with something."

"You know, you're my favorite person on this project."

"Aside from three grad interns, I'm the only person on this project."

"That too."

"Boss, I did my time. I did my twenty, saluted the flag, polished stuff, painted stuff, met new people and killed them. This professor gig is pretty good. I like it. Mary and I have a life here. Kids."

"Between you and me, just as an FYI, I was told I would have to lock this place down this week or be replaced and have the entire project moved off-campus."

"Damn, Ramirez. Something must've gotten somebody's knickers in a twist."

"I'm to be briefed later. Eighty-four days. Three months."

"I'm right behind you."

"We've done good work, Paul. The Coincidence Machine is something to be proud of, even if none of us can ever talk about it. Take my advice, get out now. Something big is coming and neither one of us want to be a part of it."

He stood up theatrically, saluted.

"General."

Sony Ramirez, Brigadier General, United States National Cyber Reconnaissance Office, got slowly to her feet.

"I'm not returning that piece of shit salute."

He grinned and dropped his hand.

"And if you ever salute me again without either one of us being in uniform? You and I are going to have words."

"Yes ma'am."

He liked Ramirez a lot.

4.04

Relaxing Picnic

His house set on a nice, wooded five acres at the end of a mile-long gravel private road. It was quiet and peaceful. He'd bought it way before he met Mary, back when he was traveling a lot. He liked the fact that when he got home, it was quiet.

So many things in life were not quiet.

Entering the backyard, Mary had spread several nice blankets over the grass. There was a picnic basket, open. As he got closer, he saw that they had the game of Clue. Mary had a word puzzle book by her side. Everybody was playing Clue but little Timothy. Tim was using the remaining game tokens to fight some important battle of the Newbury Estate. Debian was laughing. She had their Harry Potter book by her side. Probably a good luck charm. Everybody else, including Mary, looked pissed.

"Again! Again! This is fun!" Deb said, then got up danced a little jig. "Let's play again!"

"Hi guys," Paul said. He was looking back and forth to check the family emotional room temperature before proceeding.

Mary looked up, clearly torn between frustrated and happy.

"That's her third time winning," Mary said. "Bit late, huh."

"She cheats," Sal pointed a finger at her sister, "I just can't figure out how."

"That's because I'm a wizard, a ha!" She pointed an imaginary wand at her family.

They had started on Harry Potter the night before.

Paul smiled in spite of himself.

"Deb? Little Debian? I don't believe it!" He said, coming over to see the status of the board.

"It was Colonel Mustard in the Library with the Lead Pipe," Mary said. "She doesn't even use the card!"

"This is a fun game!"

"I'm NOT playing," Sal crossed her arms, "until I find out how she's cheating."

He sat down with his cloth bag he had brought, deciding that not weighing in on this was the best move.

"Kids," he looked at them, "and mom, I apologize. This picnic was my idea and I almost messed it up by being late."

"47 minutes late," Deb said.

Tim blew a raspberry but kept playing alone. He was smiling at himself for his commentary.

"It's the backyard, Dad," Sal brushed herself off, "It's not like you weren't going to come home eventually anyway."

"But I come bearing gifts!" He patted the bag, "Surprises for everybody!"

"YAY!" Deb danced around some more. Tim stopped playing, suddenly very interested.

In the bag, Paul's tablet buzzed. He tried to subtly glance over and peek, but as he looked back he realized that was a fool's game with the entire family watching his every move.

"You know," Mary said, looking at the cloth bag, "when I took off work this evening, I told them that unless the universe blew up, they'd better leave me alone."

"My universe, sadly, is a bit unstable right now."

"You need to leave?"

"No, I am here. This is where I belong. They can go to heck, harummphhh!"

He made an overly-dramatic conclusion.

"Harummpphhh!" Timothy agreed, moving army men around with purpose.

"This project's taking a lot of your time, Paul. As you know, I had a bit of extra work this week as well."

He let that one go.

"I know, I know. But we're reaching an endpoint at the end of this week. After that, no more on-call all the time. I promise."

"For a bunch of mathematicians, there certainly is a lot of drama, intrigue, and conflict where you work."

"I know, right? Academics. What a bunch of prima donnas. Like piranha."

He made a clawing gesture at the kids. Tim was enchanted.

"Rawwrrr!"

Deb laughed, "Daaaad, piranhas don't have claws!"

"Who's up for laser tag! I brought laser tag!"

"Laser tag." Mary cocked her head, "Us. Laser tag. This bunch."

"Presents! Presents! We want presents!" Sal said.

"Hey there, cool your jets little one."

He observed his family. There was no way they were going to wait any more. Another second and he would be drone-swarmed.

That thought made him smile, but the picnic would be ruined.

"Ok, enough. So we're closing down my lab next week and I managed to bring home some prototypes we made."

"Junk," Sal said

"It all works, thank you very much, Salomé Newbury. My students don't build junk."

"Nerd toys," Sal concluded. "Lucky us."

"Why don't you see what I've brought and then you can complain?"

Realizing she had pushed her dad far enough, she said nothing.

"Ray guns! I want ray guns!" Tim said.

"Close, Tim."

He reached in. He waggled his eyebrows doing his best to look like a mall Santa he saw once.

"First present is for Debian."

He handed her a blanket. In large letters it was labeled "Markov."

"It's a Markov Blanket. Handmade out of a special magic fabric."

The other kids frowned, but Deb seemed very pleased anyway.

"A new blanky! What's a Markov?"

"Inside joke, sweet. It's almost brand new. Only one in the world like it, special blended metal mesh fabric, something called a Faraday Cage. They tell me it's supposed to keep monsters away."

"Monsters?" Mary said.

"Tell you later. Next, for Tim, since he's done such a good job waiting," he cut a glance at Sal, "a graphic adventure book!"

"Mine!" Tim sprang from his toys, grabbed it and returned in one move, now ignoring his army men and digging into the comic.

"Magic Monster Blanket. Ohhh. Thanks dad!" Deb patted her new blanky, "Imma play a game on it! Yay! Just like mommy!"

They watched as she spread it out, then started putting gravels into little piles on a grid. It was oddly mesmerizing. There was some pattern there. He had no idea what.

Salomé cleared her throat, leaned back and forth. Finally she cleared her throat a second time.

Sal had been doing a pretty good job of being quiet, at least for her.

"Last, but not least," he reached in, "for you."

He handed her a necklace with a large pendant. It was white, plastic, and had a button in the middle of it.

"A necklace?"

"You might think so, but you'd be wrong. That there, Sal, is the world's first Personality Pendant. There's only one of these in the entire universe, and now it's yours."

"A what?" She looked at it as if it might bite.

"You know how you've been complaining about not being popular enough at school? Well, you wear it all the time, it monitors what's happening, then when you press the button it gives you advice on how to become more popular! Is that cool or what?"

She looked skeptical.

"Here. I wore it today. Gimme."

Before giving it to her, he pressed the button. A pleasant female voice immediately responded.

"You are eating too much fatty food. Also you fart too much in your office. In addition …"

He pressed the button again. "Look, you can turn it off too."

"AWESOME DAD!" She almost yanked it putting it on. She wandered off seemingly talking to herself, mashing the little button.

Mary spread the blanket more, getting the wrinkles out.

"What, nothing for me? You're an hour late and no flowers, no kiss, no chocolates…"

"Oh yeah, I almost forgot," he reached in and pulled out a very complicated looking set of googles, "from the mosh pit. Students loved this."

"Night Vision Goggles? Seriously? No chocolate but NVGs. I already have NVGs. Got a whole rack of them at work."

"No no no. I know that you do. These aren't night vision. These are zero vision goggles."

"They call that a blindfold. Or just broken."

"Ha ha, Mrs. Funny Person. What I mean is that these goggles have every sensor we could cram on there plus a LLM trained for vision and 3D scene mapping."

"Which means?"

"Which means that these don't care if it's light, low light, starlight, radio wave, zero light. Whatever. They have built-in hi-res LIDAR and they can use reflected light, say looking at a well-lit room reflected off a wall, to show you what's in the room."

"What?"

"That's right. You can be in the dark, not even inside the room, and 'see' inside the room based on just the light coming out of the room reflected on something else."

"Sounds like magic." .

"Pretty cool, eh Mrs. Funny Bone? Now you can go out and beat up meth dealers or whatever you folks do and be extra sneaky doing it!"

She held it out, turning it one way then another.

"Paul. Is this classified?"

"Hmm, well there's that," he put it back in the bag and handed the bag to her. "You can't let anybody know that you have these."

"Or what?"

"For everything else, nothing. For that? Piggly Wiggly," he said, knowing that this would shut the conversation down.

"What's a mosh pit," Deb didn't look up from the rock game she was playing.

"Never mind, Deb," Mary looked him, then put the bag behind her, "So you want to play laser tag? Before dinner?"

He nodded.

"I'm not playing against mom, she's a ninja or something," Sal replied.

"You're dad's the one who's a ninja."

"Donut ninja maybe," he patted his belly.

Everybody laughed or tried not to. Everybody but his wife. She finally smiled.

"Hey, you're the cop. I just teach math classes."

The notebook buzzed from the bag.

"Oops, left my notebook in there. Can I have it please."

She pulled the tablet out, looked at the screen to see if he had left message preview on.

He had.

"Sonya is asking if your presentation is ready," she handed it to him, "your math presentation, I suppose."

"She knows better," he said. "She must be worried about something."

"Mooommmmmm, Tim's climbing a tree!"

Sure enough, the seven-year old, comic in hand, was going up a tree.

"Timothy Mattis Newbury, get down from that tree right this minute!" Mary put on her "I'm mad but not really, at least not yet," voice that they all knew.

"Kid's just four, already out on an adventure," he tried to say it quiet, "takes after his old man, he does."

'They all do, just not in a good way. What are you doing?"

Debian had all the rocks in-place and was now moving the rocks around. He counted. Looked like a seven-by-seven grid.

"New game. I was watching you. It's fun! Can we do this with levels of rocks, like a bookshelf or cube? This is kinda easy, better than Clue."

Paul and Mary looked at one another.

"That's one's yours," he said.

Buzzing from the tablet. He looked at it again, guilty.

"I'll tell them that I'm ready, that the attendee list is fine, then I'm done."

He started typing. "I'll tell them not to bother me again unless exploding universes."

He continued typing.

"I'm sure Sonya's just doing that leadership thing, taking care of her troops."

"You told me."

She looked at Paul as if he had just claimed he could juggle wolverines.

"There," he pushed the tablet aside. It was a hated machine.

It buzzed again.

"Fuck," he whispered, grabbing it again.

"What now?"

"They're moving my presentation up from Friday."

"To when?"

"Tomorrow morning."

"Can I go inside? Are we done yet?" Sal was playing with her new toy.

Mary looked at him, not happy.

"You want to go inside, Dad?" she emphasized 'Dad' a little too much for his tastes, "Play laser tag? Eat dinner?"

"I want to shoot people with guns!" Timothy said.

"We will, Tim, I promise," he looked at his wife.

There was another buzzing. Thank the stars it was not him.

"Hmmm," he said, "Problems with the universe?"

Without looking at what it was, she slung her phone over 100 feet toward the back door.

"They can come get me if they need me."

That was a good idea.

He slung his tablet, doing his best to land on top of her phone. Missed it by 2 inches.

He heard her snicker. She knew what he was trying to do.

He would not dignify that with a reply.

Instead he stood up, saying, "Let's give it two hours, then I have to go."

"Avast, young Timothy!" Tim had just returned from the tree and was no doubt checking to see if he was in trouble, "We will get our ray guns, you and I, and we will defeat these horrible …. girls!"

"YAY!"

"But first!" Mary joined in, "there will be …. tickling!!!"

Mary and Paul ran off to catch the kids, laser gear in hand, to deliver some serious tickling before the vicious armed combat was to begin.

4.05

The Briefing

MINUTES OF THE END-OF-PROJECT BRIEFING
BCI
COL. PAUL NEWBURY PRESENTING
CLASSIFIED
SPECIAL COMPARTMENTALIZED INFORMATION
INFORMATION TYPE DELTA
NOFORN
EYES ONLY

Before I start, I'd like to thank my three post-grads. They do all the work around here, and without them this wouldn't be possible. Please stand. Joe Middles, Hilda Gibb, and Hank Dawson. Please, a round of applause for these great guys. I'm expecting only extraordinary work from all of you in the future.

I also want to thank you, the dozen or so folks attending demo day. I don't know who any of you are, but that seems to be par for the course for this type of work (laughter).

I love astronomy. At times I have trouble sleeping. When that happens, I take my binoculars and go to a nearby park. There I can lay on my back and watch the wonder of the universe go by. You can see all sorts of things, meet all sorts of people.

A couple of weeks ago, as I was doing this, a young girl approached me. Cute little thing. Couldn't have been more than five. She asked me, completely out of the blue, if I wanted to keep going down this road. Confused, I looked up and saw something even stranger: her mother taking a picture of both of us.

Well, I love a mystery, and this had me going. I walked over to the mom, introduced myself, explained what the girl just asked. To be honest, I was a bit concerned for the young girl's health.

The mom laughed. She explained to me that they were playing an internet game where people make bets with one another to do silly things, the girl was getting tired of astronomy (they had a nice reflector set up nearby), so they took this dare. Made ten dollars!

Sounded like easy money to me.

Now, you may be wondering what strange families in parks in the middle of the night have to do with massive supercomputing.

As the family left, I thought to myself, what if this wasn't a game? Or rather, what if it was a game, but there was some other motive behind the picture? After all, I had just been recorded in a certain spot at a certain time. That kind of intelligence, while miniscule, has value. I don't have to recount to you how photo apps have been used to discover secret bases or any of the other oddball security leaks, seemingly from innocent behavior.

Don't get me wrong. Mom and daughter were having innocent fun. The fabric of life. But our interaction also struck me as strangely anonymous, without agency. They were acting, they took the picture, but was it really them? Somebody, somewhere made that bet, right?

Who?

This work began with something I called the "Coincidence Machine." It was founded on one simple premise: are there seeming coincidences that aren't really? Everybody in the world of technology is involved in some narrative that they're starring in, perhaps several. The housewife is also taking a video series to become a doctor. The series continues to sell her on her continued involvement in order to better herself, and she happily participates. She also might be part of a narrative of some family drama she's participating in on social media. She also may be following a political movement that tells her that she's a star, or at least an important actor, in an ongoing struggle to make a difference in the world.

A young person may be part of an ongoing MMRPG with a thousand others. They also may be pinged throughout the day from a dating app, offering them another dating adventure. These are not just random pieces of data or applications. These are a form of lightweight emotional dependencies, connections. We become engaged in all activities we do because of narrative: we are presented with an external narrative that we buy into. We are entertained.

We all have these multiple narratives we're engaged in and which carry us along happily. This is being human. The universe itself can be viewed as an almost infinite number of narratives simultaneously running.

But what if we could slice those narratives a different way? Just because each of us sees these stories we're participating in as sort of a path, because it's all data we can slice it a different way. Suppose the housewife who's part of the video series to become a surgeon goes out to buy a special knife because the latest video recommended it. At the same time, the young person with the dating app passes by on their way to a date. A construction worker working a crane is texted by his wife who's leaving him, causing him to drop a large load in front of the man, who then swerves and runs over the housewife.

That's incredibly unlikely. It's a coincidence. But simply because we see it as a coincidence doesn't make it so. We don't know. More importantly, we can't know. It's measurable, but no observable. An intelligence watching a thousand people engaging in a hundred thousand narratives daily could engineer them in such a way to achieve their own ends and nobody would be the wiser. Some coincidences might not be.

You can look at people as doing their own things or you can look at humanity as little events and data that can probabilistically be joined to do other things, other narratives, things imperceptible to the average human.

The problem is that there are more ways to join up random events and data points created by our entire species than there are atoms in the universe. It's impossible. You might as well talk about demons and angels.

Until now.

Ever go out and look at the night sky? We humans have been doing it for millions of years. There's an incredible amount of interesting things out there: stars, planets, brown dwarves, novae, dark matter, dark energy, dark stars, maybe quark or strange stars, and so on. In fact many say this is the golden age of astronomy. The more we look the more we see things we can't explain, then we go back and try to figure out why we saw it. It's a great time to be alive. We are learning a tremendous amount of things about the universe, simply by looking and then doing the science.

When telescopes were first invented, most people thought they were the work of demons. Things you can't see? Up in the sky? Moving around? It wasn't natural, human, or good. It had to be evil. When the microscope was invented, people refused to believe there could be such tiny creatures all around us. If pressed and shown, they began wearing charms and amulets, unaware of how to fend off these invisible monsters. In the 1930s, Karl

Jansky was trying to solve the problem of why there was so much static on the shortwave radio, random junk. He finally realized that this was the center of our galaxy, the Milky Way. He had invented Radio Astronomy. It came from unintelligible randomness, measurable but not observable.

Current Large Language AI models, and other kinds, view the world as a set of facts provided where the machine tries to guess the next thing observed. A man buys soda one day and vodka the next, he might buy vodka soda recipes the third day. That kind of thing. But it's also possible to run the models in reverse. Given all of the things we have ever observed and say about them, what are the possible rules that apply? Instead of guessing the event, it guesses the rule. This is called abduction. Instead of a specific guess for a specific man under specific conditions, what thousand-parameter sequence of events is always true? What are the universally-true narratives? For many reasons, these would be awesomely-intricate complex and non-verbal intersecting chains, but they would always be true. We could then reconstruct reality based on how these narratives interact with other things we observe, like people.

Perhaps I am getting too theorethical.

Back to my mom and little girl. It's old news that the internet hacks people in order to get them to do what it wants: spend time on social media, argue endlessly with each other about politics, spend 40+ hours a week, basically a person's entire leisure time, playing online games. Of course, all of these people are doing what they want. In fact, they're having the time of their lives! It's just that there are other, unseen factors also at work. People gotta get paid. It's the attention economy. Like I said, this is old news.

But combining an incentive-based system with a narrative-based system gives us a whole new universe of cause-and-effect. We're like Jansky figuring out the static, only a billion times and a trillion ways simultaneously. And just like those early astronomers, the things we might see, we're not sure what does what. Is it organic, something coming out of the universal human experience? Is it something a large corporation is purposefully creating? Are there other intelligences in the universe controlling human-ity as a whole by thousands of little subtle prods that look like noise? Is there a foreign power using this? Is there some universal subconscious, a Jungian metaverse, that we're only now discovering? Are there higher-level creatures that exist in this world that are able to think and reason at levels we can only guess at? Multiple universes like this simultaneously exist on top of the one each of us lives in. What lies in the chaos?

Realizing this puts us in an odd spot.

It's like one of our neurons, deep in our brain, suddenly woke up one day and realized it was neuron, part of a larger creature. So it began studying the neurons and activities around it. Some things seemed to happen all the time. We call that physics. Some things happen sort of regularly, but not predictably. We might call that soft-science. There are things that are connected that don't make any sense, but yet exist. These are things like dark matter. We know something is going on, but not what. Somethings are mostly imagination. That might be astrology.

There's all sorts of stimulus happening in the universe, from the activity of intelligent life to quantum collapse functions. The connections are never, ever going to be clear because we're just a neuron. But we can observe. We can watch and start mapping out the subconscious of reality.

Just like when we first saw stars in the sky, now we're asking ourselves: is there a universe where ideas, dreams, thoughts, tangible objects, and plans communicate with one another, a universe higher than this one? At a greater level of intelligence?

It's not that we don't know. It's not that we don't know what we don't know. We never can. Nobody could see the random radio noise from the galactic center, any radio waves at all, until we had advanced enough. We are infants. We don't even know what the hell is going on around us enough to begin trying to figure anything out. Our eyes are just opening. But they are opening.

What we asked was this: can there exist a world of creatures, gods, monsters, aliens, demons, and goblins in the space between words? Not worlds, words. Concepts. In the mist of our dreams and subconscious? Can we now, just like our ancient ancestors just begin to see these little lights up there, wonder what's happening? Can we be the next Karl Jansky?

Or to make it much more practical, could an enemy use the internet in ways impossible for us to understand or describe but still be able to detect?

Frankly, because an enemy could use this as much as anybody or anything else, we're stuck having to figure this out before somebody else does.

We are Breakthrough Counterintelligence Initiative, and that's our mission: to see if we can build the world's first internet telescope. Or microscope. We don't really have a name for the instrument we're building since nothing like this has ever existed before. When it's just us, we call it the Coincidence Machine, but it's doubtful that name will stick.

Crystal Ball might be better, or Palantir. We are seeing things that should be impossible to see.

The reason we're receiving funding from the Intelligence Community, and thank you very much, is that the unknown is always a potential threat. A meteorite killed the dinosaurs. Microscopic organisms killed tens of millions of people last year. Even when there's no super-intelligence at work, every time we start exploring The Great Unknown in some way we never had before, we find that it's responsible for bad things where before we had no idea what was going on – or worse, we thought we knew but were wrong. I repeat: it's the Golden Age of Astronomy for just that reason. We're finding stuff that we thought we knew but we didn't. Places where we are completely clueless. Good times.

So the first step is simply figuring out if such a prototype instrument is possible. That was our project. I'm happy to report that we believe it is. If you'll look in your packets, you'll see our lab notes in Appendix A. Appendix B is a sketch of plans to take this to the next step.

I want to stress two points.

First, simply observing something is a long, long way before we can begin to understand it. Look at how long we saw stars, and even with the best modern gear we're still busy naming new things we see and figuring out how it all fits together. We anticipate that any new instrument used to observe a completely different universe will track along similar lines. Plan on seeing a lot of interesting things long before we can understand them. That's just life.

A sidebar: what to call any of these things we might observe. Demons? Angels? Gods? Aliens? Galaxies? Memestorms? Thoughts? Whims? Dreams? Here we also have working names which probably won't stick. Our job, we tell ourselves is to observe super-intelligent hyperdimensional concepts living in the Jungian Metaverse. Remember, our instrument is farming the internet for data, but the internet hooks up to every other aspect of our lives, both commentary and measurements, from cooking recipes to raw SETI data, raw data from space telescopes, so we're really farming humanity's complete understanding of the universe. In totality. All of knowledge. It's not just humans. It's not just people. It's not just data. It's everything, how it all relates. There's nothing that we don't know about that's not in there.

Hyperdimensional rules, creatures, and phenomenon aren't going to be so easy to name!

Second, without an established nomenclature and some kind of reproducible cause-and-effect theory, even if we observe something in the HJM, Hyperdimensional Junigan Metaverse, we don't know if we're looking at a tiny rock or the cause of syphilis. We just know we're looking at something. If we can get that far in my lifetime, if we can just see, I'll die a happy man.

This was team Alpha of the Breakthrough Counter-Intelligence Research Initiative, Phase I. I will now take questions.

• • •

Paul looked around. The small SCIF they had managed to bury beneath the college was packed with dignitaries. He guessed it was evenly split between legislative aides, military brass, and spooks.

Sonya hovered in the background, her kid up on stage and appearing in his first play. Though they both knew this wasn't his first rodeo.

A 20-something in the front row, Paul guessed congressional staffer, raised his hand.

"If there actually is anything to observe, and it exists in hundreds or thousands of dimensions, how could you ever begin to start naming something like that? What's a name for a thing between words? With those other scientific fields, we had pre-existing concepts: a planet looks like a circle, a bacteria might look like a snake, and so on. We started with analogies everybody already knew. We don't have any names at all for these kinds of things, not even close."

"Right. I've been thinking about that," he said, "and while I have a couple of tentative ideas I don't have anything I could hang my hat on, just wild speculation."

An older man in the back row, he guessed military, shifted in his seat. "Speculate then."

This was going off the rails. The last thing he wanted to do was sound like a nut. He looked back at Ramirez. She nodded.

"In English, we have a word for something that can't be expressed in words: ineffable. Since we've already named it, I looked into the history of how things that couldn't be described were communicated. There were a few methods, but mythic storytelling is currently my top candidate. In the movie Titanic, it's not just that the ship sank. There's much more to it than just the words. Stories tell us things that simple names and declarative statements can't, ineffable things."

He wanted to stop. He couldn't help himself.

"Right now we're looking at this new tool as a counter-threat ISR, a way to detect attacks. At some point, however, and not too far in the distant future, we'll be able to put everything in there, all the words, thoughts, and observations people have ever made about everything they've ever done or seen. Using LLMs and constructivist logic, at that point we'll be able to find and use things in the universe none of us could ever have imagined. Could ever possibly imagine. If that's not mythic storytelling, I don't know what is."

"With that I'm going to close out before I sound like even more of a nut than I already do. Thank you for your time."

He went directly to the back of the room as they filed out, standing unconsciously at parade rest beside Ramirez.

The young aide who had earlier asked a question stopped by.

"You never told us."

"Told you?"

"What you said to the young girl who asked if you wanted to keep going down this path."

"Ha! Oh, that. Well, I looked around and saw a couple other telescopes set up along our walkway. I told her of course! It's a great path! Look at all the amazing things there are to see! I see you've got a scope. I love my binos. Isn't astronomy fun?"

"Excellent. I love astronomy too. Hopefully you encouraged her."

"I hope so. They seemed nice."

The man wandered off, the last to go.

"How do you think it went?" he asked Sonya.

"I'll ask them to strike the Q&A session from the minutes."

"That bad, huh."

"No. Not at all, Paul. You did a great job. This project is something to be proud of. But you are correct when you note that Q&A can take you places that look pretty silly. Best leave that to the Phase 2 project, if there ever is one."

"Word?"

"Your guess is as good as mine. We'll see. Won't be long. By the way," she gestured and another older military man walked over, one that he had missed. "Paul Newbury, I'd like to introduce you to George Endelman."

"Endless Man?"

"Old Berry?"

The two men broke into smiles.

"You two know one another?"

"George was my CO back when we played in the sandpit. Best commander I ever had. Present company excluded."

She shook her head, amused.

"And Old Berry here was constantly telling us historical tales, not a bad XO. He liked hearing himself talk."

"I thought you were retired?"

"Well, Old Berry, gotta make a couple bucks somehow."

Paul looked back and forth between him and the General, trying to figure out the pecking order. A rank. Anything.

But there was nothing.

"Paul, George will be our security and liaison with local law enforcement regarding the recent events. George, come with me. I'll show you around."

He winked at Endelman before he left. Endelman winked back. It was very good news.

Watching them go, as they disappeared up the stairs the tiny SCIF seemed bigger again. The old, ratty beaten up projector was still running.

He went over to turn it off. He hated lying to people.

Because when he told the little girl that he loved the path he was on, she said, and he'd never forget it, "That's the wrong answer, Paul."

How'd she know his name? If he had mentioned that? They would have thrown him out of the room, or worse, chased down the girl. Probably just some kind of facial recognition at work. That stuff was everywhere. Getting out over his skis was the one surefire way to kill this before they even got started.

4.06

Counseling Debian

"You go talk to her," Mary pointed out the back door, "I told her she'd just have to wait until her father got home."

Fearfully, he pushed the back door open and went out, WWI soldier going over the wall, into a cloud of mustard gas. Certain death awaited.

He remembered being a kid and having his mom say, "You just wait until your father gets home!"

There she was, little Debian, playing something. He was the father. He had gotten home.

This ought to be good, since he had absolutely nothing up his sleeve.

I'll be damned, he thought, she's set up that rock game of hers in 3D. What size was it? Eight by Eight by Eight.

"Hey kiddo, mom says you punched your sister in the face."

She frowned, not looking at him, continuing to move her rocks around.

"She was being bossy. I don't like that."

"Well Deb, I don't like that either, but we can't just go around punching people in the face."

"We can't?"

She glanced at him quickly then returned to work.

"No, sweetie, sadly we cannot. People will start thinking very poorly of us. You don't like Salomé being bossy. Other people don't like you punching Sal in the face. What if they punched you?"

Oh, he thought, this was looking good. A little bit of reasoning by analogy.

"She's a bad person, just like the monsters."

Fuck me.

Their Harry Potter book was over there, laying off to the side. Was it the right thing to do to let her read anything she wanted? Shouldn't you control access, have a bedtime, and all that?

He thought back on the little girl in the park, then his presentation earlier.

There was a lot to consider.

"Sal says I'm a weirdo."

"Debian Newbury, I can absolutely assure you that you are NOT a weirdo."

"See? Sal's a bad person, like I said."

Oh my god, he was fighting a Kung-Fu master.

His old CQC instructor said you either change tactics quickly or die.

"Monsters, huh. Like we were talking about?"

She nodded, continuing on. She must have had half the driveway in that grid, little rocks in little boxes.

"Now Debian, no fibbing, have you actually seen one of these monsters with your own eyes?"

She stopped. No. Continued.

She was so cute and sweet, even when she was kicking his ass with logic. He felt like a carrot being eaten by a bunny. He thought again of the presentation.

You don't always share everything.

"You know, I see patterns and invisible things too. We all do."

That stopped her. She looked at him carefully.

"You do?"

"Sure! I won't stop pumping gas unless the price matches certain numbers. Your mom sees faces in clouds. Ever tell you the story of John Nash?"

"Story time! Story time! Where's the book?"

"Think I can do this without the book. So a long time ago, there was a man named John Nash. He was a brilliant mathematician, he loved puzzles like the one you have there. He loved breaking codes like your dad does. And he could spot patterns in all kinds of things other people couldn't, that's what made him so good at all those other things."

"So he was a weirdo too."

"Well yes, but not that word. Find another word instead of weirdo. He lived a really long time ago, when we were at war with these really bad guys."

"Neat! Were they dinosaurs?"

"No Deb, not that long ago. Anyway everybody was really excited and really scared about these bad guys, and Nash started seeing clues to them everywhere he went."

"Nobody else could see them?"

"Nope. They think it was because he was under so much stress and emotion. Although he had some trouble, eventually he got better and we still think of him of being a great mathematician and codebreaker."

"Retard."

"Excuse me young lady. Where'd you hear that word?"

"Sal."

She looked at him as if to say, see? Bad person.

Having a big sister couldn't be easy, he reminded himself. Stress is a tricky thing for anybody, especially a seven-year-old.

"Anything you want to tell me about what happened at Piggly Wiggly?" Mary had asked before sending him on this obviously suicidal mission.

"Nope. Sad thing. Mentally ill. Very sad. By the way, they brought in some new guy…"

"Endelman," she studied him, "got it. He already called. Meeting him tomorrow."

Stress is a funny thing.

Watching her, though, Deb didn't look stressed. She looked happy. Debian was like a puzzle-solving vacuum cleaner, sucking up knowledge and then playing with it in her own way.

Maybe happy was the way to go.

"I love you kiddo. Did you know that?"

She nodded slowly, thoughtfully. She had a wonderful smile.

"Maybe one day I can play this game you've made."

"Yay!" she didn't look back.

"I don't know, we'll see. It looks very hard."

"Nyah, it's fun, Dad. I'll show you."

"I almost forgot, the best part of the John Nash story, the part they don't tell. Not only did he make it through his problems, he ended up very happy."

"But how," this stopped her. He had her full attention. "Did he go blind? Stop seeing things?"

"No hon, he didn't. I won't lie. He had a really bad time there, but he eventually realized that it didn't matter."

"What didn't matter?"

"The patterns he saw. He still kept seeing invisible things the rest of his life. He just realized that as long as he wasn't doing anything bad, it was just something he could see and other people couldn't, and it bothered them when he talked about it. So he stopped. Died a happy man with lots of friends."

She was dubious.

"We can both do that too! In fact, that's what everybody does for the most part. If you're pumping gas and the number ends up on the lottery that night, most folks wouldn't say anything even though they might think there's something really sneaky going on. That's okay."

"Hmmm."

"It's just a matter of not saying everything you think. Think of the great scientist Isaac Newton. There are some folks, tetrachomats...."

"But they still locked him up, right? Nash?"

"Yes."

"Did he get fired?"

"Yes."

"Did he keep his family?"

"No."

"So he might as well punched them all in the face."

See? Bad person. She nodded again, conclusion reached, then went back to playing.

"Hmmm. Does seem that way, doesn't it."

He scratched his chin.

He watched her play for a minute or two in silence.

No denying it. She was happy as a lark.

"What do you see, exactly, Deb? Specifically. Use details."

"I dunno. Monsters. Like invisible monsters."

"Now Deb, if they're invisible, how can you see them."

Now she scratched her chin.

Score one for da.

He glanced at the Harry Potter book she had taken to carrying around. Maybe that's where all this was coming form.

"Like wizards? Trolls?"

He tried to think of the monsters in the story.

"Puffle-griffs?"

She looked at him as if he were not meeting expectations as a dad.

"Like Voldemort?

She nodded quickly. Dad was finally catching up.

"He who cannot be named."

Ok, then, there you go.

"AIEEEEEEEE!"

They heard Tim's scream before they saw him. He came running around the corner just as fast as he could, in only his underwear, holding out a large plastic sword, and charged into the brush.

"Dad, what did you do when you were an army man?"

"Well, I got to wear cool clothes. I got to travel. I got to meet people."

She thought about this for a minute, still playing her game. He could hear Mary start screaming for Tim from inside the house.

"And that's it. Hmmm. I see." She emphasized her conclusion with a firm nod, subject closed.

He didn't think she believed for a minute that this was all he did, and he wasn't about to talk about anything more. He'd die first. No more army man talk.

He glanced back at Potter, picking it up.

"Let's see. How far have we gotten so far?"

"Page 376," she said, not missing a beat.

"How about this: For the next week, every day you don't hit anybody..."

She was already getting excited, knowing where this was going.

"AND you don't use bad words like weirdo or retard? I will read an extra 30 minutes every night."

"YAY YAY YAY YAY!!!!"

"But wait, little one. This is just to help you get into the habit. After the week, we go back to normal. And then if you hit people or use those names? There'll be NO reading for a whole week."

She stood up. She was smiling and getting ready to explode.

"Deal?" He stuck his hand out, did his best serious dad look.

"Deal."

"Shake on it, kiddo."

She shook, also putting on a serious face.

"It's been an average of 37 minutes per night. An extra 30 minutes will put us past an hour! AWESOME!"

She began that victory dance she'd picked up somewhere, wiggling around and waving her arms wildly.

God he loved his kids.

4.07

Flying Deb

"Are we going to get ice cream after this? What happens if the engine turns off? Are we all going to die?"

Paul smiled at his daughter. They were in a cruising configuration at 3,000 feet in his small plane. Debian was obviously on-fire, excited about everything going on around her. Her first flight.

"Yes, nothing, and yes, but probably not today."

"What do all those gauges do? How do you know if something's wrong?"

"Nothing's wrong, sweetie. See here, look around. We're up in the sky! Here, you take the controls."

He let go of the yoke, looking at Deb. This was her moment to either freak out or respond, and he'd bet good money on how this was ending.

She immediately took the control, not moving but in charge. Observing.

"That's great, Deb. Now move it a bit to the left and right, not up or down yet, but get a feel for how it works."

She did as instructed, becoming even more wide-eyed as they went along.

"See? No monsters here. Nothing to be afraid of."

"I'm not afraid."

He cocked an eyebrow.

"Monsters are just kid stuff, Dad. This is science."

"It is indeed, little one. Say," he pointed outside, "How fast do you think we're going?"

"Pretty fast."

"That's odd, I wouldn't think so. Here, this gauge here tells us Knots Indicated Airspeed, or kias. What's that show?"

"111 kias," she said.

Surprisingly, she was calming down. He could see her eyes darting among all the gauges and knobs, soaking it all up.

"Good. Now, if you're flying the plane, and you are, what do you think you should be looking at?"

"That gauge? The kias thing?"

"Maybe. But what if you fly into a mountain? How would you land? You just can't keep looking at one gauge."

"Imma look at ALL the gauges," she said, then she immediately corrected, "but that wouldn't work. Gauges don't show where mountains are, right dad? Or other planes."

"Not these gauges, no."

"So what am I supposed to look at or do? I can't just keep flying without moving anything. I want ice cream! Gotta land."

She needed more deep things to spend time on and Paul was going to give them to her.

"That's why we have language, kiddo, like right now when we're talking and using gestures to one another. Wouldn't you like to know how to fly the plane?"

"Right now, yeah Dad. Duh."

"And how could I tell you without some kind of words or gestures? Not all creatures speak, badgers don't have language, and they do just fine. So why us?"

"I dunno. 'Cause we're not badgers?"

"I hope not! We've been thinking about this for years, and our best answer so far is that language exists to teach, learn, and use tools. See this? This airplane is a tool. It's one of the most super cool tools around. People have dreamed of flying ever since they saw birds. It's magic. We're magicians now."

"So if the engine goes off, am I supposed to talk to the plane? Do badgers have planes?"

"Don't be a smartass. I want you to think about tools and language. This will give you a much better answer, one that you can keep with you wherever you go in life."

She sighed loud enough that he could hear it over the engine. She was just starting to pick up her older sister's sigh.

"Ok, you want the easy answer? If the engine goes off, you make this kias number 63kias, then you land the plane. Easy. Simple."

She considered that.

"No, I want the REAL answer."

"Ok, let's say we're a bunch of cavemen. We live in a caveman family. But there's a Sabre-Toothed Tiger outside eating the other cavemen!"

"Yikes! Let's kill it! Can it be a bear, though?"

"Not a lion? Ok, it's a bear. Now I come home, caveman daddy, and I've learned how to make spears. I can't kill the lion by myself, but all together? If we had spears? Our caveman family could kill the lion."

"Bear."

"I mean bear. So I don't have words, but I sit down with you guys and grunt, gesture, and show you how to make a spear. Now here's my point: Deb, maybe you used a bone. Maybe mom used a tree. Maybe Tim made one with just a long rock, and so on. But they were all generally like spears."

"We go outside and hunt down the bear. Know what happens?"

"Tell me! Do we get to keep it as a pet?"

"No, but we do kill the bear, so we are happy. We have bear burgers for dinner and your brother Tim gets a new bearskin coat."

"Are we going to kill bears with the airplane? Do we have guns?"

She was enjoying this far too much.

"Watch it, kiddo. Does it matter that everybody made a different kind of spear?"

"No."

"See this gauge here? It's a number. If the plane is structured correctly, we can use that number to this tool, this airplane. We can do things like fly at optimum speeds or climb just the way we want. But what if the plane isn't structured correctly, say there's something getting in the way of the hole this gauge works on?"

"It would go to zero. It would be broken."

"No, sweetie, it would not. Numbers never lie, but definitions always do to some degree or another. It's important to know that to stay safe. If this gauge is broken, it may be zero, it may be too high or too low, it may be correct and slowly start being more and more wrong. We can't go outside and inspect the plane while it's flying."

"If we had a parachute."

"And a good grip, maybe," he admitted, "but most of the time not."

"So now you're going to tell me not to use that kias thingy? You lied?"

"Sure, use the gauge. Good pilots use everything. That's your answer. There is no one thing. We could cover all the gauges and I could land the plane just fine without them. I would look around outside, listen to the sound of the wind whistling over the fuselage, notice the angle the wings too with the horizon. Or we could cover just a gauge or two, or break a gauge."

"That's 'cause you're real good."

"No, sweetie, that's something most serious pilots can do. That's because it's the assembly, the evidence tree, the matrix of data, that comes together to help me fly the plane. It's never just one thing. Thinking that it's just this one thing will get you killed. The bear will eat you!"

She laughed. He took the wheel again.

"Here, let me show you something."

He turned the engine off.

"What are you doing, Daddy!"

"I'm going to land the plane, just like I said, without looking inside at all."

He winked at her. She began studying the gauges anyway.

He began the long, slow spiral to the small uncontrolled airport he had spotted earlier. The winds were a bit gusty. He estimated 10-15 at about 205 degrees. Plenty inside the safety range.

But thank goodness for the gusty wind. As they got closer on final, the gusts bounced them around a bit, heightening, he hoped, Deb's emotions. Finally, there was enough wind that he managed to land on one wheel, allowing the other wheel to pivot around and drop as they slowed down.

He glanced over at her. She looked like she had just witnessed him parting the Red Sea. He nodded, the master. God, he loved being a dad.

"See? Nothing to it. The airplane is a tool. I needed the tool to get to the ground. Whether or not any of that other stuff was 'correct' or not doesn't matter. My spear is just fine, thank you, no matter how I made it."

"But today it was nice and sunny, You could see."

She learned quick.

"That's right. If things had gotten more complicated we would have to have assembled more complex sequences, dependency trees, matrices, and so forth to land. Maybe we might even have to use the instruments, or even new ones, like gyroscopes, or radars. Even then, though, we're always cross-checking. It's the graph that holds the value, like a spiderweb, not the gauge or the number. Those things lie. But taken all together they can't lie. All definitions are wrong to some degree, sweetie. It's the overall shape of the airplane in a given context that causes the airplane to fly, not some gauge or another. It's not that simple. It's a lot more fun than that."

"But it was simple for you, Dad. You just looked outside and steered. I guess our bear was easy, I mean not very precise."

He noticed that she struggled with "precise," but only a bit.

"Ha! Exactly! We had a very imprecise bear today. Small planes are understandable, easy. Spears are easy. And we had fun. You know, you could do this. It's not hard. People flew airplanes without gauges for a long time. As you learn more about flying, your meaning matrix can become more complex. Then gauges become more important. Big planes can get very complicated! You get to fight better bears. super-bears."

"Let's go again! Now! Now! I wanna try!"

"Maybe one more time."

"YAY!"

4.08

Fencing In

"Newbury, you make a piss-poor landscaper."

Paul looked up from his work to see Mary wiping her brow. They were in the front yard.

"Thanks, boss," he said, "Only twenty more post-holes and we'll have one side of the yard covered. We are a machine."

"Privacy fences don't grow out of the ground, grunt," Mary was obviously enjoying herself, bossing him around.

"I can always dream," he said, "You know, as hard as this is, I'd rather do another three days of fencing instead of presenting to dignitaries like yesterday."

"Dignitaries – math dignitaries."

"Yeah, you know, sponsors and such."

"Want to talk about it?"

"The flying went great. The kid's addicted. She's a natural."

He didn't tell her he'd let a seven-year-old land the plane. Some stories were best told slowly.

"She managed to stay on-task?"

"Did she ever. There are dozens of instruments and controls in there. It was like taking her to Disney World. In fact, it was better. We may have a pilot in our future."

"Did you know she's drawing pictures of monsters?"

He stopped. He stuck the post-hole diggers in the ground.

"I guess we need to talk about that."

'The kid is troubled, Paul. Our kid."

"Is she, though? Or simply imaginative?"

"Imaginative."

"Do you know what our other kid Salomé told me this morning?" He waited for her to take the bait. When she didn't, he kept going anyway. "She told me that from now on she had to wear her red socks to school everyday. The red socks made her more popular."

"It's that stupid pendant you bought her."

"Why Mrs. Newbury, I do think you might be becoming a luddite in your doddering years. It's just a toy. Geesh."

"And Sal's not seeing monsters everywhere."

"How's training the new guy going?"

"Martin? He's okay, I guess. Never met a piece of junk food he didn't like, but folks love him. And he's smart. Getting people on your side is half the battle in police work."

She stopped what she was doing.

"And you're changing the subject."

"Who me?"

He gave her a sly smile. Shook his head. They knew each other far too well.

He picked the post-hole diggers back up, looked at the next hole.

She was having none of it.

"Met your guy. That Endelman is a piece of work," she continued, "Where'd you dig him up at? Never seen anybody so helpful and so completely useless at the same time."

"Yeah, he's good," he struck the ground as hard as he could. It didn't seem to make much of a dent in the hard clay.

Changing his mind, he looked down the row of post holes left to dig.

"This is a lot more work than I thought it would be."

"We have a system. Stick to the system and we'll get there. Looking at everything left to do is only going to discourage you."

"Right. Learned that a long time ago. Always a mistake to look down when doing things like jumping out of airplanes. Just stick to the system. Trust it."

"You know, I've been doing police work for a long time, Paul. We have protocols for dealing with troubled kids. They work."

Ignoring her. "I wonder if we're building this fence to keep people out or keep them in. I forget."

"We should take Debian to get evaluated, see why she's starting to become obsessed with monsters all of a sudden."

"Can't we just let her be creative, see where that goes? Hell, she might be on her way to becoming a great abstract painter or something. We don't know."

"You're right. We don't know. And we should. That's why she needs evaluating."

"But what if we're wrong? Should we really be sticking her on a track like this when she's only seven, for chrissakes?"

"What if we're right? Do we really want to end up with her medicated, institutionalized, or worse having known that we could have done something sooner? Prevented it?"

"I'm just not sure the kid needs a protocol. Or an evaluation. Maybe she just needs more room, better toys."

"Ok, I'll buy that. Answer me this: can you live with yourself if you're wrong."

"Ah fuck," he crossed his arms. He frowned. "This parenting stuff is turning out to be a lot more complicated than I imagined."

"You want for me to take her on my own? I can do that. But we really need to be on the same page about this. It's important."

"No, you're right. Let's take her for a time or two to somebody, have them tell us what's up. I take it you know somebody."

"I know some people."

"You know some people."

He looked down. His energy was gone.

"Meanwhile? You dig three more holes and you could get lucky later."

He jumped in the work with as much gusto as he could manage.

"I dig three more holes and the only thing I'm romancing this evening is a heating pad and single-malt scotch."

4.09

Wrapping Up BCI

"What do you think about my running a bakery?"

Brigadier General Sonya Ramirez stood behind her desk sorting papers out. Paul could see that on them were pictures of houses.

"Would it have a flagpole?" Paul said.

"In the front."

"Then I approve."

He stepped closer, looked at the stacks of housing pictures.

"Looking for houses?"

"Time I'm moving on, Paul. Don't let moss grow under your feet and all of that."

"Got any front runners?"

"This one," she showed him a picture of an old, stately house.

"Looks like a great retirement, Sonya, although I seriously doubt you're going to be sitting on the porch sipping mint juleps."

"No, I have a partner. We're looking to start something, a business. We just need a location and, well, a business."

"There's that. I've got it all figured out: I'm headed back to teaching. Can't wait. Got midterms coming up and I'm onto several promising new lines of research. Kids and I are even talking about a startup, who knows? It's a good field to be in."

"Well, that's it, Bed and Breakfast," she said, picking out one and beginning to stack the others.

"A partner? Sonya, is this looking to be permanent?"

Ramirez gave him a stern look.

"Hey, boss, you're retiring so I get to use 'Sonya' and ask these kinds of questions. Says so in the book. Like the normal people do."

"The book, huh. Yes, We've been dating for several months and it's looking good. Started living together. She's a nice person. You'd like her."

"Well then, let's do something! You guys come to the house. I make a mean spaghetti."

The ice broke. She smiled, but just a little bit.

"I'd like that. Plan on visiting us. It'll give me a date to push along all these decisions and I make a mean hamburger. We're going to keep in touch, right?"

"Absolutely! I'm still going to be doing research in computational psycholinguistics, you're going to be in the area. You know," he tried his best Humphrey Bogart, "This could be the start of a beautiful relationship."

"Speaking of carrying on, that's why I asked you to report first thing. We're done."

"Yeah, I know. It was a good project."

"No, I mean we're done. There's nothing else. This is the last time we'll speak here, or be here."

"What? Isn't there a report or something? The military and there's no weeks of paperwork to wrap things up?"

"Shocking, I know, but those are the orders."

"But all this stuff." he pointed around the room, "who's packing up all this stuff?"

"Endelman was here two hours before I got here, already starting in on it. I offered for us to help but he'd have nothing of it. I can't tell if he's hard-charging or just a controlling asshole. The man is preternaturally friendly. He's like a diabolical Mary Poppins."

"Not sure those are mutually-exclusive conditions. He was a good CO. If he's pushing you off, I'm sure he's got orders too. I just find it hard to believe we're not recording more. So much research and data, and we're leaving it as what, a Powerpoint?"

"Turns out there was a lot of recording going on all along," she held up a listening device, "The first rule of trusting people is never trust people. I imagine nothing else is needed."

"Nice," Paul looked at the device, "Now I feel like I'm in a Soviet Spy Novel. This is really classy."

"Paul, you haven't taken anything out of the SCIF, have you? Any gear, papers, or so forth?"

He thought about all the stuff he'd taken home, the listening device.

"Not at all. Of course not, General."

She tapped the picture of the house.

"You sure you don't want the promotion? I told them you're the best person to have it."

"This job? I thought there was no job."

He could see her tense, but she kept looking.

"There's that, isn't there."

"You're getting sloppy in your old age, Sonya," he said.

"Perhaps so," she said, "My mind's elsewhere. There's a reason people are forced to retire."

A knock.

"Hey, you guys want any cannoli? I've got a box. They're good," Endelman stuck his head in.

"My stomach says yes. My gut says no." Paul stuck his hand out to shake, "Endless man! Good to see you. Getting settled in?"

Endelman nodded. "I am, although it looks like we're not going to be working together much at all."

"That's what I hear," Paul nodded indicating Ramirez but stayed focused on Endelman, "so there's nothing? There's nothing left to do? This is it?"

"'Fraid so, Old Berry," he patted Paul on the shoulder, "Old man. I'm also afraid that there'll be no more research on the BCI side of things. Theory and stats, you're good. Write, publish all you want. Counter-intel and threats, red area. Avoid at all costs."

"But I'm still a professor, right? You guys aren't asking me to resign?" He looked back at Ramirez. She had no answers. Then back to Endelman.

"Of course!" He held his hands up in surrender, "Hey, I just work here. Passing stuff along. Sure you don't want any cannoli?"

"I can still work with my interns? I'll need to read them out of the program. Is that okay? And why all the secrecy?"

"We're just being extra careful. You know the military. We love the fucking military and the military loves fucking us. That's the way it always goes."

Paul laughed in spite of himself.

"Okay, alright, Endless. But who do I ask if I'm concerned about where the red line is?"

Endelman pointed at himself, "That'd be me. You've got my contact. Just ping me and say you'd like to go fishing. We'll meet and sort it out. Nothing recorded or transmitted. Got it?"

Endelman studied them both.

They both nodded.

"Good! I hate these long goodbyes. Why don't you both take the rest of the day off here. I've got it from here on out."

He gave them a friendly wave and left. For some reason Paul felt the man hovering just outside the door.

"You heard the man, Colonel," Ramirez said, "I guess we are officially off the project. It's all being mothballed now."

She came around the desk, took him by the elbow. "Let me buy you an early lunch. I can tell you about this new house we're buying."

They left, but before Paul made it out, he looked back at the office.

"I guess so, Sonya."

4.10

Diagnosing Debian

"There's nothing wrong with Debian, but I can't be sure because she scores off-the-charts in so many areas. There are a lot of blank spots in our evaluation, so let me tell you what I know."

His nametag said "Dr. Sykes." The older man sat behind an expensive desk, templed his fingers, and looked at Mary and Paul over them.

Mary reached for Paul's hand and held it.

"She's extremely good at spatial reasoning. Never tested anybody like her. She has a numeric memory and is able to mentally-manipulate symbols at a depth we can only guess at."

"That's what I thought too, doctor," Paul said, "She just sees a lot that other people can't. Like she has a new kind of eyeball: gifted."

"Perhaps so," the doctor placed his hands flat on the table, "You posited that when you brought her. But have you ever thought about what it would be like to have a new sensory organ? As I recall from med school, there have been people throughout history with better than 20-20 vision. Bound to happen. A lot of folks have bad vision so the laws of chance said that eventually there'd be people with what we might call super-vision. 10-20, or even 5-20 Such a person could see things 20 feet away the way a normal person would see something five feet away. They can make out so much detail it's like a built-in zoom for the eyeball. Can you imagine having a five or ten times zoom vision everywhere you went?"

"That sounds actually pretty nice," Mary said, "Who wouldn't want vision like that?"

"Well, as it turns out, most people. These people were branded witches, burned at the stake, shunned from society. It sounds great until you realize that these people could see the craters on the moon. They could make out people climbing trees on distant mountains. They could see the moons of Jupiter, just by looking up in the sky. Can you imagine being a seven-year-old in the Dark Ages and trying to explain planets and moons?"

"Not good," Paul glanced down at the desk. Sykes' desk was a monument to money and precision.

The doctor continued.

"Worse, there were also people who saw fairies and angels, gods and demons, or thought they did. They were just as convincing, in fact history has shown us that they were more convincing, probably because they were making things up as they went along, not reporting random stuff nobody had ever observed. Weird stuff moving around nobody else can see? At best it's boring, quirky. Major battles between good and evil that the audience is participating in? That's excitement everybody can get in on, whether you can see it or not. There's nothing required except emotional commitment and a very small amount of imagination. And it didn't take long for others to make up more parts of these stories, then the stories started getting assembled into longer narratives, myths, and so forth."

"So Deb's crazy, I mean making things up?" Mary squeezed his hand.

The doctor crossed his arms in front of his chest.

"Like I said, I don't know. In this job we're always on the outside looking in. Occam's Razor tells us that most likely she's just very imaginative and really has convinced herself that she sees these monsters. We'll be proceeding from there."

"I wanted you to know, Mr. Newbury, that I honestly considered your ideas. There's just nothing we can do about that, even if you're correct. We have to proceed as if, and I stress IF this might evolve into dysfunctional behavior. That's a long ways off, and we've just gotten started. So let's take it slowly. Most highly-creative people who think they see things that aren't there do just nicely in the world. A lot of creative kids have imaginary friends. Their world isn't as detailed as Debian's. They just need to learn to control it. This has been happening naturally over the centuries, so nature is on our side. I am very optimistic. She's a extremely special child."

"Timothy called me a pootie-head," Debian told them the minute they both got back home.

She seemed kind of happy about it.

"Well," Mary said, "He's little, so he's just learning."

"Pootie Head!" Tim yelled from the other room, "Pootie head Pootie head, Pootie head!"

Mary sighed.

"I'll get him."

They gathered them together in the living room, sitting cross-legged in a circle.

"You kids may know that we took your sister Debian to a doctor to get her evaluated."

"What's wrong with the little freakazoid now?" Sal stuck her tongue out at Deb.

Deb smiled.

"At least I'm not a witch."

"Pootie head," Tim said silently to himself, conclusion reached.

"What?" Deb saw them all staring at her, "I can't use the word witch now? Is that bad too?"

Deep breath in, deep breath out, Paul thought.

"Salomé," he said, addressing his oldest daughter, "is that okay with you? Can Deb call you a witch? Are you okay with this type of picking?"

"She can call me anything she wants," Sal cleared her throat officially, as if she were giving her first speech to the House of Commons, "I am above such childish name-calling. At least I'm not a clown."

Deb had been wearing an awful striped shirt. She smiled, quite pleased with herself.

"I am the clown, witch."

"To get back on-track," Mary said, "The doctor says that Debian is fine, but we should help her use her imagination in ways that don't involve hitting,"

Mary frowned.

"Or name-calling."

"Pootie-head."

"Aside from some pre-approved loving monikers, I guess." Once again, Paul felt he had wandered off-the-script. Not for the first time that day, he thought that being a dad really should come with an instruction manual.

4.11

Disappointing Joe

The dirt was piled high in places against the construction materials. Paul sat with one of his students in the middle of the ongoing work for the future Freedom University botanical gardens.

"So that's it, then?"

Joe Middles was not happy with the news Paul had for them. Paul had found each of his three interns separately and told them the news about the project shutting down. None had taken it well, but Middles was taking it the worst.

"That's it. It was a good run, Joe." he said, "I'm happy to write you a recommendation. I hear Saylor's got a great program they're starting up. It'd be a good time to get in on the ground floor."

"Sounds a lot like starting over," Joe said.

"Meh, just look at this like a beta run. Nobody gets it right the first time out, and there's nothing wrong with what we did. We can take everything we learned and go to round 2. You're looking at this the wrong way."

"What about all the prototype hardware?"

"Gone."

"And my research papers?"

"Gone. As far as I know, the day after demo day they locked it all up and carted it off. Welcome to defense research."

"You don't understand. Some of that material had nothing at all to do with our project. It was research I was going to use to build a spin-off. I knew the project was going to end. I was trying to plan ahead."

"Oh," now the pushback started making sense, "Non-project research papers? Didn't you make electronic copies?"

"Normally, fuck yeah, but we were told not to use anything but approved devices in the SCIF, so I wrote them all out by hand."

"Joe, Joe, Joe. Why didn't you tell me?"

"My own stuff. Was going to tell you as soon as I reached MVP and saw market traction. Even planned on getting you in on the ground floor. But now? Starting over? It's gonna be a slog."

"Sure that nothing you wrote is related to our work? You sure it's okay?"

"It's causality trees, eigenvectors, Von Neuman machines, and statistical inference, hyperdimensional explanatory models, but that's all bog standard stuff. All I'm doing is creating better red-team/black-team test protocols using advanced GANs."

"Ok, Middles. I hear you. I've got it. I know what you mean, and I can explain it to Sonya, but you wanna translate that *exactly* how you'd like for me to present it? It's going to be so far past them I'm concerned you're never getting those papers back, and I can slant it a lot of different ways. What should I say?"

Joe Middles thought for a moment.

"It's an AI model for cyber-security, helping folks secure their systems and make sure the crypto-currency they invest in isn't broken."

Paul nodded slowly.

Seeing the difficulty, Middles added.

"The only real overlapping part between the secret stuff and what I'm doing is that I'm also talking about using the internet for intelligence, but only for commercial intelligence, not national, and only to make sure security and crypto is working, not check for intruders. I'm just a company guy, nothing spook here."

"Hmmmm. I like it. I can see why it might have commercial value."

"Well, I'm getting out whether I get them back or not. This would just save me years of work. I really need this, Professor Newbury."

"Tell you what, Joe, I'll see what I can do."

"Thank you."

"No promises."

"Gotcha."

"And from here on out, it's Paul. No more of this Professor Newbury nonsense."

He smiled, a pro-forma smile, then stood up from the masonry stack they had met on, patting Middles on the back as he rose. He had no idea how he was even going to get near getting those papers back, but he knew that he owed the man that much.

Leaving, he couldn't admit to himself that no matter how either one of them explained it, there was no way Joe Middles was ever getting those papers back.

4.12

Pendant Taking

The final pins went into the ground, securing the volleyball net in place.

"Now, we play." Paul said, "Let's get 'em."

He looked around, hearing the kids off in the backyard. It was still early morning. They had enough time for a game or two.

"Yo! We're ready!"

The almost constant burbling and yakking of their interaction stopped and he heard before he saw them running around the corner of the house.

"Woot! Rolly Ball!" Tim yelled, jumping at the ball Mary held.

"Deb, you think me and you could take mom and Sal?"

Debian looked at her mother and older sister as if she had never seen them before.

"Easy, daddo."

"The clown and the old coot will be a piece of cake, mom," Sal said, touching her pendant.

Paul noticed Deb was wearing yellow socks. He also noticed Deb enjoyed her sister picking on her, both of which were new.

Changes.

"Young Timothy," he said, "you are what we officially call a floater."

"Floater!"

He motioned for the ball which Tim gave him.

"You can play on whichever side you'd like."

The game went about as he had expected. Debian had no idea how to set him up and Paul wasn't about to spike Mary or Sal even if she did. So they tossed the ball back and forth amicably. Paul tried out a little trash talk which neither girl took up but Tim loved. Tim spent the rest of the day saying he was going to stomp them good!

They took two breaks between games, and each time Sal walked off, talking to herself.

"She's doing that quite a bit," Mary said.

"Yeah, perhaps that pendant wasn't such a good idea."

Mary handed him a water.

"You're going to need to fess up some more stuff about that project of yours or we're going to have to take you in for a statement. Martin's got a bug about it."

"What project. Project's over."

"Having that Endelman character show up wasn't a good move."

He nodded.

"Agreed. Wasn't my call. Nervous sponsors, I guess."

"Smells to high heaven of something black, definitely not kosher."

They heard Sal yell at herself. He couldn't tell if she was talking to somebody on a phone or just practicing.

"She does that a lot," Deb said, "8 times today so far."

"She does, does she," Mary observed, "You want to look into this present of yours? Came from that lab of yours and that project of yours that doesn't exist."

"It's internet surveillance, that's the project. Happy? With my past and the topic you should be able to guess who the players are. I never worked in Boy Scouts."

"And this was a good idea," she pointed to Sal, still talking to her pendant.

"Not so much, really," he admitted, "but it's the kind of commercial product that's fairly common anyway. Half the net is rewarding you for being quasi-famous and the other half is teaching you how to become quasi-famous. It didn't seem like anything especially new, just cute."

He looked at his daughter pacing.

"And it was cute. I thought she'd like it."

"The witch loves it," Deb said.

"You are not part of this conversation, young lady," Mary said, then "Well, I can fix this right now."

She picked up the hammer they had used and went over to Sal.

Paul couldn't make out the exact words, but Sal sadly gave over her pendant. Mary placed it on a rock and smashed it with the hammer. The she rubbed her hands together, making a show of a job done.

Sal ran away crying. Deb started to go after her, but after a few steps went over to where Tim was playing in the grass instead.

Paul thought that was a good move on Deb's part. He didn't want to be around either Sal or Mary that moment.

He wandered over to Timothy as well, hoping to get in on some good army men action before dinner.

4.13

Endelman Explains

"Nice tat," Mary said to the man sitting across from them.

On his arm was a tattoo of the Roman God Janus.

He ignored her comment. Instead he looked back and forth until he was sure they were listening.

"In 2012, U.S. Intelligence realized that the secret NSA base at Pine Ridge in central Australia had seriously been compromised. The cyber attack wasn't on the servers or the satellites. The problem was fitness trackers. Service members, by wearing fitness trackers and doing daily exercise, were providing staffing, scheduling, and even knowledge about which buildings on the base performed which operations. All because people wanted to be fit."

George Endelman took a sip of his mocha. Paul had called in a favor to the man to meet Mary and him at a local coffee shop.

"Back in the dinosaur days," Paul had told them both once they sat down, "when George and I were in the service, George had a presentation he gave to senior brass about technology and security. I asked him to give you the short version. Hopefully it'll help clear the air."

So far Endlessman was on a roll, which Paul had hoped would happen. If the pattern held, he'd be having to shut his old boss down before the man spoke into the early evening, all without saying very much.

"The average Londoner," Endelman continued, "is recorded 33 times, by video cameras, between the time they wake up and the time they make it to work. Cyber security professional have the 10-10 rule: whatever you kept secret online ten years ago will be available and public ten years from now. You may not know it; companies wouldn't dare let people know; but it's out there for those who know where to look. Systems are commonly hacked in various ways, including both by technical means and deliberately by disgruntled employees looking for revenge. The time the data is stolen and the time the data is decrypted can be, and usually is, many years apart. Nothing lasts forever, including promises to keep your secrets secret."

"So you've left the service and now you help people keep secrets," Mary said.

"No, not at all," Endelman said, "Don't do secrets. In the business I'm in, that's the main problem: people act like little infants lost in the woods. Who's the bad guy? Who's the good guy? What did I do wrong? What are my special secrets? Where do I keep them so they'll be safe? I am so afraid. And so on."

Mary looked surprised.

"I must have missed something,"

"We yearn for much more simplicity than the universe is able to provide. Nobody did anything wrong at that base wanting to be fit. No Londoner is doing something wrong just going to work in the morning. Twenty years ago, the United States Office of Personnel Management kept all the secrets they could on everybody with a job for the U.S. Know how they found out they were hacked? When a company came in to demo software that detected hacking. That's how. The demo discovered they had been hacked for years, all of that data gone. Nobody knew. Nobody would have ever known."

"So they should have done a better job?" Paul asked, trying to help set the man up to draw this to a close.

"No. There is no good or bad guy. There is no 'I did the right thing to be safe' or 'I screwed up'. There's no moustache-twirling villain trying to sneak into your cell phone or hack into your bank account. Folks need to stop being such morons. Companies and the government aren't trying to take your data. They don't have to. Nobody cares. You're doing that for them, each moment that you're alive. Play a coloring book game on your phone and it records everything you're doing and sends it back to the app maker several times a second. There's no evil villain or good guys or anything you might see on the movies. It's just humans, being recorded and recording each other every second they're alive. And they're happy to do it to themselves. Hell, they don't have a choice even if they wanted one."

Paul made the "let's move this thing along" gesture to his friend.

"Oh yeah," Endelmand said, "Which is the point. It's the data. The data is neither good nor bad, it doesn't want to help or hurt you. It just exists. If you're starting a new company, odds are you're not looking to collect special data. They already do that. Instead, you're looking for patterns in all that data they already make and trying to find ways to hack their reptile brain, give them more of the stimulus they want."

He pushed his coffee away, obviously struggling with himself to wind down. The man is definitely self-aware, Paul thought. Paul wondered how much of this "I could talk all day" thing with Endleman was just a front. He suspected most of it.

"Think of the data as an ocean, a limitless sea. Each second, most all of the billions of people alive on this planet record their actions, thoughts, conversations, dreams, fantasies, purchases, movements, friendships, enemies, and so on, creating data as they go. Each little bit is a drop dumped into that endless ocean. The drops are so small you barely see them, invisible. Trying to think of whether your little drop is good or bad or where it might go or do is so far beyond the point as to be laughable. Nobody cares about your tiny bits, but that doesn't mean the ocean has no value! Far from it. There are endless depths and riches there, and without all those drops there'd never be the ocean to begin with. It's just that we, frankly, suck at figuring out where each little drop might go or the billions of places it eventually might end up. It's a ludicrous and impossible thing to expect any human to figure out. It's the data, the ocean of data, it's not you or some evil villain or person. Those drops, once made and put in the ocean, will live centuries after you're long gone, doing all sorts of things you'd never be able to imagine now. All possible because of the data, the ocean that we all made."

"And this is why George is here," Paul nodded, willing the man to nod along.

It worked. He nodded.

"That's right," he said, "I'm the data guy. My job is not to keep secrets or protect against some imagined adversary. I'm just the data guy. The Foundation, the folks that pay both Paul and me, want to make sure that the none of the data collected in their research ever gets recorded. Anywhere. Ever."

"And that's why you've been helping me," Mary said. Then almost as an afterthought. "So much."

"George is a little more excited about it than I am. I'm just a simple professor," Paul said, realizing he was pushing it even as the words came out of his mouth, "That's why we called him 'Endless Man', him and that endless sea schtick. But we agree on the overall shape of the problem, and if he seems, hmmm, less than helpful, that's the reason why."

Endelman nodded. He remained silent. Paul continued.

"My schtick isn't security. My research is about predictive things: facts, opinions, events, data," Paul said, "Most times the internet knows how you're doing, why you're doing it, and what you're doing next long before you ever do. That's what fascinates me. There are things there we could never imagine."

There was no mistaking. Mary and Paul both saw the murderous look Endelman shot at Paul in the split second before he regained composure.

"Yeah, he does the nerdy stuff, all the history and math. Oldberry is the context guy. Little ol' me? Just a humble janitor."

Mary looked at both of them as if they had tried to sell her a piece of the Brooklyn Bridge, but Paul could tell that it also seemed to work. She realized now both the general nature of the things he was working on and how serious it could be. That was the goal. He could never tell her without Endelman finding out all about it and lots of serious pain coming their way. But he knew he could give out some of the details with Endelman right there and there'd be nothing for the man to discover.

Mission accomplished.

He wondered how many more favors he had left to ask with his old friend before he ran out.

4.14

Putting Deb's Fire Out

He had no idea how long the fire had been burning before he caught it. Long enough to cover about 100 square meters. Debian just stood there looking, watching it continue the slow burn across the backyard grass.

He grabbed the Markov blanket he'd given his daughter, poured water over it, and ran to the center of the fire, swatting out and suffocating it wherever it could be found.

She just stood, watching as he worked, not disinterested but not really involved, either, the way one might eat lunch while watching construction workers painting a roadway.

"Debian Ada Newbury!" he said, finishing up putting the fire out. It wasn't too bad, but a little more and the fire department would have to have been called.

"You know better than to build fires."

He knelt down, studied her. She smiled at him.

"I know, dad, but the fire cleans. I had to do something about the darkness."

It was daytime. There was no darkness.

He was completely out of his depth here. What to do? Should he take Deb somewhere? Call Mary at work? Call the doc?

He decided to sit down. He patted the ground beside him.

"Sit down, kiddo. Let's talk."

She sat, still smiling.

"Well, that's better," there was nothing better. It seemed like the right thing to say.

"What's our next book, daddo?"

Sigh.

"You know what?" he looked around the yard. It wasn't too bad. "This backyard needs a fire pit. It needs a place we all can go, with adult supervision, and build fires. Wouldn't that be nice?"

"Sure! I can help gather rocks!"

Deb sprang to her feet and started searching the yards and nearby woods for rocks, bringing them back and beginning a small circle.

Paul stood up, wondering if he should help. His daughter didn't look unhappy, scared, or angry. She didn't look troubled in any way. She just wanted a fire, so she built one. The darkness and cleaning stuff? Probably that book they were reading.

He went over to the woods, grabbed a couple of rocks.

"I've got just the perfect book for us," he said. He placed his rocks and went back for more. "It's a famous one. Fahrenheit 451. I think you'll love it."

"Yay! Can we start it right now, before everybody else gets home?"

"We can start it as soon as we finish this," he pointed.

Going back for another round, "And then I've got Fire Lizards of Talos IV. It's a little bit more cerebral, but I think you'll like it too."

"And maybe I could read that one for you?"

He shook his head confused.

"You think you could do that, sweetie? Read?"

"Sure! I've been practicing!"

He kissed his sweet child on the head. They were done.

He gestured to the back door. They started walking.

"You know, reading about fires is hella lot better than setting them."

"I know that, Dad." He thought she sounded like a teenager. Too soon!

"No more fires without adults, got it?"

She stopped them from continuing their walk inside. She looked back at the fire ring they had just created.

Sad?

"I guess."

"We should probably keep this between ourselves, too."

She frowned at him like he was a toy that had suddenly broke.

"But why, dad?"

"Space, kiddo. You need space. I love you. I'm giving you space to grow up."

He winked and shot her a smile.

"Now, let's grab the couch and start on this book! I'm going to tell you about a completely new type of fireman!"

"Last one in has to get the cookies!" Deb took off.

He let her win. Everybody deserves a win now and then.

4.15

Playing The Game

Paul looked across the small table, evil intent in his eye.

He shifted looking about the room, then cut to his wife.

"First thing I'm going to do, then…."

Mary looked concerned.

"Is kill the dwarf."

She raised her eyebrows as if to say "Are you sure?" but that's not what she said. Instead, she looked to where Paul had just been looking.

She looked worried.

"That's you. You're the dwarf."

"It is? Yay!" Timothy said, pushing his figure forward. He sprang from his chair, assuming a bad Kung Fu stance.

"A HA! Come at me shopkeeper guy!"

"What's his Armor Class again?"

"Paul, now that you've wrapped up your project, you're going to be spending more time at home? You know, the doctor gave us some other games to play with the family."

"I'm almost done. Need to get some papers that were 'accidentally' snatched up by Endelman. Last thing on my list."

"Debian, have you and dad started keeping logs of any of the things you might be seeing? With your drawings?"

Deb looked at her dad, then back to her mom, then back to dad again. She said nothing.

"Somebody want to tell me what the clown and dad were doing building a firepit bin the backyard? Are we going to start having campfires?" Salomé said.

Paul looked at Debian. She was dressed normally, but somewhere she

465

had found a bright orange handkerchief which she had tied around her neck. She smiled and adjusted it in response to her sister's taunts. Well, at least she wasn't wearing clown noses. Yet.

"I guess we're both moving on," he said, "Me from my big project and you and whatisname from that supermarket thing."

"Martin. Beau Martin. And no, we can't quit. We got orders to let it go and close the case."

"I must have missed something in logic class. If you've got orders to close the case, then that's quitting, right?"

"Martin's the new guy. It's his first case. I don't think I could make him give it up, and I'm not sure I'm inclined to."

"Did it ever occur to you that your meddling is actually changing the situation you're trying to fix, often in unpredictable ways?"

"That's what I do, Paul. I don't meddle. Can I stop being who I am? Could you? Ever occur to you that things just don't fix themselves when left alone and you wish hard enough it could go back to normal?"

"Endelman's a janitor. Trust me, you and Martin don't want to start looking like something that needs cleaning up. He's good."

"You know, crew, we've made it back to town. This is probably a good spot to stop for the night. You guys go get ready for bed. Dad and I'll be right up."

"Booo!" Tim had two favorite words, "boo" and "yay" Paul yearned for this phase to pass.

Grumbling, they got up and left.

"You know, I've got work to do," Mary said, "at least being the police, when I find out things and go through procedure I know I'm making a positive difference in the world. You take care. I don't meddle."

Paul didn't look up. He heard the front door slam. He heard her car start.

He sat at the table in their little kitchen. The sounds of tree frogs, crickets, and faraway dogs barking could be heard muffled and far off.

Eventually, and slowly, he began putting the game pieces away.

4.16

Raining In

It was raining. It had been raining all morning, getting heavier as lunch approached. There was not much to do.

"Aren't you going to come to my room?" Sal stood in the doorway to Deb's room, hands on hips.

"Did you call me?" Deb looked up. She was sitting cross-legged with a big book open in front of her.

"No."

"Then why would I come to your room?"

"I came to your room, didn't I?"

Deb paused for a moment, failing to come up with an adequate rebuttal, then shrugged and went back to her book.

In reply, Sal cocked her head, loosened her stance, and ambled over to her sister. Failing to get any new response, she plopped down beside her.

"Dad and Mom have chores for us, but they're busy arguing."

It was very important that Sal knew this and was able to tell somebody.

"Shouldn't you be polishing your cool kids clothes for school or something?"

"I thought I might offer you some fashion advice. Looks like you need it."

Deb was wearing a red bandanna, white blouse, and sky blue pants.

"You look like a flag."

"You look like a witch."

"Clown."

"Witch."

Sal held up what she had been holding behind her back. It was a small figure holding up a hammer to the sky.

"You left this doll in the living room," Sal studied it.

"That's not a doll, that's a figurine. It's Thor."

"Looks like my dolls I used to play with, only uglier," Sal almost said, "like you" but held back.

"There's a difference. That's Thor, Norse God of Thunder. That's an Action Figure. You wouldn't know."

Sal turned the doll in her hand, looking for batteries or a string.

"Does he say anything? Do something?"

"No, silly. You collect them," Deb pointed to half a dozen more on her top bookshelf. "But they can do all sorts of things. You just have to have imagination."

"I've got imagination. More than you do, clown. I've got imagination enough I don't need to read books all the time for help. Or learn smart stuff. You know, even if you stuck to one color, you could look just as silly and be better coordinated."

"No, it's not just imagination. It's the books. You use imagination and the stories in the books. Together."

Debian looked at Salomé, disappointed.

"Toss me," Deb held up her hand and her sister tossed the figurine over. She caught it easily.

"See? Coordinated," then she made a loud raspberry. "Phpppttttt!"

Sal sighed quite dramatically, looking to the sky, then slouched.

"You're going to take a lot of work, little freak. What do you got there? Harry Potter? Ya can't read! Will you stop it already with trying to impress Mom and Dad? You can't make up for being weird by being smart."

"And you can't make up for being boring by being cute."

"Takes a lot more smarts to dress and act creatively than it does to read and do math, clown. I have what they call 'Savior Fare'. You do not. You are a simple peasant."

"You're about as creative as a robot person," Deb gritted her teeth but tried to appear to keep reading. "Not much. Robot person."

"Well you ARE a robot person," Sal spat, "full of wires and circuits and they're all broken! And that's why Mom and Dad had to take you to get fixed. Because if we can't fix you, we're going to have to get rid of you!"

Deb began weeping and trying to hide it, her little body shaking back and forth as Sal watched.

That broke it.

"Hey Deb, clown, you," Sal said, completely at a loss for words. Sal was afraid.

"I didn't mean it," Sal said, "You need to calm down. I'm sorry. I was just playing."

Somehow her confession made Deb cry even harder. Sal heard her parents moving around downstairs.

Sal looked around the room for something to talk about or play with. The shelves were mostly bare except for models of spaceships Dad had helped Deb build. At least Sal thought they were spaceships. Couldn't comment on something she didn't know about.

There was one bookshelf with a few dozen books. On the right were big and scary-looking books. Sal didn't know anything about them either. On the left were smaller books, but they were ones she had never seen.

"Guess we can't play 'I spy'" she said, mostly to herself.

Surprisingly, Debian answered.

"Not unless we're on a trip," she said, wiping her nose, her sobs finally coming back under a bit of control.

"Ever play the 'Isn't That Interesting' game?"

"What's that?"

"It's like I Spy, but you point out the item, pick it up or read it if you like, then make up a story about how it's so interesting. Watch."

Salomé went to the big books and pulled down the heaviest.

She held it out in front as if she had never seen a book.

"Know what this is?"

"Lexical History of Pre-Nomadic Tribes In The Near East."

"No, it's not. This is actually one of the original bricks they used to build the pyramid! Isn't That Interesting?"

Deb started to disagree but changed her mind.

"I guess so."

"Now you do one."

Debian thought for a moment.

"See this book in front of me?"

"Harry Potter?"

"No. It's actually a secret message sent from beyond time!"

Sal frowned. Deb continued, trying to pick up steam. "By Morlochs living in The Barrier!"

Deb couldn't come up with more.

"Isn't That Interesting?"

"Nice. Yeah, I think so!" Sal said. Deb had completely stopped crying by now.

Sal got another book, set it on the ground, then took the figurine from Deb's hand as she watched carefully.

"Now see, Debian, sit here," Sal patted beside her, the book laying on the floor in front of them, "I will show you the proper way. This is Zeentor, Chief of the BooBoo Tribe…"

"That's Thor."

"Zeentor. Hang on. So the book Zeentor is standing on is actually the history of his peoples and their journey across the…"

"That's 'Have Spacessuit, Will Travel'."

"THEIR JOURNEY ACROSS…."

Lightning struck nearby, lighting up their world. There was no rolling thunder. This close there was just a loud click or snap, then what sounded like an explosion in their driveway.

Sal dropped the figure and hugged Deb.

"AHHHH!" she screamed.

"You kids okay?" Mary yelled from the downstairs.

"Sal's a Fraidy Cat!" Deb yelled back.

Sal went to the door, eager to get the comfort of her mom, unsure of whether to admit it or not.

Deb ignored her. Salomé found herself getting very angry. She was not going downstairs.

Salomé noticed her little sister being brave.

"I'm fine, mom! It was loud, that's all!"

"Whatever."

She breathed a sigh of relief. She stood in the door, looking at her sister. Deb sat quietly. From time-to-time she hummed. She kept parsing through the book bit-by-bit, not even reading to herself but still reading.

"Stupid shit clown robot," she mumbled to herself, hopefully not loud enough for Deb to hear.

Compared to the two girls, the room seemed very empty and silent, the only sound was water gurgling down the front of Deb's window as it overflowed the gutters.

"I don't need anybody to play with me anyway," Debian said without looking up. She moved the figurine over closer so it could help her read.

Sal felt pain, but she did not know from where. Slowly she shuffled back into the room to where Deb sat.

"I'm sorry," she said. She looked at her shoes, then her sisters.

"Those are pretty sweet shoes, Deb. I should've told you that instead of picking on you."

Deb nodded. She smiled at her.

'You can still call me clown. I want you to call me clown."

Sal smiled. Deb continued.

"I didn't know you were so scared of lightning. You know the entire thing is just a big heat engine with a lot of friction creating static …"

"You can call me witch. But no more nerdy explaining things to me. You're not allowed. That's a rule."

Now Deb smiled. "Okay, witch. But why not have fun with it, just like everything else? We can play Isn't That Interesting."

Sal was quite puzzled. How could you use something like a storm?

Deb took the Thor figurine, then walked over to the window. Sal saw her kind of counting, chanting or something. This went on for a few seconds. Finally she spun around and held the Thor figurine stretched out directly at Sal's face.

"Behold the power of lighting!"

The biggest flash of lightning Sal had ever seen was accompanied by thunder loud enough to knock books from the shelves.

Deb smiled.

"See? Nothing scary."

Salomé's eyes widened. Her bladder felt weak.

"Come on, sis," Deb said, "Let's do another."

"Another what?" was all she could say.

"Another game! Only this time let's make new rules!"

Sal shook her head. Her arms went limp. The world was not adding up. For the first time in her life, Salome Newbury had become so surprised that her brain had shut down.

Deb waited patiently.

Sal shook her head again.

"Rules? What rules?"

"How about this: We each pick the item for the other to read."

Slowly things were coming back.

"Sure. I guess so. What do you pick for me?"

Deb reached inside the book and took out a folded note.

"Do this one! I saw mom writing this the other day but I can't figure it out. Maybe it's He Who Cannot Be Named! Or Zeentor!"

Sal looked at the note.

"Oh, that. This is just cursive, Deb. You'll learn about that soon enough. Cursive's a grown-up thing."

"So what does it say?"

"Hmm. Let's see."

Sal stepped back. She cleared her throat. She held it still folded, awards night and Salomé had the important job of announcing the winner.

"Here, ladies and gentlemen, for the first time only, is the deep dark secret of the Newbury house, discovered by our Number One detective, the Debster. With help from Zeentor."

"That's me! I'm Debster!"

Sal put her finger on the note as she read. Her finger was shaking.

"Subject continues to hallucinate monsters or other creatures not in evidence. Shows little attention to personal hygiene, especially when it comes to clothes selection. She seems to have no friends and take little interest in making friends…."

Sal stopped.

"That's a dumb old note, Deb. Probably some kind of police stuff for mom."

The two sisters looked at one another, the unspoken truth hanging in the silence between them.

"You're the person ain't got no friends." Deb said

"Maybe I am. At least I'm not a weird-o-saurus."

There was no emotion in their voices, only sadness.

Slowly, Debian got up and went to her bedroom door. She pointed to the hallway outside.

"Maybe it's best if you leave," she said, looking much older than her older sister, "I have important things."

Deb's lip quivered. Again.

Sal slowly went to the door. Her eyes were on the floor again.

As she approached the threshold with her younger sister in it, she looked up.

There were tears in her eyes.

"I can't, Debian," she said, then, sniffling a bit, "You're right. I don't have any friends or anything to do."

Deb shifted in place. She glared at Sal, unable to come up with anything to say. After all, Sal was agreeing with her.

Seeing she was making a bit of headway, Sal added, "I'm lonely. Will you be my friend? Please?"

There was a slam from below. It sounded like a couch had fallen.

"Well you can just go to hell!" they heard their mom.

"That's NOT what I meant, Mary!"

"Sssshhhhh!"

The voices became less distinct.

The girls looked at one another. Worry.

"You didn't know that was going to happen?"

Deb continued, "the lightning? I scared you again. I'm sorry."

"Things are not going well." was all she could say.

Deb thought for a moment, then grabbed a few more Action Figures and another book.

"Here," she put them on the floor, "Sit."

"Look, it's all got to go together: the books, the figures, the fashion, the storm, the mommy, the daddy. We gotta throw everything here in the middle."

Sal sat slowly. She looked at Deb as if she were watching a high wire act at the circus.

"We need a new game." Deb said after many minutes of listening to the rain slowly subside; the muffled yelling fading away.

"What kind of doll is that?" Sal said, pointing to the figure.

"Not a doll. Remember, not a doll. Action figure."

"Ok, what kind of action figure is that?"

"Well this one's Loki. He's Thor's brother. I have a lot more Viking figures on the top shelf. Want more?"

Sal shook her head no. Who was this person?

"Can we play with those?"

She pointed to a cardboard box of barbies she had given Deb years ago as a hand-me-down and as far as she knew Deb had never opened.

Deb shrugged. She got more action figures from her shelf. She had hers. Sal had hers. The standoff began.

Sal went over, reached down, and pulled out a half-dozen figures from the unopened box. She had no idea what any of Deb's were, but she knew hers.

"So they can all go together? Does that work? And we can dress them up?"

Debian raised her eyebrows, not yet committed.

"So," Sal said, "we'll use you wonderful action figures also, but we can make up anything we'd like. We don't have to use their actual names or anything. And we can use mine too."

Deb grumbled.

"Can it be a story?"

"Maybe," she said, "But only if we have fashion. We must have fashion. It's not a story without fashion. Everybody knows that."

Sal started in on a long and engaging tale of Sarah Sylkies and how she became the most well-dressed person at school, even if she did grow up poor and was hated by her evil stepmother. Deb helped out by providing both the school opposition and advice from Gandalf MageWizard, the school principal.

It was almost an hour later, as the rain slowed down to just a trickle, when they traded places, Deb in the lead, and she finally began telling her sister about The Darklings and how they sailed from distant and strange shores on ships of dreams and wishes.

4.17

Deciding To Steal

The group sat in silence at the table outside the campus coffee shop. It was mostly empty. The upgrades to the overhead pedestrian walkway over the interstate hadn't been finished yet, so students were forced either to use the walkway without permission or come across the railroad tracks.

Coffee was important, but there were other places to get it. Business was slow. Good.

Paul sat with his three postgrads, Joe Middles, Hilda Gibb, and Hank Dawson. They had been easily chatting up until the point they sat down, then realized that something serious was coming. Next door a sign read "Family Life Center! Opening Soon!"

"Would you look at that," Hank said as the couple next to them got up and left, "And they didn't give a tip. Those assholes didn't even leave a tip. How can people live like that."

The man had been wearing bib overalls and a baseball hat. The couple made a point of not hearing Hank as they exited.

"Lot of bad things and people in the world," Paul offered. He was frowning too.

"Some people just cheap bastards," Joe agreed.

"Yeah. People are assholes." Hilda growled.

"Ok, then, what's everybody got?" Hank said, tossing in a dollar bill to the middle of the table, "Let's fix it. Make it better. Pitch in."

Joe and Hilda each tossed in a dollar. They looked at Paul.

"Don't look at me. All I've got is a twenty. And I'm on a teachers' salary."

Hank took the money over. He checked to make sure nobody was around.

"Paranoid much?" Joe asked.

"Just don't make a big deal of it, that's all," Hank said. "Sometimes you can do the right thing without anybody having to notice."

Nobody noticed a man 50 meters away looking in a storefront window. A small directional mic pointed at them from underneath his jacket.

As he sat down, Hank stuck out his chin and grabbed imaginary overalls, making fun of the people who just left. "Country Bill goes to the big city," he said, "Too cheap to tip."

Everybody deliberately did not look at Paul. He ignored it.

"I'm here to tell you guys to keep your noses clean and follow the end-of-project rules. We do that and everything will be fine. Consider this your fatherly lecture."

"How's this nose look?" Hank pushed his nose up making a pig snout, "Clean?"

"What about those materials Hilda and I need back? What do we do for those?" Joe said, "You ask them?"

"First I need to know that you're going to follow the rules."

"I won't tell anybody and it's as if the entire project never happened," Hilda crossed her arms, "But I'm getting those papers back."

There was a pause as they gathered their thoughts, sipped their coffee.

A police car pulled into the parking lot. Two men got out and went inside.

"You need to forget this. All of this," Paul said.

"You gave your word," Hilda said, unable to say more, then, "we need them."

Hank was perpetually unwilling to accept any obstacle thrown at him. He shrugged life off.

"How about creativity? I've been wanting to write a book. They can't stop us from doing that."

"Don't know, Hank. I know I made promises when we started," Paul said, "That's on me. Don't know about books."

"It's been four years of work," Joe said, "A promise is one thing. Four years is something else entirely."

Paul just nodded. Joe leaned in.

"Is this the kind of career, is this the kind of professional you want to be?"

Hank was still having none of it.

"You guys really need to lighten up."

Joe started to reply. Paul cut him off.

"Look, this would be funny if it weren't so deadly serious," Paul said, "You guys aren't in a Three Stooges movie. This is real life, and there'll be no more work on this of any kind. At all. And yes, I believe books are included, sorry Hank."

They had to get this, Paul thought, had to.

"But what if we find out how to get them," Joe asked, "The papers. What if they're not in a classified facility at all? What if, perhaps, somebody might have airtagged them? And they're just sitting around, nearby?"

Hank said, "If we can find them, we can take them back, right? They're sitting in a park or on a desk somewhere."

"Why don't you three start a company? You've got enough talent to make a fortune." Paul sounded a bit desperate to himself. He took a breath as they considered.

"I can find you some seed money, get you some great advisors." He said.

"That's not a completely bad idea," Joe said, "I'll need to think about it."

"Papers," Hilda said, digging in, "I want my papers. What do I need to do? Can I join the military? Take a secret oath or something."

"You? Blue-haired hater of the system? Military? No." Joe replied.
She didn't like that.

"There," Joe tossed out some rolled up blueprints on the table, pointed.
Paul was beside himself.

"You shouldn't know this. This shouldn't be happening."

Joe looked like an undertaker.

"I'm taking my papers back. They're here," he tapped the blueprints, "and I'm going to go get them. You can get yours too, Hilda."

Paul looked at Hank. Hank was not even paying attention, instead playing something that looked like cow-clicker on his phone.

"I'm begging you. It's a bad idea."

The two officers returned from inside the shop, a man in handcuffs.

They put him in the car as the three watched.

"What if nobody knows?" Hilda said

"Meaning what?"

"What if we get the papers and nobody knows it happened?"

He spread the blueprints out, "This is easy."

Paul sighed. He put his hand on the papers but did not look at them.

"Things are not always what they appear to be."

"Uh-huh," Hilda wasn't buying it, Joe neither.

"This information can't exist," Paul said.

"Great. Then we won't tell you," Joe replied. "Things you don't know, don't exist, right? Is that okay?"

The conversation died off. Without realizing it, they all stared at Hank.

Eventually he shrugged and stood up.

"All right. If that's the way you want it, got my own deal. I'm not playing this no more."

He carefully pushed his chair back in place, made a point of leaving a tip, and left.

Once he was out of earshot, Paul looked his remaining two students over.

"Hank made the right move. This is serious. Are you aware of how serious it is? There's no going back once we start down this path, grab those papers. You can never tell anybody what happened."

"I'm in," Joe said, "one and done. Once it happens, it never happened. Hilda?"

Hilda considered, twirling her coffee with the red plastic mixer.

Leaving them behind, Hank began mumbling to himself, "Don't need nobody's permission to do nothing."

Hank didn't walk fast. He started and stopped, a man in a war inside himself.

The man never heard the rest of the conversation. He packed up the rest of his gear and was actively tracking Hank as he left.

"Ain't asking nobody nothing," Hank continued talking to himself, heading up over the overpass.

The man who had been watching put away the recording device. He closed in behind Hank, slowly.

The remaining three paid no attention.

"Like Hank with his book idea," Joe said, picking up the thread, trying to convince his old professor, "we'll get them back without anybody ever knowing we wanted them. That make you happy?"

"This is bad," Paul said. He looked at the two students. They trusted him. It hurt.

Joe was not buying it.

"But sometimes you have to do good things so that nobody knows you've done them," Joe said in reply, quoting Hank.

"Gimme this," Paul said, rising. He grabbed the blueprints, balled them up, took his cup to the trash can.

Along the way he dropped a twenty on the still unbussed table.

Hilda and Joe watched Paul leave, them followed along behind, wandering where he was going.

On the unfinished walkway, Hank didn't see the man walking up quickly behind him. It was only when the man bumped up against him, hard, that he realized that anybody had paid any attention to him at all.

It was too late.

The few people that saw the fall or heard the sickening thump or screech of tires began screaming when they saw Hank's body on the pavement twenty-feet below.

George Endelman slipped away into the empty mindless busyness of a university campus at work.

4.18

Showdown

There was a large flying saucer on the roof of the store.

In front of it, silhouetted in the streetlights, two short gray figures stood, looking out over the empty city street. One was pointing directly at Mary and Beau's undercover car. They were trying not to be discovered.

Under the saucer, a sign said "LGM Comics."

The subtitle was "You Never Saucer Good Deals!"

Mary sat in the plainclothes car looking at the sign. Beau Martin came back to the car from around back.

He got in the car.

"It's the van we were looking for alright." he said, "Caterers."

"Good," she said, "Now we watch."

Martin reached into the back seat, got a paper bag. He pulled out something wrapped in foil and began eating.

"You eat like this?" She pointed.

"It's good for the digestion."

"It's your second super burrito."

Martin smiled. He patted his burrito as if it were a favorite puppy, then returned noshing on the bread. "Keeps my blood sugar up."

"It's 2 am!"

He stopped.

"I know. I know. Maybe I should have brought a snack."

She frowned watching the man go back to chewing, inhaling the tube of cholesterol, gruntling.

"We've got work to do with you, Martin, if we're going to make a detective out of you instead of a blimp."

"Are you saying I need to get in shape?"

"I'm saying you're getting into a shape, just not the one we want."

She looked up to see an old beater drive by them and turn into the alley beside the store. A minute later they heard voices, car doors slamming shut.

Martin tossed the burrito into the back seat and started to get up. She stopped him.

"Somebody's here. Could be plotting, destroying evidence. This could be it. Who knows?"

"We watch."

"Shouldn't we at least go see who they are? Run the plates?"

There was a tickle in the back of her mind. Something wasn't right.

"Patience, Martin. Patience. There's only one entrance to that parking lot. We'll get the plates on their way out."

He hesitated. He looked in the back seat at the remaining food.

Her look told him no.

She squared her shoulders.

"I know you've been taught as a patrolman to remain calm and follow procedure, but it's going to be even more important if you want to be a detective. We don't write speeding tickets. Now and then events will provoke us, sometimes deliberately. It's always the rules. Always."

She looked at him wiping his mouth with a napkin that she had never seen him use.

"We stay icy. That's our job. Even more so than street cops."

She moved her hand calming invisible waters in front of them.

"We have to be the ones that play it strictly by the rules," she said, "Evidence. Procedure. Step-by-step. This is the way."

Tickle.

"How can anybody divorce themselves completely from emotion? We're all human."

She considered for a moment. In a voice much quieter, she said "Sometimes it can be a struggle to divorce yourself from logic. I'll give you that."

"I'm going to take a peek," he said, "Don't worry, they won't see me. I just want to identify the car and maybe see how many there are."

He was back at her driver's side window in fifteen seconds.

"They're carrying documents out the back."

Break-in? Fleeing jurisdiction?

"How many?"

"Two, maybe three."

Tickle. She decided. That was it.

"We're going in."

"Shouldn't we call for backup?"

"Normally yes," she said. He groaned as she explained,"99% of the time yes. This is that one-in-a-million time that there are some things you don't know. I've got a bad hunch and need to follow it."

"What fresh, tasty, farm-fed bullshit is this? Rules? Always rules?"

"Trust me, you don't want to know. Those are my rules. This is on my authority. As far as we care, either this is a break-in or the owners are here at 2 am. Either way, we have reason to go in."

"Evidence? Procedure? Step-by-step? Where'd all that go?"

"My authority. Stow it. I'll un-fuck later."

The front display window was lit up. The rest in darkness.

Comic books lined the window, prostitutes on display in the grand mall. The names called out, "Weezer Volume 1", "Arkatron: Uprising on Xenos."

Behind the window she could just make out some colorful life-sized superheroes.

She tested the door. It was unlocked. She thought of Debian.

She was aware that beside her, Martin was hyper vigilant.

She stepped through the door. An icy calm descended. Her old friend. Her pulse slowed, her vision narrowed, her focus became the room, the entire situation. She listened.

They both entered as quietly as they could, determined not to give themselves away until they knew more.

In the far back she could make out flashlights. Muffled voices.

Heavy thumping from the back of the store. It sounded like somebody moving a refrigerator, a body, or a safe.

Martin pointed that way.

She nodded.

"Fuck, this is heavy!"

"Loser! Watch my feet!"

"Shhhh!"

Mary pointed to the left. He nodded.

Two groups.

Strange. Sounded like kids.

"Quiet" A new voice. An even tone. Older.

Did she recognize that voice?

She looked at her partner. His hands were shaking. His right hand was close to his service pistol.

She caught his glance. She shook her head, then made the gesture again: calming the waters. Stay icy.

He jerked his head up and down in a nod. Could be problems there. Too late, though. Mission must continue before we lose tactical initiative.

Stepping forward, she brushed a display. It fell over, making a splash.

"Somebody's here!"

"Run!"

Martin started running to the back of the store where he indicated earlier. So that was his plan. Sounded good. She ran the other way, to the noises on the left, hand on firearm.

It was a cautious run. She carefully adjusted her pace making sure she didn't hit anything else. Quiet like. Icy.

More noises. 5 meters. She drew her pistol. She saw a figure, a form in the shadows. It looked inhuman.

Something big and heavy flew by her head.

She shot the figure. Center of mass, like always.

"Stop!"

The figure moved. She shot again, this time a bit to the left of center of mass.

"Police!" she added as the figure collapsed on the floor.

She could hear Martin taking his chase outside. It was spinning out-of-control as predicted. There would certainly be a lot of un-fucking to be done.

She cut her light on. Creeping forward, she listened and scanned as she approached the prone form.

Lying on the floor was a life-sized figure of Superman. It had two bullet holes in it.

Lying beside it was a man holding his left arm. It was an older man.

It was her husband Paul.

"What are you guys doing here?"

Nothing.

"Now you're what, part of a B&E crew?"

Nothing.

It was worse than breaking and entering. Much worse.

It was lying.

She held her pistol to her husband's face. Her face had no emotion.

"You're going to tell me why you're here and what's going on or I'm going to shoot you in the head."

Her voice had no inflection. Her eyes had no emotion.

Icy.

Calm waters.

His eyes widened. He looked at her, the gun, back to her.

"We're just here investigating!"

Nothing.

"The docs! The project docs!"

Nothing.

"We figured out they're here!"

Nothing. Her grip loosened.

"Mary, good god! It's me! Paul!"

Her face broke. She puzzled. Her face reassembled back into nothingness.

"I'm doing what I said! Your husband! The papers!"

"Boss?"

Martin had come back, out of breath. Beside him was a teenage girl, maybe 20, blue hair and nose ring. He had her cuffed and was leading her by the arm.

"Boss?"

She put her pistol away. She looked at him.

"You may need some stitches in that left arm," she said to Paul.

She stood. She brushed herself off.

Paul stared at her in disbelief. He grabbed his wounded arm. He sat up.

She turned to Martin. Time to pivot.

"Officer Martin," how would you evaluate the evidence that brought us here tonight?"

"Brought us outside?" he said, "Solid. I think the case was looking good."

"And inside," she pointed around, "does anything here strike you as being out-of-the ordinary, perhaps criminal?"

Picking up what she was putting down, he shook his head no. Paul stood. He was still holding his other arm.

"The door was open," Paul shrugged. "The backdoor was open."

Nobody believed it.

She looked back at the front door.

"The front door was open also."

"You mean there's nothing?" Martin said to her, then looked at Paul. "What about the van?"

Paul was confused.

"We'll find out that was just parked there," Mary concluded, "We'll find nothing suspicious."

Paul nodded once, looking at her, his face crestfallen.

She checked her surroundings again. She got it.

"You mean you guys thought we were attackers?"

Martin was confused.

"Attackers?"

Paul gave up looking at his wife.

Mary grimaced. She shuffled. Physically shook herself back into the present. It was like watching a far off person come back to a home they'd left, wandering around, wandering what had gone on in their absence.

"We've been punked. We were fooled," She concluded.

Martin shook the girl with one hand like she was a life-sized doll.

"What?"

"None of this ever happened. Let her go."

"There was a third one. He got away."

"Release her. Release her before somebody else shows up to this Masterful and Wondrous Charlie Foxtrot."

As he cut her loose she addressed the young lady.

"Ma'am, young lady, I am very sorry that you were involved in this, um, police action tonight. Please do not talk about this to anyone as you may be in danger if you do."

"Can I talk to my professor?"

A stern Mary looked at Paul.

"Professor" she said. She did not look back.

Paul looked away. She turned to the girl.

"Yes."

The girl moved, then stopped. She was a deer in their flashlights. Then she ran towards her friend.

"What a mess," Martin said.

"We need to put all of this back to the way it was, hope the bullet damaged nothing obvious."

"It was a paint can," Paul said. "I threw a paint can at you. It was a stupid paint can."

She looked behind her. Sure enough a brand new paint can had rolled next to the comic book racks. Eggshell blue.

"I'm sorry."

She grimaced. She looked back to Martin.

"Let's get moving. This place isn't going to clean itself up."

Nobody said anything over the next 30 minutes as the three of them cleaned up.

Martin was the last one out. Paul and Mary stood in front of the store, mourners waiting on a hearse.

"Wait a minute."

They both turned. Martin pointed.

"What were all these important docs of the professor here doing in some comic book store?"

4.19

Betting

It's an odd thing when close people disagree deeply, Paul thought. Lightly disagreeing over things, like leaving the toilet seat up, could cause all sorts of noise and drama. Deeply disagreeing could cause nothing. Silence.

That was the way the evening went when they got home. They did the things that couples did, but they did them without interacting, without life. The next morning was the same.

It was graveyard quiet all the way home from work for Paul later that day, much like it had been icily quiet that morning before he left

Paul hated the quiet.

Tim met him as he got out of the car.

"Are we going to kill mom today?"

"Excuse me, what? No, Timothy, we are not killing your mother."

"With the ray guns, silly!" Tim held out the laser tag gear from the week before.

Tim ran off to the backyard. Puzzled, Paul followed.

"We've got some hard decisions to make."

He processed Mary's words before he took in the scene. What kind of decisions?

Laid out in their yard, like last week, was the picnic blanket. Various games were scattered about, along with a picnic basket.

Tim ran off waving his pistol high and shouting, "Pew! Pew! Die!"

Deb jumped up, seeing him, and ran over.

"Are we going to play Clue! Let's play Clue!"

He heard Mary groan.

"No, kiddo, I don't think anybody wants to play Clue with you. I'm sorry."

He patted his daughter's back.

"Decisions?" he looked at his wife.

"Yeah. Which game are we going to play before dinner." she said.

"Hmmm. He walked over. Games."

"I thought I'd surprise you."

"It worked. I'm surprised."

He plopped down. Mary suddenly turned serious.

"I got the preliminary report from that accident yesterday. Afternoon."

"I heard. Hank."

"Yeah. Hank Dawson. If I remember, he was one of your interns."

"Was? Did he die?"

"Not expected to make it. They should have walled off that construction site weeks ago."

"Kids would have just jumped over it."

"Last night. You didn't mention it. All your interns were there. Except him. Except Hank. The remaining ones."

"I didn't think it was relevant."

"Yeah. Say, weren't you there when it happened? He fell? See Hank yesterday?"

"What do you mean by that?"

"Nothing," she waved him off, "Just making conversation. Weren't you meeting with your interns that afternoon?"

"Wrapping things up."

"That's right. Wrapping things up. Math things. Before you had other things to do. That evening."

"Decisions." he concluded.

"That's right," she sadly smiled, looking out over their options, "Games. Pick your poison."

"Not sure if I'd be much fun."

"Come on, Dad!" Sal looked at him over the top of a notepad she held, "Let's play!"

The Great Pendant Disaster must have blown over.

Paul looked with great uncertainty at his wife. In reply she simply shrugged.

"Paul," she said, "It's just that there's a lot going on. Piggly Wiggly, the thing last night, that Endelman character, the meeting. I'm sorry if I carry my work around with me."

"That's a long way from an apology."

She nodded.

"I owe you an apology. I can never apologize enough. But I also owe you an explanation. I like thinking of my job as solving puzzles in order to protect the innocents in life from evil, but in reality, I'm good at what I do because I'm a clerk."

"Serious."

"I'm just a filing clerk, hon. I sweep up the mess and dirt and crap, give it all labels and reports, and send it into the big gears of justice. But I'm good at it. I have to solve and sort, clean up."

"Is that the apology?"

"I apologize. I should have controlled that situation better. That was my job. It's just that the mess I'm responsible for cleaning up seems to be growing faster than I can sweep. For the first time, this one case, I feel like I'm losing track of where my next steps should be."

"That was bad, Mary. Really bad. Please don't do that again. That was crazy bad."

"I swear. I won't."

He looked around. The kids were getting anxious. They didn't like all the grown-up talk.

"Ok. I accept. But I have a condition."

Her eyebrows raised.

"In return I want you to understand that I never really had control over anything. Whatever you need to do, whoever you need to find, it's not me. I'm not your guy."

"Agreed. Fuck!"

She stood, pointing out into the woods.

"Timothy Mattis Newbury! Get your ass over here! Don't go wandering off again! Stop being a little asshole!"

"Corn hole," now Paul stood as well.

"What?"

"Corn hole," he pointed. "Let's play corn hole. It'll be fun."

"You sure? You don't do so well at it. We have other options."

Paul looked around at the assembled activities. "Clue, Battleship, Monopoly, the D&D dice, playing cards…"

"We'll just keep the stakes low."

Did his best to smile, still shaken from the night before. His footing was weak.

"Ok kids! Guys versus girls again! Form up!"

As they assembled, Paul said "What do you guys want to play?"

"Army men! Dress up! Sudoku! Go!"

He scratched his chin. "Okay! Corn hole it is, then."

Deb raced over and picked the bean bags before her sister could get there.

"Mine! I get to go first!" Sal said, "I'm oldest!"

Deb blew her a raspberry. Timothy laughed, picking up his bags.

Maybe things were working out, Paul thought.

"Betcha ten dollars I can throw this bag right through the center of the hole," Deb taunted Sal.

"You kids don't even have ten dollars," he said, "and you shouldn't be betting money. It's illegal."

"How about who gets to go first?" Sal countered.

"Sure."

Debian didn't even look like she was concentrating, Paul thought later. She just pivoted on one foot, like a marionette, and casually tossed the bag, looking the other way, showing off.

It went right through the center of the hole.

Days later he wasn't even sure if she actually looked first. It seemed as if she was just tossing dirty clothes into a corner.

"HEY!" Sal was incensed. "Lucky! MOM!"

The appeal of last resort.

"Takes after her dad," Mary said casually, "She's got all kinds of things going on we don't know about. She's probably been practicing, Sal."

"Have not!" Deb protested.

It's just going to be more of this, isn't it, he thought. Mary telling me I'm wrong because I'm keeping so much from them and my trying to keep all of my promises I've made to everybody at the same time. None of it working very well.

"This is stupid," Tim kicked a dirt clod, "Dad promised me we were going to kill a bunch of people later."

"Maybe so," he tossed the boy's hair, "looks like we're going to get killed anyway, just at corn hole. Maybe later? Mom and Deb are good."

"Let's play spies! Or assassins!"

"You mean Mafia, runt." Sal said.

"Witch!" Tim stuck his tongue out, then waggled his hands beside his head.

"I can't give you what you want." He didn't look at Mary, "I don't have the power to open up completely."

"Why?"

"Because we'd all be Piggly Wigglied, that's why."

"Then we'll deal with that when it comes, sweet."

He looked. She stood arms akimbo. Fierce. As much as he wanted to be the hero, he always thought that Mary was the real hero in the family.

Paul was a mere functionary.

"Poke her!" Sal yelled.

"I'm not going to poke her."

"Let's play poker, dummy! I mean Dad."

Momentum, he thought. Getting them all going somewhere was more important than picking out each mistake. He let it slide.

"Well okay, kiddo. That's a real game for you. But what are the stakes?"

"MONEY!" Tim yelled.

"More reading time!" Deb yelled.

"New shoes!" Sal added.

"Then that's what you'll have. Sal, run in and get our penny bowl and bring it out. We'll split it up. Tim? If you win you'll keep the pot. Deb, if you win? An extra hour of reading time this week."

"Two hours!"

"Okay. Two hours. And Sal?", she turned to listen, "If you win you'll get some shoes. But nothing expensive. Deb, go get the card table. We'll put it in the grass, play cards like the Indians did."

Deb ran off.

"What do I get if I win?"

He looked at Mary.

"What do you want?"

"You know what I want. Answers. To everything."

He looked down at Timothy, eagerly awaiting his instructions to get the game started.

"Okay. But the flip is also true. I win, you let it go."

"Agreed," Mary said, then spit on her hand, "Shake."

And like a couple of twelve-year-olds, they shook on the bet.

Tim was very impressed. He had no idea what was going on.

Tim lost the fastest, which was what he expected. On the first hand, Tim pushed all in (once they explained to him that he could do that) and lost with a bunch of nothing. He was beaming, and seemed happy enough to go play on his own, listening to them as they went.

Deb was ferocious, as they all expected. He caught Sal glancing at Deb's cards just before she raised Deb out of the game on what he suspected was a bluff, but he decided to let them work that out. Deb didn't complain much. Instead, she milled about as the remaining three played, very curious to watch all of the cards and bets, no doubt in order to fix whatever mistake she thought she had made.

"We should invite that new guy, Beau whatisname, and his wife over. It'd be good to do joint family things."

"Beau Martin. I'm not sure that's a good idea."

"Really?"

"Taking some time. Wife left."

"Apologies. I didn't know."

"I just found out. Beau is a total slob, and he's got this good old boy Columbo thing going, but I've never seen anybody as dedicated as he is to the job. Intuitively clever and smart, the heart of a bulldog. I had to make him take time off."

"Well that's good. I'm glad you found him. He might work out."

"Good for me. Not so much for Beau's marriage."

"Let me help you play, mom," Deb was reaching for Mary's cards.

"No, young lady. This kid," she pointed at Deb standing behind her.

"Takes after you," Paul noted.

"You going to bet, Dad?" Sal looked as if she might explode having to wait on the old people to do stuff. Paul thought this was becoming a regular look for Sal.

"Read them and weep."

He laid his hand down, took in the pot, and smiled at Sal.

"Young Salomé, when the student is ready, the master arrives."

"I don't know what that means, daddo, don't like it."

"Probably not," Mary said, "do you know what young Debian here did this morning?"

"Do I want to know?"

"I had all of these cases, you know, the ones we've been talking about, spread out on the kitchen table."

"She didn't see anything, did she?"

"No. None of that, thankfully. No, she asked if she could help solve my puzzles."

"Puzzles! Yay!" Deb jumped up and down a couple of times for emphasis, throwing her hands up into the air.

"Ha! She probably could! That little rascal."

"Yeah. Paul. She probably could."

Debian wandered off towards the house, embarrassed by all the praise.

"Just you and me now, bucko."

Paul did his best "winning gambler" smile. His pot was about twice the size of his wife's. Wouldn't be long.

"I guess it is," she agreed. "I believe things have just gotten serious."

"Yeah." he remembered the wager. "I guess they have."

They played for about an hour. Tim eventually wandered off to the woods again, on some great new adventure now that his parents were locked in combat. Sal began writing in her new diary, obviously disappointed at how things turned out.

Debian came back. Paul didn't notice. She stood behind him.

Mary kicked his ass. There was just no other way to look at it. He was usually a much better gambler than she. With each hand his heart sunk lower and lower into his stomach.

He never saw her glance over his shoulder, never heard Deb standing behind him signaling her mom.

"Hell of a thing to lose on a poker game," he said as the final hand closed. He felt like he did when he first heard that his mom and dad had died. Empty.

"Care to make it two games out of three?"

Mary was not amused.

"I'll set something up with the General. I mean Ramirez. I'll do it soon. But I really want you to think about where this is going. Before we get there."

"I'll play again, but not for those stakes," Mary said, "Come on kids! One more game!"

"YAY!" Deb appeared out of nowhere, behind him, ran over and set beside her mom. Sal and Tim obviously couldn't be bothered. Nobody felt like nagging them.

So the three of them sat in a stony silence, sizing each other up, making careful move after careful move, all of them wondering where this game was headed.

4.20

For Immediate Release

Pre-Dawn Attack Presages New Warfare Style

INDIVDIA - U.S. SOCOM forces executed a pre-dawn attack today on a programming group linked to organized crime and terrorist activity. No further details were available from the Pentagon.

Retired General Albert Smithboggy, USMC, commented on the raid for a local paper.

"We are a warrior species," he said, "and there are two truths regarding internet technology. The first is that ever since the first Sever was brought online we have been busy at battle, attacking one another constantly in the background, where the average citizen would never notice. The second truth is that eventually this warfare was going to go kinetic. It already has, of course, but perhaps this is the first time people take notice."

"But probably not. It's hard to get folks interested in these things."

#

4.21

Coming Clean

"This is a graveyard," Ramirez said, walking Paul and Mary into the backyard of the ancient house, "but we'll make something bigger out of it. Better."

She pointed at the barren ground.

"There's dozens, maybe hundreds of corpses underneath us, and at least twice that number of arms and legs without a torso. Pieces."

"All I see is an old well and some cobblestones," Mary said, "Where are the grave markers?"

"Ah, there's the rub. They didn't make any. All happened too quickly. If they'd made the markers we probably wouldn't have been able to buy it."

"Cholera? Plague? Smallpox?"

"War, Mary. Muskets and cannonade. During the Civil War, one April there were a thousand people out in the front yard, all doing their level best to exterminate one another."

"But why no graves? Why bury them here? Why no graves? How can you tell?"

"Nobody could tell. The battle, of course, was very small and it's commemorated by a little bronze plaque out there on the roadside," she pointed, "but folks had long forgotten what had happened to any casualties. There were so many during the war that it was easy to lose track of the details. When we started the paperwork on the house, that's when we found out."

"How?" Now Paul was interested.

"Hospital. This house was converted to a hospital, which made sense since it all happened right here. Surgeons used the rooms and the yard here to patch up the wounded, wrap up the dead, and chop off various pieces of humans that might cause trouble later."

"Yikes," Paul said, "So they just dug a big hole?"

"We don't know," she pointed, "They threw a lot of stuff down that well. That's why it's been blocked off. Going through the yard we found old surgical gear, miniballs, and so forth. That led us to the well. Once we pulled the first, um, selection of mixed remains, we just put them back and covered it all up. The dead deserve to rest."

It'd been three weeks, not one, until Paul had been able to set up his promised conversation with the retired General.

"With respect, Sonya is it?" Mary studied her.

Ramirez nodded.

"With respect, General. I'd like to avoid history if at all possible today. I just listened to more war history from this guy than I ever wanted to. Help me. Please help me."

"Hey! And I was just getting started!"

"I know!"

"You know, dear," Paul put a weird sarcastic inflection on 'dear', "we could always hang around a couple of days, visit some of the sites…"

"Yaaaa. It's never enough, is it? No matter how much history you study, there's always more."

"My guess is that's why Paul likes history," Ramirez offered.

"Yup," he agreed, "You can take the same thing, look at it a hundred different ways. It is endless. Like everything else, I guess. But history's more fun. Doesn't fight back. Take the time…"

"I find it best to distract/redirect when he goes on one of these benders," Ramirez said.

"Hard work, yard chores, things like that do wonders."

"Guys. Don't like being treated like this."

"Well Paul, I'm glad somebody remembers things. Everything now is bowdlerized or memory-holed. I suspect I'm the same way. I'm not sure how much help I can be. My memory isn't what it used to be."

"I'm confused," Mary said, looking between them, on the alert, "Are you two going help out or not?"

"We're going to help," Paul was firm. He looked at his friend and old boss Ramirez. "Mary has a hard time dropping things."

"And Paul has a hard time being honest."

Paul quickly shook her comment off. "That's not fair."

"No, it's not," she said, "he has a hard time being open."

"Maybe I'll have a post-retirement career as marriage counselor,"

Ramirez replied. "No, Mary, I'm going to help, but I also want to offer you an out. This is dangerous ground."

She clutched a leather satchel she had been carrying.

"If you're serious about this, and I mean deadly serious, I have a collection of handwritten notes I've made after retirement. I was hoping that one day, maybe twenty years from now, it'd all be declassified and I could tell my story. Paul and I have been part of big changes in the world, changes that had to remain secret."

"I'm serious about this. As a heart attack." Mary said.

"I don't see any other way, Sonya. We're going to have to push through this. Somehow."

Ramirez moved to sit at an old picnic table, rotting out in-place about 20 feet from the well. The ground was rocky, barren.

They sat.

"First, how are you adjusting to regular life, Paul?"

Paul looked at the well. The other two tried not to.

"I find it's not the operation of changing that's tough."

"Good."

"It's what to do with the pieces that are left over."

Ramirez shuffled a bit uneasily. Paul looked around the table and at her satchel.

"Armed?" Mary asked Sonya.

"Good eye."

"Looked like a Baretta, 9mm," Mary offered, then "I spotted it earlier. Sorry. Old habit."

"No worries. Yes, we've had some break-ins nearby. I thought being armed was prudent."

"Ok," he said. He did not say "Bullshit" but that's what everybody at the table heard.

"Paul, the project isn't being shut down."

"It's not?"

"No," she looked between the two as if hoping one of them would stop her, "It has to do with that incident in Pixbury. Have you heard of it?

'The Mall shooting? Pair of active shooters? Been all over the news. They set a fire, I believe."

"Well yes, but no."

"I am interested in the 'no' part," Mary cocked an eyebrow, "this should be interesting."

Ramirez took a deep breath.

"Paul's group isn't the only one, or at least it wasn't to begin with. We had another team embedded in the mall, actually. Turns out malls have a lot of open and available space and the facilities are great. So we dropped in a team, walled off the space as if nothing was there, and had them use the back entrance. Worked fine until it actually started working. They were using a different strategy than alpha team."

Mary began to speak but Paul waved her off, wanting to hear more.

"Of course we don't really know if it ever started working. We just know that the reports were good and they were given a go-time. Then the assassination team showed up."

"We didn't hear anything about an assassination team," Mary said, "It would have been in NCIS even it were extremely confidential. This was just a couple of nitwits dressed up like ninjas."

"No, not really. They were ex-SPETNAZ. Seven. Large for that crowd. Arrived looking like painters, so nobody questioned when they started going into areas under construction."

"They killed the team? Our team?" Paul was incredulous, "A foreign specops team killed a bunch of Americans on American soil?"

"No. They were foreigners, sure, but they weren't foreign. Still working out the details. We were able to go back and determine that they were all freelancers. They were living in the U.S. and somebody paid them using cryptocurrency. That's all we know. We're guessing they didn't kill them right away."

"How?"

"We gave the team a panic button. Due to the excess caution exercised by my mirror General on that team, we even had a Rapid Action Team standing by. They deployed, with orders to use any force necessary to stop the attack and bring out whatever live team members, assassins, or gear that they could. We were ready, prepared, or so we thought."

"Sounds like a complete tits-up goat fuck."

"It was. Got worse. Sometime after the action team deployed, there was a crowd, a flash mob. Several thousand people showed up expecting free hundred-dollar gift cards. Coms went down – we still don't know why. By the time we got a second team in 82 people were dead and half the mall burned down. The tech gear had been phosphor grenaded."

Ramirez threw up her hands in a "what are you going to do?" gesture.

"Holy Mother of Christ," Paul said, mostly to himself.

"Yup. And still it gets worse. Once the assassination team was mostly taken out, we believe our action team tried to shoot their way out through the mob, the only way to secure the research. Their orders were to secure research no matter the cost. There were most likely other assassination team members sprinkled in the mob or it might have been a completely separate team – that's why you'll hear eyewitnesses talk about killers in ninja gear, by the way. That was us. The assassin team were painters and suburbanites, not geared up in battle rattle."

"Fuck me," Paul said, "All those people? And we were the ones? United States soldiers?"

"Now are you beginning to understand? It was a hell of thing to cover up and we're still working through the forensics. I'm not proud of this. It wasn't my command, but I'm responsible."

"Good that you're not bothered with ego," Mary said.

"Paul, the project isn't being shut down," Ramirez said, "it's being locked down. We're escalating as much as we possibly can while moving even further under the radar."

"I didn't want to know that," he looked at Mary. "I didn't want to know any of this."

"This isn't academic playtime any more," Ramirez said.

"Are you folks done with your pow-wow?"

They looked up to see a trim, 50-something lady peeking out the back door.

"It'll be another hour or so, honey," Sonya replied.

"I'm sorry," Mary said. She cut a hard glance at Paul, who gave a "who me?" look in return. "Do you two have plans?"

"No, no. You're fine. This has been planned. Crystal's just eager for our dinner tonight. It's our three-month anniversary."

She shuffled around her papers, trying to find something to do, obviously embarrassed by personal conversation.

"Sonya," Paul said, "Is she cleared? She have a TS-SCI?"

"Cleared? Ha! She's my real-estate agent. And fiancé. I guess that makes her safe enough. But no, don't spill your guts."

"So you keep these papers locked up? You make sure she could never discover anything from work?"

"No." It was a final statement.

After a while, Mary finally spoke.

"Why are you doing this, Sonya? Really. Why. Why tell us?" Mary said.

"Because," she started, "I like and respect Paul. He's the only operative I know with multiple PhDs who can kill a man with a k-bar and never make a sound. Then give a calculus lesson."

"Killed a guy once with his boots. While he was wearing them." Paul caught himself. "Not that I can tell that story to anyone. I'm sorry, ma'am."

Ramirez nodded at him. "And he wouldn't. Mary, he would go his entire life and never tell you diddly squat about any of this. That's why. That's the kind of man he is."

"An asshole."

"Yeah, sometimes, sure. He's a good asshole, a leader. They all love him. He deserves a happy life. You both do."

"And that's it," Mary said, "that's all. That's the entire story."

"Yes. Well, aside from Janus Group."

"Janus Group? My old operations group? Thought those guys were long gone."

He looked at his tattoo.

"We're spinning it back up," she said, "we've already had several operations in the states."

"Elimination." Mary did not ask.

Ramirez nodded.

"And that's it," Paul said.

"There's the Manhattan Project and then there's this. We're at an entirely different level. In a way the subject itself is self-censoring, which helps. I don't know any more details than what I've told you. That is it, friends. That's why there isn't any more project, at least as far as anybody here is concerned. Never will be."

There was more uncomfortable silence between them.

Having enough of this, Paul finally said, "You know, funny story, that reminds me of the story of the Nazi Werewolves that were created near the end of World War II."

"Not now." Ramirez looked sad.

Mary patted the table in front of her as if keeping it down.

"You know that I'm a sworn officer of the court, right." It was not a question. "I have an oath."

"All of us here have sworn oaths, Mary, to the same government and judicial system you have."

Mary's phone rang. She held up a finger and stood, taking the call.

All she said was "I see." and a minute later, "Thank you."

Paul and Ramirez both spent the minute in self reflection.

"That was work," Mary said, sitting back down, "Hank Dawson just died."

She straightened her outfit, crossed her arms, got serious.

"What you've told me should at least be handed off for investigation by somebody. Can we bring in the FBI?"

Paul had not seen such a murderous look on Ramirez's face. He was reminded again of what a hard ass she was. He found it not as pleasant this time.

"Absolutely not. Never. Listen here, young lady," she poked a finger at Mary, "you have my word that the appropriate people have been notified and that's all you'll get."

"Mary, we've done what you've asked for, right?" Should he beg? He didn't know. He would if he needed to.

"There's more." She added nothing else.

His eyes went back to the well.

"It's like history. There's always more, Mary," he finally said. "When to stop?"

"My guess is that this is why Mary likes being a detective."

Ramirez may have smiled. He couldn't tell.

"This is it," he finally said, "I've come here. come clean. I've brought in a really nice person and good friend and put her life in danger and she's come clean. I'm done."

This time Ramirez did look worried.

"Paul, come now. Enough with the dramatics. You're not like that." She considered Mary. "Can I offer a solution? Or at least a path?"

They both studied her next words.

"You can't take this anywhere else. I care about you, or at least Paul, and Mary, you through Paul. It's in all of our best interests never to speak of this. If you trust me, how about I arbitrate. Got nothing much else to do. Mary, think about it. Paul, chill out. Something about this sits wrong with you, if you can be patient enough? Come back. We'll talk. The only question is if you trust me or not."

Ramirez cut a glance at Mary.

"I trust her," Paul said, looking back to Mary, "I trust her with my life."

Mary took a deep breath. She looked as if she was almost going to laugh. She smiled. Finally she looked back to Ramirez,

"If Paul trusts you, that's enough for me. I trust you."

"Good. It's done."

The Newburys left the old mansion the same way they came in, Ramirez waving goodbye from the front yard, Crystal by her side, Paul happier with every passing mile.

After a while he looked at Mary.

"Did that settle it? Is that what you wanted? That's all there is."

Mary seemed to ignore him at first, instead staring out the passenger side window at the farmland and cows in steady procession. She bit her nails.

Finally she said, "I don't know."

Watching the car leave, Ramirez slowly took out her cell phone and thought deeply about the call she didn't want to make.

4.22

Bargaining

The Appalachian Trail wound slowly down the mountain, through tall trees and over streams and gullies cutting into the valley below.

The man made his way slowly, gingerly through the Autumn leaves and across the small glade sitting next to the shelter.

Paul Newbury waited. Joe Middles trumbled his way to the wooden structure, swatting at gnats and mosquitoes while he walked.

He looked perfectly miserable.

Joe pointed at him.

"I should have brought a pack."

"This? I'm just breaking out the gear and taking it for a run, making sure it's okay. Don't really need anything for a small day hike like this."

Joe swatted again, "Three hours? Some water might have been nice."

Without looking, Paul reached around to his pack and tossed Joe a canteen. Then, after Joe finished chugging, he threw him a tube of bug juice.

"Oh wow, prof, you're a life saver!"

"Here, gimme," he took the items back, "Now, eat this."

He handed Joe a protein bar.

"Thank you, thank you. A thousand times thank you."

Paul couldn't help but smile at the younger man struggling with being outside.

"Does this mean I still owe you for that pizza the other day?"

"Absolutely, twenty bucks," Joe said. He smiled at Paul, indicating that his complaint was just for show.

"Sure you don't want to stay out on the trail for a while, Joe?" Paul pointed to the shelter they stood beside. "We've got a nice shelter here, place for a fire and everything. We don't have to go back."

"Delivery?" Joe looked around but saw only trees. "Do they have food delivery here?"

"Unlikely. But it looks like somebody's been here recently," pointing at the fire pit.

"Long gone, though. Probably went into town. Somewhere with delivery. Internet. Life."

"Oh yes, Joe, this is really living primitive. We may have to build a log cabin or hunt a bear in order to make our way out."

"Bear?"

"Don't worry, I have a pocket knife. I'll fight any bears we need to fight. I wouldn't worry about bears, either, there are worse things out here than bears."

Paul looked to the woods as if rage zombies were about to come running out.

Joe was unsure if Paul was serious or not. He moved in closer. Paul finally laughed.

"You really, really need to get out more, Middles. See the sunshine."

"Got technology for that. Don't need the sun. I'm moving to C-ville this week, anyway. I don't think the sun goes that far north."

"I imagine."

"Prof, it's all good news. Landed the funding to do that security startup we were talking about. You in? This is it. We're here. It's all starting. We're about to make it big."

"Hmmm," Paul crossed his arms, "Might be good to change things up, try something new. I could still do a commute, or we could move. I am interested, I'll let you know."

There was a small snap of a branch breaking, almost imperceptible.

"I thought I heard you," Paul said to nobody in particular.

Joe looked around. There was nothing. He looked back to Paul, his face saying "Is this another joke? Are you pulling my leg again?"

In return Paul ignored him. He made a beckoning motion to the woods. "Come on out."

An older man appeared. He was thin, muscular, had a square jawline and stood taller than either Paul or Joe. He was wearing a light jacket in the cool fall air.

He was smiling. He looked like somebody seeing a long lost friend.

"I never was good at hide-and-seek, Hiya Paul! Oldberry!"

Paul nodded at the man.

"You should have worn moccasins," he said, "dry leaves are tough. You know that."

Seeing that Joe was confused, Paul continued.

"I guess you two need formal introductions. Joe Middles, George Endelman. George, Joe."

"Who's he?"

"George is my old boss. I think he's picked up some work in the area."

There was a questioning look. George caught it, then nodded.

"Out for a walk. Yeah. Oldberry and I go way back. You guys like a cold beer?"

Joe was startled.

"Sure! I'd also like a motorcycle! You two know each other?"

Endelman handed Middles a beer from his light pack he was wearing.

"You went hiking. With cold beer." Paul said

"Never know when one will come in handy."

The breeze increased. Paul made as if he were cold.

"Too cold for beer."

They heard voices, another party coming down the trail.

Joe looked back and forth between the two men, picking up on the tension between them. The young man began to look seriously frightened.

"You know, George, Mr. Endelman, it was nice meeting you. And funny running into you, Professor! Probably time for me to get back for Jeopardy."

Endelman didn't say anything. He just shook his head no.

Placing his hands on his hips, they both could see the pistol on the shoulder strap beneath his jacket.

Paul looked at Joe as if to say, "See? Here's the real bear."

Joe deflated.

"Think I'll take one of those beers after all," Paul said.

Endelman tossed him one.

"We go way back, Paul."

"We do, George. You owe me one. More than one, actually."

Endelman stopped smiling, got his own beer out. Nodded as he drank.

"I think you've saved my life half a dozen times," he said.

"Seven, counting that time in New York. But I'm not counting."

Endelman pointed the beer at Joe.

"I know you. I don't know him."

"He's with me," Paul said simply, then, "I vouch for him."

Endelman now took a good look at Joe.

"If he'll vouch for you, I'll accept that. For now. But you're running out of favors, Oldberry."

Relieved, Joe hurried to leave. George stopped him with his hand.

"But there are conditions. Not so fast."

"Whatever. I'm in. I vetted for the project. I'm good to keep secrets. The professor told us."

Joe looked to Paul in desperation.

"It's not that simple," Endelman appraised him even more, like a tailor sizing up a new suit, "do you know anything about a break-in downtown the other night? A comic book store?"

Paul could see the battle going on behind Joe's eyes. He knew Endelman could see it too. His current guess was that Joe hadn't crossed the line. Yet.

"Nope."

"Whatever papers there might be, it's not just that they don't exist. NOTHING exists, about anything or anyone in the last four years. You don't live here. You don't correspond with anyone here. This time in your life is a black hole. I don't want to see or hear anything about you in regards to your work here. Got it?"

"Yes sir."

He let the man pass. Before leaving, Joe looked back, wanting to see if Paul came behind him.

Endelman stuck his hand out. Paul puzzled.

"What's this?"

"The twenty bucks I owe you," George said.

"Give it to the kid."

He handed it to Joe. Joe looked again at Paul. What should I do?

"Now we're even for the pizza. Get lost."

He didn't need to be told twice, although he was. Joe left as fast as his dignity would allow him. Paul idly thought he looked like a speed-walker.

They both watched him go. Paul caught the tension in his old boss' shoulders as he watched.

"You lied. You haven't decided anything," he concluded.

George turned back.

"Didn't we make a deal?"

He pointed up the trail where Joe had gone.

"No. You just didn't want to take care of him here, with my watching."

Endelman shrugged.

"Would have ruined a good beer. This is a bonding moment we're having."

He pointed the beer at Paul.

They heard more voices. They were getting closer.

"Busy trail," Paul said.

"Not too bad," Endelman looked around, "Nice choice."

They waited. The voices didn't get closer, instead fading away. Whoever they were, they had not come down to the shelter.

"I need the work, Paul," Endelman said, "It's good money. It's not personal."

"George. Let me help you. We've gone through worse in the past. We've got this."

Endelman shrugged again, went back to drinking his beer, much more slowly this time.

"I guess it's a good thing Hilda wasn't here," Paul finished his beer, turning it upside down to drain. "My other kid. Hilda Gibb. Have you seen my other student? You know, the one that didn't fall off the overpass?"

George raised his eyebrows. He smiled again.

"You won't be seeing her, I don't think. For a while, at least. Maybe forever."

Paul let that one go, instead shifting gears.

"Are you responsible for what happened to Hank, George?"

"Right now? Right here?" Endelman pointed back and forth between the two of them, "You want to do this? You and I aren't even supposed to be talking. We're not interacting. At all. I'll end up on the other side if I'm not very careful. These folks aren't chumps. There are a lot more folks that would come after me. After all the war we've had, there's a deep bench of folks ready to take my job. We're nothing. Little specks."

"Passing through," Paul indicated where they had heard the voices.

"They're having a good day," Endelman agreed, "It's almost like they weren't here."

"Have pity on me, George," it was time to go balls-to-the-wall, "My wife wants to shoot me, my oldest daughter hates life, I'm not sure if this professor gig is going to work out, my middle daughter is losing it. It's not just me. It's not just you. Not everybody's in this like we are. They don't deserve this."

When he looked at his old friend, he could see the Endleman had grabbed his pistol.

He hadn't pulled it yet.

"I don't do pity," Endelmen was a death head. "You know that."

"I know," Paul said. He looked at the old fire pit. "But you pay your debts, don't you."

Endelman also looked at the fire pit.

"We'll all be gone sooner or later."

Paul looked back. He had an idea.

"You know, Endless Man, you're forgetting your tactical training."

"This should be good."

"What are the first things we learned? Terrain, fire, maneuver, but the best of all? Time? If you've got time on your side, just wait it out."

He saw the man's hands relax.

"We've got time on our hands. Stall for thirty days. Give Joe and me and my family some space. We'll scatter. If you don't hear anything, if there's no more heat? Give it six months. Let's play the time card, my friend. Slow walk it."

Endelman walked over, looked at the fire pit as well. Slowly he relaxed. Paul could see Endelman was really relaxing now.

"Let's give it a shot," he said, smiling, "That's an excellent idea, Paul! Thank you."

Paul smiled back. "Don't mention it."

Endelman started leaving, but stopped.

"Next time? You won't see me."

"I know, George. I know."

Endelman left.

Paul sat very still in the gathering gloom of the twilight. He listened to the older man pick his way through the forest continuing, at a distance, to stalk Joe Middles who was about a half mile ahead. He knew his old boss without even thinking about it, instinct.

He would have to leave soon; either leave or hike after dark. The sounds of Endelman finally faded off.

He stared intently at the burnt out embers in the old firepit. Some person or group had a hike, an adventure. It was an adventure by people he would have never known, going places he could not imagine.

He rose up. He dusted himself off. He made his way back home, one step at a time.

4.23

Caterers

"You mean this was an actual plantation?" Mary asked, looking at the ancient house, "and hospital?"

They were back. They brought the kids.

"That's right," Mrs. McKenzie (call me Crystal) said, "This was an alive, vibrant place. First built in 1804, McKenzie Manor was constructed both by slaves and Irish indentured servants. They made the bricks right here. Look at this. Can you imagine that this is over 200 years old?"

Paul gleefully rubbed his hands together. He tried to ignore the fact that Mary and he had been here recently and pretend it was their first time, for the kids. They told the kids it was about time they met dad's old boss. He took another picture with the disposable camera he had bought at the convenience store ten minutes ago.

"Back then, kids, this land was the frontier, the great unknown. This was Indian Country."

Sal looked as if she had caught a bad smell, perhaps a skunk. Tim was all smiles, examining the brick Crystal had, then looking over at the stack of other bricks. Deb poked around behind a pile of debris, beer cans, food wrappers, for what, who knew.

"There is a lot of junk around here," Ramirez said, following Paul's glance. "Crystal and I have spent most evenings cleaning up some of the more recent trash. There's still a lot of work left."

Crystal nodded. She was about Sonya's age, curt, professional, black, and wore a business suit. She introduced herself as president of the local preservation society, owner of the only real-estate firm for miles around.

"Debian Ada Newbury, put that road flare down!" Mary said. Before she could get to Deb there was a pop-pop-pop behind her.

"Mom!" Tim said, "Wow! Firecrackers!"

Mary wheeled. "Where did you get matches?"

She grabbed a large stack out of his hands. Tim did not approve, but knew enough to be quiet.

"Come on, kids," Sonya said, "Let us show you the attic. You know what they have there? Secret slave holds!"

"Wow!" Tim said.

The attic was huge, like the rest of the house. As their eyes adjusted to the deep gloom, Crystal continued.

"The McKenzies were the first ones to build and maintain this property," she said, "and as slave holders in the newly-formed free state of West Virginia, it was not unusual for federal raiding parties to come by, looking for food, provisions, and anything else that might be of use, including slaves. So they hid here."

In the wooden floor of the attic they could barely make out a dozen or so squares that were a slightly different color. Crystal took a pry bar and pried one up. It covered a hole about six feet deep, built into the floor of the attic.

"As far as we know, none of the slaves were ever found," the black lady continued, "They were all freed at the conclusion of the war."

"Fascinating." Paul said. "And did the McKenzies fight in the war? North or South?"

"Yes and no," Crystal said, "They wanted to fight for their property." She smiled. "But this entire area was overrun, several times by both sides. If they left they would have lost everything. So they formed McKenzie's Rangers."

Tim stopped admiring the old logs that made up the house.

"What's a ranger? Get masks? A horse?"

Paul glanced at him but continued with Crystal, a man on a mission.

"Like Quantrill's Rangers? Jesse James? Brigands? Pirates?"

"Pirates!"

"Exactly, although not as successful. Or notorious." She said. "Although they did manage to burn Chambersburg to the ground."

Crystal kept smiling, unable to determine her next facial expression. The smile lingered. Finally Mary spoke to Sonya.

"So," she said. "You two are working here every day?"

Sonya cut a quick glance at Crystal.

"That's right."

"Your last name is McKenzie," Sal said.

Sal had spent her time staring out the one window in the attic but now seemed interested. "Are you related to the people who built this?"

"You might say that," Crystal said. "I imagine many of my ancestors spent long hours hiding in these very holes."

As they looked at the holes again, she continued.

"I'm staying here." She straightened her suit. "I'm living here. With Sonya."

"Why that's awesome," Paul said. He gave a knowing smile to Sonya. "You two been doing this, er, reconstruction for long?"

"Since I bought the house," Sonya said.

She looked at Crystal and smiled.

"So far so good."

"Hey mom," Sal said, still looking out the window. "Why are there caterers here?"

"It's just hamburgers today," Crystal said to Sonya. "We didn't order hamburgers. Caterers?"

"Probably the wrong house," Sonya agreed. "Come on, kids, let me show you one of the *three* kitchens. Can you believe it? This one even has an *elevator.*"

Sal visibly grumbled but managed to follow them down the narrow back steps to the first kitchen.

"I'll go help them out," Crystal said, heading out as soon as they all assembled. "Probably another wedding up the road at the Vicar Mansion and they got the street address wrong again."

"Probably the wrong house," Paul agreed. He winked at the kids. "And who needs caterers, anyway? We've got some yummy hamburgers. I think we might even have an authentic 19th century rhubarb pie for dessert!"

"I think I just threw up a little bit in my mouth," Sal said.

"Salomé Carlisle Newbury. You be polite, young lady." Mary said.

She looked at Paul.

"She's your child."

Paul did a quick kid check. Tim was looking at the old light switches, no doubt trying to figure out how they worked. Or how to take them apart. Sal was busy taking fire from her mom.

"I have long suspected that she is," he said. He continued to scan. "Sadly."

Deb was still, which wasn't at all unusual for her. But Paul thought she also looked contemplative, perhaps listening to something.

Far away he heard a very quiet creak. It was a board creaking on the front porch. Deb looked at him. Nobody else had noticed. Then … again. Every adult tensed a small bit.

"What are we going to do if it's not caterers," Mary said to the General, although she stared at the far wall.

"Not a good time for company," Sonya agreed. She looked at Paul. He thought she looked very sad then, sadder and more frail than he'd ever seen her.

"No ma'am," he said. "It's not."

Paul frowned. He began to grimace as well, but instead he caught himself. He checked his kids again.

There was another creak. This time all of the adults reacted.

"I need to get something out back," he said, grabbing the recently confiscated firecrackers from his wife, "I'll be back in just a minute. Why don't you guys go ahead and start the burgers?"

"What?" Deb asked.

He smiled. "I've got a surprise!"

Paul was only gone a minute. He returned to the old kitchen to find Mary and Sonya keeping the kids busy with cooking chores.

As he entered, as if on cue, they stopped. Looked at him.

"You've got a bit on you," Sonya said.

He looked down to see blood spots on his sleeve.

Rubbing it, he nodded towards the front of the house but looked upstairs.

"I think it's the newspaper that's here!" He said. "Just what I was hoping for. Which of you kids are up for hiding in the slave hold and getting your picture taken! By the newspaper? Wouldn't that be neat?"

"Not me," Sal said, "That's stupid."

Mary looked at Sal. They all knew that look.

"Sounds good." Sal said, immediately correcting and now completely in charge, "what's taking you guys so long?"

Thirty seconds later they were back in the attic they'd just came from. The kids happily climbed into the holes, but didn't close them. Only Deb lingered, still caught in whatever thoughts she had. It looked like a broken whack-a-mole game.

Sonya lifted her shirt. There was a subcompact 9mm Baretta, complete with silencer. She put it back.

Paul looked to see if Deb caught it. If she did she didn't let on.

"Deb, dear," Mary said. "You should get in the hole. You want your picture taken, don't you?"

There was the unmistakable sound of sound-suppressed gunfire from the front yard.

"What happened?" Deb asked.

Sonya started to leave, but Mary grabbed her.

Mary's eyes saw everything and nothing. Her posture stiffened. If there was some human in charge of things they weren't working her body at the moment. Paul started doing a room scan again.

"No." She said to Sonya.

Sonya stopped. She did not take her gaze from Mary. Mary's expression was etched in stone.

"What happened?" Deb asked again.

Sonya glanced over.

"To whom?"

"To the McKenzies. Did they win in the end?

"No dear," Sonya said to Deb, but she looked at Paul and Mary.

"They lost, dear. They scattered to the hills, fighting when they could, but eventually they were all either hunted down and killed, or ..."

She backed up, pulling at Mary's grasp. Mary let go.

"Were assimilated." She said, "One family could never fight millions."

"Kiddo, get in the hole. This is a big deal even for Mrs. Ramirez. Don't ruin it." Paul said. He winked at Deb.

"I need to check on Crystal," Sonya said.

Neither Paul nor Mary had anything to say. Sonya waited, but neither moved. After hesitating again at the stair door, looking back at the family again, she left. Quietly.

Paul never saw her alive again.

They both immediately turned their attention to the children. All three were in the holes but all three had their lids up and were peeking.

"Was that a gun?" Sal asked.

"What?" Paul said, going over to them. "Well, Mary, I think they've figured it out. They've guessed it."

"They have," Mary said. Her expression did not change.

She kept looking at him. He smiled some more.

"It was the newspapers, and the caterers too. There was going to be a big party. We had set this up as a surprise and I didn't want you to figure it out."

Sal looked at her father. Her eyebrows raised.

"Prep work for an upcoming movie," he said, feeling more desperate and trying to control it. The kids could make Paul scared the way no other thing on Earth could. He barely paused for breath. "It's guerrilla shooting, where they just show up and get everything on one take without making a fuss or anything."

"Well, we told them that you kids would love to be the kidnapped kids taken hostage by the evil psycho killer."

He made a menacing look.

Mrs. Ramirez and Mrs. McKenzie are playing the henchmen! Isn't that cool?"

"Dad?"

"We wanted to catch you by surprise," He said.

"Paul," Mary said.

He looked at his watch. Eighty-three seconds. Time running out.

"But dang, they started it too early! Do you think you kids can hide extremely quietly until you're rescued? You have to act like you don't know what's going on."

"Dad, Mom's making me," Sal said, "Don't wanna be in some dumb history movie."

"Newspapers too? Getting your picture in the paper? There's a couple of famous actors."

"You two get down!" Salomé was nothing if not firmly ambivalent.

The two siblings hesitated.

"Now!"

All three lids closed.

Paul could hear a very quiet voice of Deb.

"But who's the bad guy?"

"Shhhh!"

Paul and Mary held their breath, waiting to see if they had settled down.

There were no more sounds.

They heard more sound suppressed gunfire out front, followed by the front door opening and people running through the house.

Mary held her fingers to her lips.

Quiet.

They looked at the floor, daring the sounds to come at them.

A small brown ant crawled out from Paul's boot. It slowly made its way to the window.

Mary ground it out.

They heard more doors slamming. Some quiet talking as if people coordinating their work, perhaps through radios.

His heart pounded in his chest. Mary's eyes darted around the almost dark attic. He could hear Tim softly crying. Deb was quiet. Sal poked the lid to her hole up, only an inch or two, peering out in the darkness to find her parents.

Paul glared at his eldest daughter. This was going to escape containment.

She hid again.

He looked back to his wife.

Mary cupped his face. She was mourning. They both thought the same thing.

This was never going to work.

He went to Tim's hole, lifted it.

"Hey Timbo, isn't this going to be the most awesome game ever?" He whispered.

He stopped crying, wiped his nose. Looked up at his dad.

Paul leaned in, sharing a secret.

"You know, I'm pretty mad at these yahoos for ruining your surprise. Aren't you?"

Tim slowly nodded.

"So how about when they finally get here to shoot the scene where they find you, how about we reverse the plan on them? Show 'em good!"

God help him, he thought, he was using his own children as pawns.

He saw Mary sigh.

"What?" Tim whispered. Tim the co-conspirator. Innocent murder shone in his small eyes.

He handed Tim the disposable camera he had brought with him.

They heard a muffled whomp, a low-intensity flash bang.

"When they find you, you jump out at them, scream. Flash them with the camera and run at them, then out of the house. That should scare the bejesus out of them, wouldn't it Mom?"

Mary nodded. Her frown lessened.

"Run out," she said to herself.

"Cool!" Tim said. Tim was always his go-to kid for mayhem.

His door shut. Paul saw that Sal's was still cracked. She was still watching.

Mary went to her, whispered. Slowly and quietly Sal got out of her hiding hole. She followed her mom to the far corner of the attic. He joined them.

Before he could reach them, though, Sal left by the back stairs.

He looked at his wife. He leaned in. He struggled to maintain a whisper.

"What?"

She simply shrugged.

"I told her to run to that convenience store we passed, five miles back."

"You what?"

"You know …"

Another door shut in the house below them.

After ten seconds of silence she continued.

"She the best runner in the family of all the kids, Paul. My money says she's a better runner than whoever these guys are, even if they're operators."

Paul counted the seconds to himself, as Salomé, his oldest, snuck out.

They distinctly heard the back door slam, followed by a male voice.

"Hey!"

He looked at her. What have you done?

"Back door!"

A second voice.

"Give it up. You'll never get her. She's gone, man."

There were a couple of shots.

Paul and Mary huddled, squatted, as if being close to the ground could make themselves less conspicuous.

"We should go after her," the first voice said.

"Nyah. All that means is that the rest of them are in the house somewhere."

Mary made a gesture: see?

He shook his head.

She leaned in.

"That worked, Paul, just not enough. I don't know how many there are, guessing a handful, but that conversation means they can't deal with multiple targets simultaneously."

"What are you saying?"

"I'm saying they need a good punch in the face, make them commit their reserves."

"Huh?"

"We need a bigger diversion. I can do it."

He was sure he had something to say. He did not get a chance to say it.

"You stay here. Listen for me. You'll know it when you hear it. Get the kids to safety."

He nodded. It was simple. It was done.

She also disappeared down the attic steps.

As soon as he was sure she had made it down the steps safely, he went back to the kids.

As expected, Tim flashed him with the camera, completely blinding him. Old infantryman trick: in combat keep one eye closed to prevent flashes from blinding you. He managed to shush the boy before he started screaming and running.

Maybe that was a piece of luck.

Deb was still lost in her thoughts, but she allowed herself to be led out of the hole.

"You okay, kiddo?"

She looked at him. She nodded. She went back to ignoring him.

"Ok kids, I have been lying to you a bit."

Tim began speaking but Paul hushed him.

"It's a long story. Right now I need you both to do me the most super serious favor ever. It is, no kidding, very bad if you don't do exactly as I say."

They both looked at him.

He made a shushing sound.

"Follow me. Be as quiet as Superman could possibly be. Quieter than Spiderman even."

He could see Tim struggling to respond. To his credit the boy remained silent.

"We are going to sneak like little mice to the steps here." He pointed. "And then I'll make a hand gesture and we're going to sneak completely out of the house."

They continued to stare.

"Nobody can hear or see us. Got it?"

They nodded.

There was a terrible racket, as if a bunch of wine barrels had hit the floor and crashed together. He suspected that's exactly what it was. It was followed by yelling.

Pop-pop.

Almost.

A thud.

He tensed.

The unmistakable smell of cookstove gas came over them. She must have hit the mains, opened them. That was his wife: nothing halfway.

That was not good. It was more not good.

Worse was the sound of a machine gun, probably an MP-5 or an Uzi. He idly wondered if any operators still used Uzis. Tough gun. They should have brought a Hush Puppy, a Mike Kilo Two-Two, the only truly silent gun. Then it would have been even tougher on them.

Must have been rushed.

The gunfire stopped, the crashing stopped, and eventually the sounds of yelling stopped.

Was it time? Would the time get any better if they waited?

He distinctly heard, "Anybody check the attic?"

"Dad, there's only three of them and they're all in the basement."

Deb. Deb poked him. "Right now Mom's got them there."

"How can you know that?" He whispered back.

"I counted their steps," was her only reply. She spoke as if this were something everybody did. "The basement has seventeen steps. One of them walks with a limp."

He thought about it. He could hear their steps, just barely. It was an old house. That's how he knew they were there. It was possible. Perhaps he was not focused as much as she was.

He looked at his middle child.

They heard a door creak far away. Her eyes went up.

"We have 47 seconds depending on their speed," she said, "The one with the machine gun is now outside. Front porch going to van."

Debian paused. Listened.

"Dad. One's coming towards the basement steps. Second one is reloading."

Tim looked at Debian as if he had actually met Superman.

Paul patted her.

"You're really a miraculous little girl, kiddo."

They started leaving, but Deb whispered on her way out, perhaps to herself or perhaps to the house.

"Not a kid. I'm Super-Bear."

They made it as far as the woodpile. He considered that a win even if they all died here. He wouldn't have put any money on them making it this far.

It began raining. Heavily. But of course it did. Noise might be helpful. How could he use that?

He heard a sound like somebody banging on a steel drum from the treeline. It was followed by yelling from inside the house.

They were quickly soaked.

Mary.

It was time to run the other way. Ground clutter would be doused, silent. Whoever left was around front.

Where was Deb?

He looked up, peeked over the woodpile, to see Debian Newbury standing like a statue in front of the house.

In her hand was a lit road flare.

"RUN!" he yelled, and he did not have time to grab her. She'd have to come.

It wasn't five seconds later when the house blew up. He felt the wave of heat over take him. He was carrying Tim now. He didn't remember picking him up.

They had fallen down. He wondered why he wasn't on fire. He thought about the Leidenfrost Effect, where a layer of water can protect for brief seconds against tremendous heat.

A second piece of luck.

Looking back, he didn't see Debian. Then he realized she was standing right beside him.

She was smiling.

"Why'd you do that?"

"Because Daddy," she said, "now we win, right?"

4.24

Final Warning

They left the kids with the sitter. The sitter had been planned and waiting when they got home, and they both were too keyed up, even after the long drive home, to spend any time sitting around.

Mary put the kids to sleep. Paul didn't know how and he wasn't going to ask. It wasn't ideal. He didn't object. He couldn't. Something had to be done to give them space to think and they weren't about to call any-body. Else.

The rain that had been forecast for that evening just missed their house. Instead, the heavy clouds had blown through and opened the sky up around sunset for a beautiful starry evening.

Paul carried his binoculars. They walked into the park. He didn't feel like using them.

Mary carried her gun in a holster on her hip.

Neither really knew what they were doing or had any plan, so after walking about 100 yards they both stopped. They looked at the trees, the path, anywhere but each other.

"How long do you think it'll be before somebody shows up?" She looked around as if they might show up at any moment.

"I suspect never, Mary. There might not even be a crime scene."

She didn't reply right away, looking him up and down. Finally she said, "Shouldn't you be armed? After this afternoon?"

"Who says I'm not."

"My bad. I forgot that there's you," she pointed up and down as if show-ing off his fashions, "and then there's *you*. One living inside the other."

"Man of many mysteries." He chose to ignore the jab.

"This I'm beginning to see," she said, "and we are going to eliminate those mysteries, Paul. We have to."

"I am," he thought to find the right word, "committed to becoming an open book. We agreed. I showed you. There are also mysteries we need to let go."

She slanted her head and concentrated.

"Maybe. I have a proposition, Paul: would you agree to sorting and keeping track of them, as long as it was in private, no records, no electronics, nothing but us talking?"

Paul shuffled, uncomfortable.

"Maybe. Maybe. But it has to stop here, with us. It's not the solving that's the problem, Mary, it's the communicating, with anyone, that's not going to work. Trust me."

"Endelman, right?" not getting a reply, she continued, "Aside from the ongoing mystery that is my husband, there are a dozen other acts of violence and mayhem that I need to get out of my system, one way or another. I have to do this. Even if we only talk and it goes nowhere."

"I get it, Mary. Really I do. But I'd ask you to consider that we don't even know what we don't know."

"How does that make any…"

"Paul. Paul Newbury."

He recognized the voice. Directly behind him. How could somebody have snuck up on them? Who was it?

They both spun, facing the danger. Both of them reached for their firearm.

It was an eight-year-old girl, pigtails, glasses. She looked as if she was trying out for the school play. Behind her, about 30 yards, was her mother, cell phone in hand.

"Paul Newbury."

It was the girl from his story the other day, the one he had used to explain BCI. Seemed like decades ago.

"Yes?"

She cleared her throat.

"Are you going to continue down this path, continue in this direction?"

She shuffled back and forth, looking up, trying to remember her next line. She was obviously self-conscious. It was her first time in a school play.

"There's danger ahead," she finally remembered, quite pleased with herself.

Beside him, Mary looked around, trying to find danger. Paul didn't like Mary's look.

Well, this was the thing, wasn't it. Mary wasn't going to stew very long. Trying to make peace with her by explaining there were more messed up things than she could possibly imagine? Telling her that? Having her truly and deeply understand it? The would be like trying to put out a fire by throwing kerosene on it.

"Why don't you run back to your mom. I'll be along in a minute with your answer."

The girl looked as if she were not prepared for this answer. After a moment of indecision, she ran back.

"Kid must've been talking about the path being out ahead," he glanced at Mary, "and suddenly I think you're going to punch me in the nose."

Mary remained silent.

He could hear her tense.

"Ok, ok. Another Paul mystery. We can put that on the list. They just go on and on."

She looked at the girl.

"More bullshitting. From my husband."

He let go. "I had that project. We've talked about it. It's done. It deals with discovering and communicating in ways we could normally never perceive. This looks like an example of that."

They heard "Flight of the Valkyries." Looking over, the girl's mom was getting a phone call.

She smiled.

Paul looked back to his very skeptical wife.

"Ever watch the movie 'The Great Escape' with Steve McQueen?"

"What does this have to do with…"

"Bear with me."

"Ok. You do these things at the weirdest times."

"True story. In World War II, allied prisoners had an obligation to try to escape from prison camps if they were captured and became POWs. The Germans, of course, couldn't let them escape. Why can't you just be happy, they'd ask. You can wait for the war to end, stay safe. But the allies couldn't, so they set up an elaborate scheme of tunnels, earth-moving, forged documents, and so forth. Their goal was to break every man out of that prison camp, Stalag Luft 3."

"We're not surrendering."

"And the hell of the thing? They almost did it. They struggled, were caught several times, but they managed to put together the biggest prison break in modern times. Hundreds could have gotten out. That's why they made the movie about it. But all movies suck at history."

"Do you have some sort of point?"

"They were caught, of course. Only a couple of people made it to safety. Romantic fiction is wonderful. It's the heroes against the villains. But the first thing they teach you in POW school is that your main goal is to survive. Everybody breaks under torture, and simple determined, quiet survival is the only thing that will work, and even then it's a long shot."

"We're not prisoners, Paul."

"The Germans machine-gunned the prisoners who planned the Great Escape. No more prisoners, no more escape attempts. Simple. Aren't we? Prisoners?"

"Good grief," Mary finally said, the way a mom might congratulate a child on putting his shoes on backwards. "Here we go again. You're really something. You've found your calling, Paul. You're a natural born professor."

"Thank you. And you're my fierce natural born warrior cop."

She let it go.

She started to reply then stopped. Paul filled in the empty space.

"I've always been better at giving orders, pontificating, than I have been at listening, taking orders."

"This I know. Wow, you really are getting it all out, opening a vein, it looks like. I'm quite moved. Now, watch me do this on my own."

He stood stunned, as she went over to the little girl and her mom.

There followed some animated conversation. Mary showed her badge, the mom explained, Mary gave the kid a piece of candy, the mom handed over her phone, Mary studied it, the mom explained some more. Finally she gave the phone back, made a gesture for them both to stay there, and came back.

Seeing that he was observed, Paul gave a weak wave and smile to them both. The girl eagerly waved, arms over her head. She was waiting. Her mom was much more circumspect, waving at Paul as if he might be an escaped lunatic.

It was a possibility he had considered for some time.

"No luck, huh," he caught her before she could even start.

She steamed.

"You want to do a full trace on her phone, contact the company that runs the app, don't you."

Cautious nod.

"Be my guest. You won't find anything. I can save you the effort. Oh, you'll find the company, sure. But they'll just point to a proxy user, a hacked tunneling, a dozen participants, each doing a tiny bit and not realizing it. The list goes on and on. You and I, clever people that we are, could hide something with one or two levels of hiding. When you can automatically hide things as deep as you want? A hundred and forty-two levels deep? You could spend the rest of your life and still not find the answer to this one question, your extremely small and simple question you have right now: who sent that message, paid for that chore? By some random little girl?" Her eyes cut him. He sighed deeply, shrugged.

"It's an unbearable task for you, trivial to certain others."

He thought again.

"Give me a second," He began walking over to the small girl and her mom.

He knew she was following slowly behind him. It didn't matter. He put on his best smile.

"Good to see you, and you too, young lady! I'm glad you guys are out again."

"Mom says we're going back to get our telescope."

Paul looked up. "Crescent moon tonight. You'll love it."

The woman looked a bit puzzled, not sure what to do.

"You two are free to leave, get your scope. We're sorry to bother you. We've been having some cyber crime, oddly enough, in the park late at night. You were just in the wrong spot at the wrong time, that's all." he patted the girl's head, looking at her mom, "reminds me of our oldest daughter."

"What do you say!" the kid was firm, "What's my answer?" she looked to her mom, then back. She was playing her part in the play and dammit he had to say his line too.

"Your answer? Heck no! You tell 'em we'll go a different way. The safe way. Put that in there." He pointed at the mom's phone.

"Yay! We got an answer!" the girl was ecstatic.

Mom pulled out the phone as they slowly left. He heard the kid saying, "That dumb man thought we had to enter something. Bet he's never even played." They heard the cha-ching! sound of money hitting the mom's account.

"Good job," Mom said, and then they were gone.

Paul turned to leave too.

"Where are you going?" Mary was having none of it.

She spoke to his back.

"Fine. I'm going to go arrest them, take them in for questioning."

"I can't let you do that," he stopped.

"You can't WHAT?"

"I believe this meeting is over." He put his hands in his pockets.

"Weren't we having a conversation?"

"No. No, Mary. Not anymore."

"Well," she pointed to where the mom and kid had went, "let's ask them some more questions. Maybe you can image their phone or do some science-y stuff. It's a lead."

"What lead? You want to argue with an 8-year-old? Interrogate an already frightened mom? Maybe rough them up some?"

He shook his head no. It was too much. Mary was too much.

"I have my orders," staring at the ground, scared to look at her, "We both do. We just got them."

"Your orders. You're quitting."

"No, Mary, I am not quitting. I'm just not going to dig a tunnel with you, that's all. Some folks need to know when they're defeated. I'm not taking my family over the wire to get machine-gunned, virtually or otherwise."

"Fuck you."

She left.

On the way out, several paces behind her, he threw his binoculars in the trash can.

He doubted he would ever come this way again.

4.25

Burn Baby Burn

The monkey screamed at them as they came into the house. The monkey hid in the little shelves beside the front door.

It always screamed at them. Last year, Salomé had decided to go on a diet. After a lot of household drama about eating disorders and social appearances, it was decided as a compromise that they would buy the monkey.

It was a little plastic monkey. You put it in the refrigerator, or perhaps on a kitchen shelf. The idea was that when you disturbed the monkey, it would scream at you, thereby reminding you that you should be careful what you eat.

Nobody in the ongoing family drama was happy about the monkey except young Timothy, and he wasn't even part of it. As soon as the monkey arrived, Tim discovered that he could place the little plastic toy anywhere in the house and it would scream at people as they walked by.

This was lovely.

Everybody hated this. The more they hated it, the more Tim found it hilarious. The Great Monkey War had just began. Paul knew better than to take sides too early.

He smiled and then was immediately saddened by the smile.

"How the hell are we supposed to deal with THAT?" Mary asked. She threw her pocketbook in her chair.

He hung his coat up, careful to avoid the monkey. She continued.

"It's smoke, that's what it is," she said, "we're fighting smoke. We can look all we want and there's nothing there. How do we fight smoke?"

"We don't. I told you."

She went to hang her coat up. The monkey screamed at her.

"I hate that fucking monkey."

"Yes. Me too."

He studied the monkey. Horrible thoughts went through his head.

"It's for Sal. The monkey's for Sal. It's Sal's monkey."

"Sal's not here."

"I know. It's Sal's monkey."

She stepped back, pointing at the monkey as if it just appeared in a magic trick.

"Can we not somehow kill, hide, or otherwise defeat it?"

"It's Sal's monkey." He said again trying to avoid the real question.

She turned on a dime and went back to the kitchen.

"Where's the fucking fireplace lighter?"

"The what?"

"The long lighter we have for starting fires. Green. Long." She made a gesture showing length.

Gave up.

"Dear Mary, you cannot set Diet Monkey on fire," he said. He realized that she was not listening, "I forbid it."

Please come back, Mary.

He tossed it out, gauging the impact. There was just no coming back. The storm was still gathering strength and had not struck yet. He stood, a tiny ant watching it approach.

She tossed their junk drawers, target not found. Giving up, she turned back to him.

"I'm not going to. I guess I'll have to look in the bedrooms."

She started up the stairs.

"Careful. Sitter and the kids are sleeping."

"I know," she said in a muted voice.

He followed along behind her. He whispered. "Lighter? Why?"

"You're not going to like it."

"Probably not," he agreed.

In the master bedroom, he told her that the lighter had run out and gotten thrown away months ago. She did not believe it. It was a lie.

She started for the other bedrooms, where they were sleeping, but he stopped her by clearing his throat and glaring.

He sat on the bed. He held out his hand in a peace offering.

"Here. Matches. Use the matches. Why the rush?"

She sat next to him. She patted him on the knee. She was calm and that bothered him even more. Once she had returned to him that evening, began talking, he had thought her angry, but he realized now that she was sad, terribly sad. The shell was angry. The inside was empty.

"Things move on, my love," he said.

She kissed him on the cheek while getting up.

"That they do. Catch up."

He sat on the bed a while longer, wondering if there was something he should be doing. Deciding no, he went out, finding her in the kitchen.

She was writing a note, making a list. Always with the notes and lists.

Running out of subtle options, he went direct.

"What are you going on about?"

She got up, glanced back at the small white note. She looked him deep in the eyes.

"We are going to have to make some changes. Nobody is going to like them."

"What's new?"

She smiled then, a wan smile, admitting he was right.

"We've been together a long time, love," she said, "a long time. Through thick and thin."

"Twenty years now."

"Yup."

He looked at her.

"You were there when my parents died. Don't know how I could have ever gotten through it without you."

She nodded.

"And you too, the kids being born, and my parents dying, and all the problems in our careers, the trouble tonight? Looking crazy? Your sister's cancer."

He shrugged. "We've always done it. Somehow we've always made it work."

"We've made it through the changes."

She looked down a moment, frowning. He noticed her emotions fighting more and more to get out, being held in. The ice.

"But things still exist," she said, looking him in the eye.

"I don't follow."

"They're still dead, Paul. My parents. Yes, you were there. I was there. We comforted one another, but feelings aren't reality."

He gasped.

She took his forgotten matches and left into the backyard.

Something was going on out there. When he finally went out, logs were in the fire pit.

"So a fire?"

She ignored him. Instead she went in the house, returning moments later with her laptop computer.

She tossed it on the logs.

Was this a prank? Her laptop?

She went in and returned a minute later with their TV. On the logs.

Her manner was wooden, like the logs.

His tower. The streaming box. Mesh Wi-Fi. She kept going in and out.

"A fire tonight, wow. I love campfires. I should get some pictures."

She grabbed the phone from his hand and tossed it on the wood. She tossed her own phone.

"There can be absolutely NO electronic devices that can communicate or record in our home."

He frowned, watching.

"Ever," She adjusted the pile.

She went in several more times, returning with the cordless phones, his laptop, the toaster oven.

He had just bought that toaster oven. It had Bluetooth, AI recognition of what you were cooking to update the grocery list.

She stopped, staring at the pile.

He stepped towards her.

"Because whoever they are, whatever they want, whatever it is," he paused. "We know for a fact our electronics are being used against us, right."

She nodded. She did not look at him.

"Well howdy fucking doody then," he said, much louder than he should have, "I'm with you. This family, we're all going cave man."

She bent down with the matches and started the fire.

After several tries, still she could not get a fire going.

"Logs are too big." He pointed. "The gear is fire resistant. Put some fuel on that."

She left for the shed.

"Why are you guys fighting?"

He turned back to the house to see little Debian and Timothy standing side-by-side in the suddenly cold night air.

"We're just talking about stuff."

"You both were yelling," Deb said, "All of our stuff is in a pile."

Mary returned with the gas can that held the kerosene.

"It's nothing to worry about," he said. "Sometimes grownups get upset for weird reasons, that's all."

Behind him he could hear Mary beginning to dump the kerosene all over their electronics.

"But mom's burning my computer!" Tim yelled. "My only computer. My brand new computer!"

"It'll be okay, Timbo," he said. He winked. Tim was immune to his tricks, though. The kid was growing up.

He stepped towards the boy, then checked behind him to see if Mary was backing him up.

She caught the hint, and as the fire took off she turned to both of them. Her turn was mechanical.

"You." She started then her speech stopped. She started again, "You will not be unhappy for long."

Ice. Oh boy.

Tim cried harder.

He knelt down to the children, began to hug them.

"It'll be okay, kids. I promise you it'll be okay."

Tim cried harder. Deb felt like rigor mortis. Like a board.

He tried to hug them a bit harder, but he ended up looking at the spectacle that was their mother, burning all of their worldly possessions in their backyard.

"I know," he said, "How about a family campfire? Been a while, right?"

"No."

"Just like in the good old days." His voice trailed off.

"The children need to go to bed." Mary said. There was nothing in her voice except a dark emptiness. A null set.

"Can Mom read us a bedtime story?" Deb said.

Paul smiled at Mary but dared not look back at Deb.

"That's a great idea."

Mary had gone back to tending the fire. She ignored them.

"Can't I do it? I love telling bedtime stories."

"Mom does it better."

"How about if we both come? Is that okay?"

Mary frowned for a minute, considering.

Something beeped at her feet. She kicked it in the fire.

"No."

Tim had stopped crying. They all huddled by the backdoor looking at Mary, their mother. The fire.

Finally she spoke.

"Your father and I need to have a conversation," she said to the fire.

Behind him, Tim began crying again. He could feel his daughter tightening back up.

The night was empty.

"Okay then," he slapped his thighs and stood up. "Your mom? She'll probably be along in a moment. Meanwhile? Do you know what I have? Wow! You're not going to believe this!"

The kids looked up to him.

"I've just found out about this incredible story, on the way home tonight, and you won't believe what it's about. It's about vampires, that's what. And they're on Mars!"

Deb lit up. Tim looked at him askance, but allowed himself to be herded upstairs to their room.

"We can talk when I return," he said as they left.

If she heard him, she did not acknowledge.

Arriving at their bedroom, They could see the raging blazes reflected on the wall. He tucked the little ones in, wondering how the sitter or Salomé could sleep through this.

Very formally, tucked in her bed beside her brother, Deb said, "I want to hear about the vampires."

Tim looked away from them steeling himself, but Paul saw his face as it changed from happy to sad to curious as the story unwound.

He loved this time with them, weaving fantasy out of whole cloth, their minds joining together on fantastic adventures. It was the one thing he could do the best, weave fantasies, and it was the one thing that seemed to calm them the most. All of them.

Over the next half hour the fire outside died down and Deb and Tim drifted off to sleep. He made sure their breathing was deep and regular before leaving, and he kissed them each on the head very carefully.

He tiptoed down the steps and out into the backyard.

There was nobody there.

• • •

No fire. No Mary.

He reached for his phone.

No phone. He looked again at the embers.

He called her name, not too loudly because he couldn't wake the kids again.

He wandered around the back yard, looking at spaces far too small for her to be in, calling her name. The fire was dying down, going cold.

He hurried to the kitchen. Was her coat still there?

The monkey screamed at him.

It was there.

He went outside. Surely the cars were there.

The cars were there, thank god.

How about her pocketbook?

He came back in. The monkey screamed again.

Her pocketbook was gone.

He went back to check the cars again. Maybe she was *in* one of the cars.

The monkey screamed. The cars were empty.

He came back to the kitchen.

The monkey screamed.

He stood, looking around as if he were a medium calling the spirits of a long-lost loved one. He stood for a while perfectly still, watching the monkey.

He saw the notepad on the table. She had been writing something.

He sat down.

• • •

Hours later, he sat alone in his kitchen. He sat in the dark.

He gripped the note tight in his fist. He remembered the note. It was very short.

...

"I'm dead. Don't come looking for me."

4.26

Carrying On

They did come looking for her, of course. Right after he saw the note, Paul called Beau Martin.

There were two main efforts, each one spanning about two weeks. They interviewed him several times. They interviewed the kids. They luminoled the house.

Never did find anything. Took years for them to finally admit it was a cold case.

Beau got to be a bit of a friend. He'd come over in the evenings, play games with Paul and the kids. Sometimes they'd go visit him. He and Beau had nobody. They made the friendship work.

They put out a nationwide search. Nothing was ever found.

The pain never died. Paul could feel it each day, lurking in the back of his mind, coming out now and then in waves like a tide of sorrow held off by household chores, by mediocrity. But it never went away.

Instead, he found things to do. He had managed to keep his job, so he taught. The kids had continued to drive him nuts, so he continued to love them. There were fights with Sal, there were many, many events with Debian, and there were promised adventures with Timothy that never happened.

Through it all, he could feel the pain. He missed his wife. He believed deeply in his heart that if she still lived, she missed them too.

He did not know, not for sure. He didn't know anything.

But it faded. Slowly, it faded.

He kept all electronics with telemetry out of the house. He forbade the kids from having any.

At first it was because he was convinced that one day, perhaps today,

Mary would come back. It was just as she left it. He kept her clothes. He kept her things.

He kept the faith.

He kept his integrity.

It was many, many years later when he finally lost both. His faith and integrity didn't disappear. They stopped being there. He stopped noticing, and one day they were gone.

Just like Mary.

In the same dank, dark kitchen, sitting at the same table in the same seat, he looked up at the beautiful brilliant young woman Debian had become, many years later, one of his two precious children remaining, holding a knife at him, nothingness in her eyes.

He remembered.

And he cried.

4.27

For Immediate Release

New Research Center Site Approved

Town council in closed session last night approved the construction of a new research center in the former 500-acre Holder Manufacturing lot left vacant in the fire last year. The new site is expected to bring several hundred new jobs to the area. Major funding for the construction will be provided by the McKenzie Foundation.

No further details were available at press time.

# # #

V. ALGORITHM'S END

"Is humanity's just God's mistake? Or God just a mistake of humanity?."

Nietzsche

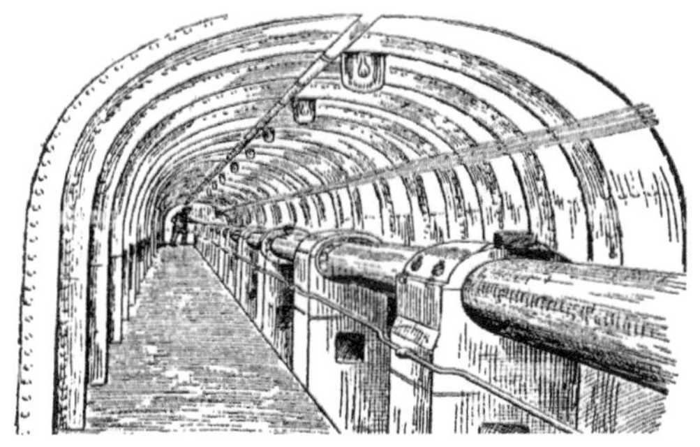

5.01

Homecoming Turnaround

Paul knew they were going to kill him. He just had no idea how long they'd toy with him first.

When he saw MELLO for the first time he feared it would be a long and painful death.

After driving up a serpentine, beautiful, paved drive, through manicured fields, well-hidden sensors, and automated defense systems, he read the small sign out front:

MELLO

In much smaller letters underneath:

Multi-modal **E**mergent **L**arge **L**anguage **O**bservatory

There was another sign, much bigger, cheap metal, with bright red letters on a white background. There were copies of it at several spots along the security fence.

"Use of deadly force is authorized beyond this point"

There was a huge observatory-like dome in the middle of the modern building.

A dome.

It was an observatory, so it had to have a dome.

Very funny. I'll be killed by somebody with a sense of humor. The day's looking up.

He'd bought a burner phone the day after he left. He didn't know why. He thought he was just too used to always having comms in the field.

He activated it. Within two minutes he got a text message telling him what to do. The messages were always anonymous.

He threw the phone out the window.

He tried four more burners after that, always with the same result.

Guess he wasn't going to have a radio.

He'd left home because it was the best choice to keep Deb and Tim alive, hopefully safe. Maybe all of this chasing after him was drawing the heat off.

It was worth a shot.

He gave up on phones. People started approaching in random places, like when he got gas, went to the bathroom, stopped to eat.

They always had messages.

None of the people knew anything, of course.

"Go to MELLO."

He ignored them.

The local police, wherever he was, started checking him out when he slept at night. Somebody had called in a suspicious car.

Anonymous.

He started parking further away from the road.

He really didn't know what made him finally change his mind. Each night he slept in his car wherever he ended up. He didn't have a plan. He made his way by using a random number generator in the morning to pick his direction.

Before going to sleep, and first thing when he woke up, he got out the picture.

He had agreed to one family picture a year. One family picture should be enough for anybody, he'd said. They complained in various ways, of course, but it had been settled. When each picture came out, he'd laminate it and carry it with him until next year's picture. Old ones went in the scrapbook.

Like a religious ritual, daily he'd study it. Sometimes he'd caress the picture as if the people were real.

In the last one, he had stood behind the kids. The two kids. Salomé was not there. He only had two kids.

Salomé was not there.

He didn't cry. As bad as losing Mary had been, the last few months was... it was...

His feelings had blown through grief and sorrow and he now floated, alone and powerless, somewhere in some universe where feelings didn't exist.

It finally occurred to him that he didn't want to live in that universe anymore. He'd come back and do whatever needed doing. One way or another, that post-sorrow, deep abysmal pain had to go. He would excise it.

He approached the building. It was the MELLO facility. Mellow, like they're all really chill here.

Very funny.

A stoner manned the small structure that served as a guard shack, or at least there was a guy who tried to look like a stoner. He had long hair, an unkempt beard, was generally slovenly, and wore a white t-shirt with a large marijuana leaf.

He was an operator. Paul could tell by the way he carried himself. The guy was no more a stoner than he was.

The guard knew that Paul also had been in the shit, although no words were exchanged. You just knew.

Noting the sophisticated security setup, he couldn't help but glance around. There would be backup somewhere. Maybe snipers. There might be multiple players with all sorts of toys. Anybody trying to rob this place would find things getting very interesting, very quickly.

He gave his name to stoner dude.

Five minutes later he was surprised to see the person who came to meet him. He couldn't believe it. It was Hilda Gibb, a student intern from back in the day.

He smiled. If she recognized him, she didn't show it. Instead she mechanically walked him through the sign-in. No hello, no welcome, no handcuffs, no nothing.

He let it drop.

They walked into a large, open industrial warehouse/factory type open floor. It looked like just any modern manufacturing plant: lots of activity. Very few people.

She took him to a small manager's office with a large window, metal table and metal chairs.

There was a black leather folio on the table.

"I saw a lot of bots back there."

"We're 95% automated."

Ninety-five percent. It had been what, twelve years? He had started the project even earlier. He started with him and three kids. He was looking at one of them.

She saw him reminiscing.

"We eat our own cooking here. The tech we use for the observatory is the same tech that runs the automation."

She smiled, but very little. It was a hairline crack in a large granite slab.

"Not that it matters, of course. The observatory covers all tech, all science for that matter. Everything. It was deemed a waste of resources to try to isolate it."

My god, he thought, he'd passed fifty robots of all types on the way in, and a handful of humans. How much money had they dropped in this? It would take months just to get caught up on the technical progress, much less the overall program.

Gibb had done well. She was a cold fish, and always had been, but she'd done well.

Somebody had to run this. He was surprised at himself for having an emotion, pride. He was glad it was one of his students. He was also glad he was far, far away from this place. He wanted nothing to do with any of it.

They did not sit. She stood facing him. She held up her right hand.

"Please hold up your right hand."

He did so.

"Repeat after me: I Paul Newbury, do solemnly swear (or affirm) that I will support and defend the Constitution of the United States against all enemies, foreign and domestic; that I will bear true faith and allegiance to the same; that I take this obligation freely, without any mental reservation or purpose of evasion; and that I will well and faithfully discharge the duties of the office on which I am about to enter. So help me God."

Holding back surprise, he did so.

She shook his hand.

"Congratulations, Colonel."

It was perfunctory. It was done.

Pointing to the folio, she said, "Your orders and commission papers. I will now brief you."

They sat.

"Hilda? It's you, right? Don't you remember me? Paul? Professor Newbury?"

"I remember you," she said. Her voice was flat. She sounded like she was reciting something from memory, not meeting an old colleague she'd worked with for over a year.

She'd had always been cold, standoffish even. When they had parties she wouldn't come and when they had events where she was required to attend she never mixed. Seemed worse now. Command had worn on her.

A klaxon sounded. Overhead lights dimmed. Red lights flashed.

He looked out into the facility. Two men ran by in combat gear, full battle rattle, each carrying a MP-5.

He raised an eyebrow.

"Perimeter drills," she explained, "Twice daily. Random times."

"To keep people from getting in or to keep people from getting out?"

"Both, and you'll want to remember."

"Remember that they're just drills?"

"Remember that they use live ammo."

"Do I get a badge, some way of indicating that I'm safe? How do they tell who's who?"

"One is being made for you right now. It's good that you're in this room with me. We'll need to set you up some network accounts. Of course, you won't be needing any of these."

She tapped her belt. She had a McGuffin in a holster.

Paul tried to remember his walk to the room. Everybody he met was wearing McGuffins.

He tapped his chest.

"You aren't all using Inserts by now?"

"It was deemed both too expensive and too permanent," she recited, as if remembering a memo, "Budgets."

"How many inserted people do you have here?"

"You're the only one."

He almost asked how they managed to get into the historical data, the evolving communication system, the keys to the meta-model. The switch.

He didn't. He caught himself. He took a deep breath. That was it. That was the solution to the mystery. He pushed himself back in his chair, startled but trying his best not to let it show.

They didn't do those things. They couldn't do those things.

That's why he was here. That's why he was still alive.

He was alive because of his insert, his embedded McGuffin. They couldn't duplicate it, and they couldn't get it out of him without killing him and destroying the McGuffin.

It was working as designed.

They needed him. The heart of the system must have been running wholly on autopilot. They couldn't get in.

What was she thinking? Time to start pushing back, find out.

He cleared his throat. He pointed to his collar. He made a gesture as if to show her that she had food on her collar.

She looked. She didn't see anything.

He pointed again. He explained.

"Your rank insignia. It's wrong, twisted. Used to happen to me all the time."

Her lips tightened. She fixed it.

In the distance he heard gunfire. He heard the unmistakable sound of a concussion grenade.

If she heard it, he couldn't tell. Her face was a moonlit lake.

Maybe they used targets? Perhaps they had some kind of indoor range?

"We're in agreement. I don't want to be here," he blurted out without thinking, acting on instinct, then followed up with "I don't want to be in your hair. How about you find somewhere quiet to park me? I'm happy to help out, from a distance."

Gibb put her fist in her hand. She squeezed it. She stared at him hard. He saw no spark of life in her eyes.

"I don't want you here. I don't think you're up to the work. I don't think you're anything but trouble. I'd throw you out on the street if I could."

"But?"

"We have orders, Mr. Newbury. We all have orders."

"This is quite the…." took him a second, "unhappy welcome for my unexpected re-commissioning."

"You have quarters already assigned. We have uniforms prepared. The officer will escort you when you're ready."

She pointed at the door. Presumably somebody was waiting.

"Great," He just wanted to go hide. It was like meeting death.

He had an odd thought that she almost looked like she was in agreement.

Gibb showed frustration. She stood. She had made some sort of decision. Now she was making her play, whatever it was.

She pointed to the door. She walked over. She opened it.

"There's the door. Tell you what: I'll make a deal with you. Walk. Just walk out and I'll forget this ever happened. I'll report you never showed up."

Now he stood also. Could it work? Was it a trick?

He studied her. She looked like she was expecting him to say yes. It might not be a trick, but it wasn't spontaneous, either. This was her attack vector, playing it hard and then offering him an out, figuring he'd take it.

He took a tentative step forward.

"Tempting, isn't it. It's all yours. It's forgotten. Today can be forgotten." She smiled again.

"Just take it."

He took another step.

It was a door, but it wasn't a door. He knew that, whether she did or not. His only choice was between stepping through that door and having a quick death or playing along for a long one.

He had been getting the messages. She hadn't, at least in any way she fully understood.

He chose.

He stood at attention.

"Colonel Gibb, I think it's time you briefed me on my mission."

She gathered herself, obviously not expecting that.

Was she sad or angry?

Both?

"Tomorrow you'll get the tour. In short, you're to be my number two, my executive officer."

"Your XO? What happened to the last one?"

"There was an incident at Disneyland. We can talk about it after you've had your tour."

Disneyland?

"Fine. But I'll need some freedom to maneuver. If you want me to manage, let me manage, let me have enough leeway to make a difference. We need to be clear on that."

"Negative. You won't have it. You'll be XO, I have no choice in that, but you're going to be on a very short leash. That is something I can control."

"Understood."

Worth a shot.

"Did you bring any personal effects?"

"Just this," he got out the picture.

He looked at his family picture again, touched it, the one without Sal.

Her voice had a flicker of humanity.

"Family."

"Yeah."

He placed the picture on the table as if it were a bug he'd just caught.

"You can't contact them."

She's right in ways she doesn't understand.

"You're right. I can't."

He took it back and put it away.

She was still ice.

"I have a favor to ask."

She was going to say no again, but he cut her off.

"Just a favor. You can say yes or no."

Waiting.

"I am grieving. I would like to grieve."

"Get to your favor. What do you want?"

"I don't want to be surveilled electronically. I would like some privacy. At least not constantly."

He corrected his posture. He was in the military again.

"I would like some dignity."

She took her glasses off. She inspected them for particles of dust which she did not find and in all likelihood did not exist. After some thinking, she put them back on.

"I'll make sure your quarters are clear and you're not specifically tagged for anything."

"Your word."

"My word. But everything else, everywhere else, you'll just be like everybody else."

She gestured around the shop.

It was unsaid.

We are all watched, of course, constantly.

She waved the outside officer in.

He looked at his new escort. She was young.

"Show me to my quarters then, miss…"

They started walking.

"Parsons, sir. Right this way."

The corridors were painted matte white with chrome trim. It felt antiseptic. Getting in the elevator, he realized that he'd only seen a small portion of the whole facility. This place extended many floors beneath them.

The doors closed.

"Any good restaurants in town?" he was trying to find some sense of normality. He was trying to make a connection. He was trying to find another human somewhere.

She replied without looking at him.

He thought she looked as if she thought he was trying to trick her. Unsure.

"We don't get to town much, sir."

"Guess I'll have to find out for myself, then."

She shot him a glance and then returned to straight ahead.

"I'm not sure the Colonel has gate privileges ... sir."

He found himself in the odd position of being in charge of his own prison.

As the elevator reached the floor and the door opened, she finally looked at him, really looked at him.

She struggled with some overwhelming emotion, fought to keep it down.

"Please ignore the screaming."

She looked back to the doors, now open.

"It never stops."

The corridor stretched out.

5.02

Worrying Debian

"We're not going to kill these park rangers. Smoky Bear would be mad," Sam whispered.

"Smoky Bear isn't real," Deb said.

"And these two aren't ninjas. They're just out inspecting the trail. doing their job. Stop being so paranoid."

Deb and Sam were huddled behind a rock over two-hundred feet from the man and woman park rangers in the creek bed below. Sam had found Deb behind the rock after waiting a half hour for her to return to camp and finally going to look for her.

He was thankful he approached in the right way. She didn't look good.

"They have radios," Deb said, as if that explained everything.

"My grandmother has radios, yet she didn't parachute into Normandy with the 101st on D-Day."

"They're encrypted. This is our chance to gather more information."

He gently pushed her against the rock.

"No more, Deb. We're not capturing more people and doing that thing again."

He didn't want to say the words. Somehow not saying them made it easier to live with.

"Then we'll die."

"Okay. That sounds good. Let's die. Can we at least die slowly? Does everything with you have to be a full frontal assault?"

"Perhaps you could go down there and perform some card tricks, create fake paper flowers, or tell jokes. Take your tip jar."

"Beats busting them in the head or whatever else you've got planned.

They're just park rangers, for goodness sakes. You know, friendly, happy, helpful people?"

"There are two of them. That's suspicious."

"Oh yes. Yes. Of course. Three would be even worse. And four? Total woodland warfare. Horrible. Quick, let's build a small cannon out of things we find lying around."

"Two indicates that the mission is serious. Haven't you ever wondered why there are two pilots on all commercial planes?"

"I guess I always thought there were a lot of controls."

"No. One pilot can fly the plane. In fact, many planes don't even need a pilot at all. It's for judgment, resilience, cross-checking."

"So, you think these two are pilots? They seem to be missing an important piece of gear: a plane."

"No, asshole. I think they're doing something important."

"How about one of them is training the other. That's important."

"Might be true," she glanced back at him, but only for a second before returning to watching the pair, "but I doubt it."

"Jeez, Louise."

They heard a radio squawk sound from the couple down below.

Deb jumped.

"It's okay. It's just a radio. Look, they're smiling. They're joking. They're not interested in anybody."

"How can you know that, they're 123.7 feet away through dense woods."

"I looked, that's how. Did it ever occur to to you that you might be wrong?"

"No, but I have a hope that one day you will be right. It's my dream. For your self-esteem."

"I'm not sure how you'd ever know."

The two rangers started walking off.

She pointed.

"Is that what you want?"

"Compared to what?"

They were at the top of a wide creek bed about eighty-feet across, in dense weeds and brush, hiding behind some large rocks.

Dried leaves and sticks littered the wooded ground, leftovers from the previous Autumn.

"Debian, we wouldn't make it twenty feet without sounding like an angry gang of escaped circus gorillas."

"If we could just make it to the creek bank."

The rangers kept getting farther out. They were now becoming difficult to make out at all through the trees.

"Impossible."

She stepped forward. The sound she made was obvious. There was no getting around the condition of the ground. She reversed course back to where Sam was still hidden.

"We could run at them. One of us could provide a diversion."

"You know, it's possible just to talk to people. Talking's good. News flash, talking actually works in most cases."

"And all they would do would be talk back."

He had no reply.

He could see her gripping the rock. Her knuckles were white from the stress.

"Let's play this out. What did you think would happen if you got what you wanted? Say we catch them."

"I would know what to do next. We would both know."

"Ok, assuming that's true, what do you think would happen to the people these rangers were talking to on the radio?"

She hesitated.

"There could be several courses of action based on…"

"Don't give me that hand-waving probability tree nonsense. Correlate the top dozen or so and generalize."

She frowned, clearly unhappy with this turn of events.

"They would come looking for them."

"And?"

"Fine. They would come looking before we could move to next steps."

"See?"

"Maybe. But there's still a large unknown as to what information they have."

"Fine. Assuming all of that, do you think you should be making these decisions for me? Do you really feel like you should be doing all of this thinking and deciding on your own?"

Her resolve wilted.

"No. You are right."

"I'm right. It's a miracle."

"Fuck you."

"Excuse me?"

"I have Tourette's Syndrome."

"No you don't."

"I might. Could be sudden onset."

"SOTS? There's no such thing as Sudden Onset Tourette's Syndrome."

"You don't know."

He was getting more worried. Dark lines were under her eyes. Her skin was pale. She looked like a boxer that had just went a dozen rounds. He believed they called it 'punch drunk'.

"How much sleep did you get last night?"

"Two hours, seventeen minutes, 14 seconds."

"This isn't good for you, this constant tension. It's no good. Have you been doing your exercises?"

"No."

"Chicken. Do you want me to say it?"

"No."

"You still want to rush these two?"

"Yes."

He wasn't giving up.

She wasn't giving up either.

"What happened last time we launched one of these assaults of yours?"

"We came here. We got the information to come here."

"And how do you think the gang is doing?"

"What do you…."

"You know what I mean. How's Jupiter, Steve. How's Jim?"

"Not well. They were injured by us, both physically and emotionally."

"And you think continuing this blind aggression is worth it no matter what the costs to others?"

"No. I do not."

"I miss the guys. Don't you?"

"They lived in a junkyard."

"Sure thing. In a secret headquarters. They wore costumes."

"I miss them too."

She looked back, clearly frantic the two rangers were leaving.

"I'll make the decision if you can't."

She began going after them.

There was no choice. He had to physically grab and restrain her. He had to stop her.

She looked at him, betrayed.

"Let me go."

"No. Not until we settle this. Can you just wait a hot minute. Can I ask that?"

"Let go."

He did so.

She turned to leave again.

"Please?"

She stopped and turned.

"Well?"

"You can do what you want. I'm not trying to stop you. As your friend, I only want to make sure you understand the risks you're taking, that's all."

"Sam, you have a point. I am taking risks for others and I shouldn't."

He breathed a sigh of relief.

Sensing danger, relief turned to caution.

"When you tell me I have a point is when I really start getting worried," he tried to lighten things, "I'm right and I have a point. All of this in one day."

"I think we should split up. I'm no good for you."

"What? After all of ...."

"It's me. I get a plan or decision stuck in my brain and I have to execute it."

She paused, cleared her throat.

"I'm not good at telling people why."

"Seriously? You're doing the 'it's not you it's me' thing? And at the same time you're admitting that what you're doing is not important?"

"No I'm not."

"That's what I'm hearing."

"On the contrary, what I am doing is extremely important."

"So," he cleared his throat and looked around the woods as if expecting to be in a crowd, "where's your copilot? I don't see a copilot anywhere. Important missions need a cross-check. Your argument, not mine."

"I hate you."

"We'll work on it."

He rubbed his hands together. Glorious victory was his.

"This'll be fun. Let's go pack up the camp, junior copilot."

She walked with him, but Sam thought she looked like she'd rather eat nails.

He also thought she looked relieved. He would never mention it and she would never admit it.

It was understood.

"Here's the deal, fly girl, I'll let you create a checklist for us. You pilots like checklists, right? Well, you create the list of things you want to do. But on each step, before we take it, I get approval or modification rights for the next step. Agree?"

"But I get to pick?"

"With my ongoing agreement and modification."

He pointed at her for emphasis.

"I get to modify, approve and have an equal say. Partners."

"You are truly annoying, Samuel Featherstone."

"I've practiced."

5.03

Core Of Conflict

"Feels lonely. Where are all the people?"

"Don't need people below level seven."

Gibb and Paul began their tour on the lowest level, the core.

"In fact, we don't allow people below level seven."

"Nobody to deliver equipment? Nobody to do quality checks? Fetch broken bots?"

She shook her head no.

"People are extraneous here, at best a nuisance. It's no different than any other modern warehouse. In those, humans wear headsets. The computer tells the people where to go, what to get. We've just eliminated the people."

He was standing on a floor the size of a superstore. The ceiling was fifteen-feet above him. Black server racks twelve-feet high stretched out as far as he could see. Lights were flashing on all of them, Christmas at the server farm, no tree needed.

No people needed.

"It doesn't seem right."

"And yet it is. All possible inefficiencies have been removed. I fully expect that the bots will adapt and evolve to run faster, have more arms, increase throughput."

"Expect? You don't know?"

She waved it off.

"Why would I know how the core and the bots plan on evolving? Oh, I suspect I could find out, but why bother? It knows how to self-optimize. That's all we need from it."

"My telescope. My internet telescope. You finally built it."

"We did. All grown up and performing like wildfire. And this is just the appetizer. Instead of bits and bytes and switches, come with me, let me show you the real action."

They went back up. On the way, he noticed that Gibb's uniform looked precisely squared-away. He could picture her this morning checking herself out in the mirror, making sure there were no errors.

His uniform, as always, was immaculate. He didn't miss his time in military service, but he did miss the magic of the uniform. It was the angles, the creases, the accoutrements welded into exactly the right place. It was just right.

He was correct.

He put the uniform on and he said something, both to himself and others, without having to make a sound.

They walked to the spot in the middle of the building where he had seen the dome. Perhaps the dome was actually being used for something.

"You backing me up?" She didn't look at him.

They were outside a steel door. A sign said, "Observatory."

There were many red warning signs.

"I have no quarrel with you, Gibb. You give the orders. I'll stick to them."

She started to open the door but hesitated.

"Are you going to help now so you can rebel, destroy things, betray me later?"

He pushed past her into the room, eager to see.

As he passed, he quietly said, "I'm helping so I can die on my own terms."

It was a large, circular room. It was true. They actually were using the dome for something.

"Giving up complete control of your life is one of the sad side effects of military services."

She joined him at his side.

"I didn't ask to go back in, to come here."

"You weren't invited, yet here we are."

Around the edge of the dome was a walkway, a mission control. It was a hallway about five meters wide. There were chairs and consoles in the circle. Nobody was sitting in them.

His mouth hung open in amazement.

"I'll follow orders, stay on a short leash like you said."

He would have agreed to anything just then.

The hallway was encircling a huge glass sphere. The sphere must have been twenty meters across.

It was the biggest true holographic display he'd ever seen. It may have been the biggest ever built.

"I don't want to spend a lot of time with you, Newbury."

He stepped forward to get a better look at what was inside the sphere.

"I just want to be left alone. You can leave me here."

"Can't do that."

"Why."

"Orders."

The blobs floated in the large observatory, each several meters wide. Blob was the only word he had for what he saw. "Balls of colored smoke with sporadic lightning" might be closer. Giant squishy squeeze toys, the type people use for stress relief.

There were three of them, red, green, and purple.

Although they drifted slowly, they more or less floated, spheres of smoke with tentacles bobbing in some five-dimensional ocean.

The ocean.

Paul could see tiny, almost imperceptible specks of white, each about the size of a pinhead all throughout the twenty-meter globe. Baby rain. It reminded him of the kind of day where it was raining, yet it was not. Instead, you could see tiny droplets of water floating all about, rain that never fell. Aviators called it BR, from the French word "brûme" meaning mist.

Baby Rain.

He remembered how interstellar gas worked. The gas between stars, like in the Crab Nebula, was invisible up close. It was so small, yet stand far enough away and you get beautiful nebula. Dots close up. Clouds far away. Smoke with a purpose. This entire sphere could be its own little speck of light if you stood far enough away. Wait. "Far away" wasn't right. Like a cube drawn on a piece of paper, what he was looking at was an almost infinite dimension plot projected into three dimensions. He was the ant looking at the cube drawn on paper and trying to imagine what a real cube would look like. Or a tesseract.

He couldn't. He could see but he really couldn't comprehend. His brain didn't work like that. Nobody's did.

The first telescopes were like that.

Here, however, at this scale, you could choose either to pay attention to the small specks or see through them to the blobs.

"That's the Three Stooges," Gibb said.

He turned back to her.

She shrugged.

"We didn't know what else to call them."

He looked at the nearest workstation. On it was an old, weather-worn paperback of *The Great and Secret Show*. It occurred to Paul that the idea of a universal sea of ideas and feelings you could explore had gone from fanciful fantasy to science in the space of his lifetime.

He went immediately back to the observatory. He felt like a man on the beach watching a four-thousand foot tidal wave approach. His destruction. Everything he knew would be wiped clean. It was beautiful.

The specks were a cloud, a noise fog, completely filling the chamber, each perhaps their own sphere or collection of spheres. Who knew how far down the scale went?

Wait. No, that wouldn't work either, he thought, there was no scale. That was just another bullshit three-dimensional term.

The view was a recursive fractal. It went forever. The giant sphere he was looking at could be found an infinite number of times in the mist it displayed. That's because it's both concepts and ideas.

Every now and then in the mist a few specks would light up as little tiny lightning bolts the size of a sewing thread went between them. Sometimes dozens would join together in a larger bolt of tiny lightning. A long thread of perfect white, then gone. Burnt into the retina. Fading out.

These brief connections were the normal things people thought of when they thought of the universe: a new idea gets popular and a huge engineering feat is accomplished. A supernova creates four stellar systems, in the process the pressure wave slightly alters the movement of other stars in that galaxy. Alien civilizations come to life, fight one another, and are gone. It's all a barely visible, itty-bitty flash of lightning in the sphere.

But it existed on the internet.

One dot might be Socrates. One could be Jesus.

Wait. Unlikely. The mind kept heading down wrong pathways even when it knew there were wrong. At the heart of things, this was not a map of things and people, this was a map of ideas and sensations. Maybe everything he knew fit inside of just one of these dots, his own tiny universe. His own glass sphere, an atom across.

Words failed. He still struggled to find them.

Decades ago, quantum physicists proved that everything was connected to everything. Quantum Entanglement was the term of art. The experiments were clear: we saw things as being beside one another. I am local to this chair. You are local to your room. But there is no locality. I throw a ball in the air and I slightly affect the rotation of supermassive black hole in the center of my galaxy. A butterfly flaps its wings and on the other side of the world a tornado forms.

Maybe some things were improbable. Unlikely that I would think of a giraffe and a giraffe would suddenly appear. Maybe we just thought so. But we know for a fact that they're all linked. The idea of something being local to something else was long dead. Was it possible to see it all at the same time? Perhaps.

People and instruments observe things and talk about them online. Both the minds and the measurements are all mixed together. His observatory was the first effort to link everything that we can possibly perceive and ask the computer: what things might be linked to what other things that we would be interested in exploring more?

It was the mind of God. Paul was looking at the mind of God. Of course words failed.

He could see, but it was impossible to get oriented to see where he fit in. What's inside of what? What causes what? Everything was in there, all the secrets.

You couldn't just push a button and get an answer, though. It was more complicated than that.

"Markov Blankets," he said simply.

"Perhaps."

Grouping things into blobs and dots at various scales was the job of something called a "Markov Blanket." Their purpose was to use math to find a boundary between something alive and the rest of the world. Your body is a Markov Blanket formed by your skin. Inside your body are organs, also protected by Markov Blankets. Inside of those, cells. More nested Markov Blankets.

A Markov Blanket was determined by math, by statistics, but the overall idea of this display was defining life itself without humans being involved. Inside this thing is me. Outside is the rest of the world. If you violate the Markov Blanket enough, I stop living. Markov Blankets were the boundaries between life and other things. All life had Markov Blankets.

Paul was asking, where are the living things?

That's why he'd given little Deb a blanket with the term on it. She was a special, unique little person, at least to them. She was their own little Markov Blanket they had made.

"What's the average nesting depth inside these things? Have you done a polymer chain analysis?"

He could tell that Gibb had no idea of what he was talking about. And she was the student who did the original work of applying polymer and protein theory to nested Markov Blankets.

What?

She looked worried, confused. It was like she was waiting for somebody to give her the answer and the answer wasn't coming.

He went back to the cloud. She began talking, as if waiting for him to look away.

"I expect us to have morning meeting every day at 0700 hours," she said, "during these meetings I will decide your activities for the day."

"Is there a command staff or other executive meeting I should attend?"

"Let me be clear: your orders are to NOT schedule or attend any other meeting without my approval. Clear?"

He watched the Three Stooges float.

"Clear. When I'm not meeting with you or following orders, do I have free run of the facilities?"

"You do not."

"Could you please reconsider that?"

He had to get back to this room. There was a lifetime of work in this room. A hundred lifetimes.

"No."

Lightning, a large bolt, flashed from one of the three big blobs to another. It quickly faded.

"What's that?"

"We don't know. It took us years just to ever see these major transient flashes. They're nanosecond scale or below. We had to code a slow-motion system to make them observable."

"If I could just touch the controls," he stepped forward slightly.

"No. Not unless you can give us some labels. Labels would help us make more sense of it all."

"Labels won't work here, Gibb. Remember all that work we did going through the papers of Charles Sanders Peirce? Labels require an observer.

We have so many observers combined that we have none. That's why it works. All we have is quadrillions of points of sensor data and thoughts."

"The sensors have names. The measurements are numbers. The people have names. Their thoughts," she stopped, realizing that unless vocalized or typed somewhere, thoughts did not have names. Intelligence did not require language.

"And anything we can see at this scale, whatever scale it is, consists of untold numbers of these things linked in ways we don't consistently understand."

"So," Gibb was trying to recover, "If we could add labels we could begin understanding. That's why we need them."

"You're missing the point. Take any one of those lightning flashes. Or take any one of those tiny specks. Each of those might consist of a million other points all in a brief web, like a big tumbleweed. We got no names for stuff that complicated. And it's always changing. Even if we had a name for one, and we don't, by the time we applied the name it would be a different thing entirely."

He shifted a bit, trying to approach it differently, wondering why he needed to explain this to his formerly brilliant student.

"What we think of as reality is just consistent patterns of transformations between the dots, not the dots themselves. Category Theory. You know that."

He pointed to the Three Stooges, the huge blobs of tricolor.

"Now those are interesting. I'm assuming they've been around for a while. Whatever your nesting system is, looks like it's found some things that while super complicated, can stay grouped together as one big blob. Wonder why. Another universe? A large civilization? A type of feeling every sentient being possesses? Gravity?"

"Does that mean you'll help, not just follow orders, actually help?"

He looked around at all the work, the controls, the data. It was his lifelong dream, now realized before him.

"I'll help."

"For starters, could you at least get the zoom working?"

"If that's the old console, it should be this slider here."

He moved a slider up and down. Nothing happened.

"Must have lost the software linkage. Here you go. Easy fix."

He started typing at a terminal below the console. Red text started scrolling up the screen.

Security breech.

He thumped his chest with his fist twice, as if clearing something from his throat.

A beep. More text streamed up. This time it was normal.

He stood up. He turned to Gibb. He smiled.

"Must be nice," she said, indicating his insert.

"You forget it's there."

"I don't."

"Any luck working around these?" He pointed to his chest and the Insert placed in there, hoping the answer was no.

"None that were both successful and sustainable. Viable."

He thought of Stetson Parks. That horrible shooting. He'd almost killed Deb. That kid was reckless.

How many more Stetsons were there?

"Come with me," Gibb said. She led him out into the hallway.

They went to another level. The level reminded him of a hospital. It was clean, sterile.

Walking to a window, she pointed.

"If you want to help, here's where you can start. Half my staff is in the infirmary."

He saw a woman begin writhing in pain on a cot. A medic came and gave her a shot. The woman went to sleep.

"Most make it out and back to duty. Not all, though. We've recently acquired some research data on the biological effects of direct exposure to the Stooges. If it can be applied, it could save people, put them back in the game."

"So they can go back to work 'acquiring more research'"

A curt nod.

"I'll take a look at your research, but first I need to know what you mean by 'exposure to the Stooges'. Take me there. Show me how that works."

"I can't."

"Why."

"It'd kill you."

He waited until she decided to offer more.

"After much trial-and-error, we've created something of a two-way interface with the model. We're assuming with the Three Stooges."

"This I have to see."

"Not without a death wish you can't. Five minutes per day. Any more than that is extremely unhealthy, even terminal."

"How can a computer interface kill you?"

"We don't know. There's a lot we don't know. We also don't understand what the interface is telling us, assuming it's trying to communicate. We only know there's some sort of back-and-forth going on. The crypto gear tells us that."

"Well, if it's any kind of communication at all, I'm sure we can work some sort of natural language…"

She interrupted.

"We're not even completely sure about the five minutes."

"I don't care. You want my help, we're going to have to start with exposure. This isn't medical. A drug is not going to do it. My instinct tells me that we're going to need new learned behavior, and that means getting into the mix with whatever they've done."

She looked at him. She was skeptical.

"Gibb, this is something I can do. Let me do something."

"Very well. We're going to need to head back down."

They headed towards the elevator.

"Smile, you're going to Disneyland. Parsons, over here," Gibb said

He saw Parsons coming over.

"On us."

"Do you think I need a guard? Is the tech that secret?"

"We both need her. She's our safety officer."

Parsons looked displeased and worried, like a child asked to take out a big pile of vomit from a shared bathroom. It quickly passed.

The doors shut.

At the bottom they entered another corridor at least the length of a football field. Soft LED lighting strips ran along both sides at the top of the walls.

It was all white. It looked new. The floor was shiny. It was recently polished.

The only exception were the controls and items fulfilling the purpose of the area. Everything of import was outlined with one centimeter navy blue strips.

The blue made a long line of rectangles on both sides. There must have been 20, 30 of them.

They approached the first one.

First he saw the observation window. It was blacked out, the kind of glass that could darken or lighten with a switch. He wondered if these were some sort of interrogation chambers.

"Start the clock," Gibb was mechanical, certain.

Parsons went to a large, chrome button besides the glass. She hit it and faced away from the window. She could see the clock, but not them or what they were looking at.

A five-minute countdown began on an antique LED clock above the button. Parsons watched it closely.

The window became transparent.

Inside was a room without furniture. There was only an easy chair. A 20-ish woman in uniform sat in the chair. She was watching a TV on the wall.

She was wired up to the maximum, he thought. He had never seen or used that amount of biological telemetry. Looked like an old sleep study, or a one of the primitive lie detectors.

She looked like a monkey in a mad scientist's evil experiment.

The TV show was disturbing.

At first glance it looked like an old cartoon from the previous century. A teddy bear type character walked from right-to-left with an old-fashioned painted background, like on the roadrunner cartoons he used to love.

Almost immediately he rejected that impression.

The bear was wielding a sword as if leading some imaginary infantry charge. He was wearing a black armband with a swastika on it. In the background, now that he noticed, the woods were on fire. His clumsy round feet began sparkling in a randomized rainbow of colors.

The cartoon had a caption. It was in a stencil font as if the army had painted it on. He didn't know if it was part of the show or had been added later.

"Bo-Bo Goes To Prison."

He jerked back.

"Is that a…"

"You and I are actually seeing subtly different images, although, once again, we don't know why."

"Okay, but cartoons? This is the bee that got in all of your knickers?"

"We call this Disneyland, in much the same way as the U.S. Military called the Mideast The Sandbox for many decades. A cute name covers up a terrible truth."

He turned. He began walking to another rectangle, another room.

"Are they all like this?"

Surprisingly, she grabbed his arm to stop him.

"Only one per day," she searched her mind, "It's never been successful otherwise."

"Fascinating. And these images cause death?"

The sound of a whooping alarm began. There was a flashing light on a station ten meters down the hall.

A man in just his underwear, wires trailing, ran from his room screaming at the top of his lungs. Paul couldn't make out the words.

He thought again of Stetson.

He ran right towards them, target locked. His face was red. He was sweating profusely. Paul thought if the man had a knife he'd cut them into little bitty pieces.

Before turning it on himself.

He had murder in his eyes.

The running man somehow got the advantage of Parsons, probably because of his complete and utter insanity. The two began wrestling on the ground.

Paul started doing mental calculations. Could this be a setup? A test? Looking at the struggle, she very well might lose her firearm.

Then it would get very interesting.

"Newbury, Aren't you going to help?"

Gibb was running to an alert button down the hall.

"Attack our own people?"

"That's an order."

He bent down and easily grabbed the man in a sleeper hold. He lifted him from the fight by his neck.

Seeing that he was ending it, Parsons pushed off. Her firearm lay on the floor just inches away.

He stared at it. He had a short fantasy about the pistol and it was gone, a leaf in the wind. He went back to choking the man out.

Before he grabbed him, Parsons had banged the man's head on the floor several times trying to stun him. His head was bloody and getting worse.

Gibb stopped heading towards the alarm and slowly walked back, as if this were the plan all along.

"The time!" Parsons yelled, abandoning her pistol and any decorum and scrambling for the metal button, hitting it again.

The window went black.

The clock read three seconds.

"That's why we need a safety officer."

"Freedom to roam the facilities," he said. He demanded.

"Done."

"I want a sidearm."

He pointed to the unconscious man.

Gibb looked to Parsons, but only for a second. Decision made.

"Done."

Paul looked to the now-dark glass, trying to orient.

"Why isn't she coming out? The subject?"

"They get twenty minutes. We're pushing the session times. It's the only way we can get more data."

"Why haven't you slowed down the interface, delayed the responses, changed the medium?"

"We've tried things."

Vague.

"How about sound-proofing the place, at least? Every time one of these happens, it destroys the entire experiment."

Gibb was quiet. He thought she looked like a schoolgirl having given her mom an unfortunate report card.

Stoic.

Parsons started gathering herself and her gear back together. The man snored.

He'd be back up in a minute. As she watched, Parsons zip-tied his hands and feet.

"If it's this bad, why continue with all of this? How can you be making any progress?"

Gibb looked at Parsons. Gibb was clearly uncomfortable speaking in front of her subordinate.

She doesn't want to look bad, he thought.

Let's test that.

"It was determined," Gibb began answering his previous question, "that some sacrifices had to be made."

"Why didn't you know about the polymer and protein-folding based nesting algorithms? You did the initial work on it, Hilda. It was groundbreaking."

She pulled at her collar.

Now he was on to something.

"It was good work. You were a great student. What happened?"

"I am Colonel Gibb to you. You have use of the facility and can arm yourself. If you want me again, set up a meeting. I will see you at 0700. Now I have more important things to do."

He didn't know if that was a snit. He didn't want to keep making her do that.

"Ma'am," Parsons secured the man to the wall. She clicked her radio twice. It was some sort of signal.

Moving back, she winced. Parsons had clearly been injured.

"Let me help you."

"I'm fine."

"I'm helping. That's an order."

He positioned himself under her shoulder and they began limping off together.

"What's your first name?"

"Bea."

"Ok, Parsons. Show me the way to your quarters."

It wasn't just one Stetson Parks. They were making a platoon of Stetsons.

The light continued. The hall continued. The screaming continued. They both continued down the hall and into the heart of things.

5.04

Accepting Opposites

Dawn came slow. Nature did too. Sam and Deb struggled with both their nature and their growing awareness as they struck camp and made their way up the mountain and into a rocky minefield surrounded by nothing but trouble.

She looked well-rested. He was relieved.

It was either that stupid deer or imaginary bears that caused all of the problems, Sam realized later. They would have been better off taking the time to build a giant catapult.

He should have known trouble was coming when he asked her, only about a hundred meters up the trail, if this wasn't the best morning ever for a hike. The day was beautiful, spectacular. It was great.

She'd smiled and said how much she loved nature and hiking. She said that if he wanted to take the trail instead of walking direct to town that was fine by her.

It only got worse after that.

"I don't mind being attacked by bears. You and I can handle most anything we meet."

He thought of stopping the hike, but he was having too much fun.

"Who said anything about bears? It's a beautiful morning. Bears don't want anything to do with us."

"Just running you through your decision-making process."

"I don't see a bear. I don't worry about a bear. No bear. No worry. Good enough?"

"Absolutely. We're going to have a great time."

"We are."

"Even if we meet a bear, which we won't."

"We are, and we won't," he started working through the options of where this was headed, "Would you like to see a bear, go to a zoo perhaps?"

"Nope. Just checking."

He decided that one day he was going to invent a befuddlement meter. He also knew deep in his heart that Debian would be the one to break it before he could make his millions.

Time to change direction before the symposium on bear statistics began.

"How long did you flight instruct?"

"Three years. Did you ever get a chance to teach?"

"No, I was a lifeguard. That's about it."

"That's a skill."

"Mostly read programming and cryptography books. Got a good tan, though."

"Don't you sell yourself short, Sam. You're constantly saying and doing things I don't understand with these amazing results. You're a teacher."

"Well, if we ever get into a water balloon battle, need to learn the breaststroke, or find ourselves in a chicken fight, I'll be sure to pitch in with thoughtful instruction."

"Don't bullshit me. Your observation about attack versus observe was spot on. We're going to need a listening post or a hideout, maybe an AirBnB room, once we get there. Perhaps a treehouse."

"I'm glad to see you in a good mood," he thought he'd enjoy the Debian sunshine while it lasted. Maybe they truly had turned a corner? They'd certainly been through enough. "I hope you're not taken back by the conversation I'm giving you this morning. You know, the talking and chit-chat and such."

"Start whenever you'd like. I'm the one making things tough on you."

"But. But. You don't mind talking about the beautiful day, the mountain, the trail, anecdotes, all that?"

"Whatever you need to be your best person."

"I'm already my best person."

"I mean just don't get distracted by frivolity."

He frowned.

"I'll do my best."

"I know you will."

It was some sort of head injury. Had to be.

"What do you think of this new checklist system of ours? Do you remember yesterday and the checklist approval talk?"

He thought about asking her how many fingers he was holding up. Too pushy. He'd try subtle.

"You know, I've reconsidered. It's a good idea. I look forward to getting started."

He stopped. He looked at her. He narrowed his eyes.

He'd seen this before. Projectile vomiting could happen at any moment. Her head might begin spinning around in circles.

"You do? My metaphor worked? The flying thing? It actually worked?"

"We've been much too rash, Sam. We obviously need a chained dependency graph decision-making system."

Ah. There she is.

"Not sure I'd go that far but I'm feeling good. You know, golly durn, I feel we're headed in the right way."

Eyes still narrowed, he looked. Golly durn almost got her going, but she held back. The dam held. Something was definitely wrong.

Surprise, surprise, she did smile, just not at him. Her mouth hung open in amazement. Was he that funny? She pointed behind him to the trail they'd been heading up.

There was a little deer.

The fawn was munching on some fresh shoots of greenery in a large rocky field. The fog had just started to lift from the mountain so they couldn't completely see her. It was obvious she was very young.

Enthralled, they tiptoed closer, then closer still. The mother was nowhere in sight. Sam began wondering if the fawn was okay. He wondered if there really was a mother.

He continued on closer and closer, with Deb right behind him, each of them in awe of the little animal.

After they had traveled quite a while, they got within 15 meters or so of the deer. It looked up.

It didn't run. That bothered him. Maybe it was tame. It wasn't right not to fear man.

He raised his arms wide, the way you're supposed to do when encountering bears.

"YA! YA! Run on off now!"

It was gone before he finished the sentence, in a flash, covering hundreds of meters of rock like a scared, giant, starving rabbit. The little white tail bounced up and down zooming still smaller and gone.

As it reached the edge he finally saw the mom.

There was a split second that he thought about waving, as if the deer would somehow wave back. The kid's okay, mom! I looked out for her.

Then they both were gone.

"Why'd you do that?"

"I was worried about her."

"Now how do we get back?"

He looked around the mountainside.

There was no way back.

Somehow in their excitement, bit-by-bit they had tiptoed themselves right into the middle of a huge field of boulders lying on the side of the old mountain. Each ranged in size from pebbles to toasters or even the occasional Volkswagen.

They were hundreds of meters from anything that looked like a trail, or trees, or grass.

"Shit," he said.

"Yes."

She put her hands on her hips.

She looked around, then repeated his observation.

"Shit."

"Well…" he stepped forward as if knowing where he was going. He pointed in the general direction of the trees. "We'll just take a look at the tree line. We'll find the gap the trail made, where we came out."

"There's no gap."

He looked harder. How could they have gotten here from the trail and not be able to see the very selfsame trail they'd arrived on?

"I don't get it."

"Switchbacks. We were going through switchbacks up the mountain. When we saw Bambi here, we just kept walking straight."

"So?"

"So there's nothing to see. The trail wherever it is, would be far enough behind the tree line to be invisible. Maybe if we were ten feet tall we'd see it. Maybe."

"Shit."

"Yeah."

"Haven't you been counting steps? Can't you give us a vector or one of those airplane things? A compass heading to get out?"

"Yeah. I can give us a pretty good angle to find our way."

"Good."

"Our way back down to where we came from."

"Bad."

"Bad. Wrong way. Lose a day on mountain. Bad."

"Shit."

"Yeah. I don't wanna do that."

There was a loud POP! like a firecracker, the echo shot out and slowly died away.

His skin goosebumped.

"Gunshot."

He looked at her.

"Rifle."

"Afraid so."

The deer were long gone.

"It is hunting season."

He frowned.

"Afraid so." He didn't want to think about that anymore. There was another shot. He rubbed his hands together, trying to gather some momentum in any direction besides what was happening to those deer. "Let's take advantage of our situation. Now that we're in a bind, we're going to need to work our checklist."

"What checklist?"

"The checklist," he pointed to all of the rocks as if that explained it, "We're lost, stuck. We need to find our way out. Let's do the checklist, like we agreed."

"There's no checklist. It's just a bunch of rocks. We don't have a checklist."

"What do you think we've been doing all this morning, with all of that fun, chit-chat, and friendly conversation?"

"Nothing at all, that's what. I thought you were just trying to impress me with how cool, calm, and casual you were."

"Banter. It's called banter."

"Ok. So what. Who cares."

"We're establishing a rhythm and social protocol to negotiate future disagreements. Didn't you get the human manual when you arrived?"

"Funny. We're still lost. And stuck."

"Ok. So what."

"We're going to need to create a checklist." She pointed "An optimal path."

"For a bunch of rocks? The checklist is about how we pick a direction, make decisions."

"Decision? Easy. That way," she pointed to the top of the mountain, "We know we're eventually going to the top. There's the top."

There were over 200 meters of dangerous boulders stretched up the hill until the trees began again.

"I'm not sure you understand what a precarious situation we might be in. Going up might be very bad."

He pointed.

"Those rocks could come down on us. That would be an ouchie."

"Ouchie. Are you trying to be cute?"

"Trying."

"Try harder. How much hiking have you done, Sam?"

"I don't know. A couple dozen times maybe."

"We went every weekend when I was a kid."

She appraised the hill for a second time.

"I'm not afraid of ouchies. Those rocks are secure."

She did a doubletake.

"Although that one rock doesn't look right."

"Very interesting. Odd rocks. I'll take a note. Shame there aren't more. We could use them for trail blazes."

"We have engineering skills. You have engineering skills. We need to use them to get back."

"Well, unless you have a way to construct a catapult and brought along a backpack with a parachute, the problem is much simpler than all that."

She didn't look convinced.

"You think we're going to math our way out?" he said, "this is very simple. This is how people get lost. They either don't stay where they are or they end up going around in circles. It's stay or go. If we go, we need to go straight So it's two choices. We just need to pick one. This is about as easy as it gets."

"Sure."

She pointed up, "There."

"I disagree, Deb. I think we go back the way we came."

"You're wrong. Hang on, let me check my checklist," she pointed to an imaginary spot in front of her, "Yep. Wrong. Still wrong. Checklist says so."

"Funny. We shouldn't argue. Why don't you go your way and I'll go my way? As long as we stay in earshot, whoever finds their way out first just calls out to the other?"

"Excellent idea. I agree. Looks like that bantering thing is working out for you."

He eyed her warily.

"Really?"

She started walking up. He turned back and began gingerly feeling his way along.

Getting out was proving a lot harder than getting in.

"Yikes!" he heard her scream.

He looked over his shoulder. He could still see her. She was frozen staring at something on the ground.

"What is it?"

She didn't hear him so he increased his volume. Still nothing, so he yelled.

"Snake."

He couldn't hear her at all, but he knew what sound she was making.

"Be very still. Back off slowly."

She was already doing that.

He met her when she had backed way about five meters. He'd gone as fast as he could given the unsure footing.

There was a large rattlesnake on a large rock where she'd just been standing.

"Whoa."

"Yeah."

"I almost didn't hear you."

"Yeah. Splitting up isn't going to work either."

He sat. His shoulders slumped.

"Good thing we've got the old team back together."

She slouched down next to him, relieved to be away from the snake.

"Yeah. Good thing. Now the old team needs to get out of this mess. One way or another."

"Ok, ok, decision trees," Sam said, "If we can't decide then we can't decide, right?"

She stared at him blankly.

"So we can decide NOT to decide, right?"

"You're not making sense. How does this system of yours work?"

He pulled out a coin and showed it to her.

"We'll flip."

"This entire morning we make no checklists, we perform no analysis, we make no plans. This entire morning. For this."

She pointed at the coin.

"A coin."

"We can NOT decide, right? We have to go some way, and there are only two options. Tell me, what's wrong with using a random number generator to choose between two equally arbitrary options?"

"I don't have time to explain it."

He shut up. Either she would continue or not. He crossed his arms.

Finally she said, "Fine. Heads."

He flipped.

"Heads it is, so we're going upward."

He thought she might argue, but instead she said, "not back to the snake."

"Of course. Just pick a direction around him."

"It was a female, not a 'him'. What sort of path-finding algorithm should I use?"

He fought back multiple responses. He swallowed. He looked at the clouds going by. He thought of the beach. He did whatever it took not to get into this with her.

They heard a rustle. Large amounts of brush were being moved aside as something came through, somewhere far below them.

"Think that's a bear?"

"I think that's people."

"Me too."

God he couldn't tell if she was messing with him or not. He tried poking.

"I don't think any bears are stupid enough to mess with us. They have no coins."

She smiled.

Smiled! Bingo! Called it!

Then she nodded agreement, "Stupid indeed, but I also think meeting people would be worse than meeting bears."

"Maybe."

Fuck.

"Let's move."

They scrambled up, then began the serious scrambling over uneven rocks that getting out would entail.

It didn't work too long.

"Debian, you've picked three directions in the last four minutes. Could you just pick one and stick with it? I'm trying to watch my footing."

"I've picked six directions in the last 273 seconds. Are we going to use this system of your or not?

"Yes, but …"

"Ah, fuck it. You stay here. I'll get to the edge on my own."

She turned and stomped off.

He looked up from his feet after her, this time with several things he wanted to say, things he had to say. She was in for it now.

He didn't have time for that, though, because before she was 10 meters away, she'd fallen down. She was holding her ankle and yelling.

"Come here," he said, which was stupid because he was going to her.

He hurried over.

"You okay?"

"Yaaaaa! You think?"

"Let me."

He knelt quickly and felt her ankle.

"Ouch!"

She was starting to calm down. He suspected she was more surprised than hurt. He knew better than to say it.

"No swelling. No bone. Not much tenderness."

"It hurts, numbnuts."

"Still have your cheery disposition. I'm guessing it's heavily bruised, maybe lightly sprained."

"What now? How does your monster master cross check system handle injuries?"

"Coins wouldn't work. There's too many options. That was just for picking who got to pick a direction."

"So we're back to arguing."

"No, Deb. I'm not going to argue with you. I'll carry you if I have to. How did you plan on solving problems like this? What was your master plan?"

"We never got there. We never finished dicking around with your stuff."

"What should we have done instead?"

"I told you, dipshit," she rubbed her foot some more, "we needed to create a multivariate decision tree analysis based on risk. How else would you act rationally? How do you think planes work?"

"But there's a simple checklist…."

"There's a book of checklists, and each one is just a condensed version of a risk analysis decision tree."

"I know the tech and math, Deb, but we're not going to have the time to go through all that work and map creation while hiking across a mountain."

"Don't you already have one started?"

She tapped her head.

"What the hell have you been doing all this morning, mentally practicing your breaststroke? Getting a tan?"

"I thought you liked the way we were going."

"Well yeah. I was encouraging you. I was being a good instructor, getting your confidence up."

"Getting MY confidence up. You fear Park Rangers and think that some rocks are actually spies. Imaginary bears bother you. You think I'm the one needing confidence?"

"I'm not doing this," she gritted her teeth, obviously wanting to fight. "Especially with a lifeguard."

He shook his head in disgust. He looked at her feet, then his. He saw the size of the rocks, felt the problem deeply. He felt how she must be feeling.

"Come on, fly girl."

He turned his back and scooted in a seated position back towards her. "What?"

"No, we are not going to be creating risk decision trees today. We are also not going to be doing differential calculus or manifold diagramming. Instead, space cadet, I'm going to teach you how to play chicken."

"Chickens. I don't like chickens. What…"

"Climb on my shoulders. I'll stand. Your new height will let you see further. I'll carry the weight. Now shut up and get on."

She did.

The game of Mountain Chicken continued for another hour. Sam hauled Deb around on his shoulders. Deb pointed the way she wanted to go. Sam mostly ignored her and went the way he wanted, but not always. She didn't seem to notice the difference.

They eventually found the trail again just at the peak as Deb had wanted. There was an overlook providing a look at a lush, colorful valley and mountains. It was a panoramic view, the kind people put in their living rooms.

Putting her down, she propped herself up on a rock and started rubbing her foot, but not wincing as before. He broke out their rations.

She didn't continue fighting. Maybe it was enough that she had pointed and he had acted, even if not always the way she'd liked. He didn't want to ask.

He stretched his sore muscles and enjoyed the view. He enjoyed the silence.

"Are you happy?" She asked. "Now we can move on to establishing a secret hideout. It can be a place to put all of our gear."

"Yes," he looked back to her, "yes I am."

5.05

Caving In

"One thing's for certain," Sam said to the new, empty, fresh, cold, dark hell he found himself in, "It's either figure a way out or die."

It was pitch black.

There was a shuffling sound off to his right and behind him. It sounded like things being moved around, maybe a grunt.

He stood perfectly still. He wished for any kind of sensory stimulus. A breeze would be perfect.

He decided not to speak or make any more noise because he was afraid of what might happen in response.

"Those boards were not as sturdy as I thought," Deb's voice said from behind, "We must have fallen into a cave."

Sam was extremely pleased that she was alive.

"You said we needed a hideout, Deb. Now we're buried underground in the dark. Nobody knows we're here. This has to be the best hiding place ever."

"I knew there were caves and mines, this area's replete with them. Before settlers moved past the Mississippi, Virginia used to be the major producer of gold in the colonies. It's still coal country. There's even plenty of Uranium. I knew the boards were old, but I had no idea they were dangerous."

"This is not good, and by not good I mean bad," he said to the darkness. "Got a light?"

"No."

"Get on your knees, then. We need to start feeling around. We need to be methodical."

He got down. He heard her behind him, crawling to catch up.

"Have you ever done any cave exploring?" She asked.

"Spelunking? Took a tour once."

"Did they teach you anything?"

"Yes. I hate caves."

"Not so fond of any places without light myself."

"Well, Deb, cheer up. Blind people do this all the time."

"We're not blind. We've never done this."

"Let's see," he was trying to remember, "they use echoes, sticks, memorized landmarks they can feel and hear. Saw a blind guy riding a bicycle once. You know, I bet that a blind person could use the rocks around themselves to construct a map. That's it, Deb. You can make a mental map. You should be pretty good at that."

He waited as he heard her shifting around.

"There are too many rocks. Statistical noise."

"Did you even try? How about really odd rocks by shape or feel? Could be you could improve your categorization…"

"If you'd like to describe the ontological system I need to use to adequately categorize thousands of rocks in a cave you've never visited, such that we could effectively use k-means clustering, or even gaussian…

"Ok. You are correct. You should go back to the geology lesson."

He heard a sniffle.

Another.

"Sam. I'm afraid."

"I am too. We'll work it out like we always do. We just need to keep listening to each other, work the problem."

"The problem is that we're going to die."

"That's the stakes. We don't know the problem yet."

He heard another sniffle.

"I have allergies."

"I know."

She grunted.

"Hey, I've found a candle."

"See there? Things are already looking up."

"Unless you want me to eat the candle, things are not looking up. No matches."

"Keep searching. Less talk, more work."

A minute later she said, "Ahhhhh."

To Sam it was the surprised reaction of a person who just realized that they'd sat in cold water.

"What is it?"

"I found something over here. It's big."

"I'm coming."

He started towards her voice.

"And Sam? It's got bones."

"Let me see already."

Although he could not see, he could feel enough to be sure that they had found a body, or at least what was left of one.

"No soft tissue," he keep feeling, "No smell. It's been here a while. Feel around, see if you can find a backpack, clothes, pockets, anything we could use."

"I'm feeling around in total darkness," she sounded as if she were making a diary entry, "over a dead body, in the hopes of looting it."

"What's the matter? Didn't your mother tell you that there'd be days like this?"

"My mother is no longer with us, Sam. She hasn't been since I was a small child."

"I'm sorry."

"I found a water bottle. Empty. Nothing else over here, just a stick and a watch. Neither work."

"Here we go," Sam announced, "Swiss Army knife."

"Be very useful if we have any cans to open or fish to scale."

They searched around more. They found nothing else.

"Great. It's moving along. We have more information."

"We have a corpse."

"We have somebody who came through. He's not in a pile of dirt. We have a candle. I think there's no avoiding it."

"What?"

"This is manmade. Wherever we are. The ground is mostly flat. The boards were covering a mine, not a cave entrance."

"You are correct. This is information. We've fallen into a mine."

There was not much emotion in her voice.

"If it's manmade, that means that there's a system. It's not all just random. We need to figure out what it is. We're going to have to move faster," he said, "we need to get up, move faster, walk around. Time is of the essence. The problem has changed."

"The faster we move, the quicker we lose track of where we came in."

"There's that."

"And the easier it'll be to fall over something."

"Didn't you say that guy had a hiking stick?"

"He did, here," she prodded him with it, "So what?"

He stood.

"I'll use the stick as a cane. The stick can be a blind person's cane."

"You're going to hurt yourself. You've never done this before. This is a very bad place to learn."

"Have some faith."

He made some small steps, shuffles really, mimicking what he thought he remembered from seeing blind people on TV.

"Here. Got it. Already we have something new. Our progress continues."

"What?"

He bent over, picked it up.

"Found a crowbar."

"You plan on using that to light my candle?"

"No, smartass. I don't know yet."

He could feel Deb's discomfort building up some sort of steam for an explosion.

She was a pot of boiling emotions with too tight of a lid.

He needed to redirect her before a meltdown or a blow-up. Deb could handle the complexities and uncertainties of the entire world, but then something out of the blue would cause her to hang.

"That's what you are. Sam. You're a collector of oddball tools that neither you nor anybody else know how to use."

"Always on your game, Deb. We're going to have to work on your Theory of Mind if we're going to get that candle lit and get out."

"And now you've invented up some new theory to explain? Probably another of your dumbass distractions."

"I'm not that smart. A Theory of Mind is the thing that every baby has. Even you. You have it. It engages mirror neurons in your brain to allow you to imagine being another person."

"I don't like people. I don't like their neurons."

"I know. Trust me, I know. That's not the point. There's a candle here. You have it. There's a body. There was a person. That means somebody, another human, had a candle and planned to use it, otherwise it wouldn't be here. So, Theory of Mind. Pretend you're that person. If you were that person, what would you do with your matches?"

"Put them in my pocket and go home."

"Other than that."

"Can you give me a hint?"

"This isn't a puzzle. I don't know the answer. This is what you call an interactive creative exercise."

"Sounds corporate."

"No. It's a game. It's just a game. You like games, right?"

"A game. I love games. Why didn't you say so? What are the rules?"

"Hmmm. The rules. I'm not sure that…"

"So we can determine who wins. I can create a probability matrix."

"It's not that," he scratched his head. He made several ums and ahs, "The rules. I must admit that you have me stumped. I don't know."

"You want to play a game, yet you have no rules."

"You're right. Silly me. I apologize."

She started clicking with her mouth. It was the clicking sound somebody might use to call a dog. It went on for about a minute.

Did he break her?

Deb with her mouth clicks sounded like a skipping record.

"Are you going …"

"Shut up."

He listened. She went on for another two minutes.

Finally she spoke. It was almost a whisper.

"That's no good."

He waited. Surely this was going somewhere. He pictured shaking her in the dark, trying to get her to respond. Maybe she would start clicking again? Finally the silence broke.

"Based on the echoes, this, wherever this is, is part of a larger network. You were correct. It could spread for miles."

"Can we keep some tiny spark of optimism? Optimism might be all we have."

"We got rocks. That's it. Wait."

He had to do something about this negativity.

"Of course we've got rocks. It's a mineshaft, a cave."

"No, wait. I mean certain rocks."

He heard her crawling off. With the rocks again.

"Are you going away to find more rocks? Because I'd like to come along."

In reply, a miracle.

He saw a spark.

"How'd you do that?"

"Flint. Rocks make sparks. Sparks make fire."

She banged them together again. Sparks flew.

"I can do this. We can do this. Here, let me help."

It took the better part of an hour, but eventually they got the candle lit.

Looking about, they were in a small room, perhaps a break room for miners from two-hundred years ago.

There was a large pile of dirt. They had fallen straight down. The mineshaft had sealed itself behind them.

On the walls were the oldest phones Sam had ever seen. He guessed they were from 1910, 1920. Old ragged cloth-insulated wires led down to other tunnels. The phones must have been some communication system for somebody. Somebody long gone.

Following the wires, he saw their options.

There were too many options.

Heading off in six directions were six other tunnels.

Each went as far as he could see.

Deb looked around.

"We could still fall to a lower level."

"And don't forget that there could be another cave in. More sparks. Need more sparks."

He smiled a dumb, crazy smile. He sat down and crossed his legs Indian style.

She sat down across from him. She looked worried.

"Something funny?"

"Yeah. The more we know, the worse it is."

"Perhaps I should blow out the candle?"

He actually considered the idea.

"No," he finally said, "darkness may be comforting, but it's no way forward. Movement is life."

"I've got it. I know what we should do."

Deb slapped her palms on her legs. She stood. She began walking off down one of the tunnels. She'd made it about a hundred feet before he caught up and stopped her.

"Why this way?"

She moved past him and started pushing on a support holding up the tunnel back from the way they came.

"Be careful."

"Because I want this to cave in."

As she said so, tons of dirt cascade down narrowly missing them and blocking the way they'd come.

She pointed at the walls.

"Sam, our elevation hasn't changed. That means we're still close to the surface. We didn't fall that far. By walking northwest I was walking where the topography would make us even closer to the surface."

"I don't see. Do you now see the surface?"

He moved the candle around.

"No, but I see four more tunnels leading off."

She was right. She hadn't explained to him how she knew where northwest or how she'd memorized the topography without them having a map.

"Look there."

Two more skeletons in rags were propped against the wall. Neither had any tools.

"They were probably with that other guy," she pointed back the way they'd came. "They made a decision. They got closer to getting out. He didn't. Sam, let me decide. I'll get us out. Movement is life."

"You want to decide? Fine. Enough. No more. I'll let you decide. We may die here, but we'll die the way you decide."

He was serious. As the words came out of his mouth, he realized he was serious. The news came as a terrible shock.

They walked down one of the tunnels a ways further.

"Hold this," she handed him the candle.

She began pushing on the wall again, not ready to give up on her idea even if it was the end.

He watched. He felt vaguely numb.

The wall came down as before. As before, she'd managed collapse the wall in such a way that they were not harmed.

The candle blew out.

"That sucks," he said.

"Get the rocks back out again. We'll have to start over."

"I thought you had them."

They were in the dark again, only this time in a much smaller space. No magic rocks.

"We're probably going to run out of air," Sam said, "so there's that to count on."

"At least we'll not starve."

"You're getting the hang of this optimistic optimization strategy," he laughed. It was a dry, short laugh, void of humor, "Perhaps a bit too late."

"I have many talents," she said. Her tone was void.

"Sometimes I think that we really suck at this kind of thing, you know?"

"You said that we should work together more. Use resources. Be like blind people."

"I know I did. I said we should listen more, work the problem."

He thought.

"Weren't there some old phones? Didn't we see phones?"

"Yes, but they're old timey cave phones. They're easily a hundred years old. I can guarantee you that they're not connected to anything outside."

"Well why can't you do one of your tricks, then. One of those weird things you do and get us out of here. Make a map of the wires in your head or something."

"What do you think I am, a trick pony?"

"I think you're the most amazing and incredible person I've ever met, and every time you look deep inside yourself, these things happen. I don't understand them."

He cleared his throat. If they were going to die, he had to find out.

"So what are you, Debian? What really ARE you?"

He could tell she was thinking. Finally, in a tender voice, she replied.

"All I can do is give you some kind of analogy. I will try."

"I'll take it."

"Suppose that we are three-years-old, growing up in a house we've never left. One day, through some cleverness of our own or magical intervention, we get a landline installed.

The landline is truly a mysterious and magical item. For us, it allows us to do things we've never before imagined, like get a pizza. We've never had one or seen one before. We know nothing about them. They're just fun. We manipulate our new telephone in various ways and various things happen. Sometimes nothing happens. Even that's fun.

But here's the thing: we've never been out of the house. Sure we poke around on the phone and cool things happen, sometimes nothing, but nobody's ever called us.

All we know is the phone, and we really don't know that.

Do we want the phone to ring?

Sam started processing it aloud.

"So, you and I are in a house. You're afraid of somebody calling you on the phone. What would you be afraid of, your subconscious?"

"No, you misunderstand, Sam. It's not just us. It's everybody. It's all the people in the world in this house. Humans have only been around the briefest second living on the tiniest dirt speck. That's our house. We are babies, toddlers. The phone has nothing to do with me. The phone is something everybody else is using."

"I'm trying, Deb. There's this phone. So the house is all the people that ever existed. Why are we talking about phones? Are extraterrestrials trying to contact us?"

"No. It's worse than the visitors. Much worse. Because, Samuel, I'm the one person who doesn't need a phone. I've been outside. I can go. I've looked around. And now I'm back, and I don't want to tell anybody about it or ever open that door again."

"You want to know what it was like? Picture a baby caveman, perhaps a Neanderthal from fifty-thousand years ago. Drop them in the middle of a busy modern downtown street, with traffic, cars, flashing lights, and so forth. The baby could deal with new types of living creatures. Childhood is, after all, full of strange and new alien things. But this experience would be total overload. It's madness.

"Stay away from intelligent communications technology, Sam, the kind that allows the instantaneous sharing of thoughts. You've been punching the buttons on it for a while. We all have. You've been getting some pretty cool results. I can assure you that you don't want to be there when somebody eventually calls."

"And that's those things that you don't like talking about."

"Yes."

"I understand better, I think. I believe you. I believe in you, Deb."

He said it twice to make sure he was feeling it.

"I can't help us. I'm afraid."

"I'm sorry. I guess I'm not listening enough to be helpful. I'm not you, Debian. I'm not inside your head. I'm trying."

"Maybe you should do one of your exercises. Clear your mind. Might give us some new ideas. A new spark, like you said."

They had ran out of things to say. Sam thought hard about being a better listener. She deserved that. He had failed them. He needed to relax through that feeling if he was going to become useful again.

As he did so, in the silence he heard voices and cars.

"I hear them. This way. Follow me."

Fifteen more minutes of crawling, each one punctuated by slight rock falls threatening a larger catastrophe. Finally they felt a breeze, finally they saw light through a crack. Finally they got out.

"Found it. By listening. You were right."

He was shaking.

"Let's give up the underground stuff, Deb," he said as they finally broke free. "For now, let's keep everything above ground."

"How'd you know the general direction of town?"

"I could hear voices and cars."

"I could not. There were no sounds."

"Guess I have better hearing."

"There have been fourteen incidents where you have done and perceived things that did not match up to my sensory input."

"If that's your way of saying thank you, you're welcome. I'm also the only person here that seems to be able to conduct reasonable chit-chat."

"Smalltalk is pointless."

Standing on the hill, the lights of town two miles away were pretty.

"Instead of us solving the case of Deb's missing social skills, how about we just be happy we got out. We got out. Let it go."

Deb did not respond.

They headed down the hill, this time being very careful about where they walked.

She was unable to let it go.

5.06

Killing Trust

Like most people, Paul Newbury was capable of murder. He never expected, however, that before the day was over, he would have to murder somebody who trusted him.

Major Parsons was right at Paul's side, though, and that meant something had to be done, whether Paul liked it or not.

The meeting was only a short walk from the base. He had given his word to Gibb and Parsons that he was not going to run off.

Adventure Park was a very small slice of a very large 40,000 acre purchase the federal government made decades ago. The entire purchase covered a long gorge, one of the biggest east of the Rockies. Where they were headed it was hundreds of feet deep. It stretched for miles.

In compensation for the hundreds of homes and farms that were seized, there had been fair payment and the promise of a wonderful park. MELLO had been built almost dead-center of the acreage, with access to the town, the cliffs, and the nearby deep water of the Little Friendly River.

A lake had been built. The government said it was to be for fishing but in reality it was for reactor cooling. No fishing had ever taken place, no camping, no hiking.

One tenth of the area, as promised, was eventually made into a state park.

Nobody had said how big the park would be.

It was not well-maintained.

After twenty years, they put in a scenic trail. There was talk of future improvement.

Promises can be kept and broken at the same time, Paul thought as they walked.

The walk was less than a mile. He missed the outside.

"Shouldn't we be driving, be more mobile," Parsons looked around as if the squirrels might come from the trees in an attack pattern.

"Come on, Parsons, I'm sixty-years old. I'm not going to get very far."

They entered a large gravel parking lot. It was empty. A sign announced the park and invited all comers to various outdoor recreations, none of which were actually available.

"I read your jacket, Parsons. Aren't you due for promotion?"

"Yes sir. Next up would be command, assuming I make it."

"You've got almost perfect marks. That'll help. Your test scores show high ability in both creative and strategic thinking. That'll help too."

"If you say so, sir."

"I've been looking for a number two."

"You're already a number two."

"Things change. Once you reach command, you'll learn that you have to nurture a cadre, a kick-ass staff, as you work your way up. They come along until it's their turn."

"If you say so," she paused, "Sir."

"I'm not bullshitting you. It's been that way since Caesar, probably. You don't promote the man, you promote the staff."

He rubbed his chin as they walked to the path, taking the lead, only glancing back at her.

"Stick with me. Let's see if we can make a command team happen."

"If the Colonel says so. I plan to stick to you. I'm not letting you get anywhere."

It wasn't the same. It was close enough.

"Has the Colonel been briefed that we're here to see Joe Middles, the billionaire entrepreneur?"

"I have."

They started down a small paved path from the parking lot to the deep woods.

"Where's his car?"

Parsons had a good point.

He looked back. Nope, the lot was empty.

"Joe and I, we go way, way back. I trust him. If he doesn't have a car, it's for a good reason."

She frowned.

"Relax, Parsons. There's no ambush here."

"If the Colonel says so." was all he got.

He smiled, not letting her see it.

There was only one path. It trailed along the steep cliff. There were half-circular overlooks every half-mile, a total of four. Each one backed into the path and mountain on one side and hung out of the ravine on the other. They were little concrete half-moons hanging off a steep, wild cliff.

"Isn't it a bit irregular meeting an important industry contact in a park?"

"You think so? How should it be done?"

"There are strict protocols for this kind of thing, sir. It avoids ethical problems."

"Maybe. Admittedly, I've been gone a while. Let's suppose you're absolutely correct. See? I think you'll make excellent command staff one day. You already got started."

"Thank you, sir. So why aren't we following the rules?"

Paul stopped his leading and talked to her.

"Because without relationships there are no industry contacts, that's why."

"And with bad or non-existent protocol you'll destroy the very industry you're trying to engage."

Whoa. Parsons was something else. He felt like he was getting to know a human hand-grenade. She was both impressive and not just a little bit scary.

"Right again, Parsons. But take care of your people, whether inside or outside. That has to come above all else. Everything depends on that."

She frowned again.

"If you say so, sir."

She was agreeing with him, but her tone made it clear that she hated everything that came out of his mouth.

Joe Middles did not look well.

They found him in the first outlook. He was sitting and staring off into space. His eyes were vacant.

Joe jumped up when he noticed them.

His expensive John Ford suit was crumped and dirty. He hair was uncombed. He looked like he had slept in the weeds. He had visible bandages on his head and arms.

He came to meet them. He had a bad limp.

"Joe," Paul said, "Joe Middles."

They hugged.

Letting go and holding him off, "What the hell happened to you, Joe?"

"Got into a fight with an employee."

"I see that."

"I lost."

"I see that too."

Joe was pale and gaunt.

"When's the last time you ate?"

Joe looked around. He counted on his fingers.

"Two days ago."

Paul looked to Parsons.

"We got any snacks? Give them to him."

He didn't think she'd have anything, but, being the good boy scout, Parsons had both snacks and water.

Middles began inhaling them.

Twenty seconds later, "I also have an arrest warrant out for me."

That was a surprise. Parsons stepped back. Paul stopped himself before he joined her. Joe was Joe.

Catching her step back, Paul was going to reprimand, encourage her to be more human. That kid needed to relax a bit.

Parsons was perfectly squared away, from head to toe. She was the picture of military perfection.

Middles was unshaven, ragged. It wouldn't surprise either of them to smell booze on his breath. He seemed to have no idea of this; or else to purposefully be ignoring his appearance. Instead, the expression on his beat-up face was powerful. He was in charge. Joe Middles looked like he'd just walked into an expensive nightclub.

Between the two, Paul felt like a tourist going through a homeless camp next to Buckingham Palace.

"Joe, come on. Let's get you back to base. It's not that far, we can…"

"I'm fine here. I'm not going anywhere."

Middles looked around. For a brief moment Paul thought the man believed he was in a night club, or a boardroom.

"In fact, let's wrap this up, Paul. I have some other things planned this morning."

Both of them knew that was bullshit and both of them respected and liked each other too much to say anything.

Middles checked his watch. Paul guessed that the watch cost about ten times the value of his house. Yet here he was, looking like this.

Joe was really getting into a rhythm now, pacing back and forth across the small concrete overlook.

"You were right all those years ago. We never could get the Inserts cracked, although we were close at the end."

"We succeeded too well," Paul said, thinking of his own Insert.

"So I decided to find a way around them."

Parsons was right behind him. Now Paul was getting nervous. Paul couldn't unload this information on her.

"How did you …."

"We used the tech we created back in the day."

"The tech that you promised me and Endelman you'd never use."

Middles stopped. He straightened his expensive clothes. He looked like he was performing his next lines. He was dignified. He was a concert pianist called in for an encore.

"No, I did not. It's parallel construction. I used the same system the FBI uses."

"It is …"

"Let's say the FBI uses secret intelligence methods to find out that you are a criminal, they can't charge you because that would give away their secret methods, right?"

"Right."

"But they still know you're crooked, that you're a criminal. Knowing that you're a criminal and that you are committing these certain crimes in this certain way, they know what they need to prove, they know how it all ends. So, in parallel, they start with no evidence, just a "guess" about how you're a criminal and here's how you commit crimes. They pretend they never saw the intelligence. From zero, they construct a completely new case using none of the sensitive material. It's a criminal case that is constructed in parallel to how a real case would work. Once they're done, it looks like just any other case. Nobody knows they ever spied. The secret stuff remains secret and is never mentioned."

"But everybody is guilty of something," Parsons said, as much to her surprise as anybody else's, "If that's the way it works, why don't they use parallel construction to put us all in jail?"

"Only used in special cases, that's why, but that's besides the point. I decided …"

Middles looked at his old friend. Paul thought he looked like he was deciding how many cards to play.

"I decided to re-construct the Coincidence Machine and the Jungian Metaverse Explorer using parallel construction and stick it all into a portable AR rig."

Now Parsons was engaged, "What are you two talking about? A young what?"

"He's talking about things above your pay grade, Parsons. Step back fifty feet or so."

"I'm not going anywhere."

"That's an order. I'm in an enclosed area. You can watch me just as well from there."

She backed away. She watched them carefully each step, never turning her back to them.

Joe was talking about a way to go inside the sphere, to walk around through normal life but see the sphere at the same time, overlaid.

Paul leaned in.

"You're saying that you have a wearable Augmented Reality system that will let you see, hear, and otherwise participate in the universe's superintelligence while otherwise just walking around?"

"Yes, but I've been afraid to test it. Well, mostly afraid."

"Why?"

"The first person that tested it killed themselves."

"From what I've seen, that makes sense, Joe. This information changes everything. You're doing things you shouldn't."

"I know."

Middles wobbled. He looked close to fainting. Paul caught him.

"When I leave," Paul said, "let me send you some food. I have to give you provisions. Allow me that."

For a flash the desperate vulnerability appeared on Middles' face, then was gone.

"Please," Middles said in a low voice. He resumed looking as confident as he could. Paul was sad. He was not impressed at Joe's bravado, at least not in the way Joe wanted him to be.

"It'll be done."

Through the woods they heard sounds. They heard people talking but they couldn't make out the words.

"Is that voices?"

"Kayakers. They love to shoot the rapids."

Paul looked to the river. It was supposed to be down the cliff there somewhere. He couldn't see anything. It was too overgrown.

"Unnerving, Joe. Voices from nowhere," he thought again of the homeless camp. He wondered if his friend had tried the AR gear but wouldn't admit it, "Feels like the trees are talking to you."

"It's a beautiful spot."

He'd known Joe for years, but his friend was off. This wasn't the super-confident genius go-getter he had mentored. This was a play actor, playing a billionaire in a poor community theater production. Something deep had cracked inside him.

Why was Joe here?

"You want a deal."

"I want a deal."

"If you've got the gear you say you have, replacing billions in research and development? You got a deal. You can write your ticket, Joe. We can work something out."

Middles looked around as if surveying a vast empire. Paul began to feel sorry for him.

"I'll be right here. Take your time. You'll probably want to bring an acquisitions team. I have a very busy appointment schedule, of course, but I'm in no hurry for a deal."

"You want to negotiate. A billion-dollar deal. From. An. Overlook."

"It's all I've got right now. I have other plans, of course. This is the right spot for now."

Parsons was standing a ways off at Parade Rest.

He couldn't tell if she heard or not.

He suspected she had.

He lowered his voice a bit. He spoke to her without looking at her.

"What time is it, Parsons?"

"Fourteen-hundred hours, sir."

She didn't bother looking at a watch.

Like most people, Paul Newbury was capable of murder.

Fuck.

She wasn't out of earshot.

Time to refactor.

Breathe out.

"Joe, I don't see this working. They'll just come here and pick you up."

I can't go into town or I'll get arrested," he replied.

"Right on that account," Paul started studying their environment more.

For being so close to MELLO, the ravine, the heavy woods, and brush, it all came together to isolate them. You could be dozens of meters away and if you were quiet, didn't move, used cover well? Nobody would know you were there.

Joe could do none of those things.

"Joe, you're not leaving until we get you squared away. We're going to get you situated. I don't want to have to worry about you."

"Don't worry about me, Paul. I'm doing fine."

"You're anything but fine."

"I'm exactly where I want to be."

He needed to bring Parsons in closer.

He motioned her over.

"Parsons, isn't there a patrol that covers this area?"

"Yes sir. Thermal, night vision, and motion detection. Twice monthly, I believe."

Joe and Paul, friends for years, looked sadly at one another, beloved family members saying goodbye for the last time.

They were both thinking the same thing but neither of them said it. Checkmate.

"Joe," he said carefully, hoping the other man would pick up on the hint, "I appreciate your taking care of our, um, mutual acquaintances. That was a good deed."

Parsons leaned in again, interested.

"Anything for a friend." he rubbed his sore jaw.

"They're both, um, quite full of surprises."

Paul shot a quick glance at Parsons. She was still a rock, only now a closer rock.

"They definitely keep you guessing, doing things you don't expect."

He thought of his letter opener.

"They're in town."

Now he backed up.

"Could you say that again?"

"Our friends. Saw them on the way in. I expect it won't be too long before they're paying you a visit."

"That's the last thing in the world I wanted to hear, my friend."

"Then you're definitely not going to like the fact that I suspect one of them, you know which, can crack the Inserts with little or no gear. Don't ask me how."

Paul felt like a deflating balloon, the last holdout of some child's birthday party, slowly sinking in a faraway unnoticed corner.

He furrowed his brow. He looked quietly at the stone floor in front of him. Slowly, he began smiling, not looking up.

Decision made.

Breaking a human neck is never as easy as it seems in the movies. First off, most people don't have the strength to exert the lateral force required to be sure of the deed. It's not done with some two-handed slap dance during a choreographed fight sequence.

You have to be sure to get the appropriate leverage. Heads are not supposed to do that, so they tend to snap back into place. If you lift somebody's head off their spine only to have it snap back generally into the same place, people tend to get angry about these things. That's why in Close Quarters Combat training (CQ) they teach you to never use it as an initial attack vector unless forced to.

Although it had been years, Paul remembered most of the maneuver. He had the element of surprise. With a brief bit of unpleasant struggle and noise, he got the job done.

Joe only screamed once.

He looked at his dead friend on the ground, Joe's face turning blue.

"I loved this man like a son."

In one motion, he bent down to pick up Joe Middles' body in a fireman's carry. Paul walked over to the edge of the overlook and tossed his former student into the dense brush and weeds far below.

He turned to his escort.

"Parsons, I made the Command Decision to terminate this man. I deemed the risk of even his continued existence to be too great. Pick up his gear."

She looked to where he had thrown the body. He did not. He never wanted to look there again. The corpse had already rolled into deep hiding in the tangle as if it never existed.

"Parsons, you have two choices. One, you can report everything exactly as it happened. Two, you can say he came at me with a knife and I defended myself."

She thought.

"Which one would you choose, sir?"

"I'm going to remember that I defended myself against a dear friend who lost his mind and came at me with a knife," his voice broke a bit but regained it, "I can't live with anything else."

He started to leave but changed his mind.

"You write it up any way you want. It's your decision. It was still the right thing to do and I still couldn't live with remembering how it actually happened."

Gathering the lost stuff Joe had left, they both went back up the trail.

They were half-way back when she stopped him.

"There was no car in the parking lot."

"That's correct."

She looked around.

"There was no Joe Middles."

They continued back, each thinking their own dark thoughts.

5.07

Perching

"Mos Eisley, a wretched hive of scum and villainy."

"Samuel Featherstone, read maybe three good science-fiction books in his life but knows every line of Star Wars and Monty Python."

He didn't bother responding. There was too much to see. But he had to ask.

"What are you currently, reading, perchance?"

"Transformer Resistance Wars, Three Phase."

"Electronics? History of circuit theory?"

"Multidimensional Wizard Psychics."

"Hmm," noncommittal.

"They're quite angry."

He let it go.

A steady breeze blew up the mountain over and through them. It was getting chilly.

They had found the perfect hiding and scouting spot. It was the most annoying, impossible-to-ignore spot around. They were at the top of the biggest mountain and at the base of a giant tower sticking up from the peak.

Perfect place to hide.

As they continued their hike it looked like they'd entered a very large wilderness area. They thought about finding a road but Deb had pointed out that you didn't have giant towers with microwaved repeaters and cellular gear unless you had a direct view of civilization.

So up they went again, eventually reaching a fifty-meter square dirt clearing at the top. The way up and the surrounding area was as wooded, thick, and rocky as their hike had been all along. A single, old, barely visible dirt road led up to the site.

In the middle of the clearing was a five-meter chain-link fence with a padlock. A signal shed the size of two house trailers was directly at the base. On the tower, the roof of the building, or in the center of the clearing they could be seen for hundreds of square miles. But with just a bit of concealment, like inside the shack or along the tree line where they currently were, they were both invisible and had a commanding view.

Down the valley a half-dozen miles away was the small town that they'd traced her dad to.

"This isn't even Mos Eisley," she said, "It isn't that big."

He nodded. He held up his binoculars.

"Dozen stoplights. About fifty commercial buildings. That's not bad. Smaller is better for us."

"Seven. There are seven stoplights and 43 commercial buildings, depending on the classification system."

He kept looking.

"With our binoculars we'll be able to spot your dad, if he shows up."

"WHEN he show up, you mean." She took a hesitant breath, "it'll be getting cold at nights."

Sam found the more time he spent with her the more he enjoyed it. He had no idea why. Both the enjoyment and his perplexity made him smile.

She saw him smile, so he thought he would play with that, see where it went.

"You know, I watched a show on the science channel about surviving in the arctic. If there are two of you stranded out in the cold weather and you're concerned you might freeze to death?"

He chanced a look.

She had the same look that she had before she had punched him in the face.

"They say to build a fire, of course. Silly people."

He smiled and nodded to himself as if agreeing to yet another round of endless breadsticks for the entire table.

Looked back to her. Her face was frozen. He yanked back to staring straight ahead again.

She was faking that anger. He knew it.

"Or you can strip naked and get in the sleeping bag with each other. There's always that."

If Debian Newbury had caught fire that moment and began ascending into heaven, Sam would have been less surprised.

She laughed. She had a nice laugh.

"Building a fire might be easier for us, though."

"Pam told me that."

Was that anger? Continuing right away would be good.

"Pam. My therapist. I had a therapist. Part of being an orphan, I guess. She used to tell me to stop and smell the flowers. It was an easier happiness than intimacy, at least for me."

He picked up a small flower.

"Turns out she was right. Little flowers everywhere up here. Did you ever do therapy, Deb, you know, related to all your family things?"

"No. Dad was a hard ass. He was a real character."

They both knew she was lying.

Sam only frowned. She looked at her shoes, then reached down to get a flower of her own."

"Sounds like Pam was a smart lady."

She took a deep smell.

He sniffed again.

"Fred, that's my second stepdad, found Pam by randomly searching around online. I think he just called until he found somebody who'd take me. I was a bit of a problem for a while."

She was slightly smiling to encourage him on. The smile started growing cracks.

"Timothy and Salomé were my therapists I guess. Dad too. They kept me out of trouble, they did."

She did not want to meet his glance.

"Wow Deb. Living in the same place. Same family. You had a real life. I envy you."

"If you knew me, you wouldn't."

"Hey, we don't have to talk about everything, you know. There are standard decision-making tools. Like we have a random number generator. We can use prediction markets. Stuff like that."

"How about semantic maps? Decision trees? Is that going to be too much mental work?"

She could have said that a hundred ways that would have been ugly. It seemed somehow kind.

"No, God help me for saying this, but our ontological mapping system is misaligned, probably due to some deep epistemological paradoxes. Whew! See! I do speak Debian!"

"We're too different. We can't agree on stuff. I speak Sam too. But we're also pretty smart. Made it this far, didn't we?"

She looked at her rubber chicken which she had gotten out and was instinctively holding. He saw her start going through her exercises.

He waited.

She finished and put it away.

Screwing up her courage, she said "It might be fun, Sam."

"Let's work on the here-and-now, young Padawan. I'm afraid the Force is not strong with us."

She reached for the chicken but stopped, instead turning to the view.

"My brother might be down there."

"Timothy, right? That's your brother? Does he work with your dad?"

"Nyah. He was just a kid. Eighteen now. He's gone."

Sam waited for more but as the minutes ticked by he got impatient.

"Did he run away?"

"He … I don't know … I don't know what to tell you, Sam. He was there. We argued and such, but no more than normal. Then he was gone. Dad might know. Or not. … It was like Dad didn't know ….. It was like nobody knew. He was gone."

"That's messed up. Didn't that happen with your mom too?"

If she'd heard him she ignored him, instead saying, "We're going to need to start getting things set up before it gets dark."

The wind carried the screech of a hawk.

"Raptors," she said.

He looked up but could see nothing. A second screech sounded from behind them.

"Two of them," he said, "must be hunting."

"Raptors," she said again, "the real ones, not the movie ones."

"Not as exciting as the movie."

"Perhaps. Depends."

The closer hawk screeched again.

"On what?"

"On whether you're a rabbit or not."

"Our rabbits are down there," he pointed, "we've got those pictures of your dad. We have our binoculars. We're going to need to set up a watch schedule."

"Then what?"

"Then we start logging."

"How are we going to make it to town if we see him? It's fifteen minutes by car."

"And we don't have a car."

She nodded agreement.

Far below as they looked, they saw the sparkles of a blue light. Sam searched for it with the binoculars.

"Looks like somebody's getting a speeding ticket down there."

She looked through hers.

"Yea. Four-lane switches to a two-lane. Classic speeding trap."

"Good money for the town, though, in something like that. Especially a small town.'"

She put the glasses down and grunted.

"I guess so. How many times does it take for it to be bad? A thousand? At some point, it's just a trap, highway robbery, right? They know something's wrong with the engineering and signage. At some number, it switches from being safety to being negligence. They're just taking advantage of people. How many?"

Deb always came up with these things. He knew that if he gave her any sort of number as an answer, it would be open bar, so he didn't.

"We've been here before. This began with you and I meeting in a conference room."

"It began with my dad and I sitting at our kitchen table."

"It began right here in front of us," he pointed at an imaginary person, "and we kept getting closer and closer. Now we've ended up here."

He gestured to the town with his binoculars.

"Miles and miles away, using binoculars to see thousands of little people run about their normal lives, trying to spot the one set of things that'll make sense of it all."

"Don't despair. It's here, all of it. We're narrowing it down."

"Ok, so we're narrowing it down, then what?"

"We catch my dad, that's what."

"Catch? Be honest. You mean kidnap. Ok, sadly I'm with you. So we kidnap your dad. I think he has the answers too. But you haven't answered the question we both asked, then what? Another town? Another mountain? Another dad? Does he come with us? What happens to your dad? And no matter what happens, how can it ever end here?"

"I know you can end it, Sam. I know you can."

"Have you lost your mind? How can that be?"

"I can't describe it. I just know."

"I think I know why."

"Ok."

"You know I can solve things … because I'm good with bears."

He winked. She grimaced.

"I have a new worry about you, Sam."

"What."

"I worry that you will accidentally fall off the mountain. Accidents happen. You could fall. Accidentally."

"Point taken. Didn't do a lot of dating in school, huh. Don't strike me as the Prom Dance kind."

"No. You?"

"No. Had a lot of study."

"Me too, lot of study."

"You know," he began. He shut that down and started again, "I can see a lot of pain with your mom. It's okay to share pain. We don't have to go with the bears and punches and mountains and all that. It's okay to share pain."

She crossed her arms and tensed up as if picking a fight, but he knew that whatever she was fighting, it wasn't him.

"She left a note, did I tell you that? They say she killed herself. Is that enough pain? Would you like to hear about the bloodied mess they found my sister Sal in? Maybe we can renew our time at EigenCorp."

"Anger. That's anger. That's not pain."

"How do you know? How can you possibly know what I am feeling?"

He stared sadly at her dark, defiant eyes. He knew what she was feeling. He knew.

"I'm sorry. I was being presumptuous. I'm better than that."

"You are better than that, Sam. I know it."

"Thanks?"

"I mean that sincerely. I enjoy your company. I miss my family. You make things easier."

"We seem to have run completely out of families in our lives."

"At first I though you were drugging me, putting something in my food. That's why I liked you. I have determined, however, that I actually like you."

"Guess I lucked out."

"We both did."

His stomach knotted. The pain, so sudden in the onset, continued. He had to do something about it.

"I cheated at Cybercon," he blurted.

"You cheated to get your job at EigenCorp? What? How? How could you cheat to break into a locked system, that's the definition of cheating. Cheating means breaking the rules. You were supposed to be breaking the rules, that's what breaking in is."

"No. I manipulated the administrators. Took them out to dinner. Got them to give me their hardware keys."

"Sex? You mean sex? You took people out for sex, then what, drugged them? Even then, Sam ..."

"No, no, no. It's not like that. That would be shitty as hell, but inside bounds. No. I just asked them."

Deb shook her head a couple of times as if she had water in her ears. She frowned. She cocked her head in curiosity.

"Some kind of drugged hypnosis? One of those magic deals of yours?"

"I don't want to talk about it. I don't know. I got their hardware keys, broke into the system, then reverse-engineered how an outsider might do it. Then I put everything back and broke in normally. I wrote that part up."

"It doesn't work like that. Those algos are open-source for a reason. You know that. The only thing that's secret is the hardware keys themselves. There should be nothing to find out."

"Topology of the network, configuration deviations of the protocols on the machines, that's what. Yeah, each lock is completely secure, but everything has a tiny leak somewhere. Take a dozen locks, hundreds of machines, thousands of app configurations and so forth. Make a map of all the pieces..."

"Yeah, if you got an entire admin staff to paint a God's eye picture, but how could anybody ever do that?"

"I just asked them, that's how. Then I told them to forget it, and they did."

He'd finally stunned her into silence. She stared at him. Her mouth hung open. Sam felt creepy crawlies running all over his body. The knot was gone. This was worse.

"Sam, that's starting to make ..."

"Shut up."

She smiled but said nothing. Sam felt like he'd just been caught masturbating in high school by somebody who hated him.

"Now it's my turn to ask you never to mention this," he said without looking.

"If that's what you want, then I won't," she said, "I was just guessing anyway."

"Guessing. Hmmmm," he said, "Quick test. Without telling me, pick one of each of these two choices: left-right, up-down, one-two, over-under. Got it?"

"Yes."

"Ok, mine are left, up, two, and under."

"Right, down, one, over."

"That's what I thought."

"What."

"Given any two choices, we instinctively pick the opposite of one another."

"That's not true."

"Yes. it is. You're doing it right now. Don't be in denial."

"I'm not in denial."

"Just making it worse."

"Fuck."

She began to argue before realizing she was being punked. Instead she said, "Let me review. We are heading into some sort of crisis with not only my dad, but perhaps many others."

"I don't see where we have a choice."

"We both agree that we need to be open and make decisions together for this to work. It's too important otherwise."

"Again, no choice."

"Yet we can't agree on much of anything else."

"I don't think so. But that's not the best part. The best part is that even if we just make random guesses, we'll always disagree."

"We are broken and in desperate need of repair."

"That's good. You should go into counseling."

"I lied, okay. If you're going to insist, I lied."

"Huh?"

"I lied when I said I didn't have a counselor. You could say I told the truth. I didn't. I had a psychiatrist, Dr. Sykes."

"It's okay. I'm okay with that. You don't need to talk about it."

She continued on without responding as if once the dam had burst the water had to gush out.

"He gave me meds. He taught me some things about the way I am."

She looked left-to-right, nodding her head as if agreeing sternly, yet sadly with a large group of others who were not present. Sam pictured a doctor, perhaps this Dr. Sykes, speaking to a committee deciding young Debian's fate. Yes, yes. Very unusual case. It's all so very sad, gentlemen."

It was the kind of thing that would grind on Debian for years and make her mad with rage.

But what, exactly, was sad?

"Dr. Sykes was a crook, of course," she said, "Cheated on his wife, over-charged the insurance, dubious test scores. I made up my mind," she nodded again to herself, "I was never going back there again. And I didn't."

He felt perhaps it was time.

"Let me ask you, Deb, did you stay away because he was a crook or because the process was painful?"

He placed his hand on her knee trying to comfort her.

She jerked back as if shocked. Maybe it wasn't time yet. He continued as if nothing happened. He took his hand and pointed at the city below.

"See that town, all those people?" There's a lot down there, a lot of pain, I'm afraid it's going to be worse than this Dr. Sykes of yours could ever dig out.

She looked back to him. He thought she looked like a lost little kid in a K-Mart waiting with the manager by the front door.

"I seem to be especially broken, Samuel. Wherever I go, even to the top of a mountain in nowhere, the pain follows me."

"Believe me or not, I feel the same way. We all do. Life is pain and suffering, sickness and death. Buck up."

"You wouldn't make a good counselor," she waited, "believe me or not."

Wink.

Wink.

"Probably. Just saying that some things you gotta go through. Nobody asks or cares if you want to or not. Everybody's gotta go. That's one of them."

He pointed.

Their smiles faded.

They enjoyed the silence. Debian eventually said, "You're right, this is going to be painful. Perhaps neither of us is ready for it."

"Deb, we need to communicate. I mean really communicate."

"I can't."

"I can't communicate for you. This is something you're going to have to do on your own."

"There are things that you can do that I can't," she said, "and don't you ever say that I said that to anybody."

"Who hurt you?"

They both watched the town. It slowly got darker.

Finally he said "We're going to need to set up noisemakers, make a decision about picking that lock or not, it's either the tree line on inside the shack. You choose."

He rose slowly, waiting for an answer. Not getting one, he set off on his chores.

It was several minutes later her teeth gritted and her lips thinned, when she finally stood. Her body clenched as if in a strong wind.

She was alone on the mountaintop.

"I know exactly who hurt me."

She got out the lock-picking kit.

"I don't know at all," she continued to nobody.

She turned for the gate but didn't move yet.

"I'm going to fucking find out."

She started towards the gate. The lock would be easy.

"I'm going to fucking find out and fucking fix it for good."

Her voice was lost in the wind and oncoming darkness.

5.08

Nothing

Nothing happened that morning.

Martha Simpson loved fried chicken. Deal Smith was an avid girl-watcher. Louis Evers was deeply afraid of spiders.

None of this was interesting to them the day they met the man who wasn't there.

Martha was sitting out on her front porch enjoying the morning sunshine when he walked by.

"Say, can you tell me the way to Town Hall?"

"Sure thing," she pointed.

Next door the neighbors were frying chicken. Wow, she thought, was that the most enjoyable smell ever? Before she finished replying she got up and went inside. She spent the next few minutes deciding whether to go visit her neighbor or order food to be delivered. She decided to order.

Deputy Smith was the next to see him. There was a very unusual man walking down Main Street.

Smith pulled his car over and rolled down the window.

Before he could ask the man anything, at least *perhaps* before he could ask him anything, a convertible full of young girls in swimsuits sped by. They had to be doing 40 or 45 in a 20.

He had to do something about that. It was his job.

He chased them and spent the next half-hour issuing them a stern warning. Nobody was hurt, but they really needed to be more careful.

Louis Evers spent the most time with the man. Evers was working the Clerk of the Court desk when he came in. He must have spent five minutes answering questions, although Louis didn't remember what they were.

Almost as soon as the conversation was over, Kikky Mackers brought in a huge box of giant spiders and dumped them on the counter! Mackers had been mad about his property taxes for years, and for years had threatened to give people a piece of his mind if they went up again.

Mackers dumped the spiders all over the counter. Louis screamed and ran away as fast as he could. He hid in a closet for an hour until they finally coaxed him back out, assuring him that they'd all been cleaned up.

Nothing unusual happened that day, really. Simpson's neighbors had been planning a chicken lunch for weeks, talking with her online group about the best recipes. The girls were having a Senior Skip Day, a tradition that went back as far as anybody could remember. They had been busy texting one another for a few days about the best place to swim. Mackers had been scheming his revenge for months but never spoke a word, instead searching online for the best way to disrupt local government, researching who was afraid of what, where to buy scary spiders, and so on.

All of these things, while unusual, were also the types of things that happened everywhere. Everyday. Enough, perhaps, to be noteworthy.

Brains were funny. A man would drive to work and suddenly his car break down. Getting out, he realized that he had no recollection of the boring, repetitive part of the past hour, his driving. Now that his car was broken, however, he had to plan a way to get to his destination.

If you'd asked any of those three, or a dozen more people in town, nothing happened that morning. They walked to school. They patrolled town. They sat on the porch. They went to the grocery store. If you pressed them quite hard, they would remember something. The neighbor fried chicken. There was another case of young speeders. That jerkface Mackers finally went too far and got arrested.

Anything else, though? Nope. Nothing happened the day they met the man that wasn't there.

5.09

Increments

The leather satchel sat in the corner of the room.

As Paul worked through the day's reports and plans, from time-to-time he'd look at it.

Whatever happened to Joe Middles, the answer was in that bag.

Joe had become a danger to himself and others.

As a student, Joe had always been cautious, clever. Paul had even thought of him as Machiavellian at times, a little too clever. Joe was the kind of guy that no matter what happened in life, you knew he'd come out on top.

Yet the man he'd met the other day was delusional, suicidal.

Given what Paul had learned about MELLO, the observatory, and the things being observed, exposure was the most likely answer.

The satchel sat there.

Paul thought of the death reports he'd read, the woman writhing in the infirmary, Parsons almost getting killed, all of them almost getting killed, by the temporarily insane man.

The field work.

The gun lying on the floor.

He got the satchel. He placed in on the table in his room.

He still kept working. Maybe with it closer more ideas might come. He felt the leather.

As he worked, he thought, of all things, of the Bataan Death March.

On 9 April, 1942, Japanese forces had fully surrounded allied forces on Bataan and were breaking through the lines. Defeat, and death, were imminent.

Something almost unheard-of happened. Over 75,000 people surrendered to the Japanese.

The Japanese did not believe in surrender. Warriors who surrendered were less than human. Yet here they were with tens of thousands of prisoners. What to do with them? What do you do with 75,000 newly acquired animals you didn't want?

He looked again at the satchel. What to do with them?

So they marched them over 65 miles to various camps for imprisonment. Sixty-five miles through dense, wet jungle was difficult for healthy, well-fed people. It would be many days, most likely over a week.

These prisoners were neither healthy or well-fed. Many were injured. They were stripped of their possessions and told to march. March or die. The choice was simple.

He opened the satchel. He did not reach inside.

The men were captives for over four years, at least the men who made it through the march. They were the Ghost Soldiers, men who lived constantly at the border between life and death, inhabiting neither world.

Reaching in, he pulled out some electronic gear. Earpieces, thick black glasses, the kind the military used. A charging wire.

There was no doubt in his mind that whatever was going on with the observatory, it was deadly.

And here he had a tiny observatory in his hand, one he could wear.

What to eat?

It was a simple question. Marching through the jungle, no food or water, watching men fall out and get shot or bayonetted, you either found something to eat or died. But who knew about all these plants? Was the water okay? These men had no experience, but they were starving.

Since they were a large town on the move, they asked the doctors.

The doctors didn't know either.

Paul got out his stopwatch. He set the countdown timer for five seconds.

So the doctors came up with a rule: find something, keep it, hold it in your hands. Did your hands go numb? If so, throw it away. Now rub it lightly on your lips? Feel anything bad? Throw it away. Touch it to your tongue.

It kept going until they finally ate it, they finally found something that would keep them alive.

The process was very simple. Tiny steps with safety checks. It was the only way they were going to live.

He put the VR gear on, hitting the countdown clock.

Five seconds later he ripped them off.

He was alive. He set the countdown clock to four hours for his next effort.

The choice was simple. March or die.

5.10

Shooting The Shit

A fifty-caliber, 12.7mm, 292.8-grain BMG round will cut that girl-scout into two pieces, Parsons noted as she set up the Barrett M82 Sniper Rifle. She was on the roof of the local bank, looking out over the lower part of town.

Down below, Sam was taking in the morning sun. He was walking and thinking about the fun he'd planned today. All he had to do was offer to buy a car and scare some kid. It was acceptable to fail at both. In fact, he wanted to fail at both. He couldn't be happier. Maybe he could make faces or yell at the kid, assuming there even was a kid. He'd offer the car salesman $15. They'd laugh. They'd scream. They'd curse. However it turned out, Deb would stop this endless pestering about his so-called powers of persuasion.

He promised her that he'd try, though, and that was that. That was the deal. Even if he somehow achieved both goals, once completed, the argument would go away. They could move on to whatever the next argument was.

Sam loved performing and entertaining and wasn't afraid to fail.

It'd be fun.

The Barrett snapped into place and Parsons began zeroing in on the used car lot.

The wind had just a touch of chill to it. The day was warm, but not overly so.

Fifty-feet below and a hundred and fifty feet away, Sam began whistling.

He read the sign on a travel agency as he walked by.

"Discover Alaska."

There was a picture of a bear eating a fish from a river, snow-capped mountains in the background. The sky was crystal blue. You could smell the perfection.

They never showed the bears eating people. All you got was the dream.

He'd long dreamed of Alaska. As a child, he had a list of the dozen places he wanted to visit once he became rich and famous. Alaska was at the top.

He couldn't remember the last time he'd had that daydream. Five years ago? Ten?

It was school. It had happened some time in high school.

Of all the changes growing up, he missed daydreaming the most.

Parsons adjusted the scope for windage and drop, using a laser range-finder to get an accurate distance. She needed a spotter. Sniping without a spotter is unsatisfactory. It felt like amateur hour.

She banished the thought immediately.

Gibb had told her to kill everybody at the used car lot. That order was a little too Black Ops/False-Flag even for Parsons. But she'd saluted, said "Yes ma'am." Orders were orders. The mission was the mission.

Seeing her consternation, the other Colonel, Newbury, had taken her aside before she left.

"We know there's this kid," he explained, "The kid has got to go. I'd explain exactly why but it'd kill you."

Was he serious? Was this some kind of test? A kid? Shooting a kid?

"Shoot the kid. Leave the rest," he paused, realizing he had just con-tradicted her previous order, "There's a slight chance somebody else will assist. Maybe a girl. Or a boy. Early 20s. But don't wait. Don't count on an easy out."

"Yes sir."

"And Parsons, know that doing the right thing sometimes can be unpleasant, even disgusting. But never compromise. You're asked to do your duty, not perform moral calculus. Got that? We all start becoming moral philosophers and this is no longer a fighting force."

"Yes sir."

"Motherfucker," She moved the rifle around. The position wasn't going to work. The morning sun was overwhelming the shot sight, reflecting off storefront glass.

The mission wasn't looking or feeling very professional.

She moved to the other corner of the bank roof.

Downrange, Sam walked into the used car lot. There were three people: a salesman, a girl scout, and her mom.

Deb got one right again, dammit.

He heard the kid doing her spleal as he walked up.

"Supporting your local scout can help children receive a better education."

The man nodded. He looked like a man who was very well-practiced at being kind.

"Sounds good," Sam offered, interjecting himself into their conversation, "I'm always up for a good cause. Aren't we all?"

The salesman grinned. The man had a smile of knowing friendship. They were best buds at a Ruritan dinner joking about the rubber chicken they'd just eaten.

"Be careful my friend," he said, "It is a good cause, but last year they took me for $400. I had to sleep on the couch for a week."

"Ouch."

"My wife ate the cookies."

"Double ouch."

"No more than a hundred dollars, kid, okay?"

The two began haggling.

"So you don't care about children? You're going to leave us, the girls of the town, all to starve?"

Damn, she was a tough one. She took no quarter.

Her sharp language reminded Sam of someone else.

Somehow or another, Deb had gotten it into her head that he could really persuade people. Really. Like if he were the Amazing Featherstone and had his own flying carpet and such.

The only way it was going to be settled was a dare. The dare was that he had to buy a cheap used car at a ridiculously low price and get some rando kid to leave the car lot while he did so.

He had no idea how she knew a kid would be there, but there the kid was. His plan was to run the little girl off, but watching her tear into the car salesman he realized it might be tougher than that.

That's good. So what? Failing was good.

He won the bet by losing. As long as he tried.

Failing with the car salesman shouldn't be too tough, since Sam only had fifty bucks and the man looked both sane and sober. Sam thought he also looked quite clever. He just didn't show it.

Sam viewed the morning ahead as a performance, one of his magic shows. It was a fool's errand, sure. He stopped being worried about looking like a fool a long, long time ago. He was going to pour himself into the act. A good performance was 90% attitude.

Up above and hundreds of meters away, Parsons had a much simpler job. Shoot the kid at all costs unless somewhere, somehow, somebody else takes care of her. She wondered a bit how the Colonels knew the kid would be there. She didn't wonder too much. Her job was pulling the trigger, not selecting targets or assigning missions. Newbury had been right. Do the work.

"Hey mister, how about you? Would you like to participate in nurturing the future of our children?"

Sam snapped out of it.

What a line. That girl must have several of those she's practiced. He pictured her in front of a mirror at home, memorizing a dozen or two lines, honing each one, preparing for big day of selling.

He looked mom and girl over. The girl was extremely earnest and hard-working. The mom was extremely tired and frazzled. They'd already been at it for hours.

"Why are you here?" he blurted to the kid.

"To raise money for ..."

"No, I mean why here, right here at this car lot right now?"

The girl held up her phone.

"It's my cookie app."

"Huh?"

She began reciting the sales pitch, no doubt something she'd read online.

"Using a sophisticated model, the Cookie App takes your location and previous sales and tells you how to maximize your effort."

She stressed "sophisticated" and "maximize." They were new words and she was quite proud of them.

Thinking him a bit daft, she summarized.

"Helps me sell more."

"How?"

She held the phone at arm's length, the first time she'd really thought of how things like this might work.

"I dunno. Magic."

From atop the bank building, Parsons watched the conversation play out. All was happening as she was briefed. If the targets could just move around a bit, she'd have a good shot.

She'd take it.

The roof was uncomfortable, but she was used to being uncomfortable on a stalk. The wind was gusting. That sucked. The sun was peaking in and out of the clouds. That sucked. Her position wasn't that great. Suckage number three.

Sam could smell the blossoms in the wind. He nodded absently.

The day still had a pretty good chance.

The girl was saying something else. Sam wasn't paying attention.

Perhaps ignoring the girl would work. Let her and the salesman tire each other out and then she'd leave, off to her next victim.

"Why don't I talk to somebody else. You seem busy," Sam said to the man.

"Sorry, sir, it's just me today."

As the salesman responded, he looked behind Sam. A large propane truck pulled into the lot.

The driver rolled down the window.

"Just leave it over there, Saul," the salesman yelled.

Sam watched the driver get out, then limp his way to the diner across the street.

He didn't look well.

Seeing Sam's compassion towards the driver, the girl approached closer and made another run.

"Buying cookies can help the poor. Don't you care about poor people?"

"Now dear, that's a little much. Be honest with the man."

"Well I'm poor, and it'll help me."

Watching the girl argue with her mom, seeing himself in every person on the lot, it all fell apart. Sam stopped having fun. He saw the constant negging and nagging and how it hurt relationships, he remembered why he was into computers instead of street (and professional) busking and cons. Once you went dark, there was no place to stop. It was endless. It was one thing for a little girl to go all cutthroat. Part of growing up. It was something else entirely when Sam did it. This wasn't hacking a computer system. This was straight up stealing. It wasn't right to be fooling these people. Cars and cookies. Whether it was small or large, it didn't feel right.

On the roof, the girl scout's head was in the crosshairs. Parsons began her count. To herself she recited the shooter's mantra, BRASS-F. Breathe.

Relax. Aim. Slowly-Squeeze. Follow-through. At the last minute she pulled up a bit. The silenced 500-meter shot missed the girl by six inches and took out a chunk of pavement 100 meters behind them.

Fucking downrange. She should have gone with a smaller caliber.

Below, Sam decided to meditate, look inward. He'd promised Deb he'd give it a try, and now seemed as good a time as any. He began doing the exercises he had been teaching Debian. Plus, the girl was getting on his nerves. Even the salesman looked like a lot of work. They were ignoring him. Sam needed the concentration.

As he listened to the continuing cookie bartering and negotiation, he reached out with his mind. There were no other words for it. He did so by maintaining a focus, clearing his thoughts, and drawing himself, the focus, in to a smaller and smaller dot at his center. Reaching the zero point, Sam Featherstone disappeared and his self-awareness became a fuzzy blob that slowly and tentatively began spreading around them all.

He'd experienced the feeling before while meditating, of course, but over the years it kept getting stronger and stronger. It was why he didn't meditate anymore. It had become unpleasant.

There was a threat nearby. It was something with pain, accuracy, and cunning.

Gun? Knife? Spear?

It shook him to the point that he snapped out of it. As he did so, a huge hunk, the size of his fist, plopped out of the pavement down the street.

The girl, her mom, and the salesman didn't seem to notice. They kept haggling.

He reached in his pocket. He handed the girl his money.

"Here, put me down for some cookies."

He gave her the fifty.

"I don't even know your name."

"Don't worry. I'll catch up later."

"Hey! You kids! Get away from there!" the salesman yelled.

He looked over to see a few young boys on bikes, chatting and horsing around beside the tanker truck that had just arrived.

The man waved them off.

"Get going before I call the cops! You hear!"

Tinkering some more with their phones, they finally put them away and rode off, still laughing and cutting up.

"Motherfucker." Parsons said for the second time.

Now there were some new kids in the way. Some bunch of kids on bikes cutting up. There was too much movement in the target area.

Of course, she'd had the shot the first time, right? But she pulled up at the last minute, right?

"Fucking target noise," she said to nobody.

Suckage number four.

Sam's money disappeared in the girl's hand faster than any trick he had ever performed.

Now he had no money.

This was stupid. Deb had him faking himself out, punching at ghosts. He was imagining his own enemies to fight and deal with. Feeling guilty, he made up his mind to try the meditation thing again, only differently.

Parsons also made up her mind. She felt no guilt. The mission was more important than all other considerations. It was time to buckle down and get serious before this got fucked up beyond all recognition.

She reloaded.

Quickly going through the mediation again, Sam didn't feel. Instead he did something akin to mentally stomping his feet. As the diffuse bubble began, he tensed up and released all his energy. It was a shout. He turned it all off like a switch. He angered himself out of his own thoughts.

He wasn't really trying so far, but he had to at least half-way try. He had to be honest with her about it.

The shot went wide this time, and it was nothing she had done. It was like she had a miniscule seizure, unconscious jerk, right at the last moment.

Odd.

She'd never had that happen before. She lost the shot. It ricocheted off a brick wall and knocked out the windshield of a car in the far lane, again far downrange. The car swerved quickly, running into two other cars.

Fuck.

She hoped the driver was okay. The other drivers.

She could have killed somebody.

Off the rails. This op had officially gone off the rails.

Admit it. Fubar. The op had gone fubar.

"Get the hell off my lot!"

As Sam came back he saw the formerly happy man, the salesman, now all red-faced and angry.

"You little hellion! Get out of here!"

The man's face was beet red and he was shaking his fist at mom and daughter.

Was this the same friendly man he'd just been talking to? Yelling at the girl?

The mom looked like she was going to hit the man in the head with her purse.

What had been said while he zonked out for just a few seconds?

All three of their phones rang.

Looking at them, Sam thought this might be the only time in his life he was going to get into a fight with a girl scout.

They rang some more.

"You guys going to get that?"

It was like talking to a wall, or the air itself.

Parson started packing her rifle up. Something was wrong here. She was going to find out what.

"How about I give you $50 for that car," Sam pointed behind him to a lot full of cars and no car in particular.

He smiled. He didn't smile at the man, he smiled to the man. He tried to thrust out his smile through the man's anger, through his head. You. Feel the smile.

"Done," the man said, suddenly looking quite pleased with himself. He looked as if he'd just learned a major investment had paid off.

The wind picked up.

What was pleasant became suddenly cold.

Reaching the ground level and leaving, now Parsons had to decide if she was going to break cover and go talk to this girl. Should she follow her and her mom? Perhaps she could assist the new guy that had showed up, right on schedule. That would be against orders, but it seemed to her it would get the job done.

She knew that whatever happened, she wasn't going to be shooting any more. Something was wrong. If she couldn't shoot, no matter what the reason why, shooting even more wasn't going to help anything. Time to improvise.

The car wreck was becoming quite the spectacle for folks. As she stood by the corner of the bank, more and more people walked by, gawking. Traffic stopped.

She could neither stay nor go.

Over in the lot, Sam was getting desperate. He'd already caused a car wreck and a fight and he really had no idea how. The girl and the mom were still angry. The salesman looked like somebody had pushed the pause button while he smiled, as if he were waiting for some new gesture from Sam that would make him even happier. That was more disturbing than all of the other strange things happening.

He had to fix this. Should he push some more? Push more? Was that a thing? To push?

This was messed up.

Parsons decided to walk towards them in order to fit into the flow of the crowd. She still hadn't decided whether to engage or not. She got the feeling she was crossing some line somewhere, but as long as the mission ended in some way that was planned, technically she thought she was still good. Still, it all didn't sit well with her.

She should have been briefed better.

She'd have to decide soon.

Life had gotten much too crazy for Sam by now. He just bought a car which he didn't want with money he didn't have. For a price that made no sense.

He also had to do something to make mom and kid happy before they turned their anger on him.

He envied the girl. Wouldn't it be great to be a child again, selling cookies. It sounded incredibly more fun than all the nonsense he'd been up to lately. Safer. He missed the simplicity of childhood.

Oh well, maybe he could make the daydreaming magic happen again?

"ALASKA!"

He said it. He felt it. He pushed it. He regurgitated it.

Parsons immediately pivoted right and walked into the travel agency. She was determined to buy a ticket to Alaska.

"Let's go to Alaska," the mom said to her child.

"Can we go right now?"

"I don't see why not."

"Yay! I want to see the bears!"

He watched the mom and child leaving. They were holding hands. His mouth hung open. When he finally did look back at the salesman, he was gone.

He didn't know where the man went, but he had a pretty good guess.

Being alone, he saw no point in staying in the lot, mouth open. He left. He felt broken somehow, beaten.

It worked. He didn't know how or why it worked, but somehow, it worked. But how did Deb know the girl would be there?

He didn't complete the paperwork for the car. He didn't go inside. He didn't want to know if his luck would continue working or not. It was bad enough already.

"How?" The word "how" keep repeating in his head, bouncing around.

He bumbled his way back, passing Parsons as she left the travel agency. Parsons was shaking her head as if trying to clear her vision.

Parsons was having similar thoughts. How. There was no doubt that Colonel Newbury had better situational awareness than anyone else on the base, but how? He never got out. He never went anywhere alone. He only left the base once, and that was with her. How had he known about that tall kid? She had missed an easy shot. How.

Having shaken off this sudden Alaska desire, she found what she was looking for. The propane truck.

Nothing suspicious. She kept searching. She looked where the biker kids had been playing.

There it was. It was an improvised thermite bomb. It had a push-button trigger. Regular explosives, at least the kind these kids could buy, wouldn't cut through the steel on the tanker, but thermite on the nozzle would work fine. It'd be a spectacle.

And where the tanker sat was directly behind a busy service station. She saw a fuel truck driver, hose in hand, filling the tanks up just fifty-feet away. Another large fuel truck waited behind him.

In the middle of a busy town, near other fuel storage locations, it'd kill hundreds, thousands.

Where did that leave her?

How?

She took the bomb.

Twelve-year old terrorists? A biker gang with bicycles? And why the girl scout and not the kids? The girl was the triggerman? A girl scout? A tall kid?

None of that added up either.

How.

It was also obvious to her that Gibb and Newbury had completely different operating styles. and that Newbury and Gibb didn't get along at all.

She hoped she was not around when the inevitable showdown arrived.

But she was.

5.11

Checking Out The Mates

Paul was never going to let the thing from another planet anywhere near his field of vision. He trusted those assholes about as far as he could throw them, and frankly the soup wasn't that good to begin with.

He sat at the cafeteria table with an old style VHS tape movie in one hand, still in its original wrapping, and a spoon in the other. His trusty moleskine notebook to the right of his tray, a large bowl of minestrone front and center.

Although the room could easily hold a hundred, there were only about a dozen there, including two heavily bearded men who were serving food. A large banner hung over the entrance.

"Stirs-days Thursdays!" and "You could win a classic horror movie! No purchase necessary!"

A pocket chessboard was competing with the lukewarm soup for his attention, at least when he wasn't doing the actual work, the reason he came to the cafeteria to begin with.

He had to get a better handle on base operations.

He looked at his hands. He put the items down. They were still shaking. He hoped nobody noticed. 1900 hours was a good time for a dinner, right? Quiet? His project with the AR gear could be kept secret in his quarters, right?

He hoped.

Then Gibb and Parsons arrived.

He had made it up to thirty seconds at a time with the gear Joe had left him. He woke up with memory loss. He was numb in the extremities. He was shaking. He felt like he had the flu.

But he was not dead. His body still worked.

Aside from the tremors.

It had been working. The plan had been working. He just needed to take some time apart, tweak the titration schedule a bit.

Looking at the stack of papers in the chair besides him, so far the files did not paint a happy picture.

Reviewing base records while eating wasn't the restful break from what was going on in his room that he had hoped for.

In his quarters, as in his previous life, at least things tracked. Events were logical and sequential.

The more he looked at the administrative status of the base, though, the more it didn't track.

Things were done out of order. A response might arrive a week before a problem had been identified. People came and went and there were no gate records. He didn't believe that for a minute. There was a COIN operations team. Somewhere. Orders and information went back and forth through at least a dozen different names and terms, none of which he could find. He didn't know if he should keep tracking them down or not. He didn't know if he could. The dozen mysteries could easily transform into a hundred if he kept poking at them.

That was the heart of his problem: there were so many moving pieces, so many things going on, and it was only him. Which parts should he investigate? Where should he make his move? Where could he hurt the most, find out the most?

He had some sense of the endgame. He wanted to fix what he could even if it meant a huge sacrifice to do so.

The problem was there was just too much to fix. There was too much wrong. Having too many choices can be much worse than having too few, he knew. This is why when you buy a service online you only get a few options: free, basic, professional, and premium. Everybody takes free until they're stuck having to pay for it. Then they look at the table. Three choices, right? Premium is insane! Who would spend that much? So then they're choosing between basic and professional. Let's face it, who is going to admit that they're average?

You only appear to have choices. The game is rigged.

There's really no choice at all. Although it's rigged to make money, the deeper truth is that human life's like this: the illusion. If the vendor had provided a hundred switches you could turn off or on to get different prices, nobody would buy anything. There would be too many choices.

Should he choose?

People wanted the appearance of freedom without actually having to do the mental work it requires to choose.

Given his druthers, he wouldn't choose at all, but there was so much evil here in addition to dysfunction. He was brought out here against his will and here he was going to fight.

The action reports sat on top of the stack.

His problem wasn't that this bloodbath the paperwork documented was unjustified. It was. He had no doubt it was wrong. His problem was that it wasn't wrong in the right way.

Militaries screwed up. In fact, most anything they did was a screw up. Reading back through history, it wasn't amazing that the U.S Army won battles. When it won, it had an huge industrial base advantage. It almost had to win. No. What was amazing was that it won at all. Most everything it did was seriously dysfunctional.

So, like all organizations, instead of working on flexibility and adaptiveness, it increased the documentation required. It may still screw up, but as long as the docs were right it was obvious that the screw up had to happen all along and thank goodness we have the docs now to prevent it from happening again.

The system validated that people always did the right thing. If something bad happened, docs changed the system so that the next people will still always do the right thing. That was the purpose of large systems of people that nobody wanted to admit. The people are never wrong for the job, it's just that the system hasn't been perfected enough. Maybe we need a new class.

So when he started this paper chase of figuring out how these orders to kill so many people came to pass, how he ended up here, it always ended up with one person.

Himself.

Somehow, Paul Newbury, or at least some simulacrum of Paul Newbury had been running the base all along, making the decisions and screwing things up royally.

It was deeply disturbing, not because he'd been framed, but because the paperwork never framed people. It had never worked like that.

The bureaucratic paperwork system was broken, and deep in his heart it made him very afraid.

He looked at his new-won prize. The light gleamed off the plastic.

"It creeps! It crawls! It strikes without warning!"

The lady was screaming on the front. Behind her, several official-looking people were also screaming.

Was screaming an option?

He rarely screamed. He'd been in pain and surprise, of course, many times extremely so. But as he got more experienced, it all seemed so repetitive, even the horror.

No. Screaming was not an option for him.

He picked up the most recent action report. He added the inventory movement summary.

He started through them again.

No, this would just lead to more frustration.

He placed them back. Without completely singling it out and putting it on the table, without committing, he searched the stack of paper in the chair next to him. He moved Gibb's SRB to the top.

Idly he flipped it open. It had been the first thing he had been interested in, of course. He'd already gone through it once.

Gibb had a very interesting career. Coming in with outstanding test scores, over time she had slowly ratcheted down. Her light dimmed.

The creative thinker became less creative. The decisive student became the nebulous leader. Options became threats. Opportunities became problems.

He wasn't sure if her career had done this to her or she'd just changed, deviated.

Whatever it was, it was a loss.

He watched the two of them, Gibb and Parsons, finish up in line. Gibb was holding court, looking around making pronouncements. Parsons was dutifully trailing along. No doubt her sharp mind was recording every jot and tittle.

He looked back to the chess set. He emptily toyed with the idea of pushing a pawn. Queen's Gambit Accepted was always difficult to play through. He was beginning to feel a little out of his depth.

Hearing his name, he looked up. They were both looking at him.

He nodded. He felt he had to do something or they'd be over, ruining both the game and the day's review.

Looking down to the game, he ground his teeth. These false orders were taxing his thinking, taking over, as much as he desired to work above the fray. Why was Gibb, always wanting to be in the spotlight, allowing such a thing to happen, somebody else taking credit? What supporting documents he could find of her culpability, whenever he could find them, were shabby.

Without looking back up, but wanting to, he realized that Parsons didn't know. She'd stand there alongside her boss, maybe for years, soaking up this terrible leadership and buying into a world that never existed.

Bad apples ruin good ones.

It was not just some paperwork problem in the cloud. Real people were suffering directly in front of him.

Twenty years from now he'd be gone but the impact on Parsons would still be there.

Motherfuck if this wasn't a job for an XO.

He was the XO.

He finally looked up. He had lost.

He waved them over.

"Parsons," he said as they approached carrying their takeout dinner, "I just read your after-action report. That was a nice piece of work the other day."

She frowned.

"Sir? Ma'am?"

"I haven't reviewed it with her yet, Newbury. Let's just say I found it creative, perhaps excessively so. Parsons, we'll talk later."

"Yes ma'am."

"It's just a difference of opinion, Parsons," he said, "no worries."

Gibb interrupted.

"Not at all. We are in complete agreement."

The girl was obviously confused. Did her two bosses agree that she'd done a good job or not? Paul tried to patch it up.

"The Colonel's right, obviously. I'm still mostly civilian. I'm working on it. Bear with me."

Relief.

"Yes Sir."

"You can leave, Parsons."

She looked to Gibb for approval as he continued.

"XO business. Above your pay grade. Now beat it."

"Ma'am?"

Gibb looked at her watch.

"1100 hours tomorrow morning at the gate. Remember, civilian clothes only."

She clicked her heels.

"Ma'am. Sir."

As soon as she was out of earshot he addressed Gibb.

"How in the hell could I have been issuing orders at this base six months ago when I only just got here?"

Gibb darkened.

"Ma'am," he finished. God, that woman was pedantic.

"I don't know. We started receiving information about eight months back."

"Didn't you question what was going on?"

"Immediately and forcefully. I was told it was over my pay grade and I was given secret orders that were clear and unambivalent. They're in my safe."

"But I wasn't even here. I didn't exist here."

"Frankly I didn't know if you were even alive or not. My guess was that you had left and they were using your identity as a cutout, a fake, much the same as we have inflatable tanks and radars. The enemy expected a commander, so you became the commander. We had quarters, uniforms, daily logs, doctor visits, and every other possible proof of Paul Newbury that we could create. I never thought you'd actually show up."

"What happened to the last XO?"

"Disneyland, like I said. He thought he could spend time with the experiment on his own terms. It was undocumented and out of bounds."

"So he went crazy, attacked people?"

"Worse. Since he did it on his own, I was the one that found him."

"In his quarters?" he thought of the gear back in the satchel in his room. By the table.

Suddenly he didn't want to look at her.

"I found him in the core at 0231 hours when he missed a security drill and I had to fill in. He was coding something. We never could tell. He was nude. He was painted head-to-toe in blue and red. Somehow he'd made a spear out of the wooden dowels we use in the closets."

She stopped. She waited.

He finally looked.

"I shot him. It didn't kill him, so I shot him again."

"Did he attack?"

"I shot him. Let's leave it at that."

Oddly, none of this had been mentioned in the paperwork he had been reviewing.

He put the chess set away. The game was lost. His concentration was lost.

"I'll be taking over records management from here on out."

"The hell you will."

"You have no choice."

"I'll throw you in irons, put you in the box."

"I suspect you will. I'm doing it anyway."

"I don't think you're seeing it, Gibb."

"Too much for my puny brain?"

"This has nothing to do with you personally. This is a professional issue only."

"I've been doing this for years. Just how long again have you been back for?"

"Perhaps if I could show you using actual files...."

"Sure, go down to records and start pulling things. You'll find that you can't get very far without my signed orders. In fact, I believe they're under orders to arrest you if you even try."

"That's a nice move. That's what I would do."

She smiled her wolf smile.

Check.

He pulled Gibb's SRB from the chair and plopped it down on the table.

"How'd you get that:? They weren't supposed to ..."

"And they didn't. I'm sure if I had showed up during normal hours, they would have arrested me."

"But you didn't."

"Because I didn't have to. I anticipated that move. I went in the middle of the night. And with...."

"And with the XO keys and run of the base, you can get anywhere you want to."

And mate.

"As I should. Exactly. Now, listen, this is what we're going to do."

She sat down. He wasn't sure whether she was going to spit on him, stab him, or bite him. He didn't care which.

He kept going.

"I will be managing records work on the base, as I said. That's after all part of my job."

"Not if I …"

"In fact, according to all this documentation, I've already been doing so."

She began again but he ran over her.

"Relax. This is not about control. We, you and I, have a severe problem here. All this fakery and misdirection is fine, but I'm not clear after investigating what the hell is actually going on here."

"Look around. That's what's going on."

"I mean how it all works. The system's a mess. There's no consistency and the linkages are all wrong. I'm only trying to do my job better. We need a grip on things. You need a grip on things if any of us are ever going to do our job effectively."

"And that's …."

"That's all," he finished for her. "You want that. You want to do a better job or not?"

She nodded.

"Then get the hell out of my way and let me get back to work."

It was the first time he'd ever seen her confused. She looked away, as if to get up, then back to him as if there were something there.

He finished.

"Ma'am."

She shuffled off. He thought he heard her talking to herself.

Eventually Paul also left the cafeteria, left his meal half-eaten. He took the thing with him. He still wouldn't look at it. He'd seen already the damage sensory input could cause. He'd felt it.

Nope. Not watching. He made that decision.

You take your victories where you find them.

He was bothered enough by what he'd seen already, the deals he'd made, his plans for the next few days.

Space monsters weren't that bad, even real ones.

When you finally meet the devil, he always turned out to be much better and much worse than you could possibly imagine.

He whistled a bit, trying to bolster his spirits. The song died out quickly. He continued regardless.

5.12

For Immediate Release

Assault Team Sees Man 'Fly Away'

Bergville, KY, Members of a special tactics and weapons counter-terrorism unit testified in an open Congressional hearing yesterday that they witnessed a wanted Bergville man 'fly away' two years ago.

The hearing was a follow-up to the long-ago 2023 House Oversight subcommittee on UAP Investigation. In that hearing, retired intelligence officer Maj. David Grusch testified that as a result of being tasked to investigate all UAP-related programs, his conclusion was the United States had both been aware of, engaged with, and had captured, intelligent beings previously unknown to mankind. He further testified under oath that the U.S. likely has been aware of "non-human" activity since the 1930s.

Secret Services agents conducted an early-morning raid on a farm just outside Bergville, according to testimony. Encountering a lone man sitting on a second-story porch, the man "flew away" as they attempted to apprehend him.

"We assumed that there was some new form of Jet-pack in use," agent John Walker said, "but after filing the report and doing the forensics, we couldn't explain how he left the site."

Other witnesses testified to other unusual cases

involving law enforcement and suspects. On one occasion a woman appeared to walk through a brick wall. On another, a room containing only a baby caused officers to fall asleep, waking almost an hour later with the baby missing.

"This is becoming the law enforcement version of Project Blue book and the big UAP flap back in the day," Congressperson Daniel Jack said in a telephone interview, "Like those, this kind of thing most likely has always gone on and modern telemetry is just making it harder to ignore. We need to figure out what to do about it."

Since the 1940s law enforcement has famously been involved in UAP stories, professor DJ Howards, author of "Good Cop, Dumb Cop" explained in a recent telephone interview, "and whenever it got out, it always ruined the careers of those involved. By the 1950s we can see evidence of LE agencies, just like other military and intelligence agencies, actively suppressing reports and data. There's no conspiracy. Things like this just make them look stupid. People don't like to look stupid. Agencies don't like to look stupid, so they don't do it. When's the last time you saw a press conference where they said they didn't know something, or they did something they admit was stupid?"

Howard explained that modern media, with demons, angels, aliens, flying saucers, and magic has created a pre-existing narrative that such stories fit into. People aren't comfortable experiencing something they don't understand and can't reproduce, so the witnesses or the reporters talking to the witnesses stick the experience into one of these preexisting myths. It's the only way the information can be shared for public consumption. Others then attack the myths instead of the experience, creating much ridicule and shame. The initial observation gets lost.

"The word 'alien' doesn't mean what we think it does," he said, "it's not people from another planet, people from Mexico. It's just things we experience that we have no reference for. Non-reproducible intermittent phenomenon is an extremely tough concept for many."

"We're making a mistake assuming that alien things will appear alien," he said, "truly alien things won't appear like anything at all to us. You ask a dog to look at a clock. The dog doesn't bark at it. It's not scary or stupid. It's just something that's always been there in its stimulus range (and out of it) but it doesn't mean anything. The dog suddenly doesn't start wondering how to build clocks. That's the true meaning of the word 'alien'."

Hearings will continue until Friday.

# # #

5.13

Lions

"Grab it or get out of the way," Sam told Deb, "Either way, that stocking cap's gotta go."

He shot a look at the older lady across the mostly-empty bin. She had her eye on the stocking cap. She was slumped over. She had palsy. She was also closer to the pure wool stocking cap than he was.

And she had quick hands.

They were at the secondhand goods store. It was going out of business. It was crowded.

"Why are we competing with people we don't know for things we don't want?"

Deb grabbed the hat anyway. Already in her basket were men's socks and children's party balloons. She put the hat firmly in the back.

"Because they're on sale, Deb, that's why. If we're going to spend time out in the woods on your scheme, we're going to need extra clothes, and lots of them. As long as they fit, doesn't matter what they are."

He noticed the items in her basket.

"Not sure we need balloons or a badminton set."

"They were on sale."

"Don't you want to prepare for the next step, continue your big master plan? The outdoor part?"

"No. The plan won't work." She looked around. She was worried about something.

He noticed the size of the crowd. They were talking too much.

"You're right. We should be careful of what we say."

She pulled him over to the side, out of the endless river of shuffling bargain hunters.

"I don't see why we need to be in commercial combat over used items of such a bland nature," she crinkled her nose, "Why not just buy bulk fabric?"

"What's the difference? Let's just take advantage of the situation we have here. We can always put things together in new ways. It might even be fun."

He did not want to start a fashion discussion with Deb.

"Especially with the weaklings," Deb stared at the older lady from earlier. The lady pretended to ignore them. "There's too many people. We will end up competing for subpar items. This preparation work requires consideration. We should have a discussion as we go along, not a free-for-all."

"You might have a point. Let me check. Perhaps there's another shop nearby. Less crowded."

As he left, Deb looked at the bin in front of her. She poked at a couple of items as if expecting them to move.

"Excuse me," Sam said to the obviously over-worked lady trying to restock before the shelves were destroyed again, "are there any other secondhand stores around?"

"Hmmm," she rubbed her chin.

"No sir. Not until Hattersfield and that's about ten miles past the secret government base."

"There's a secret government base?"

"Yup. MELLO, The one we don't talk about. Say, if you or the missus are looking for work. I think they have a job fair coming up. It's good pay."

"Yes, yes," Sam picked up the thread, "I had forgotten the name, but we're here for the work. We're looking for interview clothes, actually."

"Try aisle seven. Good luck!"

She went back to stocking.

"Nope," he said, returning. He started looking through the same bin she had been poking at before he remembered he was directed to go somewhere else, "Follow me."

"I want you to tell me what happened to the girl the other day," Deb joined him at aisle seven as Sam tried to look interested in thirty-year-old suits.

"Be specific. I want you to tell me exactly what happened."

Sam shot back.

"I want you to tell me why you just announced that you don't want to continue on your own plan."

"I feel things have changed. It's not going to work anymore."

"You feel."

"I don't feel. I see. I see that things have changed."

"Once again: I don't understand you, but I believe you."

"So what happened?"

"The other day? Unlike you, I didn't see anything. I don't see things. I feel very confused about how weird it all was. You may be the only one able to make your way around in all of this craziness."

"You are broken. We need to fix you."

"That was very helpful. Nice chat. I'm glad we did this."

He walked off, mumbling.

He eventually found himself next to the entrance with his back to the door, looking through a bin of chemical lights. They might come in handy no matter what they ended up doing.

He heard rather than saw the two women come in directly behind him.

"Parsons, we're looking for two twenty-somethings, a man and a woman. We find them, we hand them off to another team. I wanted to take this chance to talk to you about your recent performance."

"Yes ma'am."

"But not here."

"Yes ma'am."

"And watch what you say, it's crowded…"

The voices faded into the general miasma of greedy, slow-moving, hypnotized shoppers.

This was trouble.

He used the reflections in the store to look at them as much as possible as they blended in.

They were browsing, but they really weren't really shopping for anything. Instead, they were looking up every now and then to check out the crowd.

Fortunately, with the going out of business sale, the place was packed. It would be difficult.

He watched the two lock into a rigid search grid, front-to-back, then right-to-left.

With the size of this crowd and the pair's almost clock-like progress, he thought it was a simple math problem to stay opposite them in the store. Using reflections as a cross-check, it shouldn't be too hard to stay out of sight.

It was possible.

For a while.

They'd need to wrap up the shopping fairly quickly, though.

Main problem: Debian.

His stomach sunk.

Getting her to do anything on a good day was like giving a cat a bath using a shop-vac.

She seemed to get into moods, either locked into some cockeyed plan she wouldn't give up or wanting to do the opposite thing that he wanted to do.

Today looked like mood two, opposite day.

Joining her again, he pointed to a sign on the wall.

Help Wanted.

"There you go, Deb. Maybe we could work here while figuring out what to do next."

"I picked this for you to wear."

She held up a suit. It did not have clowns or flashing lights.

It was just a suit. It was an old suit. She had picked out a suit.

Debian Newbury.

For him.

Wow, opposite day was getting far out of hand this week. He thought about checking her for a fever, but she would probably hit him.

So he went in the changing room.

She waited.

"I am not very impressed yet," she called out to the curtain, "I'm waiting to be impressed."

Sam came out in a dark, hooded, all-weather jacket.

"I found this while I was in there."

"It's a jacket. It's not a suit."

"It's more than a jacket."

"It's a black jacket. Is there more than that?"

He opened it up, revealing several layers and many zippers.

"See? You think it's just a jacket, but this actually has four different interchangeable layers. It allows for thousands of different configurations."

"16."

"16?"

"Sixteen combinations. Four layers, each with two possibilities, off or on. 2^4=16. A nibble. That's not even a hundred combinations."

"You're always entertaining, Deb."

"And you're not wearing the suit I gave you."

"Each layer?" He moved his hand up and down, as if selling the suit on an infomercial, "Check out the double-stitching, the breathable fabric. Notice that each layer is reversible. Each layer can either not be worn or worn. If worn, there are two possible configurations, in any order. Four layers."

"So?"

"The state space for each position is all of the remaining layers. It's 9C4."

He assumed the gloating look of an old man who had just won \$1.50 at Pinochle in a retirement home.

"Would you like to do that math?"

"It's not nine C four, but the answer you're looking for is 126."

"Point made. I'm buying this jacket."

"Asshole," she said to the curtain as he went back in to try on the suit she'd given him and it was her turn to walk away muttering to herself about how he was doing the problem all wrong, and how a hundred was nowhere near a thousand.

"30," she said, loud enough for nearby shoppers to notice.

Laughing and still enjoying his victory, he came out minutes later holding the suit. He bumped into somebody.

"Excuse me,"

He looked. He looked again.

"Do I know you?"

The lady smiled. Sam thought she had very clear eyes.

"Guess I just have one of those faces."

The woman moved on, but Sam was pretty sure she'd blushed. He was also pretty sure he'd seen her recently.

He found Deb over in one of the far corners deeply involved. She was shuffling items around in a deep bin. It was a large box of furry things. In her basket were several large beach towels, the kind that had beer cans, dogs, rock bands, or naked ladies on them.

"What are you looking at?"

She didn't respond. She was absorbed in sorting through whatever it was. He read the sign.

"Used wigs and toupees: \$5."

"I'm going to make some pillows," she finally said, pulling out a bright red wig and sticking it in the basket, "You had a good idea that we could combine things into new things."

Sam remembered that silence was golden. He became very interested in carefully reading all the signage nearby.

When she finally finished, her basket looked like a bunch of tribbles just returning from Spring Break. He said, "So how much money do we have left?"

"Not a lot. We need to do something."

"It can't be very public. We're already doing too much, out and about, mingling. This is not very low profile. We don't have the gang anymore to shield us."

"I told you already that I could decode the Beale Treasure messages…"

"No. We are not going to go digging for buried treasure, even if you know where it is. That's out of the question. No more underground. We need to find something else."

"Our problem has an easy answer. The answer is you. What happened with the girl? What did you do? Can't you just give it another shot?"

"I don't want to have this conversation, Debian."

"Please."

Please? That was also new.

Oh well.

He took a deep breath. He hummed quietly, trying to look as if he were performing magic. He closed his eyes. He rubbed his head deep in pretend magic thought. It was a mannerism he'd seen a mentalist do one night in Vegas.

Suddenly he popped his eyes back open, as if overtaken by psychic surprise.

"I have a feeling. I sense there are two dangerous people here. We're going to have to make our escape. There is danger."

He moved his arms about slowly as if feeling something invisible in the air.

"The feeling is strong."

Deb looked around as if expecting to see little sparkling stars orbiting his head or dancing unicorns.

Sam had no idea what she expected.

There were a hundred people here.

"How did you know that?" she lowered her voice, "Can you feel the other people's feelings?"

"I know that because I heard the two talking as they came in the door. I just bumped into one of them, ok?"

She made a sad face. It was almost a pout. Could Deb pout? What the hell was going on in the universe?

He continued.

"My super magic powers says let's get the hell out of here. So lay off."

She started moving her head around, trying to see them. Sam thought she looked like a baby playing peek-a-boo. Yikes. Pretty soon everybody was going to notice this barnyard chicken-like thing she was doing with her head bobbing about.

Yikes.

"I think I see them too."

"Can you please not look directly. Please. Can you stop that."

"Doesn't matter."

"Why."

"Because they've stopped looking."

"Great."

"Now they're just staking out the exits."

"Awful."

She stopped her terrible gawking.

"But it's probably the maximal search pattern. With only one entrance, they can wait for people to come to them."

"I'm impressed," he said.

"You should be in control of all this. With your thing."

"Oh my god, girl. You don't seem to be able to move past this thing, this conviction of yours."

"I don't know what to do. Without your help, I can't decide on what's next."

Sam looked left and right.

"Then I'll decide for us."

He thought she was going to laugh at him.

"What kinds of decisions could you possibly make on your own?"

He started to get angry. She continued.

"I'm not trying to insult you, Samuel. I'm just saying that you can't see where you are, right?"

Samuel?

She pointed to all the people.

"You're like the rest of these."

"I'll deal with that later. For now, I have an assignment for you. I want you to find some way of sneaking out the back door. I'll catch up with you in the alley later."

"Without paying?"

"Give me half the money,"

He took it.

"I'll leave a big tip. It'll all work out. Okay?"

"Why?"

"Because I'm going to go over there and talk to our two new friends, that's why."

He walked away with purpose and calm. He didn't dare look back.

"Either of you have the time?"

Sam was wearing his best "Howdy stranger" face.

Both of the women looked at their watch.

No cell phones. Interesting.

"4:17," the younger lady said, the one he knew from somewhere. He realized that it was the woman he'd just bumped into.

"Thank you. Lost my cell. Need to catch the bus."

He hoped there was a bus. The town had to have some kind of bus.

The older lady smiled at him.

"You know, I think I've seen you around, how about you?"

She looked at her younger partner, trying to remember.

"Bea?"

The younger lady cut her eyes at the older lady. Sam saw some fear or anger there. But it was only for a second.

"I don't know." Now the younger one took a second for a lookup, "Hilda. I saw him earlier near the changing station. He certainly looks familiar."

Sam would bet that neither one had ever used the other's first name until just now.

"Now I know!" the older one said, "You were in town the day of that big car accident, weren't you?"

Sam saw the younger lady positively struggling to control her surprise.

He tried to help. He felt sorry for her.

"Maybe. Seems like I heard something about a fender-bender," he looked to the older lady, "I don't recall you, though."

He looked again at the younger woman.

Travel Agency. It came to him. That's where he'd seen her. She was coming out of the travel agency, shaking her head. That day. He remembered feeling guilty for some reason about it.

Acting on instinct, he kept this to himself.

The older lady patted him. She was the loving grandma, although she couldn't have been more than 45.

"I guess it's true what they say. It's a small world after all, isn't it?"

Sam was feeling uneasy but couldn't tell why. He was interested in this feeling so he thought he would play with it.

"You two must be from MELLO," he said, using the new word he'd heard while watching them for a reaction, "I hear they have job openings."

"I don't know if that would be such a good idea," the younger lady said. She looked clearly worried that he might keep asking.

"Don't sell the man short now, Bea. We regularly hire groundskeepers. What sorts of skills do you have?"

The younger lady was now visibly disturbed.

"Oh heck, it's a lot of technical nonsense, ma'am, unless you know computer science."

"That's what I got my PhD in. Try me. I'll do my best to keep up."

Sam's face turned crimson.

"Well, the usual. NNs, LLMs, MDLs, quantum cryptography, discrete determinate non-linguistic semantics, reverse-engineering ICs, I advanced number wheel based posit standards by ...""

She held her hand up.

"That's enough. If you know half of that I'm interested. Where'd you study?"

"Freedom University."

"You don't say! Paul Newbury."

"How'd you know?"

"You're going to love this," she said, dodging his question, "Can you meet me at the gate tomorrow morning, say around nine?"

Sam smiled although he felt deeply like he'd just lost something important.

"Deal."

They shook.

He left. He tried to still look interested in shopping. He tried to figure out what just happened. It was good.

He thought it was good.

The two women left the store a little while later, each with a bag of things they didn't want.

"Picking up Featherstone was a nice move," Gibb said.

"Thank you, ma'am."

"I'm inclined not to write you up for failure on the mission the other day. You were being observed the entire time, of course."

"Thank you ma'am."

Gibb studied her eyes closely.

"I'll use Featherstone to leverage Newbury. The Colonel seems to have taken quite the liking to you."

"Yes ma'am."

"But that's the last freebie you get, Parsons."

"Yes ma'am."

"I may have some more unpleasant work for you, and it's likely to involve the Colonel."

"Yes ma'am."

"Is that going to be a problem?"

"No ma'am," Parson said without hesitation.

On the other side of the store, Debian Newbury waited in silence by the dumpster. From time to time she stamped her feet back and forth.

Sam joined her. They headed in the opposite direction.

"I believe that I'm going to need you near me for at least the next few days," he told her, "and you're not going to be able to be there."

Deb explained to Sam using perfect logic why this was the dumbest move she'd seen him make so far, and she'd seen a lot of dumb moves from him.

Sam was quiet.

Eventually, Debian was too.

5.14

Worrying On The Mountain

"He knows something's wrong," Sam said as they hid in the woods watching the signal house on top of the mountain.

The faded orange truck had been there an hour. During the days, they had replaced everything as it was and took their spot in the woods. About an hour after getting back from town, the man had shown up.

"He knows nothing," Deb replied, "everything is perfect. He's just no good at his job."

"You want to talk about it," he finally said.

"There's nothing to talk about."

"You're afraid."

"I fear no man."

"Thank you, Conan the Destroyer."

"I'm certainly not afraid of getting into MELLO, finding Dad."

He narrowed his eyes and studied her, wondering how far to push it.

"You're afraid of your dad."

"That man cannot hurt me again. I won't allow it."

"Did he ever hurt you?"

"Well no," she looked around the woods as if wanting to run off, "why haven't you ever dated? Don't tell me it was studying."

He squirmed.

"It was too easy."

"Okay, I'll believe you were studying."

"He knows we're here."

She kicked a rock, "maybe so, but even if he suspects there are kids or somebody around, he won't do anything."

Sam stared at the truck as if the truck had answers.

"Let's just say nobody ever turned me down. I ended up hurting a lot of people. But don't think for a minute I'm letting you change the subject."

"What subject."

"Exactly. You don't want to find your dad."

"How can you say that? The only thing I've been doing since this all started was trying to confront my dad."

"Sure, you'll confront him, you'll catch him, you'll interrogate him, you'll turn him over to authorities." Now it was his turn to kick the same rock, "Did I miss any euphemisms?"

"You are being stupid again."

"But what you don't want to do, what you can't do for some reason? Talk to your dad."

"You're full of shit."

"Maybe. But he knows we're here."

It took two more hours. He finally left.

They packed their stuff back into the shack, made dinner, and went to sleep.

Neither one said anything.

The next morning Sam took off in his new suit while Deb pretended to sleep and waited for him to leave.

5.15

Welcoming Sam

"Fourteen," Parsons said, joining Paul staring out over the lake, "There have been fourteen terminal civilian incidents since the facility was constructed."

Paul looked over Victory Lake, the manmade lake in the back of MELLO that fed the reactors. He was not ignoring her, but he didn't feel like looking at her, either.

"Just say killed, Parsons. We killed people."

"TCIs, sir, Terminal Civilian Incidents. Operational Security Requirements. What else could we do? The land is clearly posted."

"We could have not tried to weaponize things so fast, that's what. Lethal force protecting a dangerous weapon is justified. Lethal force protecting the things we're working on? It's both too much and too little at the same time."

"Perhaps if Colonel Gibb could be retired, transferred, promoted. If she left, we could change our posture, sir."

"I'm still not sure if Gibb is an obstacle or a tool. Maybe we can ask her. Here she comes."

He squinted.

"Who's that with her?"

"I believe it is Samuel Featherstone."

"I know Sam."

"He wanted a job."

"Joe was right," he said, finally looking at Parsons, "It wasn't going to be long."

"Tell me," he continued, still watching them come over, "When you started your career, did you ever think it would get so complicated?"

"No sir. You?"

"At first, no. I just got to kill people and blow up things. Life was good then, simple. I started mastering the career and diving deep on computational dynamics, applied philosophy, and information warfare."

"Ruined it for you?"

"At first? No. But it did eventually. And it didn't stop with just ruining my career."

He rummaged around in his mind, unable to continue. Parsons was worried.

"Sir?"

"Don't let that happen to you, Parsons. That's all."

They didn't speak again for the five minutes it took Gibb and Sam to arrive.

When they got there, Paul stuck his hand out.

"Sam Featherstone. It's truly good to see you, son."

Sam shook it vigorously.

"Professor Newbury."

Sam cocked his head, noticing Paul's uniform and unsure of what name to use for his former teacher.

"No, Sam, it's Colonel Newbury now."

"I see that."

"New job. I felt it was time to try something different."

Inside his mind, Paul kept repeating, wishing he could make it true: Please don't mention Deb. Please don't mention Deb. Please don't mention Deb.

Paul could see the young man struggle to start a conversational rhythm.

"Me too, er, Colonel. They say everything's always changing. I guess they're right."

"That's true, Sam," he finished the handshake just a few seconds too long, "Although sometimes I would like to find this 'they' that are always saying these things."

Winked.

"Can't never seem to find them," Sam's smile turned up, happy for the small talk.

"Sam, I thought you already had a job."

"I did," he said, "There were personality conflicts."

"I can't wait to hear all about it," Gibb smiled. It was a smile with no teeth. "We're going to have a great time talking about your work and life history. It'll be fun."

"Parsons and I were just talking shop," he said to Gibb.

"That's what I know. You two were talking about security incidents," she seemed especially proud to know things she wasn't supposed to, "why don't you tell us what happened during out last TCI."

Parsons looked at Sam but spoke to Gibb.

"Ma'am. I don't think Featherstone's been cleared."

"Relax, Parsons," Gibb said. Her smile stayed in place like a clown's smile on a funhouse entrance, "There's nobody here but us chickens."

Now Parsons looked at Paul for help.

He looked back to the lake. Unable.

"But ma'am," Parsons continued.

"I insist, Parsons," Gibb said, "I insist."

Paul gave a quick nod to release Parsons. He hoped Gibb hadn't seen it but he was sure she had.

The younger woman assumed Parade Rest. She spoke, staring straight ahead.

"April 15th. 1715 hours. A family of four, two males and two females, were observed setting up a campsite on the far side of Victory Lake."

She stopped, as if hoping that would be all.

"Go on, Parsons," Gibb said.

Looking uncomfortable.

"An undercover team was sent to warn them off. The team posed as park rangers. The adult male and female indicated that this was their traditional family land going back seven generations. They had been promised camping rights."

"And?" Gibb seemed excited, teased, waiting for the next words.

"And later that night a team was sent over to remove the family and any evidence they had been there. It was a TCI."

She stopped again, looking back and forth between her two bosses. Neither demanded that she continue.

So she stopped. She relaxed her posture and assumed a more civilian stance. Her shoulders were noticeably lower than before. Wrinkles were visible around her eyes.

Parsons no longer consisted of right angles.

"I'm not sure what the point of that was," Paul said to nobody in particular, "Say, Sam, what kind of job were you looking for?"

"Groundskeeping?"

Sam looked at Gibb.

"Although she did say something about computers."

"Mr. Featherstone looks extremely qualified," Gibb had decided to ignore Paul's jab. "A former student of yours, isn't he?"

"That's correct."

"And he worked with your daughter. I believe her name is Debian?"

"I've never seen the two work together. Debian doesn't get out much."

"I take it there's no swimming in the lake," Sam said, "what with the TCIs and all."

"There are a lot of rules, young man. A lot of rules. We're going to go over every one of them until you know them by heart."

"So what happens if you break the rules?"

Parsons took that one, "I think you're going to find that this becomes a much more difficult situation than 'personality conflicts'."

Paul looked down briefly, ashamed.

"I'm sorry, Sam."

They heard the klaxon sound from the building, startling them from their conversation.

About a dozen armed men appeared that were previously in hiding and began a security sweep.

Paul saw Sam's concern.

"You'll get used to it. Security drills. Like the monthly bus to town, the place has a certain rhythm and mood to it. You might even find it pleasant."

Paul's words were happy. His face was sad.

"Eventually."

Sam took it all in stride.

"If you say so. Fortunately, it's not too far to town to walk. I love a good walk. It energizes the soul."

Paul's mood went down another level.

"We don't get out much," Gibb said, "Gate privileges and town passes have to be earned. You'll get used to it all in time."

Sam looked at Parsons.

"I know I've seen some of the facility people around town more than once recently."

"Sam, let's get you settled in," Paul looked back to Gibb. Could he remove the boy from this torture?

"I assume he's one of our new groundskeepers, then?"

"Not at all," she said, "My plan was to bring him inside, make him my personal assistant."

She patted Sam's shoulder. He was a horse she'd just bought.

"I'm going to keep you close by."

Parsons perked up.

"Ma'am, security protocol prevents …"

Gibb stopped her.

"Protocols have just been overridden."

Gibb dared Paul to say something.

"Any questions, Parsons?"

"No ma'am."

Paul had questions. Too many.

"Is this the last of our, um, new hires for a while?"

"Not at all. I've got another special opening that I'm saving for just the right person."

They all knew what she meant.

Whatever you called it, Sam and Debian were going to be taken hostage. Gibb was going to be the jailer.

There was a bit of awkwardness as the implications sank in.

"But, we have a world-class cafeteria," Parsons said.

Everybody suddenly found Parsons very interesting.

"Taco Tuesdays is to die for. Mostly it's international fusion. They make this risotto …"

She stopped, realizing she was the center of attention.

Parsons cleared her throat and addressed each of her supervisors.

"Sir. Ma'am."

There was a thump-thump of flashbangs nearby.

"The sound of lunch?" Sam said.

"Grenades, Sam. They do that a lot, but like everything else, you'll get used to it."

Paul felt the lie hang uneasily on his lips.

He couldn't live with that.

"If we're going to be honest, let's be honest," he said to the others, "Sam, this is a secret military base. I'm not saying we're prisoners, but we're not leaving."

"But I'm just a groundskeeper," he looked at Gibb, "I can be just a groundskeeper, right? I don't need any special attention."

"Too late, Featherstone."

Gibb watched Sam closely for a reaction.

He kicked the dirt. Paul watched Sam shake his head in disgust.

"In the spirit of openness, I have a problem with joining organizations," he said.

"Not being able to commit?"

"Leaving. I keep joining organizations I can't leave."

No.

The thought came as clear and loud inside Paul as if it were the voice of God.

No.

It had to stop sometime.

"No ma'am," Paul said and all activity stopped in the conversation. They looked at him.

"Colonel Gibb. This is unacceptable," he continued, "I find no justification for your actions under any military standards or precedence that I'm aware of."

Gibb turned to him directly.

"Is that insubordination?"

"No ma'am. That's my resignation. You have the tender of my commission. I'd appreciate it if you'd let me finish...."

Gibb was incensed.

"You. An hour. Report to my quarters in an hour."

She looked all of them over.

"Alone."

They watched her leave, each of them wondering what their future might hold.

Parsons finally spoke.

"I wonder who the new XO will be."

"What's an XO?" Sam asked.

"I think I'm looking at her. Congratulations, Parsons."

"You have to be kidding me. Can I turn it down?"

"What do you think? Do you think I had much of a choice? I was happy with a career teaching amicable lug nuts like this one."

He nodded to Sam.

"Thanks prof."

"You're welcome, Sam. So, it looks like I have an hour. Anybody have any options or ideas?"

"You could beg forgiveness," Parsons said.

"Not going to happen. Sam?"

"Unless boss lady really likes card tricks, I'm drawing a blank."

"You know, maybe she had a point. I could start a mutiny."

"I am not resigning my position or engaging in a mutiny, Paul."

He noticed her use of his first name. The implications were clear.

"Nor would I want you to. This is my hand to play out one way or another, not either of yours."

"I want to stay positive," Sam said, "But this day is not at all turning out like I had thought."

"Tell me about it," Parsons said, "I could use a vacation."

For some reason she thought of Alaska. And a bear.

"The military is just a machine," he said, "a tool, like a computer. It works according to rules, as Gibb loves to remind us."

"One day I'd like to know what these rules are, Paul. My commanders keep explaining them, but each time they explain it to me, it's always different."

"You might be right, Bea," he used her first name, "I'm just not sure I want to take that step."

"How can I be right, I didn't even say anything."

"Who's your commander now, right now?"

"Gibb."

"Your direct commander."

"You, sir, at least for another hour."

"And if I were to institute charges against Gibb, instead of resigning?"

"Well, sir, I suppose there would be some process for that."

"And your job would require you to listen to me, in the absence of a JAG, to conduct that process. Instead of Gibb, I mean."

"He's good," Sam said.

"I'm beginning to see where the Colonel's going," Parsons said.

"And?"

"And frankly I like it."

"It's settled, then."

Both Newbury and Parsons assumed a much more military posture.

"Major Parsons. You are ordered to detain Colonel Gibb immediately. Use force if necessary, up to and including deadly force. She's to be held in her quarters without communication until further notice. Let's stop her from making this command even more of a sick, rabid, disgraceful joke than it already is."

Parsons said each word with the kind of finality one might if they were getting married.

"Yes. Sir."

She strode away. Her walk was deliberate and focused. She had a hand on her sidearm.

Watching her go, Sam said, "I guess you don't need any new groundskeepers?"

"We need a lot, Sam, but you should probably leave. This is your time. I'm going to offer you what they offered me. I can walk you to the gate right now. It'll be like you never came."

"I'm not going anywhere," he replied, "I think you, of all people, know that. You probably can guess that I have a lot of questions…"

Paul shushed him by pointing his finger to the sky.

Sam understood.

"So, there's more technical work I can do."

"There is," he pointed to the building, "Let's get you through orientation first. We're going to get this project back on track if it's the last thing we do."

He thought again of their security posture and the TCIs.

They both started walking, but Paul stopped after just a couple of steps.

"Last chance, Sam. You can walk out now. You need to know that none of us may make it out of here alive."

Sam's perpetual smile dimmed.

"I expected no different. Let's roll."

5.16

Rockstar Rehab

Paul Newbury looked like a rock star headed toward rehab, not the leader of some secret facility.

Sam didn't know if that was going to make screwing the man over easier or harder.

He'd finally made it to see his old teacher after two full days of "Initial Orientation". "Initial Orientation" consisted of being locked in a room while CAI (Computer-Assisted Instruction) bots drilled him over and over again on all the things he couldn't do.

He left with an access badge, but not much else. He was on his way to the quartermaster, but thought it'd be wise to first stop by, maybe say hello, get a better grip on where Paul's emotional leverage points were. Everybody had them.

He remember his teacher fondly. His memory was nothing like this.

The door was unlocked, so he entered.

It was awful.

The furniture was cheap hand-me-downs for a cheap, hand-me-down hotel. There was a small, round, fake wooden table at the foot of a small, lumpy hotel bed. There was a faint whiff of antiseptic.

The first thing he noticed was how perfect Paul's uniforms were. There were about a half-dozen, all pressed and pristine in plastic dry-cleaning bag hanging in a claustrophobic mirror-walled closet.

Then he saw Paul. His pants were halfway down, his underwear still on. He was lying on the cold, tiny little cheap-ass tiles hotels put around their sinks and bathrooms. There was a leather satchel under the sink, wires hanging out. A pot of coffee was mostly empty. A mostly empty bottle of scotch stood next to it. A single Styrofoam coffee cup was on the paper alongside a paper notepad and pencil.

As he entered and shut the door behind him, he saw that the notepad was full of madman scribbles.

Unconscious Paul lay shivering.

Sam ran over and knelt. Pulse strong. Beady sweat. He shook him.

"Professor Newbury?"

The eyes popped open. The shivering stopped.

Sam watched as his breathing steadied.

After a dozen or so breaths, still not looking, "Sam? Is that you?"

Now he looked at Sam. Sam thought his old teacher was expecting an angry bear or some other monster.

"It's me. Here we go."

He helped him get into a sitting position. All the time he looked at Sam as if they hadn't just seen each other two days ago.

"Why are you here, Sam?"

"You hired me. Remember? What have you been doing here?"

Paul slapped himself. It wasn't the "oh gee I forgot my umbrella" type of slap. No. He slapped the living shit out of his face. Did it again.

Sam was going to physically restrain him but he stopped himself then looked as if for the first time seeing him.

"Oh yeah. I remember."

Sam thought Paul sounded more than just a little bit drunk.

"Let's see," Paul closed his eyes as if remembering. His head slumped. Was he asleep?

His head popped back up.

""You were at EigenCorp, weren't you?"

"I was. I worked with your daughter there."

"Debian. How is Debian doing?"

Hmm. That was a hell of a question, he thought.

"She's concerned about you."

Paul looked wistfully off, as if seeing Deb in the shower. One of his eyelids began drooping.

"I'm also worried. Should I call a doctor?"

"Bah. Nothing they can do for me, Sam," his eye stopped drooping, "might as well call a witch doctor or hold a prayer meeting. I just need a little time, that's all."

Paul fell completely over. He gently began snoring.

Startled, Sam reviewed his options.

There was no way this was going to look okay for him. He may be witnessing this man's death. A death without answers could kill Deb, he knew. He had to keep her alive. Anything it took.

He shook him gingerly.

"Professor?"

"Yeah yeah yeah okay yeah okay…"

The man thrashed around, shook himself awake, then looked at Sam as if nothing had happened.

"Sam. Good to see you."

He realized he was repeating himself, shook a bit more.

"You caught me a bit out of sorts."

"I see that."

"I've been doing some research. Strictly hush-hush. Not without side effects, it seems."

Paul looked up at his uniforms hanging as if they were shaming him.

"I'm here now, professor sir. Let's get you sorted. Some food, water, maybe a nap? You'll be good to go."

Sam desperately hoped his bullshit wasn't showing.

There was a beep. From somewhere, this disheveled, barely conscious man pulled out a radio.

"Speak."

It was like a different person. Paul hit that one-syllable response like a hammer hitting a nail, direct, sharp. Bang.

"Sir," the voice came through, "Over the last twelve hours, we've been tracking an anomaly in the core."

"Explain."

Bang. Again. No slur. He could almost feel the effort Paul was expending.

"Energy surge, high resource usage, cycle time, storage growth, they're all headed off the charts. We wouldn't have noticed if extra shipments hadn't started showing up at the loading docks. Hard to ignore a dozen tractor-trailers lined up on the main drive, sir."

"Recommendation."

Sam saw him slump with that last one. He didn't know how many responses the man could cook up.

"None sir. Just reporting."

Paul began to reply, stopped, gritted his teeth, then "Roger. Out."

He put the radio back and fell over. He was still awake, though.

Sam helped him slowly back to sitting.

"What was that?"

"Nothing. Here, help me to the bed."

His knee bent, then went back.

"Good. Thanks."

Did he think he was already sitting on the bed? Paul stayed conscious but said nothing. Sam sat beside him, tapping his foot. Sooner or later he was going to have to make a decision.

"Fair bit of automation we have here, Sam."

"Saw that coming in. Fair bit of rules, too."

Maybe things were working out.

"Fair bit of automated rules, too. That's how they getcha."

With two fingers, he jabbed at the cheap tile floor. They get you. Ants? Termites? Should he ask?

"People not watching them," neither man looked at the other, both staring straight ahead, "We're gettin' better. Tryin' to."

Now he pointed at his own head. He tapped it three times.

"It's what folks think they know. Much worse than not knowing. No way around it, though!"

Was this a joke? He looked at Sam as if he'd just delivered a punchline. Sam thought he'd go with the old repeating last word trick.

"Nope. No way around it," he agreed.

"'Cause brains! That's why!"

Sam sighed. He began to mourn his old teacher, but he knew that being sad wasn't going to save him now.

He considered. He had a grandma that had a stroke. This reminded him of that. The conversation started to feel almost musical. It was like the word boxing with the drunks he'd do at the soup kitchen. The pitter-patter, the pattern, the lilt. This man's neurons were firing, there was an electrical dance. He was invited. Paul would probably not remember it.

"But what are you going to do, right?" Sam joined in. He tried to sound with an identical tone and inflection as he had heard. It was close.

"That's right," Paul agreed, "Whatdya going to do?"

Seemed to be working.

"Can't shoot 'em, right?"

Paul cut him a look. Paul lowered his voice as he replied.

"No, not all of them. You can't. You know what, you can't even try! That's because they're invisible."

Sam began to feel very sick.

"Say, did they issue you a pistol yet?"

What?!?

"Pistol? We get guns?"

"Not guns. Pistol."

Paul absent-mindedly blew a raspberry.

"And not you," he examined Sam, "definitely not you. I don't think you're going to be here long."

What did that mean.

"Professor, I'm here until we finish this, but I have a stupid question."

Right guy to ask, he thought.

The man's hands were shaking so hard he looked as if he were being electrocuted.

"Wat?"

"What IS this place?"

"The mind of God," Paul said firmly, resolutely. HE smiled and looked straight ahead, not even seeing Sam.

Sam gestured back to the liquor bottle.

"How much of that have you had to drink?"

"Looks like almost all of it," there were a couple of laughs like coughing. Paul's smile got even wider. Sam thought of a jack-o-lantern.

The smile left. Sam watched him key the radio.

"Jamison, how big is the anomaly?"

The reply was almost instantaneous.

"Well, of course we don't know sir, we can't go down there, but it's twenty percent of base power and growing."

"Interesting. Out."

He put the radio back down.

The lights were on somewhere, Sam thought, "You guys have some programming issues, something I can help with?"

Paul began to giggle but stopped.

"It's the robots," the old man finally said, "They're building things."

"What kinds of things?"

"Nobody knows! Right?"

Slapping his knees, surprising Sam yet again, Paul pushed himself to his feet. He wobbled uncertainly.

"How's Debian? How's my daughter doing?"

"Better," Sam replied. He didn't know whether to say "Better than you" or "Better than she used to be." He wasn't sure which answer was true, if any of them were.

Ooof, what a smell!

"Let's get you cleaned up."

Paul looked down at his shorts, stained with urine.

Sam gently helped him clean up, organize his affairs. He didn't want to leave the bathroom, though, changing his mind. Sam suspected he was afraid of another accident.

Neither man spoke during this.

Just as Sam thought about broaching the subject of Deb again, Paul started talking. It was without context, as if he were in the middle of a story.

"Killed him I did. Broke his neck and threw him off the damned cliff."

Paul looked to Sam as if he had just finished a long story and Sam was supposed to react.

He nodded slowly and looked very serious. What else could he do?

He said nothing.

"I know, right? Terrible."

"Terrible," Sam returned the serve, "Sir."

The sir got Paul's attention. Let's go with that.

"Sir. Professor Colonel Sir. I'm going to need a better explanation of what's going on here if you want me to help."

He lifted Paul's chin slowly with his hand, made him keep eye contact.

"You want me to help, right? You remember that? Did Deb have anything to do with this? Did she help you with the programming?"

"Debian? God no. She's beyond all of this. Much. More Important."

His eyes twinkled. Sam watched him try to grab a conversational thread, a gymnast jumping off one swing and midair looking for another to catch.

"You see, Sam, I was building a telescope. Did I tell you that? Well, it was kind of like a microscope, or a mirror, really."

"So you see things. You see things here. That's nice."

Sam looked around the room as if there was something to see.

"All the time. All sorts of things. Just like my little Debian did."

"Are there displays, windows? Can I see things too?"

"Of course man, of course. They're everywhere. Too many, in fact. I'll take you."

This man couldn't make it to the bathroom and he was offering base tours. Sam nodded again seriously.

"Facts, programming, logic, reason. We're men of science are we not?"

"We are."

Paul looked at him conspiratorially.

"Sam, honestly, based on science, how rational and logical do you think any of us are?"

"Not very. Honestly not at all. Programming has shown me that real logic and reason and what we call logic and reason aren't even close to one another."

"Exactly, my man. Science."

He gave Paul another nod. Maybe with enough nods his old professor would return to Earth.

Won't remember any of this, he reminded himself.

"Met a man this morning," Paul continued, "at least I think it was this morning. I think it was a man. Would you like some bacon?"

"I'd love some."

"Big and brown. Top shelf. And be lively with it."

Sam went over, grabbed the big brown object, brought it back.

He was confused

"Novum Organum?" he read.

"Sir Francis Bacon. It was a mistake, of course, just like"Principia Mathematica", but a very useful one, let me tell you that."

Sam thought his former professor was going to launch into a lecture. Instead, he caught himself. He smiled wanly, a child caught passing gas while the parson visited who knows enough not to giggle.

"You can keep that, Sam. I regret I don't have a Principia for you. Sorry."

"Looks very valuable. Beginning of sciences, right? People used to be very superstitious. I …"

"Samuel," Paul interrupted, "Do you believe in ghosts, demons, angels?"

Sam blurted, "I don't know. I guess not. I guess it depends on what those names mean."

"Exactly! Now you're getting the hang of it!"

"I am? Sir?"

"How's Debian doing?"

"Sir? Since you last asked?"

"Right. Any change?"

Sam looked around the room.

"No? Sir?"

"Chinese had three of them."

"They did."

He had no idea what the old man was babbling about. This was a waste of time.

Paul looked at him as if he could read Sam's mind, as if offended.

"Book burnings. Purges. Oh sure, we've done amateur hour in the west along the same lines. The burning of the Library at Alexandria, the odd fanatical religious fire burning across the land. But the Chinese were centralized, organized. Long before we ever were."

"Deb said you liked history," he hoped Debian would never see her dad like this.

"But the Chinese did it right: burn all the scrolls, kill all the scribes, banish the families and teachers. All that knowledge? All that culture? It just disappeared like it was never there. But the rest of us are learning, Samuel. We're getting a lot better. We can erase a culture now and ninja edit it all so that it never existed."

"I can't tell you the number of times I've thought the exact same thing," maybe he could chat the guy out into the hall, find an aid station.

"You know, when this is over with," he pointed, "We're going to need a new one, even if they' don't ninja edit out this one."

Sam looked at the ancient tome.

"A new book? Like one of those modern language translations?"

"No, no. A replacement. A Novum Novum Organum. Ha! I guess you'll have to do both. An organon also."

"My job should be to start writing books?"

"Don't be an idiot, Samuel 'You' as in somebody. You should be on the lookout for somebody to write replacements. They're going to be needed."

Damned coot sounded sane. But hell, the words just didn't make sense. Progress?

"Um. Yes?"

"I mean it. Can't go all the way back to the Dark Ages or Stone Ages again, can we? Ha!"

The laugh sounded as if Paul was shouting at somebody. Something.

Sam began thinking of Paul as a radio playing an old-timey drama where Sam wasn't even part of the audience.

"We can't go back to witch doctors."

"That's it."

"Do you need a witch doctor?"

"No. I need you to pray with me."

"But I don't pray."

"Neither do I, but it's going to work."

"How would we…"

"This is it. Hold my hand."

He did so.

"We're going to close our eyes, control our breathing. We're going to focus on health and stability for the rest of our day."

"If you say so, okay," Sam closed his eyes.

"I'm going to recite the Greek Alphabet."

Paul responded before he could complain.

"I feel like somebody should say something."

A wink's as good as a nod in a dark alley, Sam thought. It wasn't worth asking about.

There followed one of the weirder five minutes of his past year, and his past year had been full of weird minutes. They breathed. Paul spoke ever so often, drawing out and droning his Greek letters.

Reaching Omega, it was over. Sam opened his eyes.

The Placebo Effect was powerful. He felt a lot better, like he had the best sleep of his life. Paul looked a lot better. His old professor looked …. normal.

Who knew?

"That's what I was afraid of," the older man stood. He was no longer so old or frail looking. His hand did not shake. His footing was firm.

"Wow," Sam said, "I feel a lot better."

He stood also. It was the power of prayer. By God if it was that good he was ready to join a monastery.

His old professor looked at him as if suddenly afraid again.

"This is terrible," he said looking at Sam.

"Feeling better?"

"No. My god. Too many random variables now."

He pointed at Sam as if Sam were being used by a teacher as a bad example to the rest of the class.

"I hoped," Paul started, "No I feared. I worried that this would happen."

"So now the tour? You can show me this place?"

Paul shook his head no.

"No, no. Not now. I have some urgent things to attend to. Oh no. The anomaly."

"You're better? Okay now?"

"It's a horrible tragedy, Sam. I feel great. Tell you what, why don't you go talk to Gibb and get some background from her. It's not like she has anything else to do. We'll catch up in the next day or two, I promise."

Paul started taking Sam to the door.

Sam was suddenly running out of time.

"Don't you want to hear about Deb? Maybe we could go meet her? I know where she is. It's very close."

Paul looked at him as clear-eyed as a preacher on Sunday morning.

"Very much so. With all of my heart. But now I've got to do this. I have no choice."

He opened the door.

"And Sam? There's always three. Look for the third one."

"Sir?"

"I'll explain later."

Sam closed the door. He left, lost in thought. He wasn't sure that the professor would make it through the night, much less a couple of days. Something really sick there.

Random thoughts popped into his mind as he walked. A sea shanty, "What do you do with a drunken sailor?" It turned out, nothing. Clint Eastwood, "It's a hell of a thing; killin' a man. You take away everything he ever had and ever would have." Ozzy Osborne, "All aboard the crazy train!!"

Sam felt like the dog that caught the car he was chasing. Now what.

Back in the room, Paul cleaned himself completely up. He drank the rest of the scotch.

He got the gear back out from the satchel. He set up at the table again, gear and notepad in hand.

There would be no stopwatch.

He took a very deep breath and let it out slowly. He thought of their prayer.

He had a note to write and a deal to make.

Time was running out.

Chaos

Hilda Gibb had to be the biggest piece of shit that Sam ever gave a taco to.

The woman also had cats on the brain.

He sat her dinner tray down on the table in her room. Her room, the prison.

Sam thought it was a pretty nice prison.

There were ceramic kittens as salt and pepper shakers. Paintings of kittens were on the wall. The light switch overs had cats on them. He had to get a stuffed kitten out of one of the chairs to sit across from her.

"Why choose us?" he said. "I need to hear it from you. Why have you been chasing us?"

He had decided friendly banter and ice breakers weren't going to work with Gibb. He went straight to the point. Sam thought she'd respond to that. Perhaps nothing would help. He had to try.

"We all have orders, Mr. Featherstone," was all she said. She started eating, obviously enjoying herself, her food, the attention.

"That's not good enough."

She stopped, as if considering whether the meal needed additional seasoning.

"Hmph," she responded. She put her taco back down.

"Perhaps it doesn't matter. After all, nobody would believe you. You're never leaving here like you are. You want to know a secret? It wasn't all us. Some of the things you experienced were us, but others weren't. We've long had a relationship to the McKenzie Foundation, for instance."

"Happy Valley Pickles?"

"I said I would explain a bit more, mostly because I feel sorry for you, not spill my guts."

"Just tell me about the pickles."

"Hmmph," she gestured again in frustration.

"We have a paramilitary group that performs an active defense. They intercept and take care of threats before they make it here."

"Janus Group."

She cocked her head and shrugged, as if to say maybe yes and maybe no. He knew she meant yes.

"Deception and misdirection are a critical part of the job we do."

There was a knock on the door.

"That should be Major Parsons," she said, "Enter."

"Checking in on you two," Parsons said, entering, eyeing Sam warily, "The Colonel was concerned that something might have happened."

"Just talking," Gibb replied, "Featherstone's safe. Newbury needn't worry."

"I'm good." He said, "I thought a little friendly conversation might help me understand everything that's happened, that's all."

"Oh, okay," was the reply from Parsons, "Interrogation. I don't do interrogation that well. I need remedial classes."

"It's not interrogation. It's just a conversation."

Gibb interrupted, "Aren't all conversations interrogations?"

She addressed them both.

"I want something. You have it. You try talking first. We are either going to chat, or," she reconsidered what she was about to say, "we do things. Other things. It's up to you."

He rubbed his face.

"I don't think either of you understand me at all."

"The feeling is mutual," Parsons said from behind him, "Civilians."

"I see you like cats," he knew that continuing to frame this as an interrogation was a disaster.

He pointed to her bed where a fake kitten was napping. As he gestured, it woke up and began licking its paw.

"Incredible realism, isn't it," Gibb said, "The more I interact with it, the more I can't tell it from a real cat."

"Why cats?"

"Kittens. I love them. Cats are predators. They stalk. They hide. They work together to hunt, even housecats. Did you know that?"

She smiled at the kitten as she continued.

"Kittens show the promise of all of that. It's the potential, but it's not yet there. They love you."

"Cute."

"And they'll surely fuck with you, just enough to let you know that potential is always there."

He walked over to the bed, hoping he wasn't crossing a personal line. He didn't think so. Gibb didn't strike him as the kind that had any personal lines.

He petted it.

It began purring.

"Why not get a real cat?"

"Kitten," she corrected, "Why would I?"

"To see it change, to grow up. I like kittens too, but I like watching them grow, explore."

He stopped and stepped back a bit, still looking at it.

He tried again.

"Surely everything must grow up, mature, change."

He studied the simulacrum kitten. He began petting again. It was relaxing. Its back scrunched and it continued purring, responding to him.

"Why? This creature is programmed with the behavior of all kittens everywhere. It's perfect. To me, there could be no better kitten."

He thought of arguing, but sequestered the impulse. How could an unchanging thing ever be real? Even mountains change.

Arguing was no good. He was tired of arguing.

"I'm a simple person. All I want, all I ever wanted, was to code, to program. I wanted to use math to unlock secrets. I wanted to make something of myself."

"Sam, don't sell yourself short. You're here, right? I bet that you're the Aide-de-Camp to Newbury. Isn't that something? Isn't this it? You've made the Big Time. You're playing in the major leagues."

"No. I don't want anything to do with the Army. I don't want to be part of a place with tons of secrets to keep. Secrets are corrosive. I just want to be left alone to do my thing. Clear my name. Do my thing. Why does it always have to be so complicated?"

It wasn't a question but he got an answer anyway.

"Perhaps you make it that way. You should consider that."

This was pointless.

He turned around.

"Bea, I'm not making much progress here. Let's leave and let the Colonel here stew in her own juices."

There must have been a signal, he thought later, or a hand gesture. Or worse.

He started to leave. He stopped, though, realizing Parsons was not coming along.

"I'm not going anywhere," she said.

He turned in surprise. She crossed her arms.

"And neither are you."

Gibb smiled. Sam decided he didn't like it when she smiled. Nothing good ever came after that.

"Report."

Sam stood in amazement listening to Parsons report.

"Newbury has put out communications to his daughter as we suspected he would. The unknown anomaly in the core is continuing to grow. He's looking into it. We're getting calls from a local sheriff, wondering where all the Newburys are. I don't know how he came up with us."

Gibb stopped her.

"I'll handle that. It's been too long since I spoke to the Governor. How are the Three Stooges?"

"Newbury keeps saying that we need to tune something called a 'Markov Blanket'. This is beyond me, ma'am."

"I'll handle that also. Good work, Major."

"Thank you, ma'am."

"I guess I'm back to grounds keeping?" he said.

"That's not in the cards for you, Sam. You know that."

"It was worth a shot."

"Walk with me."

She left her pretend prison like McArthur returning to the Philippines. Happy, victorious, but not just a little bit staged. This was her moment, Sam thought.

They started walking, Gibb in front, then Sam, then Parsons.

"You know, Major," Gibb said continuing and not bothering to turn back, "I'm happy to help you with those courses. I used to teach interrogative techniques at the academy."

"Thank you, ma'am. I look forward to it."

"Maybe I should sit in," he said mostly to himself, "I don't seem to know much about it."

They walked a short distance from Gibb's quarters. Parson had her left hand on his shoulder. Nothing overt, just a clear indication of who was in charge.

They came to a place that looked like a baby viewing area in a maternity ward. No, it was a series of viewing areas. Sam remembered the music practice cubicles he'd seen in college.

Approaching the first one, Gibb said "Start the clock."

Parsons hit a big square metal button on the wall, the kind used to open doors for handicapped people.

A five minute countdown began on the display just above.

"You asked why you were here, why all of this," Gibb said, "You're here because we need to advance our integration technology."

Looking into the room, Sam saw an airman sitting in an easy chair watching a TV.

That was the only thing in the room that was normal.

The man's scalp and body were wired with perhaps hundreds of electrodes. He wore glasses that had laser sensors that closely monitored his pupil dilation and eye movement.

Looking at the screen, Sam saw what at first he thought was a cheap horror movie. There were pigs, writhing in filth, but large. Grunting, digging, rooting. Realistic. Great FX. Giant pigs. Each must have been four or five feet tall. They had heat vision, he noticed as one of them vaporized a board. As he watched, they burned down their barn and escaped, only to find lizard men wearing backpacks coming out of the farmer's house. A blue sun hung on the horizon.

He could hear no sound, but whatever sound it was, the man jerked back in horror.

"You're here as a programmer, Sam," Gibb said. She seemed happy to finally tell him, "somehow we've run across a computer program that hacks into people's brains directly. Any more than a few minutes of this each day and people die. We want you to help us figure out why."

"You've got experience with the models, you've got experience with the social issues and human factor, you've got experience with most all of the wetwork."

She looked at him closely now.

"You've even got experience with all this weirdness we keep running into."

He looked back to the TV, then to the man watching. The man was now flinching at irregular intervals. Were they shocking him?

"You wanted to code. You wanted to program. You wanted to figure out things nobody has. That's exactly what we want too. We're good. We have no quarrel with you."

Parsons squeezed his shoulder.

Down the hall, four orderlies appeared from one of the rooms carrying another man.

The man was twitching and jerking as if in a seizure.

"Is he going to be okay?"

"BWAAA!" the man yelled as they disappeared, carrying him around the corner.

"He'll be fine," Gibb said, "A little sedation, a couple of days of light duty. You won't even be able to tell that this happened."

"Used to be a lot of screaming," Parsons said from behind him, "Quite distressing. So we started soundproofing the rooms. It's much better now."

"We lost seventeen men before we established the protocols."

He thought he heard another scream from the man, now much father away.

"It was dark times," Gibb said.

"From where I'm standing right now, it looks like even darker times," he said.

"I lost my husband," she said.

That was that. He certainly couldn't fight these people. Gibb looked ready to jump on a hand grenade for whatever her cause was. She was committed no matter what.

Why was Parsons doing this?

He remembered being trapped in the mine with Deb. He thought of his old roomie Stetson, the wires to the brain, and all the terribleness that resulted from that.

Pops gutting those kids.

Deb shooting Endelman.

Deb said he was the answer. Deb said he could change things.

He didn't understand her. He believed her, but he didn't understand her.

He relaxed, meditating. He brought his center into himself again. Once there, he cast himself on Bea. He had no other words for it.

Why was she doing this?

He pictured a series of briefings. Colonel Gibb was there. Sometimes others. He couldn't make out the details. He was dreaming somebody else's dream. The conclusion was clear, however, and visceral. The nation, your friends, your family, your job, your freedom are all at risk. You will have to fool these people to save them.

Can you do it?

Sam felt her deep revulsion, but Bea Parsons had a kind of purity he could only admire. Looking in on her thoughts like this, he felt like he'd taken her on as a lover.

Of course she could.

She only wanted to do the right thing.

He broke.

"It's important to do the right thing."

He looked away. He didn't look at her. He was ashamed.

"Yes, it is," she said in the most human and vulnerable voice he'd ever heard from her, "but it's not always easy."

If she only knew.

"You'll cheer up when your friend Deb gets here," Gibb said.

Was Gibb happy? Sarcastic? Mean?

He almost asked her what she needed Deb for, but he now knew better. Whatever she said, assuming she said anything, would be a lie.

Fuck it. He had to know.

Rape.

The word appeared without warning in his brain.

He made it go away.

Reaching out just a little bit, he began to see Gibb, really see her.

He didn't want to do this anymore. He hated himself.

Maybe if he asked, she would think it, even if she lied. He wouldn't have to go further. Please no more pushing.

"What do you need Deb for?"

He didn't know if she replied or not. He was too stunned by the vision.

Deb was on a hospital bed. Machines were monitoring her life signs. Machines were adjusting an IV to keep her semiconscious. Her head was shaved. Under bandages, wires went directly into her brain. The walls all around the room were showing dozens of those crazy stories, 24 hours a day.

"YA," he felt shocked.

"It's not that bad," Gibb said, continuing whatever else she'd been saying.

"You know, Major," she addressed Parsons, "I've been thinking. We may need to bring an entire QRT here. Things are likely to get a little spicy."

"Just say the word."

"Needs some thought. I'll let you know."

"Ma'am," she pointed to the clock, "We only have about a minute left."

"A minute until what?"

"Insanity."

Gibb pressed a button. The window went dark.

She smiled for no reason he could determine.

"Good news," Gibb said, "Debian Newbury is at the front gate, asking about the Janus Group. That girl is not anything if not predictably stubborn."

If she only knew.

A terrible chill came over him.

He needed answers. He needed to change directions. He needed that right now, before it was too late.

They had something. He needed something. We do things, other things. It's up to you.

"Parsons," he turned pleading, trying to stare her down, "They're lying to you. She's lying to you. Can't you see that?"

Parsons looked at him as if he were trying to con her, as if she had been briefed this exact thing was going to happen.

"I don't think so. Nice try, though."

He turned to Gibb.

"This is wrong. You have to stop doing it. It's all wrong."

From behind, Parsons spoke.

"Doing the right thing can be unpleasant, even disgusting."

He turned back to her as she continued.

"You know who told me that? Paul Newbury, that's who. Your old professor. Be careful who your heroes are. Be careful which side you pick."

"You fucking morons," his anger welled up, "He's not my hero and I'm not choosing sides. Fuck, I'm here to get the damned bastard, not help him."

"So you're on our side, then," he heard Gibb, "We want to get him too. See?"

Confusion, fear, hate, frustration all spun around inside of him, fighting for dominance.

"Come on, Parsons," Gibb continued, "Let's collect the girl at the gate and then take Newbury out."

He didn't know exactly what they meant by taking Paul out but he could guess.

Gibb's words from before kept destroying him: They have something you want, so you try talking first.

Aren't all conversations interrogations?

Taking a deep breath, he pushed out to Parsons all of the fear, hate, and loathing he felt. Stop Gibb at any cost. He fed the chaos. He pushed the chaos.

It was three seconds.

It couldn't have been more than three seconds. She drew her sidearm and shot her boss.

Gibb dropped like a sack of wheat.

Parsons looked insane.

He knew he had to stop her or she would take out as many people as she could find.

He had done something very wrong.

Happy. Where's your happy, Bea? Go to your happy. Make yourself happy. Forget this.

She smiled and put her gun back. She walked away. She looked like she'd just finished a load of laundry and was going to get more quarters instead of somebody who'd just gunned down their boss in cold blood.

The klaxon began sounding.

The base went into lockdown.

Hiding Gibb was much tougher than he imagined. Using her arms, he managed to drag her the hundred feet back to her quarters before the chaos really began out in the hallway.

He shut the door behind him. The base had orders to leave her alone. Would hiding here work?

He opened her closet. Maybe he should put her in there. Maybe he should go in there.

As he was hiding the body, he saw it. Most other people would not.

It was an earpiece, a tiny camouflaged earpiece, the kind that stage magicians use to have their assistants secretly help them. It blended perfectly in with her ear.

He picked it up as if it were a bug. He held it close.

A deep voice.

"Colonel Gibb, you're due at the core in fifteen minutes. Make sure Featherstone is dropped off and secure at Disneyland before you proceed to the core."

He flung it across her room as if it were on fire and burning his hand up.

What did Gibb say? Orders. We all have orders.

He thought she meant orders in the generic sense. Army people follow orders. But he realized now that she meant literally. She was getting orders minute-by-minute, hour-by-hour, and immediately following them.

He started scrooching his butt back into the closet, in shock.

He was afraid of reality.

Somebody had answered the phone. These people not only answered the phone, they were trying to set up a call center.

Outside, he could hear men running around, doing whatever army men did. They didn't yell as before. He had to really listen to hear them.

Somehow that made it all worse.

He made it to the closet and pushed himself to the back wall.

He could picture Gibb getting order after order in her earpiece, dutifully following each one, doing her best to stand out as a superior officer. What a tough duty assignment. She should be promoted. She was a real trooper.

He started pulling the closet door closed.

He'd kept winning and winning. He ran into problems in life and he would overcome them.

Each time he won, things got worse.

He'd won his way into a dark closet, waiting for a bullet.

He could run. He could take out one or two. He knew that now. But he couldn't take out everybody. He couldn't turn off security cameras, or find booby traps.

So he sat, shaking, his knees to his chest, afraid to stay and afraid to go.

He felt his own heartbeat. He closed the door.

He lived in a very dark place.

Outside, the kitten watched. Waited.

$$5.18$$

Delivering

Sam would have given anything to be with Deb again.

Then they delivered her like a pizza.

Shivering in the closet, in the dark, lost in despair, he heard a knock at Gibb's door.

Maybe it was something else. Another noise. Could be the structure settling. He'd always heard people talk about the structure settling. He supposed it could make a sound like that.

There was another knock.

Maybe they'd go away.

He got out of the closet. He stood facing the door.

He didn't get out because he was brave.

He got out because he didn't want to die sitting down.

"Colonel Gibb," somebody spoke.

They'd go away. He'd be quiet and they'd go away.

Then he heard the most fucked up thing ever.

"Yes."

It was the voice of Gibb. Dead Gibb. Dead Gibb he had just drug into her own bathroom.

Gibb with the hole in her head.

Back there.

Marley was dead to begin with: there is no doubt whatsoever about that.

He'd gone insane. That was the only answer. Just like the prof. He knew Gibb was dead. Her corpse was completely lifeless as he drug her. He would know. He checked twice.

"What do you want?" dead Marley spoke again.

Did he dare turn around to look at the bathroom, the body, the result?

What the hell was back there?

What rough beast, its hour come round at last, slouches toward Bethlehem to be born?

"We have prisoner Debian Newbury," from outside the door. "Reporting to your quarters as orderd, ma'am."

"Leave her. I'll take responsiblity."

"Yes ma'am."

The door opened and Deb came in. She held up her finger to indicate silence while she made sure the guards were out of reach.

"Like my little ventriloquist trick with the kitten?"

"Deb!"

"Sam!"

The two ran towards one another. Each had their arms open, glad for the fierce loving hug to come.

They did not hug.

Instead, as they get about a foot apart, each stopped. They realized what was happening.

Wariness and fear overtook them.

Unable to complete the hug, unable to abandon the hug. A foot away, each pivoted left and right, tilting, their arms forming different angles with each other. They couldn't get the exact correct angle.

Without the proper angle, of course, humans were not allowed to hug. Everybody knew that.

The dance of the nerds might have continued all night, but Deb finally stuck her hand out.

Sam shook it.

He used both hands though. He didn't give up smiling. No way.

"I am so glad to see you. I missed you."

"I've missed you terribly, Samuel."

She closed the door behind them, looking to make sure the hallway was empty first.

"Dad?"

"Down in the core. Restricted area. Deb, how in hell did you make it here?"

"What do you know about Janus Group?"

"Later. Focus. How. Are. You. Here."

"I let them capture me. We're the security experts, Sam, that's our job. EigenCorp didn't hire us for our good looks."

"You got in the system, didn't you. You got into their system and then turned yourself in. That's some Trojan Horse work right there. How did you ..."

She hushed him.

"A bit. I got in a bit. Only a bit. Not so fast. Enough to get sent down here and fake Gibb's voice. That's about it."

"Well, it's enough for me," he was still smiling ear-to-ear.

"I'm a little confused about Gibb. Is she here?"

"In the bathroom."

"Tie her up?"

His face fell down. The knot returned in his stomach.

He shook his head quickly from side-to-side, afraid.

"So you did the thing, right? You did the thing," she studied him.

Nod yes.

"I'm so sorry."

"Don't want to talk about it."

"Then we won't," and she moved on to other things as if they'd just discovered his zipper being open or her underwear showing. It was bad. It hurt. Embarrassing. Water under the bridge. Let's move.

In that moment, something changed inside of Sam.

"How'd you know Gibb wasn't here?"

"It's complicated. Her bio signs weren't showing up anywhere in the facility."

She continued.

"How'd you get into her quarters?"

"Complicated. How'd you know I was here?"

"I didn't. I just wanted to be dropped off at the best spot possible."

"Which would be the commander's quarters if she wasn't here. They'd leave you alone here."

"Yes."

"Nicely done."

"We're back. Best next move?"

"I trust you. You decide. I'll follow, like always. I've done enough damage."

"No, you decide, I'll follow. I'm the one trusting you. Finally. Something I should have done months ago because ..."

She looked up, rummaging around for the appropriate word to finish her thought.

"Moron."

He smiled even more, in spite of the desperate situation. She always could make him smile.

"If this is going to be one of those relationships where they spend an hour trying to pick what to eat or what to watch on TV, I'm nope-ing out right now."

"Relationship? We have a relationship?"

"Baby steps, young Debian. Baby steps."

He looked around the room for options.

"Your intuition was spot on. We should have everything we need here. I say take the computer and hack into the network. That firewall and DMZ's fucked up. They always are."

"I was wrong. My plan. I don't think that's going to work."

"Why not? Who's going to interrupt the boss? And if they do, you can use your trick again."

"I won't. I can't."

"Why?

"No computer."

He checked again. She was right again. He just assumed that anybody's living quarters would contain some kind of computer. Not that kind of place.

"Well, we still have a few hours, maybe even a day until somebody gets worried enough to come."

"No, Sam. I heard them talking. I blew that too. This is just one stop on a full day of activities they have for me. I'm on a tight schedule whether I'm in Gibb's quarters or not."

"How long?"

"With surety, ten minutes. With luck, fifteen."

"Then we gotta leave," he pushed past her and opened the door.

Following him out, Deb started taking it in.

"What is this place?"

"I was told a secret military base."

"Looks empty."

"I was also told a telescope, an observatory, a mirror, and a window."

He counted them off as he listed them.

"They don't know," she said.

"But you know what it really reminds me of?"

"A hospital."

"No. Hitler's bunker. The war was over but they still wanted to fight. They had to dig themselves into the ground to do it."

"There has to be a stairway around here somewhere. Let's use that. Let's find the back door to this place."

"Not going to work. The base is on lockdown. Plus the stairway is enter-only. Only one exit."

"Top floor."

"Top floor beside the guard shack if I remember correctly."

"We're going to have to do something else."

"Stay or go," he shrugged.

"What's up with all those windows and the blue rectangles?"

"You don't want to go there. That's some evil mad scientist stuff."

"Mad scientist?"

"Probably exaggerating. But whatever it is, it's bad. It's some sort of audio/visual stimulation system they've stumbled across. Hacking into people's minds."

"With this kind of hardware? They're using Markov Chains, LLM, MDLMS …"

"Yes, yes. I don't need the list. Looks like it. It's so stupid. It's stupid scary as fuck. Trust me."

"I'm going to go look anyway."

"But Deb, you can't. The lady said it might kill you."

"Looks to me like they're just observation rooms."

"They said they were exploring how the sensory input could damage people, even kill them.

"You trust me."

"With my life."

"Then let me do this."

"You're in charge, like I said, no disagreement, but will you let me help you? Can I watch and help?"

They both knew what kind of help he was talking about.

"I wouldn't try doing it without you."

They went to the nearest one.

Watching her and not being able to see inside the glass, he hit the button.

She made no face at all.

He didn't know what to think about that.

So he waited. He looked at the timer. He struggled to be patient.

After two minutes he felt like he had to do something.

"You okay?"

"Yup."

She still watched, uninterested. She was not frozen. He'd seen her plenty of times frozen, but this wasn't that.

She was simply bored. Vacant. A whale watcher told her to look in a special place and she'd be sure to see the whale breech. Meanwhile, time ran on. No whale.

She was waiting and waiting, but whatever she was waiting for was not happening.

Another two minutes.

"Hey, you alright?" again.

This time she did not respond.

Was she going to be angry if he stopped her? Or was she going to be angry if he didn't stop her?

He was going to stop it. He couldn't help but remember what he saw inside Gibb's mind: Debian in the hospital bed, the sensors, the screens, the medication.

He had to stop it.

He hit the button closing the window.

"That's enough."

She smiled. She turned to him.

"Oh well, we tried. Worth a shot, right?"

Sam thought her mood seemed light.

Nothing happened.

"Will you tell me what you saw? Did you figure out how the base operates? Have you been in touch with a true AGI?"

"Sam, don't be stupid. This entire place is just a computer system. That's why I could hack into it. There's nothing magical going on here."

She pointed to the glass, now dark.

"Boring, maybe."

She fully addressed him now, arms crossed.

"You really should calm down. Programmers have been doing this kind of interactive thing for a long time, since ELIZA and the talking horse. This is just a different and extremely more complex configuration of stuff we already know, generative AI storytelling. There may be something coming through the system, but the system itself is pretty boring."

"Well dammit, what did you see, then? You're not answering the question."

She hesitated.

No, he concluded, she was not in distress. He didn't have to do that thing.

"Just some stupid fantasy documentary how-to video. They were explaining how to make a phase cannon."

"So we can make a phase cannon?"

"Got any antimatter?"

"No."

"Then no."

"So, to recap, we have nowhere to go, but we can't stay here. We could go to the guard shack. And with a little antimatter we could build a phase cannon."

"Correct, but an important piece of information is that we can go two different ways. We can use the steps or the elevator. We're not completely out of choices. It's not like we need lawyers, guns, and money."

Maybe that room had messed her up pretty badly after all. Lawyers and money? She was not operating as programmed. That's what she would say. He knew.

"Were you able to see if this facility had preprogrammed response systems, scripts?"

"Sure, why?"

"Wonder what happens if multiple things occur at once?"

He calmly walked over to the wall and pulled the fire alarm.

"Let's find out."

Nothing happened. Again, nothing happened. After a minute or so, Sam admitted it.

"That was disappointing. You'd think a fire would have more excitement."

There was a pounding. It sounded like a drum.

"Drums?" he asked.

"The doors," she said, "They can't get out. The people."

She was correct. One door being banged on became two doors, then three.

Pushing Parsons. Pulling the fire alarm. Sam had managed to lock all these people into rooms where they'd die in the next few minutes.

Through the racket, they heard a soft hissing sound.

It got loud enough that they were unable to ignore it further.

"Not good," Deb said.

"Halon fire suppression?"

She checked the hall again.

"Not without masks. Not without a server farm to protect. Something else."

"Sleeping gas? Smoke? Some kind of pressure differential system?"

"I briefly saw something about an intruder gas system. With the proper McGuffin or Insert I could have found out. But not without them."

"Whatever it is, it isn't good."

"I suspect arsenic or cyanide."

"Not good."

"There's also nerve gas, perhaps a blistering agent…"

"Thank you. Let's just leave it at not good."

"I'm running out of ideas, What tools do we have?"

"Our brains."

"Ok, lets work with that. We know we can hack our way in to the central system. You've already done it."

"Briefly."

She pushed the button for the elevator.

"Who knows? How about trying that again? If we put our heads together, we might make it further."

Could he somehow save these people?

"We might. But not without an insert. You know that. That's why they work. We couldn't make it far enough to shut this place down."

"There's that."

"And one thing I know, Sam, without a doubt: we're going to have to totally shut this place down or destroy it to get out. This thing they're watching is everywhere. It's not even localized to this building. This base doesn't contain anything. It shows things that are already out there. Shutting it all down would at best create a shadow that we might work in, some room to work."

"Ha." It was a bitter sad laugh. "So best bet, we make a shadow to get ourselves out. Once out, we're right back to where we started, just without this one particular building or computer."

"Correct."

"And we still don't have your dad. This might be time to start thinking more about an end game."

They both knew what he meant.

She smiled. She winked. By god she winked at him.

"Smile. Cheer up. Remember the mine? Whatever happened to your Optimistic Optimization Strategy? Movement is life? Remember any of this?"

"I don't know. Lost it, I guess."

"Watch this," stepping inside the elevator, her fingers danced over all of the buttons. In a second or two, all of the control lights inside the elevator were flashing.

"What'd you do?"

"It's now in Command Mode. We can go to whatever floor we want to."

"Great. Maybe we can visit the cafeteria before we die. It's taco day."

She swallowed. She swallowed hard.

He could tell something big was coming.

"You didn't ask me what computer I used to hack in here."

"I guess, let me see … Wait, what computer did you use?"

"My hands," she looked as if some awful, vile thing was coming up inside her, "I can touch things, feel the logic behind them."

"Always thought you were more than some cheap, knock-off Aspie Sherlock Holmes."

"Don't start."

"I won't. God, that was too much. I wanted to say I'm sorry and instead I'm trying to start a fight. I should be apologizing."

"For what?"

"When you told me back in the junkyard that these things were com-ing, you meant real, literal things."

"Of course."

"I'm sorry. I should have listened."

"And when you told me, back at EigenCorp, that you had a special way with people, you really meant that you had an preternatural ability with others?"

"I guess. I didn't know it."

"I should have understood."

They stood in the elevator.

The doors closed.

Neither pushed any buttons. They just stood staring straight ahead.

Finally Deb spoke.

"I'm afraid, Samuel. I'm trying to be positive, but I'm afraid."

"I know."

"Aren't you?"

He started to laugh but caught himself, afraid of how maniacal it would sound.

"Afraid? I am beyond fear. I'm going to die. You're going to die. It's like it already happened."

"No. You misunderstand. I'm not afraid of this," she waved her hand around indicating everything, all reality, "I'm afraid of this."

She pointed to her heart.

"I know, Debian. I know."

"How do you deal with it, without going insane. How can I deal with it?"

"Look around. Look where we are."

The elevator was empty.

"Left is right, dark is light, sane is insane. A hospital is a bunker. A telescope is a movie theater."

He punched the button to take them to the bottom, all the way to the core.

Looked at her as the elevator began moving.

"And down is the only out."

5.19

Transcending

It all moved like clockwork. It moved like the clockwork of a ticking timebomb.

Sam was glad there was no bullet to the head that awaited them when the elevator doors opened. He was glad the walls didn't electrocute them and poisonous gas wasn't released. He was glad the flying robots weren't actively trying to behead them.

It stopped. Everything had suddenly stopped.

But why'd it have to be so dark? The flashing light had stopped. The awful alarm sound had stopped. As they reached the bottom, the lights went out. All they had in the smoke filled corridor ahead of them was little red emergency LEDs every fifty feet along the ceiling.

There was no deadly disaster waiting for them.

It turned out to be worse.

As they stepped into the corridor, something fell out of Deb's pocket, hit his foot.

"Sorry."

He picked it up. It was one of her paperbacks.

"Flying Tickle Bunnies of Thermos Four?"

"A classic."

"I wouldn't read it if it came with free bunnies — or a free thermos."

"Probably way over your head anyway."

Up ahead they saw a man sitting.

Paul Newbury was busy behind several consoles. He checked to see who was coming in. He managed a quick look while he kept typing.

Seeing the both of them, he did a double-take. He squinted.

"Debian?"

She only glared.

He was already back to typing again, but managed to look a second time.

"And Samuel."

Sam took a step forward, then looked back to see if she was actually going to come along.

She took one step.

"When I told you to bring a boyfriend home, this isn't exactly what I meant."

"He's just some schmuck."

"That's right. That's me." Sam nodded with a stupid smile. He pointed to himself with both hands, "The Schmuck."

He was willing to take the hit and insult if it would keep the peace. The air felt electric.

Seeing the silence, he kept at his patter.

"Isn't it great we're all here? Why don't we grab a seat and talk over things?"

Paul kept typing as if nothing had been said. Perhaps another shot?

"There's nothing like a good family heart-to-heart. Am I right?"

He looked again at Deb. Her eyes were locked on her dad.

"Or not," Sam said, "we could always skip the catching up part."

They heard a door slam, a hard clank.

He looked back down the hallway, to the door they'd just come through.

There was a white, glowing cloud around it, perhaps it had floated over there? A plasma? Smoke? How would it glow?

"What the hell is that?" he asked the room.

"You don't want to know," Paul continued working.

"I know," Deb said, but she added no more.

The cloud dissipated.

Where the cloud had been, the metal now appeared to be welded shut.

They were welded in.

Paul finally completely stopped.

"That, boys and girls, was my decision being made for me. I'm doing the best I can to shut this place down."

"Don't tell me." Deb continued looking at the door.

"We are now trapped," he said.

Although the power was off, in the silence Sam felt a gentle dehumidified breeze pleasantly waft over them. The air smelled vaguely like hospitals or a fab.

On the far side of the floor, behind racks of servers and shelves of gear, two-hundred feet away, they could hear bumping and clanking. There was the sound of electric motors.

Even though the power was off, it was obvious something was being built back there. By something.

"Let's check out the back wall. Might be a door, or another room back there."

He started out on his own, leaving the others.

"Don't do that," Paul spoke deadpan cold.

"Why not?"

"I just don't think it would be … healthy. That's all."

A quadcopter buzzed by, one of a dozen they'd seen in the last few minutes. It was carrying a basket of some kind of material.

Following close behind were three bipedal bots, all in a line. They all had tools.

Nothing happened.

It was like the humans didn't exist.

Paul continued not working. He seemed resigned to something.

"This is as far as I go today, right here." he said, "I won't be leaving with you."

Every muscle in her body tensed.

"Remember the breathing. Do the count," Sam said.

She continued being tense all over. He could see the muscles in her arms as if she had been sculpted.

"Do we need to get out the chicken?"

Paul looked perplexed at Sam's remark, but instead of commenting reached down and handed him something.

"This is my satchel. Inside are key project papers, there's data on a disk there too. Some things."

He stopped. To Sam the man looked suddenly regretful. Sam saw a man who, on his way to work had just gotten out of his car to discover he had ran over a beloved puppy.

"You'll know how to decrypt it."

"You. Are. Coming. With. Me."

Each word from her was a spit, a chop, an attack. A punch.

Now Sam was getting concerned.

"Come on, Debian. You need to relax. Move through it. Breathe. No more Deb robot. You can do this."

She began a smile, then stopped, as if testing out a new car. Seeing that it worked, she looked at him, worried.

Behind her eyes, he could feel her pain. There was something deep there. Hidden. He watched. He reached out and felt. She took two deep breaths, finally relaxing, fully.

She looked normal, as if nothing had happened. They had both just seen a human reboot.

"Young man," Paul said, "I think that's the most amazing thing I've seen, and I've seen something amazing things lately."

"It's a chicken thing."

"Ignore him. He's an idiot."

He started to agree again but decided he'd had enough abuse for one day.

"Let go of it. Stop trying to control everything, Dad," she sounded calm, casual, "Let me make the decisions for once."

"I think you're going to have to," Paul responded.

It was a wan smile he gave Sam. Paul had the smile of a man on his deathbed, doing his best to cheer up his visitors he hadn't seen in years.

"I've yet to throw any puzzle at this girl that confounds her. And I'm a pretty good puzzle-maker."

Sam looked at his companion as if he'd never seen her before.

"She's one of a kind."

"Got the best of both me and her mom."

"Bullshit." Deb said and no more, as if the word 'bullshit' was the universal magic word to make people shut up.

In the distance they all saw the reflections of what must have been arc welding. There was a large grinding sound, as if somehow heavy equipment had made its way this far down.

"The bots are constantly moving, buzzing about. It's like working in a beehive," Paul said.

"What are they building?"

"I don't know."

"What's in the folder?" Deb pointed.

There was a manila folder pushed off to the side, obviously not included in the papers her dad had given Sam.

"I gave you the satchel."

She reached for it. Paul put his hand on hers.

"We don't have the time."

Slowly, bit-by-bit she started pulling the folder from under his hand.

He didn't stop her, but he didn't look her in the eyes either.

She opened it.

Pictures fell out. They were the kind of pictures you'd get from a private detective, surveillance pictures taken from a distance.

"Nothing much here," Sam said, "That's just a bunch of pictures of Shotwell, the FBI agent."

"That's my mom."

She threw the photos down, still staring at them.

"My mom's still alive."

Sam was getting the creepy crawlies about this place. Something was very wrong, extremely wrong, more than he'd ever known.

"This could be a bad time for us to visit," he said, "we could.."

"Shut up or I will hurt you."

"Got it."

Sam could both watch and feel in his mind her freeze up again. Dammit. Again she became the robot.

Paul made a cross gesture, the way Catholics did. He took a breath, then jumped up, right into her face.

"Darklings! The Darklings are here! The Darklings are real! They're real! Goddammit, you've got to…"

At 5:31:07 PM on Tuesday afternoon, eighty-feet below the ground, in a top-secret government facility, Debian Newbury shot her father Paul in the head with his own pistol.

The event was recorded.

The man made no movement. He collapsed, a puppet no longer with his puppeteer. His carcass sprawled across the chair he had just been sitting in. Blood spurted from his open wound to the floor.

A puddle formed.

There was a low hum that began rising in pitch and volume. It was the sound of a large HVAC system spinning up.

"Hmm."

No response.

The lights came on. After a second or two the flashing red lights began again.

So far no alarm.

Lucky.

"Didn't take them too long to break through that roadblock,"

He looked at the door, welded shut. Trouble was coming from some-where. He wished he knew where.

Time to move.

He pulled the body a few feet away. He got out his knife.

They were going to have to gut this man, her father, like a fish if they were going to have a chance of getting out of here. Deb could crack an Insert, but she needed the Insert in hand to do it.

Her head cocked. Deb looked like a dog with a problem. Things were happening that were totally unexpected.

"Deb."

She cocked her head a bit more.

"I'm sorry," he said to what was left of Paul.

He began cutting and sawing. The blood was still oozing.

She collapsed to the floor as if her string had also been cut, but there had been no gunshot. The reboot had failed. Deb had BSODed.

Whatever was there, whatever Deb was doing, he'd get to that in a minute.

First things first.

Blood covered his arms. He hand slipped as he struggled. He began sweating.

Paul's intestines spilled onto the floor.

He cut it out the way Pops had shown them both just a few weeks and many millions of years ago.

A minute or two later, holding the bloody mess in his hand, he began his next job, Debian.

He looked up and down her limp form, checking for breathing, bleed-ing, movement.

She looked okay.

He dropped the Insert. Without her, it was useless anyway.

The clock was ticking.

Gently he scooted over to sit close to her but did not touch her. It didn't feel right, even holding her hand would somehow just keep pushing her down, he knew it.

He scanned her again, top to bottom. Had he missed something?

How'd he end up with this girl? How'd she end up with him?

He saw the corner of the paperback sticking out.

"I've read it."

He could feel her shifting, but it wasn't enough.

"I read the Tickle Bunny book."

She moved, but her eyes didn't open.

"It was good," he continued, mostly to himself, "I thought the hero bunny was quite brave when he faced down the Ice People."

Activity. Her eyes opened. She looked at him. She was uncertain, confused.

"You did."

"I did. I almost cried to be honest. It takes something special to keep pushing on when it's all gone."

She sat up.

"He did have two lucky rabbits feet, Sam."

"He did. Well, he was a Tickle Bunny, of course. But what he really had was hope. That's what did it. I need you to have hope."

She looked to the terminal her dad had just been using, then back to Sam.

"I'll try."

"That's all I ask."

She sat up, got to her dad's seat, ignoring the blood and gore. He shifted position to be at her side.

He picked up the insert with his left hand. He was unsure.

He didn't want to shove that awful thing that had just been inside her father in her face. Yet. Yet if he didn't do it, she couldn't continue. She needed the insert. She was the only person alive that could crack one.

He decided to hold it out to the side, make it visible, obvious.

She saw it. She took a deep breath. She took another.

"I. Do. Not. Want. That."

She was fixed on it. She dared not look where it came from.

The puddle had gotten much bigger.

"The bunnies would have never made it."

She flinched. She didn't reach.

"Hope, Debian. We cling to hope."

She snatched it from his hand and plugged it in.

For a moment he wasn't sure if she'd start working or not.

"I need you to get this."

She saw him but didn't speak.

He continued, "I've got you. I need you to get this."

She began.

He didn't want to say any more. He didn't want to nag. Her emotional position was too precarious.

Five minutes turned to ten. He had to do something. It could be a minute. It could be an hour.

"Exit. We need to leave." he reminded.

She held the bloody insert in her lap, the probe plugged into the terminal. Her fingers flew. Sam idly thought she must be typing 200 words per minute, or more.

Her typing sounded like rain.

He looked, curious.

Hexadecimal dumps flashed by. It was so fast. He could barely tell they were numbers. It was far too fast for him to read.

She was pattern matching and processing at a speed he'd never seen before, even in a computer.

Perhaps a bit of prodding.

"So, I've got the satchel. I've got the papers. I've got the disks."

She kept going, a hard rain on a fierce afternoon ahead of a dark cloud.

"Deb."

Wait.

"Debian."

Time to push.

He lightly placed his hand on her shoulder. She flinched, but only slightly. Code kept scrolling by, her fingers flying. He thought he saw some assembler. She was raw dogging a system hack in assembler, both creating and exploiting an attack vector in real-time, for chrissakes.

"Door. We need a way out. Find us something, maybe a crawlway, or even an emergency exit. A sewage drain. A large crack. A cave. Something. Anything. Please."

She jerked to a stop and looked straight up at the ceiling, thinking.

He took the hand back.

"Deb?"

She rose out of the seat. She slowly walked over to the stone wall. She examined it like it was something different from just an empty plane of blank rock.

He crossed his arms. He started feeling for what she was thinking.

There it was.

Inside her head was numeric chaos. Lighting flames from the quantum foam.

He couldn't track the individual thoughts, but he could help calm her.

He reached out. He soothed.

She stood still, but placed her hands flat, shoulder height, like she was trying to push the wall away.

This couldn't go on too long. There must be some urgency along with the calm.

Push.

Just as he was deciding to give up, switch tactics, to let go and go looking for an exit on his own, he noticed something about the spot where her hands touched the wall.

There was a soft blue glow around her hands.

He rubbed his eyes. Surely there was some sort of hallucinogenic, a defensive mist at work.

Something.

Now her hands were dark, oddly so, as if her hands and only her hands had gotten four shades darker.

The soft blue spread out, not as a glow, but now as faint lightning-like tendrils. It was just above the limitations of his eyes ability to see them.

Or maybe he was seeing them through her eyes? Maybe none of this was real?

"Are we…."

As the lightning tendrils reached a certain distance, they flashed, from almost seen to sun-hot. The entire floor flashed as if a giant sky strobe light had just gone off. For an instant, they were white-hot spider webs of fire. They didn't fade. They dug. They disappeared into the rock, without changing it.

At the same time, he heard a giant exhaling, perhaps a fifty-foot giant was letting go of their breath, happy to be put to work.

And it all stopped. No blue. No sound. Even the construction work and HVAC stopped. He could hear them both breathing. She rocked back and forth lightly, as if testing the cement. The world held its breath.

"Deb … I …."

It was a CLICK – POP! He remembered that for the rest of his life. A CLICK when the wall just failed to exist anymore. There. Gone. A POP when the air rushed in to fill the void where the wall had been.

There was a huge hole, a tunnel, at least 20 meters deep. In the back of it he saw part of the old mine.

Slowly she dropped her hands, looking at the gaping hole she had created.

Her head turned.

Now he knew something he hadn't before.

Sam knew what Debian Newbury looked like when she was scared.

5.20

Sunsets

They stood in the cave, admiring the sunset
"We know now."
He looked at her. She was not crying.
A lone tear stood guard halfway from her eye to the floor. She shivered.
He looked back.
Some time passed until he said, "Everything's going to be different"
No response.
He heard her shallow, ragged breathing, the sobs.
Finally she said, "Is it?"
"You'll want to see the letter."
The sun continued to set.
"I need you," she said.
There were more tears.
"Debian, you've saved my life. You're part of me."
Insanity. Total insanity.
Slowly, she took his hand.

• • •

PAUL'S LETTER
I'm glad it was you.

We never meant to keep secrets from you. There were no answers to be had, there was nothing you could do. We wanted you to be happy.

My sweet girl, there was never anything wrong with you. I'm beginning to understand that you're a horrible danger to yourself and others and I wish we'd all known that earlier. You might always be. I am sorry. I would have carried this burden for you if I could have.

I tried.

I have done what I could.

I made a deal. I was promised that you can decide to walk-away. I've given you that. Neither you nor Sam will be harmed if you do so. Now you have something I never had: a choice. Use it wisely.

Find your brother; he needs you.

It's okay not knowing, my heart. We never knew about any of this before we started, and knowing will just lead to another Great Unknown. It never ends. Not every puzzle needs you to solve it. The best ones don't.

Some games are best lost.

Live a life you can look back on and be happy.

I love you.

Dad

THE END

TO RECEIVE YOUR FREE EBOOK
(AND OTHER GOODIES)

NEXT IN THE SERIES

A PREVIEW OF DB MARKHAM'S NEXT BOOK, FINAL LIGHT

A Bad Day

THE WORST PART OF Tuesday wasn't writhing in pain, having flames shoot from her head, voiding her bowels and dying in screaming agony in front of a crowd of cheering onlookers. No, the worst part of Tuesday for Beverly Castler was finding out that the afterlife began in Newark, New Jersey. What a dump.

Warden Smithers led off the festivities with a 3am visit. She had been told to dress to expect important visitors.

Entering her cell, Smithers saw that Beverly did not disappoint. Perfectly put-together grey hair, a business suit of dark grey and white, fine, expensive antique jewelry, and always the razor-sharp predator blue-grey eyes. The Murdering Madame of Manchester sat perfectly upright in her chair in her room, moving only slightly to acknowledge him as the guard passed Smithers through.

To others, Beverly Castler was an extremely bad person who also did extremely good things. To herself, Beverly was an extremely good person who also did extremely bad things. Best described by one reporter as a "cross between Martha Stewart and Hannibal Lechter", she was sixty-two, the oldest woman on death row, the woman serial killer with the highest body count, the woman two-dozen books had been written about, and the only woman the state had given a closed trial including sealed records. She was also the only woman Smithers ever met that was both loved and hated by everyone she met.

It was unnerving. Her effect on himself and others reminded Smithers of how deer must feel trapped in oncoming headlights: interested, scared, bemused, fearful, and frozen.

Dead.

"Warden Smithers, how good to see you," She smiled warmly. She pushed forward a gift-wrapped box, "This is something for Lisa. Not much, but all I could do."

"Lisa? My wife?" he managed.

"Of course! Her birthday is coming up this week, she's forty-three if I remember correctly, and if I'm not mistaken next week is your twenty-second anniversary as well. Best wishes to you all. Made this myself," she pointed to the small box, "I've got another gift coming next week."

"Beverly, I have another letter for you," he pulled out the envelope.

"Let's see, press, writers, TV, bloggers, victims, death row advocates, potential suitors? Personal delivery, must be special."

"It is," he opened it and got his glasses out. "It's from the mother of little Timothy Beavers, the one you flayed alive and put into the stew for customers visiting your house of prostitution."

"Oh dear," she said, "I imagine it's quite negative, dark, and dreary. Little Timothy was such a sweet boy."

Smithers didn't know how to take that. Instead, he held it up, "Should I read it?"

"Heavens no! I get several of those a week. I don't blame those poor souls for being so unforgiving. I hope the letters help them, bless them. Don't we have more pressing business?"

"You probably won't have time later," he paused for just a second, then put the letter away. He slowly rose from her table, ushering her up. "Today's a big day. We've got a surprise."

"Something's wrong, I can tell, Lucas," she said, "Governor's finally visiting?"

He nodded, but slowly. She finished standing.

"And I suppose he's ready to deal, hence all this middle-of-the-night shenanigans. That man is so tiresome. Always has been."

He began walking her down the hall. He let her go first. There was no point in giving up manners, even at a time like this. She smiled as she noticed his consideration.

"I'm not so sure about that, Beverly," he managed again, the words coming rougher and rougher. He was walking beside her. He'd witnessed more than twenty executions, but nothing like tonight. "You might be wanting to make your peace with the maker."

"Oh don't be so drab, Lucas. If the Governor's here, things are looking up. Trust me."

Reaching the end of the hall, he pointed to the left.

"Why that way?" she asked, "The interview rooms are to the right."

He said nothing.

"Lucas, even if they're here to kill me, the execution chamber is also the other way." she was a kind matron indulging a minor slip-up on his part.

He could say nothing. Instead he pointed to the left again. They began walking to the door at the end of that hall. The old one.

It was an ancient metal door, part of the old prison that hadn't been renovated with everything else 20 years back. The old chrome knob was dented, scruffy, weathered, scratched. They were visiting something of a museum piece, something the guards would bring friends in to see when nobody would get in trouble, something Law Enforcement still joked about when finally apprehending a killer.

A black plaque on the door. It read "Old Sparky."

"In here," he opened the door and they both went in. He closed the door behind them.

They were in a semi-circular room with windows for walls. Curtains had been drawn over the windows. The smell of old leather and dust hung deeply in the moist air.

In the middle of the room was something that looked like it might be a dentist's chair straight out of an old western. It was covered in an old black drop cloth. Smithers flipped a switch. Fluorescents flickered to life. Along one wall was a row of switches. She thought that it looked like something out of an ancient black-and-white horror film.

"Old Sparky? Seriously?" She smiled while shaking her head and tut-tutting, a school marm amused at some expected but lame juveline hijinks. "I know better than that. What kind of charade is this? Some kind of mind game? I'm scheduled for lethal injection, and that's over a week from today."

Smithers pulled the cover from the chair. Cockroaches scurried for cover from the harsh light.

"If the Governor thinks this negotiating tactic will work, he's got another thing coming."

She sounded firm, but not as firm as before, Smithers thought. He could see her body tighten as if she had just read his mind.

A cold chill ran down his spine. It wasn't the first time Beverly Castler had that effect on him, but he suspected it was the last. He hoped. Goosebumps overtook his arms and shoulders, threatened his back.

"Beverly," he said, walking over to the curtains, "I'm 53. I've been a warden for eleven years now. I've seen a lot of things."

He pulled the rope opening the curtains up.

"But yours is the first surprise execution I've ever witnessed. May God have mercy on your soul."

She took a step back, as if attacked and preparing to defend herself.

It was the first time he'd seen The Gallery like this. The Gallery was usually a somber place, with extra security to prevent outbursts, people dressed like a wedding or a funeral, each side either for the victim or the perpetrator.

Not tonight. Instead, it looked like a party box at a Super Bowl game. Somebody had set up a keg of beer. There was a snack table. A dozen or so people milled about in street clothes. When the curtains opened, cheers went up in the audience.

"Is this even possible?" he wasn't certain if she was asking herself or him.

"You really don't think Epstein committed suicide, do you?" He let it go right there. There was no point in torturing the lady. Her end was coming soon enough. This was part of the job he didn't like thinking about, much less talking about.

She grabbed her broach absent-mindedly, still processing the scene in front of her. She looked at the chair, then back to him.

They heard a knock on the glass.

The Governor always looked like a cross between a shoe salesman, an accountant, and a lounge lizard, except when he was in his cups, which Smithers gathered was most every night. Then he looked worse, like the devil's own version of those things.

He smiled a hello, then tapped at his breast pocket, indicating Smithers' next task.

As the Governor went around to the side door, Smithers withdrew a folded paper.

"I have here a commutation of your execution. You'll still serve life, but next week just before your Execution Day the Governor will announce that now is a time for healing. You can live."

The Governor entered the room. Smithers finished, "It's the best deal you're ever going to get."

She ignored him and instead stared down the Governor. "What do you want, George? Another child to rape? Maybe some more disabled kids ramped up on crank and PCP fighting to the death so you and your cronies can bet on them?"

Now it was the Governor's turn to step back, but Smithers noticed that he recovered as quickly as she did.

Smithers wondered if he had the right person in custody.

"We need to know where the rest of the tapes are, Bev," he said, "You give us the tapes, this all goes away."

"You're going to put this in writing?"

"Right here," he took the paper, "You tell me, I'll sign it. Smithers can witness. It'll be on the Attorney General's desk come first light."

She sat, she actually sat down in the electric chair.

"I have your word."

The Governor nodded somberly, or at least as somberly as he could given the circumstances, "There's nothing in this for me or you if the tapes go away. Even if you come out and try to blackmail me, nobody will believe you. Or hear you for that matter. You have my word."

She considered, toying with something in her pocket.

"Let me see the paper."

The Governor put it on a clipboard, started handing it to her, then stopped.

"The tapes?"

"Sign it first, asshole."

The Governor signed, gave it to Smithers who witnessed it. Now the Governor held it from her again.

"Your turn. Sign it and it all goes away. Where are they?"

"My lawyer's office," she took the clipboard, "in his safe. Like that'll do you any good anyway. You didn't say I had to deliver them, only tell you where they were."

She began signing, humming a happy tune.

"Great," the Governor said. The two men began strapping her in. She had no time to protest. "Let's get this over so we can hit some clubs."

The Governor held her shoulder as if saying goodbye to an old friend.

"But you said."

"Politicians say a lot of things, sweet," the Governor obviously was trying to impersonate Castler, "Your little mind doesn't believe everything it sees now, does it? Poor dear."

"But I'm not prepped. My head should be shaven. Should have had a last meal."

"That'll just make it more entertaining," the Governor said, taking the clipboard back.

He took the commutation letter off and slowly ripped it into pieces, obviously savoring every moment. He dropped it on the floor. Somebody else could clean it up. Such things were beneath him.

"I really wish I could take a picture of this," he said, then smiled again, "Keep it in my special album. But tut-tut," he wagged his finger, "Taking videos and pictures of bad things is a naughty thing to do. I think you know that now, or you will in a minute or two."

"You don't think I have more papers?" she asked, "You think that was all?"

The Governor got out the cap, started to blow the dust off of it, then changed his mind. The dust would be better.

She continued.

"You don't think I mailed myself videos, audio? Put things, things you don't want to come out, in a safe deposit box only I know where?"

Smithers helped the Governor get the ankle contacts wet. They started attaching them to her ankles.

The Governor stood.

"We only have eighteen people here, the witnesses for the execution," he said, "Oh, I could have easily brought in a hundred. What was your final death toll, at least the ones we know about? Eighty-four, wasn't it? Yes, yes, I could have filled the room up several times over."

"George, I'm giving you this last chance. Don't do the wrong thing." she said.

They began applying the cap.

"Sadly, though, I had to limit it to those I could trust with absolute secrecy," he said, "See that lady there?"

He pointed to a frail lady in the gallery. She didn't have a plate or a cup. Instead she stared into the execution chamber as if looking into hell itself.

"That's my sister," The Governor said, "You don't know. You wouldn't know. Adopted. She's had a hard time with drugs. That's how she lost her two kids."

"It could ruin your career," she added.

"And that's how you ended up with them, at your home, under your care, in your program. I believe they were numbers thirty-nine and forty, at least by our count."

"George."

If he heard her he didn't indicate it. Instead he went over to the switch.

"They were two that you burned alive in the incinerator. Any last words?"

Smithers could could see Bev's body tense. She looked around the room, then out into the audience. As she observed them observing her, her body relaxed. Her smile returned. She was the lady in charge.

"Of course," she said, as if she were giving a prepared a speech for the local Rotary Club, "This all reminds me of a little girl I was counseling once. She had a lot of difficulties adjusting and was dealing with PTSD from an absolutely horrible upbringing."

She looked off as if remembering the moment. She nodded to herself, at least as much as she could.

"I always tried to counsel them, you know," she smiled wistfully, "And every so often one would take to it, make good, end up with a scholarship or become a doctor or whatnot. These are our victories. I cherish those. They are so precious."

She turned to look at them.

"But she did not. So I took to more aggressive therapy using the cattle prod and slow acid burns. Eventually skin flaying. I kept hoping beyond hope that it would take. Poor thing. I do love the little ones," she nodded, "and then, sadly, one day it looked as if it wasn't going to work out. I remember quite clearly her telling me that God loves me and no matter what I did, there was always a chance for Heaven for all of us."

"Castler," Smithers hated interrupting but she had to be reminded that this couldn't go on forever.

"You know what I told her?" now Beverly became fully happy, "I told her to go fuck herself, that's what. Then I threw her in the wood chipper. She made the nicest sounds."

She looked at the Governor and Smithers, her smile still there.

"You can all go fuck yourselves, and I'll see you in hell."

Electrocution was not painful. Beverly remembered reading that somewhere. It was true.

Of course, to those in attendance, her eyes popped from her skull, her head caught fire, she thrashed around tightening her entire body into a rock each time the switch was thrown. From the outside she made quite the sight, thrashing in pain. But from the inside, nothing. The audience was allowed in, each one taking a turn at the switch. She voided her bowels, her bladder. She began to smoke, a hotdog left on the griddle too long.

To Beverly Castler, there was a click, a bright light, and all was gone. She had been turned off.

Silence.

Her eyes opened. There was no choir or heavenly singers, not that she expected one. No devil waited with a pitchfork. No flames. No clouds.

Instead it was Fleetwood Mac.

A bright placard sat on a table announcing "$20 Margarita Mondays!" and several other mixed drinks, all fruity with bright colors. There was music, people talking all around her.

The table was small, square, made of fake wood. She sat in one chair. Two others were empty. As she looked around, she saw a bar. On one side of the bar was a large glass window. Beyond the glass she could see large commercial airplanes pulling in and out of the gates.

People were crowding in, milling about, and crowding out. Almost all had roller luggage. In the background some pop singer of a hundred years ago sang about pain and loss. There was somebody making a gate announcement. A large paper banner hung over the bar. It read "WINKIES NEWARK, THE BEST LITTLE BAR IN JERSEY!!!!" Underneath, another sign said, "TRIVIA NIGHT!"

"Who you got to screw around here to get service?" she heard from beside her off to the back.

Glancing back, there were a couple of middle-aged women. They glared back at her.

Excuse me, she wanted to say, I just got executed. Very sorry to bother you. Assholes.

She turned around to the bar again.

Beverly Castler didn't go to heaven. Beverly Castler died. She didn't go to hell. She was not reincarnated. Instead, she ended up in an airport bar in fucking Newark, New Jersey.

The day had really driven off a cliff.

The Ride

FOR LEM, HIS DAY ended in being abducted by drug runners in a magic truck full of corncobs and cocaine. It didn't seem right to Lemuel

Rickenbacker that it started with desperately wanting to boil the children in hot oil, but it did. Perhaps that was the punishment. There was also the matter of why anyone would want 24,000 pounds of chicken beaks and an assortment of items including a pile of rusty tricycles and three pairs of brand-new Canadian Sauna Pants.

...

www.ingramcontent.com/pod-product-compliance
Lightning Source LLC
Chambersburg PA
CBHW020533310726
48979CB00014B/2314/J